TRAPPED
The Erinnan Legacy

Treason and Truth
Book 3 of 12

J.A. Cauldwell

<u>Dedication</u>
For Gary
The answer to your question is
Quite a lot!

Character lists and notes on world building
are at the end of the book

THE ERINNAN LEGACY

TREASON AND TRUTH

FROM THE PAST COMES MAGIC, FROM THE PRESENT, DANGER, GRADUALLY COLLIDING

<table>
<tr><td>1</td><td>TREASON</td><td>5</td><td>THROWN</td></tr>
<tr><td>2</td><td>TERA</td><td></td><td></td></tr>
<tr><td>3</td><td>TRAPPED</td><td></td><td></td></tr>
<tr><td>4</td><td>TRAGEDY</td><td></td><td></td></tr>
</table>

STORIES FROM ERINNA

EVERYBODY HAS A STORY AND SOMEBODY KNOWS IT

Standalone stories that may link to characters from other series.

TIES

For freebies, The Court Newsletter and to see more details and information on works in progress, please visit https://erinna.co.uk

TRAPPED

From the past comes magic, from the present, danger, gradually colliding.

Forty years after rebellion raged, Landis House lies in ashes — with the future of greater consequence than any past. The home of King Adeone's closest friend and Defender, its destruction feels less like tragedy and more like strategy. Accident or arson?

Tradition binds Prince Arkyn's and Prince Tain's fates with the empire's, and now they have to face that future. As Prince Arkyn shoulders the weight of official life, Tain must prepare for a destiny he doesn't want: Justiciar of the Empire.

Meanwhile, Lord Scanlon unearths secrets and targets loyalty within the empire. He's not just playing politics. He's attempting to clear the board and no one is safe.

Unrest has learned patience as daggers sleep and secrets waken.

Copyright

Trigger Warning

This book is set in a pre-Victorian-inspired world with elements of fantasy. It includes references to difficult themes such as loss, hardship, and moral dilemmas. Some events explore the consequences of harm, societal oppression, and personal struggles, including grief and guilt.

This book is written in British English. The lack of Z might keep you awake but we like U. If you prefer a different flavour of English, I hope you find your next read soon.

Maps

THE OEDRANIAN EMPIRE

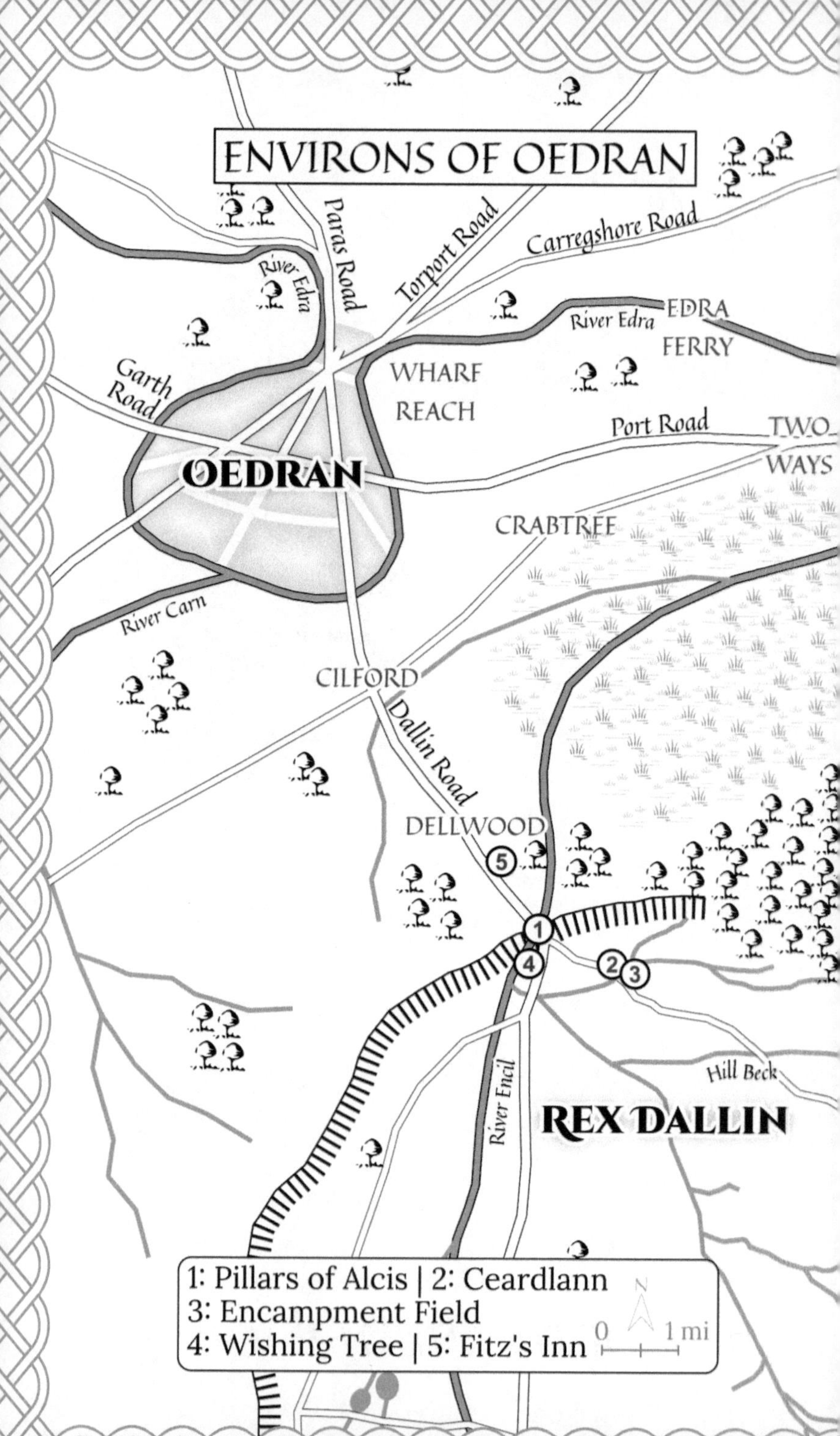

ENVIRONS OF OEDRAN
Paras Road
Torport Road
Carregshore Road
River Edra
River Edra
EDRA FERRY
Garth Road
WHARF REACH
Port Road
TWO WAYS
OEDRAN
CRABTREE
River Carn
CILFORD
Dallin Road
DELLWOOD
5
1
4
2
3
River Encil
Hill Beck
REX DALLIN
1: Pillars of Alcis | 2: Ceardlann
3: Encampment Field
4: Wishing Tree | 5: Fitz's Inn
N
0   1 mi

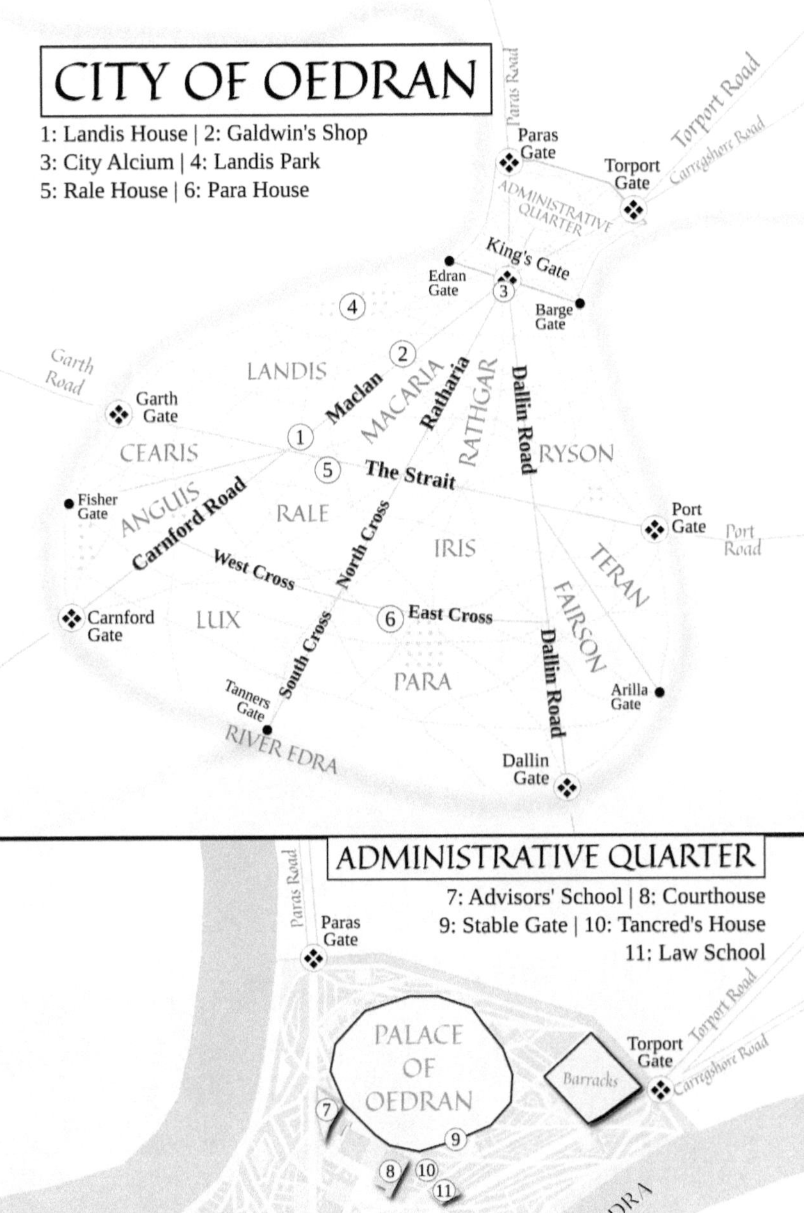

CITY OF OEDRAN
1: Landis House | 2: Galdwin's Shop
3: City Alcium | 4: Landis Park
5: Rale House | 6: Para House
Paras Road
Torport Road
Carregshore Road
Paras Gate
Torport Gate
ADMINISTRATIVE QUARTER
King's Gate
Edran Gate
Barge Gate
Garth Road
Garth Gate
LANDIS
Maclan
MACARIA
Ratharia
RATHGAR
Dallin Road
RYSON
CEARIS
The Strait
Fisher Gate
ANGUIS
Carnford Road
RALE
North Cross
IRIS
Port Gate
Port Road
TERAN
West Cross
East Cross
FAIRSON
Carnford Gate
LUX
South Cross
PARA
Dallin Road
Arilla Gate
Tanners Gate
RIVER EDRA
Dallin Gate

ADMINISTRATIVE QUARTER
7: Advisors' School | 8: Courthouse
9: Stable Gate | 10: Tancred's House
11: Law School
Paras Road
Paras Gate
PALACE OF OEDRAN
Barracks
Torport Road
Carregshore Road
Torport Gate
Edran Gate
The Pike
King's Gate
RIVER EDRA
Barge Gate
N

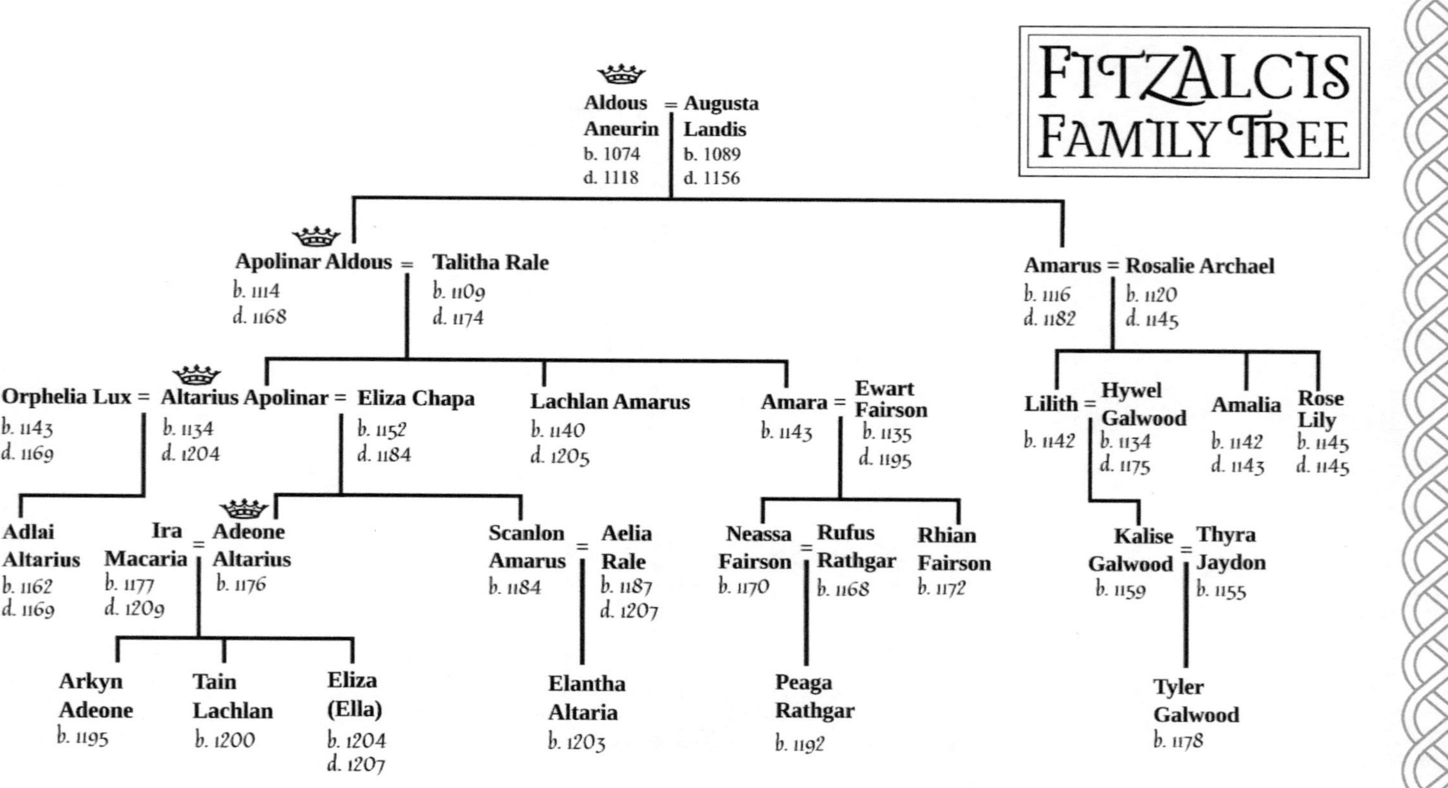

FITZALCIS FAMILY TREE

Aldous Aneurin = Augusta Landis
Aldous Aneurin b. 1074 d. 1118
Augusta Landis b. 1089 d. 1156

Apolinar Aldous = Talitha Rale
Apolinar Aldous b. 1114 d. 1168
Talitha Rale b. 1109 d. 1174

Amarus = Rosalie Archael
Amarus b. 1116 d. 1182
Rosalie Archael b. 1120 d. 1145

Orphelia Lux = Altarius Apolinar = Eliza Chapa
Orphelia Lux b. 1143 d. 1169
Altarius Apolinar b. 1134 d. 1204
Eliza Chapa b. 1152 d. 1184

Lachlan Amarus b. 1140 d. 1205

Amara = Ewart Fairson
Amara b. 1143
Ewart Fairson b. 1135 d. 1195

Lilith = Hywel Galwood
Lilith b. 1142
Hywel Galwood b. 1134 d. 1175

Amalia b. 1142 d. 1143

Rose Lily b. 1145 d. 1145

Adlai Altarius b. 1162 d. 1169

Ira Macaria b. 1177 d. 1209 = Adeone Altarius b. 1176

Scanlon Amarus b. 1184 = Aelia Rale b. 1187 d. 1207

Neassa Fairson b. 1170 = Rufus Rathgar b. 1168

Rhian Fairson b. 1172

Kalise Galwood b. 1159 = Thyra Jaydon b. 1155

Arkyn Adeone b. 1195

Tain Lachlan b. 1200

Eliza (Ella) b. 1204 d. 1207

Elantha Altaria b. 1203

Peaga Rathgar b. 1192

Tyler Galwood b. 1178

CHRONICLE

1168
Accession of King Altarius
1169
Bayan Rebellion
1175
Altarius marries Eliza Chapa
1176
Birth of Adeone
1184
Birth of Scanlon Death of Queen Eliza
1203
Scanlon marries Aelia Rale, Birth of Elantha
1200
Birth of Tain
1195
Birth of Arkyn
1193
Adeone marries Ira Macaria
1204
Scanlon drops title of Prince Birth of Ella Accession of King Adeone
1205
Death of Prince Lachlan
1207
Death of Princess Ella and Aelia
1209
Death of Queen Ira. Promotion of Wynfeld
1211
Arkyn undertakes Terasian Review. Roth murders Portur.
1210
Gad attacks King Adeone at the Guild Banquet
1209
Triniculum Plan. Haster life-bound
1211
Anonymous notes left. Secretaries dismissed.

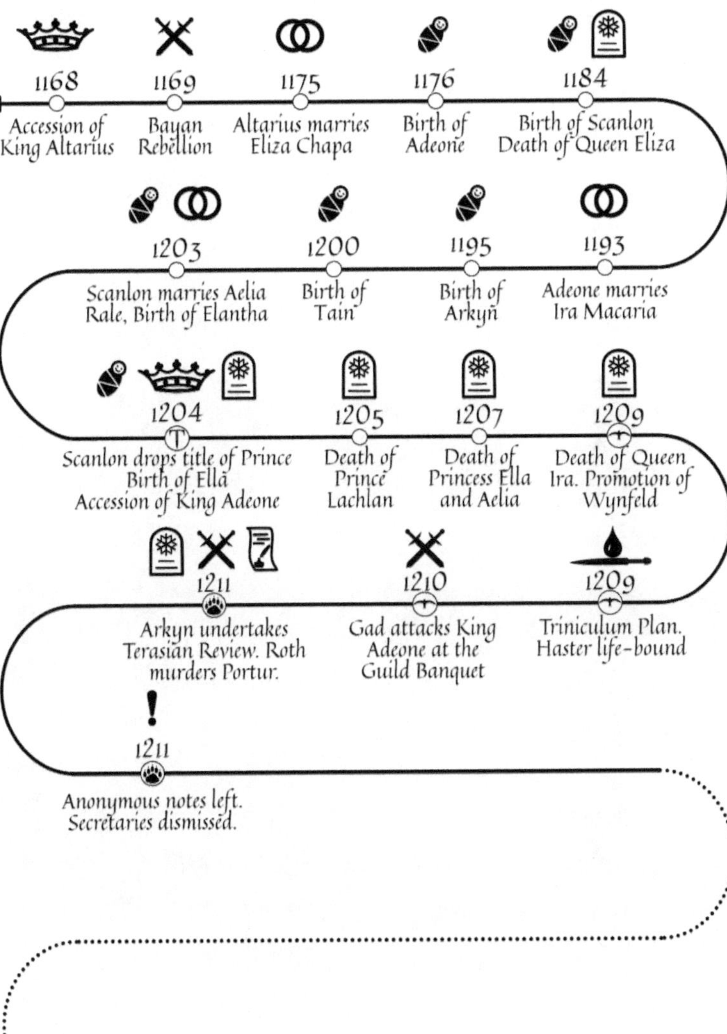

TRAPPED

PART 1

Chapter 1
REBELLION
1169
EXTRACTS FROM THE DIARY OF
PRINCE LACHLAN AMARUS FITZALCIS

Hexadai, Week 3 – 20th Cearal 1169 – Day One

Hardly had time to breathe today. I warned Alt, but he didn't want to listen and now rebellion in Bayan. Lilith and Galwood missing! Stupid idiot. Why didn't he rescind that blasted tax? He knew people weren't happy. Just because he's King doesn't make him right! I suppose this is day one of the rebellion...

Tretaldai, Week 4 – 24th Cearal 1169 – Day Five

Conscription Day. Aluna, it's hard watching; each man is someone's father, brother or son. Most came but there were enough arrests to keep me busy – won't be me though. I've decided I'm going with Alt to Bayan. Ewart's also coming, but he's sent Am to Tradere; I'm pleased, just wish Alt would send Orph and Ad to the Rex Dallin, it'd be better for them. I know the city needs a leader but he should be protecting his family. Dunius is Representative...

Imperadai, Week 6 – 11th Tradal 1169 – Day Twenty

They came out of nowhere! How did they know where we were? I'd fifty men with me, no more. We were lucky to win, whatever I'll tell Alt. Lost enough men though – Lord Iris and young Julius included. Ig is badly wounded; Alt is furious. Don't even know all the names of those lost. Names... Time is short for writing; that council was heated. Initials safer now. CS, LN fought well. Capt. P is trying hard to prove himself. Why? What's he hiding? Alt's listening to everyone at last but he's got the General for a reason, let him strategise.

Cisadai, Week 7 – 16th Tradal 1169 – Day Twenty-Five

...Can't stop thinking about L, hope she's alive. Could have been Am - bet the rebels are glad it isn't, I am. Trying to find a crack to open up the cit. Lord C or M would be best. Maybe C's son - must find him though...

Tretaldai, Week 7 – 17th Tradal 1169 – Day Twenty-Six

C's son walked into camp, asked to speak to Alt. He's our chink. Hope his father doesn't realise his son's joined us - let alone is honour-bound. Capt. P seems to think night is dangerous. Alt's ordered a guard to be in my tent at night... S is rather a pretty one too... I'll try to keep him.

Pentadai, Week 7 – 19th Tradal 1169 – Day Twenty-Eight

Three men dragged by Capt. P into Alt's tent. Alt asked me to judge, he forgot it's military law within the camp's confines and would have been even if they weren't soldiers, soon put him right. Not sure I'd have convicted TT without far more evidence... CS and LN were traitors - no wonder they survived that ambush... C's son should have made Garth... Alt's methods of execution might be traditional but rather brutal. Didn't take long for the men to kill the traitors, anger all round. Bodies moved to the camp's extremities; won't take long for nature to feed. Alt ordered the traitors' names proclaimed in Oedran for a year. The families who raised them must take some of the blame; if we lose this fight, we lose Bayan and worse comes to Oedran...

Imperadai, Week 8 – 25th Tradal 1169 – Day Thirty-Four

...We march on Garth. I've got Cmdr R and a company to distract the walls. Alt's going for the main gate. Alcis bless us, we'll need the moons' help if C's failed...

Septadai, Week 8 – 28th Tradal 1169 – Day Thirty-Seven

Not had a moment to write. Bayan's ours. Citadel fell quickly. C's father killed. M defected before we attacked. All other lords to be executed. City Guard disbanded.

Rebels taken have been hanged. Men tracking down others. Best news: L and G found. G looks ill but Alt's naming him Exarch. L simply looks drained. Sent word straight to her father. He made his normal sarcastic reply but he was relieved. Just have to secure things and head for Oedran. Orph must be pleased. Ad will be wanting all the stories…

* * *

Cisadai, Week 32 – 23rd Anapal 1171

I never appreciated in 1169 how much damage we did, especially as it wasn't proved. To have family die of shame and to carry on facing the world. He handed those coins back so apologetically; I wasn't insulted, how could I have been? Tried to talk to Alt. Am intervened; she reckons we owe him - even if it hadn't been L.P. involved. I reckon she'll get what she wants, as always. Anyhow, I'll see him again in a couple of days when he's had time to think… There's something in his eyes…

Chapter 2
A NEW ERA

LORD SCANLON THUMPED a wall. He couldn't return to Ceardlann, to the Rex Dallin, to the place that had been the FitzAlcis' retreat for six centuries, to where privacy was guaranteed. Banned and banished because of others' actions. Adeone had manipulated his father. King Altarius would never have taken such action without provocation. Scanlon stopped pacing. Maybe, just maybe, there had been provocation but it wasn't of his making. His character had been moulded by others' teachings, then tainted, tarnished by events of others' making. Adeone was punishing him for them, for wanting to be himself, to act how he wished; he wanted Scanlon to be as lax and soft as he was, as flippant and as scornful about the traditions of the empire. Well, he wasn't going to conform. Whatever had happened, whatever was between them, he had his principles and he'd stick to them.

With rage still coursing through him, he decided on his course of action. A half-formed decision became defined. He'd put out feelers for discontented souls, those who feared the changes Adeone would make, but now he *would* pursue his plan of becoming king. Adeone couldn't be allowed to wreck their forbears' work or the ideals of iron control, which had forged an empire from disparate lands.

The door opened and his wife entered. He glared at her. She must have known what would greet him on his return from Terasia.

Seeing anger in his gaze, Aelia said, "Welcome home. I'm sorry I wasn't here; Her Grace asked to see me."

"What a welcome indeed! You *should* have warned me!" Seeing her puzzled expression, he scowled at her. "You mean you didn't know we've been *banned* from the Rex Dallin? Or rather that I have. He refused to give *me* entry!"

"Who did? Not Adeone, he'd never—"

"No, not him, he hasn't the spine to," spat Scanlon. "It was in the requests and bequests."

"Your *father* refused to give you entry after his death? Oh, Scanlon, I'm so sorry. I had no idea. His Majesty never said a word. I would have tried to warn you. What a welcome. Come, my dear, sit down, let me send for refreshments. You must have ridden hard and this has come as a shock."

"Oh, stop fussing. Have you any news?"

Aelia stepped back. "Elantha's beginning to talk, not much but definite words. Her cousins are all voluble as ever. Ella's beautiful—"

"Are *you* carrying again?"

"No, sir." Aelia dropped her gaze.

He sneered. "I'd have thought you'd have been more fertile. Your sister's had four children since her marriage. Girls are no use to me. I could cast you aside tomorrow. I need a son! Give me one soon. I'm going to be home for a time before I travel to Areal to undertake the law review."

"Could I not travel with you?" enquired Aelia.

Disdain dripped from him. "I'm not travelling with a screaming toddler. You'll stay here and nurture our child to be obedient. I'm going to the Courthouse. Be ready to receive me this evening."

Within a fortnight, Scanlon was fretting; by the time another had passed he had decided to travel to Tradere before returning to Areal.

Aelia was glad to see him leave but worried about a few snippets she'd overheard. Her husband was simply annoyed; he *couldn't* be contemplating usurping his brother, could he?

* * *

In Tradere, Scanlon decided he couldn't live at the Palace of Oedran. He needed somewhere he could plan without questions being asked, a house in a secluded spot. He sent for his new advisor, employed in the last week.

"Bantling, find me a house, somewhere in Anapara. One that's private. See it's large enough to maintain my status and family but not so large that I *must* entertain."

"Very good, sir. I'll see what we can manage."

Scanlon jerked his head in dismissal. He ought to adopt an honorific. He'd lost the obligatory 'Highness' when he became *Lord* Scanlon instead of *Prince* Scanlon, but he ought to be addressed better than 'sir' or 'my lord' by his staff. He was FitzAlcis and the chief official of the empire.

Two aluna-months later, Bantling returned. The Justiciar's Administrator had a word with him which resulted in raised eyebrows and questions that weren't answered.

Scanlon looked over as his administrator announced Bantling. "Well?"

The advisor gave a short bow. "We've found a house that might suit you, Greatness: Black Hills. About a day's ride to the north-east of Oedran, in the Raven Hills. Secluded, surrounded by a good-sized wall, enclosing the whole estate as well as the house."

"Who holds it?"

"Your landlord would be Lord Atgas, sir."

Scanlon pursed his lips. "I'm FitzAlcis *not* a tenant! His Lordship will relinquish the house if it suits."

Bantling took heed of the tone. "Very good, sir. I'll approach his son. The current Lord Atgas is elderly and Lord Abbas is running the estates."

"I'll expect an update within the week. You've already spent far too much time on this."

A week later, Bantling re-entered the Justiciar's office to find his employer disciplining his manservant; the whip cracked, flesh parted and blood ran. Bantling winced, noting the man's scars. This wasn't the first time Scanlon had taken such measures.

When Scanlon had dismissed the manservant, Bantling asked mildly what he'd done.

Scanlon put the whip through his belt. "He was inquisitive to the point of insolence. You have a report?"

Bantling swallowed. "Lord Abbas says that he's happy to come to some arrangement and, should you wish to view the house and estate, he will make it available whenever you wish."

"I am not your equal! You will address me correctly. You were employed with specific conditions, were you not? One of which was that you are unattached. How long have you been married?"

The spacious room was suddenly claustrophobic. "A year, Greatness. I needed the job, sir…"

Letting the thong hang loosely, Scanlon pulled the whip from his belt.

Bantling's eyes tracked the thong, his feet rooted to the spot. He took a steadying breath as Scanlon padded towards then around him. *'Prey,'* he thought. *'I'm prey…'* He jumped. The icy caress of the whip's heel touched his sweat-soaked neck. Would he die whipped or beaten?

"I shall ignore the fact you've lied to me," hissed Scanlon, "but I shan't forget. How old is your son now? Six aluna-months, I believe…"

The sound of a dagger being unsheathed. Maybe that would take his life, his son's life, his wife's life. No, Scanlon wouldn't be that kind. Scanlon liked his toys.

The Justiciar moved in front of Bantling. Faster than a cutpurse, he sliced off the advisor's belt pouch and took his dagger. "Never come armed into my presence again. Go."

As Bantling passed him, Scanlon's administrator said, "He means it, Advisor. There's no escape. He *would* find you all. Don't reject him, it would be unfortunate. To question, to advise against something means you're against him."

Returning to his room, Bantling found it ransacked. As he put things in order, he found personal papers, books, elaborate accessories and best tunics were gone, even his everyday knife had vanished.

He sank onto his bed, his stomach twisting into knots of dread. Administrator Dyer had been right. There was no escape. He had trapped himself. A dream job had become a nightmare. How had he fallen for Scanlon's easy public manner?

Chapter 3
FIRE AND FAMILY
Pentadai, Week 45 – 5th Lufial, 19th Geryis 1211
Oedran – Landis House

KING ADEONE AND LORD LANDIS rode through the Administrative Quarter followed by three palace coaches. The warm stillness of the last weeks of spring was welcome, but acrid smoke was rising as they approached Landis House. There were more people than normal congregating around the gates, craning to see what had happened. Adeone nodded to Hillbeck to clear a path.

Riding into the stableyard, there was no denying the stables had been destroyed and the old part of the house had been gutted. Hearing horses, William broke away from the group of the servants clustered in the yard. Having been Landis' manservant for years nothing much fazed him. He gave a slight bow to Adeone.

"His Highness is in the gardens, Sire, with Lady Elantha and your children, my lord."

As Adeone entered the gardens, Tain ran over exhilarated.

"Father—" He stopped, aware of all the eyes on them. "Sorry, Sire."

Adeone simply pulled him close and gave him a strong hug, relieved to confirm with his own eyes what his administrator had told him and William had inferred. Tain was safe and unharmed. "Where's your cousin?"

"With my nearcousins, but I helped with the bucket chain. I—"

Adeone smiled. "I look forward to hearing about it over dinner. For now, you're all going to the Palace." He glanced at the Landis House nurse who was walking towards them with a gaggle of children. "Thank you, Nursie. Can you see all your charges, and mine," he added ironically, ruffling his son's hair, "to the Palace. Maria is expecting you. There are Palace coaches outside."

Nursie nodded. "Of course, sir. His Highness did a marvellous job organising everyone earlier."

Adeone chuckled. "I can imagine he did." He gave his niece a hug. "Are you all right, El?"

She nodded. "It wasn't too scary."

Adeone watched them go and made his way towards the house. He took a moment to thank the moons that it was a still day as the images of a fire-ravaged city played on his mind's eye.

Lord Landis was surveying the damage glumly. "Fortunately, no-one was hurt, but I guess I was going to have to rebuild this wing eventually."

Adeone sighed. "What happened?"

"His Highness spotted a fire in the stables. Somehow, it jumped to the house. He told Clodach to take the horses to Macarian House; I hope you don't mind. Getting them out let the fire take hold, but that doesn't matter."

"Very sensible of him. Is much lost?"

"It could be worse. They stopped it where the new and old house meet and managed to rescue a lot. William knew what mattered. His Highness helped with that too. Wouldn't be gainsaid, though William and Nursie managed to keep him out of actual harm's way."

"Thank them for me."

Lady Landis was crossing to them. Her face an explanation of her thoughts.

Adeone smiled at her. "You're staying at the Palace for now. We'll sort out everything you need there. The tailor always has a few tunics made up, just in case, likewise our dressmaker. I'm sure we've some of the children's things still around as well."

"I thought it was only Festus that could read me like that, Sire."

Adeone chuckled. "The children have already gone to the Palace. Shall I leave you both to all of this? I have a feeling I'm a distraction."

Landis shook his head. "I'm pleased you're here, sir. William?"

"Yes, my lord?" replied the manservant, ambling over.

"What's everyone's accommodation like?"

"Usable for now, sir. The attics of the new house mostly escaped. Other than smelling of smoke, they seem fine. Likewise, the cellars."

Landis nodded. "Good. The King has kindly said that the family can stay at the Palace. Other than those of you who attend on us privately, the rest will have to stay here and start to clean up."

"Of course, my lord. If you'll excuse me, I'll inform your steward."

Adeone said, "Shall we take a look?"

They entered the house by the front doors. The smell of smoke was pungent, but the damage seemed minimal. Landis relaxed. He could design a new house around this. He was glad that his father's habit of keeping doors closed had persisted. Some rooms were untouched. The small stair between the drawing rooms was useable and safe. He led the way along the passage to the old house. Here, the damage was far more noticeable. Smoke-blackened walls, damp floors and a broken door. Landis peered beyond its charred frame.

"Not as bad as I expected. It looks worse from the outside for a change. I'll get men clearing this tomorrow when everything's settled."

"I'm impressed your household managed to stop the fire," said Adeone.

"Yes. I wasn't sure that the pond would hold enough. Great-grandfather had it created after a smaller fire broke out. Obviously, he knew what he was doing."

"I suppose one Landis needed sense," remarked Adeone with a grin.

"Isn't he your ancestor as well?"

"No. Queen Augusta was his half-aunt. It's her father who's our common ancestor."

"I'm glad you can remember that. I can't. I'm all right on the direct line but anything else, I need to look up. Marriages and half-family, I've never bothered to learn."

"Anything come to mind about our house being burnt down, Festus, instead of family history?" enquired Cornelia, tongue in cheek.

Adeone chuckled. "Come on, if you can't do anything else here, let's return to the Palace and see everyone settled."

* * *

Two hours later, the younger children and Finian Rale had been reassured and settled into the FitzAlcis nursery. The twins had a set of smaller rooms, known as attendants' rooms, with a sitting room allocated to them. Landis and Cornelia had been given a suite of rooms near both the nursery and their eldest children. In Adeone's words, he doubted any of them could escape the others so family life would be preserved.

He looked up as his administrator announced Lord and Lady Landis. After enquiring if everyone was settled, he led the way into his own private sitting room and waved to chairs.

"I've had an idea that I'd like you to consider, rather than reacting immediately." His lips twitched as their eyes narrowed. "Landis House isn't going to be fit to live in for months, that much is clear. Would you consider living at Ceardlann during that time? Not just the children, both of you, William, Ivy and Nursie too."

"We can't accept that, Sire," said Landis.

Adeone caught Cornelia's eye. "Does that count as an immediate

25

reaction?"

"Probably, sir, but he's right. We have no claim—"

"No claim?" exclaimed Adeone. "Cornelia, your sister married my brother. Your husband is my wed-cousin and I'm nearfather to your children. If you go back a couple more generations, we're all related. How much more of a claim do you need?"

"Ceardlann is different, sir. It's your retreat. We can use Rale House," said Cornelia. "We've Finian living with us as our ward. It's my childhood home. It wouldn't be inappropriate."

"True, but I'd like you to consider how much nicer it might be to have the Rex Dallin for the children to explore. The nearcousins could spend time together—"

"Plot together," muttered Landis, catching Adeone's amused eye.

Cornelia hesitated. "Festus has Court and other duties here."

"Yes, keeping me out of trouble. Your rooms here aren't just for tonight or tomorrow. They're for whenever you need them. I should have allocated you some before. Faran has a set. Yet my Defender doesn't. Unthinkable."

"Are you calmly going to sit there and demolish every argument?" asked Landis shrewdly.

"Yes," replied his friend. "Then, if you continue to argue, I'll pull rank on you. Not on Cornelia. Just on you."

Landis turned to his wife. "You decide. I'm going to lose and then get the blame whatever happens."

His companions both laughed.

Seeing Adeone meant all of it and more, Cornelia said, "So basically, Sire, you think we're being fools?"

Adeone snorted. "It wouldn't be the first time I thought Festus was. Now, decide for him as every good wife knows how."

Cornelia thought for a moment. "Ceardlann *would* be better, sir. That is, if the Comptroller can put up with us."

"I'm sure he won't know how to thank me," replied Adeone. "Do you think I should send him warning?"

Festus chuckled. "For once, I think that might be politic, sir."

* * *

That evening, Adeone dined with his sons and niece. Arkyn smiled as they listened to Tain explaining everything to do with the fire – how he'd spotted it, how he'd helped rescue items and then how he'd helped with the bucket chain – whilst Elantha sat toying with her food.

Arkyn whispered, "*Are* you all right, little flower?"

She shrugged. "Yes. No. Not sure. Tired, I think. I'm glad you're home. I've missed you."

"I you. You'll have to tell me everything that's happened here."

She looked at him. "Will you have time to just talk now?"

"Yes. We'll find a corner and hide from all the mayhem. I'd like to."

Whilst listening to Tain, Adeone watched them unobtrusively, reassured by how close they were. When Tain seemed to have run out of things to say about the fire, he observed,

"Anyone would think your brother hasn't been away for most of this year and I for a season."

Tain blushed. "Sorry, sir. How was your trip home?"

Adeone chuckled. "Rather less momentous than your day. El, do you want to be excused?"

Elantha shook her head. "I'm just tired, Uncle Adeone. I'd like to stay but I'm not really hungry."

"Is there anything you'd prefer?" (She shook her head.) "Then when Tain's finished, we'll go and sit comfortably and you can tell me everything he's got up to."

In the King's sitting room, Adeone settled himself onto the couch rather than his usual chair. Elantha snuggled up next to him, sucking her thumb. Tain frowned. An hour later, Elantha was yawning, though trying to pretend she wasn't.

Adeone chuckled. "Come on, little flower, you need your sleep."

"Will you— Sorry. It's not Ceardlann. Goodnight, uncle."

Adeone smiled. "I'll come and tuck you in. Tain, are you ready yet?"

Tain shook his head. Even though he was, he wouldn't admit it.

Once Adeone had left with Elantha, Tain said, "You've been quiet tonight," to his brother.

"Just tired."

"But you slept through all the excitement. How can you be?"

"You ride the length of the empire, then discover your secretary was treacherous and you'll find out. Are you pleased our nearcousins will be at Ceardlann?" asked Arkyn as images of Stuart's bloody back rose to the fore of his mind.

"Yes, but they're not Cal. Can you speak to father?"

"If I can. Cal does need time with his family as well."

"I know, but it felt odd," said Tain. "When Master Galdwin's letter arrived, Cal went really quiet; not just homesick, as he used to be, or thinking of his home. It was like he'd been told off. I don't think he expected to be back. I asked him what the letter said, but he wouldn't tell me. Father will think I'm imagining it or, worse, making it up, but I'm not, Arkyn, I'm really not."

"I believe you. Will you tell father I've gone to bed? He'll understand."

Tain was curled up on the chair, half-asleep, when Adeone re-entered his sitting room. He knelt by his younger son, saying quietly, "I've missed you."

Tain swallowed. "El—"

"Doesn't have the love of her father and she has so much love to give. I can't be everything she needs, but I can give her some hugs. Come and curl up with me. I'm proud of what you did today, though you put yourself at risk."

Tain smiled wryly. "I wasn't thinking. I'm sorry for making you worry. Can you tell me about Terasia? Arkyn said something about Stuart being treacherous."

Chapter 4
CONUNDRUMS
Hexadai, Week 45 – 6th Lufial, 20th Geryis 1211
Messenger Link

THE FOLLOWING MORNING, Adeone looked up as a chestnut flying horse appeared with a flash of green light. Recognising Inriri, Adeone accepted the magical messenger link and was faced with the smiling visage of an old friend.

"Ifor, how are you?"

The Deputy Governor of the Low Plains replied blithely, "Very well, Your Majesty, very well indeed. I hope, beyond hope, that you are also?"

"Well enough. I didn't expect to hear from you for some time."

"It's nothing disastrous, Sire, nothing at all disastrous. I had a mind to ask Your Majesty a question and thought I'd like to do it this way."

"Ask away, my friend, but tone down the flowery expressions. They're not good for my health."

"Your Majesty's wish is my command. My son, sir, is of an age to consider his future education. His mother and I have been talking with him and he'd like to train to be an advisor, in Oedran for preference."

Adeone paused. "It's not a decision for which you need my approval."

"It's one I hope you hold no objection to, Sire. It'd do the lad good to be in Oedran, as I was. We're hoping he'd stay with his cousins."

"I am presuming you've heard that there was a catastrophic fire there yesterday. Ah, I take it not. It may be best if you talk with Landis, Ifor, before making any decisions. Especially as there are already seven children in his care."

"I shall certainly do so at the earliest opportunity, Sire. Certainly I shall, if you hold no objection to Emrys being in Oedran."

"As I've said, you don't need my approval for his education."

"I realise that, Sire. I just hoped you wouldn't mind."

"Not as such. Is that all, Daioch?"

"Yes, Your Majesty, I should keep you from your work no longer."

"I wish you could. Give my regards to the Tuchlin and to… Nia."

The link broke, leaving Adeone cursing himself for feeling torn after so many years. Daioch had wanted other assurances in proposing to send his son to Oedran. Assurances that Adeone was unable to give; there was too much history there.

* * *

Landis entered the Inner Office an hour later. His frustration clear.

"What else could I do?" asked Adeone, defeated.

"He's my sister's oldest child! He's my nephew, Sire. To cold-shoulder him over incidents not of his making is unfair."

"I didn't—"

"No, you made it clear to Ifor you didn't want to know, sir. He can't help it if his wife wanted to marry you and you chose someone else."

"I think you need to be careful, Festus."

"No, sir, I'm fed up: fed up of not being able to mention my sister for fear of stirring old memories. It wasn't your fault, it wasn't hers that Ira won your heart but after so long it's not right to dwell on the pain it caused. I'm not denying I'd like to have seen you marry Nia, but you married Ira and had two wonderful sons with her. Feronia married also and her children are the world to her, I'll welcome them all into my home but I'd like to know when I present them at Court their careers there aren't over before they've begun because of our own youthful legacies."

Adeone sighed. "I broke your sister's heart, Festus. Why don't you hate me for it?"

"Because, deep down, I knew you'd never marry her, and she was looking for her heart to be broken. Father, Uncle Iris, Uncle Macaria were always very clear you couldn't marry a Landis. I don't know why, but they were adamant. Don't take out your guilt on Nia's children, please."

"I'll try not to, but the guilt is still there."

Landis collapsed onto a chair. "She made a good match with your help. Daioch will be Tuchlin. No-one doubts that."

"When is Lord Emrys arriving?"

"At the beginning of winter, Your Majesty, so he has chance to get

29

used to Oedran before he starts at the school. Julius is happy to share his room here with him, so there's no need to confuse matters with Ceardlann. If you'd rather he wasn't in the Palace, then I'll work something else out for them both, so Emrys isn't alone."

Adeone took a deep breath. "It would be a pleasure to have him here. I hope I get to meet him early in his stay, Festus, I really do. I'm just a fool at times."

Landis eyed him. "Isn't everyone? I'll tell Ifor that your apologies were profuse and that you had some weighty matters on your mind."

"Don't lie for me."

"Who said anything about lying? You're crowned; there's always something on your mind."

Adeone hesitated. "I'd be willing to bet there's more on yours today. Is everyone settled?"

"Yes, they seem to be. You do realise your kind invitation has meant that we've just put all our troublesome children together."

Adeone chuckled. "Is that any way to talk of your Prince?"

"No, but it's a sensible way to talk of my mischievous nearson. I went to see if Julius was all right before dinner. I found Tain curled into a chair, bright eyed, excited and Julius looking a little too innocent."

Adeone chuckled. "I look forward to discovering what that was about. Come in…"

Entering the office, Arkyn bowed to his father and spotted Lord Landis. "Uncle Festus, I'm sorry about Landis House. I didn't like to disturb you when you were getting settled."

Landis pushed himself to his feet. "Thank you for the consideration, sir, but I think we'd have coped. Are you too old for a hug now? We didn't get a chance with your arrival yesterday."

Arkyn shook his head, crossing to his nearfather. The months of absence fell away with the embrace. "Thank you for your letters; they helped."

"What letters?" asked Adeone, his eyes narrowing.

Arkyn smiled, dropping into a seat. "Amongst other things, explaining your angst about keeping your friendship with Percival secret."

"Ah. That. Thank you for helping dig me out of that hole, Festus."

"My pleasure, Sire." Landis was watching Arkyn carefully. "If you'll excuse me, sir, I'll go and see Lord Iris."

* * *

Once Landis had gone, Adeone said, "What's caught your thoughts?"

Arkyn hesitated. "Tain."

"You're not bearing tales, I take it. What about your brother?"

"I hope I'm not. I'm worried…" Arkyn explained everything Tain had told him about Scanlon saying that he, Tain, didn't have to be a justiciar, about Cal's return to Oedran, and his own suspicions that all wasn't well between Tain and Elantha.

Adeone heard him out. "Tain and El have never had the close relationship you have with her, but there was something last night I wondered about. I think he missed us and was jealous of her, but we can only change that by showing him that we don't love him any less because she's got a place in our hearts. I'll certainly be speaking to Master Galdwin, even if just to understand why he didn't inform me Cal was going home. Though I will give Cal some time with his family as well. As for not becoming justiciar, what do you suggest?"

"Me, father? Why?"

Adeone's lips twitched. "Your reputation for solving complex problems has just been forged in Terasia. Don't let it falter now."

Arkyn pulled a face. "I had help."

"No, you didn't. You got Iris to rewrite his reports. Come on, stop being modest. What do you suggest?"

Arkyn sighed. "Personally, I'd tell him the truth about uncle." Seeing his father's quizzical expression, he elaborated, "Tain's mischievous, but if you tell him why he's not to do something, he normally won't do it unless there's a very good reason or it won't harm or hurt anyone. Occasionally, he puts himself at risk, like yesterday, but he didn't make anyone else endanger themselves to get him out of trouble. He wanted to help, wanted to be of use... I think if you told him about uncle, that might work the same way."

Adeone sat forward. "What if it doesn't? What if he reacts badly?"

"We've lost mother, Ella, grandfather, Uncle Lachlan. I'd hope he'd want to help keep us all safe. I can't explain easily but I think his high spirits are sometimes, if not boredom, maybe, I don't know, lack of purpose in some measure. When he knows what he wants, I can't keep up with him."

Adeone chuckled. "That's true enough. So not only do you think we need to tell him about Scanlon, you also think we need to get him interested in law?"

Arkyn considered. Was that what he'd meant? He supposed it was. If Tain had a reason and a direction, would he take it? "Yes, Sire, I think so."

Adeone ruffled his hair. "We almost managed a whole conversation there without you using an honorific. So how do we get your mischievous brother interested in law?"

"Get him a tutor who can do it for us. He's never going to listen to me over this one."

Admitting it made sense, Adeone considered the traditional options: a judge from a family of standing, a Lord of Oedran who had gone through the Law School, a lecturer from the Law School, an ambitious lawyer. There were many options. The Court had been speculating that Lord Ryson would take the post, but Adeone was reluctant to appoint him, given the lord's previous friendship with Scanlon. He cursed to himself. There wasn't another Lord of Oedran who had the right credentials. An ambitious lawyer: more than he could buy such a man. He needed someone established in their career, who wouldn't be bribed, or easily corrupted, who didn't like Scanlon's regime. A judge was the more sensible option, if there was one who didn't conform to Scanlon's methods. As he whittled down the options, a face and name began to form in his mind: Judge James Tancred. He spoke the name aloud.

"You've always respected him, father. Could he manage this?"

"Yes. If anyone can get your scapegrace of a brother interested in law, it's James. He is a bit more visible in my life than Percival has been but he's on a level with him and Festus for me. He's got the right standing, he's got the experience in law, he's worked for us before and I trust him like no-one else in that profession."

"Then maybe he would be a good tutor, sir."

Adeone sat back. "What did I do without you?"

"Annoyed Uncle Festus more," replied Arkyn sagely. "I'm sure had he not got burning problems elsewhere, you still might."

"That was an atrocious joke."

"You're laughing."

Adeone dissolved into more obvious laughter, glad to be with his elder son, glad to be sharing the burdens he'd carried alone for so long.

Chapter 5
ADEONE'S MORNING
Septadai, Week 45 – 7th Lufial, 21st Geryis 1211
Inner Office

ADEONE LOOKED UP as Richardson announced Major Wynfeld the following day. Waving to a seat, the King crooked an expressive eyebrow.

Wynfeld sat down. "There's no evidence of foul play, sir. Nobody was around who shouldn't have been, nothing was out of place. If I had to take a guess, I'd say it started in the tack room. The stablehands have a small hearthstone there for heating the bran and also some of the waxes used in saddle care. It's not unusual for mistakes to happen."

"At Landis House?"

"Everyone has bad days, sir. His Lordship's grooms are all particular about his and his family's safety."

"Are you personally satisfied it was an accident, Major?"

Wynfeld considered. "Unless any evidence to the contrary is forthcoming, yes, sir. Would you like me to interview people again?"

Adeone shook his head. "If you don't have a feeling something's wrong, that's good enough for me. Did you manage to get to see your aunt yesterday?"

"For a short time, yes, sir. Thank you. I also paid Beaver a visit."

"How did he take your reappearance?"

Wynfeld caught the King's eye. "I believe he has mixed feelings, Sire. He was mindful of the restrictions for Jacobs' and Stuart's employment at the barracks. Though he was appreciative to hear he would be getting help in the form of a co-captain."

"I'm glad, though I do expect the issues of the last year to be resolved."

"He is aware of that, Your Majesty. I've asked him to investigate one of the clerks who seemed too keen to close files, thereby dictating whom we have been watching. I will have a report on that and the matters and attacks of the last year as requested. We'll keep our ears out but, if the fire was an accident, then at least it wasn't another case of treason."

"Small consolation to His Lordship, I expect," remarked Adeone.

* * *

Two hours later, Landis entered the Inner Office saying, "There's been a suggestion that my nearson might have had something to do with the fire." As Adeone stilled, he continued, "I've told the person who suggested it that if they repeat that to anyone, they'll be seeing a side of me they won't have long to remember."

Adeone snorted. "Thank you. Did Tain get a fit of mischief on him?"

"No. He was with the others from the moment he arrived until he spotted the fire. His guards were availing themselves of my hospitality in the kitchen and stableyard. They'd have seen him, or any of the children, if they'd been responsible."

"Good. Are you going to tell me who was blackening Tain's name?"

"No. They won't be doing so again. The house is a mess. I've had a stonemason round. It will need a rebuild—"

Adeone waved to the comfortable seating. "I'm not surprised. Did you lose much?"

"Everyday things. They rescued everything of value from the house and even managed to save all the old papers from our archive. Some paintings I've never seen before as well. Cornelia found one of Aelia's old sketchbooks she left at the house before moving to Black Hills and never reclaimed. It stirred a lot of memories."

Adeone smiled sadly. "I imagine it did. Is Cornelia all right?"

"Strained. Losing her father and her home – this year hasn't been easy

33

for her. Though we both agree we owe your bundle of trouble a reward."

"What sort of way is that to talk about your Prince?"

"A sensible one," replied Landis with a grin. "It could have been much worse without him. What do you think he'd like as a thank you?"

"Probably a life without lessons, but until then… I think he had his reward being involved with it all. He was still enthused by the experience over dinner last night. He had almost forgotten he hadn't seen myself or Arkyn for months. So, do you have an idea of how you'd like to rebuild?"

Landis nodded. "Yes. Relatively quickly, for one thing. I know you don't mind hosting us, but it's not that. I want most of the work done before winter sets in and slows it down again. If the structure at least can be up by then, the internal works can continue. I've a sketch plan drawn up, at least for a replacement wing."

"At least?" enquired Adeone, crooking an eyebrow.

"I'm tempted to extend the new house. Or rather wrap the now new house around the old new house, which is technically, or will be, the old house now that the old house is no longer there."

"You do it on purpose, don't you?" grouched Adeone. "What would you put in the extension?"

"My study and the library for a start. I'd need a lightwell, but that's not a problem. I'll make it into a small courtyard. My idea is that the replacement wing will mostly house my servant quarters and my steward, warden and so on. The old house was a hotchpotch of family and functional areas. If I move my study, the library and possibly the archives out of the ground floor of that wing – though, thinking about it, the archives are probably better nearer the steward – then I can get a better library and a larger study. I'll also gain more space for family rooms. We will likely need it as our brood grows, and I like to think Julius' when he's married."

Adeone smiled. "Isn't it traditional his brood would be brought up out of Oedran?"

"They're never going to Whitethorne," said Landis sharply. "I didn't send my lot there; he's not sending his."

"I know. This is all sounding surprisingly reasonable. I'm sure the masons could get a lot of it done before winter. Certainly all the footings, and that's the hardest part in winter."

"That and getting mortar to set."

"Let's hope it's a mild autumn then but, if you're here or at Ceardlann for longer, I really don't mind. Look, get the plans drawn up. Take whatever time you need."

Landis hesitated. "I do have duties—"

"I've just coped without you for a few months." Adeone's eyes sparkled.

"Ask Iris or Fairson to preside at Court for you until the Munewid. It's only a couple of days. It'll give you more time. If there's anything I need you for, I will let you know but take time to get everything in motion."

"The Petitionals—"

"Iris has managed to advise me before on the logistics for those. Festus, stop arguing. Your house has burnt down. It isn't exactly something you want to be dealing with."

"True." Landis ran a hand through his dark hair. "Thank you." He swore. "Tancred's mock trial?"

"Isn't for a week." After a moment, Adeone added, "I'd like you to escort Tain to that. With Fitz retired, I'd be happier."

"Then I shall, sir. A just reward for spotting the fire?"

Adeone snorted. "I don't think we should put it like that to him."

Chapter 6
TRIALS OF UNDERSTANDING
Alunadai, Week 47 – 15th Lufial, 8th Lufis 1211
Oedran – Administrative Quarter

A MOCK TRIAL might have seemed like a good plan to the adults in Prince Tain's life but, for him, it was a reminder of everything he didn't want to acknowledge was his future.

He left the Palace by Stable Gate with his nearfather and strolled to the Courthouse. The city always fascinated him. There was so much to watch, so many different faces from all over the empire. So much variety of life. He rarely walked around Oedran and so dawdled, asking about what he was seeing. The longer he took, the less of the mock trial he'd have to endure.

He grew quieter as the Courthouse loomed larger. His future lay within those forbidding and ornamental facades. Within that building was the heart of law in the vast Oedranian Empire. The symbolic and ancient Justice Hall was surrounded by seven others, administrating justice to the inhabitants of Oedran and, when the need called, the other provinces of the empire. The Law Library had held original decree and law documents since before Oedran had had an empire. His education on the laws of the empire had already begun, facts slipped into other lessons; just thinking about it made him bored.

Years before, his Great-uncle Lachlan had shown him around the building. He couldn't have been more than five at the time and it wasn't long before Lachlan died. Now, over six years on, the building held far more meaning. His duty lay within it and it would dictate his future. As the second son of the King, his duty, his inheritance was to assume the post of Justiciar of Oedran from the age of fifteen, taking on different provinces each year until by the age of twenty, he would be the Justiciar of the Empire. Continuing until the next second born prince turned fifteen. The idea terrified him.

* * *

The Keeper of the Justice Hall, superintendent of the Courthouse, greeted them by the rear door. He smiled at Tain and bowed.

"Has Your Highness come to keep us on our toes?"

Tain smiled back. "Not yet, Keeper. Do you think I could manage it?"

"From everything I've heard, I'm sure Your Highness could. It would do us good as well."

"Why?"

"Lord Scanlon is often busy in the empire, sir, so we need someone to keep us in order," answered the Keeper. "Which court is Your Highness visiting today?"

Landis said, "Judge Tancred has a mock trial set up in Court Six."

"That's James for you. Come on then, I'll see you settled."

Landis shook his head. "The King would prefer it, Keeper, if no-one realises His Highness is there. Would you have somewhere for the guards? I'll take care of everything else."

"Of course. Your Highness, maybe you'd care to come and have some refreshments when the 'court' adjourns or is concluded?"

Tain nodded enthusiastically. "Thank you, Keeper, I'd like that."

* * *

Tancred's eyes hardly flickered as they entered the courtroom. The only other person to notice their entry was a first-year student who was watching the mock trial. Landis glared at him as he went to rise and the young man settled back in his seat.

Tain sat beside him, grinning. "Tristan, what are you doing here?" he asked in a whisper.

"Seeing what I'm in for next year, sir."

"I'm suffering the same."

Tristan Richardson chuckled to himself. Son of Adeone's administrator he'd met Tain several times over the years.

Landis took out a piece of paper from his belt pouch and a pencil and leaned carefully on the writing slope in front of him. Completely easy with the fact that Tristan was sitting next to Tain. He trusted the young man and Tain was happy in his company.

The 'trial' was well underway. The small courtroom was packed with men. Twenty students were dotted around the scene, playing everything

36

from lawyers to witnesses to the accused. Faces showed worry, anticipation, boredom and excitement. Some were making notes, others were lazing disinterestedly in their seats. The student playing the accused was finding it amusing. He had some sort of briefing in front of him and was reading it, as his fellows argued his case.

From the simple wooden bar and desk, Tancred was tolerantly saying to one student, "Peter, I have faith you can do this if you conquer your nerves. Start again. Talk to me; ignore everyone else."

Tain watched as the lad, who was about seventeen, took a breath and fixed his attention on the judge. He managed to get through to the end of his witness statement without stuttering too much. He found his place and sat down with a sigh. Momentarily, he caught Tain's eye before looking away.

Tain relaxed; he hadn't been recognised. Glancing away, he saw his nearfather was hunched over his notes. He almost laughed. Wasn't it he who was meant to be learning something? Then, he saw the *notes* that his nearfather was making. The sketch of the court scene was unexpected, as were the doodles that now filled the page.

Landis sensed the glance. He whispered, "Concentrates my mind."

Tain suppressed a giggle. "I'll tell father. Do you do this in official meetings?"

"Yes, and, if you tell your father, I'll tickle you until you can't speak."

Half an hour later, the mock trial ended. The accused had stood his ground, thrown in comments to confuse matters, and, Tain was sure, hadn't followed the briefing, as he'd caught a warning tone in Tancred's eye and a grin on the student's face.

Tancred asked, "For extra points, what would the sentence for the crime be?" The judge's gaze swept around the court. "Someone here knows? You cannot *all* have forgotten."

Before he could stop himself, Tain said, "Three months for the first offence, six for the second and for three or more up to a year on each conviction: sentenced in either aluna-months for the alunan, or cisluna-months for the cisan. Never more than a year – unless violence has been used: in that case up to a year and six months."

Landis put his head in his hands, murmuring, "What happened to remaining hidden, sir?"

Loud enough for all to hear, one student said snidely, "His Highness *obviously* knows the law better than *us*. Why *are* we here?"

"Apologise to our Prince immediately, Lord Kenelm, or leave this court," instructed Tancred.

"My most *humble* apologies, *Your Highness*," huffed Kenelm Para.

"They are accepted, my lord," replied Tain pleasantly.

Kenelm's classmates were hiding their smirks. The heir of a Lord of Oedran, he had thrown his weight around once too often.

Tancred turned to Tain. "Your Highness, my students are rather tongue-tied today. What would the sentence be in *this* case? The defendant was under age at the time of the offence and the mitigating factor was accepted."

Tain thought. His lessons had not been so specific. Ewall had told him to read the law and memorise the sentences. There was surely something else. He bit his lip. Tancred was looking at him encouragingly and, after Kenelm's snideness, he didn't want to get this wrong. There'd been something in the law about mitigating factors: why would it be there unless it had a bearing and why would Judge Tancred have highlighted it to him unless it changed something?

"Would the sentence be three months, Your Honour? Could it be classed as a first offence?"

Tancred smiled. "Yes, sir, it could – and that is the sentence I would hand down – full marks. It would be three months; as the defendant is born under Cisluna, that would be nine weeks. A sentence I am contemplating giving young Payton for deviating from his script."

The accused grinned. "Your Honour has always maintained we should expect the unexpected in court, sir."

Tancred's lips twitched. "True." He caught Tain's eye. "As Lord Kenelm observed, Your Highness *is* here. Would you prefer to sit at the bar? It will give the next 'trial' an edge for my students and will certainly have been unexpected."

Tain looked to Landis for permission. His nearfather pushed himself to his feet by way of an answer, accompanying him to the bar, before taking up a stance behind him until invited to sit by the judge.

The rest of the afternoon passed off pleasantly. Tain found he matched the students when it came to background knowledge. The nervous student gradually overcame some of his nerves and his stutter became less noticeable. Payton played a defence lawyer and became far more serious. Kenelm, however, lounged in his seat, self-satisfied, amused and sneering. Tancred wrote 'F' at the side of his name and appended a few notes in shorthand. When the trial ended, he dismissed the students before saying,

"I hope you found that interesting, Your Highness."

"Yes, thank you, Your Honour. Why did you fail Lord Kenelm?"

"Anyone that takes the practice of law as a joke should not be practising it. I am not going to favour Lord Kenelm because he is heir to a Lordship of Oedran, and I will make that clear to Lord Para."

"So, would you fail me then?" enquired Tain, intrigued.

"I do not think I would ever have to, sir – you have the look of Prince Lachlan in those eyes. He was a brilliant justiciar. You will go far, sir."

Mischievously, Tain said, "Flattery gets you nowhere, Your Honour."

"That was not flattery, sir. I am sure His Lordship will tell you I am pathologically honest."

Landis chuckled. "I certainly can, James. His Majesty would like a word, when you get a chance."

Tancred eyed him, half amused. "Then, if Your Highness can excuse me, I have an appointment with the King."

Tain's stomach inexplicably knotted. "By all means, Your Honour."

The judge bowed and left.

"Shall we go and see what the Keeper has decided you'd like in the way of refreshments?" asked Landis.

Tain nodded. "What did he mean about uncle and keeping them in order?"

"It was a light-hearted reference to the fact your uncle spends more time out of Oedran than in it, sir – nothing to worry about."

"Surely, though, he should be here as well? This is the heart of the empire. Such a high official should be here, shouldn't they?"

Landis ruffled Tain's hair. "Maybe your uncle has wandering feet."

* * *

As they re-entered the Palace by Stable Gate, Landis grinned at his nearson. "Shall we race, sir?"

Tain shook his head. "I wouldn't want to do you an injury, but can we go through the gardens?"

"Are you asking me that to distract me from the cheekiness?"

"Yes. I could tell father you doodle in meetings."

"I could still tickle you," said Landis, turning down the path to the gardens.

"You'd have to catch me first."

"Which puts us neatly back at the beginning of this conversation," muttered Landis dryly.

* * *

The King's Administrator heard them coming before he saw them. The Audience Chamber echoed with their footsteps and Prince Tain's chatter. As they entered the Outer Office, he pushed himself to his feet. Landis rarely waited to be announced. As the King's Chief Advisor and closest friend, he had certain privileges, but as the holder of a King's Token he didn't have to tell anyone why he needed to see the King. As the King's Defender, he didn't even have to check if he was busy. To deny Landis entry, to stop him from seeing the King, was treason.

Even as he straightened up from his slight bow on Tain's entry, Richardson said, "Go on through, sirs, but His Honour is still there."

Tain grinned. "Thank you. Tristan was at the trial."

"I hope he learned something, sir. Would Your Highness like announcing?"

Tain shook his head. "I'm taking lessons off my nearfather."

Adeone and Tancred were sitting by the fireplace in the Inner Office, a drink apiece, looking completely at ease.

Seeing Tain was with Landis, Tancred rose. "If you can excuse me, Your Majesty, I have some reports to write on my students for their next tutor and would not intrude on your time with your family."

Adeone smiled. "I'll take that as an acceptance. Thank you. I know Uncle Lachlan would have been pleased. I'll see you on the first day of 1212, if not before." As the judge left, Adeone eyed his son. "I thought you didn't want to be noticed. James told me you spectacularly highlighted your presence."

Tain shuffled his feet. "I got carried away, sir. I knew the answer."

Adeone chuckled. "Between us, I'd have done the same. Festus, thank you. We won't keep you. You must have so much still to sort out. Come and sit down, Tain."

Tain sat with a sense of foreboding. There was something in his father's manner, a certain gravitas that suggested something was brewing. He watched his nearfather leave and then nervously gazed at his father as he sat opposite him.

Adeone said, "Arkyn tells me you find law boring and don't wish to be Justiciar."

Tain bit his lip. "He shouldn't have told you, sir."

"He didn't do it with malicious intent. I needed to know the rest of what you told him. There are things I've never told you because you were too young. You still are a bit for some of it, but we think that you need to know. Tain, we *need* you to become Justiciar. Not because it's your inheritance, others have avoided it in the past, but because if you *don't* your uncle will wreck the empire. He is already trying to do so in one way or another. Everything that our ancestors built, he is trying to destroy."

Tain frowned. His eyes flicked away, glancing over towards his father's desk. "Why would he though?"

"Greed, jealousy, simple psychopathic tendencies; the honest answer is we don't know; however, you are one of the few people who can stop him in the near future. You and *only* you could arrest him for the numerous times he's committed a crime."

"Why can't you order his arrest?" enquired Tain, examining his father's strained and saddened face, confused.

Adeone saw the way his son was watching him. The confusion was understandable. In Tain's eyes, he was all-powerful. "I would need a full justiciar to try him, and he is my brother – whatever else I might think about him as a person, we are born of the same parents."

"What has he done?"

Adeone considered him, remembering Arkyn's advice. "Your uncle has tried on numerous occasions to kill all of us. That is why I have you live at Ceardlann. He can't gain entry there. His laws are becoming more barbarous, his sentences longer. He is trying to engineer an uprising. It is taking all my ingenuity to prevent it."

Pensive, Tain enquired, "You still won't arrest him?"

"No. Would you arrest Arkyn if your places were switched? I might not be close to Scanlon, but he is still my brother. Then, of course, there is the problem that he manipulates others into doing his bidding. *Proving* it is *Scanlon* behind something is quite difficult when you have to go up several rungs of the ladder before anyone even knows he is involved, and proof is crucial to prevent civil war. If we act without it, we are no better than he is; people will lose trust and see us as the enemy. They will pick sides, see him as the wronged party. He's personable when he wants to be, can seem genial and beneficent when it suits him, but he is also vindictive. He hides that side of himself at my Courts, where he can find followers, especially in the empire."

Tain was still thinking. "Is this why he's hardly ever in Oedran?"

"It's one reason. Our strained relationship is another."

"What makes you think I could stop him though, father?"

Adeone smiled. "I don't think you can yet, but give it eight years and I hope you'll be a formidable Justiciar of the Empire."

Tain put his head on one side. "I can't imagine that, but I'll try my hardest, father."

"Thank you. Remember one thing, don't lose the laughter."

"I won't. Well, if Cal's around I won't."

Adeone sat back. "Yes, your brother and Uncle Festus told me he's been in Oedran. I'll have to see Master Galdwin once more, won't I? What do you—" he broke off as his administrator entered to say Advisor Chanter was waiting to see the King about the up-and-coming Petitionals. Adeone asked him to give them a couple of moments.

When the door closed behind Richardson, Adeone said, "No rest for me today. Tain, don't worry, everything will come right. We don't deal in tragedies; not whilst we can still laugh. Now, give your father a hug and go and tease your brother."

Chapter 7

DECISIONS AND DOUBTS
Afternoon
Administrative Quarter – Law School

HAVING COLLECTED HIS NOTES from Richardson, Judge Tancred strolled through the Palace. He'd trod the corridors many times over the years, but their gilt and carvings were far from commonplace to him. The worn stairs tramped by centuries of occupants spoke to him of the history surrounding him and the future yet to come. His well-heeled shoes tapped their practical way from the King's Corridor to Stable Gate without haste. Runners dodged by him, couriers on their more sober feet stepped aside, long-serving guards smiled and nodded, some even saluted. He stopped for a word with a couple – men whom he had passed the time of day with waiting on one prince's time or another. He could have left by various exits but he, like many, used Stable Gate for preference. Its wide gates stood ajar at all hours with guards in crisp tabards making sure no-one simply wandered in. His green judge's robes were passport enough to see him through with no question, but woe betide any who tried to dodge through without a badge, buckle, hat, tabard or robe that granted entry. Though, if they knew who you were, it helped. Every day at least one chancer attempted to slip past them, but even if the guards didn't hoick them back, the grooms would trip them up.

The paved city streets were reassuring after the unsettling audience with Adeone. The solid, bone aching familiarity of the street grounded him in a way the golden corridors couldn't. He'd grown up in Oedran, running around streets with his feet bound in rags instead of sturdy shoes.

A short way from the Palace and Courthouse, the symmetrical forbidding and foreboding façade of the Law School discouraged idle investigation. Walking up the steps, he recalled how scared he had been the first time he entered. The other students had pointed and jostled, laughing at his threadbare breeches and tunic. Now a student hastily held the door open for him. He smiled and thanked the young man by name. It didn't seem to reassure him.

Wandering down the utilitarian corridor, he glanced automatically into the lecture rooms when the doors stood open. If there was no lecture, students were gathered revising or talking. None were being raucous. They were probably all too shattered. The finals for the year would end on Pentadai and then it would be a different matter.

Entering a small outer office, he smiled at the scribe, requesting a word with Lord Ryson.

Moments later, the red-haired Lord of Oedran, Provost of the Law School, was saying, "James, you're just the person I need. I hear you had a visitor at your mock-trial."

"I did, my lord. Three to be precise: Prince Tain, Lord Landis and Tristan Richardson. I was intrigued by young Tristan's presence. He has obviously inherited his father's acumen."

Ryson chuckled. "So it seems. How was His Highness?"

"Very well. It is, in a manner of speaking, on his behalf that I am here. His Majesty has requested that I take the post of tutor to His Highness."

"An erudite choice," remarked Ryson non-committedly. Had the judge even heard the rumours that had placed him, Ryson, as that tutor?

"I cannot speak as to the erudition of His Majesty's choice, only state how flattered I am," replied Tancred. "I am aware this will cause issues for timetabling, as I need to tender my resignation."

Ryson shrugged. "I'll have to cope. I am not surprised that His Majesty has picked you, Judge. You've been close to the FitzAlcis for years. If you need anything, if I can help in any way, do please ask."

"Thank you. I appreciate the offer, my lord. I will write up reports on each of my students for their next tutor and I will pass over the marks from the mock trial today to Your Lordship's secretary. Payton has merit. I should, perhaps, warn you that I have been obliged to fail Lord Kenelm. His attitude was rather unfortunate: first in his lack of respect for the process and court, and, secondly, for his snide comment to His Highness. Anyone of his future stature, who cannot show common courtesy to the FitzAlcis in public, should learn it is not acceptable."

"His knowledge of law?"

"Woeful and lacking. I have seen other heirs pass through the school." He smiled wryly as Ryson crooked an eyebrow. "None of whom, including Your Lordship, took the experience as a joke. I am sorry to say Lord Kenelm showed he expected no repercussions for his attitude. I did have His Lordship apologise to His Highness—"

"In open court?" enquired Ryson, troubled.

"Yes, my lord. The comment was made in open court. I, therefore, considered it more than appropriate for the apology to be public. I hope that is understandable."

"Yes, in that case, I agree."

"Thank you. I now consider the matter closed as Lord Kenelm's tutor; however, due to his lack of knowledge and attitude toward the exam, I still am unable to pass him."

"That is your prerogative," replied Ryson. The political upheaval caused by Tancred's decision would be immense. He'd certainly receive pressure from Lord Para, but he suspected not from the King who respected the judge. The phrase '*be thankful for small mercies*' sprang to mind. "When do you start to teach His Highness?"

"On the Munewid. I will clear my office here and have reports for you by then. I should let you continue."

"Thank you. Dinner one evening?"

"That would be an honour, my lord."

* * *

Tancred walked home. The King's proposal had been unexpected and disquieting. He had thought such times were behind him. Seeing the King occasionally was very different from being a member of his staff. The lines had been redrawn. Had he been right to accept, right to once more become visible in a way he hadn't been since Prince Lachlan's death?

He entered his house and looked around its welcoming simplicity, as though he was seeing it again for the first time. The entrance hall was dim, dark wood and velvet curtains kept out the light, but he liked its wooden panelled simplicity, with its square shape and unassuming stairs. On his right, next to the door to the drawing room, a marble-topped sideboard held a vase of flowers. He should have bought more on his way home. His wife loved the simple flowers that grew in the crevices of the city and in the parks. She wasn't one for grand displays of lilies or roses, instead late daffodils brightened the hall. Seeing them made him smile.

He asked his footman if there had been any messages, as though he'd been doing it all his life. On hearing there were none, he simply nodded in dismissal. There would be time to talk with John another day.

Taking a deep breath, he entered the drawing room. His wife was sewing a small dress together. Somewhere one of their acquaintances was obviously expecting. Greeting her with a peck on the cheek, he sank into his chair, feeling the weight of the day heavy on his shoulders but not on his heart. He watched Bets for several moments. She still greeted him with a contented and private smile even after so many years. As he watched her, he saw again those years of their lives as images of the ages: running around the same streets, arguing like strangers and then like siblings, listening to her sister's impassioned voice, listening to the world of injustice around him and then noticing Bets standing quietly by, her gaze accusing him of heartlessness and being right. A loaf, a simple thing, had made him lose reason and there was her sister making him see, making him face his inner rage and he had known in that moment, as in no other, that rage was not who he was, it was not who she was. Later they talked. Later her sister died and Bets came to him to talk, to mourn, to be with the one person she felt had known her sister's voice. Soon, there had been no other for either of them. He'd looked, dreamed but she knew his soul and he knew hers.

The years passed, marriage happened, rebellion came with destruction in its wake. He had told her to leave. She and their son did not need the whispers, the accusations. He tried, how he had tried, to support them. Qualified but failing. His eyes welled at the memory. She had never lost faith in him and he had just risked the life they had again.

"Don't think on it," came her quiet reproval.

Could she read his mind, his memories, his troubled soul? They had been part of each other's lives for so many years that it would not surprise him if she could. She had seen his puzzlement.

"It's the only thing that brings tears. I'm here. I came back when I could."

He swallowed. That was true, but those years of loneliness ate away at his heart. She would think him a fool. He had survived so much before.

"I saw the King earlier."

"I'm glad he's home. Do you want to invite him to dinner? I don't mind."

"Not immediately, though at some point. His Majesty offered me the position of tutor to Prince Tain."

"What? That's…" She caught his eye. "You've accepted." It wasn't a question.

He sighed. "When His Majesty offers you a post, it is only polite to accept." He saw the flicker of fear in her eyes. "I did yield to His Majesty's persuasion."

"But… if you're on his staff, you… Did you tell him?"

"No. There was no opportunity that I thought was appropriate. Prince Lachlan may well have told him before. I can only imagine he did and that the King does not wish to raise the matter with me."

She put her sewing aside. "James, you must check he knows. If he's the man you've always believed he is, there is no reason to fear, surely?"

Tancred pushed himself to his feet, crossed to a sideboard and poured himself a rare whiskey. Resuming his place, he considered what to say. "I believe His Majesty to be a good man, to be a fair man, to be a kind one. I do not know if he could be impartial in this and that worries me, Bets. I do not wish to lose his regard."

"Won't keeping secrets from him be worse?" enquired his wife.

"Yes, but then there are many that I have kept during my time working for Prince Lachlan and whilst advising His Majesty. I would not tarnish his memories unnecessarily."

"It is your decision but, James, I would try to find a time to tell him. He respects you. I wouldn't like to see either of you hurt by something so far in the past."

"Who now can speak of it but us, Bets? Who would even think it worthy of notice? Have I not made my own life?"

She sighed. "Yes. Maybe no-one will speak of it but as you've just agreed to teach Prince Tain, there are likely others who will feel jealous or aggrieved."

He took another sip of whiskey and lapsed into the silence he was so good at. Did he want to face the jealousies of his colleagues? Did he want to carry the burden of the past to an unknown future? Prince Tain would be his pupil for three years, and it was likely he'd be a mentor for a few more after that. True, Lord Scanlon had ignored Judge Fairson from the moment he had taken the Justiciar's Oath in the Justice Hall, but not all princes treated their tutors with such little regard

Chapter 8
PASSING COMMENTS
Hexadai, Week 48 – 27th Lufial, 20th Lufis 1211
Law School – Provost's Office

TWO DAYS BEFORE THE MUNEWID, with reports and marks having been given to the students, Lord Ryson looked up as his secretary announced Lord Para. Ryson smiled grimly at his peer. Para's long face didn't speak of contentment. Presumably he hadn't got any joy from the King.

"What can I do for you?" asked Ryson after the door closed.

"Pass my son."

Direct, to the point and as expected. "I'm sorry, Para, but the rules are quite clear. Lord Kenelm has failed his second year. The mock trial was an exam. Unusual though it was, it tested the knowledge and deportment of our students. His Honour felt your son did not merit a pass. I cannot change that as I wasn't present."

"No. We all know who was though."

"Yes. I've heard several accounts of what occurred—"

"My son apologised to His Highness!"

"I wasn't referring to that incident. I was referring to the fact that Kenelm lounged in his seat, sneering at proceedings. The school's rules are clear. Proper deportment is expected at all times. Lord Kenelm is not someone who can claim ignorance of etiquette—"

Para leaned heavily on Ryson's desk. "I could tell the world about your dirty little secrets. I can't think the King would like to know of your proclivities."

"His Majesty has been aware of my *proclivities* since one of my lovers was blackmailed over our relationship some years ago. I don't think you'll get any joy by trying to extort cooperation, Para. I'm a lawyer. I'll happily have you in court for it."

"I'd never be convicted," spat Para.

Ryson shrugged. "No, but your reputation would be ruined. What you have forgotten in your haste to bully me is that I have nothing to lose. Every other Lord of Oedran has more standing than I do, in one camp or another. None of the FitzAlcis trust me. That won't change even were I able to ignore the school's rules and pass your wastrel son. I have no family left for you or anyone else to threaten. Caving into your demands won't buy me favour with the King – quite the reverse – and I don't ever want favour from Lord Scanlon—"

"You were stupid to turn your back on him."

"That is a matter of opinion. Are you so enamoured of his methods?"

"They're needed. Everyone is becoming far too soft. King Altarius would have ordered you to pass my son."

Amused, Ryson said, "Were you that close to His Late Majesty? I never witnessed it. Judge Tancred, on the other hand, had the ear of Prince Lachlan and, from what I witnessed, was respected by King Altarius. Ah, yes, there's the door. Do use it."

The slam of wood reverberated around the room. Ryson smiled, contented.

* * *

Para entered the Palace chuntering to himself. What was the point of being a Lord of Oedran if a cisan-born judge could get the better of you? He entered Court. There was only one route left open to him now to save face. Did he want to take it? Owing favours was far more troublesome than misusing people's secrets. He wandered through Court oblivious of everything. Eventually, he found his son in a private room drinking with Chander Teran. Two moments later, father and son were alone.

"Getting drunk won't help!"

"I leave that to Julius," retorted Kenelm. "So?"

Para poured himself a drink from the jugs on a sideboard, cursing. "The King won't order Ryson and Ryson won't change the mark. Were you really lounging and sneering?"

Kenelm hesitated. "It was so humiliating, father. We were playing parts as though we were little kids. Tain's a child, yet he was sitting at the bar—"

"Prince Tain will be fifteen in three years! He'll be the Justiciar of Oedran and you'd be wise to remember that and not risk our family's fortunes. We need to be careful—"

"Do we? Our side has strength. What has the other but weaklings?"

"The crown, the empire and the army. Not to mention, the General, most governors and apparently some important judges. You also know more than is good for you." Para slammed his goblet down, wine fountaining like blood against his white tunic. "Forget it all." Para cursed. He'd have to change before he went anywhere else. There were spare tunics at the Palace but they didn't have the careful tailoring of his own.

"I'm not telling anyone," remonstrated Kenelm. "Lord Scanlon might have more influence than his absences suggest, but he doesn't have people where he needs them. It's fine having people at Court but who controls who's here?"

"Hmm, let me think, the FitzAlcis?"

Languidly sipping his wine, Kenelm said, "Presiding lords, the Steward, even the guards to some extent. If the guards aren't on our side, we're in trouble."

Para's eyes narrowed. "If you don't pass your exams, *you're* in trouble. You know full well why he wanted you at the Law School. Do you want to explain?"

"Not particularly. Look, the Law School is useless. You don't need lawyers. You need judges."

"Yes, and, for that, we need more lawyers to promote."

"So, buy them," retorted his son, dark eyes flashing. "I don't see why I must make an impression to get us more men on side. It'll probably do the opposite. In three years, people won't stand on principles. They didn't when Lord Scanlon took over. They cowered and converted to his methods. To keep their jobs, they'll do the same for Tain and I won't crawl to him. He's not going to forget the mock trial. It'll always be between us—"

"Ah, you've realised! Your actions now matter."

"Yeah. Well. The law's boring. Maybe the army would be better."

"No," snapped his father. "We're putting Chander into the next available captaincy we can. If Lord Scanlon can't persuade Ryson and you move to the Advisors' School, you will have to get your head down. We might be able to persuade the Dean to put you in at second year but that's all."

"Fine. Though the first might be better. I can spy on Julius and Irvin then."

"Leave the Iris family alone," said Para. "Others are working on them."

Kenelm leaned forward. "Who?"

"Never you mind. Now, stop idling in here. Get working through Court. Your sister is doing a good job even without knowing why. Don't let her get the better of you."

Kenelm smirked. "She won't. When's His Greatness due back in Oedran?"

"Soon," replied his father dismissively.

Chapter 9
CROSSING A LINE

As THE FIRST DAY OF 1212 dawned, most people were recovering from the Munewid festivities the night before, or deep in slumber. Judge Tancred presented himself at the Outer Office and asked for an audience with the King. Richardson announced him almost immediately. The judge entered the Inner Office soberly and, seeing his mood, Adeone requested Advisor Rayburn leave. Tancred apologised as the military advisor departed.

Adeone relaxed when the door closed. "Why so serious, James?"

"I am about to disappoint Your Majesty."

Adeone got up from his chair. "I doubt that. Come and have a drink and tell me why you *think* you're about to disappoint me."

Tancred sighed; sometimes the King could be *too* kind. Sitting down, he accepted a brandy. "Your Majesty may have to find someone else to teach His Highness – at least to begin with. The gentleman who was to take over my duties at the Law School has died. Lord Ryson was not going to tell me. My son did so. They can find someone else for most of the lectures. My son is taking over some, but His Lordship is finding it difficult to locate a lecturer for historical law."

The King said, "You are, perhaps, feeling that your skills would be better used at the Law School, instead of teaching your future Justiciar?"

Unable to read Adeone's mood, Tancred was honest. "Not exactly, Sire. I feel that I have left them with few options. The other reason is rather more personal; it is to do with Ceardlann. I... It is hard to explain. You were kind enough not to rescind my permission to visit the Rex Dallin on Prince Lachlan's death – but the last time I spoke to him I promised I would not enter the valley again after scattering his ashes. I would prefer it if the last time I went was the one where I said goodbye to him. I cannot teach Prince Tain here in Oedran. I should have realised I would have to go to the Rex Dallin before today, but I did not, Sire. I am truly sorry for the upset this is going to cause."

Adeone steepled his fingers, thinking. After a few moments, he said, "As I want you to teach my son, I don't accept your resignation. Will you see if we can make it work? I'm sure Tain will like to hear he might have to come to Oedran more often and not have his tutor living in the same house."

Startled by Adeone's certainty, Tancred enquired, "Is Your Majesty sure we can make this work? I would have thought it awkward."

Adeone smiled. "Are you willing to try? There may be advantages.

You could still preside in courts as well as teach at the Law School."

"I shall try, if Your Majesty is sure."

"I am. You are the tutor my son needs."

"Then how can I deny my King?"

Adeone crooked an eyebrow. "Prince Arkyn or Lord Landis would say a 'no' would suffice. Thank you for yielding to persuasion. I'm finding it hard to trust people with my sons' welfare."

"I could do no other, Sire."

"James, I might have had to be forthright with Lord Para, but I don't need you to highlight my position."

Tancred chuckled. "My apologies, sir." He sobered. "I presume His Lordship was unhappy with my decision at the mock trial."

"You could say that. He marched in here in high dudgeon. I told him I had no rights over whom the school took or whom it chose to fail. He stormed out in even higher dudgeon and, I believe, is planning to talk to Lord Scanlon. Though, I think, Kenelm has said he won't continue with his law education with a failed year."

Tancred nodded. "Even if Lord Scanlon told me to pass Lord Kenelm I would refuse; he would make the worst sort of lawyer, Sire. I will not pass someone merely because he is the heir to an Oedranian Lordship."

"Good. I don't want mollycoddled lords. I want ones who can think. It might prove a challenge in itself. Their entitlement is extraordinary. I spend more time than I like to think about sorting out their squabbles or pandering to their prejudices."

Lips twitching, Tancred said, "I ought not to keep you from your work, Sire. I fear I have already caused complete confusion."

"It keeps Richardson busy. You know you're always welcome. In fact…" Adeone got up and rang for his administrator and requested the scroll of King's Token holders.

When Richardson returned, Adeone wrote Tancred's name on a token and sealed the small scroll with gold wax before appending the judge's name to the master scroll. It was only the third the King had issued in seven years. The other two had been gifts of King Altarius and never rescinded.

"This should make your life easier, James. Keep it safe. You're aware my office can check it and that, if you produce it, they *must* let you in to see me. That, I think, is all you have to be *told*. After all, you know the laws governing their use."

Astounded, Tancred accepted the token. Speechless, he studied the King's face.

Adeone chuckled. "I mean everything it implies and am wondering what has taken me so long to give you one. Prince Tain will be in Oedran for a couple more weeks. After the Petitionals have finished in two days' time, I will give thought to how we can overcome the issue of Ceardlann."

Tancred left, still stunned. Adeone handed Richardson the master scroll, enjoying the memory of Tancred's face. No matter how long the judge would live, he'd never become used to the fact that *the King* accepted him as a friend.

* * *

Unthinking of where he was going, Tancred walked aimlessly through the Palace. Bemused by events, he let his feet decide the route. A guard held a door open for him and he found himself in the sunshine at the western end of the palace. The air, carrying the vying scents of city and garden, helped revive him. Shaking his head to clear the preoccupation, he saw he was in a relatively private area of the grounds, between the front of the Privy Wing – housing the FitzAlcis' private apartments – and the palace wall. He'd left the building by the path that led to the Privy Gate. He would have to walk through the grounds – the Privy Gate was not one he would use unless accompanying the FitzAlcis. He doubted the guards would even let him. No, that was wrong. With a King's Token they would. He glanced up at the windows of the Inner Office, then at the tightly furled scroll in his hand. There was so much meaning in something so fragile and small.

Prince Lachlan had taken him to see Adeone when the King was barely a week old. Lachlan had been proud of Adeone, proud and relieved that his brother had a direct heir again. Adeone had been a cheerful baby and a lively child until he was nine.

All too clearly, Tancred recalled Prince Lachlan summoning him that fateful day. Queen Eliza had died in childbirth. King Altarius had collapsed. Prince Lachlan as Regent was asking him, Tancred, to take the news to Ceardlann. To take the news his mother had died to a child whose world shattered.

The Comptroller had broken the news to Adeone, but Tancred had not left. He had stayed, trying to help, though, for years, he felt he had failed. Adeone had sunk into a depression, and it had been others who had turned the then Prince's mind away from the bereavement. After a time, Tancred had realised others were better placed to help and so he had left for Oedran.

The mood in the city had been sombre for many months. Eliza had been a merchant's daughter and had felt that much closer because of it. King Altarius was distraught and Prince Lachlan had taken so much on himself that his private life fell to pieces.

Feeling inadequate, all Tancred could do was watch. He had suffered loss and bereavement within his own life and knew how it could affect people; the knowledge – and, in some part, empathy – had been marred by the feeling Adeone shouldn't have been left at Ceardlann to suffer it alone. He'd visited on a couple of occasions to try to let the young Prince know he wasn't forgotten.

Eventually, Altarius had let Adeone return to Oedran to meet his brother, Scanlon, and to resume his life and lessons, but the joy had left Adeone. Over the following months and years, he would often seek out Prince Lachlan in the evenings. Tancred, as a friend – and as a member of Prince Lachlan's staff, and then a judge – was often there. It was in Lachlan's chambers they had talked and debated, turning the reticence of youth and age into understanding and friendship. The love of life re-entered Adeone; his mischievous streak carefully encouraged by Prince Lachlan. Even after Adeone became friends with Landis, he would spend evenings with his uncle, preferring his company to many of his own age.

Since Adeone had become King, Tancred had advised him many times when specifics rather than generalisations were required. That should have been Lord Scanlon's job, but, as he was never in Oedran, someone had had to do it. Would Adeone have consulted Scanlon even had he been there? Tancred did not know. There was no love lost between the brothers. Had resentment been born when Queen Eliza died? Maybe. Whatever the start of the problem, it was now Lord Scanlon who inflamed it.

Did Prince Tain know of the situation? Tancred would have to ask. It would not do for him to let slip that the Justiciar wanted to murder the Prince if Tain didn't already know.

* * *

He was still contemplating the issue when Tain and Elantha tore around the corner. He bowed slightly as Tain slowed up.

"Good afternoon, Your Honour," said the Prince carefully.

"Happy Birthday, Your Highness."

Tain grinned. "Thank you. I thought you were going to tell me off for not having a guard."

Tancred smiled. "I am only going to be teaching Your Highness the law. Common sense could be considered your own affair. Though now you mention it, where have you left your guard? It would be wise not to stray too far."

Tain shuffled his feet. "I know, but he was too slow to keep up. He'll be annoyed with me now."

Tancred was troubled. "I am sure he is concerned solely for Your Highness' safety."

Panting, the guard appeared and spotted Tain. "You *mustn't* run off! The trouble—"

Tancred cut across him. "Guard, modify your tone! You do not use

52

the word *must* to princes.”

“I’m afraid, *sir*, I have my orders directly from the King.”

Tancred, hands clasped behind his back, considered the guard. “Your Highness, if you have no objection, I would speak with your guard alone.”

Tain smiled. “None whatsoever, Your Honour.”

“If you could wait within sight, sir, I can accompany you to your destination in a moment, if you wish me to.”

Playing an impeccably well-behaved prince, Tain said, “Certainly, Judge.”

Once Tain and Elantha moved away, the judge eyed the guard. “I am sure the King would have been interested to see and hear the manner in which you correct His Highness’ spirit.”

“His Majesty would have more to say if anything happened to the boy.”

“He would indeed but you are still not talking to, or of, His Highness in a fitting manner. If you have anxieties about his behaviour, *you* do not chastise him. You raise it with your superior officer. You *certainly* do not *publicly* berate him. Now, where was His Highness going?”

The guard looked as though he’d swallowed a lemon. “Quite frankly, sir, I’d like to know on what authority you presume to correct me?”

Tancred replied levelly, “I am correcting you on my authority as His Highness’ tutor. Now, I would like to know where my charge was going and your name. Mine, should you need it, is Judge James Tancred.”

“Luke Lyne,” muttered the guard. “*His Highness* was going to see the King. I tried to tell him the King would be busy but he wasn’t having any of it.”

“Then please make your way to the guardroom on the King’s Corridor separately. I will escort His Highness, with his permission.” He walked over to Tain. “So, you were going to see the King. Would you permit me to accompany you, sir?”

“Of course, Your Honour,” agreed Tain. “How can I refuse? You’ve prevented me getting another lecture.”

“Is his manner always so confrontational?”

Elantha whispered, “It’s normally worse than that, Your Honour.”

Tancred nodded, his mind turning over the revelation. “Are we to keep the King waiting?”

“He’ll be busy, won’t he?” said Tain.

“Have you ever known His Majesty have no time for Your Highness or Her Ladyship?”

Tain grinned. “No, Your Honour, I haven’t.”

* * *

They reached the Outer Office where Richardson wished Tain a happy birthday before announcing him. Tancred would have departed, leaving a message that he needed a word, but the King spotted him and waved him into the Inner Office. Six minutes later, Adeone managed to persuade Tain and Elantha to wait for him in his sitting room. He turned to Tancred.

"I observed an interesting scene occurring in the grounds, Your Honour. Would you care to tell me why you dismissed my son's guard?"

Tancred did so honestly, finishing his report by saying, "I have never heard a guard address anyone they were protecting in such a manner, let alone their prince, and I hope to Alcis that I never do so again. I apologise if I was wrong to dismiss the man, but I was more concerned that His Highness did not feel that he was going to receive a lecture on his birthday; especially from someone who should not be giving him one."

Adeone's face had set during the explanation. "Thank you. I think the guard is about to find he is dismissed more permanently. What's his name?"

"Luke Lyne, Sire. He should be waiting in the guardroom."

"Thank you. Are you up to keeping my mischievous son company, or would you prefer some peace and quiet whilst I sort this out?"

"Sire, he is in your private sitting room—"

"I'd hardly have suggested it if I minded. Go into my bedchamber and turn left."

* * *

In all the many years he had known the FitzAlcis, Tancred had never been in the King's sitting room. It was far smaller than he expected. The sun streamed through the windows on his left. The summer heat made a fire unnecessary; so, directly in front of him, a painted fire screen showed a rural landscape, which he recognised as a view from Ceardlann in the Rex Dallin. There were inlaid sideboards on his right and a u-shaped arrangement of two couches and a chair in front of the fireplace.

Glancing around the comfortable and intimate room, his gaze fell on Prince Tain and an impish grin. "Is Your Highness, perchance, planning some mischief I should be aware of? I would rather avoid being an unsuspecting victim."

"I'd step over the trip wire then, Your Honour."

Tancred looked down and followed the string line that was against his ankles. He smiled and carefully stepped over the line.

"Thank you, sir. I expect I was not the intended target."

Tain shook his head. "I have more sense than that."

Tancred laughed. "So instead of getting a judge who would have to take it in good part, you are planning to get the King who does not. I can see I am going to have an interesting time, sir. Might I enquire as to what is in the goblet you are busily rigging up?"

Elantha grinned. "Coloured paper, Your Honour. We're not quite so foolish as to make it liquid."

"Especially not as it takes some setting up," agreed Tain, clambering on a chair to balance the goblet carefully on the door frame and loop the string through a hook in the ceiling used for hanging a tapestry.

"It would be a shame to have to dismantle it, but are you certain it is a good idea, sir?" mused Tancred, steadying the chair.

"Yes, but only here. I wouldn't try it anywhere else, other than Ceardlann. Anyway, I can always blame Julius. He told me how to manage it."

Tancred chuckled. Was the King aware his nearson was teaching his son a few tricks? Raised voices broke into his contemplation.

"Maybe we *should* take it down if father's in a bad mood," said Tain, biting at his lip.

Elantha hesitated.

Guessing, correctly, it was Luke Lyne at whom the diatribe was directed, Tancred remarked, "I am sure His Majesty would not want something so carefully planned to go to waste."

"Are you meant to encourage my mischievous side, Your Honour?" enquired Tain.

Tancred's lips twitched. "As I said earlier, sir, common sense is left to your conscience – when it does not extend to your professional life, that is. This *is* a private room."

"I like you, Judge. So, do you think we should leave it up?"

"I am sure Your Highness knows what is best in this situation. I am lacking in experience."

Tain and Elantha looked at each other, then at the string and grinned. The shouting had stopped and, before they had completely made up their minds, there was the sound of a door opening and Tancred moved over to the windows. The King entered the sitting room, tripped on the string and a cascade of paper flew around his head. He looked up and then at Tain who beamed at him. Adeone started chasing his son around the room. Catching him, he tickled him until Tain begged him to stop.

"Are you sorry?" asked Adeone.

Gasping for breath, Tain shook his head.

Adeone carried on tickling him until he said he was. Elantha was laughing and Tancred hadn't got a straight face.

It sobered quickly when Tain, catching his breath, said, "The judge didn't stop us, father."

Adeone eyed Tancred. "I *was* hoping you'd be a voice of reason in my son's life."

Tancred inclined his head slightly. "I am sorry, Your Majesty. His Highness was grinning too much for me to intervene."

Adeone rocked back on his heels, pushing himself to his feet. "A *very* sensible reason. There's one thing I do need to make clear... In here, I am Adeone."

Tancred hesitated. "I am not sure I can take that step, sir."

"I am, so please try." Adeone collapsed onto the couch beside Elantha. He took a breath. "I haven't missed the fact you had a hand in that trick either, little flower..." (Elantha wriggled as he tickled her feet.) Half a minute later, he stopped. "Right, so now you've abused me, what else do you have planned?"

Tain smirked. "Nothing yet, father."

"I would say I'm relieved apart from the fact I heard 'yet'. Never mind, I'm sure I'll cope. James, what are you doing still standing?"

"Preventing my joints from seizing up, sir," observed Tancred, surprised Adeone hadn't realised that he hadn't been invited to sit.

"For that 'sir', you can sit down and seize up. Before you do, though, can you ring the bell for Simkins? It's over there."

Tancred did so before easing himself onto the couch opposite Adeone. Simkins entered and spotted the paper flakes though appeared to ignore them.

Adeone noticed the almost imperceptible glance. "His Highness has been taking lessons from Lord Julius, Simkins. I'll get him to dismantle the trip wire in a moment. Is there any chance of some refreshment?"

"Certainly, Your Majesty. Anything in particular?"

"A sleeping draught for my son, I think. I would like a quiet afternoon; however, as even that would have little or no effect, tea for myself and the judge and some juice for the scapegraces." He was about to leave when Adeone added, "And a dustpan and brush so His Highness can clear up."

Tancred was surprised by the last request but Tain, without being asked directly, dismantled the trick and started to pick up the larger pieces of paper.

"Help your cousin, Elantha." Adeone winked at Tancred. "They made the mess."

Tancred fought to keep a straight face and lost. "So they did, si— Adeone."

"See, you can manage it. Have you thought any further about the problem of Ceardlann?"

Tancred replied that he had not and for the next couple of minutes he and the King tried to devise a way around the problem. Entering, Simkins placed a tray on the side table; deftly pouring the tea, he passed drinks to the King and judge before passing Tain and Elantha a goblet of juice apiece. Winking, he motioned that he'd finish clearing up.

As Tain and Elantha went to sit down, Adeone said, "Kind of you though it is, Simkins, you do spoil them."

"I know, Sire," agreed Simkins, "but it is His Highness' birthday."

"Well, if you insist, I won't object. First, however, in the black cabinet at the bottom is the woodland scene box; would you pass it to me, please?"

He did so, and Adeone placed it on the table by his hand.

When Simkins had gone, Adeone said, "When I was your age, Tain, an enterprising carpenter, having heard about my tendency for practical jokes, thought I might like this. I think you might get more use out of them now." He opened the box before passing it over.

Tain stared at a collection of miniature carved bugs of all shapes and sizes, painted to appear real. He glanced at his father, then at the bugs again and grinned.

"I warn you though, your Uncle Festus is used to them," admitted Adeone. "Try them on your Aunt Cornelia. Just remember, I *didn't* give them to you. I can't imagine what people would say if they knew their King was giving a future justiciar ammunition for his jokes. They might also work well on Julius and Julia. If you remove the top layer, there are more realistic spiders than the ones you have made before."

"What did grandfather say?" enquired Tain, innocently.

Adeone became shifty. "Oh, he never found out to my knowledge – nor did your Uncle Scanlon. The carpenter knew which side his bread was buttered. He still does. I told him on no account was he to make you a set." As Tain's face fell, Adeone continued, "I asked him to come up with something more inventive instead."

"So, what is he making me?" enquired Tain with bright eyes.

"I have no idea. I'm sure you'll find out one day. Now, I've replaced your guard… Yes, I thought that might meet with your approval. If an attendant is ever like that again, you tell me."

Tain bit his lip. "You won't be too busy?"

Adeone almost swore. "Tain, get this straight, you are my *son*. The empire is my *job*. *You* are a lot more important. I have time for you whenever you need it; for any of you. My family comes first. You, Arkyn, Elantha are all more important to me than anything else. I might occasionally get distracted, but if you need me, I'm here. So, next time a guard acts in that manner, I want to know. I never want to feel that you felt you couldn't come to me. I thought you knew that."

Still biting at his lip, Tain admitted, "I do, father, but I don't want to get in the way."

Adeone ruffled his hair. "I want you to. I don't mind hiding from work for a time, always have liked avoiding it. From what your tutors have told me, you're the same. I think the judge might have his work cut out. Mind you, as he won't be at Ceardlann with you, there might be more opportunity for your skiving to succeed – mine never did."

Astonished, Tain said, "You're not coming to Ceardlann, Your Honour?"

"I am afraid not, my prince."

Adeone explained, "His Honour is still going to preside at the courts here. It will have many advantages."

Tancred shot Adeone an inscrutable look, which the King ignored.

"Oh, right," said Tain, nonplussed. "Can't I make you reconsider, Your Honour?"

Tancred never hesitated. "Not for the moment, Your Highness. You might have to find some other way of playing practical jokes on me than bugs in my soup."

"Is that a challenge?"

Raising his eyebrows at Tancred, Adeone shook his head slightly.

"It certainly sounded like one, Your Highness," observed Tancred, "but I am sure I can rely on your good judgment to see the best way forward."

Adeone smiled. "That means no, Tain. James is too polite to state it outright. Are you still wanting a celebration this evening?"

Tain nodded. "Can Cal come? I've not seen him for a while and it's his birthday as well."

"I know. I thought it best to let him have some time with his family. I'm sure he already has plans for this evening, but why don't you pay him a call? I'm sure Master Galdwin won't mind."

Tancred was thinking, *'Even if he does, there is not much that can be done if a prince turns up on your doorstep wanting to see your son.'*

Tain jumped up. "Can I?"

"I don't see why not. As long as you don't lose your guard. No running off in Oedran. All right?" (Tain agreed.) "Go on with you then. Elantha, are you going as well?"

"No, uncle. I'll get in the way."

Once Tain had gone, Adeone said, "So, little flower, what have you and Arkyn planned for Tain this evening?"

Six minutes later, Elantha left with a list of ideas and Adeone chuckled at the look on Tancred's face.

"I'm sorry; I'm afraid common sense isn't common in here and there is certainly little sense to it."

"All I saw was a close and happy family. One or two of your ideas, though, reminded me of Prince Lachlan."

"Yes, they would. They were his. Now, I must return to the preparations for the Petitionals."

Together, they made their way into the Inner Office. As Tancred reached the door, Adeone growled,

"The terror's moved my desk around. *Everything* is on the wrong side."

Tancred laughed then apologised.

"Your turn, James, I am sure will come."

"So am I, Your Majesty. I anticipate it with interest." He bowed and left with a smile.

Making his way to his office in the Courthouse, Tancred passed pleasantries with his scribe before closing the door and sinking onto his chair. He pulled out the King's Token and laid it on the desk in front of him. It was full of such meaning: respect, friendship, complications. He should have stopped the King giving it to him. He should have taken the opportunity, should have protested, should have... There were too many things he *should* have done. Maybe the most important was to leave the past where it belonged. Who but Richardson would ever know he held this mark of trust?

Chapter 10
SMITHERS
Mid-afternoon
Inner Office

THE KING VIEWED the mess that was now his desk and set about rearranging it with a practicality that might have intrigued people. Complaining about his son's inherited sense of humour would have been pointless. He'd been oddly pleased that Tain and Elantha had worked the trip-wire trick between them. It explained why Tain had accepted not attending the Munewid feast, but he wondered what else his son had in mind.

With the Petitionals the following day, the afternoon was mostly dull routine. After that, came more pleasant tasks, preparing for the celebrations for Tain's birthday. Adeone remembered his own birthday celebrations, held at Court with great pomp; therefore, he'd decided that, until they were fifteen, his sons' would be private.

He crossed to the window, watching the gardens and beyond them the glimpses of the Administrative Quarter. Smiling to himself, he wondered if Tain had managed to find Cal. Then he began to consider Lyne and how far he had overstepped the bounds. Rubbing a hand through his hair, he decided to remind the guard now assigned to his son that he would check what had been happening in Tain's day. He called for Richardson and told him that he wanted a word with the guard when it was convenient.

A couple of hours later, Smithers reported to the Inner Office, appearing

59

far too cheerful after an afternoon in Tain's lively company.

"So, did Prince Tain find Master Calumiel?" enquired Adeone.

"In the end, Your Majesty, with a helping hand from Lord Julius Landis."

Adeone stopped himself groaning. He loved his elder nearson, but he wasn't always a steadying influence. "That's a comment with a story behind it if ever I heard one."

"Master Calumiel wasn't at home, sir. Prince Tain asked if we had to return to the Palace and I said not if His Highness didn't wish to—"

"Do you think that was a wise decision?"

Smithers never blinked. "It was a nice day, sir, and His Highness was enjoying the freedom. I didn't think it would be frowned upon. I'm sorry if I made an error in that."

"I'll let you know when I hear how you came to meet Lord Julius and find Master Calumiel."

Smithers smiled. "His Highness went to Landis Park, sir. Lord Julius came up to him and then showed His Highness to where young Master Calumiel was spending the afternoon with his aunt, cousins and siblings. Lord Julius left at that point, but His Highness was invited to stay by Master Calumiel's aunt, one Madam Susan Tanner of the Macarian Lordship."

"There weren't any incidents I should know about?"

"Not really, Sire. Master Galdwin was on edge when he spoke to His Highness, as though he was waiting for something but I think it was normal nerves. Young Crispin Galdwin knocked His Highness over by accident in the park but that was all. Oh, and two men in the Administrative Quarter, sir; I didn't like the way they were watching the Prince. Something wasn't right. They pretended to be having a conversation when I looked at them."

Adeone frowned. "Could you describe them, do you think?"

"No, Sire. Verbal description isn't my strong point. I could draw them for you, though; one had a distinctive scar."

Adeone was startled. "Then please do. Hand the sketches to this evening's sergeant. Thank you for also letting His Highness be himself this afternoon."

"I liked seeing him enjoying himself, Sire. He's a good kid."

Adeone chuckled as the guard realised what he'd said. "He is. All right, Smithers, you can go. Thank you."

Adeone called in Sergeant Marsh, the senior sergeant of the King's Guard, which had no captain. Marsh saluted but was far easier than Smithers had been. He'd been guarding the King for years and, although wary, wasn't worried. Adeone eyed him for a couple of seconds.

"Has Lyne left the Palace?"

"Yes, Sire. I'm sorry I didn't notice what was happening."

"Should I discover any other guard has overstepped the bounds, I won't be so amenable. What's Smithers like generally?"

"He's good, sir, certainly one of the best of Your Majesty's Guard."

Adeone got to his feet. "He's certainly refreshing. Leave him guarding the Prince until His Highness returns to Ceardlann, please. The experience might be educational for them both. Are you on duty this evening?"

"No, sir. Sergeant Hillbeck is; unless Your Majesty would prefer—"

"No, Hillbeck will be fine," interrupted Adeone. "The Landis family are joining us for my son's birthday celebrations. It might get noisy. That's all for now."

* * *

Some time later, there was a brief knock at the door and Lord Landis entered. Seeing his friend was deep in thought he simply waited.

Moments later Adeone, looking up, smiled. "Are you ready for an evening of mayhem, Festus?"

"Always, Sire, but I also need permission to go to Macia."

Adeone sat back. *Technically*, as protector of the Macarian Lordship, he should be undertaking the visit to the Macian Isles, but Landis had taken on aspects that he couldn't at the request of his, Adeone's, wed-father. He chewed at his lip. Part of him wanted to visit Macia again. The trip to Terasia had re-awoken his urge to travel.

Landis saw it. "Alternatively, Sire, you could also come, and leave Prince Arkyn in charge here."

"I'm not sure he'd manage both the Anaparian Review and running Oedran. He isn't as fit as he was going down to Terasia. Plus, tradition dictates that he should do the review from Paras in the north – not, unfortunately, from Oedran. Anyway, your house has just burnt down. Don't you have things to sort out here?"

"I've signed off the plans and appointed a foreman. We've both got messengers if he's got questions, and Cornelia is more than happy if I'm not tripping her up. So, what's your decision, Sire?"

"You *are* in a rush, aren't you?" observed Adeone. "There was no comment on traditions changing."

Landis grinned. "I was thinking you might want to say something about the influence my elder son is having on your younger."

"Oh, that! Julius is an amateur when it comes to bad influence, but, as you want my decision, I'll give you travel leave if you take him with you."

Landis snorted. "One way of getting rid of the influence, but he starts at the Advisors' School tomorrow, so it may be tricky. Personally, I think he'll drive the lecturers grey and this time next year they'd be all too glad to get rid of him. Until then, I rather suspect the Dean might argue."

Adeone laughed. "Most of them look far too healthy. Have a word with the Dean and tell him you want to take Julius with you to Macia. When he starts to object, drop in the fact that *I* want you to take Julius to Macia. It should shut him up nicely."

"I thought you were meant to have become serious when you became King, sir?"

"When did I do what I was meant to? All right, only use it if it becomes necessary. Then tell your mischievous son that he'll still have to catch up on anything he missed and that the trip is *not* for relaxation."

Landis nodded. "I'll make sure he understands that, sir." He walked over to the decanters and poured two whiskies. Turning, he found Adeone was watching him with a wry expression. "You look like it's been a long day."

Adeone slowly wiped his pen clean, placing it carefully in its rest. He moved the document he'd signed to the side and pushed himself to his feet, ringing for Richardson and telling him that he was finishing for the day. After the administrator left, he turned to Landis.

"It's been interesting." He motioned to the chairs by the fireplace, explaining events regarding Tancred, Lyne and Tain, concluding, "I'm hoping the year doesn't continue in this vein."

Landis chortled to himself. "I must say I admire Tain; he picks the days when he knows you won't get too angry with him to pull off the annoying stunts." He hesitated. "What *exactly* went wrong with his guard, sir? You must have dismissed him for a reason."

Adeone explained then sat sipping at his drink, the stress of the day ebbing from him. What would his friend conclude? The post of *Defender of the King's Life* was usually viewed as ceremonial, but Landis had never seen it as such, and it did have some oversight of the protection of the King's heirs.

"Maybe, Sire, you should consider giving the Princes a constant guard, especially as Fitz has retired. When you picked him to oversee Their Highnesses' safety, I wasn't worried. Now I am. With your permission, I'll set up a Princes' Guard, so when Prince Arkyn travels to Paras there are guards we know we can trust. I don't think leaving their safety to the militia and Palace Guard is enough peace of mind anymore."

"Then, before you leave for Macia, I want a plan of action for the Princes' Guard."

"Before? I planned to go next week so I can return when I'm needed more for the house."

"All right, do a few notes for me and I'll see about setting up the guard. Tain and Arkyn will be leaving for Ceardlann, so we, sorry, *I've* got time. I'll stop by and have a word with Fitz. See if there are men he can recommend.

I suppose we'd better get ready for whatever is in store for us tonight."

"It's probably wise to fortify ourselves," observed Landis taking his glass.

Chapter 11

CELEBRATIONS

Evening

King's Chambers – Triniculum

THE FAMILY MEAL was uproarious, not least because Landis' eldest four children were there, as well as the Princes and Lady Elantha; the children knew that normal rules had been suspended. Tain took all the many tricks in good part – the empty pastry case he examined with interest and the salted juice he simply grimaced at. He got a nice piece of revenge when Julia found a bug in her soup.

When he could, Landis said, "You're right, my oldest is a poor hand at being a bad influence."

Adeone laughed and winked at his friend. After the meal had finished, he suggested they go and use the Audience Chamber. Arkyn, catching his father's eye, smiled conspiratorially and hung back as the others ran out.

When Adeone, Festus, Cornelia and Arkyn entered the Audience Chamber, paper was swirling around the heads of the children and two bemused guards on the dais. Wishing for the party to be private, Adeone dismissed them.

The adults perched on the edge of the dais, mediating where needed. Adeone threw random comments into the proceedings, causing confusion. After a time, Arkyn perched next to him. Adeone ruffled his hair and Arkyn grinned. This type of evening was uncommon for them in Oedran, and atypical even at Ceardlann. The possibility of getting a similar evening would be rare for a long time. Arkyn would be travelling, so would Landis and Julius. Once he began his education in earnest, Tain would realise he had to sober up. With blinding sadness, Adeone's heart plummeted; they would never have another evening where his sons could be this carefree. He watched Tain chasing his nearcousins, watched the way Elantha was dodging, laughing, her blonde hair flying, thumbing her nose at Tain as he missed catching her. His heart lifted.

"Elantha, you're disgracing yourself!"

Adeone's heart shattered. It had been too good to last. "Lord Scanlon?"

As one, everybody faced the entrant.

As though it was the most normal thing in the world, Scanlon said, "I thought I'd come and see my nephew on his birthday, Sire."

63

Tain glanced between his father and uncle's neutral faces before catching his nearfather's fleeting but unmasked suspicion. His uncle wasn't welcome. Had he been blind before? Their hostility was obvious – but had it always been obvious and he'd been oblivious or had his father stopped trying to hide it? No, his father was hiding it and it was his nearfather who showed his feelings. Tain recalled his former tutor telling him to control his emotions, control his features, never to show what he thought, what he felt. It had seemed outlandish, restrictive but watching his father and uncle greet each other, he finally grasped why. No-one watching them would know there was anything amiss. He tried to catch Arkyn's eye but his brother was watching Elantha. Her distressed eyes were betraying her as much as the fleeting suspicion had betrayed Landis.

* * *

Adeone broke the momentary silence. "So that we don't disturb the party, come through and explain how you managed to finish affairs in Lufia so quickly. Landis, join us." Once in the Inner Office with the door closed, he whipped around. "Well?"

"Well what?" sneered Scanlon. "I gave my reasons outside."

"I'd be a fool to believe them! You've never cared to be here for Elantha's birthday, so why should I believe you've come to see Tain on his?"

"Trust?"

Adeone snorted. "Such a thing does not exist in your vocabulary. What brought you here?"

"I am worried about Tancred teaching Tain. He is out of touch with how the courts are run."

Adeone stilled. "You mean with the abuse of the law? Prince Tain will be tutored by whomever I think best. That's my final word on the matter."

"You'll always get people who disagree with the judge. Unfortunately, your authority over those supposed abuses is somewhat limited. How do you cope with not being in control? I bet it's enough to make you want to sit down and slit your wrists."

"Not really. You've had a long journey. Maybe you would prefer to rest instead of putting up with the children running around."

"Is that a dismissal?"

"Yes, it is. Get out!" Scanlon left and Adeone waited to hear his steps retreat from the Audience Chamber before saying to Landis, "I want the reason he's here and your travel leave is postponed."

"I was going to suggest I stay, Sire. Shall we return to the celebrations?"

When they reached the Audience Chamber, the joy had gone and the atmosphere had become muted. Elantha was particularly downcast. Adeone smiled at her but didn't get much of a response.

He let the subdued party continue for half an hour before giving Landis the nod. The Lord of Oedran tactfully extricated his brood and they left for their rooms. Adeone gave his sons and Elantha a hug goodnight.

"Don't worry, little flower. I doubt your father will stay for long and you'll return to Ceardlann soon. Give me another hug and keep smiling."

"I'm sorry, Uncle Adeone."

"No need to be. You just look so much nicer wearing a dimpled smile. There's the dimple, just there. Go on with you all. I need to see Chapa about a headache cure."

* * *

Half an hour later, Landis entered Adeone's sitting room. "Lord Scanlon never made Lufia apparently, Your Majesty. The Sagamore received an apology but the Justiciar had to return to Anapara – not Oedran; otherwise, I am assured, he would have informed you. I'm not sure I believed him. Lord Lux had just left Lufia when the Sagamore received the message. Strangely enough, Lux arrived last week, long enough for him to have been travelling with Scanlon and for Scanlon to have detoured elsewhere. I'm rather concerned about what they were planning."

"If he never made Lufia, he can damned well go there now," snapped Adeone. "I certainly want him there at some other time than next year when Arkyn is there for the review."

Landis nodded. "I've also ordered a complete sweep of the Palace tonight. There'll be extra guards in the King's Hall so that nothing can be rigged up for tomorrow's proceedings. Luckily, there isn't anywhere an assassin can hide."

"There could be, if the entrance to the Viewing Gallery hadn't been lost."

"Thank Alcis it has been," admitted Landis.

"I still think there must be a secret lever, which I now hope stays secret. My ancestors' paranoia is working for me for once…"

Landis noticed Adeone was becoming drawn. "Well, if you'll excuse me, Sire, I'm going to have an early night?"

The King looked at his friend shrewdly. "I suppose I do have to be awake for tomorrow's proceedings."

Chapter 12
COURTHOUSE
Cisadai, Week 1 – 2nd Cearal, 2nd Cearcis 1212
Privy Wing – Nursery

PRINCE TAIN WOKE the day after his birthday with a sinking feeling. The previous day had been fun, but today would be full of lessons. He got dressed glumly. He didn't want reminding of what his future was or a day of being lectured, however nice the judge seemed.

Entering the FitzAlcis schoolroom, Tain tried not to show how much he didn't want to be there. Ewall was definite: private feelings about public duties were for private times.

Judge Tancred hadn't got any books with him and hadn't set out any writing materials. He did, however, push himself to his feet and bow as Tain entered. The Prince smiled.

"Thank you, Judge. Where would you like me to sit?"

Tancred returned the smile. "I thought, if Your Highness is amenable, to start our lessons with a walk to the Courthouse, where I will endeavour to relate its history to you. I think the day is far too pleasant for us to be embroiled in dusty tomes of law. Would you agree, sir?"

Tain grinned. "Definitely!"

Chuckling, Tancred said, "Then, I believe, guards are waiting for us. When we reach the Courthouse, the Keeper may explain any history I miss. He has a wealth of knowledge that few harness. I hope Your Highness does not mind if he joins us."

Tain swallowed. "Erm, Judge, do I get to mind? Even supposing that I do, which I don't, but would I be able to mind?"

"A valid question. In this instance, sir, I would respect your decision, as it is not crucial to your understanding of the lesson. The word *lesson* is, admittedly, something of a misnomer for our time together today."

Tilting his head slightly, Tain said, "What does father think about this?"

Tancred's lips twitched. "His Majesty has been kind enough to express trust in me. I am sure he will enjoy the story when you tell it. Shall I send for Your Highness' cloak?"

* * *

They entered the Courthouse by the huge bronze doors with their embossed tree and moon. Tancred explained one man could easily open them. Tain looked at their twelve-foot height and marvelled that that could be the case. He asked how and Tancred explained that the craftsmen had balanced them so exactly that even after a couple of hundred years they still swung freely.

"Some people think it is magic, Your Highness, but it is just good engineering."

Tain nodded. "Why is there only one moon depicted?"

"The laws are the same for everyone, sir. Ah, Keeper, good morning."

"Morning, Your Honour," replied the Keeper, moving to greet them, his long teal robes marking him out. "Your Highness, welcome back. I hope James has been explaining all the symbolism."

"He was beginning to, Keeper. He's been explaining about the doors."

"Ah, well, they are one of our more magnificent features. In a few years, you'll have a key for them, one of only two in existence. More ceremonial now, admittedly, but we still have the odd day when the Courthouse is closed."

As the Keeper talked, Tain learned about how the Courthouse had developed, forming over time into one building from many. They stayed in the atrium for some time as the Keeper explained the myths and legends surrounding the building. He pointed out the magical star stone placed above the doors to the Justice Hall that was said to bind the personifications of Truth and Justice within the hall.

"Is that really true though, Keeper?" asked Tain.

"The legends say they've been seen, sir. There's histories that mention it and there are stories that Truth and Justice weren't the only concepts personified. If it wasn't true, why would the stone be here?"

Tain considered that. "Is it actually a stone? It's not a glass made to look like one?"

Judge Tancred chortled to himself. "You would definitely make a lawyer, Your Highness."

"Apparently I get to skip that," murmured Tain.

"True, sir. As a judge, it is possible that you could find another take on the situation."

"What like?" enquired Tain, intrigued.

"Well, Your Highness, you would listen to both sides. Reading about the legend, reading the histories of the Cearcall, may give enough insight to lead to belief instead of scepticism. Within those histories it mentions that no-one but a wright can release the stone, and that, if they do, Truth and Justice would be released."

"That doesn't prove it's a star stone though."

"A valid point, Your Highness. You are now thinking like a judge."

The Keeper smiled. "True or not, Your Highness, it is the idea that keeps the Justice Hall a formidable prospect for defendants and lawyers alike. There's nothing like a bit of history, magic and myth combined to help a case along. I'm sure the judge has plenty of books on the subject if it interests you. Historical Law is his speciality. Now…"

As they continued the tour of the wider Courthouse, Tancred and the Keeper related more history and small facts discovering what Tain already knew and some of what he didn't. Eventually, a runner disturbed them and the Keeper took his leave. They continued their tour with the Law Library, where shelves held tomes of law and scrolls of rulings and precedents.

They ended the tour at the office Tain would one day use. Tancred entered and one of Scanlon's senior scribes rose.

"Is there any objection to Prince Tain seeing the Justiciar's office, Conridge?" enquired Tancred.

The scribe couldn't say no, it would one day be Tain's. "The Justiciar's desk isn't to be disturbed, Your Honour."

"Thank you. We shall do our best not too – will we not, Your Highness?"

"Of course, Judge."

Grinning, they entered the office. Tain glanced around the long narrow room with interest. On his right, tall slender windows looked out at the private Justice Garden and opposite them were shelves of books and scrolls on either side of a large fireplace, in front of which were comfortable chairs. Opposite the fireplace, in the centre of the wall with the windows, was a glass-panelled door leading out into the Justice Garden. Tain turned slightly. Immediately on his left was a large table set round with chairs, whilst opposite it, at the far end of the room, was the Justiciar's desk – behind which was another door.

Tancred, who had been in the office many times over the years, said lightly, "I do not think this room has changed in all the years that I have known it – although Prince Lachlan did have a new desk made; he was fussy about his desk."

"Why?" enquired Tain.

"Because when you are sitting at it for hours on end, sir, it needs to be right and comfortable to work at. I think Prince Lachlan found the original desk too small; he tended to spread documents out somewhat."

"It's very ornate," observed Tain.

"It is indeed, Your Highness. Prince Lachlan had a thing for prestige. The more ornate something is can signify the higher the rank of the person who owns it."

"Oh. I suppose that makes sense – though we tend to wear plain tunics in comparison to the merchants here who wear doublet and hose."

Tancred smiled. "Yes, Your Highness. The merchants are trying to display their wealth; the colour and composition of your tunics is such that you do not need to. The concept is called *less is more*. Your tunics are probably more comfortable."

"They're easy to put on. It takes Cal six minutes longer than me in a morning."

"I can believe that, sir. Have you seen enough?"

Tain glanced around the office again. "What's through the other door, Your Honour?"

"A dressing room of sorts. It tends to be a private room."

Tain said, "Oh well. Then I think we've seen everything we can, haven't we, Your Honour?"

"I think so, sir. Shall we find the Keeper? His office is opposite this one."

As they entered the outer office, Conridge rose and Tain thanked him, which made Tancred smile – no-one could say this Prince was rude. They crossed to the Keeper's office, with its dim light and dusty air, and were soon supplied with cool drinks and berries. Tain and the Keeper conversed easily. Tancred watching them saw the years ahead as clearly as though he had already lived them. There would not be many disagreements. They would sit and talk until someone reminded them that they should be doing something else. That, reflected Tancred, was how it should be and was far removed from how it was with the judiciary splintering into opposing camps. There was the 'old guard' as he and many others termed Lachlan's judges, and then there were Scanlon's judges – some of whom weren't bad; they were merely following Scanlon's methods. The empire was becoming a harsher place to live than it had been even a decade earlier. Tancred hoped the Keeper could keep things amicable for long enough to let Tain become Justiciar.

* * *

They were making their way out of the Courthouse when a youth ran up to the judge with a message from his scribe.

Tancred took it, broke the seal and read the short missive. "Tell your father I will return in a couple of hours and ask him to find me the relevant precedents list, please." Seeing Tain's interest had been roused, he said, "One of the cases I am presiding over has requested an adjournment, sir – something about new evidence."

"Oh, is that normal?"

"Normal enough. It is not a large case and I have some doubts myself about the guilt of the defendant; however, we are not meant to consider our feelings. Never make up your mind on the spot. Always listen to and examine the evidence."

"Do you ever find that you know if someone is guilty?"

"Occasionally I can be relatively sure, but I never go with my gut instinct. For instance, Your Highness, if you will forgive me, many would think that there is not a mischievous bone in your body."

"I don't have *a* mischievous bone, Your Honour. I have a skeleton *full* of them."

Tancred laughed. "With pedantry like that, Your Highness should go far."

"Thank you, Judge. Don't you want to go and sort the case out now?"

"There is still time, sir. They cannot hold the court without me."

"Really, if you want to sort it out, I won't mind."

Tancred caught the Prince's eye. "I could almost think you wanted to get rid of me, sir."

Tain was still smiling. "Not at all, Your Honour."

Tancred knew what Tain was up to; what was more, Tain knew he knew. The judge made up his mind. There was more than one way of teaching someone.

"Your Highness, it would make my life easier if I were to sort this out now; however, I do not know what His Majesty would say."

"Who'd tell him?"

"Someone would, sir. You can depend on it," admitted Tancred. "So, there is only one option: Your Highness comes and enjoys the experience of watching someone else work. It can be quite relaxing. You may even learn something that way."

Tain sighed, defeated, then grinned. "Why not?"

They returned to the Courthouse and discovered the lad who had brought the message talking to two other youths. Tain recognised him as being the hesitant student from the mock lecture. Spotting the judge, he went to run off on his errand, but Tancred called him back and sent word that Tain was accompanying him.

The judge led the way once more through the Courthouse until they reached his office and a scribe rose to greet them. Winking at the scribe, Tancred entered his inner office with Tain following him curiously.

The office had a comfortable, well-used air. Motes of dust hung in the sunlight streaming through the narrow window on their left. It looked out over a small square, several feet below them as the land had dropped away. Opposite the window was the fireplace, redundant in summer, its blackened hearth told of many winters' use. Around it, seats sagged on three well-worn leather-clad chairs.

Immediately in front of them was Tancred's desk – polished but simple in design, a complete contrast to the Justiciar's. Behind it, shelving was crammed with scrolls and books, some yellowed with age, crumpled from long use. The air was redolent with the scents of their paper and parchment.

Tain had the odd feeling the room was smiling at Tancred as he entered.

Tancred smiled back. He liked his office; it had moulded itself to him and he had felt drawn into its enveloping simplicity in return.

He turned to Tain. "Welcome to my little empire, Your Highness. It is not much but it does the job, which is all any of us can ask of an office. If you wish to, feel free to sit down. Now, if you can excuse me, I ought to examine this pile of documents my scribe has so considerately left on the middle of my desk."

Tain looked at the books and scrolls on the shelves. What sort of thing did a judge keep in his office? He found treatises on the application of law, a handful of scrolls with tags that suggest they were lists of precedents, a few seals that suggested some scrolls were actual laws and, interestingly, several history books.

Tancred pulled the list of precedents towards him and started running a finger down it. A moment later, he turned to the shelves and apologetically reached over Tain's head to pull a scroll down.

"May I read one of these, Your Honour?" asked Tain.

"Of course, sir – just be careful. Some of them are getting quite fragile and old, like me. They have been well used over the years. Some were your great-uncle's before they came into my keeping."

Tain mused, "An odd way of putting it, Your Honour – into your keeping?"

Tancred smiled; the King had been right; Prince Tain had an enquiring mind. "I consider myself a custodian of them, Your Highness. I shall pass them on at some point. I have heard that you have a passing interest in the Cearcallian Era. Am I informed correctly?"

Tain nodded. "Laioril got me hooked on the stories."

"Then I believe you might find this one of interest."

Tancred passed Tain a volume entitled, *The Laws of the Cearcall and Their Effect on the Early Empire*. Taking it, Tain read the title with interest. He curled up in a fireside chair and was soon drawn into the pre-Empire world – when there was a group of twelve people, known as the Cearcall, each with a different magical spirit, who had helped to keep peace between the lands. The book explained how the Cearcall had had an effect on the laws of the different lands and how those laws had carried through into the empire when it formed after the Cearcall was, quite literally, blown up by its own magic.

Twelve minutes later, Tancred unobtrusively got up and sent for the prosecution and defence counsel to visit him and put the case before him for an adjournment. When they arrived, they were perplexed to find the next Justiciar present. When Tancred introduced them, Tain got up and greeted them pleasantly and correctly, then excused himself, sat back down and carried on reading.

Tancred eyed the defence counsel. "Daleman, why are you requesting an adjournment?”

The lawyer glanced sideways at Tain. “We may have an alibi for the defendant, Judge. A friend who saw him in a different part of the city.”

“How has this come to light?” asked Tancred, making notes.

“A letter, sir, received by the defendant’s wife. It mentions having met the defendant that evening at the Golden Hare—”

“He might want to go to prison then,” muttered the prosecuting lawyer.

Tancred crooked an eyebrow. “Jenkins?”

“What? I can’t imagine why anyone wouldn’t want to face their wife when they’ve just been found at a brothel, Judge.”

Tancred flicked his eyes in Tain’s direction.

“Ah, erm, sorry, Your Honour,” said Jenkins with a grin. “All I’m saying is, has the defendant considered all aspects and consequences of this new evidence?”

“That is for Daleman to decide.” Tancred considered for a few moments. “Can we call this witness to court?”

“Yes, Judge,” replied Daleman. “However, he is currently in Byfa. So we need time for him to return. I have contacted him and he is willing to stand witness for his friend. He requires a fortnight to get his affairs in order and return to Oedran.”

“Jenkins, any objections?”

“None, Your Honour. Why would I object? I get a fortnight to put my feet up.”

“Then I will adjourn tomorrow for a fortnight. I will also inform the Keeper that you have time on your hands, Jenkins.”

“Your Honour, is always so kind to us,” replied the lawyer with a flourish.

The prosecution and defence left, relatively happy. Tidying the papers up, Tancred was surprised to hear Tain ask,

“Why two weeks, Judge? It doesn’t take that long to get here from Byfa.”

Tancred paused. “It is the longest the court can adjourn for, Your Highness. I have no doubt that Daleman is using the fact to give himself a bit of leeway. As no-one will be harmed by the wait, I see no reason to object. Although Byfa is only around three hundred miles away – depending on what a person is carrying, if they are riding or walking – it could take a few days or a couple of weeks. I expect, if I were to read the letter, it will have been delivered several days ago. The defendant is not facing a capital charge; however, it is always worth taking the time to verify new evidence. The prosecution, in the shape of Jenkins, obviously has his doubts about the defendant’s guilt now. If he was certain of obtaining the conviction, he would have asked for less. Mind you, it also gives him more time to come up with a different slant on the evidence – if he is certain about the defendant’s guilt. Double motives, nothing quite like it, sir."

"Are they common, Judge?"

Tancred smiled. "If you ever find a lawyer with a single motive, he is of a rare species, sir, and should be in a museum."

Tain laughed. "Would that make his motive an old one, Your Honour?"

"Ancient, sir. How is the book, if I might ask?"

"It's good. Who wrote it? It doesn't seem to be fragile."

"I am afraid to say, Your Highness, that it was a joint effort."

"Between?"

Tancred sighed. "Who am I to deny my Prince the knowledge that his great-uncle and I wrote a book together?"

Tain stared. "You and Great-uncle Lachlan wrote this?"

"We both had an interest in the early law of the empire, sir. Between us, we realised we had a lot of knowledge gathered that should not be lost. It is also the only copy in the empire. I might still have the original manuscript somewhere though."

"It's a good read, Judge."

"I am pleased you like it, sir. It has not been read by many people but I thought you might appreciate the material contained within it. I also hoped it was not quite as soporific as many of the books on my shelves."

"Could I borrow it to finish it?"

"I would rather that it did not leave this office, sir, but you may come here whenever you wish to continue reading it."

"Then, Your Honour, I'll content myself with that. Thank you."

"Not at all, Your Highness. I am sorry I cannot bring myself to let it out of my possession. Would you like a page marker for the book?"

"Yes, please. I suppose I ought to be getting back to the Palace and Ewall's more conventional lessons."

"If you will permit me, Your Highness, I shall walk with you."

Chapter 13

PETITIONALS

Morning

Palace – King's Hall

WHILST TAIN AND TANCRED were walking companionably around the Courthouse, Adeone and Arkyn were in the King's Hall listening to people who had complaints about their lives. A centuries-old tradition, the Petitionals were spread over two days, with the King's Hall echoing with footsteps and angst.

Arkyn was attending for the first time and, standing by his father's throne, felt as surreal as Tain did wandering around the Courthouse. Here was his future, shown to him with startling clarity and aching feet.

Each petitioner handed a scroll to the King and explained in a few words what the petition entailed. Adeone passed the scroll to Arkyn, who passed it to Richardson who passed it to a clerk, who recorded it before passing it to a different clerk to place in the correct box hidden behind the dais, where the petitioners couldn't see how many others there were.

Unlike many previous monarchs, Adeone made sure each petition was read and a response prepared and delivered to the petitioner. It was partly why he'd asked Arkyn to attend.

The Prince, whose trip to Terasia had left him with an astoundingly astute reputation for a sixteen-year-old, would be dealing with petitions relating to the militia. In doing that he would be learning far more than twenty briefings on the army could tell him. His time in Terasia had given him a good grounding in most subjects but military matters hadn't featured much at all, mainly because the then *Commander* Wynfeld had made sure that it didn't, with a competence that had been recognised with his promotion to Major of Oedran.

By the time they took a break from proceedings Arkyn was feeling the strain of having been on his feet for hours. Adeone asked Richardson to get him a chair and, when Arkyn sank onto it gratefully, said,

"I should have thought; I'm sorry."

"Some traditions can't be changed, Your Majesty."

Adeone eyed him, amused. "Don't tell Lord Landis that. Stay seated for the next session."

"No, sir. The only man seated at the Petitionals is Your Majesty. I'll cope, as long as I get a foot bath this evening."

"You know, I wouldn't mind."

Arkyn replied carefully, "I think it is better that I stand, Your Majesty. Many rumours start from inconsequential actions."

"That's far too true. How many petitions were there?"

Arkyn asked Richardson. A couple of minutes later, the number came back at one hundred and twenty-three.

Adeone murmured, "Yes, and far too many of them were law related. Richardson, ask the Justiciar to join us, please. As he's in Oedran, he can take responsibility for his judiciary."

Returning to the dais from talking to the guards, Landis enquired quietly, "Is that wise, Sire?"

Adeone eyed him. "That is a discussion for later, my lord. Can you assume your position as my Defender for the next session?”

“Certainly, Your Majesty, but who stands on your right?”

Adeone swore slightly. “It will have to be Scanlon. Do you mind, Arkyn?”

“Not at all, Sire. I’m not twenty.”

Landis muttered, “Traditions could be changed.”

Adeone threw him an inscrutable glance. “There’s the difference between nearfather and nearson.”

Arkyn laughed. “Maybe I have taken other lessons from my nearfather, Your Majesty.”

“Yes. Have I ever said that that’s what worries me?”

“Why do I get all the blame?” enquired Landis rhetorically.

They were still smiling when Scanlon joined them. The Justiciar bowed to the King and took in Landis’ and Arkyn’s presence. His glance at Landis was derogatory and dismissive, but his look at Arkyn was appraising.

“Your Highness, I have yet to offer my congratulations on your work in Terasia. I hear that you surprised them all with your decisions and that the province is now recovering after some rather unfortunate incidents. Oedranians, though, are pleased to see you returned to us in full health.”

Adeone bit back his retort, thinking that he’d leave his son to deal with the underlying insults, which Arkyn did.

“Thank you, Lord Scanlon, but I could not have achieved half of my reforms in Terasia without your influence.”

“Your Highness, my influence in your education has been minimal but I thank you for the compliment,” crooned Scanlon, inwardly seething, and outwardly maintaining the mask of Court that dictated that the obvious was the intended comment.

Arkyn smirked. “Compliments are often like the Terasian weather: temperamental. I prefer honesty.”

Adeone intervened before Scanlon burst a blood vessel trying to contain his rage at being shown up. “Lord Scanlon, I’d like you to attend the Petitionals, to reassure the petitioners that we work together to reverse abuses.”

“Your Majesty, I would like to, but I have a case to attend to that has been waiting for my presence for a few weeks,” lied Scanlon.

“I’m sure the Keeper could rearrange it for tomorrow, Justiciar. I feel for the defendant, but you are needed here. Richardson, please inform the Keeper that the Justiciar has been unavoidably detained.”

“Of course, Sire. Lord Scanlon, is there any message you wish to send?”

Scanlon glared. “If there were, I would tell you without you asking.”

Adeone said mildly, “I think we’re about ready to reconvene. Lord Landis, are there many people waiting?”

“About sixty, Your Majesty.”

"Then this afternoon should be far shorter than this morning's proceedings. Inform the Steward that we're ready to start in six minutes, please."

When Scanlon left after the last petition of the day had been handed over, Adeone turned to Arkyn.

"I think you annoyed the Justiciar, Prince Arkyn."

"A rather unfortunate matter, Sire," observed Arkyn, "but one that I suspect won't have a lasting influence on his regard for me."

Landis fought down a smile but Adeone, getting up from the throne, caught his eye and silent humour flashed between them before escaping as small chuckles.

"I rather suspect the same, Your Highness," replied Adeone.

"I'm sure the Justiciar accepted your views with tolerance, Your Highness," stated Landis.

"I'm sure the Justiciar has little thought for my views, my lord," replied Arkyn. "I am but a prince not yet of my age."

Adeone said, "I'm sure he's going to have far more to think on. I will make it clear I want some of the abuses outlined in the petitions reversed."

Landis nodded. "A wise move, Sire, if I may say so."

"As you have, there isn't much I can do about it. Come, we shall go and talk whilst the clerks sort out the records of today, ready for tomorrow."

The three of them left the King's Hall and Richardson, who'd overheard much of their talk, smiled to himself thinking that Scanlon might make men fear him but friendship, respect and a united aim was sometimes more powerful than all the trepidation in the world.

Chapter 14
CONSEQUENCES
Morning
Palace – Lord Scanlon's Chambers

THAT SAME MORNING, slightly calmer, Para had ambled through the Palace to Lord Scanlon's chambers in the Privy Wing. He waited patiently in the tiled antechamber whilst Scanlon's manservant enquired if the Justiciar would see him. A few minutes later, he entered the spacious sitting room and gave a slight bow.

"Thank you, sir."

Scanlon waved to a chair and dismissed his manservant. "How can I help, Lord Para?"

"A small inconvenience has arisen, sir. My son has suffered a grievous insult. He was forced to play act in a mock trial and then was failed because he saw through the charade and wouldn't demean himself by performing an unbecoming part. He rightly had more thought for his position, but I fear Ryson has sided with his examiner and won't see the ludicrous nature of the situation."

Scanlon crooked an eyebrow. "Who was the examiner?"

"Judge Tancred, sir."

"And Ryson backed him?" spat Scanlon.

"So has the King, sir. My son feels the insult gravely. He knows he can't be seen to fail and fears this will have tainted his career beyond measure for years. He'll always be seen as the one who failed. If Your Lordship—"

"What's your offer?"

"It is for your own cause, sir. Kenelm is your staunchest supporter—"

"Everyone is a staunch supporter when they want something," said Scanlon. "But is it worth it to me? Your son is obviously not working as hard as we thought in my service. Maybe he needs this lesson."

"Sir, I can assure you he has been giving your endeavours all he can. He has spotted several opportunities..." Para explained everything his son had said about who they needed on side. "He is easily bored, sir. The Law School won't challenge him enough if men like Tancred are given precedence. It is not only an insult to Kenelm's person, but men such as Tancred are weak minded from birth. They have not the lineage that breeds nobility and strength."

Scanlon crooked an eyebrow. "I have no love of Judge Tancred but I wouldn't call him weak. Misguided, yes. Dangerous, yes. Weak, no. His appointment as a judge might have been questionable, but I do not know enough about that yet. His appointment as tutor to Prince Tain is unfortunate and it would have been best avoided. I had thought the King would appoint elsewhere."

"Ryson said he's not trusted. He also said that the King knows about his lovers, but I can't believe that."

"Oh, the King knows," said Scanlon. "It's not something that makes any difference, anyway. There's no law or taboo against the situation. Who his lovers are is where the problems arise. Anyway, you didn't love your wife, so I don't see you've anything to feel superior about. Which way does your son lean?"

"He's two bastards already, sir."

"Are he and Chander in competition? Oh dear. I do hope your estates can continue to pay their dues."

Para smirked. "Mine can, sir. Teran's got too many of his own. About

Kenelm's education—"

Scanlon pursed his lips. "Go and see the Dean of the Advisors' School. I'm not minded to undermine the King today. If your son fails another exam, he can take the full weight of the disgrace and I'll add to it. You both know too much. I expect to dine at Para House tomorrow; when I hope, for all your sakes, your best behaviour is good enough. Else, I will direct your son's education more precisely myself, including chastisements for anything I deem a failure." He saw Para's face. "Your son is *not* immune from my anger simply because he's your son." Scanlon jerked his head as Richardson's messenger appeared.

Para left without a word. Hosting a dinner for Lord Scanlon was not what he'd planned. They couldn't risk any more mistakes. He crossed the Palace and collected his horse without passing one pleasantry. He rode to the Advisors' School and spoke with the Dean, a more amenable man than Ryson. Kenelm would start the second year at once.

* * *

Para House gleamed by the time Lord Scanlon entered. Para greeted him and took his cloak without a word. Scanlon had always adhered to the ancient practice that lords waited on princes.

"Welcome back, Lord Scanlon. It's an honour to have you here."

Scanlon smiled. "It's an honour to be here, my lord. I hope your cook is still the same."

"She is, sir, and has been busy preparing your favourites all day. I believe you remember my children: Lord Kenelm and Lady Malandra."

Scanlon's glance lingered on Malandra. "I do, Para. Shall we repair to your study? We needn't bore Her Ladyship with our talk."

Para motioned with his hand and led the way to the rear of the house. Kenelm followed them. Only Malandra had been excused.

Para closed the door behind Kenelm and waited. He'd done what he could. Maybe it was time his son learnt the perils of serving Scanlon.

The Justiciar said, "I understand from your father that you already have children, Kenelm."

Kenelm's eyes lit up. "Yes, sir. Two girls. Their mother is—"

"Going to help my cause and so are her children. Her children. Not yours, Kenelm. The child born out of marriage follows its mother's fortunes in law. Didn't you get that far?"

Kenelm hesitated. "Sir, they are my father's grandchildren."

"No, they are not. They are nothing and have already been collected by my men." He stepped close to Kenelm. "Consequences! If you fail again, they will be punished. Kneel." When Kenelm had knelt, he looked at Para. "You've told him far too much!"

Para whitened. "Sir, he is my only son."

"Yes, and you're not barren. Your hands, Kenelm."

Kenelm held up his hands. How had failing one exam led to the kidnapping of his children and this? He glanced at his father. Why was he so pale? The Justiciar couldn't kill him. All Scanlon could do was take an oath that he wouldn't reveal anything. He wasn't going to anyway, so why was his father so pale? When the cold steel of the dagger rested on his palm, he understood that maybe there was more to Scanlon's control. He swallowed back nausea. Would Scanlon extract a life-bind from him?

Scanlon drank in the fear rising from Kenelm and sweeping over him from Para. Blood sang in his veins. Should he life-bind Kenelm? It would certainly ensure the boy's loyalty, and Para's, but the marks wouldn't go unnoticed. The steel would remind the boy well enough. He took a truth-binding. Still with the boy's sweaty palms against his, he elicited everything that Para had revealed and then wiped the memories from the boy's mind. In a fit of pique, he bound the boy to revenge slights and to forget his children.

Para paled further. He wanted to plead, but it would make things worse. Two moments later, he and Scanlon were alone.

"Greatness, if he has offended you—"

"He has disappointed me. You swore to my cause. You bound yourself to my orders. I did not order that you were to tell your son everything I planned. This is the consequence. By Alcis, if you weren't a Lord of Oedran, I'd have satisfaction from your skin. You have endangered everything!"

"My liege, I have only ever sought to further your just aims."

"And now you will kneel!" Scanlon snapped. He loomed over Para. "You have two options, Joren. Speech or life-bind. I will take either but nothing less."

Para swallowed. "Speech, sir." Once bound not to repeat anything Scanlon didn't want him to, Scanlon permitted him to rise.

Scanlon clapped him on the back. "Let's forget all the nastiness. Come. We should dine and let your children entertain us. Your daughter is certainly blooming. Is she acting as mistress of the house now?"

"She is, sir, and it's running well under her eye."

"And they are beautiful eyes. I think I will stay the night."

Para paled. "It would be an honour, sir." Would they all suffer from Scanlon's mood?

Scanlon smiled. He had no intention of interfering with Malandra's life yet. "I look forward to all the entertainment you can provide."

By the time Scanlon left after breakfast, all Para wanted was for the Justiciar to be as far away from Oedran and his family as possible. When his steward commented on how genial Scanlon had been, he had all on agreeing. The previous night had proved to him there was no leaving Scanlon's side. They were in it until the end. Even if he wanted to turn on the Justiciar and hand evidence to the King, he couldn't. He couldn't speak the words and Kenelm couldn't remember anything of Scanlon's aims, nor could he be told them again. Their lives hung on Scanlon's favour. He didn't even want to contemplate what the fate of his granddaughters was to be. They'd probably never find out, and Kenelm couldn't even remember them. They had to work with the Justiciar. With all his moods and requests. The only way they could live was if Scanlon won. If the King discovered he'd been speech-bound he'd die for treason. If Scanlon lost, he'd die for treason for it was known he supported the Justiciar. His options had shrunk because no-one would overrule Judge Tancred.

Chapter 15
FAMILY
Imperadai, Week 1 – 4th Cearal, 4th Cearcis 1212
Inner Office

THE MORNING AFTER the Petitionals ended, Richardson got up hurriedly as Lady Amara entered the Outer Office. He gave a slight bow and considered what to say. "Lady Amara?" was the safest thing he could think of.

"I'm here to see His Majesty."

"The King is in counsel, my lady."

"No, he simply has a few people with him who will be leaving."

Richardson sighed. "I'm not sure that His Majesty—"

"Will be happy that I'm debating this issue with you. I'm sure, as an exceptional administrator, you've read the clerks' print that says that in this situation you should go and quietly inform His Majesty that I'm here. When that's done, I'll thank you for announcing me and everyone's happy."

"The meeting attendees?"

"I should have said everyone who's important is happy. Just go and tell the King, Richardson, and save your insolence for a day where I care to laugh about it."

* * *

Adeone nodded his thanks to Richardson and pushed himself to his feet. His aunt's willowy frame did little to hide the determination in her shrewd eyes. Her grey hair was far more tamed than her renowned tongue and Adeone, for all he loved her dearly, knew if she was visiting him during the day, she had something on her mind that he was meant to fix.

A moment later, he said, "Bullying Richardson—"

"Is perfectly fair, Sire," replied Amara blithely. "If it's not, why are you grinning, nephew?"

"Because he said you were in a particularly good mood, aunt. Come and sit down and explain why you're throwing highly influential people out of my office."

"Whilst you try not to look too glad about it." She sat near the fireplace, arranging her skirts carefully.

Trying to fend off the inevitable, Adeone said, "I trust you're well."

"I am. What about your son?"

"Which?"

"Don't play the pedant. Even if you're not worried, I am."

Adeone passed his aunt a drink and sank onto a comfortable chair, his head in his hands. "I am, but until Arkyn admits it—"

She squeezed his shoulder and passed him the glass. "You need this more than I do. What's happening?"

He rubbed his face. "He's never recovered fully from the flu. Chapa thinks it might have been some sort of poison, but Wynfeld can't find any evidence of it. There was seasonal illness in Southern Areal and Terasia as he passed through."

"Chapa's not stupid," observed Amara. "What else is he saying?"

"Nothing. Well, he says Arkyn should be all right with some rest."

"So you've got him involved in the Petitionals?"

"People will expect—"

"People have expected a lot of me over the years too," smirked Amara. "It's amazing how I've changed their expectations."

"You can say that again. I'm not sure I should follow your lead in this."

Amara chuckled. "Maybe not." She squeezed his hand. "You need some answers. Shall I interview Chapa for you?"

Adeone eyed her sideways. "No, thank you. I would still like him to be my doctor."

His aunt's eyes sobered. "In all seriousness, sir, I think you need to speak with him again. I dined with Arkyn last night. We had a private talk – not even Kadeem present. Your son isn't himself."

"Is he… Is it just the fact he's tiring?"

"Mostly. He didn't have an easy time in Terasia. He was telling me the stories and asking for mine, but he didn't fool me."

"No, I expect he didn't," remarked Adeone dryly.

"Telling him about Wealsman might have been kinder."

"I had my reasons for not doing so. One day, Wealsman will support him in unexpected ways. It is better their friendship formed as it did."

Amara's eyes narrowed. "Your gut instincts—"

"Are based on dreams, aunt," admitted Adeone finally. "Dreams that feel unusual. I dreamt Arkyn was tossing and turning in sleep, his hand bandaged. It was the night before he fell ill. I knew he'd hurt his hand, but there were small things I couldn't know, the position of his nightstand or the hangings on the bed. Portur changed them in 1203 before Scanlon's visit. Small details that I found were right when I was there."

"I don't suppose these dreams are telling you who is attacking your family? Are you satisfied Arkyn's household is free of traitors?"

"I have no evidence it isn't and they worked hard in Tera. Wynfeld can't find anyone either."

"Hmm. His promotion to Major raised a few eyebrows."

"Good. I intended it to," admitted Adeone.

"Just be careful." She smiled. "When do you want me to send Chapa in this direction?"

"I will send for him when I am ready, aunt. Though I'm truly touched by your care for my son."

Amara crooked an eyebrow. "I hope you weren't expecting anything else. I'm also pleased you appointed Tancred for young Tain. He's a good man, more so because his life hasn't always been easy. I should leave you to continue."

Grinning, Adeone relaxed back. "No, you shouldn't. I want all the Court gossip everyone hopes I won't find out about."

"You mean everything that you shouldn't show you're interested in," retorted Amara.

* * *

An hour after she left, Richardson asked Adeone if he had time to see Chapa. Suspiciously, Adeone agreed he had. As the doctor entered the Inner Office and Richardson left, the King said,

"How's Lady Amara?"

"Determined, Sire. She suggested Your Majesty might like a word."

"How helpful of her. Come and sit down and tell me about my elder son."

Chapa hesitated. "Ah. I admit I thought being at home would help him more than it has. I have been doing some reading and careful investigation. There are known instances of lethargies developing after illness. I am concluding that Prince Arkyn may be suffering from one. They are rarely, if ever, life threatening, but, if I am right, it will limit how much His Highness can manage. His energy will be far lower than might be expected. Some days he may struggle more than others. I think it can be managed but it will be a case of trying regimes and diets and seeing if they help until we find something that does. In time, it may disappear."

Adeone steepled his fingers. "*Was* it poison?"

Chapa frowned. "There's no evidence. I'm still perplexed by why no-one else fell ill, but it could be that they could tackle the illness more easily. It does happen. Or they could just have been lucky. Whatever the cause, though, His Highness is suffering the effects."

"If you have a regime and diet in mind, I suggest you go and talk with Edward and Kadeem. I will talk with Prince Arkyn."

* * *

Half an hour later, Arkyn entered the Inner Office listless and drawn. "You wanted to see me, Sire?"

"I always want to see you," answered Adeone. "Let's go through to my sitting room." Once there, Adeone sank onto a chair, watching his son carefully. "You're looking tired."

"It's been a busy few days, sir."

Adeone crooked an eyebrow. "Try again."

Arkyn swallowed but didn't say anything.

"Chapa has been to see me. So has Aunt Amara. You do realise she is exceptionally difficult to fool?"

"I do now," muttered Arkyn. "What did Chapa say?"

Adeone told him. "This is unfortunate, but we can work around it. It doesn't have to become common knowledge. Though I think we should tell Tain."

Arkyn swallowed. "He's difficult to fool too."

"It runs in the family. Arkyn, don't fret over it. Chapa is confident we can make positive changes. I just want you to promise me that you'll tell me if I ask too much of you."

Arkyn watched his father's face. "Why wouldn't I?"

"Don't even try that line. I know it of old – mostly through using it too much myself."

Arkyn chuckled. "Sorry, father. I will tell you if I think I really can't manage something."

Adeone's eyes narrowed. "Is that the best offer I'll get?"

"As my father, yes."

Adeone shook his head gently. "I won't be pulling rank on this one. Well, unless I think you really are ill and not telling me."

"Can we not dine with Aunt Amara then?"

Adeone chuckled. "I don't think we'd get away with that. She'd come and find us. Trust me, that is best avoided."

They sat talking until Richardson entered to say Judge Tancred was waiting. Adeone started. Everything else had put the appointment out of his mind.

* * *

Adeone greeted Tancred with a word of apology. Unfazed by his wait, the judge talked over the intricacies of teaching Tain without living at Ceardlann. Talk twisted over different possibilities including the use of messengers and Tain spending some days every week in Oedran. There were arguments against both possibilities; in the end, they decided that the easiest option was to see if Fitz had a private room at his inn in Dellwood, a mile outside the Rex Dallin bounds. If they didn't publicise the fact, it should be safe enough.

As the conversation concluded, Adeone said, "Well, James, is that all for now?"

"For myself, yes, Your Majesty, but I am feeling guilty. My actions mean that Ewall must remain in post. Is there any way he might be able to retire?"

Adeone steepled his fingers. "He has agreed to continue."

"I know, sir, and I am sorry to raise it; however, I believe that maybe something could be worked out – even for semi-retirement."

"As I have mentioned previously, I'm finding it difficult to trust people. Much as I agree that Ewall deserves an easy retirement, I can't think of anyone to take his place. Do you have any ideas?"

"I have been thinking on the matter, sir," replied Tancred. "I came up with two options if you will permit me to explain." When Adeone motioned him to continue, he said, "His Highness requires specialist tutors. I think that can be seen by all. The two options I envisaged were either a lawyer or an advisor. A lawyer for obvious reasons. Advisors are trained to some extent in law. There is, of course, another benefit in that you allocated an advisor to teach Prince Arkyn; if he is still trusted then there is no need for another person to be granted entry to the Rex Dallin. If you'll forgive me going that far, I hope you can forgive me also saying that justiciars in the past have also become regents. An advisor could provide training for that instance."

Adeone regarded Tancred for a couple of moments. "There is merit in that and is something I had foreseen. Thank you, James. I think you've not only solved one problem but have salved my conscience. I'll certainly talk to Ewall. He can have his retirement, as long as I can get an advisor for His Highness."

"Thank you, Sire. I am glad my solution met with your approval."

Adeone got up and poured two goblets of wine. Tancred took his with thanks and then followed Adeone to the comfortable chairs. He waited until the King had sat before doing so himself. Adeone smiled, Tancred was certainly traditional, but he wasn't at all stuffy with it.

"I didn't know you and Uncle Lachlan had written a book on the

Cearcallian Era."

Tancred smiled. "Not many do, Sire. It was a hobby of sorts."

"Prince Tain was talking to me about it. He found it a fascinating read. I must congratulate you on achieving the interest."

Tancred tried to shake off the praise. "It was nothing much, Sire. It was the first book to hand that I thought would not send His Highness to sleep."

"It was an inspired choice, James; so far he hasn't stopped mentioning it in two days."

"I am sorry about that, sir."

Adeone laughed. "I can stand it. Are you planning on making my son an expert in early law?"

"Not exactly, but it is helpful to understand where our laws have come from, sir, and to know the result of the more tyrannous ones, especially the fact they led to many uprisings."

"Bayan in 1169 comes to mind."

"Yes, sir – the Etanes tried to up taxes too much and the then Lord Rathgar did not stand up for his province, which was the first to be hit by the law. It was meant to be implemented with the review."

"Yes, I remember learning about it and the fact that my half-brother and his mother died of a fever when my father was defeating the rebels."

Tancred stilled. "Yes, Your Majesty. It had far-reaching effects."

"It did. I sometimes wonder what my lost family were like."

"I am afraid that I could not tell you, sir; I did not know them then. I was merely a newly qualified lawyer trying to scrape a living together."

Adeone smiled. "I know. It's just my father never really talked about them." He sighed. "I'd better get back to my desk. Thank you for your help."

"I hindered rather than helped, sir."

"James, stop blaming yourself and start preparing lessons for my son to be taught by an advisor."

Tancred smiled and bowed out. Adeone's tone had been tolerant enough. He became more sober as he walked through the Palace. He wished the rebellion hadn't been brought up: his brother had died during it. He should have told the King but, whilst the King was maudlin, it wasn't the right time. There would be a better opportunity.

* * *

Twenty-four minutes later, Tain bounced into the Inner Office, grinning broadly. Adeone got up to greet him and ruffled his hair.

"We need to talk."

Tain's face fell. "It's not about uncle again, is it? Because I've not told anyone."

"No, Tain, it's not, and I wouldn't have told you if I didn't trust you to keep your word. It's about your lessons with Judge Tancred."

"Oh. It's such a nice day, father—"

"You'll not distract me. Tancred has suggested the use of messengers occasionally, but Arkyn tells me you don't like using them. Why?"

Tain shuffled his feet. "I don't trust them. The Herald can watch them."

"The only way that messengers can be watched is if *I* order it." He paused; if he wasn't in Oedran, Scanlon *could* order it but that was a point he didn't think Tain needed to know yet. "There is a magic set up by the Cearcall that resides in the Herald's office. I have to specify whom I need watching and, Tain, I promise you, it would never be you."

"Yes, but the possibility is still there."

Adeone studied his son carefully. "All right, I accept that, but I won't spy on you. Now, what else is it?"

Tain glanced at his father then looked away.

Adeone became concerned. With a sense of foreboding, he asked, "Tain, my son, why do you *really* not like using messengers?"

Tain bit his lip and whispered, so quietly that Adeone almost missed it, "Mother was in a link when Ella fell."

Adeone managed to keep his face calm. He hadn't known that. "But your sister didn't fall because your mother was using a messenger, Tain."

"No, but I should have been watching Ella. I..." Tain started crying.

Adeone held him in a tight hug. His eyes weren't dry either. There was so much he didn't understand about what occurred when he'd visited Lufian. What had the link been about? Did it explain some of Ira's guilt over Ella's death? Why hadn't she told him, trusted him to help and not blame? Why did she keep it secret?

Tain's reticence over using messengers was a boy's fear someone else he loved would die – an understandable fear but one he had to overcome to fulfil his duties.

Eventually, Adeone said, "It wasn't your fault, Tain. It really wasn't. You do know that, don't you?"

"No. It *was* my fault. I was annoyed at Ella—"

"Who hasn't been annoyed with their siblings sooner or later? Tain, what happened that day isn't your fault. You were seven. Your mother was busy. You were a typical young boy and I should have been there. Nobody is to blame. That is what accident means. Ella fell. She would have fallen even if you hadn't been annoyed with her. That was never in doubt. You didn't push her, so you are not to blame." Adeone looked at Tain. The last sentence had struck a chord. "You *didn't* push her, Tain, did you?"

"No, but I wanted to."

"You didn't; that's what is important. I want to do quite a lot, but I don't."

"What like, father?"

Adeone smiled. "Pretend my work doesn't exist… Now that we've got to the root of the problem, will you try to call a messenger?"

"Must I, father?"

"Sooner or later, yes," said Adeone, hating himself. "You'll need them when you're older."

"What did people do before they existed?"

"That was before Ull came into the world. You should know by now, from listening to Laioril, that all they did was fight with each other. Talking wasn't as important, especially not over long distances."

"Yes, but they must have done *something*," insisted Tain.

"They probably wrote to each other. You're not going to distract me so give up trying."

"Sorry, father. I just find them annoying as well. They're all so PESKY!"

There was a flash of green light and Adeone reached out as a small, rainbow-coloured, dragon tumbled through the air.

It was muttering to itself. "Centuries in the dimension and someone finally decides to work out I exist. I mean it's lucky I like having nothing to do but after quite so long it can get *boring*. It's not like I was born to this job. Well, all right, maybe I was, but that rather defies anyone's definition of being born. I mean—"

"Aren't you meant to ask what we want?" enquired Adeone mildly.

The dragon looked at him whilst pacing back and forth on his hand. "Am I? No-one told me that. I don't know, they simply let us come out with no training. I mean, how do I flap my wings? Or flick my tail, for that matter. I mean, I don't even know whether I can breathe fire."

"You can't. Not in here anyway," replied Adeone hastily.

"Oh well. If I'm *meant* to ask you what I can do, I suppose I'd better." His head rose and he sat up on his rear legs. "What can I do for you?"

"Oh, not me, Pesky, it's my son who summoned you."

The dragon lay down, putting his head right down onto his front claws. "Great! Centuries of preparation and all I get is a stringy kid. I mean, with a name like 'Pesky' I know I'm not up to much, but I did kind of hope for something a bit more regal."

Adeone laughed. "I think we can manage regal. Prince Tain might not end up being king, but he certainly does regal."

Pesky perked up. "That's more like it. I can certainly go and flick my tail at the others in the dimension…" He seemed to think. "Which must mean you're a king."

"So everyone tells me."

The tiny dragon sat up. "Which land?"

"Whole empire. Shouldn't you have an instinct or something about this? I can ask Dragoris to get a link with anyone in the empire and I don't need to know them."

Pesky sniffed. "Oh, Dragoris is full of himself, he is. Believes the dimension revolves around him. Hardly says a word – thinks everyone can make way for him—"

Tain laughed. "You make up for him though."

Pesky shuffled round. "Are you saying I talk too much?"

"Yes. You've hardly stopped."

"You two should be right for one another then," observed Adeone.

Tain and Pesky turned to the King then looked at each other. Tain held out his hand and the dragon flopped onto it.

"So what can I do for you, princeling?" asked Pesky.

"Have a chat with Arkyn… A short one!" suggested Adeone.

Pesky perked up. "One link with Prince Arkyn Adeone hopefully coming… Now, do I flap my wings or flick my tail?"

Tain sighed. "Your wings I think."

A couple of minutes later, Adeone smiled as the opaque heat haze around his son vanished. "What did your brother say?"

"He seemed pleased to be interrupted instead of reading petitions," replied Tain, grinning. He glanced at Pesky, who was bouncing up and down on his hand. "Are you ever still?"

"No. That was fun. What can I do next?"

Adeone watched the dragon. "How about you talk to other messengers about how you should do things?"

"Good idea." Pesky disappeared.

Adeone laughed. "Tain, it appears your messenger is unconventional and, therefore, perfect for you."

Tain beamed. "Yes. Arkyn said the same. Sir, might I go and see Cal again later? My nearcousins aren't the same."

"Are you missing his company that much?" (Tain nodded.) "Then I'll have to do something about it, but don't disturb him today." As his son's face fell, Adeone crooked an eyebrow. "Without Judge Tancred at Ceardlann you're going to get more free time." That raised a sly smile. "I thought you might have realised. I don't want to rule every minute of your life, but can you do something for me with some of that free time and have a few more defence lessons?"

"I'll try. Cal's better than me at swordplay and archery, so I've got to catch him up."

"Nothing like a little competition in life." Adeone ruffled his son's hair. "There's something else. Arkyn's not well…" Seeing Tain biting his lip, blinking hard, Adeone pulled him into a hug. "Not ill like your mother was." His son relaxed. "He has a lethargy. If he says he's tired, or if Kadeem or Edward say he's asked not to be disturbed, will you respect that?"

Tain nodded. "Of course, father. He will be all right though?"

"If we keep an eye on him; he's hopeless at doing it himself."

Tain chuckled. "That runs in the family."

Chapter 16
OF STAFF AND HOUSEHOLDS
Pentadai, Week 1 – 5th Cearal, 5th Cearcis 1212
Inner Office

READING AND NUMBERING PETITIONS, Arkyn glanced up as Edward entered. His administrator had become more attentive since Doctor Chapa had had a word and, much as he appreciated the reasons, Arkyn found his concentration broken by the frequent interruptions.

"I'll take a rest when I've finished this one, Edward."

"His Majesty has asked to see you, sir."

Arkyn crooked an eyebrow. The lack of indication as to when suggested it was an immediate summons. He pushed himself to his feet as Edward answered his unspoken question.

"I'm not sure what about, sir."

"Then I don't know how long I'll be. Thank you."

He made his way to his father's chambers, half wishing the summons hadn't appeared. It wasn't that he didn't want to see his father, it was that he found it increasingly difficult to hide his exhaustion from him. His work would still be there when he returned to his office, and he'd wanted to finish it for the day. He barely acknowledged Hillbeck and Coppard's salutes as he passed. The guards in the Audience Chamber he didn't even glance at. Stopping and resting for a couple of moments was tempting, but that would start rumours, and he could hear someone else walking along the King's Corridor. Entering the Outer Office, he raked up a smile as his father's administrator pushed himself to his feet.

"Any idea why I'm needed, Richardson?"

"Suspicions only, Your Highness. I'm sure His Majesty will explain."

Arkyn gave a slight nod. Whatever it was, Richardson wasn't going to divulge details. It could be because that he didn't want the secretaries to hear, or he genuinely didn't know.

He nodded his thanks to Richardson as the administrator announced him, bowed to his father and felt his gaze sweep over him.

"Are you feeling better today?"

"A bit, sir, but it's odd; I feel fine one day and look atrocious, and the following day I feel drained and look fine."

"Then you'd better sit down. Would you like a drink so we can remove ourselves from this formal arrangement?"

Arkyn wondered what that said about the mid-morning summons. "I thought I was here for a formal reason, sir."

"That is not the point; however, if you're comfortable with it, whom am I to argue?"

Arkyn's lips twitched. "My father and King, Sire," he teased.

"Try to remove Percival's sense of humour from your repertoire... Now, how did you find the Petitionals? Did you end up with many petitions?"

So, that was the reason for the summons. It made sense when he considered it. He couldn't say that he'd found them exhausting, boring and frustrating. That wouldn't change anything. He couldn't say his altercation with his uncle had been the only enlivening thing during them. He settled for, "Interesting but also, I don't know, odd? They might take some getting used to. I've not counted exactly, but I think there were around ninety, including those handed to the clerks without the petitioners entering the hall. Maybe a few more. I'm numbering them as I go."

"That sounds about right. There are some that I've got to hand to Lord Scanlon as well, leaving me with a nice pile. I've been thinking about the ones you're dealing with; I know they all involve the militia at one level or another, some involve military law—"

"Most do, sir." Well, that at least was true. The trend had become apparent early in his perusal.

"Could you see if there's any pattern in them? Commanding officers or location, for example – any connections between the petitioners, that sort of thing; Wynfeld should be able to help."

"Gladly, sir. You're wondering if uncle is manipulating the army, aren't you? Or, at least, feeling against them," observed Arkyn.

"Yes, that's exactly what I'm wondering. I'm also not sure that sending you to Tera was a good thing – you've become too shrewd."

"I could become blind to motive instead?" commented Arkyn dryly.

"There's no future in that approach. Would you mind if I asked Advisor Rayburn to work with you on the military petitions?"

"Why should I, Sire?" Help wouldn't go amiss, that was for sure, but was it help offered or someone to check his work? He wished he could remove the paranoia when dealing with something new and unknown, but his uncle *would* seize any opportunity to discredit him, and his father had to be watchful of that as much as he did.

"Because after Tera I have been reliably informed, by people whose judgement I trust, that you don't need any advisors."

"Then they're all delusional, Sire." Arkyn swallowed. Who had been talking like that? Wynfeld? Percival? Even Daia Sansky? He half wished they wouldn't. There could only be mistakes around the corner if he and others believed him infallible. No-one was that. His father had rung for Richardson, asking him to send in Advisor Rayburn. That must have been who had been following him into the chambers. His father was saying,

"After we've spoken to him, can you give us an hour without interruption?"

The administrator's eyes twinkled. "I can do better than that, Sire – unless His Highness has to be anywhere else," replied the administrator.

Arkyn shrugged. "Nowhere other than Court; so, feel free to save me from it." He didn't want to admit that the pile of petitions would take up all his afternoon. If his father got wind of that, he'd never get them finished for days.

"Why the smile, Richardson?" enquired Adeone.

"It's fortunate that I've cleared the rest of your day and had Edward do the same for His Highness, Sire," replied the administrator.

Adeone growled, "Thank you. Tell Rayburn to join us and stop predicting my actions so well, it can get very… very…"

"Amusing?" asked Arkyn.

"Annoying?" enquired Richardson.

"Tiring, Sire?" suggested Rayburn, entering.

"Irksome!" finished Adeone, glaring at them all.

"An often underused word, Your Majesty," commented Richardson, adding, "Advisor Rayburn, Sire."

"Yes, I know that," muttered Adeone. "He just announced his arrival with 'Tiring'."

"*Annoying* was already taken, sir," observed the advisor innocently.

"That's a word that lends itself to many situations. Thank you, Richardson, that's all for now. Carry on predicting my requests."

As the door closed on the Outer Office, they were all smiling and Arkyn felt some of the weight lift as he pushed himself to his feet to greet the advisor. He'd spend a couple of hours with his father and then excuse himself. He'd still be able to get something done, but his father could think he'd be resting. If Edward wasn't hovering, he might get through even more. After the petitions were summarised, he could take time for himself with a clear conscience.

As the door closed on Richardson, Adeone said, "Prince Arkyn, I believe you know Advisor Rayburn."

"I do, Sire, but more by reputation than acquaintance."

Rayburn bowed to him. A confident bow, not at all self-conscious or hurried. Arkyn weighed up what he knew of the man. Rayburn had been on his father's staff since his grandfather's day. He had become the King's Military Advisor with his father's accession, which spoke of a level of trust and long-proved competency. He had a vague recollection that his nearfather thought highly of Rayburn, and Wynfeld had spoken well of him.

"Sir. Reputation is often a different way of saying rumour, so I'm, naturally, concerned about what you've heard, but Your Highness' reputation is now far more than rumour."

Adeone's eyes twinkled. "Rayburn, have a seat and be careful; that was almost a compliment and outside of Court. Prince Arkyn, I think you'll find Rayburn is slightly unconventional…"

Arkyn reseated himself. "Then I hope the advisor and I find we can work well together, Sire."

The advisor also sat. "Your Highness, I shall be working *for* you."

"Your point being that we shall therefore be unable to work together?" suggested Arkyn. If the advisor was that way inclined, there might be more problems. Sycophancy wasn't a harmony to success, quite the opposite.

"Not exactly, Your Highness, but you are my Prince and the relationship is, therefore, unequal. 'Together' implies equality. I hope rather that Your Highness finds no fault with my work or manner."

"Would you say, therefore, that we've got off to a good start?" Arkyn enquired wryly. The advisor was still relaxed, not at all perplexed by the situation, and Arkyn found a spark of genuine liking.

"I would hope that we've started with honesty, sir," replied Rayburn, undeterred.

"Yes, I think we've started with that, but please, Rayburn, try to tone down the pedantry when it is a common pleasantry; I tend to tear apart my speech without help." Was this why his father and nearfather rated the advisor? This complete acceptance of roles without any undertone of discontent. The straight talking without rudeness.

"As you wish, Your Highness. My apologies."

"Now that you've sorted out that small issue…" began Adeone, as they both started guiltily. "…No, no, I found it illuminating; however, Rayburn, you're aware that His Highness is investigating petitions that relate to the militia. Do you have any immediate advice?"

"Getting rid of the army would solve all the problems, Sire."

"Unfortunately, that isn't a viable option," responded Adeone with a smile.

"It's a good point though," stated Arkyn. The advisor was used to the King's ways and sense of humour. That could be good but, if Rayburn was to work for him, he couldn't allow him too much leeway so early on. If he did, his uncle would no doubt twist it, reporting that his staff were impertinent and disrespectful. "I take it, Rayburn, that what you actually meant was a simple 'no'?"

"Correct, Your Highness," agreed Rayburn. "I might suggest we'll need a summary document."

Relief washed over Arkyn. Maybe he could delegate the rest of his reading for a time. He could then read through everything more leisurely as opportunity presented itself. "You'd better ask Edward to do you a copy of the one I was writing yesterday. It's currently on my desk. Maybe you could finish it. I've been numbering the petitions and trying to find common themes to help with ordering them."

Adeone chortled at Rayburn's expression. "What's the matter, Advisor?"

"Erm, I was expecting to have to write one from scratch, Sire. It's rather disorientating to find that I don't need to."

The King nodded. "I can appreciate that. You'd better report to the Prince's Administrator, Rayburn."

* * *

After Rayburn left, Arkyn sat opposite his father by the unlit fire, talking quietly. Their enforced formality with others present fell away. The months in Terasia had forged within their relationship something deeper than father and son or King and Prince. The common aim bred understanding where before there might have been frustration. So, when Adeone suggested Arkyn's new staff should include twelve advisors, his son was comfortable saying no, where before Terasia he might have felt obliged to agree. The traditions surrounding them dictated Arkyn couldn't rely on one man, as he was wont to do, but should appoint a broad staff. At Adeone's suggestion, they decided to appoint six advisors, to placate expectations: three would be juniors answering to seniors who would answer to Arkyn. That way, he could continue to deal with fewer men. Glad for the compromise, Arkyn raised no further objection. As talk turned to memories of Terasia, Adeone revealed he wanted Arkyn to have a coach so that, if he was travelling in bad weather again, he was less likely to fall ill.

Arkyn moved to sit by his father. "Thank you."

Adeone ruffled his hair. "It's what I'm here for. Tell me if there's anything you can't face."

"I will, or at least, I think I will."

"As decisive as ever about personal decisions, I notice."

"I follow your fine example, father."

"You're not too old to be tickled," pointed out Adeone. "Or I could make you have twelve advisors to deal with."

"It might make my reports longer."

"Hmm. I suppose that's stalemate. I'd like your opinion on something else as you're here. Judge Tancred has suggested I get an advisor as a co-tutor for Tain – one who can be at Ceardlann. I wondered what you thought about Spellen. He taught you well, or seemed to."

Arkyn smiled. "I should think Advisor Spellen will face the challenge with competence, sir, and Ewall does deserve a retirement and pension. Spellen should have had enough warning about Tain's humour."

Adeone smiled at his elder son. "Is that ever possible?"

Chuckling, Arkyn got up and retrieved the jug of water from the sideboard. He topped up his and his father's glasses before sitting down opposite the King and asking what Rayburn was like to work with.

* * *

Arkyn left an hour later and Adeone returned to his desk, feeling easier in himself. There was something reassuring in his son's calm, practical manner when facing difficulties and new challenges. It reminded him that not all of life had to be a fight. Compromise could win the day. His work wouldn't wait for another day, much as he appreciated Richardson's earlier gesture. He picked up the first report from the pile Richardson had left that morning. He read the majority before asking his administrator to summon the Steward. By the time the man arrived, Adeone had read the remainder with his blood boiling. His son's example would wait for another day.

He tossed the report over the desk at the Steward. "What makes you think interfering in His Highness' household is permissible, Steward?"

"Your Majesty, I meant to do no such thing, but, now His Highness is home, does his household require four footmen?"

"Maybe you'd care to decimate mine whilst you're at it? No? You surprise me. His Highness will be travelling to Paras later this year and his household will need to be substantial enough to enhance his position and cope with his progress through the empire. Are you secure enough to manage to find men of their calibre again?" (The Steward tried to interrupt.) "I don't want to hear excuses or apologies. His Highness' household does not come under your eye. It is his concern; if there are substantiated doubts about it, then it becomes mine."

"Who informs Your Majesty of the doubts, Sire?"

"I'm rather surprised you need to ask. That's all for now." He didn't miss the dark glint in the Steward's eyes, but he didn't care. The unwarranted interference had destroyed his day.

Chapter 17

PRINCES' GUARD

Septadai, Week 1 – 7th Cearal, 7th Cearcis 1212
Prince Arkyn's Chambers

ARKYN AWOKE ON SEPTADAI wishing he was at Ceardlann but that would have to wait. He'd invited Julius to breakfast with him. Too late, he realised he should have invited his other nearcousins as well, but he'd wanted to see how Julius was coping with the Advisors' School.

His nearcousin entered with a florid bow. "What have I done this time, Your Highness?"

Arkyn shrugged. "You think I'm told? His Majesty would be informed first. How are you finding your rooms?"

"Very comfortable, thank you, sir. You won't get rid of us at this rate."

Arkyn waved him to the table, thinking, in some ways, it would be nice if it were true. There were days he felt too alone, especially when he didn't have the energy to stand at Court. "How's the Advisors' School?"

Julius pulled a face. "Different." He toyed with the fork in his hand. "How do you do it, Arkyn? How do you sit through hours of drivel?"

Arkyn chuckled. "That good. Well, it starts with a decent breakfast." He glanced at his manservant. "Thank you, Kadeem. That's all for now." When he'd gone, Arkyn said, "Drivel?"

Julius sighed. "Dank and depressing drivel. Honestly. It's like I'm Lucius' age. You wouldn't believe it."

"How is Irvin coping?"

"Much more diplomatically. Seven years to go."

Arkyn chuckled. "It could be they are covering fundamentals for a short time. Don't forget, not everyone has the King's Chief Advisor as their father, and the King as their nearfather."

"True. I'm just hoping this isn't a case of starting the year as it means to go on. How has yours been?"

Arkyn considered how to answer. "Busy. Father wants to set up a more permanent staff for me and has asked Advisor Rayburn to advise me on the petitions."

"You're getting more to do then?"

Arkyn pulled a face but didn't reply and wasn't upset when Julius changed the subject to Court gossip. None of which was particularly taxing. An hour later, he left and Arkyn breathed a sigh of relief. He enjoyed Julius' company, but he'd been less awake than expected. He poured himself another glass of water before ringing for Kadeem to clear. Making his way to his office, he found Edward and Rayburn waiting.

He nodded them both inside and sat down. "Edward?"

"The only thing in your diary today, sir, is the meeting about the new Princes' Guard with His Majesty. It's due to start in an hour. I'm reliably informed Lord Landis, is currently doing a spot check on all guards in the Palace. Much to Captain Pixney's chagrin as he doesn't know why."

Arkyn's lips twitched. "He doesn't have long to wait. Rayburn?"

The advisor smiled. "I've finished the summary document, sir, and wondered if you wanted any advice about Lord Landis' suggestions for your new guard."

Arkyn caught Edward's discreetly raised eyebrow. The advisor was taking his new role to heart.

"I'll ring if I require anything, Edward. Have a seat, Rayburn." He waited until the door closed before asking, "How do you know what Lord Landis has suggested?"

"I am the King's Military Advisor, Your Highness. On occasion, His Lordship does talk matters over with me."

Arkyn accepted that. Even his nearfather must need others' insight occasionally, and Rayburn appeared to be shrewd. Arkyn glanced at the report by his hand. His nearfather had been thorough. The plan outlined for the Princes' Guard was, to his own eye, more than acceptable and workable. Maybe it was a good test.

"Do you have any concerns about the suggestions, Advisor?"

Rayburn considered. "No, sir."

Arkyn's eyes narrowed. That wasn't at all sycophantic or verbose. It gave him scant facts to base a judgement on. The suggestions were relatively simple, it was true: one captain, three sergeants and fifteen guards. They'd answer to him on a daily basis, but ultimately to the King. They would be independent of the other official guards and militia. Along with his nearfather's proposal was a note in his father's hand saying he was thinking of Sergeant Marsh as captain, and transferring Smithers, promoting him to sergeant to watch over Tain.

"Who would you suggest as captain, Rayburn?"

The advisor never hesitated. "Someone with a lot of experience as a senior guard, sir. Can't be Fitz, not now he's retired. I expect His Majesty will pick either Marsh or Hillbeck from his own guard. It makes sense. If I were to take a bet, I'd say Marsh. He's got more experience."

"That is true but do you not, therefore, consider he might be better guarding the King?" enquired Arkyn truly intrigued by Rayburn's shrewdness. He hadn't expected him to hit on Marsh. Who would? The King's senior guard. Many would see it as a demotion.

"There are many reasons why His Majesty would choose an experienced guard and why it makes sense to do so, sir. The King – I hope you'll forgive me – cares more deeply about Your Highnesses than he does about himself. He'll want your lives protected by the best there is. Partly for the love he bears you, partly for the future you represent but mostly because he's an excellent swordsman himself and your brother still has many years to perfect the art of protecting himself."

Arkyn's lips twitched. Rayburn's conclusions were probably closer to the mark than he'd admit. "How long have you worked for the King?"

Rayburn swallowed. "Since the last weeks of 1200, sir."

"And how long do you intend to?"

"Until His Majesty no longer wishes for my advice, sir. Or until I earn Your Highness' ire, I suspect."

Arkyn snorted. "Is my reputation so formidable?"

"Rumour has much speculation to sustain it, my prince. Your work has been much admired, the new appointments following the provincial review much debated, and Lord Iris has been most complimentary."

"Congratulations. That neither avoided my question nor answered it. Do you have any other observations?" As Rayburn opened his mouth, Arkyn added, "About the new Princes' Guard."

Rayburn changed tack, chortling. "Nothing about the structure, sir. I expect the men will have background checks done by Wynfeld and Beaver. Those will be important and thorough. I suggest that more men than needed are vetted. You might like to handpick the men of the guard if His Majesty doesn't. If men are transferred from the King's Guard, and Marsh or Hillbeck are captain, then they will have knowledge of them. From the Palace Guard, you should get Captain Pixney's views. I have little doubt that Wynfeld will be available with his, should you require them."

Arkyn watched the advisor talking without fully hearing all he was saying. There was something in Rayburn's general bearing that spoke of honesty, not secrets. His advice was pertinent, to the point and made without prejudice or reference to Landis' views, which he must have known.

Arkyn toyed with his pen. "Thank you, Rayburn. That is all for now."

The advisor left with a practical half-bow. So far, he was proving, if not invaluable, astute. Arkyn re-read his nearfather's report before walking through the Privy Wing to his father's chambers, where he entered the Inner Office minutes before everyone else.

His father glanced up. "You breakfasted with Julius?"

Arkyn grinned. "Yes. He didn't seem too hungover either. Do I need to know anything else for this counsel?"

"No. I'm going with your nearfather's suggestions…"

* * *

Half an hour later, Arkyn had listened to his father outline the plans to the other attendees. Marsh had accepted the promotion. Smithers would be transferred and Landis had requested the guards were trained to the best level the General could manage.

Adeone laughed lightly. "That's better than mine, my lord."

"Whilst we're at it, Your Majesty, we'll get yours trained as well."

Arkyn smiled to himself. In reply to his father's raised eyebrow, he said, "I think, Sire, they'll also need to be fit. Prince Tain does have a lot of energy."

"Too true. Lord Landis, any comments on that?"

"I'll see they're fit, sir. Now, after the spot check I did earlier today, there are rumours going round that I think the Palace Guard are incompetent. I happen to think they do an excellent job but I like to make sure they are still capable if not proficient. My secretary told me I had more guards I liked than those I didn't. So, other than that resulting in more problems finding the men we need for the Princes' Guard, congratulations are in order – as well as my apologies for putting Pixney through today without any explanation."

Adeone made a note. "Thank you, Lord Landis. I want this guard ready in an aluna-month. Any questions?"

"One, Sire," admitted Major Wynfeld. "Will the guards accompany Their Highnesses in the Rex Dallin?" When Adeone shook his head, he said, "Might I, therefore, enquire then what they'll be doing in Oedran when they aren't guarding Their Highnesses, sir?"

"I can find them plenty to do: enhancing their skills, augmenting my guard, helping Pixney with the Palace Guard and guarding any visitors of standing. Prince Arkyn, do you wish to add anything?"

Having caught his father's eye, Arkyn replied, "One thing, Sire. Everyone here is aware of the situation. The attempts on my father's life and mine are tantamount to proof that my uncle will never give up. Now, unless he trips himself up and admits liability, the only person who can stop him dragging the empire into civil war is my brother. His safety is paramount – more so than my own. I want to know the guard are prepared for whatever scheme Prince Tain comes up with next." He ignored the glance between his father and nearfather and instead held Marsh's gaze. It would be the new captain who had to deal with his request. Marsh simply nodded by way of reply and reassurance.

The King said simply, "His Highness is right. Thank you, gentlemen. Prince Arkyn, Lord Landis, please stay a moment."

Arkyn caught his nearfather's eye. Had he spoken out of turn? Even if he had, he didn't particularly care. Tain needed protecting.

Once they were alone, Adeone added, "You didn't need to do that, Arkyn."

"Maybe not, but I wanted to. Can you imagine a world without Tain?"

Adeone laughed. "No. It was certainly a duller place. Scanlon's informed me he's going to tour the provinces again; however, I'm not sure when he's going. I want Tain and you, Arkyn, to return to the Rex Dallin for a bit. Landis, can I ask you to postpone travelling to Macia until the guard is set up?"

Arkyn relaxed slightly. Time at Ceardlann would be very welcome and if his father had made the decision, he didn't need to feel guilty about it.

Landis considered for a moment. "I'm sure the Fencible will like more time to prepare, sir. Though, given past experience, Your Highness, might I beg a favour of you? See His Majesty stays out of trouble in my absence. Keep him and Prince Tain apart. I'm not sure which is the bad influence."

Arkyn laughed. "I'm afraid I can't promise to be successful, Uncle Festus." He pulled his documents together. His notes folded on top.

Adeone shook his head in amusement. "You're losing your touch, my lord. You two shouldn't be conspiring and certainly not in front of me."

"Surely, Sire, it is better than us conspiring behind your back – at least you know what we're planning," observed Landis, straight-faced.

A knock preceded Richardson entering with a pile of documents.

"Come to keep me in condition?" asked Adeone.

"Would I presume, Sire?" replied his administrator.

Landis said, "We'll leave you to it, Your Majesty."

"You are kindness itself, my lord," muttered the King. "If you're not careful, I'll think you haven't got enough to do and locate something else."

Landis bowed. "Come on, Your Highness, I think he means it. Let's make our escape whilst the going's good."

Chapter 18
ADVICE AND ADVISORS
Cisadai, Week 2 – 9th Cearal, 9th Cearcis 1212
Palace – Landis Chambers

THE FOLLOWING MORNING, Landis lingered over breakfast. His younger children and ward were breakfasting with Tain and Elantha, but that just gave him time to brood. New situations with old acquaintances could be tricky for him.

The sight of her pensive husband piqued Lady Landis' curiosity. "What is it, Festus?"

"I have to go and see Prince Arkyn about his advisors."

Cornelia eyed him. "He's your nearson, not old King Altarius!"

"At least with King Altarius I knew where I stood. I knew how he

99

worked. I've watched His Highness grow, helped mould the man and now I have to face the official he is, not the nearson I know. Yesterday's meeting brought a few surprises."

"Arkyn will still be Arkyn, my dear. He's probably as nervous as you are. Be yourselves, that's all it will take."

"I'm not sure it'll be that easy, for some reason I feel history closing in around me."

She squeezed his wrist. "History should be left to historians. If you worry about that, you'll never live in the present but in the anticipation of future criticisms of past actions. Go and see His Highness and then you'll wonder why you made this fuss in the first place. What's more, if you're not careful, you'll worry yourself into unintentional actions."

Landis got up. "Most people would be amazed to hear it."

"Yes, well, whatever most people think, you're still a man, with all the faults of one."

Landis paused. "I'm not sure that was reassuring."

"I'm not sure I meant it to be. Go on. Not everyone in your life will flatter you."

"It might be nice if one did on occasion – or at least, one whom I'm close to!"

Cornelia got up and slipped her arm through her husband's. "My dear, flattery should not be necessary in your heart to know we love you."

As Landis watched her, his grey eyes became less preoccupied. Cornelia smiled warmly at him and put her head against his arm.

"I'd better retrieve my notes," murmured Landis, leaving her with a parting kiss.

Cornelia turned and spotted her elder son. "Julius, what time did you return to your rooms last night?"

"Mother, I'm over cisan-age."

"Yes, and looking under-the-weather instead. Have you got lectures today?" (He paused.) "Go on. Don't disgrace your father's name and, don't forget, you're abusing the King's hospitality as well. As his nearson, you ought to be setting an example."

Julius walked away mumbling. Cornelia's eyed narrowed. She could have sworn her son had said something about the fact he was setting an example, it just wasn't a good one.

* * *

Quarter of an hour later, Edward knocked on Arkyn's office door saying sonorously, "Lord Landis, Your Highness."

"Thank you, Edward. Lord Landis, I shouldn't be long." Two moments later, he shouted for Edward. "Send this to Terasia in the dispatches."

Edward took the letter. "I'll send it at once, sir."

"No, it's all right, by the dispatches is fine, the most anyone can glean from it is that Wealsman and I enjoy chess. It's hardly a secret."

Once Edward had left and closed the door, Arkyn eyed his nearfather, who had stayed standing off to one side.

"Take a seat, Landis; I'm intrigued you let Edward announce you."

Landis smiled, sitting down. "He offered, Your Highness, and I thought it prudent, as this is the first time I've visited your office."

"So it is," replied Arkyn mildly. "We'll wait for Rayburn before we start. He shouldn't be long."

Watching Landis with a penetrating gaze, Arkyn wasn't convinced that his nearfather was as easy as he portrayed. If he was honest with himself, he was wondering how to approach the situation as well. His father managed to keep some level of detachment, so he should also be able to.

When Rayburn had joined them, Arkyn said to Landis, "My lord, I believe you're here to persuade me a multitude of advisors is a good thing."

Landis shook his head slightly. "I'm noted for attempting the impossible, sir, but His Majesty has merely asked me to confirm some details."

"You'd better confirm them then."

Rayburn on the sidelines was watching the Prince's face and Lord Landis'. He realised they were both uneasy with the forced formality induced by his presence. "Your Highness, would you prefer me to leave until the initial discussions are over?"

Arkyn, surprised by the offer, said, "No, thank you, Advisor. I can't foresee a situation where you can't be present. Lord Landis?"

"I'm not at all concerned by Rayburn's presence, sir." If Arkyn was happy, Landis knew he didn't really have a choice, but it would have been easier without the advisor there.

"Good. Then you'd better continue."

Landis did so. "His Majesty has informed me that there are to be advisors added to your staff this year, sir. He mentioned that you'd come to the agreement of three senior and three junior ones. Is this still correct?"

"Yes, it is. With regards to the seniors, can His Majesty's Advisors spare Rayburn, my lord?" enquired Arkyn surprising even himself. The advisor had impressed him, that was true, but he rarely took to people so quickly.

Landis paused, normally he'd have agreed immediately but Rayburn's post as the King's Military Advisor was difficult to fill. He had been seconded to Arkyn's staff for the sole purpose of dealing with the petitions relating to the militia.

Arkyn saw the hesitation. "I take it not."

"I would have to speak with His Majesty, Your Highness."

"I shall do that, my lord, until then we had better work on the assumption that you will be returning to the King's staff, Rayburn; however, I would be interested in knowing if you hold any objection to remaining on mine."

"Not if I knew there was another advisor to take my responsibilities on His Majesty's, sir," replied Rayburn diplomatically.

"Then we'll proceed on that understanding. We'll need to list around eight advisors, Lord Landis. If possible, for the junior ones, I'd like to give the opportunity to recently graduated advisors who might be worthy of note. Give them a chance to gain their reputations."

"It would be better to wait until your staff expands a bit more, sir."

Arkyn smiled and, catching Rayburn's eye to include him in the reply, looked at his nearfather. "Traditions can be changed, my lord."

"So they can, sir; however, my recommendation isn't based on tradition but common sense. The smaller your staff, the less leeway you have for advisors who aren't experts."

"Everyone has to start somewhere," responded Arkyn, frowning. His nearfather was being unusually stubborn. Maybe he needed to stop thinking of Landis in those terms for the moment. In this situation, he was a member of their staff, not a nearfather.

"Yes, Your Highness, but your staff is a representation of your position in society."

"It should also represent my principles, my lord," explained Arkyn, trying to draw the conversation back to a professional one. "I believe in giving people a chance. I won't keep *anyone* on my staff if they don't merit it."

Puzzled by Landis' stance, Advisor Rayburn said, "Forgive me for interrupting, Your Highness, but you could simply employ one advisor of the type you describe."

"I still advise against it, sir," remarked Landis.

Arkyn got up, crossed to the window and gazed at the view across the gardens unseeingly. Landis was obviously against the idea, and decidedly so – which perplexed him. Rayburn, however, wasn't but was the advisor merely being polite? How far should he push his wishes? He wanted to give new advisors a chance but didn't want to appear too obstinate.

Sitting down and nodding for Landis and Rayburn to as well, he said, "Lord Landis, I shall compromise—"

"Your Highness, it is not necessary if you are set on the action."

Arkyn pursed his lips. "Please do not interrupt me, my lord. Two senior and two junior advisors will be appointed to my staff who are already established. One advisor shall be appointed who might assume either role, depending on His Majesty's decision regarding Advisor Rayburn. If you are retained on the King's staff, Rayburn, that advisor becomes my third senior advisor and the junior post goes to a recent graduate. Does that make sense, Lord Landis?"

"Yes, sir, but a graduate can be appointed anyway."

"You've made your opinions known, my lord, and I hope I can take advice. Do you have a list of potential advisors?"

Landis handed over a copy cursing himself; he'd annoyed Arkyn. It wasn't a good start.

Arkyn took the list, apparently at ease but had he been right to push the matter? It might be the first time they'd worked together, but it shouldn't have been a test of will.

By the end of the meeting, it appeared the small disagreement inherent to the beginning of it had been forgotten. Both Arkyn and Landis had relaxed, but there was still an odd atmosphere. Arkyn gathered his notes together.

"I shall speak to His Majesty and then you can see about appointing those named, my lord. Advisor Rayburn, whatever is decided, we shall resume our trawl through the petitions soon."

Rayburn rose. "Of course, Your Highness." On the threshold of the office, he bowed precisely and smiled as he left.

Once the door had closed, Arkyn eyed Landis; who had a strange feeling; the Prince was evaluating him and, for the first time, Landis was uneasy in his nearson's presence.

"Your Highness, I might have been too forceful earlier."

Arkyn's evaluating gaze never wavered. "You were trying to mix too many roles. Private advice is for private locations. I had given the matter of my advisors more thought than I think you realised, but I shall stick to the compromise we've reached. Now, I must go and see His Majesty, so if you'll excuse me…"

* * *

Questioning how he'd handled the situation, the walk along the King's Corridor to the Inner Office wasn't far enough for Arkyn to rid himself of his preoccupation and doubts. Landis had many years' experience in appointing and managing advisors and the demands on the FitzAlcis staff. He would have had good reasons for the stance he'd taken.

As the door closed on the Outer Office, his father asked, "What is it?"

"It's nothing, Sire. Have you got a couple of minutes? It's about my advisors."

Adeone had an inkling of why Arkyn was uneasy. "Don't tell me, Landis overreacted to the situation."

Arkyn paused. "That's the problem. I don't know if he did or not."

"Then tell me what happened and I'll see if I do."

"Must I, sir?"

"I think it might be wise if you did," replied Adeone reassuringly.

So, Arkyn explained; by the time he'd finished the recitation, Adeone was troubled.

"What was Festus thinking? I can't see anything wrong with your request; I wonder if there's something he's not telling me."

"Was I pushing the matter too far, Your Majesty?"

"I don't think you pushed it at all. I'm impressed with the compromise you reached as well. There's nothing wrong with wanting a newly qualified advisor when it's one in six. It's a good idea – especially if there's an exceptional advisor in the making in this year's graduates. We normally offer the top graduate work here anyway. I'll have a word with your nearfather. It's not easy for either of you, but he shouldn't be advising you against such actions without giving a proper explanation."

"Thank you, sir, but I think Lord Landis might be re-evaluating his advice."

Adeone smiled; having heard Wealsman's stories about how Arkyn worked, he wouldn't be at all surprised by that. "Maybe. Now, about Rayburn…"

"If you need him, Sire, then I can cope; I've just found he's someone I feel comfortable with."

"Better than Iris?"

"Different, Sire."

"That word hides a multitude of facts," observed Adeone dryly. "Look, I'll be honest. Rayburn is one of my closest advisors and one of my best, but he's seconded to your staff and I did that quite happily. If you want to keep him for the time being that's fine, but should I need him—"

"He'll be there, Sire. Thank you."

"That's all right. I thought you'd get on with Rayburn. He has an old-fashioned attitude but it's mixed with honesty and good advice."

"It must make Court interesting."

"He adapts well. I suspect he'd have adapted to working with my father also."

"Does that mean, I wonder, that he's career driven? Would he, for example, adapt to Uncle Scanlon's methods?"

Adeone paused. "No, I don't think so; he's too principled for that. I think with father he'd have found a diplomatic way of putting advice, but to work for a scheming, psychopathic lunatic is beyond him."

* * *

Immediately after Arkyn left, Adeone sent for Landis. He didn't interrupt his mood by doing anything else in the meantime. He watched the gardens, lips pursed, trying to determine how to approach the matter. He couldn't have his Chief Advisor defy his son, however close they all were in private.

Landis entered without his normal exuberance. He noted Adeone's stance. "I've been a fool, Sire."

"I want your side of what happened with His Highness."

The honorific spoke volumes to Landis. This wasn't going to be a polite chat between friends about the idiosyncrasies of their children. Landis explained as much of the meeting as he could recall without bias, without trying to paint himself in the best light, without anything but the honesty Adeone valued. He watched the King's face; it hadn't worked.

Barely controlling his rage, Adeone snapped, "If you ever undermine your Prince in such a way again, I will be looking for a new Chief Advisor! You get this chance, Landis. Terasia handed your Prince the Memini's Manuscript because of his work. You could have destroyed that hard won reputation. Luckily, Rayburn is discreet and His Highness can disassociate private and professional personas; it might be worth you taking lessons off him in that respect!"

"Your Majesty, I realise I might have been too forceful but His Highness can't have inexperienced advisors. It will be dangerous."

"Your Prince is not proposing appointing a raw recruit to the post of a King's Advisor. It's a junior post on his staff. Do I need to remind you how young and *inexperienced* you were when I appointed you?"

"I wasn't newly qualified, sir."

"You hadn't taken any work between graduating and your appointment though," Adeone reminded him icily.

Landis tried reason. "Sir, he's not proposing to appoint a future Lord of Oedran who has had the necessary social as well as professional skills drummed into them from an early age."

Adeone's eyes narrowed. "I never thought you'd be so fixed or so prejudiced. You know, as well as I do, that, apart from in small ways, Prince Arkyn is far more traditional than I ever was or am. He's not going to risk the empire for any principle and few of us can claim the same. I wish I had half of my son's ability to compromise and accept unwanted advice, for in the end, Landis, he *did* listen to you. Do you realise that he's given you a greater honour in that small fact than your actions gave him? You questioned his judgement, his right to choose who works for him; you questioned my decision to let him handle this. He's already done far more in one year working on the reviews than I ever did. He's appointed a governor and run a province, all whilst recovering from flu; it wasn't such a simple affair as his manner suggests either."

"Sire, he appointed Wealsman, who was a forgone conclusion," observed Landis with a trace of exasperation tinting his voice.

"Wealsman *wasn't* a forgone conclusion! Not for Arkyn. He knew nothing of anyone but Portur when he went south – nothing. I never told him anything; maybe I was in error there but having seen the results I don't think I was."

Landis hesitated. "I know you didn't tell him you were friends, but he would have been briefed about the lords running—"

"He wasn't! I wanted and needed him to come to his own conclusions. I didn't want my views or others' to prejudice him. Can't you see it now? He's not the child that you have to gently introduce into the world. He's found the world and matched it already."

Adeone watched as Landis' face changed from earnest reasoning to sickening realisation.

Two moments later, Landis admitted, "I'm an absolute... I don't know what I am, but I'm in the wrong. I shall try to reconcile things with Prince Arkyn, Your Majesty."

"Good! You're to apologise to him. Though don't tell him about this; he asked me not to speak to you."

"He did?" enquired Landis, startled. "We're in for an interesting few years, Your Majesty."

"Have you only just realised that?" enquired Adeone.

"Sometimes you need a reminder, sir. I shouldn't have been such a fool, Sire."

"No, you shouldn't but I think the worst thing you did was refuse to accept that Prince Arkyn knew his own wishes."

Landis clasped his hands behind his back. "I don't mean this as an attempt to dig myself out of the hole, Sire, but do you, therefore, simply want sycophants to advise His Highness?"

"No, I don't. I need people to realise his opinion is valid and he's not a child. I also need to know that my Chief Advisor recognises Prince Arkyn is his future king and can recognise when something is important and, likewise, when it is not. It is on days like today I think you shouldn't be my Chief Advisor; friendship doesn't mix well. Now, let's move off the subject before we end up arguing any further."

Landis inclined his head slightly. "Certainly, Sire, but I could do with knowing your decision regarding Rayburn."

"I've left him on Arkyn's staff whilst he accustoms himself to his other advisors, but on the understanding that I can recall him, which leads in nicely to my next point. Arkyn will be getting a young advisor on his staff by the end of this year." He watched his friend's blank face. "You'll observe the spring finals at the Advisors' School and pick a candidate who will be exceptional and can work well for your nearson."

"I don't feel I know enough of how His Highness works, Your Majesty; especially not to make such a decision for him," admitted Landis, both to Adeone and himself. Returning to the school, even to oversee the finals, was not his idea of fun.

"Then see Wynfeld. He knows."

"I'd rather not show up my ignorance quite so spectacularly and Wynfeld has become quite shrewd," replied Landis with a sinking heart. Adeone was resolute about the idea. His friend wasn't ignorant of his dislike for the school; this was his punishment.

"Are you *wary* of Wynfeld?" Adeone's amusement didn't show.

Landis never hesitated. "It's more that I've developed a respect for the Major, Sire, but wish to keep the relationship between myself and the FitzAlcis mythical."

"You mean you can't divine it fully so you don't want someone else to. I can understand that – our fathers were always cagey talking about each other, maybe it's their legacy. That aside, I mean it: talk to Wynfeld. He is definitely fulfilling the promise we saw in him."

"Yes, Sire, especially as he's opened the file on me that the Intelligence Regiment had previously closed." Landis inwardly cursed as Adeone stilled.

"How do you know that?"

"Friends in the right places, sir, and I know when I'm being followed."

"What friends?" enquired the King in a deceptively calm way.

"Does it matter, Sire?"

"Yes, it does!"

Landis inwardly cursed. Adeone's temper hadn't cooled. How many more times was he going to trip himself up?

"One of the clerks came to me with some information, sir. It came out in our conversation. I'm not sure if he was telling me with the intention of gaining favour, or if he was just stupid. Either way, I've heard that he's been replaced. Hence my comment regarding Wynfeld, the timing of his return to the city and the man's replacement is co-incidental."

Adeone's eyes narrowed. "Yes, isn't it? What else did he reveal to you, Festus?"

"Nothing, which made me wonder what his motives were. Might I enquire why Your Majesty wishes to know?"

"Are you doing anything nefarious that Wynfeld might need to report to me?" enquired Adeone, scrutinising his friend. Anyone could betray him: friends, courtiers, staff, lords – Landis met all of those.

Landis laughed. "Never, Sire. I'm being watched!"

"I wasn't joking, Landis," remarked Adeone. "Wynfeld only follows people when he has information on them."

"Or when they're close to the FitzAlcis. Your Majesty has nothing to worry about."

"Nothing that, as my Defender, might be problematic when you're being followed?" mused Adeone.

"No, Sire, nothing."

"Oh, then I can hardly tell Wynfeld to stop."

* * *

Landis left the Inner Office, his mind reeling. Adeone's displeasure and suspicion had been tangible in a way it hadn't been since the truth-fealty reading in 1210, and that had felt less antagonistic than this. He ignored Richardson and the secretaries and left the King's Chambers. He had to go and see Prince Arkyn. There was a private shortcut for the King's Advisors that ran by the Prince's chambers that would take him to his office. If Arkyn wasn't available, he could ask Edward to let him know when he was and visit that underused office. Playing by the rules might be wise for a time.

Edward took his appearance with equanimity and announced him without fuss or emphasis, as though he was always asking to see the Prince – or, maybe, he'd been expected.

Rising from his bow, Landis caught he's nearson's eye and swallowed. The door clicked shut behind him. He opened his mouth, but Arkyn forestalled him.

"Thank you, Lord Landis. The apology isn't needed."

Landis' brows creased. "I haven't said anything yet, have I?"

"No, but you don't need to. I returned to ask father about something and Richardson mentioned you were there. I could hear what is politely termed *a discussion*. Was I wrong in my assumption that you were about to make amends?"

"No, sir, you weren't, and I'd have come and apologised anyway."

Arkyn crooked an eyebrow. "Would you? I cannot believe that His Majesty's annoyance hasn't in some measure influenced your decision or timing. I knew I couldn't stop him being annoyed or talking to you about it. For which I must apologise to you."

"No, Your Highness, you mustn't. I was the fool of the moment. I suppose I forget how much you've changed over recent years."

"Everybody does. How can I make them realise?"

Landis smiled. "I don't think you have to, sir; it's the job of your staff. Maybe my problem was that I've known you since you were born and was too close to truly see the changes. I see Your Highness most days or weeks

108

and yet in that familiarity is disaster as well as understanding. It's a problem I've fallen foul of with His Majesty over the years. It's my weakness."

Arkyn was amazed by the frank statement. His surprise showed. Knowing it, he said, "Then traditions *can* be changed. You are actually admitting to being fallible… Uncle Festus, it's not easy for me either."

"I know. I should never have made it harder for you; that's not what a nearfather is. I've been asked to attend the finals at the Advisors' School this year to find a candidate who could join your staff. Until then, if your advisors require help, I will attend to it."

"Father must have been annoyed. I'll formulate some requirements if you think they'll be helpful?"

Landis relaxed. "I think they might well be, sir. Are you going to Court tonight?"

Arkyn shook his head. "I'm meant to be taking an evening off. I'll see if Tain wants to annoy me for a bit."

Landis grinned. "How is he?"

"Incorrigible as ever."

* * *

Having left Arkyn's office, Landis made his way to the Advisors' School and the Dean's office. In his mind, he replayed various interviews he'd had with the gentleman over the course of his own studies twenty years previously. The interviews had normally included the fact he had 'breached school etiquette'. They raised a small smile within him as the memories played in his mind.

As he entered the Dean's office, a secretary hastily rose, proving once and for all that Landis was no longer a student.

"I'm afraid the Dean is busy, my lord."

"I'm sure he'll welcome my interruption."

After momentary hesitation, the secretary announced him. Sometimes there were advantages to his position.

The Dean rose. "My lord, it is a while since we've seen you."

"Yes, many years. There are several things I wish to talk to you about in private." (The secretary left.) "First, I am due to visit Macia officially and would like Lord Julius to accompany me."

"That might be an issue, my lord. He is at a critical point in his lectures."

"From what I recall, first year lectures can't be called critical, not so early in the term. I can assure you he will not be having an easy time."

"Even so, my lord, I do not see how he can take time away from his studies," replied the Dean. He'd not let Landis disrupt the school again.

Landis mused, "That is a shame. His Majesty thought it was the sobering experience his nearson requires to focus his mind. I'll have to tell the

King that Lord Julius must wait to see the workings of the empire at first hand. Such an opportunity can enhance theoretical study but if it must wait, it must."

The Dean cursed himself for a fool. "I had not considered it in that light, but, you're right, the chance to gain practical experience at such a level for a future Lord of Oedran must be utilised. How long would Lord Julius be away?"

"A couple of aluna-months and if his lecturers wish to give me details of what he should be studying, I shall do my best to guide his thoughts in that direction."

"Thank you, my lord. I'll pass on the comments."

Inwardly amused by the Dean's change of stance, Landis never let it show. With his normal calm manner, he dealt with minor matters concerning the tardy deliverance of the list of recent graduates to the Palace and then enquired how the final exams were conducted. Finding no change from when he himself took them, he saw that the Dean's interest had been roused.

"I will be observing some of the finals – all, if my other duties permit me; as the King's Chief Advisor, I might be in need of more advisors in the next year or two and I'd like to see who's graduating. Court is valuable but not always illuminating enough for my current challenge."

"Challenge, my lord?"

"Did I say that? How my tongue runs away with me at times. Now, there was something else I needed to talk to you about. Ah, yes, Advisor Spellen. Will his current job be open for him when Prince Tain no longer requires his services?"

"I cannot tell, sir. I cannot guarantee that I will be Dean when he theoretically returns and, if I'm not, I can make no assurances for a future incumbent of my post."

"Thinking of retiring?"

"Why would I ever want such a quiet life as retirement offers, my lord?"

Landis gave a significant glance at the desk. "I can think of a few reasons, Dean. I shall leave you to continue in peace."

On his way out of the school, he sidestepped a group of first years, his son amongst them. He caught Julius' eye.

His son stopped, perplexed. "Father, what are you doing here?"

"Annoying the Dean. It's my new hobby. When will you be back?"

"Probably for dinner. Why?"

"If I'm not elsewhere, come and see me; I've got a bit of news I think you might want to hear, but I'm not telling you now with all your nosy classmates round the corner listening to every word. Alcis, you'd think I was born yesterday!"

He heard suppressed laughter and winked at Julius as he continued his exit from the building.

* * *

Having left the school, he ambled his way back to the Palace, entering by the Privy Gate. After the morning's altercations, he felt he shouldn't, but occasionally the use of privilege was for others' benefit. It reminded them of his position. He glanced up at the windows of the Inner Office. He had to somehow rescue the day. If the King went to sleep on an argument, it would linger between them.

He strode through the Palace, apparently oblivious of everything. He doubted the altercations of the morning had stayed truly private. His coming and going between the Inner Office and Prince Arkyn's would have been noted. He trusted Richardson and the King's secretaries to have kept anything they overheard private, but he didn't know if anyone other than Arkyn had heard the discussion. If they had, he needed to stop rumours that the disagreement mattered.

Entering the Outer Office, Richardson informed him that Adeone was alone. He entered the Inner Office all too conscious of the tension he felt. Adeone's crooked eyebrow didn't hint at lingering displeasure. Landis relaxed slightly and replayed the meeting with the Dean.

When he reached the end, Adeone said, "You shouldn't tease him."

"Why not? He put me through seven years of torture to teach me very little. I have to get my revenge."

"You mean you were omniscient before that? Sorry, did I say 'omniscient'? I meant to say—"

"Either way, the answer is probably no, Sire. I've learnt more from working with Your Majesty than the school ever taught me."

"Courtier," grumbled Adeone. "If you're not careful, I'll make you work some more with Prince Arkyn. See what he did to Lord Iris."

"Uncle Iris isn't so different from before."

"He has his moments. Though he's not taken up your adage of traditions changing quite yet. For saying that you're uncle and nephew, you're very different."

"We're all interrelated, sir."

"Yes. It's worrying. Maybe it's time to encourage marriage into Oedran from the provinces once again. Otherwise, in a couple of generations, all the Lords of Oedran will be half-wits."

"I'm not sure that most aren't already, Your Majesty," replied Landis. "Will you dine with us this evening? I'll be telling Julius about Macia."

Adeone shook his head. "I've got to get this done. You'd better ask

Richardson to join me."

Landis left wondering if Adeone had relaxed quite as much as his manner suggested.

Chapter 19
ORDERS
Imperadai, Week 2 – 11th Cearal, 11th Cearcis 1212
Oedran

FOR SCANLON it was becoming an uphill struggle to get people close enough to the King and Princes to be useful to him. Some of his men had gone missing, others were corpses and even his spies were reporting finding it trickier due to more questions being asked. Clerks he thought were secure and untouchable were being relocated, others whom he might have turned were wary and the lack of funds due to Prince Arkyn's endeavours in Tera were being felt. Having stayed for long enough, he picked Arkyn's birthday to leave Oedran. Sometimes the small things had the most impact.

The news about the Princes' Guard was sobering – it was going to be difficult to get anyone into that. Handpicked by the King and Prince Arkyn, the challenge was prodigious. He would have to play a longer game there.

On the ride to Black Hills, he contemplated his options. There was one palace official he needed on his side if he was to achieve anything and two others ideally placed to help. It wouldn't be easy to garner their support, but it might be possible. FitzRyson would have to be first.

A knife was simple, poison more uncertain, disgrace was slow but sure. The disgraced rarely held respect and without respect more would be willing to wield the knife, carry the poison, chance their hand. Maybe he'd been too narrow-minded and considerate about how he was going to murder his family. He needed new methods. If they wouldn't do it willingly, he would discover their secrets.

* * *

The ride to Black Hills cleared his mind considerably. He was greeted by his steward – a doltish, dim-witted hirsute man with impressive presence and muscle, which was all he needed of him. He didn't need his steward to start having his own ideas.

"Did you have a good ride, Greatness?"

"Yes. Ask Bantling to join me."

Bantling entered the Justiciar's study and waited to be addressed. Two minutes later, Scanlon deigned to glance his way.

"You will do several things for me. I want a way of discrediting Judge Tancred. Try through memories of my predecessor – if I can discredit them both, I might as well. Start at Prince Lachlan's death. I need to influence FitzRyson. See if he's any secrets that I can use. Next, the King is setting up a Princes' Guard; I need a way into it. Also, get Chapa talking to someone. I might need to glean information from him at some point. Finally, forget I ever ordered any of that but see my wishes are carried out. Does my cellarer have all he needs?"

Bantling swallowed. "I believe so, Greatness."

"Good. What's on your mind?"

To avoid giving the truthful answer, the advisor said, "Forgive me, Greatness, but Prince Arkyn seems to be becoming a real threat."

"His work in Terasia certainly has made my life harder, but he *is* ill so something succeeded even if not as intended. I will have to rectify his interference. Terasia was a veritable goldmine. Portur was so dim he couldn't see what was happening under his nose."

"Can't we persuade the new Margrave, Greatness?"

Scanlon laughed, mirthlessly and mockingly. "Percival Wealsman is one of the King's closest friends. There is no way on Erinna we could buy him. I'll say this much for the King, when he gets people's loyalty it takes an awful lot for them to see the error of their ways. No, I'll need some other way of financing my projects."

"People would pay for the right sort of decision in court, Greatness."

Scanlon pretended to be outraged. "Are you saying *I* should accept *bribes*?"

"Not at all, sir," replied Bantling hastily. "I'm saying we should accept them and fill your coffers."

"There is still the problem that it is a *bribe* and, if it became known, then steps would have to be taken."

"I'm sure we can arrange it so it isn't known, sir," said Bantling. "Forget I ever suggested it. You could always, forgive me, but you could always marry again. An heiress maybe, with plentiful lands, Greatness. The income could be—"

Scanlon pondered that one. "It's a shame that a lord with only a daughter hasn't been foolish, isn't it? If he'd been convicted, his daughter would become a ward. Under certain laws, she would become a ward of the Justiciar. A pretty young lady whom I'd have to protect. I wouldn't need to be tied down to marriage. Yes, I'd have to visit her lands a lot to make sure they were being managed correctly. It is almost a shame that is all a fantasy. Find me a viable way of supplementing my income, Bantling, or suffer my displeasure."

"Sir." Bantling bowed as low as he could before exiting backwards.

As Bantling returned to the small office Scanlon had afforded him, one of the Justiciar's guards said,

"Your time's coming, bantam cock. Can't avoid him forever. You're imprisoned here, you do realise that?"

"I can leave whenever I choose, and, remember, I'm the Justiciar's advisor."

The guard sneered. "Aye, and I'm there whenever someone falls from favour. He keeps you because you're too afraid to talk."

Bantling eyed the guard. "Back to your post!"

A smooth educated voice, at odds with the rough appearance of the speaker, said, "Is the Justiciar returned?"

Bantling turned. "Yes, my lord. I can enquire if he'll see you?"

"If you think it wise, flunkey. How *was* Oedran? Oh, of course. I'm sorry; he doesn't let you go in case you're forgetful of yourself. Maybe I should offer you work instead."

"My lord, I thank you but decline; I am content and required here."

As they moved towards Scanlon's office, the lord remarked smoothly, "You lie, Bantling, you *always* lie! What would Lord Scanlon say if I told him?"

Bantling's heart plummeted to meet his rising stomach. "The Justiciar is well aware of my actions, sir."

Once in his office and alone, Bantling fought down the continuing urge to be sick. He *had* to wake from this nightmare.

Chapter 20
COUNSEL

Alunadai, Week 3 – 15th Cearal, 15th Cearcis 1212
Inner Office

ADEONE SAT DOWN LANGUIDLY at his desk. The piles of documents he'd happily left the evening before welcomed him back. He glared at them; how dare they remind him of their existence so brutally? He had to deal with them, but, instead, he rang for Richardson, who entered with an uplifting smile. In Adeone's current mindset, it was merely annoying.

"Good morning, Sire."

"Is it a good morning, Richardson?"

The administrator paused. "It hasn't begun with any tragedies, sir."

"I'll be glad for that. What have I got on today?"

"General Counsel – the Treasurer has sent his apologies, sir. He won't be present. Other than that, there are no meetings arranged."

"Thank you. Ask Prince Arkyn to join us for counsel and tell the Treasurer, if he wants to raise anything, to ask to see me, but I'll expect him at the next counsel without fail. That's two in a row he's missed. What's in all these piles?" enquired Adeone.

"Oh, a multitude of minutiae, sir. I could lose most of it for today."

"That would mean it would be waiting for me tomorrow. I shall carry on regardless. What time is counsel?"

"It's in half an hour, sir. Your Majesty might like to read these first." The administrator passed the King two brief reports.

Adeone took them. "Leave me to my fate, Richardson." He flicked open the first report settling back in his chair. The report was enlightening, if not curious, on the dedication of Lord Lux as Ealdorman. The Lord of Oedran might well be one of Scanlon's supporters and caution might well be a virtue, but he couldn't sit back and let Lux walk all over expectations. Ensuring the Etanes ran smoothly, so laws could be made and amended, was not a job that either he or Scanlon wanted overlooked.

When Richardson announced Arkyn, Adeone passed the report to his son, interested to see what he made of it. By the time Arkyn had finished reading, his face had gone from polite curiosity to puzzlement.

"What are you going to do, Sire?"

"I'm thinking of roasting him," admitted Adeone.

Arkyn chuckled. "Understandable, but given the situation, sir, maybe a more subtle approach would be better. Maybe just the hint Your Majesty is aware of the failings will be enough. He can't be the first ealdorman in our history not to be seen at the Etanes for a fortnight, and the longer he's absent the longer it will take for Uncle Scanlon to get laws passed, which won't make him happy."

* * *

Half an hour later, Richardson announced the Steward, General, Chief Yeoman, Captain of the City Guard, Lord Lux and Lord Landis, then stayed in the room himself.

Adeone broke off his conversation with Arkyn, greeted everyone with ease and waved them all to the long table. His lips twitched, seeing everyone almost absentmindedly arrange themselves, then think twice because of Arkyn's presence, and wait for him to get to his chair and sit before they all took their places.

Adeone read the agenda Richardson had put by his hand. "We shall start. Lord Lux, I'm aware you need to be in the Etanes so is there anything you need to raise with me?"

"No, Your Majesty," replied Lux.

"Have there been any laws proposed in the last two weeks?"

"No, Sire."

"Any amendments requested or proposed?"

"No, sir."

Adeone pursed his lips. "I assume there are no declarations about to expire also. I better not keep you from meeting the cisan members any longer, your duties being so onerous."

Everyone but Arkyn paused, unsure why the King had reacted in such a way. Richardson didn't dare catch Landis' eye, who had glanced at Adeone rather puzzled. Lux had more sense than to comment; he bowed out, furious.

Adeone ignored the speculation. He turned to the Chief Yeoman. "Aldhouse, I'm impressed with your report, but I wonder if half of it is inventive use of numbers. Can you please send me the actual figures and not percentages? I'd like to be able to allocate expenditure more exactly. Richardson will see a couple of scriveners from my office help you out in collating the information to my requirements. Anything else?"

"Your Majesty, I'm sorry if the report wasn't to your liking," said the Chief Yeoman. "It was prepared as normal."

"It was perfectly acceptable but I require some clarification of certain matters. It's not a criticism. Now, returning to my question…"

"Sorry, Sire. I'd like to recruit a few more men, enough for another section. As we gradually take over from the City Guard, the time has once again come to up our numbers. Especially with the ban on weapons in the Administrative Quarter. we're feeling we could do with more men."

"Send me proposed figures and a full outline of recommendations and I'll read them. Anything else?"

"No, Sire."

Adeone smiled. "Thank you. Captain, how's the City Guard?"

The elderly captain replied genially, "Getting more peaceful by the day, Sire. The only thing I need to raise is the fact the annual check of the city walls is due to occur during summer; I'm trying to finalise the details; is there any date Your Majesty had in mind?"

"Talk to Prince Arkyn's Administrator. His Highness will undertake the inspection for me. General?"

"I've only one thing, Your Majesty," replied Paturn soberly. "At some point I'd like to invite His Highness to inspect the barracks, if that is permissible."

Adeone said, "Certainly. I was going to ask you to talk to Edward about arranging a date."

"Then I'm pleased to have saved Your Majesty the necessity."

"Quite. Steward, how's the Palace?" enquired Adeone, turning slightly to face the man who ran the Palace day-to-day.

"As it ever is, Sire, a contradiction. His Highness' and Your Majesty's households are their normal, efficient selves. I've no concerns about the rest of the staff that I can't resolve and the Court is behaving itself remarkably well. There have been no incidents to bring to Your Majesty's attention, strange but true."

"Are we expecting any Guests of Court?"

The Steward shook his head. "Not this aluna-month, Sire. At least none have written ahead. I believe Lady Rhian has written to Your Majesty regarding a visit in the summer, but Lord Fairson will accommodate her."

"Yes," confirmed Adeone. "I've told her that I am looking forward to her visit. We'll have to organise a few entertainments during it, and see I've a few evenings spare, Richardson. Steward, see Her Ladyship's rooms here are prepared. If she stays late one evening, I wouldn't want her to feel that she had to cross the city to get home. Landis, tell me what's on your list."

Landis said mildly, "I think that this might be one request I can't fulfil, Sire, for I have no list. In fact, for the time being, I have absolutely nothing to raise with Your Majesty. Can you accept such a fault, or shall I start inventing?"

Amused, Adeone finally looked at him. "I would rather you didn't invent more work for me." Glancing around the rest of the table, he continued, "As His Lordship has failed to provide us with anything, gentlemen, I think, for now, that is all. Prince Arkyn, please stay."

As Adeone rose to signal the end of the meeting, everyone else did likewise, but Landis, as always, was the last to collect his papers and make motions of departure. Adeone watched him levelly and he waited until the office was empty of the other attendees.

"What's your list, Landis?"

His friend smiled. "I honestly don't have one, sir, but I was thinking that Lux wasn't happy."

"There is a law waiting for him that I know Lord Scanlon has raised."

"Ah. Even so, to chastise him publicly?"

"Maybe it was the opportune moment. Anything else?"

Landis shook his head. "I think Prince Arkyn came out of that with more to do than either of us."

Adeone laughed. "True. Sorry, Arkyn."

Arkyn shrugged. "I'll cope, sir. Though inspecting the walls may be a challenge."

"You'll not be doing the whole circuit, I never do. They chose precisely which bits to show us and normally it's the bits they've repaired in the last year. Anyway, it won't be for a couple of weeks. You're going to Ceardlann tomorrow. Followed by all your nearcousins later this week. I'm sure you'll be enjoying yourself far too much to worry about any of this."

Landis said, "Can I join you at Ceardlann, Your Highness? It sounds far pleasanter than here."

Adeone snorted. "You're going to Macia next week. You must have much to arrange for the trip still."

Landis bowed. "I'll continue with that, if you'll excuse me, Sire."

* * *

Twelve minutes later, Richardson interrupted Adeone and Arkyn saying Lord Teran had requested an audience looking particularly disgruntled. The reason for his mood became clear immediately. Wynfeld had refused to bow to his privilege and entitlement. Adeone tried not to let his private feelings on that show. He could have explained matters to Teran, could have dealt with the matter quietly but, instead, decided to get Wynfeld's side of the story and so sent for him.

Half an hour later, Major Wynfeld entered the Inner Office, saluted and stood at ease, waiting. Adeone studied him for a moment but saw no hint of uncertainty. Wynfeld was confident that his actions had been correct.

"I hear you're hunting for a new captain, Major."

"Yes, sir, for the post we discussed in Tera when you were kind enough to promote me."

Adeone nodded. "I wondered if that was it. I am told that you have forgone the tradition of the commission being bought. Would you care to explain why?"

"Certainly, Sire. It is because of the delicate nature of the work. I would rather have the best man in the post to serve Your Majesty than accept the highest bidder. I have told everyone who has approached me that all names will be considered but that I will not be bribed."

Adeone regarded Wynfeld, his fingers steepled against his mouth.

Arkyn leaned forward. "Major, why mention being bribed? Has someone offered you money for yourself to accept their candidate or themselves?"

"Yes, Your Highness, they have done so."

Arkyn turned to his father. "Your Majesty, the bribing of such high officials is a serious offence. Would you permit me to investigate the matter alongside the petitions?"

Adeone caught his son's mood. "Would you reveal who tried to bribe you, Major?"

"If Your Majesty or His Highness asked me, Sire, I could do no other. Yet the uproar might be far out of proportion to the initial misdemeanour."

118

"True. As a Lord of Oedran, Teran, do you think it a wise course of action?"

Teran never hesitated. "Your Majesty, I am no advisor, but I would say that it might have long-lasting repercussions."

"Not quite as long lasting as finding out which members of my Court have tried to bribe officers of my army: lordships could be lost for it..."

"Then maybe it is better, Sire, to forget the whole matter," suggested Arkyn. "Lord Teran has made his feelings known and Major Wynfeld has responded with an explanation that is acceptable."

Adeone nodded. "I tend to agree, Prince Arkyn; however, I still have to decide whether to allow the Major to appoint a captain in his own way."

Arkyn was grave. "We have never had cause to doubt Major Wynfeld's decisions before, sir. If his appointment doesn't work this time, then I'm sure the Major would be willing to try more traditional methods next time."

Adeone crooked an eyebrow. "Major?"

"I'm more than content with that, Your Majesty."

"Teran?"

"I see I have no option but to agree," grumbled Teran.

Adeone said, "There is always an option; however, I think that the Prince's suggestion is the best solution. Thank you, gentlemen. Major Wynfeld, I do want a word with you about the barracks. Lord Teran, I shall see you at Court soon."

Teran left with a blank expression but easily readable body language.

"He's not happy," observed Arkyn once they were alone.

"No, but the threat of facing charges for bribery was effective. Well done, your audacity is remarkably well honed," observed Adeone. "Wynfeld, choose whom you want for the job and if anyone else tries to bribe you start a list going. Sooner or later, they can take the consequences."

"Sire, can I explain something? I'm not averse to commissions being bought. This one though is for the intelligence regiment and I'd rather no-one sneaks in funded by a traitor. I've a list of men who have put their names forward for a commission, new to the army; could I pass it to Your Majesty? Most I know nothing against, they seem good men: the sons of merchants, mostly. I'd like to see them in Your Majesty's army."

"I'm sure spots could be found for them," remarked Adeone. "Pass the list along by all means, and give a copy to the General. We'll keep an eye out as to which captaincies are becoming vacant in the provinces. If any turn up through the petitions, Prince Arkyn will let you know."

PART 2

Chapter 21
ON THE ROAD
Cisadai, Week 3 – 16th Cearal, 16th Cearcis 1212
Palace – Service Courtyard

THE FOLLOWING DAY the carts were packed, the Rex Dallin drivers would be waiting at the ford, their charges were safely together and Simkins and Kadeem had been released to attend to the moving of personal possessions to the Rex Dallin.

Lips twitching, Kadeem said, "What would we do without moments such as these, sir?"

Simkins snorted. "Come on, let's go. The sooner we're there the better for us."

Kadeem swung himself up in to the saddle of his horse and nodded to the draymen. "Ready? Come on then."

Simkins, mounting his horse, smiled to himself. The young manservant of Prince Arkyn had certainly changed since he'd started in the King's Household. There was an assurance that Simkins recognised as being the result of travelling abroad with the Prince. Once they were through Oedran the guards with them halved and Simkins caught up with Kadeem.

"So, how are you? How's the household?"

"Same as ever. I think Thomas and Alan are anticipating a break whilst we're in the Rex Dallin. Or they will be until they see the list of jobs that I've left for them."

Simkins laughed. "Cut them a bit of slack. They'll work better for it."

"I do. They both worked hard in Terasia, especially Alan. He'd make a good manservant; I don't think the Prince's household will keep him long."

"You'd be surprised, there's more status to being a footman to a prince than a manservant to a minor lord."

Kadeem grinned widely, turning slightly in the saddle. "I'm sure I can't imagine what you mean, Simkins."

Simkins eyed him. "That's the first time you've not called me 'sir', are you getting complacent?"

"Not really, I just thought if I was going to be sarcastic, I might as well be informal."

Simkins laughed. "I think His Highness has had an effect on you."

"I think it might be mutual, sir."

A short while later Kadeem said, "How's your family? I've not seen them in a while."

"They're much the same. I've got to find Harry and Hazel a position soon. They can't live at home all their lives."

"I wouldn't have thought there would be much trouble in that, sir."

"No, but it's putting them somewhere where they aren't at risk, so to speak. It's a shame His Majesty isn't setting up a household for Prince Tain this year. I flatter myself but I think Harry could do well in it."

"I'll keep an ear open."

"Thank you," replied Simkins.

"If it wasn't for you, sir, I wouldn't be Prince Arkyn's manservant."

"I loathe to correct your flattery but it was your actions that brought you to the attention of the King."

"Someone still had to tell him who I was," observed Kadeem, "and I can't believe the knowledge simply arrived straight in his head."

"You have learnt a lot recently. I hear though that Prince Arkyn's satisfied with you."

"I hear the King is with you, sir."

Simkins took the hint. "Sorry. Have you found a masseur?"

"I'm getting close. There are a couple who have come forward. The Major is currently checking them for me."

"Shouldn't you talk to Beaver about such checks now?"

Kadeem made a noncommittal movement with his head. "His Highness trusts the Major; it is better that it is his name on the report."

Simkins absorbed the information with interest. "The Major seems to have come far since he first appeared."

"We all have it in us, sir."

"That was annoyingly philosophical, Kadeem. We *don't* all have it in us to rise from sergeant to Major of Oedran in three years!"

"No, because we're not all in the army. Is it only three years? It seems longer. I became the Prince's manservant at about the same time. It makes you wonder what the next three years will bring, doesn't it?"

"No. I'd rather not think of the future. Live for the day, especially in current times. Have there been any more attempts?" enquired Simkins.

Kadeem hesitated. "Not provable but it's amazing how, sometimes, when plans are changed you hear of an incident occurring."

"Yes, it is. Be careful in Paras."

"I intend to be. Did you enjoy travelling with His Majesty?"

"Yes," admitted Simkins. "It's nice to see the empire but *only* when we reached our destination. The travelling part I'll happily leave. Terasia, Gerymor and Serpent Isle are the worst by far. Though Serpent Isle isn't, in a sense, too bad because most of the trip you're on board ship. Paras is a week and a half at an easy pace. I liked Areal and the Low Plains, they're a couple of days. Tradere's not too bad, only a couple of days more."

"They sound better... Of all the places we stayed at on our trip to and from Terasia I liked Amphi – the stress of moving slipped away there."

Simkins smiled. "That's because the Governor of Areal has years of experience of the FitzAlcis descending. You don't need to inform him of anything other than current wishes. He knows all the protocols and follows them seamlessly. Arriving in Tera this time was pleasant. I found that I needed to do very little there."

Kadeem nodded. "Warning would have been appreciated but we had been there for some months already."

"It was more than that. I think Lady Wealsman's influence was marked and Lord Wealsman's of course... Hang on, who's this?"

An older gentleman rode up – ignored the guards and manoeuvred his horse into step with Simkins and Kadeem – saying, "You know my inn actually rattles when you lot pass by?"

"We've not passed it yet," said Simkins. "Morning, Fitz. How's life?"

"Somnolent. Can't get used to retirement. Thought I'd come for a bit of mayhem."

"Are you telling us you don't enjoy it?" enquired Kadeem amused.

"I'm saying that sometimes I wish there was something more. I've had years of traipsing around after the FitzAlcis. It's a matter of honour that they don't traipse without me."

Simkins said, "They're not traipsing far. How's the inn?"

"All right. I suppose I'm getting used to it," replied Fitz. "Whether the locals are getting used to me is another matter."

"The amount of times that you've sat in front of the bar, they should have been used to you years ago."

Kadeem chuckled to himself and listened as the two friends and former colleagues bantered. He glanced over his shoulder, nothing amiss with the carts. It wouldn't be long before they were at the Pillars of Alcis, the entrance into the Rex Dallin. There, they had to change drivers, normally farmers from the valley helped. After that, they had to get to Ceardlann and unload. The carts would remain there until the FitzAlcis had arrived. They'd then return to the Pillars and the waiting draymen would take them to Oedran. Would Fitz continue to Ceardlann or return to his inn, so that the draymen could have a drink whilst they waited? It was one reason the inn existed in the lonely village, whose road led to a place few could enter. It was there to provide accommodation and victuals to FitzAlcis staff who couldn't enter the valley but had to be close. Was that why the

King had wanted Fitz to run it? Having a friend and former guard captain watching and listening, picking up the gossip, would be invaluable, and Kadeem began to wonder about how crafty the King could be.

Chapter 22
CHASING RABBITS
Midday
Oedran – Galdwins' House

LATER THAT DAY, Calumiel Galdwin was moodily playing with the stew on his plate when a voice hailed for attention in the shop. He looked at his father.

"They can wait, we're eating. Stop playing about and get it down you."

Cal returned to his food and had taken a spoonful when a voice he recognised said mildly,

"Excuse me for disturbing your meal, Master Galdwin; I wonder if I might have a word?"

Cal jumped up so quickly he almost fell over. He hurriedly bowed.

King Adeone watched the fair-haired lad, amused. "What's the hurry, young Cal?"

"Won't you sit down, sir?"

Adeone glanced at a simmering Master Galdwin.

"No, thank you, Master Calumiel. I have been sitting all morning and will be in the saddle this afternoon. It's better that I stand. The Princes are outside."

Realising the King wasn't going to be leaving without speaking to him, Master Galdwin nodded and watched Cal leave in search of his friends. Madam Galdwin chivvied her other children out, leaving Adeone and Master Galdwin facing each other.

"I've been informed you sent for Calumiel a few weeks ago," said Adeone. "Might I enquire why?"

"It was a private family matter, sir."

"Will your private affairs now allow him to return to the Rex Dallin?"

"I don't mean to be disrespectful but—"

Adeone's tone, although still calm, took on another dimension, "Galdwin, I believe we had an agreement."

"Yes, sir, but his mother misses her eldest. That is the long and short of it. Cal needs to learn the business too. He is my heir and of the age to learn it."

"Yes. I would remind you that whilst my sons are at Ceardlann I do not get to see them."

"Yes, Sire, but I suppose the difference is you *could* visit them if you chose. We can't visit Cal."

Shaken, Adeone said, "You have caught me out in an inexcusable fault, Master Galdwin. Richardson!"

A couple of moments later, the administrator had left writing materials and been dispatched to the Palace to fetch two True Dallins, and Adeone faced Master Galdwin.

"I will allow yourself and your wife entry to the Rex Dallin whenever you wish it to see Calumiel. Your other children also will be allowed entry whilst they are under cisan-age. I hope that sets your mind at rest."

Stunned, Master Galdwin still managed to grumble, "It does and it doesn't, you could say. There is still the slight problem of him learning the trade, sir."

Moving Cal's abandoned plate aside, Adeone sat ready to take notes. "What are the important aspects of your trade that can be learnt outside of the shop?"

Galdwin paused but registered something in the King's manner that told him to answer honestly – after all, his uninvited guest could call on every expert in the empire.

Adeone made copious notes whilst Master Galdwin detailed everything from fibres to finished cloths, from supply to sale. He filled two sides of parchment and asked for clarification on several matters before wiping his pen clean saying, "Apart from the fact I found that a fascinating insight into a trade I know little about, I have a proposition to make to you..."

Disorientated, Master Galdwin sighed; he knew the King's propositions of old and hadn't expected him to grasp the subject so quickly.

"...It comes in two parts. The first is that I will appoint and finance a tutor for Calumiel to teach him all those skills he can learn away from the shop, if you wish you may have a say in that tutor but the man will have to meet the same strict standards set for my sons'. The second part is that Prince Tain will soon spend more time in Oedran, shadowing the courts. Master Calumiel will return here during these periods to learn anything else he needs. Will you accept that?"

Master Galdwin considered. If the King meant it, Cal would be more than a match for anyone. He made up his mind. He might not like being involved with the FitzAlcis, but he'd accept it for the good of his family.

"Yes, sir; I don't see how I can refuse."

"Thank you. I would not have Tain grow up alone."

"But, Sire, he would never be *alone*, surely. For a start, Lord Landis' children are currently living with you."

"I'm afraid, Master Galdwin, that he will be very much alone. Arkyn has been taking over the Provincial Reviews and is therefore travelling. I can't have Tain in Oedran and Ceardlann is, by its nature, isolated. His Lordship's family *are* living with us but only for a few months. Tain needs a confidant; Lady Elantha is too young and too close to the source of the problem to be that."

"The problem, Sire?"

Adeone swore gently. "Forget I ever said that, please, Master Galdwin; it was an unguarded utterance."

"Certainly, sir, but I take it you are referring obliquely to the fact that your brother is getting, shall we say, dangerous?"

Adeone stared at him, "Master Galdwin, how—"

"It is relatively common knowledge he isn't content as Justiciar, Sire. For Oedranians at least, you might as well proclaim it. I'm sure we had one of his men in here one day, trying to catch me out selling silk cloth against the law."

The two men stared at each other with an unprecedented understanding between them.

Adeone said quietly, "That is the true reason you are reluctant for Cal to be with my family?"

"When my cousins disappeared, Sire, I lost my closest friends. I don't want him to suffer like that."

"Master Galdwin, please believe me when I say I do everything I can to make sure your son is not in danger – as much as I can do for my own children and niece."

"I believe you. It's just hard to accept my eldest might be in danger."

At that moment, Richardson reappeared; Adeone passed Master Galdwin the two True Dallin.

"Keep those safe, please. They don't work without your name being on a scroll also; however, if a traitor gets hold of both a token and the scroll, you can imagine what could happen. Now, the last thing I will say is that if ever you, or your wife, need time alone, for whatever reason, send to the Palace, I will gladly have the rest of your children in the Rex Dallin for as long as you need."

"Thank you, Your Majesty. I appreciate the gesture."

"Well, Master Galdwin, do you want to tell your son and wife? I'm sure he'll like to know we've been conspiring about his education."

Master Galdwin led the way. There'd been a side of the King he hadn't realised was there: a man worried for his sons' future. He'd thought the King could get anything by ordering it and had resolved it wouldn't include his cooperation. Giving way to common honesty and a wish to do what was right by his eldest son had surprised even him. A unexpected, grudging respect for Adeone was forming. They found Cal outside talking to Tain and Arkyn. Tain and Cal looked in apprehension at their respective fathers. Adeone smiled, but Master Galdwin was his normal serious self as he said,

"Go and pack your things, Cal, and quickly; you don't want to delay the King. I'm sure he has more than enough to do. Would Your Majesty and Highnesses care to come inside and wait?"

"Gladly, Master Galdwin, but we shouldn't keep you from your work or hurry your goodbyes."

Half an hour later, they were on their way to the Rex Dallin.

Master Galdwin's frame of mind wasn't helped by his seven-year-old son, Crispin, asking when Cal would be back.

"When he's learnt something. You've got the shoes to clean."

* * *

Ceardlann was in muted uproar because of their arrival. The stone and timber house welcomed them back with reassuring familiarity as the Comptroller, chief official of Ceardlann and the Rex Dallin, greeted them.

"It's good to have you home, Sire. I hope you had a good ride."

"Good enough, thank you, Comptroller. I might need a headache cure but other than that I think I'm fine." Dismounting, he handed Pursuit's reins to a groom.

"I hope the headache's not too bad, Sire. I've got some refreshment for it."

Adeone laughed. "Always prepared. Shall we go in?"

Entering the large antechamber, the Comptroller asked, "Where's Lady Elantha, Sire?"

"She's been feeling a bit off colour with a touch of summer cold. Doctor Chapa thinks that it's better she stays in Oedran for a bit." Picking up a drink and a piece of cake he continued, "Shall we adjourn to your office, Comptroller, and leave the terrors to take over Ceardlann?"

They spent a pleasant half hour talking about everything and nothing before Adeone decided he wanted some true solitude. He strolled through the busy stableyard before heading for the path to the forest and a longer walk. The Comptroller watched him go with an odd sort of affection.

An hour and a half later, holding himself up on the doorframe, Adeone half hobbled, half hopped into the Comptroller's office.

The Comptroller hastily got to his feet and offered his arm. "What happened, sir?"

Adeone shook his head at the offer of assistance, collapsing onto a chair. He hooked a stool around with his good foot and raised his injured one, so it rested on the seat. "I've twisted my ankle, bloody stupid thing to do. Oh, don't worry; this was a genuine accident, for once."

The Comptroller rang the bell and asked Joe, the senior footman, for a couple of bandages. When they arrived, so did the housekeeper.

She bobbed a curtsy. "You're still getting into trouble then, Sire."

"I like to keep you busy, Susan. How are you?"

"Well, thank you, sir. What have you been doing this time?"

Adeone chuckled. "Walking. Problem was, I didn't notice the rabbit hole. Before I knew it, I'd gone and twisted my ankle."

"That was daft. You should always watch where you're going." Whilst she was berating her King, as though he was still a nine-year-old boy, she was also feeling over his ankle to make sure that was all he'd managed. Smiling, she said, "All I need now, Sire, is for Lord Landis to pop his head round the door and tell me it wasn't his fault and I'll think I'm back twenty-odd years."

"For once, it wasn't. Surely, though, my younger son keeps you busy? He manages it with everyone else."

Susan laughed. "Aye, you could say that. His Highness and young Master Calumiel have turned some of my hair grey, that's for sure. Now, if you could just lift your leg a bit, I'll get it bandaged."

Adeone did so. When his ankle was secure, he smiled in thanks at Susan before saying, "Don't let the scapegrace run *too* many rings round you."

"I won't. No more than I let his father."

When she'd gone, Adeone was still chuckling. "I can't understand what she meant by that last comment. Can you, Comptroller?"

"I wasn't paying attention, sir. I've found it safer."

Adeone gave him a sideways look. "Hmm. I'll hobble out of your way."

"Lady Landis is in the drawing room, Sire. Should you wish for more conventional conversation."

As the King left, the Comptroller chortled to himself. In Oedran the King was *the King*. Few people dared speak to him with anything other than respect. At Ceardlann he let quite a few of the staff take liberties. To his staff, it made him a person, not a figure of terrifying authority. He'd effectively blocked any influence Scanlon might have had at Ceardlann through former ties; for Scanlon had never let anyone forget who he was.

* * *

Adeone hobbled to the drawing room. Cornelia rose, took in the fact that he was limping, looked concerned but then raised an eyebrow when he blushed, asking if he could join her.

"Certainly, sir. Might I enquire why you're hurt?"

He told her, adding, "Go on, say it; it's the type of daft thing you expect."

"I wouldn't presume. I leave that sort of effrontery to my husband. Did you have a good ride from Oedran?"

Adeone eased himself into a chair. "It was pleasant. The children were chatting incessantly. Young Cal is here, by the way."

Cornelia smiled, picking up the embroidery she had been doing. "I'm pleased about that. I'm sure His Highness will be as well."

"He certainly seemed to be making up for lost time. It means there'll be one more terror to give you a headache."

"One more or less, I'm sure I can cope. I'll have seven here, so I should apologise to you for the headaches."

"I'm coping," said Adeone lightly. "Is everything ready for their arrival?"

"Yes, sir. Thank you. We've created room for everyone and also a small sitting room for our brood, so yours can get peace should they want it."

"I'm sure the children will be fine. You might be the one needing somewhere peaceful. How's Lord Rale doing?"

Cornelia considered; she and Festus had taken over the care of Finian when her father, his grandfather, died. "He's being no trouble. A bit quiet but I think after my lively brood anyone would seem quiet, sir. He's thinking about studying law. Would you have any objections as his formal guardian?"

"You mean other than the fact he would come under my brother's direct influence? I'm sorry, Cornelia, but I need as few lords under that influence as possible. If he continues to live under your roof, however, and you keep an eye on him, then see how he goes. He might change his mind anyway."

"Probably. Thank you. There's still two years before he comes of cisan-age. I don't want Festus to get too mired with responsibility. He's got enough to do."

Adeone sighed. "Yes. I'm truly sorry about that, although I don't know what I'd do without him most of the time. Are you going with him to Macia?"

"No. I'll stay here and see to the house and children. Festus told me you said you'd help if I needed it."

"If there is anything I can do let me know, Cornelia. Always, not just with the house."

Lady Landis smiled to herself, sorting out a new thread. "I'm sure Festus will."

"I'm not. That's why I'm asking you to. When's the house due to be finished?"

"External works by the end of autumn, then internal by the end of winter."

He watched Cornelia shrewdly. "Do you think the workmen have given themselves a margin of error?"

"I'd be a fool not to, sir. Why?"

"Oh, nothing." Seeing she didn't believe him, he added, "A small plan I'm cooking up."

"Do you need a kitchen maid to try the recipe on?" enquired Lady Landis demurely.

Adeone laughed. "Maybe. Once Festus is elsewhere causing trouble for me, would you have any objection if I spoke with your foreman?"

"Why should I mind that, Adeone? I'm a lady. I don't tend to deal with the workmen."

Adeone guffawed. "Right. One day, *a long time ago*, I might have believed that. Then Ira told me everything you were doing whilst I borrowed your husband for official duties."

"That was unfair of Ira. I thought I'd kept up the pretence nicely."

"You did, do even. How's Ira's nameling doing?"

Cornelia smiled; she and Festus had named their youngest for the late Queen. Talk turned to the children and soon a knock at the door heralded Tain. His father sighed at the bright-eyed expression his younger son wore.

"Can we go for a ride before dinner, sir?"

Adeone smiled. "Of course. Just make sure you're back *and clean* before seven this evening. I need a quick word with Cal before you go."

"Right, father. Can't you come for the ride?"

"I'm afraid not. I've already twisted my ankle chasing a rabbit down a hole. I can't imagine what I'd manage on a ride."

Six minutes later, Cal entered and bowed. "I understand you wish to see me, Sire."

"I certainly do, young Cal. Close the door. No, Lady Landis, stay where you are by all means. Now, Cal, you've obviously gathered your father has reservations about you being at Ceardlann. I've convinced him you can learn your trade nearly as well here, as in Oedran, and I've agreed to appoint a specialist tutor for you. It might take me a few weeks to do so; I'm sure you *could* cope without lessons for that long but, in the meantime, you're going to share Tain's tutors once more. Also, apparently you are getting extremely good at wielding a sword. Have you told your father?"

Cal shifted his feet. "No, sir. I thought he might disapprove."

"Probably wise. Never lie to him about what you do here but if there is anything which you are learning, that comes to his attention, that he doesn't wish you to learn and that subsequently he lets me know about, then I will have to see it is no longer taught to you. I trust you understand. How did you find Darky on the ride?"

"Fine, sir, thank you."

"Good. Whilst you're with us, he's yours to use. All right, go on. It's nice to have you here."

"Thank you, sir; it's nice to be back." Cal bowed out.

Cornelia's lips twitched as Adeone caught her eye. Innocently, she asked, "Were you encouraging Cal to be duplicitous, Adeone?"

"I'm sure I recall telling him not to lie," replied Adeone with a chuckle and a glint in his eye.

Chapter 23
CLOTH MERCHANTS
Imperadai, Week 3 – 18th Cearal, 18th Cearcis 1212
Dellwood – Fitz's Inn

WHEN FITZ SHOWED Tain and Cal into the room set aside as a schoolroom, they found Judge Tancred seated comfortably in an armchair reading a scroll. He rose and bowed slightly as the Prince bounced in. Tain grinned, curling himself into an armchair. Tancred smiled at Cal and nodded to another. Perplexed, Cal sat, glancing sideways at the table and chairs.

"I have never been able to teach anyone in a formal atmosphere. Fitz was kind enough to provide more comfortable arrangements," explained Tancred. "How was your ride?"

Tain grinned wider and started chatting.

Rather intrigued, Cal listened. Ewall had been formal and the judge was the opposite. Tancred managed to get Cal involved in the conversation and soon they were talking about the way colour and cloth defined their social hierarchy.

The basics didn't take them long. Most information they had gathered from observation growing up. The FitzAlcis' clothes usually had scarlet, emerald green and gold in them. The lords all had a blue stripe; wide for *the* lord and narrow for the other males in his family. Only the FitzAlcis and the lords could wear silk. The price of velvets and satins of other threads meant the cisan couldn't usually afford them, so although not debarred were rarely seen outside the alunan. Gradually, the judge outlined the clothing laws, discovering Cal had learned the majority from working alongside his father and observing what was happening; Tancred filled in gaps and gave the young boy some pointers into the tricks the Aulnager and yeomen used to check the law was being adhered to.

"How often are the checks made, Judge?" asked Cal anxiously.

"As often as the Aulnager wants them to be. As chief cloth merchant, he understands the trade and his fellow cloth merchants. The outcome of any investigation is written in a ledger in the Guildhall, and can be viewed on application by anyone. The merchant is allowed three chances before prosecution: each time he fails a black mark is put against his name. Each time he passes, if any black marks are recorded, one is scratched off. The Aulnager is saying everyone has a bad day."

Tain laughed. "That's kind of him."

The judge smiled. "Most people deserve a second chance. It can be worth tempering our justice with kindness where appropriate."

"Surely, Your Honour, if the law isn't followed people will mock it."

Tancred chuckled. "Most do anyway, Your Highness. Those who get caught are unwise or unlucky; however, if you are too rigid in implementing it – for example, by prosecuting every cloth merchant for a minor infraction – then there would be unrest, even an uprising. No-one likes tyranny. At least if they are laughing at the law, they are not killing anyone because of it. Sometimes it is more advantageous to turn a slightly blind eye. On occasion, a word in the right ear is all it takes for people to mend their ways. I do not mean threats; those can be as bad as following the law to the extreme. No, I mean, a simple acknowledgement that people have noticed the law has been broken is often enough. Always be careful. You are there as a custodian of the law and its power, not as the ultimate enforcer. You will be the ultimate judge, where you lead others must follow, but it can be seen throughout our history that subordinates will magnify the mistakes of their superiors. Conversely, they can also magnify their good."

Tain chewed at his lip, considering. He was about to say something when there was a knock at the door and Fitz entered with a loaded tray.

"I thought, after a couple of hours of learning, you could all do with some refreshment."

The judge said, "Thank you. Has it been a couple of hours?"

"Yes, Your Honour. How have you coped with His Highness?" Fitz's eyes were twinkling as he looked at Tain. The Prince grinned back as he reached the tray.

"Oh, well enough. There has not been a joke in sight."

Tain offered the judge a drink. Tancred took it with thanks and, catching a warning tone in Fitz's eye, sipped it.

Without grimacing, he observed, "It seems I will not have to tell Your Highness that I like salt in my juice. I thought you might find the practice unusual, but I suffer from a salt deficiency."

Tain's face was nonplussed as the judge finished the juice. Fitz chuckled to himself as he left. Tain enjoyed the reactions he got from people, but he wouldn't know how to handle that one, being unable to laugh at it or congratulate himself.

Tancred chose some bread, cheese and an apple and sat down, leaving the Prince to work it out on his own.

Chapter 24
HOUSE AND GUARDS
Tretaldai, Week 4 – 24th Cearal, 3rd Middis 1212
Inner Office

LORD LANDIS AND JULIUS set off for the Macian Isles on the same day that the Aulnager handed Richardson the shortlist of candidates for the post of tutor. Adeone, meanwhile, waited until Landis was out of Oedran before summoning his friend's foreman.

The gentleman was shown into the Inner Office and gave one of the shortest bows the King had ever received. Adeone motioned for Richardson to stay before turning to the foreman.

"I understand the footings for Landis House are almost complete. How long until you finish the walls and roof?"

"Same amount o' time as I told Her Ladyship last I spoke to her, sir: end o' autumn."

"What's your margin of error in that?"

"Don't work with errors, sir. Never have, never will. End o' autumn it'll be"

Adeone said levelly, "Let me put it another way, Colban; is there any chance you could complete them sooner?"

"If we can, we will, sir. Can't tell what the future holds."

Adeone sat back, fingers steepled, now regarding the foreman more seriously than before. "Richardson, please leave us for a moment." Once he'd gone, Adeone eyed the foreman. "You don't like my interference, am I correct?"

For the first time, the foreman appeared uncertain, but carried on in his normal manner. "You could say that, sir."

"I thought I just did. Now, I want the honest answer. Why?"

"Honest answer?" The foreman caught the King's eye and now there was a slight glint in his. "Well, sir, I think that Lord Landis is paying us and that means I answer to him or Her Ladyship on this job."

"You don't think my position stands for anything then?" mused Adeone.

"No, sir. Not on this job, it doesn't. Not to me. Not to my men."

"Normally I'd say 'good'. You need to be certain whose paying you and why. Nevertheless, I *did* promise His Lordship I'd help to oversee his affairs whilst he is overseeing mine in Macia."

"Her Ladyship copes, sir."

"She does, extremely well," acknowledged Adeone. "Now let me explain my reasons for disturbing your day… As a *friend* to Lord and Lady Landis, I would like to help. Let's cut behind the problem that I'm not paying you and get to the truth. You would be the first foreman in history not to leave a margin of error in a project of this size. If everything goes according to plan, when *could* you finish the house structure by?"

"Current man power: end o' the autumn, sir," replied the foreman, his lips twitching.

"Right. If I don't get an answer to my next question, that isn't, or cannot be construed as, insolent, then I will speak to Lord and Lady Landis and advise them about this meeting. I assume you understand the implications."

"Now you're talking my language, sir."

Adeone had to stop himself from smiling; threats always had some worth. "Good. My question is, how many extra men would you need to get the walls up by the end of summer?"

The foreman gave a number.

Adeone noted it. "Do you have all the specialists you need on site?"

"Course I do, sir. Part o' me job. It ain't just the men. It's the ashlar we need, the mortar and so forth. His Lordship's particular about all o' that."

"Yes. I expect he is. Which quarry are you using for the walls?"

"Carregshore, sir. We ship it down to the port, then up the Edra. It takes time."

"See the quarry has all your requirements—"

"Already does, sir," replied Colban.

"Good. As it's my quarry, I'll give orders they are to fulfil the request as soon as possible and make sure they can. I'll also see you get the extra men you need."

"Who'd be paying 'em, sir?"

"I will, which means next time I ask questions, you'll answer them, without procrastination, prevarication or insolence. Is that understood?"

"Once I find a dictionary, sir."

Adeone had enough. "Remember to whom you speak! You may go."

The foreman gave another miniscule bow and left.

Moments later, Richardson entered and saw the King's face. He closed the door. "What would you like doing about him, Sire?"

"I want you to get Wynfeld to investigate him, then I want you to see he has the extra men, equipment and resources he requires," replied Adeone. "Here's the list. After that, you had better make sure he understands that when I ask questions, he answers them. I don't mind craftsmen, I don't mind people who are blunt, I do mind people who realise they are being insolent and don't alter their behaviour. Then if he doesn't get the house walls finished before the end of summer, get my lawyers to charge him for breach of verbal contract. I'll hold him to that."

"Very good, Your Majesty. Lady Landis was wondering if you have a moment."

Startled, Adeone said, "Of course I have." Seconds later, he rose to greet her. "Cornelia, you weren't waiting for long, I hope."

"No, Sire. I told Richardson I didn't mind waiting until you'd finished your meeting. Was it our foreman I saw leaving?"

"Yes, he's advised me he'll get the walls finished by the end of summer."

"Erm… thank you, sir. I take it he wasn't too rude? He can be blunt."

"Nothing I couldn't deal with. What brings you to Oedran?" Adeone moved out from behind the desk and over to the more comfortable chairs. He waved Lady Landis to one.

She seated herself whilst replying. "I came to see Lady Elantha, sir. Well, more accurately, I came to see if she was well enough to return to Ceardlann. Apparently, Chapa is satisfied she is."

Adeone nodded. "Yes, he told me this morning. I was half thinking of accompanying her to Ceardlann myself tomorrow morning, but if you would be so kind…"

She smiled. "Come anyway, sir. Have a break."

"You sound like Festus," grumbled Adeone good-humouredly

"Penalty for having married him, I think. Consider it anyway. I'm sure Their Highnesses would like to see you."

"I'm sure they would. If only so Tain can escape lessons. I'll think about it, Cornelia. Come to dinner with me. I have to go down to Court later, but I'd be glad of the company."

"Then of course I will, sir. Now, I mustn't keep you from your work."

* * *

After Cornelia left, Adeone took an impromptu walk to the barracks. The day was blustery but warm, and, during the walk across the Administrative Quarter, he was pleased to be outside. Maybe a ride to Ceardlann *would* do him good.

Wynfeld rose and saluted on his King's entry, hiding his surprise.

Adeone seated himself and motioned for the Major to do likewise. Tongue in cheek, he asked, "Keeping busy?"

Wynfeld's eyes glinted. "The background checks are certainly helping with that, Sire."

"Yes, there have been a few, haven't there? There's another list here that the Aulnager passed to Richardson this morning. It's for a tutor for young Cal Galdwin, so the person must be trustworthy enough for me to let them into the Rex Dallin. Now, truth be told, I was sick of sitting at my desk so thought I'd come and see what's happening about training the men shortlisted for the Princes' Guard."

"Quite a lot, Sire. Might I suggest we go to the training area? I believe Marsh and some of the men are there now. Given time, they'll be extremely good." He held the door open for Adeone.

"Not too much time, I hope. What exactly are you training them in?"

"After Prince Arkyn's advice, the two-hundred-yard dash in full armour, Sire."

The King laughed. "Yes, that is needed. Can they manage it?"

"They're getting better. I suggest, sir, that Prince Tain isn't told they've been trained in the pursuit for a time. After that, it's intense weapons training, sir, until the men are decent swordsmen, pikemen and archers."

"Anything dirtier?"

Wynfeld was momentarily stumped. "Sir?"

"Major, traitors never fight fair. Get the men trained in all the tricks that the low-life of the city use. If needs be, send them into the wharves, unarmed, and tell them to pick a fight with the largest stevedore they can find. If nothing else, you'll know the good fighters. Next, train them in reading a map for ambush locations. I believe your cartographer is sent copies of all the maps held by all the forts in the empire. Get a few copied. Start with the route His Highness will take to Paras. Run your eye over them. I know you're good at spotting such places. See if the men come up with the same. Look out maps of the cities as well."

"Right, Sire. Would you like them trained in the skills our scouts use?"

"I hope that wasn't a facetious comment."

The Major, extremely serious, said, "Not at all, Your Majesty. I've suddenly realised they could be useful."

"Then get them trained. It will give them skills for when they are not guarding Their Highnesses. Get them trained in intelligence work also."

The remainder of the walk to the training area was conducted in silence. Captain Marsh saluted when they reached the training yard. Motioning for him to carry on, Adeone watched the swordplay for some time before turning to Wynfeld.

"The aggressors are being too kind, Major. Few assassins carry swords. They prefer daggers. Swords are too noticeable, especially after I banned them in the Administrative Quarter. Carry on with this but see the Custodian of Oedran Prison. Tell him you want people who can wield a knife and know the tricks. Then make sure they can't escape when they help with the training. Whatever else, remember that traitors don't fight fair."

"Very good, Sire. What would you suggest we offer the prisoners to obtain their cooperation?"

Adeone regarded him. "I'm sure you'll think of something, Major. It might also be worth considering that, once their sentence is spent, they could be useful informers." Lips twitching, he asked, "Is anything wrong?"

Wynfeld, who'd been eyeing his King wondering if he'd always had a bent for duplicitous dealing, said, "No, Sire, nothing. I have realised that we're going to need a new training regime."

Adeone nodded. "Though not a completely new one, Major. Please tell me if you ever think my ideas won't end in the best result."

"Thank you, Sire," replied Wynfeld. How many more ideas did the King have for collecting intelligence?

Chapter 25
MEMORIES
Imperadai, Week 4 – 25th Cearal, 4th Middis 1212
Rex Dallin – Ceardlann

WHEN THEY ARRIVED at Ceardlann the following day, Elantha left in search of her cousins whilst Adeone greeted the Comptroller. Tain and Cal were at Fitz's with Judge Tancred, so Adeone sent word he was at Ceardlann. Lady Landis excused herself and went to oversee preparations for a more formal lunch than was usual.

Enjoying being alone and without work, Adeone entered the Great Hall, looking around with affection. The wooden panelling held a sheen from the polish; it gave the room a pleasant ambiance lacking in the Palace of Oedran. He sat in a chair, absorbing the atmosphere, remembering the times he'd visited with Ira just after they were married. Arkyn, Tain and Ella had all been born here; Ella had also died here. Had that really been five years ago? She'd have been eight this year. Her death had been the day his life had changed. Lady Aelia had also left them that day. Ira's illness, then her death two years later. After three years, the scar across his heart still bled despair. Would he ever escape the feeling, the feeling of wanting to run from the world and hide, of wanting to return to before his brother had shown his true colours, to before Ella had died?

Images played across his mind. He and Ira here with Landis and Cornelia: evenings of dancing and laughter, carefree in nature. No children to fear for whilst loving them with every resonating fibre of his being. No lost days to mourn. No future fighting to outmanoeuvre his brother.

He rose and moved to the large floor-to-ceiling window behind the dais. Idly, he watched the small garden, enclosed by different wings of the house. He'd not entered it since Ira died. It held too many memories of youth and hope, of happiness and early love.

Tain ran into the hall. Adeone held out a hand to him and the Prince, noticing something he couldn't name in his father's manner, walked over soberly and stood quietly by him.

Adeone put an arm around his shoulder. A couple of minutes later, he glanced at his son to see Tain watching him with concern.

The King smiled sadly. "I'm sorry, Tain, I was maudlin."

"That's all right, father. It happens to the best of us."

"That's a very adult comment, my son. Whom have you been listening to?"

"Uncle Festus, father."

Adeone shook his head. "I should have known. Your nearfather has a lot to answer for."

"He says the same about you, father."

"Does he indeed! He's right, but it doesn't mean he should tell my sons that!"

Tain grinned widely and his father gave him a belated hug, ruffling his hair. Tain smoothed it down, exasperated.

Adeone chuckled before saying, "Shall we find somewhere in the gardens to hide? You can tell me what Tancred's been teaching you."

* * *

Once in the gardens, Adeone sat on the grass with his back against a raised flowerbed. Tain sprawled on the lawn in his favourite position, legs kicking at the air, hands picking at the grass. Adeone turned his face contentedly to the summer sun as his son chatted away.

When he could slip a word in, Adeone said, "I thought you found law boring."

"I did, but there're so many different aspects."

"Yes, and you get to ask a lot of questions. You've always enjoyed that." He chuckled as Tain pouted in mock offence. "Ask away. It's how to learn and it keeps people on their toes."

"Is that what you do, father?" enquired Tain innocently.

"Of course. No point having the tag 'King' on the front of your name to sit there and listen."

"But I won't have that tag."

"No, but you'll have one equally as useful. You should read some of the unofficial history in the Diary Archives at the Palace. They extend to before the Fall of the Cearcall. All our family history written down and stored there – protected by a magic set up by the Cearcall to prevent anyone else reading

140

it. You should start adding to it soon."

"How, father?"

"Start writing a diary. Every time you complete a volume, whether that is monthly or yearly, deposit it with Thomkins, the diary archivist. It'll give him something to do."

Tain grinned impishly. "So do you think I ought to give him the last two and a half years' worth I've written then?"

Adeone eyed his son. "You've kept that one quiet. I didn't know you were keeping a diary."

Tain nodded enthusiastically. "Maria thought it might help after…" His voice trailed off and Adeone, knowing that he meant the death of his mother, simply smiled sadly as he asked,

"Did it, does it help?"

"Yes, father, but if there's somewhere they can be safe, then they ought to be there, oughtn't they?"

"Yes," agreed Adeone. "Next time you're in Oedran, I'll introduce you to Thomkins. He's a cheery old cove."

Tain smiled. "I'd like that. Father, when are you returning to Oedran?"

Adeone groaned. "Probably sooner than I thought. I've just spotted Richardson's messenger… All right, Launfal, I'll speak to him." Two moments later, he was in a link. "Go on, what's happened this time?"

"I'm truly sorry, Sire, but you're needed at the Palace. There is a situation developing and Pixney thinks it might be better if you were here," explained his administrator.

Adeone eyed him. "What sort of *situation*?"

"The guards discovered their lockers were searched, sir."

Adeone thought, *'Thank you, Festus!'*, who'd searched the lockers during the spot check. Although what he actually said was, "I'll be there soon. Meet me at the stables." When the link broke, Adeone found his son watching him with concern. "What is it, Tain?"

"You're going again, aren't you? And one day you'll never come back."

Adeone ruffled his hair. "The assassins will never get me."

More normally, Tain asked, "When *are* you coming again?"

"Not sure. Soon, I hope. Give me a smile I can take with me."

Tain's smile was wan and worried; it held none of the normal life Adeone was used to seeing. His heart breaking, Adeone left for the stables.

Chapter 26

SEARCHED

ADEONE REACHED the Guards' Corridor in the Palace and viewed the wreckage in the locker room. It wasn't Landis' spot check the men had discovered. By his side, Captain Pixney explained they'd found the mess that morning. The King reassured the muttering guards he'd investigate and sent for Wynfeld.

Whilst the Major searched the locker room for evidence of the perpetrators with his infamous competence, Pixney received a piece of Adeone's mind. He wasn't happy at having been required to return from Ceardlann but, as the captain pointed out, the guards would never doubt the King's word, however much they might doubt other officers'.

Adeone forced himself to calm down; being irate would never help the situation. Instead, in a lucid moment, he decided to split the locker room. The King's Guard and Palace Guard had shared the same one for years, and he was willing to bet Scanlon had been after information to use against the forming Princes' Guard. There weren't many who would have the audacity to target his guards. Having spotted Smithers waiting to collect his possessions, he asked Pixney to send him in.

When the captain saluted and left, Adeone glanced around the office. It had the bare, utilitarian air of all military offices. There was no ornamentation. The desk was solid wood without carvings, the filing cabinets the same. Shelves ran alongside one wall looking odd devoid of their scrolls and piles of paperwork. Adeone reached for a blank piece of parchment from a stack on the desk; Richardson's or the Major's work, no doubt. From his belt pouch, he retrieved a small pen he carried around with him. He'd written half a page of notes on what he'd ordered and his reasons for the orders before Smithers entered.

Adeone acknowledged the salute and ran an eye over the guard. He was fitter than he had been when was guarding Prince Tain. The reports the King had received about him were all good. He'd also had the guard closely watched, more thoroughly than the guard knew, although Smithers had suspected he was being observed; however, his gaze wasn't hostile or wary but as straight as ever. The guard stood at ease waiting for the King to speak. Adeone continued to watch him for a couple more minutes and was impressed. Smithers' posture and gaze never changed. There wasn't a hint of anxiety there. Here was a guard with either a clear conscience or one who was good at hiding his guilty secrets. Adeone eventually smiled.

The King said, "You're sensible. Tell me, was your locker searched or merely messed about?"

"I'd say it had been searched, sir," replied the guard without emphasis. "It is a bit of a coincidence that my rooms received the same cack-handed treatment. Your Majesty's spot checks don't leave the traces these idiots did. Good luck to them. I don't keep secrets they'll find."

"How many secrets do you have, which could be used to coerce you?"

"None, Sire."

"I hope that's true. I can tell you as well that I had nothing to do with the searching of your rooms."

"Thank you, sir. None of the men, to my knowledge, believe you had anything to do with last night."

"I can assure you I didn't. Now, I haven't invited you here for a chat about the responsibility for the outrage committed here last night but rather to commend you for your hard work over the Princes' Guard."

"Thank you, Sire. I'm simply doing my job."

Adeone smiled. "Remarkably well from the reports I've received. I'd like to make you a sergeant of the guard. Would you accept the promotion?"

Smithers took a moment to reply. He hadn't expected that. "I can hardly refuse, Your Majesty; if you think I am worth it."

"I wouldn't offer it to you if you were not, Sergeant. You will, under Captain Marsh, be in charge of Prince Tain's safety. I hope you're fit. I'd be glad if you kept the promotion private for the time being."

"Thank you, Sire. I hope I can match His Highness' energy."

"Thank you. That's all, Smithers."

* * *

By the time Adeone rolled up his notes, all he wanted to do was to get lunch and unwind for half an hour. As he was leaving for his chambers, Wynfeld asked for a private word. Once in the Inner Office, Adeone poured them both a drink and pointed at the comfortable chairs. Wynfeld hesitated.

"I'm meant to be having a morning off, Major, and therefore have no wish to talk across my desk. Just sit down."

"I'm sorry your morning was disturbed, Sire."

"It wasn't your doing, and Richardson's feeling guilty enough for everyone. What did you need to see me about?"

"We found nothing substantial, sir. I shall leave everything else and not disturb your morning further."

"Tell me. I appreciate the gesture, but you might say it's now superfluous."

"I was simply going to request an audience to discuss the state of the intelligence and training regiments, and any concerns that Your Majesty might have regarding them."

With studied deliberation, Adeone put his glass on the table. "What makes you think I have any? And what makes you think I wouldn't have already raised them?"

"I know Your Majesty will raise issues, but I also suspect I've been left to come to my own conclusions, and now I'd like to see if they match, Sire."

Adeone steepled his fingers, taking a couple of moments to formulate his reply. "See Richardson and, Wynfeld, I thought I asked you to find a commander and extra captain."

"I am working on it, sir."

"Good," said Adeone, "because I've forgotten what Captain Beaver looks like. I hope your new duties aren't too onerous."

"Not at all, sir. I'm enjoying the challenge."

Adeone finally smiled. "Good. I see you've relaxed as well."

"Sir?"

"Nothing. Let me top your glass up and we can turn the conversation to less official matters."

Wynfeld pushed himself to his feet. "Let me fill the glasses, Sire, you're having a morning off."

Adeone laughed. "So I am."

* * *

Once Wynfeld had left, Adeone sat contemplating the events. Scanlon had never openly shown his hand before. Had he meant to this time? If not, there would be repercussions for the men responsible. He consulted a list kept securely in his desk. Scanlon was at Black Hills.

Idly, Adeone tried to put himself in his brother's shoes. If Scanlon had wanted his interest in the guards known, he'd have to commend the men who had done an excellent job at proving it. If he hadn't, he'd want someone to take out the mistake on and the easiest person would be the one responsible for it. Adeone made a note and carried on thinking.

What had the men found? Was it anything of interest? Most of the higher guards, those in the King's Guard, had been briefed about Scanlon's plans. Would they be silly enough to keep incriminating material in their lockers?

He'd wait for Wynfeld's report. He had no doubt he'd receive a detailed one as soon as the Major had chance to put pen to paper.

Lord Iris unintentionally interrupted Adeone's thoughts. Would Prince Arkyn like Lord Irvin's company for the Anaparian Review? By the time Iris left, he'd been given the task of reorganising the Guards' Corridor to make way for a new locker room for the Princes' and King's Guard, and Adeone stopped worrying. With Lord Iris in charge, everything would go smoothly.

* * *

Wynfeld had returned to the barracks via Court. He called Beaver into his office. Keeping his subordinate officer standing, he enquired, "Anything occurring I should know about?"

"Not that isn't already under control, sir."

"When was the last time you took the evening report to the Palace?"

Beaver hesitated. "Erm…"

"When was the last time you *spoke* to His Majesty, Captain?" enquired Wynfeld icily.

"Er…"

"Do you think being Captain of Intelligence with the remit, therefore, of protecting His Majesty that that is an acceptable response? No, Beaver, it isn't! What's more, I don't like being informed by His Majesty that he's forgotten what you look like!"

"Sir—"

Wynfeld wasn't prepared to listen to excuses. "You will never be taken seriously if you aren't seen! You deliver the evening report to Richardson and wait for His Majesty to read it – from my experience, that is normally straight away. Before you start telling me that you don't have time, you *make* time. As the previous Major said to me, I will not tolerate my officers making a mockery out of the militia. Nor will I tolerate you making a mockery out of the intelligence regiment!"

"Sir."

"Is that all you have to say, Captain?"

"Don't really think there's much more I can say, sir. Your feelings are clear. When I've a co-captain, I should find it easier to see the outside of my office."

"Yes, and don't lie when I ask you if anything important or significant has happened in the city again. I *have* heard that Lord Scanlon visited Lord Ryson when he was here. Do you know why?"

"Not exactly, sir, but they were friends."

"*Were*, Beaver, *were*! We might not be certain if they are anymore, which is why you do everything you can to find out anything that happens. You might be interested to know that they tried, or at least Lord Scanlon tried, for reconciliation. Now, you do what you can with that and for your information. Lord Ryson informed me of the incident with the opening words '*I expect you've already heard, Major, but…*' I don't like being put in that position. I had to answer that you were collecting such intelligence and I had yet to read your report on the matter. Please make sure I can be honest in that statement by seeing I get a report to read regarding the incident."

* * *

Adeone lingered over his lunch, turning over the morning's events, those at Ceardlann and at the Palace. Tain's fears sliced at his heart, but it warmed him that his son would reveal them. There wasn't much he could do other than continue fighting by outwitting his brother's schemes.

He re-entered the Inner Office, unable to tell anyone what he'd eaten. Richardson had been busy; his desk now had paperwork in a neat pile. The top document was the standard midday report and, having read it, he rang for his administrator.

"Ask the Major to check if the yeomen on the Torport Gate saw anyone being escorted from the city earlier today. My brother won't have been happy about last night. Then can you discreetly inform the Comptroller that I am planning to visit Ceardlann tonight, please? I'd like it to be a surprise for Prince Tain. He was disappointed when I had to return. Did anything else happen this morning?"

Richardson's lips twitched. "Only one thing, Your Majesty. I'm not sure if I should pass it to you though. I remember a lot of mischievous moments coming after correspondence from the gentleman, and he's in more of a position to make it official mischief now."

Adeone laughed. "If you don't hand me Percival Wealsman's letter, Richardson, I'll… think of something!"

Grinning, Richardson handed over a letter from the Margrave of Terasia.

When he had it, Adeone motioned for his administrator to leave and broke the seal. He didn't stop smiling until he'd finished reading. Even then, the grin continued to light his features for a couple more minutes. He and Percival might talk over messengers occasionally, but it was about official matters. His letters were full of unofficial chatter and news – a wealth of information on one of the most distant provinces.

Adeone picked up a pen to answer the letter with equally innocuous gossip. It took his mind away from the day's events. Sealing his reply, he rang for his administrator.

"See that gets to Terasia quickly, please, and if the tramp of boots I heard was a courier with Wynfeld's report, you'd better bring it in."

Two moments later, Adeone was reading the report. They'd been right only certain lockers had been *searched*. The Major outlined measures for making sure it never happened again, at least in the near future. Adeone made notes beside the suggestions and told Richardson to arrange a meeting with Wynfeld and Captain Pixney. He'd talk through the suggestions then. He eyed a timepiece before asking Richardson to see that everything was ready for his return to Ceardlann at five, and to extricate him from Court then if he hadn't returned already.

* * *

Court was busy but not crowded. Adeone had passing conversations with several people before spotting Lady Julia. The ladies with her drew back as he crossed to them.

"So, my lady, this is where you hide. Walk with me, if you will." Once they were further away from listeners, he asked, "Have you heard from your renegade twin?"

Julia laughed. "Do I have one, Your Majesty?"

"I suppose that would depend on your definition of 'renegade', wouldn't it? I can amend it to 'troublesome', if you'd prefer."

"Oh, *that* twin, sir. I think I can safely say he is too busy to talk to me."

"I believe I warned him it would be no break."

"I believe you did, sir, several times."

Adeone gave his neardaughter a sideways look. She had the grace to blush as they both laughed.

Adeone said, "Now, my dear, do you have a dance card all marked up for this evening?"

"No, sir, I'm quite free."

"You haven't captured the hearts and minds of the young lords?"

Julia murmured, "Do they have any, sir?"

Adeone shook his head. "You are certainly Festus' daughter. If you wish to accompany me, I'm riding to Ceardlann at five on an unexpected visit."

"I would be honoured to, sir," replied Julia.

"Good. I'd like your company. I shouldn't keep you from your friends any longer. I'll come and find you when I'm ready to leave."

Julia once again curtsied as Adeone moved off. She returned with serene features to her smiling friends.

One of whom said, jokingly, "The King favours you, Julia."

"He is my nearfather, and we are living in his homes, Malandra," replied Julia. "It would be rude to not speak with me, would it not? And the King is never rude, not to me."

"Yes, but to others—"

"Is that any of our business? He is the King," warned Julia politely.

"I suppose not. So, whom are you dancing with tonight?"

Julia smiled. "No-one. I'm sorry to disappoint you but I'm going to have an evening away from Court."

"Got a better offer?" enquired Lady Malandra Para.

Julia laughed. "I'm hardly likely to admit it. So, whom have *you* got *your* eye on?"

They talked the next couple of hours away. It intrigued the ladies with Julia when the King made his way over to them once more. Adeone had a few words with all of them before he and Julia left.

When the King was out of hearing, Malandra said, "I'd say that was a better offer. Do you think he'll marry again?"

Lady Indria Iris shook her head. "I think he'll be forever grieving the late Queen."

"Pity, all that going to waste."

"Malandra, shame on you...!"

Chapter 27
EVENING AT CEARDLANN
Evening
Ceardlann

As SOON AS they were clear of Court, Julia shared a glance with her nearfather and broke into spontaneous giggles. His lips twitched but he didn't join in. If the Court wanted gossip, they could find it in anything. Something as harmless as leaving with his neardaughter, who was a guest in his residences, wouldn't get them very far.

By the time they reached the stables, Julia's giggles had subsided. She rarely traversed the Palace in her nearfather's company and his taciturnity had unsettled her. She took her riding cloak and gloves from her maid with a smile of thanks, donning them swiftly. A groom led over her mare, Drifter, and helped her mount.

Adeone swung into the saddle with familiar ease. Pursuit nickering to him. He smiled, patting his horse's neck. He could feel Pursuit's wish to gallop, but that would have to wait.

Riding through the city, Adeone glanced at Julia. At fifteen she had a lively curiosity that Court hadn't tempered, and a love of life that had never been quenched. He smiled to himself, remembering the baby she'd been, the young girl Ira and Cornelia had despaired and laughed over and now the young lady she was.

They crossed The Strait before his thoughts had settled themselves and were beyond the Dallin Gate by the time he said, "Do you enjoy Court?"

She glanced at him. "I enjoy the company, Sire."

He crooked an eyebrow. "Is that all?"

She laughed again. "It's strange without Julius. Not that I'm complaining," she added hastily, "but I'm used to him being there to annoy."

"I won't tell him you miss him," said Adeone innocently. "Far be it from me to interfere in your sisterly reticence. I was surprised you were there alone."

Julia shrugged. "It stops me getting under mother's feet, sir. She's got enough on with the little ones and the house. I also thought the Comptroller might be grateful for the peace."

"He's had Tain living there since 1209. I'm not sure he knows what peace is anymore."

She exchanged a wry look with him. "I can't imagine what you mean, Uncle Adeone. Tain's always so calm."

"With absolutely no mischief encouraged by his older nearcousins," Adeone mused dryly.

"Well, we're all said to take after our fathers, sir."

Adeone laughed aloud. "I believe we deny knowledge of that."

"Yes. Mother never lets father get away with it."

Once in the Rex Dallin, Adeone glanced at Julia. The ride had put colour in her cheeks and her eyes were bright.

"Shall we race to Ceardlann?" he suggested.

"Wouldn't that be rather indecorous, Uncle Adeone?"

"What else is a nearfather for? Come on."

Minutes later, they clattered into the stableyard laughing. Dismounting swiftly, Julia tried to straighten her hair.

"Give up. It's not like it matters here," said Adeone, giving her a one-armed hug. "You're a better rider than I remember."

"I've had more practice, Sire, and Drifter is a good mare."

"She is. She still has a bit of fight in her, which for you... Ah, evening, Cornelia. How are you?"

Lady Landis gave a brief curtsy. "Well enough, thank you, Sire. I see you've found my daughter."

Adeone's eyes twinkled at her. "I didn't realise she was such an absent daughter."

"She has her moments," admitted Cornelia. "I hope she's been polite."

Adeone chuckled. "I always find her company refreshing. She has been the model of propriety."

"I'm pleased, sir. Julia, go and change for dinner."

Adeone watched his neardaughter leave, his eyes bright with mischief. "She does you proud, Cornelia. Mind you, I can also see Festus in her. Do you know where Tain is?"

"In his sitting room. No doubt planning another scheme," replied Cornelia, lips twitching. "The last was going and watching for foxes and badgers up in the woods."

"It's educational, I suppose. Did he go?"

"I believe so – there was a muddy trail that wound its way to the night nursery and some innocent grins, Finian's amongst them."

Adeone laughed. "I deny all responsibility for Tain."

"It might be a bit late to do that," said Cornelia with a chuckle.

"True. I shall go and alert him to my presence before someone else does. What time did you order dinner for?"

"I thought seven, sir. Elantha and Antonia could join us then as well."

Adeone walked quickly through the house, entering his sons' sitting room without knocking. Tain was curled up in a chair with his back to the door. Cal spotted the King but at a sharp look stayed where he was; however, Tain noticed the stillness in his friend and half turned. Adeone stepped to one side, crept up on his son and tickled him for several moments before being floored by a hug.

When he'd got his breath, Tain exclaimed, "You said you didn't know when you were coming back!"

"I didn't *know*. I thought I might. Then I found I could, so I did."

"So what happened in Oedran?"

"The normal: an event instigated by your uncle that nearly caused a riot."

Tain frowned. "Is that normal?"

"It's not always unusual. I see you've not grown out of asking questions during the day."

"It's the only way to learn, father."

Adeone chuckled. "Haven't you been taught that it is impolite to use the King's words back to him as a pert reply?"

"Yes, but this is Ceardlann and everyone says I'm like you were."

"Hmm. I can tickle you again. A little bird told me you've been out at night and up to the forest."

Tain shuffled his feet. "Yes, father, but we *were* careful."

"Good. Did you see anything?"

"No, sir."

Adeone watched him blithely. "That's not on, is it? I think you'll have to go again with more expert help. How about I ask the head forester to take you out at night? He knows the best spots and will make sure you get to see something. He knows an awful lot of forest lore as well. Go out with him during the day, when you can. He can teach you how to track animals and, if you wish, how to hunt as well."

Six minutes later, Adeone said, "Come, shall we go down for dinner?" Tain nodded and Adeone turned to Cal. "Is there anything you need?"

"No, sir, thank you."

"You need a better sword," said Tain.

Adeone looked at Cal steadily. "Do you, young Cal?"

"I'm not sure, Your Majesty. Something feels wrong with the one I'm using. Maybe if there's another one not being used that I could try…"

"I'm sure we can find one somewhere. A swordsman, like any skilled man, needs the right tools."

Cal whispered, "Thank you, sir." Be grateful for what you've got was one of his father's favourite expressions.

Adeone noticed the quiet tone and let it pass. "What had you got planned for after dinner?"

Tain replied, "Playing a board game, sir."

Adeone smiled. "Mind if I join you?" He didn't ask Tain but Cal.

Rather surprised, Cal said, "Not at all, Your Majesty."

They'd reached the large antechamber and Cal held the door open for the King and Tain. Adeone entered and scanned the room. Elantha ran over. He swung her up into a hug. At eight years, she was getting heavy; his back twinged but he ignored it. Arkyn turned, seeing his cousin run across the room. He stopped mid-sentence, startled.

Adeone grinned at him. "I take it nobody told you I was here?"

Crossing to him, Arkyn said, "No, father, they didn't!" glancing at Cornelia and his chuckling nearcousins.

His father gave him a hug. "I expected at least one of them not to keep the secret. I see I did them a disservice."

Once the greetings were over, Adeone spent time talking with Arkyn. "Iris asked if you'd like Irvin's company for the Anaparian Review."

Arkyn smiled. "He's attending the Advisors' School."

"So's Julius and he's in Macia. I'm sure something could be arranged. From what you told me, Irvin would enjoy the time in another city."

"He certainly would, sir, and I'd enjoy his company."

* * *

Tain rolled over, exasperated; his thoughts wouldn't stop chasing themselves and it must be midnight. He didn't want to disturb Elantha or Cal, but he shouldn't stay in bed; he should find something to do until he was tired.

Entering the sitting room, he stood for a moment, disconcerted. His brother was sitting in the window-seat gazing at the stars.

Without moving, Arkyn said, "I won't be long, Kadeem."

Tain grinned. "You really shouldn't assume."

"What are you doing up?"

"Sleepwalking. What're you thinking about?" asked Tain as he sat at the other end of the window seat.

Arkyn sighed. "Mother. Wondering what she'd make of me."

Tain swallowed. "I often wonder the same thing. I mean, look at you, talk about disreputable."

"Sorry, is there a mirror in front of you?"

151

"It might give me a better view."

Arkyn grimaced. "I know the feeling."

Tain laughed, then went pensive. "Father's told me about uncle. Do you think he had anything to do with mother's death?"

Arkyn gazed at the stars again. "No. Mother's illness couldn't have been created by poison. Whatever we wish, her time had come to join our ancestors." After a moment, he said, "There is something so peaceful about the stars."

Tain wiped his eyes. "Yes, it's because they can't talk."

"That might be it. Have you ever thought of taking lessons from them?" asked Arkyn, pulling out his handkerchief and offering it to his brother.

Tain took it. "No, I shine enough without them."

"Other than at archery."

"I'm getting better. Not right on target, but at least I've stopped taking out birds."

Arkyn laughed. "True. So why couldn't you sleep?"

Tain bit his lip. "Does uncle really want to kill us? And to take over the empire?"

Arkyn shrugged. "Apparently so."

"Oh. Father thinks that I can stop him."

"I know. Does it bother you?"

Tain sighed. "Yes, because I can't. I don't know anything—"

"Glad you admit it at last."

"Ha ha. I meant about what he's doing, how I could stop him—"

Arkyn considered that. "Do you think I knew anything about the reviews before I went to Terasia?"

"You knew more about that than I know about this."

"It's why you've got lessons with the judge, Tain. You're twelve, you're not meant to know *everything*. Surprising though that might seem to you."

"I follow your fine example, brother."

Arkyn grimaced. "That's only going to get you into trouble. Are you still worried about being justiciar?"

"Yes. Are you about being king one day?"

"No, I'm not worried; I'm stoically terrified."

Tain smiled. "Glad it's not just me. I know I won't ever grasp the law."

"Give yourself chance to grasp things slowly. Don't expect to wake up one day knowing everything. I'm sure the judge would tell you it's taken him a lifetime to know all he does."

Hugging his knees to himself, Tain covered his bare feet with his night-tunic. "He already has, but surely more is expected of me."

Arkyn gave a non-committal jerk of his head. "Perhaps, but you'll have lawyers to help."

"Or hinder. Have you got your advisors yet?"

"Most of them. To tell the truth, I'm nervous of them."

Tain said, "You'll be fine, Arkyn. Terasia gave you the Memini's Manuscript, so you can't be completely hopeless!"

"Damned by faint praise."

"But it wasn't faint, Arkyn, was it? They gave you the manuscript. What an honour is that!"

Arkyn groused, "Not them, idiot, your comment!"

"I'm your brother; does that mean I'm meant to be complimentary?"

"No, thank Alcis, because that would work both ways."

The door opened, and Kadeem entered. In answer to a raised eyebrow from Arkyn, he enquired,

"Would you like a hot drink, Your Highness?"

Arkyn smiled. "I think I would. Tain?"

Tain nodded. "Please, Kadeem. If it's not too much trouble."

"No trouble at all, Your Highness," replied Kadeem with a smile.

"What's it like, having a manservant?" asked Tain once he'd gone.

"Not so different to Maria looking after you. No, I suppose that's wrong. It is different but nothing I can put into words. Kadeem's more philosophical than Maria ever is for a start."

Tain laughed. "Yes, I've noticed."

"What have you been up to today?"

"The same as ever. I like Judge Tancred but Advisor Spellen's very different to Ewall."

Arkyn raised his eyebrows slightly. "Yes, isn't he? Not quite so laid back, and that's saying something. Ewall wasn't informal by any means. Spellen knows his stuff though."

Tain sighed. "Why can't we have an easy life?"

"They don't exist."

Tain bit at his lip. "Can't we run away from it all? I'm actually scared of the law. I shouldn't be, but I am."

Arkyn shook his head. "It's not the law. You fear the unknown, like me. I suppose we've both got to get to know it."

Tain went quiet and gazed out the window once more. After a couple of minutes, he murmured, "For what it's worth, I think she'd have been proud of you."

Arkyn smiled sadly. "She'd certainly have been proud of you. I suppose we have to try to be the men she always hoped we would be."

Tain nodded but, before he could reply, Kadeem had re-entered with two steaming beakers of milk and honey and some biscuits to dunk in them.

The brothers moved over to near the fireplace. The warmth of the drink combined with the fire meant it wasn't long before both Arkyn and Tain were yawning. Tain fell asleep.

Arkyn watched him fondly. "I'll be with you in a minute, Kadeem; I'll just get Prince Tain to go to bed."

"Allow me, sir, it would be a shame to wake His Highness."

Arkyn opened the door to the night nursery as Kadeem carried Tain in. Quietly he drew back the covers so that Kadeem could put Tain down and was touched by how carefully his manservant tucked his brother in.

* * *

Once in his own bedchamber, Arkyn said, "I haven't helped my brother's fears tonight."

Kadeem passed the Prince a night-tunic. "I'm sure you have, sir."

"I'm not. He fears the future so much."

"It's understandable, sir, and, if you'll forgive me, you have also feared the future over recent years – even in a small measure still do. Is it, therefore, unusual that His Highness also worries about it?"

"Do you mean that if I hide my feelings, he'd be less anxious?"

"No, sir, I didn't mean it like that. I was trying to say that, as brothers, Your Highnesses are likely to share certain traits," explained Kadeem.

"I suppose that's logical," admitted Arkyn. "Do you think Prince Tain will ever become reconciled to what his life will be?"

"Over time most people become reconciled to their lives, sir. I'm sure His Highness will be no different. It is primarily a case of having the support of those around us which helps. Can I get you anything else, sir?"

Arkyn sighed. "No, thank you, Kadeem."

"Then may your dreams be pleasant, Your Highness."

Chapter 28
SLOW DEATH
Pentadai, Week 4 – 26th Cearal, 5th Middis 1212
Anapara – Raven Hills – Black Hills House

SCANLON PACED AROUND HIS STUDY at Black Hills, frowning so deeply that no-one dared stay in the room with him. Events at the Palace went beyond belief. If the man responsible wasn't before him soon, there would be more repercussions.

Two hours later, a tentative knock at the door revealed three of his household and between two of them another man.

Scanlon simply snapped at that man, "Well?"

"Nothing of interest, Greatness."

Scanlon drew himself up; his tone cold, hard and sneering. "No. I know that. I have already been told that. I have already been told what happened; what a complete and utter bloody mess you made of things. I told you to *search* the lockers! I didn't tell you to destroy the locker room or the captain's office. I didn't tell you to make it so obvious that the King had to be involved. Who were the two men with you?"

The man, swallowing, named them. Lord Scanlon *never* wanted the names of people who did the jobs he needed.

Scanlon sneered. "One was your son? Your only son?"

"Yes, Greatness," replied the man, barely audible.

"You shall watch as he is executed for the fiasco. You needn't plead, it has no effect. Bantling, make it slow and painful. I'll watch. Then castrate the other two. If they don't have the balls to do a job well, then they won't have balls for anything else. I will not tolerate stupidity and lies!"

It was cold hearted and level toned. Only a fool would have tried to reason with him. Bantling bowed as Scanlon turned away. He'd never witnessed such a rage before.

The father of the condemned was carried out; Bantling also left, though someone would have to calm down Lord Scanlon. Random executions wouldn't help, but nothing would talk Lord Scanlon out of this one. It would have to happen and remain as private as possible. There was no doubt word would escape, and a healthy fear of Lord Scanlon was wise. He didn't forget and he didn't forgive, and anyone messing up his plans would suffer. Bantling made sure the cellarer knew what had to be done and left. He didn't like Lord Scanlon's methods, but it was far too late for him to escape. If he left, he would immediately be hunted and found – there'd be no escape from the scryers. A slow death wouldn't cover what he would suffer for running away. He couldn't escape, couldn't run, couldn't hide. Lord Scanlon got absolute loyalty or people were tortured. If he, Bantling, were to kill himself, that wouldn't make any difference. Lord Scanlon would make his family suffer. He shivered, remembering the tone Lord Scanlon had used; he didn't care about anyone or anything, but he got what he wanted. There wouldn't be another disaster for a long time. Great Alcis, he had to hope there wouldn't be. Suborning people into becoming traitors wasn't easy. Blackmail and threats didn't always work. Every man was different, and every approach had to be devised carefully. Then there was the other scheme that the Justiciar had brewing. Getting a man of the right calibre for that one would be difficult and challenging. He didn't have long, and Lord Scanlon knew he hadn't found anyone yet.

Then there was the information the Justiciar wanted. It was getting dangerous. He had to complete both or find out what it was like to suffer one of Lord Scanlon's more inventive punishments.

Chapter 29
INSPECTION AND GUARDING
Imperadai, Week 5 – 4th Tradal, 11th Middis 1212
Administrative Quarter – Barracks

GENERAL PATURN AND MAJOR WYNFELD met Prince Arkyn at the gates of the barracks hoping the inspection would go well. Once the initial pleasantries were over, they walked through the barracks passing several men, all smartly turned out with clean jupons or tabards, polished greaves and breastplates; so, when they passed a raggedy and ill-dressed man who saluted, Arkyn raised an eyebrow at Wynfeld.

"One of the intelligence regiment, sir, going out on duty."

Arkyn stopped and jerking his head at the soldier summoned him. "What character are you meant to be assuming?"

"Dock worker, Your Highness."

"Then next time, grab your cap from your head; only a soldier or guard salutes. If you're dressed in character, be that character. Also, you've no river mud on your boots and no knife in your belt. Your belt would be better to be old rope than that fine leather. A few pointers that might keep you alive."

The soldier swallowed. His eyes flicked to the Major's blank face then back to Arkyn. "Thank you, sir. I'll sort it."

As they carried on down the corridor, Wynfeld remarked, "He was also wearing a signet ring."

"I thought I'd said enough, Major. Was that set up?"

"No, sir. I'll make sure they're not that lax again."

"Good. General, I think we'll start in the training yard. What training is taking place today?"

Paturn inclined his head slightly. "Hand to hand combat, Your Highness. Men of the training regiment against another regiment."

Arkyn surveyed the sanded training yard with interest. The Major motioned to Captain Edmonds, who gave the order to halt, before shouting the men to attention. It took them several moments to adjust to Arkyn's presence. When they did, the salutes were exact.

Arkyn nodded in thanks. "I shouldn't stop your training. Please, carry on."

Edmonds saluted and gave the order to continue. Arkyn's sharp eyes swept across the men and eyed their skill with scepticism.

He turned to the Major. "Which half are the training regiment?"

"Those with the armbands, sir."

"Hmm. I'm not convinced by their skill. Either they're purposefully letting blows through or they need training themselves. General, is this the only training area?"

"For this, yes, Your Highness," replied Paturn stolidly. "It holds around a hundred men. The small yard is more for officer practice."

"Where are the stores?" enquired Arkyn.

"Other side of this yard. Between here and the parade ground, sir."

"We'll go there next, if we can do so without interrupting the training."

The General hesitated. "Sir, our itinerary—"

Arkyn cut across him, "I'm *inspecting* the barracks, General. Surely you wouldn't try to prevent me from seeing an area?"

The General stood straighter. "Not at all, sir."

"Good. Then maybe you'd care to lead the way."

At the stores, the Prince asked, "Do you have all you need, Sergeant?"

The sergeant in charge said, "Mostly, sir, if there wasn't something to moan about, it wouldn't be the army."

The General glared at him, Major Wynfeld gave a polite cough but the sergeant didn't look abashed.

Arkyn said, "Quite, there is always something; however, I'm assuming, possibly incorrectly, that you have no major concerns about the state of your stores?"

"Your Highness, you're correct. I have no major concerns. Other than the fact *the Major* is now eyeing me like his new hobby."

Arkyn chuckled. "I'm sure he can appreciate your honesty. Carry on."

"Sir." The sergeant saluted and watched Arkyn leave, swearing in the privacy of his head. He'd be on fatigues for a month for that slip up.

Once out of hearing, Arkyn said, "Leave the sergeant be, Wynfeld. Nerves can be many things."

"Sir."

"I mean that, Major. It'll worry him far more, for a start."

By the time Arkyn returned to the General's office, both Paturn and the Major were wondering what the Prince's report to the King would be. From working with his Prince in Terasia, Wynfeld knew that whatever Arkyn said or commented on during the inspection, the report would be an honest and astute summation of his views and would probably be more positive than the General currently expected.

Arkyn took a drink from Kadeem. "How many men could the parade ground train, General?"

"It took about five hundred in 1169, sir."

"Mm. I'm wondering if it's worth swapping the two areas. What are your thoughts?"

"It's never been done, sir, because of the problem of stopping that many men fighting if tempers get frayed."

"That's a good point but how often has a riot started from training? Thank you, Kadeem, you can go."

Kadeem left with the General's batman.

Paturn became more forthright. "Never, sir, but we've never given it the chance of starting. I must advise against the plan. I would have to stand opposed to it, even in front of His Majesty."

Arkyn said, "Major, could you send me the training regime, please? I'd like to understand it before I make any recommendation to the King. I must say though I'm impressed by the men's display. Their armour is sparkling. How much warning were they given?"

The General replied, "Two days, sir, and most didn't require the time."

"That is reassuring, but I'll not give you as much warning next time. General, regarding the empire, do you hold any concerns?"

"Not that I haven't already reported to His Majesty, sir."

"Good," replied Arkyn. Should he show he'd understood the reproach? No; the General might have been unaware of it himself.

After his Prince left the barracks, Wynfeld turned to the General. "Why did you rebuke His Highness, sir?"

"The empire is the King's domain. Much damage has been done in the past by princes forgetting that. He didn't realise anyway."

"I think he did, sir. I've seen him ignore comments before instead of causing disquiet."

* * *

Adeone read the formal letter of apology from the General and wondered if any official would survive their first encounter with Arkyn without needing reassurance.

Having read the letter twice, Adeone summoned Paturn and eyed the elderly man as he entered and saluted. He tapped the letter on his desk, raising an eyebrow.

The General explained events at the barracks, honestly and without obvious bias.

Adeone listened carefully. It was revealing and interesting for him to hear how his son faced responsibility. As the General finished, he said, "Firstly, General, I'm not angry, this time. Secondly, thank you for your apology and explanation. There are several things, however, that I need to make plain to you. Prince Arkyn holds my absolute trust and knows the threats that plague us. I do not keep empire matters away from him because of those threats. I am under no illusion about my mortality and I am not going to leave my sons unprepared for their future. If your Prince asks you a question, you answer it. He is far more conscientious than I ever was at his age. How did you realise you might have overstepped the mark?"

"Major Wynfeld informed me, Sire. He understands Prince Arkyn remarkably well."

"Yes," said Adeone dryly. "He stopped my son shattering at the time of Queen Ira's death. He was there at a crucial moment for your Prince. After working together in Terasia, they have an instinctive understanding of each other as well."

Paturn considered. "Then I think I should step aside, sir, when it comes to guiding the Prince. The Major appears to be the better person."

Adeone waved the General to a chair. "No, I don't agree. You can teach Prince Arkyn much but remember that he doesn't always show what he's feeling – even to me – but once the language is learnt, it is well worth knowing. Do you think Prince Arkyn will make a good king?"

"When his time comes, sir; which I hope and say will not be for many years."

"I'd prepare yourself for the change sooner – it's coming; I can feel it in my bones."

"Your Majesty, I shall only prepare to celebrate your next birthday and the many after that."

Adeone smiled. "Don't be blind or a courtier, Paturn." He relaxed in his chair. "There are times when I watch Wynfeld listening to and guiding my son and I wonder what makes men follow and respect Arkyn so highly. Terasia handed him the Memini's Manuscript. After centuries of refusing to hand it over, they tamely gave it to my son."

"The why is immaterial, Sire. What you need to remember is that you have had more influence on His Highness than you ever give yourself credit for. He *is* your son and no-one doubts that. Respect given to His Highness is respect given to Your Majesty."

Adeone sighed. "I sometimes wonder. Arkyn is far more traditional than I am, Paturn."

"No, sir, he has your outlook, but maybe his approach is mellower. He allows men to change—"

"Are you saying I force change?" enquired Adeone, his lips twitching.

"No, sir, but men see your requests as an order, a proclamation, a direct instruction. Prince Arkyn lets men decide to follow him and they do."

Adeone frowned. "Yes, but *why* do they follow him? Wynfeld would march to the ends of the empire for him, without question. I'm not so sure he would for me."

"Does it matter, Your Majesty? Prince Arkyn commands loyalty without realising it. As long as he never realises what he's doing, the empire will love him."

Once the General had gone, Adeone sent for Arkyn. When his son entered the Inner Office, the King said mildly, "The inspection went to plan then."

Arkyn blushed. "I didn't mean to cause any trouble, Sire."

Adeone chuckled. "No, but as Paturn has kindly said, you're definitely my son. Come and tell me everything that happened."

* * *

At the barracks, Paturn sent for Wynfeld. "Major, tell me why His Majesty thinks you have more respect for the Prince than himself."

Wynfeld frowned. "Really, sir? I respect them both equally—"

"They are not equal, Major! The King is your liege, not his son. Such preferences in the past have led to rebellion. If His Majesty has noticed, others will have done. You are charged with protecting the King; do not, through concern for the Prince, neglect your duties. I'd rather not have to listen to His Majesty wondering what is behind your preference. His Highness' life is important. The King will probably tell you it's more important than his, but we do not need an underage king."

Paturn watched Wynfeld leave, hoping the King's fears his life was ending were not as accurate as other thoughts had been.

* * *

The following day, Adeone, Arkyn, Paturn, Wynfeld, Captain Marsh and Captain Pixney were once more closeted in a meeting. It was a warm day and the meeting was mellow as befitted it. The General and Major said they had no reservations about letting the men of the new Princes' Guard out of their care. The Major said that he had learnt things from the unusual training methods the King had suggested and it might be worth training a regiment up as an elite force, for whatever the future held.

Adeone, who'd been thinking the same thing himself but had waited for someone else to suggest it, added it to a list. The General caught the King's eye; knowing full well what his monarch was up to, he'd worked for him for long enough.

Pixney informed the meeting the new locker room was ready to be used and would be in operation from midnight. There would be guards stationed in the corridor throughout the night as a deterrent against another search.

The King nodded. Anything making his brother's life harder had to be a good thing. He made another note on the parchment by his hand.

He listened to all the reports with interest before asking for concerns: the only one raised was that the guards being highly trained might get bored easily with disastrous results. He outlined the guards would augment the King's Guard whilst they themselves received more training. They'd also be used by the Major to help train up an elite regiment.

The Major showed surprise, then shook his head. How long had his King been thinking about that one, simply waiting for him to suggest it?

Adeone continued explaining that the guards could act as overseers for different areas of the Palace, thus taking some pressure off Pixney and his sergeants.

The captain nodded; he'd certainly be glad of the help. Being the only officer was extremely stressful when he had three shifts to oversee.

With a handful of guards patrolling the corridors, instead of standing in them, the Palace would be a lot harder to infiltrate and corrupt. Not that Scanlon would ever use devious methods to corrupt the guards, thought Adeone wryly; he'd just go for simple ones like torture instead. Subtlety had taken one look at his brother and gone to hide a long way away; it didn't want to be used by him. Adeone appreciated the gesture; blatancy was so much easier to spot.

Rotas for the Princes' Guard would be delivered by the guards to the King's office, Prince Arkyn, and Major Wynfeld as well as Captain Pixney. It wouldn't do for Scanlon to get hold of them and work out a method of attack around them. Scanlon would no doubt deduce a lot from observation but Adeone wasn't going to make it any easier for him.

* * *

The following day dawned and found the new Princes' Guard in place. Arkyn carried out an inspection of the Oedranian city walls giving his guard plenty of practice. He felt relatively safe with them. Not quite in the same sense as he had when he was with Fitz, but he had exuded experience *and* competence. Arkyn found the walk round the walls both tiring and exhilarating, but was pleased when he returned to street level and the coach that his father had insisted upon. He returned to the Palace and reported to his father before having a peaceful afternoon with no duties to perform. Returning to Ceardlann the following day, he took Cal's new tutor with him: a former aulnager called Annatto, who seemed reserved but without that reserve being oppressive. He explained his sons had taken over his business and he was quite happy to let them. That made Arkyn smile slightly. What sort of retirement Annatto would have teaching Cal he didn't know but he doubted it would be staid.

Chapter 30
BOOKS AND GIFTS
Cisadai, Week 6 – 9th Tradal, 16th Middis 1212
Palace – Lord Landis' Office

LORD LANDIS LOOKED UP as his private secretary entered his office carrying a simple wooden crate. As members of his staff went, Redford was less deferential than some and quieter than others. He knew what his job entailed and didn't let Landis get in the way of him doing it.

"Do you have a moment, milord?"

"You should know, Redford," replied Landis amiably. "Especially if you've got by Atlem. What's in the crate?"

"I went to Latimer's and found a few books and scrolls for your library."

Landis grinned, pushing himself to his feet. "Tell me you've found another copy of *Places of the Cearcall*." Crossing to a comfortable chair, he nodded for Redford to sit opposite him.

"No such luck, milord. I think you've the only copy of that. I found a nice copy of *The Flora of Southern Anapara* and a decent scroll of *The Last Days of Ull* by Hanes of Mynedfa. I'm thinking it might be nice to add to the children's collection. It's not long, but it explains how Ull formed Cisluna before falling to his death. I thought it might intrigue Master Lucius."

Landis sat down and pulled the crate of scrolls and books towards him. "I have no doubt Master Lucius would be enthralled by the idea of Ull stepping into nothingness and falling to his death after sending all the surrounding rock spinning into the heavens to form Cisluna. What ideas he'll get from it, I dread to think."

Redford chuckled. "I've often wondered what Ull thought as he fell."

"It probably wasn't polite," replied Landis dryly. He picked up the rolled parchment. "We're sure this scroll isn't unique?"

"Ten a darl, sir."

"Then give it Master Lucius." He delved into the box again, pulling out a black, leather-bound book. "Redford, I know I said I appreciate unusual texts but *The Uses and History of Obsidian* is quite obscure."

His secretary smiled quietly. "I wondered about Lord Daioch, milord."

Landis snorted, opening the book. "I doubt he needs this. He's could no doubt write it." His eyes lit on a paragraph.

The greatest minds concluded that Ull's action, in removing all rock from the country, was the reason stone could not exist there. The earth would swallow it, trying to regain that which it had lost. Without stone, there was no ore, and without ore the people learned to live without metal until they had become almost allergic to it, if not in actuality in mind. Any stone or metal was sucked into the earth as though an unendurable weight was placed on quicksand. This had become known to the rest of the empire as Ull's Curse, but to the Low Plainers it was Ull's Blessing for they came to value what they had so much more including rare, highly prized woods and obsidian from near Ull's Watchtower. Obsidian had been formed in the heat of the blast Ull had caused. A rock more like glass it was used by scryers to utilise their hue. One obsidian mirror could pass through many generations and hands but to break a scryer's mirror was said to blind the destroyer.

"Never mind. We'll add it to our collection. That way, should my wed-brother ever visit, I will be able to debate with him. I'm sure His Lordship won't know how to thank you." He pulled out two novels and crooked an eyebrow.

"Bit of light relief, milord. *The Memor's Dream* is meant to be good."

"I suppose we all need relief sometimes. What's this? *The Social History of the Cearcallian Age*. I presume you had a good reason other than to save me from insomnia?"

"Their Highnesses seem to be interested in the Cearcall, sir."

Landis sighed. "So they are, but I doubt the origins of alunan and cisan interest them overmuch. Mind you, I suppose it would help Prince Tain understand some laws."

"It also has some passages explaining the way people began to believe that the moons control our destinies, sir. I originally expected it to be dry and, as Your Lordship rightly said, a cure for insomnia but it's intriguing. The dual months I knew must be because of the moons' cycles, but I hadn't realised that it was only in certain lands where they became common. Some continued with only alunan months and they had many names. Often, they persisted until the land was drawn into the empire. Sometimes until the Perandoria that gave us our current names."

"Sounds like you should be the one to read this then," said Landis passing it over with a smile. "Add it to your own collection. I'm sure Judge Tancred, as an expert on historical law, can give Prince Tain all the lessons he needs. Anything else?"

"A *History of King Atgas*, sir, and the illustrated copy of *The Flora of*

Southern Anapara."

Landis lifted the history out of the box. Again, it was a bound book, though the carved leather cover was looking a little bedraggled. He put it to one side. Histories of the Kings of Oedran were interesting, but he had many. Occasionally, they mentioned his ancestors. The book at the bottom of the box was bound on the short edge, its cover a wonderfully patinated brown leather. The title embossed and gilded had little wear. Either it had been carefully handled or re-gilded recently. He opened it with almost exaggerated care. The illustrations were exquisitely drawn with fine lines and painted with watercolours. "How old?"

"Certainly more than fifty years, milord. Latimer guessed at closer to a hundred. I bartered him down, but we both knew its worth."

"It is beautiful. Leave it out the next time His Majesty visits. He does appreciate beautiful items." Landis briefly considered giving it to Adeone at the Mundimri, but there was a part of him, a small insistent voice, that said he wanted to keep it for himself even more.

* * *

In Eyllyn on the Low Plains, Lord Daioch's mind was also drawn towards gifts for the King. He'd enjoyed his years in Oedran, mainly thanks to the friendship he'd formed with Adeone and Landis. Since returning home, since becoming Deputy Governor of the Low Plains shortly after Adeone's accession, he'd been careful to keep the memory of the friendship alive. The wed-kin tie to Lord Landis had strengthened their relationship, but Adeone had so many calls on his time it was easy to let the personal become professional.

He'd spent several hours with an artist, describing his idea. Adeone's dislike of flamboyance was well known but he still appreciated beautiful objects and it was a careful line to tread.

The craftsman, who was now working with the artist's sketch, was skilled and careful. The gems Daioch had sourced were locked away until needed. They wouldn't accidentally be dropped for the earth to consume them. The floorboards here had cracks large enough to swallow the stones. Carefully laid canvas covered the floor under the workbench. Now the wood-inlay work was complete, the gems and obsidian would be next.

Watching his design come together, Daioch missed vital aspects that would cause the beauty in the piece to be forgotten and wreak havoc on his life.

Chapter 31

CHILDREN

Pentadai, Week 6 – 12th Tradal, 19th Middis 1212
Ceardlann

THREE DAYS LATER, recognising he needed to spend more time with his younger son, Adeone reorganised his meetings and went to Ceardlann. The house welcomed him warmly and, before he'd even dismounted, he was smiling to himself. He felt he was returning home and that his life in Oedran was merely one of his many varied and vivid dreams.

Entering the house, he nodded to the Comptroller, who'd crossed to greet him. Recognising the King's mood, the Comptroller bowed slightly and left again.

Whistling softly under his breath, Adeone went to find Tain. His younger son welcomed him enthusiastically before politely insisting on finishing his lessons – which left Adeone nonplussed but unwilling to crush the enthusiasm. He left again with a word of congratulations to Spellen, who explained it was Tancred's work. Once alone, Adeone shook his head, amused. He'd always thought James would have an effect but not necessarily so soon.

Making his way to his private chambers, he heard Cal's voice and entered the room it emanated from. He smiled both at Cal and Annatto before staying to discover what Cal was learning. By the end of the boy's recitation, Adeone was impressed, not only with the tutor but with Cal's attitude. Lord Rale interrupted them, asking Cal for some swordplay.

Once the boys had gone, Adeone enquired, "How has Master Calumiel been coping, Annatto?"

"Very well, Your Majesty. He'll make a good cloth merchant. He is an exceptionally quick learner."

Adeone said gravely, "Yes, he's had to be, I think. Now, just a word of warning, do not tell Master Galdwin that his son has weapons training, please. You've seen what the world can be and I think eventually Master Calumiel might well find he needs to defend himself. I wouldn't be doing my duty to him as a kind of guardian if I didn't teach him the skills he might require later in life, but I feel Master Galdwin wouldn't want it."

"I'll not breathe a word, Sire."

"Thank you. I know that Master Galdwin will find out at some point but the further into the future, the better. Now, I really do want to know the truth – is there anything you need or want?"

"No, Sire. I've never been anywhere so welcoming or helpful in my life."

Adeone smiled. "I'm pleased. Now that I've lost you your pupil, I must

165

see if I can find my first-born. Just ask if you ever need to see me.”

The former Aulnager bowed as the King left. It was heart-warming that the King concerned himself about Cal’s welfare. Then again, he reflected, the King seemed to worry about everyone’s welfare, as though he had nothing better to do.

* * *

Adeone tracked Arkyn down to the area designated as a training yard. The Prince was standing watching Cal and Finian fight. Adeone leaned next to him on the fence.

Arkyn grinned. “This time someone told me you were here, father.”

“That was kind of them. How are things?”

“Tain’s working too hard; other than that, the same as ever.”

Adeone nodded. “Yes. What’s got into him?”

“It’s since you were last here. He’s hardly played a prank since.”

“That’s not like him. I’ll have a word, just to make sure it isn’t anything worrying. I doubt it will last.”

“No, I must admit, I thought that as well.”

The King looked sideways at his son with raised eyebrows. They both laughed.

“Before you go to Paras, I’d like you to speak to Chapa. Your exhaustion does appear to be getting better slowly, but I’d like to make sure that he is happy for you to travel. You’ll take it in easy stages and I’ve told the Domini that you’ll be there a week before you start doing any work towards the review. I’ve told him it gives you time to see Paras.”

Arkyn relaxed. “Thank you, father; although I’d probably have been all right. Is Lord Irvin accompanying me again?”

“Yes, I managed to make the Dean of the Advisors’ School see sense. I had to tell him, however, that Irvin would be in meetings with you to see the workings of the empire at close quarters. I then told Irvin who, I must admit, took it well; for saying all the time he’ll lose from perusing the documents in the library there.”

Arkyn smiled. “I’m sure he’ll cope, sir.”

“He’d better. Then I’ll have your report to look forward to – with annotations!”

“I cannot imagine to what you are alluding, sir,” replied Arkyn with supreme innocence.

Adeone eyed him. “No, you can’t imagine, simply because you *know*! You don’t need to *imagine*. Just come back with it yourself, this time, and talk me through it.” Adeone focused on the fight occurring in front of him. “I see Festus wasn’t lying. Cal *is* very good.”

“He’s a better swordsman than I am, father. Especially now I don’t

166

have stamina for the fight."

Adeone patted his son on the back. "It'll return."

Arkyn didn't reply. The lethargy had taken over every aspect of his life. He had no energy for anything other than necessary duties. He had the good days and the bad days but always there was the nagging feeling that the bad would get worse but the good never better. He knew he had to talk to Chapa again but half of him didn't want to, didn't want to admit there was still something wrong with him, nearly a year after he fell ill.

"How's Uncle Festus getting on in Macia?"

"He's not finding any major problems. You should have a reasonably easy review in a couple of years. Apparently, Julius is keen to get home."

Arkyn chuckled. "Yes, I've had a letter from him. He might not enjoy the meetings, but I believe he's found compensation in Macian rum."

Adeone stayed for some time watching the young Lord Rale and Cal training before nodding to Arkyn and leaving for the house to greet Lady Landis, who had her daughters and Lady Elantha with her. He left for his study with the intention of unwinding where he wouldn't interrupt anyone else; however, he seemed to do nothing other than sort out the lives of the children under his care that day. Maria asked to see him and politely pointed out that Lady Elantha was getting too old to share the old nursery room with Tain and Cal. Adeone suggested she shared with her cousins, and Finian and Lucius moved to share with Tain and Cal. It was all very well trying to keep family units together in the Palace, but Ceardlann was so much smaller. He was sure the children would work it out between them. What Tain and Cal would teach Finian and Lucius was something he decided not to think about. Maria left contented, though Adeone realised that he ought to find a manservant for his younger son, sooner rather than later.

Having spoken to everyone else, he had a word with Elantha's governess. When she entered, she was obviously apprehensive.

"Is there anything concerning you regarding either Lady Elantha's learning or her welfare?"

"No, sir. If there were, I'd speak to her father."

Adeone stilled. "Have you had much cause to do so?"

"No, Sire. He contacted me recently to say he was unhappy with Her Ladyship's deportment at the Palace but that was all."

"What did you do about that?" enquired Adeone, trying to keep his temper. It wasn't her fault Scanlon was being nasty to Elantha.

"I spoke to Her Ladyship, Your Majesty."

Adeone crossed to the window so she couldn't see his face. Composing it, he turned back. "Lady Elantha is under my care, Clayton, and, although I acknowledge Lord Scanlon's paternity, you answer to *me*. I am the head of her family. I have had no qualms about Her Ladyship's conduct, whether that is here or at the Palace. The incident which, I believe, the Justiciar was referring to was my younger son's birthday party. It was a closed family affair. There weren't even guards present. Now, I'd be glad if you will give me your assurance that you will in future correspond with only myself over Lady Elantha's care."

The governess visibly relaxed. "Gladly, sir, but he is her father."

"As I said, I am head of her family. There is also the fact of the ban on any communication with Lord Scanlon for the inhabitants of this valley, under the terms of my father's requests and bequests. What is the name of your messenger?"

The lady paled. "I… I don't know how to call one, sir."

Adeone explained and watched as Mistress Clayton called the name *Yilan* and a black calindat – a cat with a snake's fangs and tail – appeared.

"Now you have your messenger. Call her and ask for a link if you need to speak with me."

"Thank you, Sire."

"There is no need to thank me," snapped Adeone. "I shall watch to make sure that you are not in contact with Lord Scanlon without my approval. You have broken the rules of living here. If you break them again, I shall find a different governess for my niece."

The governess blanched. "Very well, Sire."

Once the governess left, Adeone found himself a drink and sat, gently simmering. The woman had been a fool. Why he'd given her a second chance? He wasn't normally so tolerant when it came to Scanlon and Ceardlann. Drastically reducing the number of people with access to the valley might be wise. As soon as the Landises left, he'd remove the right for Lord Rale and the Landis servants, other than William and possibly Ivy, Cornelia's maid. He'd also see if all the household he'd moved from Oedran were needed, or if the house could revert to running with valley descendants. They were born into fealty. Some even said it was a life-binding one – although, as none of them had died in suspicious circumstances for many years, he didn't know if it was true. He couldn't remove the Galdwins' permission; they'd kept quiet about it and he hoped they would continue to. He was still brooding when Tain interrupted his solitude.

Adeone allowed himself to be disturbed and spent an enjoyable couple of hours listening to and talking with his son. By the end of which, his thoughts had resolved themselves. He'd remove permission for every non-essential person when it came to the household – that probably left Maria and the tutors – and he wouldn't give permission to anyone else for a couple of years. When he appointed a manservant for Tain, the gentleman would stay in Oedran. One of the male members of the Ceardlann household could act as a manservant in the valley. He'd also have a word with Arkyn; if Edward wasn't needed at Ceardlann, he'd request the administrator stayed in Oedran, even if he didn't revoke his permission. Kadeem would have to stay with Arkyn to make sure he didn't overdo things. That would about halve the people with permission or general access.

He'd have to start the hunt for a manservant for Tain soon. The chances of finding another man like Kadeem at the right time were slim. That was the sort of luck you had once. Maybe the Steward could help. He'd tell him when he returned to Oedran on Alunadai.

* * *

Three days after his return to Oedran, Adeone managed to send for Tancred. The judge sent his apologies, saying he would be teaching Tain for the next couple of days from Fitz's. Adeone accepted that readily enough. It would be worth waiting to see if the judge noticed Tain's enthusiasm waning.

Tancred half suspected why the King had summoned him. He wasn't overly worried about Tain's new-found enthusiasm; however, it would have to be carefully controlled. Tain was a passionate boy and anything he became interested in was all consuming. Following long held beliefs in not making the life of administrators any more difficult than normal, he asked Richardson when would be convenient for him to see the King; therefore it was Septadai before he presented himself at the Inner Office.

For once he was kept waiting whilst Adeone and Arkyn finished their final official meeting before the Prince departed for Paras and the Anaparian Review. When Arkyn left, he stopped and apologised to Tancred. The judge simply told him not to worry and that he hoped the Prince would have an enjoyable and productive time in Paras.

"I'm sure I shall, Your Honour. Before I go, I must congratulate you on the interest you have engendered in Prince Tain for the law."

"Without His Highness' capability to absorb new experiences with a will, it would not have been possible, sir."

"Judge, you do yourself a disservice. I am, however, keeping you from your meeting with His Majesty."

Two moments later, the King greeted Tancred pleasantly and passed him a drink without asking. The meeting would be as informal as Tancred could allow. Adeone was perfectly easy and Tancred tried to match it but years of habit took over.

"My sincerest apologies for not making it sooner, Sire."

169

Adeone sighed. "James, I'm hardly going to complain because you were teaching my son. Sit yourself down. Now, how are you finding the scapegrace?"

"His Highness is a pleasure to teach, sir."

"Even with the practical jokes?"

Tancred chuckled. "Oh, I think they fell rather flat, one way or another. There has not been one for the last couple of weeks. I think His Highness is seeking easier prey."

Adeone gave Tancred a tricky look. "I'm impressed, James. I've never known my son to give up so quickly. Might I ask what the secret is?"

Tancred laughed, a warm laugh. "I simply took the 'jokes' in my stride, Sire. I told His Highness that I had a salt deficiency or that paper flying round my head reminded me of celebrations. I am expecting something else at some point."

Adeone's eyes twinkled. "I wouldn't be surprised. I *am* impressed though. Now, His Highness seems to have developed an enthusiasm for the law. You are to be congratulated on that. It's not long since the prospect was abhorrent to him. I must ask, though, whether you think it is a healthy enquiring interest or a dangerous, all-consuming one?"

Tancred weighed up his answer. "I think, Sire, that His Highness' current interest will be short lived, or rather it will wane to a less zealous pursuit naturally. I am trying to make sure that he doesn't become fixated by the law alone, but His Highness is a passionate boy. I remember another prince very like him."

Adeone smiled. "Yes, I'm sure you do. Can you keep a close eye on the situation, please? Having been the same kind of prince, I know the pitfalls. Let me know if you become troubled."

"I certainly will, Sire. That is, I will let Your Majesty know. It is not a given that I will become troubled."

"Thank you, Your Honour. You've just proved you're a judge," replied Adeone wryly. "How are *you*?"

"I am well, thank you, sir. I hope Your Majesty is as well."

"Oh, I'm fit as a fiddle. After all, I'm so busy you might as well say I'm highly strung."

Tancred chuckled. "I am unsure that all the hours you spent in Prince Lachlan's company as a child were—"

"Wasted, is what you want to say, I think."

Tancred caught his eye. "Most certainly, sir."

"Coward."

"Or courtier, sir."

"Is there a difference?" enquired Adeone innocently.

"Not that I have ever found."

They settled down to talk about everything and nothing of any importance with replenishing glasses and reminiscences to keep them going.

* * *

Tancred walked home contemplating the King's concerns. He turned into Judges Row. The wide street with its whitewashed limestone houses was far removed from the dingy wharf alleys of his childhood. Stables at one end, within their own small compound, and the yeoman house at the other gave a feeling of affluence and security. The judge walked up the steps to his front door and glanced automatically at the delivery box. There was a loaf, various vegetables and a wrapped package of unidentifiable origin. The last made him pause. He leaned down and picked everything up.

Once in the entrance hall, he placed it all on the sideboard, as John crossed to take his cloak. He didn't move to acknowledge the footman. He stared at the collection of items as his blood ran cold.

"Why are these delivered so late, John?"

The footman frowned. "'Tis unusual, sir. I'll ask cook."

Tancred shook his head. "Could they have been delivered this morning?"

"We'd have noticed, sir. The lad normally rings the bell or knocks."

Tancred undid the parcel, a nice piece of brisket in waxed paper. His blood didn't warm. "Destroy all this, John. Do not, whatever you do, eat any of it. Also, I want you or Maisie to collect our food from now on. Go out to the markets or butchers and bakers yourself. Never shop too often at the same place and if anything is unavailable, go to the Palace and talk to the cooks there. Upper Hall or the King's chef."

"Your Honour, that's rather—"

Tancred held his gaze. "I am teaching the next Justiciar. There are various people who would rather he learned his trade from others. Even as a member of the King's retinue, I am under threat. I do not wish to find that any of my household have died as a result of poison. Some men are unscrupulous enough to put others at risk."

"Very good, sir. Thank you. I'll see to it."

Tancred divested himself of his cloak and crossed to the drawing room. His wife was once more sewing.

"Who is expecting?" asked Tancred with a smile.

"Widders' youngest daughter. Hasn't he mentioned it?"

"I have no recollection of it."

Bets smiled. "She's due in the next few weeks. I called on her today. With two already tripping her up, I said I'd finish these for her. She thinks it's a girl; I'm not convinced. Oh, and I called by the butcher's on my way home. I thought we could have some brisket for dinner tomorrow when

Thomas is here. I've even persuaded cook to do you a mushroom sauce to go with it."

Tancred laughed and rang the bell. When Maisie appeared, much to the two ladies' confusion, he said, "Tell John your mistress ordered the meat, so it should be fine." Once the maid had left, he explained.

His wife shook her head at him. "You should have asked."

"I did not wish to worry you," replied Tancred, easing himself into a chair with a brandy for company. "Do you think I am overreacting?"

"Yes, but I understand why. I'm sure John and Maisie will like getting out in the mornings. How was the King?"

"He simply wished for a talk about Prince Tain's education. I was able to reassure him that all is well."

"Have you told him yet?"

Tancred put his drink down. "I cannot believe he does not know. His men delve into everyone's background before he appoints anyone to his personal staff. Even Lord Landis has been investigated in the past."

"How do you know—?"

"His Majesty has told me. That all being the case, why would he not be aware of past events?"

His wife put her sewing aside, holding his gaze. "Because he has known you for so long, has he even considered there might be something?"

Tancred swallowed. "Do not force me, Bets. I would prefer to let matters lie."

She picked her sewing back up. "I do not mean to force you. I just don't want to see you hurt in all this."

He leaned forward, gently removing the sewing from her unprotesting fingers. Kneeling in front of her, he buried his head in her lap. Her hand rested in his hair.

"Why does it still shadow our hearts and lives, Bets?"

She had no answer for that. Why did anything resonate through the years? Why did the past haunt the present? She wanted to say that he had taken the job, that he had accepted when it would have been prudent to refuse but she couldn't. Her husband respected the King too highly to jeopardise their relationship in that manner. She ignored the knock at the door, not wanting to startle him. He rarely showed such frailty and affection. She doubted anyone but her had seen this side of him in years. Maybe no-one ever had. Her eyes fell on a vase painted with a field in autumn and a river running by. Her heart lifted. They hadn't had much when James had come home with that, but she treasured it more than he could ever know. Adored that in the impulsive moment, he had thought of her enjoyment over anything else.

"I love you," she whispered. "Love you no matter what, James. I won't mention it again." (He didn't move but his shoulders relaxed.) "Dinner must be ready."

Reluctantly, he sat up and she saw the traces of dejection in his eyes. She slipped a hand against his cheek.

"I'm here. We'll leave the past where it belongs."

He turned his head, kissing her palm. "Thank you. I thought to invite His Majesty to dinner whilst Prince Arkyn is away."

"Will he have time with Lady Rhian visiting?"

"We will discover that by whether he accepts an invitation." He eyed the pile of sewing. "How many clothes *are* you finishing?"

"I'm not sure. May was looking harassed; so, when she started to put things together, I let her youngest distract her and picked up her work bag. I'm sure she'll appreciate it when she's had a rest."

Chapter 32
LANDIS HOUSE

Septadai, Week 9 – 7th Lowal, 21st Tradis 1212
Landis House

TWO WEEKS AFTER Arkyn set off for Paras, the day was warm, but there was the faint hint of autumn in the air. It wasn't long until the Munpyram and with its cooler days. The end of summer was approaching quickly and with it the deadline Adeone had agreed with Colban over Landis House. He'd had various reports from palace specialists impressed with what they'd seen. Intrigued, he told the foreman to expect him and Lady Landis. They could inspect the works together.

That Septadai, he and Cornelia rode through the gates of Landis House. Grooms ran forward to take the horses as they dismounted. Adeone nodded to the head groom before turning to the foreman. The man barely bowed.

"You've certainly made good progress, Colban." Adeone was looking at the rising walls in front of them. The wooden scaffolding still obscured much of the building but from the gaps he could glimpse pleasantly proportioned windows, lintels and keystones, dressed stone and internal divisions.

"Yes, sir. We hope everyone will be happy."

"Good. Then, Lady Landis, shall we inspect the works? Whilst I try to keep up Festus' style of remarks."

Cornelia caught his eye. "There's really no need, Your Majesty."

Throughout the tour, Adeone made sure Cornelia was leading. The plans for the building hadn't given a proper feeling for what Festus was trying to achieve, but he found the house impressive, appreciating Festus' sense of practicality and grandeur. They walked into the room that would become the study and Adeone immediately felt, even as a shell, that this was a room where Festus would be relaxed, and where they would, no doubt, spend many an hour talking. There was a door into the new library and one to the hallway on perpendicular walls. A fireplace was opposite the hallway door. He recognised the flattened arch of the carved surround. Festus had reused it from the old house. It made him smile. His friend pretended not to be sentimental, but there were hints he was throughout his practicality. The windows looked out onto gardens which would be redesigned once the building work was finished.

"I think you'll have to prise Festus out of here with a crowbar, my lady."

Cornelia smiled. "Oh, I was planning on leaving him in here, sir. I might let him out for meals."

"Not throw away the key?"

"I wouldn't deprive Your Majesty of his help, only myself of his inanities."

They finished the walk round the shell of the house, before sitting in the old drawing room, which had escaped the fire.

"The men have done a good job so far," observed Adeone. "He's even got the roof struts up on the back portion. I wasn't expecting that."

"Nor I. I must thank you, sir, for your help."

Adeone said, "I got involved for mischievous, if not selfish, reasons."

"Yes, sir, but it was kind all the same. I wonder how long it will be until it's finished."

"I don't know. Do you think Festus will let my interference continue? I can lend you any specialists you need to help, and general labourers too."

Cornelia chuckled. "Do you want to get rid of us, Sire?"

"Aluna, no! But this is your home. It's a pleasure to have you staying with us. Part of me wishes you'd be there permanently. The company has been lovely."

"Thank you, sir. I'm just afraid the noise has been somewhat more than you're used to."

Adeone shook his head. "It's done me good, a lot of good. It's stopped me wondering what else is happening in the empire. Last year, I spent more time worrying about Arkyn and Tera than anywhere else."

"You weren't alone in that, Sire. Festus even suggested riding down there himself. The only thing that stopped him, I believe, was the fact that Wynfeld was down there and Wealsman was Acting Governor."

"I never knew that. I keep finding out more that he does and thinks."

Cornelia smiled. "He's always been like that though."

"Yes, I'm immensely privileged to have him as a friend. I still remember him approaching me, in the Palace gardens, when I was rather depressed, and enquiring, as though it was the most normal thing in the world, if I wanted to accompany him on a ride. I said I didn't think my father would let me. His reply was if you don't ask you never know. He simply went to see my father, who was rather surprised but said as long as a couple of guards went as well, he couldn't see the problem."

"Yes, he told me, years afterwards, that he didn't know how he dared approach King Altarius in that way as there was an odd constraint between his father and yours."

"I didn't know either," admitted Adeone. "It's strange, thinking back. It was the start of the greatest friendship of my life, and not just of friendship. He caught me watching Ira. You were with her, weren't you?"

"Yes, sir. Ira couldn't believe you were interested – especially not as you only really danced with her for days. The Court was agog watching. I remember your father got to hear of it and the Court was buzzing when he said that as long as you were happy, he couldn't understand what the fuss was for."

Adeone smiled sadly. "He always seemed so distant with me."

"Ira told me, long after we were all married, that the old King never showed affection. She also told me, though, that Altarius spoke to her when he was dying. He asked her to look after you and said that he loved you very much, but you reminded him too strongly of Queen Eliza for him to show you just how much. It was a wound he couldn't open."

She glanced at Adeone. There were tears in his eyes but for which person she didn't know, his mother, father or wife. They were all dead now.

"I'm sorry, sir, I shouldn't have mentioned it."

Adeone blinked the tears away. "Maybe not, but I'm glad you did. Ira never told me any of it. I suppose the time was never right. I wish I'd known before. I always thought my father was morbidly paranoid because I was his eldest surviving son – maybe he was, but for more than that reason."

He crossed to the window, examining the view. Cornelia watched him, feeling inadequate in the situation she had helped create.

Adeone sighed a deep sigh. "It is all in the past, though, far in the past."

Cornelia half whispered, "I'm sorry if it caused you any distress."

"Don't be. I'm all right. I shouldn't reminisce. I always find the present so hard to live with when I return to it."

"Why?"

Adeone swallowed. "Even with friends and family, I am sometimes lonely. There is much, as a king, people assume I have. They never stop to think about the isolation it brings. Even my sons are taught to address me 'correctly'. Surely 'father' is correct enough for any situation. I'm put on a pedestal and, like any statue, I have to present a fixed image to the world. Unfortunately, I'm flesh and blood."

Cornelia rose and, crossing to him, put a hand on his arm. "We know that, but, to keep you safe, we have to observe convention. If we don't, who will?"

Adeone turned to her. "I'm being foolish."

"You're not. You're being honest. Something that is challenging in situations like this."

"Thank you. I shouldn't be troubling you."

"Nonsense, of course you should," replied Cornelia. "I wish there was something else I could do. Have you ever considered marrying again?"

"I'll not do that to Ira's memory. I can't see myself settling down with anyone else. It would, for one thing, be hard to explain everything to someone. The boys would become unsettled as well..." He swallowed, eyes searching her face. "This has become a sombre conversation. Shall we change it?"

* * *

An hour later, they left for the Palace. Adeone felt decidedly free, as though the talk with Cornelia had closed something he didn't even know was open. He decided to take a ride round the city before heading back to the Palace. They exited the Maclan onto The Strait, the main east-west road through the city, and made their way east towards the Port Gate, planning to take Portside, which ran alongside the city wall, up to the Administrative Quarter. It should have been an uneventful ride, but there was a small cavalcade entering at the Port Gate. Adeone reined in to see who was arriving. It had to be someone of standing with the palaver occurring. Spotting a more than welcome face, Adeone smiled and shook his head in mock disbelief. Spotting the King, the entrant bowed in the saddle.

"Warning might have been nice," quipped Adeone.

"At least I'm early and not late, Your Majesty."

"It does make a nice change. Now, which way were you planning on heading first, my lord?"

"The Palace of course, Sire. I have a report for you."

Adeone groaned. "You are sometimes kindness itself, Lord Landis. First, send your luggage ahead of you. We're going for a small ride to look at your house."

Landis glanced at his friend, perplexed. "Why, Sire? They'll not be far past the footings."

"I have my reasons, my lord."

"Let me locate my wayward son then, sir."

176

* * *

When Landis saw the house. He had all on keeping a neutral face. Colban, surprised, showed him and Julius around as Cornelia and Adeone once more went to sit in the old drawing room.

Landis entered half an hour later, his face a picture of restraint. "It's a shame my study isn't finished, Sire."

Cornelia chuckled. "Julius, we're just going to take a walk in the gardens."

Once alone, Landis eyed his friend. "Why?"

"I need to explain? Fine. I complicate your life. You've been attacked multiple times in my service. For once, I saw something I could do to help. Not cause more issues for you. Just help. I've supplied the men—"

"Yes, Colban explained that bit."

"Good. He's an interesting gentleman but a remarkably efficient one. Are you angry?"

Landis collapsed onto a chair. "How can I be? I want to be. Part of me wants to be. But I can't be."

"I'd understand."

"Oh, it's not because you're King. It's because I understand your impulse to help and you've not actually changed any of my orders. You've not interfered in the house itself and, let's face it, that must have taken some self-control. Thank you."

"Not at all. The help is there for as long as you want it. If they can get the roof on by the end of summer, which was the verbal contract I had, then the plasterers can start and hopefully that should be dry by the time the weather really changes. Everything else can then take its time."

Landis' eyes narrowed. "Thank you, sir. I'm certain now that one morning I'll wake up to discover my whole life has been reorganised without my knowledge."

"I did that to you years ago. Come on, we'd better get back to the Palace before Richardson sends a search party for me."

Chapter 33
FAMILY MATTERS
Late Afternoon
Inner Office

ADEONE AND FESTUS REACHED the King's Chambers, where Richardson welcomed Landis back pleasantly, then, when the door had closed on the Inner Office, cancelled everything that the King was meant to be doing.

Meanwhile, Adeone poured two drinks, pointed at the comfortable chairs and, sitting down, told his friend everything that had occurred over the weeks he'd been away. Simkins interrupted them after a few hours to ask them if they wanted any food. Adeone's stomach rumbled at the mere suggestion, protesting it had been hours since he'd thought about it. Half an hour later, Adeone and Festus were tucking into a substantial meal. Landis started yawning soon afterwards.

"You're losing your stamina in your old age," joked Adeone.

Landis yawned more broadly. "Will my King be gracious enough to let his official get the sleep he needs in that old age?"

Adeone eyed him, lips twitching. "If only so I don't strangle the courtier out of him. Go on. I'll go down to Court.

The Court had heard Landis was home and, once the curiosity about his early return had waned, Adeone found himself oddly relaxed. He was passing through the Anaparian Room when he found he was asking a lady if she'd like a dance. Rather startled, she accepted. For the first time since Ira had become ill in 1207, the King found himself dancing. He ignored the hush radiating around the Queen's Hall.

His partner said lightly, "We're being watched, Sire."

Adeone's lips twitched. "Don't worry, I'm used to it."

"I can't believe that, Sire."

"You're slipping, Lady Rhian. Surely your mother has taught you to be more cynical."

"That's one way of putting it, sir."

Adeone chuckled. "I'm sure you have many more, cousin. The thought of Lady Amara has moved many to inventive language."

"Mother has many hidden qualities and always seems to get the best out of people," murmured Rhian. "Shall I tell her you were asking after her?"

Adeone caught his cousin's eye. "Certainly, my lady. It is a while since I talked to my aunt." He smiled. "I *am* glad to see that you've arrived safely."

"I came to tell you earlier, but Richardson mentioned you were talking with Festus."

Adeone chuckled. "Ah. Probably best for your sanity to have avoided us. It's good to have you here. I hope you'll come and keep me company over the Court Supper?"

"Thank you. I'd be glad to. I visited to get all the family news."

"You mean the Court hasn't already informed you? That's remiss of them; I find out what I'm meant to be doing from them.

They were both laughing as the dance ended. Adeone escorted his cousin from the floor and continued to talk to her for some time. It wasn't often he managed to. They knew each other passably well, but Rhian had grown up in Tradere on the Fairson estates that her father had managed for his family.

Adeone found his contented mood continued throughout the rest of the evening. The talk with Cornelia had certainly laid a couple of ghosts to rest. He found he couldn't get the energy together to even wonder why Lord Lux and Lord Anguis were deep in discussion in an unfrequented corner.

* * *

Two days later, Adeone found that Landis had some additional information for his report. Groaning, the King held out a hand for it.

"Apparently you were dancing," observed Landis handing it over.

"Surely the Court can find more interesting things to talk about!"

Festus snorted. "Tradition dictates that gossip about the FitzAlcis' takes priority and – unfortunately, for you and yours – I don't think it is a tradition that can be changed overnight, Sire."

"If Percival Wealsman was here, he'd say to put a proclamation out stating that gossiping is an indictable offence."

Landis laughed. "Yes. I wonder what he'll make of the news."

"He'll smile and enquire what the fuss is about. Are you merely here, Landis, to ask questions you already know the answer to?"

"Not exactly, sir. There's one where I don't know the answer: are you all right? Cornelia is worried she might have upset you the other day."

"Tell your lady I'm perfectly well. I feel content with life at the moment."

"I told her you would be. Although I don't know what she said to you."

Adeone explained what had happened at Landis House.

Festus understood both why Cornelia had been worried and why Adeone was content. He also, with a flash of inspiration, understood why Adeone had been dancing. He smiled as his friend finished explaining.

"I don't mean to interfere, sir, but Cornelia might be right. Why don't you marry again? Ira would never have wanted you to be lonely."

"I don't want to damage Ira's memory."

"That's not the only reason, is it, sir? You know her memory would never be forfeited if you remarried."

Adeone glared at him, but Festus didn't lower his gaze.

Adeone weighed up possible ways of stating his reasons. "I don't want to alarm Scanlon into drastic action. If I remarry, he'll be afraid another heir will be born. It would endanger the life of any wife I might take. I won't risk someone's life simply to ease my loneliness, Festus. That is all I shall say on the matter."

"Forgive your blundering friend."

"If he stops pretending to be a courtier and also, as he's revealed his real motive for coming, if he takes away the addendum to the report and finds somewhere else for it!"

179

Lord Landis lifted it off the desk. "I might feel unappreciated, Sire."

Adeone said seriously, "I'll appreciate you far less if you *don't* take it away with you."

Landis laughed. "Consider it done, *Sire*."

"Stop using titles to emphasise your actions and leave me to work."

Landis rose. "I'm yours to command, Sire."

Adeone picked up a document. "Then I'll see you this evening."

* * *

Landis left the Inner Office in a contemplative mood. He walked through the Palace to the Court and was intrigued when Lady Rhian asked to speak to him. They ambled out into the sunshine and had done almost a full circle of the Imperial Garden when Rhian sat down and motioned for Landis to join her.

"How's Adeone?"

The way she asked at once told Landis she was worried. "He's fine. Just doing what he does best by acting randomly to confuse people."

"It must be something to do with being FitzAlcis; my mother is the same."

"I hadn't noticed."

She glanced sideways at him. "Age hasn't improved you at all."

"You and the King are in agreement there. How are you coping with the rumours, my lady?"

"By smiling, and pointing out the King is my *cousin*. It's amazing how people leave me alone after that. Why did he dance with me?"

"Because he felt content with life for the first time since Princess Ella passed away. How long are you staying in Oedran for, my lady?"

"The year. Stop changing the subject. It won't work."

Festus sighed. "It was worth a try."

"I'm sure it was. Is he truly content?"

"Yes, he is. Why? Don't tell me you've developed a soft spot for someone after all these years."

She laughed. "I'm just concerned; as anyone should be. Especially with the situation in the family."

Festus nodded. Neither of them needed to elaborate on that.

Rhian said, "Scanlon approached me a while ago, started trying to persuade me that Adeone wasn't being an effective king. Oh, not outright, not so much that I could report him for it but that was what he insinuated."

Festus stilled ever so slightly. "What did you do?"

"I told him that, whatever his *personal* opinions, the empire was thriving and Adeone was liked and respected by all *true* subjects of it."

Festus whistled under his breath, then checked himself. Laughingly he said, "You are certainly your mother's daughter, my lady." He became

180

serious. "Be careful."

"I will be but don't expect me to watch the Justiciar undermine the King."

"I never have and never will. My lady, don't think I'm trying to change the subject, but would you do something for me? Will you keep your ear to the ground, both here and in Tradere? We need everyone we can get to keep an eye on the situation and I have a feeling that no-one will read your mail."

She looked at him, amused. "Are you trying to recruit me to a spy network, Festus Landis?" Seeing him blush, she laughed to herself before whispering, "You're getting slow. I've been passing Major Wynfeld information for a couple of years already."

Landis groaned. "I should have known."

Rhian winked but her face sobered quickly. "Festus, could you do *me* a favour? It might put you in a difficult position, though, because I'd like your word you won't tell Adeone."

Landis hesitated. "If he suspects and asks, I'm bound to reply."

Rhian watched the gardens, obviously thinking. After several long moments, she said, "Very well. I'm worried about Neassa. It's one reason I visited. I think her marriage to Rufus is souring. Can you keep an eye out?"

"Of course, though I have no love for the Rathgars."

"No. Nor I, even though they're wed-family. I never did trust Rufus' motives in pursuing Neassa, but now… I don't know. Something feels like it's changed, and not just the weather. It's getting cool. We ought to complete the walk before people think there's something dubious happening. I mean, we wouldn't like to have to disillusion them, would we?"

They gently sauntered into the Palace talking of nothing more momentous than the fact autumn might arrive early and hoping it would be a kind winter.

PART 3

Chapter 34
PARAS

THE DAY LANDIS RETURNED to Oedran, Prince Arkyn entered Paras. Greeted at the gates by a welcoming party of city officials, the absence of the Domini intrigued and displeased him. The Chief Merchant welcomed him and, after the pleasantries had concluded, they rode through the city with the merchant pointing out landmarks and explaining its history. He was knowledgeable, but Arkyn listened to what he wasn't saying as well. People moved aside for them more nervously than those of Oedran, and yet without the speed of those from Tera. Arkyn smiled in thanks at them and received half-frightened bows in return. Why? Was the entire city on edge for his visit?

Riding through the ancient castle gatehouse, Arkyn examined it with interest. Once the seat of FitzAlcis power, the forbidding walls around the wards were still well maintained. The capital might now be Oedran but Paras Castle was formidable. Assessing it, Arkyn knew he'd never want to lay siege to it and understood why Bayan had never captured the city.

The Domini of Paras was waiting to greet him. Arkyn dismounted and handed Ponder's reins to one of his guards, walking forward until he was clear of the melee created by horses, grooms and his companions. The Domini moved to greet him and the Chief Merchant did a smooth introduction before bowing and moving away. To Arkyn's astonishment, the Domini knelt.

When he was standing once more, Arkyn hissed for the Domini's ear alone, "My father is King! You do *not* kneel to a prince, Synclare. Is that understood?"

The Domini swallowed. "My apologies, Your Highness. Your—"

"I did not ask for your apologies! I asked for your assurance."

"I understand, Your Highness."

"Good. Might I introduce you to my companion, Lord Irvin Iris?"

The Domini greeted Irvin pleasantly before Arkyn accepted introductions to various officials. Entering the keep, he took in its stone grandeur.

"Where's my office, Your Excellency?"

The dedication to duty intrigued the Domini. "If you'll follow me, Your Highness, I will show you. We chose a room that gives you a good view of both the city and the sea."

"Thank you for the consideration, but I will be reading documents more than perusing the view. So, tell me, Synclare, any murders occurred here that I should know about?"

The Domini frowned. "Not that I know of, sir. I can always check."

"No need. I'm sure I'd have found out by now. No plans to murder me in the offing?"

Shocked, the Domini exclaimed, "I should hope not, Your Highness!"

Arkyn turned to Irvin. "This might be less eventful than last year."

Irvin struggled to keep a straight face. "It wouldn't take much, sir."

They continued for a couple more minutes in silence. The walk up flights of stairs and along long draughty corridors tired Arkyn more than he allowed anyone to see. The Domini obviously thought he should be as high as possible. For the view or to keep him out of the way?

A guard on one chamber saluted as they approached. Arkyn acknowledged it, turned to Marsh and gave him a significant glance. Marsh motioned to the two guards with them and the Paras guard stepped aside, glanced at the Domini and left.

The Domini opened the door, moving aside.

Marsh coughed. "Your Excellency, as your guard was on the door, you go first."

The Domini glared at Marsh, insulted by the insinuation there might be an assassin lurking. Haughtily, he entered the office.

Arkyn following took in an opulent room. Tapestries showing historic events brought a warmth the stone corridors lacked. Rugs covered the floor and an ornate desk stood below a window looking out to the calm sea – a contrast to the feelings of those in the room.

Arkyn crossed to the desk, removing his cloak and riding gloves. "Marsh, that's all for now, thank you. Edward, I'll need writing materials. Lord Irvin, please stay with us." He waited for the door to close behind Marsh and for Edward to set out paper, ink and pen. "Domini, Lord Irvin is here both as my companion and because His Majesty believed that His Lordship would benefit from the experience of watching the workings of the empire at close quarters. He is to be afforded every opportunity to observe those workings. He will also accompany me in many different meetings to scrutinise them – starting with this one." He seated himself as Edward moved aside. "I hope Your Excellency is aware of how serious your blunder was—"

"Your—" started the Domini.

"No! I will not listen to excuses. There is no excuse for such an obvious insult to His Majesty. Certainly not from his own Representative.

Your Excellency has placed us both in an invidious position. When you leave this office, you will immediately write a letter of apology to His Majesty. You wish to object? By kneeling to me, Your Excellency suggested to all present that the King was dead. Would you prefer that I deal with it under that guise? No. I thought not." Arkyn saw Irvin and Edward were also still standing. He motioned for everyone to sit. "Domini, my guards will be on every door into my chambers and their orders will override any given by a senior officer in the regiments here. When it comes to my safety, they act autonomously. I shall need to talk to the commander of the fort soon about several issues that might arise during my stay. I will also need to talk to your guard captain. Next, is there an official itinerary for my stay?"

"Yes, Your Highness. I have a copy in my office for yourself, and your administrator."

"Please see they reach us within the hour. I will study it and see if it needs altering. There's a fortnight until my advisors and clerks arrive from Oedran. I will complete all initial interviews during that time."

"Very good, sir. I have arranged to be there during each of them as well."

Arkyn watched the Domini appraisingly. "That isn't how the review process works. I will speak to your officers without your presence."

"Your Highness—"

"There are no options on that. You'll have more than enough to do. I see from your face that you still wish to protest; I advise you against that course of action."

"I must still object, sir."

Arkyn pursed his lips. "No objection will change my mind. Only if His Majesty were to instruct me otherwise would I let you attend. Feel free to contact the King over this matter."

"Thank you, Your Highness."

"I suggest we clear up this dispute immediately. Contact the King."

The Domini, in a fit of bravado and surety of his own position, did so.

In Oedran, Adeone exited the link; his face wasn't a pleasant picture of contentment. He contacted Arkyn.

"Are you annoying the Domini already, son?"

"The feeling is mutual, Sire. He knelt as soon as he saw me."

"He's a bigger fool than I thought. Your grandfather appointed him in 1204, a few years after the last review. I had my reservations but could do nothing. He deserved a chance. I've told him I support all your decisions. He is to abide by those decisions as he would mine – it seemed to disquiet him."

"Yes, he looked a bit nonplussed."

"Arkyn, don't be afraid of your instincts. Have faith in yourself."

As the link broke, Arkyn refocused on the room. The Domini wasn't there. He raised an eyebrow at Edward.

"His Excellency stormed out, sir."

"Send one of the guards to tell him to return." Arkyn glanced at Irvin. "Sorry about this; I envisaged a different beginning to this review."

"Hopefully next year will be less problematic, sir."

Arkyn snorted. "That's what I hoped about this year."

* * *

A couple of minutes later, Kadeem entered with Alan, the latter carrying a laden tray.

The manservant said, "Refreshments, Your Highness. I asked Edward to keep the Domini outside whilst you partook, sir."

Arkyn smiled a devious smile. "Thank you, Kadeem. You couldn't have timed that better had I ordered you to." He took a goblet of water from his manservant. "Have they shown you where my private rooms are?"

"Yes, sir. A couple of floors below this office and on the other side of the keep. I'm trying to locate—"

"My office needs to be closer to my chambers." Having taken a drink, Arkyn put the goblet on his desk. "Where has Lord Irvin been billeted?"

Kadeem became solemn. "Out in the city, sir."

Arkyn swallowed a bite of fruitcake. "I don't think so. There should be ample room for him here. What is the Domini playing at?"

"I'm trying to find out, sir. Of your advisors, only Rayburn has been given rooms here."

"That is more understandable." Two minutes later, Arkyn continued, "I think you can clear, Kadeem. On your way out, you can tell Edward that I will see the Domini."

* * *

A moment later, Arkyn said, "No, don't sit down, Synclare. Why did you leave?"

"I needed a breather, sir."

"Then you wait and request one. You never storm out of my office again. If you do, you will never see the inside of a governmental office again. Is *that* understood?"

"How can it not be, sir?"

Arkyn stilled. Every bone and muscle in his body under minute control. Edward, from behind the Domini, watched, worried, and then glanced at an unnerved Lord Irvin.

Slowly enunciating every syllable, Arkyn said, "If I ask if something is understood or not, you will answer either with a positive or a negative. If you are obtuse again, I shall take measures and will deal through your deputy for this review and I will not be subtle about it. My office will be transferred closer to my private chambers. Lord Irvin is to be accommodated within the keep and not billeted out to the city; however, I will allow some of my advisors to reside there. Please see my orders are carried out and I receive the itinerary as soon as possible. You may go."

The Domini left chuntering to himself.

Arkyn glanced at Edward. "Something tells me that he isn't happy with that ultimatum. It is the end of the matter as far as I am concerned. Only if he annoys me again will I carry out my threats. As I have a week without plans, I shall leave you to arrange my office and Lord Irvin and I will find my chambers."

Chapter 35
PRIVACY AND PROTECTION
Late Afternoon
Paras Castle – Keep

THE WALK through the keep gave Arkyn more pause for thought. Everyone they met was extremely wary. Arkyn had never experienced this level of nerves from everyone he met. As they reached his chambers, Marsh was giving the guards orders. Arkyn nodded to him and entered his rooms. He walked directly into the sitting room. That worried him. Normally, there was an antechamber. He chewed at his lip and rang for Kadeem. The manservant entered, and Arkyn raised an eyebrow, glancing around the room.

"I'm trying to resolve the issue, sir. There are very few antechambers in the keep."

"What happened to the FitzAlcis chambers? There must be some."

"I'm tracking them down. Can I get you anything, sir?"

"Not for the moment, thank you. Just do what you need to."

"Sir." Once outside, Kadeem cursed. It was a complete mess. Had the Domini's castellan, or the Domini himself, had the forethought to contact the King's or Prince's staff, the situation would never have arisen in the manner it had. He told his deputy to be on the alert for the bell and left the Prince's rooms to find the castellan.

* * *

A runner showed him to a small cramped office, where a gawky man somehow managed not to knock the piles of paperwork flying.

He watched as Kadeem entered and pointedly closed the door. "What can I do for you? I am assuming you are one of His Highness' household."

"I am. Though never assume it. There have been many tricked in the past into becoming traitors by that mistake. For your information, however, I am Kadeem and my deputy is Thomas. If you need to liaise about anything, you come to us first. Now, there are some slight issues that need resolving. Firstly, Lord Irvin needs accommodating in the keep."

"Yes, the Domini was vocal about that. Mind you, he's been going round like a bear with a sore head for days."

"Why? It isn't the first time a member of the FitzAlcis has visited since he became Domini."

"No, it isn't. Shall we say that he's used to it being Lord Scanlon?"

Kadeem appeared to ignore that. "His Highness wants this review to go smoothly. After the events that greeted him last year, I was hoping he wouldn't have anything to worry about here. Where are the official chambers for the visiting FitzAlcis or representatives of His Majesty?

The castellan opened a drawer and pulled out a plan. "Here." He pointed to chambers near the Great Hall, which included an office. "The Domini insisted His Highness wouldn't want to be disturbed by the comings and goings. He sees His Highness as a youth who will wish to laze around leaving the work of the review to others."

Kadeem nodded. "He might have been enlightened today. I shall leave you to arrange matters, but I expect those chambers to be ready by tomorrow evening. See Administrator Edward about His Highness' office. Good day, Castellan."

"Good day, Master Kadeem."

Once the door had closed behind Kadeem, the castellan swore. He'd told the Domini that the Prince would expect the correct chambers, but the Domini hadn't wanted to listen. He went to see the castle guards and told them what they needed to move. At least it kept them occupied.

* * *

Kadeem, meanwhile, walked through the castle to the corridor currently housing the Prince's rooms. A captain was remonstrating politely but firmly with the guards.

He walked over to the scene. "Can I help, Captain?"

Recognising Kadeem's white tunic and scarlet edged belt, the officer relaxed. "I'm Captain Jones. The Domini informed me that His Highness wanted to see me but, *apparently*, he's resting and not to be disturbed."

"I will check. Please wait here."

Kadeem found Arkyn was smiling at a story Lord Irvin was telling. Hating having to break the moment, he mentioned Jones was waiting.

"Show him in please, Kadeem. Lord Irvin, I hope you'll excuse me. Stay by all means." A moment later, Arkyn rose in greeting. "Come in, and take a seat, Captain. I apologise if my guards were obstructive."

"Thank you, Your Highness. I'd have been more concerned if they weren't."

"How long have you been in Paras? Wynfeld said you were at Garth with the Exarch before."

"I was, sir. I've been here since the beginning of the year."

"Then I hope you've found your new posting rewarding," replied Arkyn. "Now, I need to tell you formally that my guard acts independently. Please concentrate on protecting the Domini, but any time he and I are together, Captain Marsh's instructions will override yours."

"That is expected, sir."

"Thank you. So, is Paras as rich and fulfilling as you could wish?"

Jones caught the Prince's eye; neither of them paid attention to Irvin's confusion.

"I always feel that there is more to discover in any city. More than can be found by any one man in any one lifetime. They are always evolving. I'm finding out quite a lot about this one."

"What like?"

A few minutes later, Arkyn said, "Thank you, Captain. I shouldn't keep you any longer."

After Jones left, Arkyn became thoughtful before ringing for his manservant. "I am curious to know what the Domini thought I'd be interested in, Kadeem."

The manservant nodded. "I shall chase the itinerary, sir. Your Highness, could I have a word in private? I'm sorry to presume..." Once the door had closed behind a retreating Irvin, Kadeem explained, "I've spoken to the castellan. He mentioned that the Domini simply views Your Highness as – well, sir, you'll have to forgive me – as he would any youth. He's expecting the work for the review to be carried out by others and that you are simply here as a figurehead. That you'll '*laze around*'. I'm sorry to speak out of turn, sir, but I thought you ought to know as soon as possible."

Arkyn motioned for Kadeem to stand in front of him. "If anyone ever says anything like that to you again, you know what you do...?"

"Keep it to myself, Your Highness?"

"No, you do exactly what you've done and *stop apologising* for it. I think I'll have fun proving the Domini wrong. Tell Edward I'd like a speech preparing for the first banquet they have arranged – for once, I'll even use it. You'd better let Lord Irvin in."

Shortly afterwards, Arkyn took the itinerary from Edward and read it. There *was* a banquet that evening. "I'll have a meeting with you and the Domini first thing in the morning about the schedule from then onwards. For now, see you set enough time before the meeting with the Domini for us to go over it. Is there a speech prepared for tonight?"

"Yes, Your Highness." He passed over a scroll. "It's rather standard, I'm afraid, but should certainly confuse the Domini."

"Good. I feel like a bit of fun. Thank you, Edward. I shouldn't require anything else today."

Edward left. Arkyn smiled and unrolled the scroll. As Edward had said, it was a perfectly normal speech of arrival. He let it furl itself up once more. Then, with a word of apology to Irvin, rang for Kadeem.

"There is a banquet, Kadeem. It starts at six and is going to be a long one. Can you lay out my full formal wear please? Has word come regarding Lord Irvin's chambers?"

"Only that they have found appropriate rooms, sir. His Lordship's manservant is currently seeing to arrangements."

Arkyn turned to Irvin. "We've a couple of hours before the banquet. Do you wish to relax in your own rooms?"

"Only if Your Highness no longer requires my presence, sir."

"Well, you'll need some time to get ready for the joys that await us."

"Then I shall be glad not to rush, sir."

Arkyn smiled inwardly; Irvin was turning into something of a courtier. "Go on then. Full formal – mantle as well." After Irvin left, Arkyn sighed and looked at his manservant. "Peace and quiet at last. Quick work on Lord Irvin's chambers, Kadeem."

"Thank you, sir. Is there anything you require?"

"Just wake me up half an hour before the banquet, so I don't look like I fell to sleep."

Once Kadeem left, Arkyn twisted round on his seat and, kicking off his shoes, lifted his legs onto the couch. He shifted until he could lie with his head on the arm of the couch, stared at the ceiling and drifted off.

Chapter 36
KENSAL
Early Evening
Keep

Irvin found his rooms before deciding to stretch his legs. He wandered to the ground floor of the keep and examined the wall tapestries.

A voice at his shoulder said, "The Bardic Tapestries depicting his rise to fame during the Age of Tyranny, commissioned after he helped restore King Arlis to the throne."

Without turning around, Irvin replied, "Thank you. I was wondering what they depicted. I'm Lord Irvin Iris."

"Lord Kensal Parchi; I was going to be your host, but I understand my services are no longer required."

"I'm truly sorry for any inconvenience."

"Oh, there's no need to be. I half suspected it would happen. The Domini has his moments of foresight, but this wasn't one of them. What drew you to the tapestries?"

Irvin grinned and turned. A shortish young man stood beside him. "General interest in the empire's history. How do you know what they are?"

"Other than the fact I live in Paras? I'm studying our history. There are anomalies in the tapestries. For instance, they show two star stones, yet the Bard apparently had one. It is a question that all the historians here want answered since I pointed it out. The threads are faded, but I think one at least was green, the other possibly grey, which would make sense as his descendants still have that stone."

Irvin's eyes lit up. "I've heard the city is a centre for historians. I was hoping to get chance to look round your libraries."

"I'm sure it could be arranged. His Highness won't require your presence every day, will he?"

"I'm not certain. I'm training to be an advisor. His Majesty thought the trip might benefit my studies. I am here to observe the workings of the empire at close quarters. Lord Julius Landis has recently gone to Macia with his father for the same reason."

"Then we'll have to manage what we can when you're not with His Highness, which you are not now. Would you like to see the Castle Archives? They're a couple of minutes' walk across the wards."

Irvin was torn. "I have to get ready for the banquet."

"It won't take long and you'll have time to change. Come on."

* * *

Irvin entered the archives curiously. Kensal had a few words with the librarian, who said laughingly,

"Don't be surprised if not everyone shares your enthusiasm, my lord. And the official scrolls are still out of bounds."

"You're no fun anymore, Ketin."

"Sorry. No chitty, no entry. You know the rules."

"Much good they do anyone." Kensal walked over to Irvin. "Being a future Lord of Oedran is all the credentials you need, apparently."

"Yes, it has some benefits. What did he mean about the official scrolls?"

"Oh, a lot of these archives are copies or histories written from the original documents. The official scrolls are those original documents. I've been trying to gain access for the last couple of years."

"Why are you unsuccessful?" asked Irvin, reading some of the scroll tags.

"The Domini won't grant me permission. I've found discrepancies before now in documents, as I spotted the anomaly in the tapestry; I think His Excellency feels threatened. He has an interest in history but not in being proved wrong."

"Is there a cataloguing system for all of this?"

Kensal shrugged. "Not one that Ketin ever admits to. Now, what are you interested in?"

"Don't tempt me. I should return and change for the banquet. You'll need to dress as well. Won't you?"

"What's wrong with what I'm wearing?"

Lord Irvin looked him up and down. His well-made, crumpled linen tunic looked comfortable but didn't declare a lord wore it. A worn leather belt and ink-stained pouch only enhanced its serviceable, everyday aura.

"His Highness likes to see people in formal wear on formal occasions. He says it helps give him warning. Your tunic isn't appropriate and your clothes are an integral part of showing respect at Court."

Kensal sighed. "I don't really... That is, formal and me – we're in different libraries. I guess I'd better race home and change. I'm trying to remember if I even own a formal tunic."

"If your man is worth his pay, you'll have one even if you never wear it."

* * *

An hour later, Irvin reached the Great Hall and spotted Kensal looking rushed. Walking over to him, he noticed that people's eyes followed him with interest.

"You do own a formal tunic then, Lord Kensal? You even have a mantle."

"Apparently. Do you know where you've been seated?"

"No. I assume somewhere on the dais."

"We'll check." Quietly, he added, "With the Domini involved in seating arrangements, it is never safe to assume anything."

About twelve minutes after they located their adjacent seats on the dais, Arkyn and the Domini were announced. After being introduced to several more people, the Prince caught Irvin's eye. Excusing himself to Kensal, Irvin made his way over to Arkyn.

The Prince said, "Who was your companion?"

"Lord Kensal Parchi," replied Irvin. "He was to be my host. Ironically, he's studying the histories."

Arkyn chuckled. "Maybe I did you a disservice by insisting you're accommodated here."

"It's better than grandfather getting to hear about it, sir."

Arkyn raised an amused eyebrow. "I suppose that's true enough. I should apologise to Lord Kensal for the upset."

Two minutes later, Kensal was politely saying it didn't matter and hadn't put him out at all.

"Lord Irvin tells me you're interested in history, Lord Kensal."

"I have my moments, sir."

"Don't we all? I developed an interest in the Cearcall a while ago."

Kensal visibly perked up. "Really, Your Highness?"

"Truly. A gentleman I know told myself and Prince Tain stories for hours. It got both of us reading more."

"Well, sir, if you'll permit me, I'll gladly show you our libraries here."

Arkyn caught Irvin's eye and smiled conspiratorially. "I would take that most kindly, my lord. Now, if you'll excuse me, I believe the Domini requires my presence."

Kensal bowed slightly in answer.

When Arkyn had moved off, Irvin said lightly, "I forgot to mention His Highness' interest, didn't I?"

"Yes. What was the smile for?"

"It is a long story." Had Arkyn done that solely to protect him from his grandfather's remonstrations?

Half an hour later, they were all seated and Arkyn had made the prepared speech. It made Irvin smile. The previous year Arkyn had delivered more impromptu speeches than prepared ones.

They were eating when the Domini said to Arkyn, "I noticed you spoke to young Kensal Parchi, Your Highness."

"Yes. He is interested in history, I understand."

The Domini said, "Yes, sir. He keeps asking for permission to see the official scrolls, but – at barely twenty and with a habit for wishing to prove others wrong – I don't think it would be responsible to allow him access."

"Would you deny *me* entry?"

"No, Your Highness."

Arkyn found he was interested despite himself. "Yet I am only seventeen. We all must start somewhere in life. Lord Kensal's passion for history is notable."

The Domini sighed. "I'm sorry, Your Highness; I warned him not to talk incessantly about it."

Arkyn frowned. "He didn't; I instigated the subject and I would not stop people talking about what interests them. We need experts and no one man can be an expert in everything. We need to listen to others to learn. Now, I understand your market day is Pentadai…"

Talk wandered into other reaches and Arkyn, glancing along the dais, was amused to see Lord Irvin and Lord Kensal deep in conversation and everyone around them shaking their heads.

Chapter 37

EYE ON THE FUTURE

Tretaldai, Week 10 – 10th Lowal, 3rd Lowis 1212

Inner Office

OVER TIME, Adeone heard the full details of Arkyn's arrival in Paras and noted exactly what his son *hadn't* told him. He'd had doubts about Lord Synclare's competence, but he hadn't expected the man would make such a fool of himself. To not house Arkyn in the FitzAlcis chambers was unbelievable. Should he contact the Domini and explain how annoyed he was? He cursed to himself. Arkyn would be fine. He'd make his feelings known as only he could.

Richardson interrupted the King's contemplation by enquiring if he could see Lord Iris. Glad of the distraction, Adeone agreed.

"Come in, my lord. What can I do for you."

The elderly Lord of Oedran seated himself but waited until Richardson had left before saying, "Sire, this visit is under my remit as your Deputy Chief Advisor, rather than as a Lord of Oedran."

"Landis hasn't been up to anything I don't know about, has he?"

"No, sir, not that has come to my attention."

"That's a shame; I like to catch him out. All right, my lord, I'll stop teasing. What can I do for you?"

Iris took a breath. "I've been contacted by the Domini. His Excellency doesn't believe that His Highness was responsible for the Review of

Terasia, Sire. He thinks I did it all and His Highness' illness was a ruse. I have put him right, but his attitude was not what I would have expected, and his manner of expressing his views was unfortunate. I think he might benefit from other work, Your Majesty."

Adeone watched the lined and wrinkled face. "Hmm, do you? That's rather interesting. You've seen many governors come and go in your time, haven't you, my lord?"

"I have seen my fair share of them, yes, Sire. I'm sorry if—"

"Iris, I'm pleased you've raised this..." Adeone explained everything that had happened, concluding with, "As you can see, he's not endeared himself to me. One mistake I can forgive, but a catalogue of them is rather harder. I was going to see what conclusions Arkyn came to before I made any move."

Iris nodded. "I think that would be interesting, sir, but His Highness won't have a season to choose the new governor this time."

"Point taken, my lord." Getting up, Adeone went to examine the view from the window. "Why did he doubt that it was Prince Arkyn who did the last review?"

Iris pushed himself to his feet. "I believe he's simply prejudiced by the Prince's age, Your Majesty. If I hadn't been in Tera, I might have found it more difficult to understand. What occurred there last year was rare. As long as His Highness doesn't fall ill this year, sir, such problems may well resolve themselves."

"True. Was that all, Iris?"

"Concerning Paras and the Domini, yes, Your Majesty."

"Concerning something else?"

Iris watched the King's tired face. He'd obviously been worrying about things more than he'd admit again. "It can wait, sir. It's not at all important."

"If it's not important, let us sit more comfortably, whilst you tell me."

"Sire, I would be happier remaining as we are, if that's permitted."

Adeone frowned. "Of course, my lord, but what is it?"

Iris hesitated. "I've been giving things some thought since I returned from Tera, Sire, and would like to retire as your official advisor. I feel I'm getting too old to give Your Majesty the advice required."

Adeone walked over to Iris, whose face was stricken on hearing himself asking to be released from his lifelong duty.

The King said, "I'm getting Your Lordship a drink. Come and sit down and stay sitting, even if I'm on my feet detaching the decanter."

Once they were seated, Iris eyed the King uncertainly. "I'm sorry, Sire."

"You don't want to resign in your heart, do you?"

Iris sighed. "An Iris has been an Advisor to the FitzAlcis for many generations, sir."

"Traditions can be changed."

"My nephew has a lot to answer for, Sire, and that expression not least of all," said Iris, frustrated. "I would like to recommend my son to your staff but I can't in all honesty. Since he graduated, he's not exactly excelled. My grandson would, if he'd put his ridiculous pursuit of history aside. I'd happily stay until I could recommend him to you, sir, but I feel myself slowing down. I cannot attend Court as often as I would like and I feel my advice is suffering for it; therefore, I think it best I resign."

Adeone steepled his fingers. "If you think that I'm going to let one of my best advisors, and the longest serving at that, walk away because *he* thinks he's past it, you've another thought coming. Especially when his latest advice matches my thoughts so exactly. *No*, listen to me, my lord. I couldn't care less if you attend Court only on the days that you must preside there; I'll miss you being there, yes, but, if that's all you can manage, that's all I will ask of you. You were my father's closest advisor—"

"What works for one may not work for another, Sire."

"Nonsense. You've never yet given me bad advice or let me down. I'll not let you walk away when it costs you so much."

"The things in life that matter most are rarely painless, Your Majesty," observed Iris, crestfallen.

Adeone sighed. "I know but I'm not in the habit of forcing pain on people. Please accept that you'll be an Advisor to the FitzAlcis until you greet your ancestors? We *need* you, Lord Iris – now more than ever."

"Sire, in all conscience… There are men far better than I to take my place by your side."

"I don't accept it. Nor would Landis, nor would Arkyn." He paused, seeing a determination creep over Iris' face. "Very well, if you must, you must, but don't ever tell me you're going because you want to; I'll never believe it. Thank you for all you've ever done."

Iris knelt. "Sire, I can see no other way. You must be served by the best and I no-longer think I rank amongst those."

Adeone leaned forward and slipped his hand under Iris' elbow. "Get up please, my lord. I think I've just had an idea. Would you accept a ceremonial post?"

"It rather depends on which, Your Majesty, but I'll probably have to register some protest," admitted Iris, before pushing himself up.

Adeone laughed. "It'll take too much energy. What do you think about King's Counsellor? We've not had one for about a hundred years."

"Sire, I meant to resign, not accept such precedence," said Iris, astounded.

Adeone eyed him. "I mean to be sensible every day, but always fail.

That's your nephew's fault too. Will you accept the post?"

"What of Festus, though?"

"Let him do all the work and I'll find another Deputy Chief Advisor."

Iris looked at the King. "I… Thank you, Your Majesty; I don't know what else to say. I can face myself now."

Adeone smiled. "No, my lord, thank you. It's long overdue. I'll get the proclamation drafted and inform Lord Landis. I'll always value your advice whenever you choose to give it."

Chapter 38
BUTTERWORTH
Pentadai, Week 11 – 19th Lowal, 12th Lowis 1212
Paras

THE ANAPARIAN REVIEW moved smoothly into its first stages once the Domini had overcome his ageist attitude enough to accept Arkyn wasn't going to be hoodwinked. He organised several banquets at various intervals during the initial fortnight and made every effort to ensure the Prince had a good time.

Arranged by the dais and on the doors, the Princes' Guard's sparkling armour lent grandeur to a spectacular sight, with Captain Jones and his deputy, Sergeant Butterworth, augmenting their ranks as required. Having talked some more with him, Arkyn had found Jones to be excellent at his job once he had understood that the captain's bluntness was simply his manner. He hadn't spoken to Butterworth and, with the strict military hierarchies and prejudices, didn't expect to.

On guard duty in the Great Hall, Butterworth watched everyone present: guests, guards, servers and pages. One lord caught his attention; one seated at the lower tables by choice. There was something uncomfortable in his manner and an odd shade around him. He would stop and glance around, hunting for something. Once, he looked directly at Butterworth, but the guard's eye-line was above and beyond him. Butterworth's eyes continued to rove. Six minutes passed before he realised he'd not noticed the lord again. He scanned the room for him, but he'd vanished.

The following day, on a gut instinct, he spoke to Captain Jones.

"Sir, is it possible for me to speak to His Highness? I think I need to warn him of something."

"Of what, *Sergeant*? I'll pass the message on."

"It is… I can't…" Butterworth stammered before remembering Wynfeld's warning in Tera to keep his utilisation of Ull's Legacy private. "Sir, I think Major Wynfeld would rather I spoke only to the Prince."

"The Major isn't your immediate commanding officer," retorted Jones.

Butterworth swallowed. "He's yours, sir, and I'm not too certain that he's not mine, unofficially. They put me on a ship and sent me here with no option or discussion."

Jones snorted. "It is the Major's trademark; I'll give you that. I'll reconsider, but that's not a promise you'll get to speak to His Highness."

Butterworth saluted and left, inwardly seething at Jones' obstinacy.

Two days later, Butterworth spoke again to the captain. Caught at the close of a banquet, Jones was terse and bad tempered.

"Sergeant, your duties do not include seeing His Highness! If you have concerns to raise, you tell me or Captain Marsh. I'll see you in the morning about this. I've had more than my fair share of issues tonight and I've got a long report to write so, basically, get out of my sight."

Butterworth saluted and left, swearing as soon as he was out of earshot.

When he went to report to Jones, the sight that met his eyes was one memory would never erase. He tiptoed forward. The mess was unbelievable. A minute later, he locked the door and went in search of Captain Marsh.

* * *

In Oedran, Wynfeld wondered what to do. His King would want answers, but would it be wise to tell him what had occurred? Prince Arkyn would surely do that. He sat in his office for mere moments before acknowledging that whatever Prince Arkyn did, he still had to answer to King Adeone and this didn't rank amongst minor matters. He walked over to the Palace and asked Richardson for an audience.

Wynfeld and Adeone had barely passed pleasantries when there was a small shimmer in the air as Fafnir appeared. A few moments later the link formed.

Arkyn said mildly, "I'm sorry, Sire. I hope you weren't busy."

"Not at all. Wynfeld had just been announced."

"Oh, then he's probably told you—"

"He's not told me anything yet. What's happened?"

"Jones was murdered last night and Butterworth has concerns, unspecific as always, but he thinks I'm being watched malevolently."

Adeone paused. "Who murdered Jones?"

"They don't know. It wasn't pleasant. Slashed across the back and then stabbed multiple times. He wouldn't have seen his attacker, or at least they don't think so, but it's odd, sir, he was killed in his office; therefore, he probably knew the person or, at least, was expecting them."

Adeone absorbed that. "What are Butterworth's exact concerns?"

"Simply that someone has been attending the banquets and watching the dais malevolently."

Adeone sighed, exasperated. "This is why it is better not to trust in magic; it's always so damned indeterminate! What's Synclare doing?"

"Apart from assuring me that everything is being done, probably not much. He talks a lot and acts little. I wish I could find another Wealsman; I'd advise the Domini's removal without a second thought."

"Then find me a new Representative."

"Sire, you can't mean that. It's only my opinion."

Adeone snorted. "Your opinion merely confirms my own and others, including Lord Iris. Anyway, even if it was *only* your opinion, I'd say the same. You learnt far more than you realise in Terasia." Seeing Arkyn wanted to argue, he continued blithely, "Do you feel safe in Paras now?"

"I don't feel unsafe, sir, but I also don't feel comfortable. I trust Marsh and my guards. I trust Butterworth, but things are sometimes missed."

"I don't think they will be. Can you finish in a cisluna month?" enquired Adeone.

"I should be able to, sir. Most of the preliminary work has been done. Finding a new Domini might be harder."

"I'll send you a shortlist by special rider. Arkyn, don't get too worried. Let others deal with the investigations. I rather suspect that they'll find nothing. Just get the review done and get home, please."

Arkyn smiled. "Your wish, Sire, is my command!"

Adeone caught his eye. "You've been listening to Rayburn."

"He's teaching me a lot, Your Majesty," admitted Arkyn innocently.

"The sooner you're here, the better," growled his father.

Arkyn chuckled. "How's Tain?"

"The same other than his enthusiasm for learning hasn't yet waned."

"Should we encourage it to? The more he learns, the better."

Adeone nodded. "Yes, but there are limits to what's sensible. Was there anything else, or shall I let Wynfeld tell me what you just have?"

"Of course, I should have had more consideration."

"Why? I'd rather talk to my son than the Major of Oedran, whoever he may be."

"Wynfeld might be getting concerned."

Adeone shrugged. "Is Wynfeld ever unconcerned? He's been worried since about two sentences into our initial talk at the gates of Oedran. It seems wrong to let him be anything else." He sobered. "Do I look grave enough?"

"Until anyone sees your eyes, sir. I shall let you talk to Wynfeld."
Arkyn gave Fafnir a nod.

Adeone merely winked at Arkyn as the link broke.

The King found the Major of Oedran standing exactly where he had been when the link formed. "Take a seat, Wynfeld. Richardson!" His administrator entered. "We're not to be disturbed. Can you personally copy out the list of candidates for the post of Domini and send it to Prince Arkyn today? I've told him he'll have it as soon as possible." When the door had closed, Adeone turned to Wynfeld. "The murder of Captain Jones is unfortunate. What was he working on that meant someone wanted to kill him?"

"It wasn't anything that he's confided to me or, to my knowledge, to Captain Beaver. It's more likely the fact he was a spy, but I can't say that for certain."

"What do you make of Butterworth's summations?"

All too aware of his King's views on Butterworth's spirit as a Sensor, Wynfeld said, "There might be something in it, but I don't know what. I could talk with him and see what he remembers."

"Do so. I'm still not comfortable using Butterworth, Wynfeld."

"I realise that, Sire, but he has proved he has his uses."

"Yes, at confusing the issue," retorted Adeone. "If you're happy, then I suppose that's all that matters; as long as I never have cause to deal with Butterworth directly. I have the oddest feeling that we will never find Jones' murderer, but you'd better tighten your circle of protection around His Highness: discreetly double his guard. I think he'll be in Paras for a cisluna-month more and I've agreed to him finding a new Domini."

"Very good, sir. If I might have sight of the shortlist, I'll forward His Highness any information we hold on the candidates."

"Then see Richardson. I want the list on its way tonight, Wynfeld. It doesn't give you much time."

"We'll cope, Your Majesty."

"Good. Oh, and, at some point, I'd like what you know about Lord Kensal Parchi. I was acquainted briefly with his father, all too briefly, but Lord Kensal has become an acquaintance of Prince Arkyn. Apparently, he's studying the histories at Paras."

Chapter 39
SCRYING

IN THE SMALL SITTING ROOM she and Julius shared, Julia curled up in a chair with a novel. Her nearfather had gifted her several when she turned fifteen and their stories enchanted her. Within the pages of the leather-bound volumes were worlds of beauty and strife, where good triumphed and evil burned. Words wove the stories and played images in her mind. Places that she'd never seen lit her imagination, places that had never been were as real as the streets of Oedran.

Her brother's manservant entered. "Lady Malandra's called by, my lady."

Julia smiled. "Thank you, Adam. Show her in." She scrambled to find her page marker, moving books and detested sewing aside. She bent to look under the table when a cough made her look up. Adam handed her the marker with a knowing smile.

"I'll bring tea, my lady."

Malandra smoothing her skirts out as she sat down, said, "Why do you read so much?"

Julia shrugged. "Why don't you read more?"

Her friend considered that. "There's always something I don't understand. My governess didn't think reading much use to a lady."

"My father would never have let ours get away with that," said Julia. "I just wish he could have lost the embroidery lessons as well. Mother eventually gave up, but there's still the odd thing I'm meant to do." She glanced with hatred at the pile next to her. "I'm meant to set an example for my sisters. I've always admired her optimism."

Malandra chuckled. "Pass it here. You read to me and I'll do your embroidery. We'll both be happy then."

Half an hour later, Indria joined them. By the time Julius entered, they had settled into their afternoon.

He lounged in the last free chair, watching Malandra's quick fingers. "You know, sis, if I told mother who's doing your sewing, she'd make you unpick it all."

Julia threw him a withering glance. "You wouldn't want Malandra's efforts to go to waste."

He chuckled. "You're right, so I guess I'll say you were all chatting nonsensically about Court gossip. I'll bribe Adam to back me up."

"He doesn't accept bribes," said Julia. "Haven't you got lectures or something?"

203

"Not so you'd notice. I don't suppose anyone fancies a ride?"

Julia's eyes narrowed. "Haven't you got someone else to bother?"

"The Princes aren't here, Irvin's in Paras and Finian's at Ceardlann; so, no. Sorry. Malandra, take pity on me."

She looked at him appraisingly. His eyes reminded her of a lost puppy. "Maybe tomorrow, Lord Julius, if someone else comes as well."

Julia looked between them. "Fine. I'll take pity on you. Indria?"

Irvin's sister nodded. "Let's make it a picnic; the weather's lovely."

Julia and Julius shared a glance. He said, "Ask mother. I'm sure the kitchens won't mind."

"Why me?"

"She'll be less suspicious."

* * *

Scrying, Landis cursed; he could walk the streets of Oedran through his mind's eye, but the results were hazy, fuzzy and useless compared to the old scrying bowl. He swore. He couldn't get one made; the suspicions would be rife throughout Oedran and especially the Court if word escaped. The fog shifted. A delicate hand was on his shoulder. He pulled himself clear of the steam and mopped his face. His eldest daughter stood beside him.

"Haven't you learnt that my room is sacrosanct, Julia!"

"Sorry, father, but mother told me to come and see you—"

"What have you done this time?"

"Nothing, sir, but I wondered if we – Julius, myself, Malandra and Indria – could take a picnic up to the Wynwood Meadows for the day."

Landis sat back. "I can't see why not, as long as you're sensible."

"Thank you. What were you doing?"

"I have a cold coming on."

Julia hesitated. Obsidian suggested otherwise. "I won't tell anyone, father, but are you a scryer?"

Landis pursed his lips. "I have explained, Julia."

"Of course, but I wondered if I could ask you how you find out if you've got a Ullian spirit or hue?"

"I suppose one just knows; I haven't myself experienced the uncertainty."

"That doesn't mean you don't have one, father," said Julia.

Landis paused, impressed. "What are you trying to tell me?"

"I think I may be a wordsmith."

Landis' eyes never left his daughter's face. "Interesting. Why?"

"Words lose their ambiguity, pedantry is second nature and I have an aptitude for anagrams."

Landis chuckled. "It could just be that you're bright, Julia."

"I just thought that, if you are a scryer, I might have inherited something."

"Not from me. There's no proof that Ullian spirits and hues pass down families. I wouldn't mention your suspicions to anyone. Let whatever it is develop and, if you're interested, have a search in the library when we're back home. I've collected a few texts over the years on the Ullian Legacy. They may be of interest. Your nearfamily have certainly thought so."

Julia smiled. "Will you give my love to Uncle Adeone when you next see him and tell him we're all wondering when he'll be dancing again?"

"I will give him your love. You should know better than to speculate about other matters. Talking about dancing, though, I've noticed you've been doing a lot more recently. Should I add up what I can afford in a dowry for you?" he teased.

"Not yet, father. Humourless popinjays most of them. But I think Julius is eyeing up Malandra..."

Landis went grave. "Really?"

"But not seriously, father."

"Good. He's not marrying a Para. Not when Lord Para is one of Lord Scanlon's associates. Be careful what you say around her, Julia."

"I will, but Aunt Aelia married Lord Scanlon and—"

Landis took his daughter by the shoulders. "Do you think your aunt's death was an accident, Julia? Do you? If you do, you're in a minority. She chose to end it. She was pregnant as well. Can't you see? Lord Scanlon is systematically destroying everything we hold dear. I've been attacked; your nearfather was nearly killed, as was your nearcousin. One of Wynfeld's men was murdered yesterday in Paras, in the castle's keep. The threat isn't an illusion of the Jeci of old. You've *got* to be careful; you've got to watch what you say and whom you talk to. I know children may choose their own paths but be aware of putting others in the way of danger."

Julia nodded. "I shall be, father. I'm not oblivious to the problem—"

Landis forced himself to relax. "I'm sorry, but you're still young—"

"Don't I know it! Everyone's condescending, patronising and assumes I'm ignorant." She saw his stricken face. "Not you, father, but at Court it's like they're sneering at me for wanting to be me. I'm never going to be a natural lady of the Court. I can't abide the witterings of my fellow ladies. Yet if I try talking to anyone with even an ounce of brain, people jump to unsubstantiated, offensive and ridiculous conclusions that insult my intellect and presume character traits better suited to common whores. I admire Lady Rhian for telling the world she's not getting married. It must have taken some guts..."

"And Lady Amara's influence," murmured Landis.

"...I just wish people would believe me when I say all I want is decent discussion."

Landis chuckled. "I believe you and, Julia, I'll respect whatever you decide is your future; however, to stop you becoming quite so bored, use your obvious intellect for the good of the empire. Try a little spying on the side; it's a rewarding hobby."

"You can't mean that, father."

"I do. Let people believe your attitude is changing and listen hard. I'm sure you'll find out more than you realise. Oh, and has anyone introduced you to Lady Rhian?"

"No, father, the chance hasn't presented itself."

"Then next time we're all at Court, I'll do the honours. I think the two of you will get on well. Now, I'd better continue."

"Of course, father, thank you for the chat. I've heard scrying can be draining, though, so don't work too hard." Seeing his face, she hugged him. "I won't tell anyone, I promise."

Julia entered her sitting room. Her brother was there alone, working at a small desk.

"Permission granted by father. Oh, and you're not marrying a Para."

He glared at her. "Who said I wanted to?"

"Your doe-eyes. Don't hurt her."

Julius frowned. "I wasn't going to. I just wanted a bit of fun."

"You're allowed all the *fun* you want. We're not. Be kind."

He blushed. "All right. Sorry."

Chapter 40
DIARY ARCHIVES
Hexadai, Week 12 – 27th Lowal, 20th Lowis 1212
Inner Office

ARRIVING FROM CEARDLANN, Tain half ran into his father's office and Adeone, in the middle of a meeting, shook his head, apologising to the attendees; seeing them, Tain also paused and apologised. As one, they rose and left to wait until the King had finished greeting his son.

Adeone sighed. "Did you even hear Richardson?"

Tain sagged, "No, sir," then brightened up, "because he was here, with you taking notes."

Adeone paused. "That's my rebuke undermined. Never mind, these things happen. Did Cal return with you?"

"Yes, sir. He's at home. Can he come to dinner tonight?"

"Let him have some time with his family, Tain. You see him every day; however, you can invite him here tomorrow afternoon, before you return, and run riot around the Palace for a few hours. I intend introducing you to Thomkins in the morning. Knowing your habit for asking questions you'll be in the Diary Archives until well past lunchtime."

Tain grinned. "I must have got the habit from somewhere, sir."

"If you're not careful, I'll quiz you on what you've been learning, or are meant to be learning."

Still grinning, Tain said, "Feel free."

Adeone eyed him. "Hmm. You're not meant to call my bluff."

"Sorry, Sire, the fault is mine—"

"Is that Tancred's influence or Spellen's?" grumbled Adeone.

"Both, sir, but you must have approved what I'm being taught."

"Right, that's it, out you go." Tain sagged and Adeone gave him a one-armed hug. "I don't mind but, by the looks of you, you galloped through every muddy puddle you could. Go and get cleaned up. I'll finish depressing everyone who's waiting and then we can have some time together."

* * *

The following morning, Adeone led his son down a well-worn spiral flight of stairs into the basement of the privy wing and a long low-vaulted room. Brick lined, it was warm in the light of lanterns, but shadows swallowed the light and regurgitated unease. History could be felt but time had no place. An elderly man got up from a small table at their entry and bowed rheumatically.

The King said, "Morning, Thomkins."

"Good morning, Your Majesty, Your Highness. I hope the sun shines."

Adeone nodded. "It's a nice enough day; once we've left you in peace, you ought to get out and enjoy it a bit."

"It's the stairs these days, Sire. I takes all my time to get up them but that's no matter."

Adeone smiled. "I wish there was some way of bringing the sun to you, but I know from experience that if I suggest you retire, you'll give me a look. Now, Prince Tain has a couple of volumes to hand over. Maybe you could give him the tour? I'll leave you to get acquainted."

Tain glanced at his father. "Aren't you staying, sir?"

"No. Come and find me when you're done. Thomkins, I'll see you soon."

The old archivist smiled. "Of course, Sire. I hope your day brings you something to note."

When they were alone, the archivist said, "Well, Your Highness, welcome to the Diary Archives. No-one's sure how old the actual archives are, they were built during the Cearcallian Era but that's as far as we know. The diaries of all your family, who care to add to the archive, are here for at least the last four hundred years and possibly more, but I can never seem to find the time to go to the back and see what's there. This will be your area, sir. There's a nice set of shelves and it's marked with your name. If you just want to put what you've brought on there, I'll see to filing it properly later. It'll go on the top, but I've always got a step if you can't reach to retrieve it yet. Now, there are some peculiarities to this place. No doubt His Majesty has told you that no-one other than a FitzAlcis can read any of the material here due to a magic set up by the Cearcall."

"Yes. But, how does that magic work?"

Thomkins smiled. "We don't know, I'm afraid. Maybe one day someone will solve it but I quite like the mystery after all these years. I came up here from Terasia forty-nine years ago this year and I've never regretted it. The mystery is spice to my life. Not only can I not read the diaries I catalogue and archive but neither can Your Highness if the writer is still alive. It is also considered a violation to read anyone's whom you have known well. I suspect though, for you, that would cover the late Queen's. She added regularly to this archive, but others haven't. Your grandmother only ever added one scroll and the current Justiciar hasn't handed me anything at all. That's the way of it."

"Have you ever asked him for any?" enquired Tain.

"No, Your Highness, it's not my place to. I guard what's been given; I don't request it – if you didn't give me another scroll, that would be that. Now, let's look. Here's your brother's and father's... This was Prince Lachlan's, and this King Altarius' – they both contributed but inconsistently: sometimes more, sometimes less. I don't much know the habits of people further back because I wasn't here, and the gentleman I took the job over from wasn't in a position to give me much information, you might say. Tragic, that was. It was said he got lost in the further tunnels, but he was never found. I don't think there are that many side alleys off this room for him to have got lost in, but you never know. The room certainly goes out beyond the actual walls of the Palace. You can tell where the break is. The roof gets wet and we can't keep anything at that end for fear of it rotting."

"Then why isn't it bricked off?"

"Keeps the air fresh, is what I was told, Your Highness. Now, you can come down here whenever you like and read any of the older diaries. You might find interesting snippets in them. I know that Prince Amarus, last Justiciar bar one, was a regular contributor... His diaries might be of interest. He retired to Ceardlann after Prince Lachlan took over, but he was an interesting man. I don't remember him too well because I took this job on after he'd retired, but the one time I met him was memorable. He had much the same outlook as Lady Amara has. She was named for him, of course, as you were for Prince Lachlan."

"Lachlan's only my middle name."

"Aye, Your Highness, but a notable one to bear. I should leave you to look around. Take this lamp but be careful with it, please. I don't want the whole place to be on fire during my watch. You'll find tables scattered at intervals if you want to read anything."

Tain grinned taking the lantern. "Thank you, Thomkins. You really don't mind?"

"Not at all, Your Highness, the company will be good for me."

Chapter 41
THE PALACE
Afternoon
Palace – Privy Gate

CAL WALKED TOWARDS the Palace. Why did he feel apprehensive? He'd known Prince Tain for three years, but this was something altogether different. He'd never dealt with the FitzAlcis in Oedran during what might be called normal times. When he and Tain had become friends, they'd met at Macarian House during Queen Ira's illness. He'd lived at Ceardlann with the Prince and that couldn't be normal either, for the house was their refuge and you only required a refuge if your normal life was different.

Cal nervously approached the guard on the Privy Gate and handed over his invitation. The Ceardlann guards were all relaxed but this one was straight as a poker and openly suspicious. The guard eyed the young boy in front of him and took the proffered letter. He read it with a sceptical eye and noted the signature; all suspicion disappeared from his gaze in an instant and he stood straighter, disconcerting Cal even more.

"That's all in order, sir. Do you know your way or shall I ask someone to show you through the Palace?"

Cal swallowed. "Erm, well, I don't know my way…"

"Not to worry, youngster… sir. I'm sure there's someone around here that does."

* * *

A couple of minutes later, a courier was showing Cal through the Palace.

"What's your name?" asked Cal eventually.

"Craig, sir."

"I'm Cal. Why does everyone keep calling me *'sir'*?"

"Because you're a friend of His Highness, sir. Not to address you so would be an insult, if not to you, to His Highness."

Cal frowned. "I can see how it might be an insult to me, if I minded – which I don't – but why would it insult His Highness?"

"It just would. I know it would, but I can't explain why."

A voice behind them said mildly, "It is because, Master Calumiel, if one is disparaging about a friend of a prince one disparages that prince's judgement. If one insults the friend of a prince and the prince comes to hear of it, there may be repercussions through the loyalties of friendship."

Cal turned and smiled. "Thank you, Your Honour."

"Not at all. Are you going to see His Highness?"

"Yes, sir."

"Then I shall take myself elsewhere. I rather think I would be in your way. Maybe you could, however, pass on my greetings to His Highness?"

"Gladly, Judge, and I don't think you'd be in our way at all."

"Nevertheless, I should not interrupt His Highness' plans."

Tancred watched the visitor and guide continue their walk through the Palace smiling to himself. He went in search of the King.

* * *

As Richardson announced Tancred, Adeone caught the judge's eye and could only smile in welcome, for Tain was talking in a never-ending stream. Finishing the monologue on the Diary Archives, Tain grinned at the judge.

Adeone finally managed to say, "Come on in, James. I think you've arrived at an opportune moment." He ruffled his son's hair. "I might not need a headache remedy now. Were you after this terror?"

"No, Your Majesty, but I believe Master Calumiel might be. I have just talked with him on my way here."

Tain jumped up. "I'd almost forgotten! Sire, can I..."

"Go on." Adeone watched his son leave. "As you weren't hunting for your charge, James, I guess you were after me?"

"Yes, Sire. I rather suspect I was."

"If it's only suspect, let's find ourselves a drink, as the topic can't be too arduous."

Once sitting down, on invitation, Tancred said, "As I mentioned, Sire, I came across Master Calumiel. He was asking a courier for clarification on why, if he isn't addressed correctly, His Highness may be insulted."

"Ah. Surely Spellen has explained such things?"

"So I thought, sir, but then I wondered if Advisor Spellen has ever truly considered Master Calumiel as his pupil or even someone who should have matters explained to him. I should not wish to disparage the advisor or his abilities, but the incident I overheard troubled me."

"I can appreciate why, as I can appreciate why you've spoken to me. I shall talk with Spellen. I had thought my instructions regarding Master Calumiel's education had been clear, but maybe further clarification is required. At any rate, it will stop me wondering exactly what Tain's next plan is."

Tancred smiled. "I have not heard His Highness planning anything for a while, Sire."

"No, neither have I; it concerns me slightly," said Adeone, grinning and topping up his friend's glass.

* * *

Tain half ran through the Palace to the nursery rooms. The guards on the doors saw him coming and held them open for him with a small smile.

He stopped and tutted. "No salute?"

They saluted.

Tain grinned. "Now the door's closed."

The senior glanced in amusement at the Prince. "Can't manage everything with only two hands, Your Highness."

Still grinning, Tain mused, "There's always a foot, Smithers, but I'll live with it."

Cal bowed as his friend entered and was surprised not to receive a reproachful look.

Tain said, "You're actually here!"

Cal smiled. "I am. What was that with the guards?"

"I was annoying Smithers. It's a rewarding hobby. So, what shall we do? I know, I'll show you the Palace. Other than the Court – which is boring anyway. We could sneak into the King's Hall though, if we time it right."

"Sounds good to me, sir. Oh, I saw Judge Tancred on my way here. He sends his greetings."

"Yes, I just saw him; I was with father. Come on, let's tell Maria where we're going."

Maria eyed her charges, hands on hips. "Very good, sir, but remember we're leaving for Ceardlann in four hours. I'd like you here in three, all right?"

Tain nodded. "I'll try to remember, Maria, and Cal will remind me."

Maria glanced at an innocent and intent Calumiel. "I've heard *that* before." She changed her posture and smiled warmly. "Go on with you then and don't spend too long in the kitchens."

Tain grinned. "You know all my hiding places, Maria. It's not fair."

"Life rarely is, Your Highness."

211

Once in the corridor, Tain said, "I think she meant that."

"Yes. So, did you go to the Diary Archives earlier?"

"Yes. There must be hundreds of years of my family history there and none can read it but us. Historians must curse that, but I find it fascinating. Oh, this is the Privy Wing. It's like our house, I suppose. Family and close friends stay in this part of the Palace and we've all got apartments as well. There are private kitchens on the ground floor and other servants' rooms. There're guardrooms but the only offices are ours – or rather His Majesty's and my brother's."

Guards snapped to attention with a rapidity that made Cal jump. Tain, however, appeared oblivious to it and half ran up a flight of stairs, grinning. At the top a courier hastily got out of the way and Tain nodded in thanks but other than that no acknowledgement passed, whereas at Ceardlann he always said thank you. They entered a corridor with tall arched windows along one side. It felt airy and open but there was an undertone to the atmosphere Cal noticed immediately.

"Is this the King's Corridor, sir?"

"Yes. How did you guess?"

"By nothing I could ever put into words, Your Highness."

"I didn't think you'd ever run out of *those*!" murmured Tain.

They reached the Audience Chamber and Tain said, "Hillbeck, you know Master Calumiel, I think."

"By sight, yes, Your Highness. His Majesty's still here."

Cal marvelled at the ornate Audience Chamber with its painted scenes and looked at its dais in awe of what it stood for. Here was a reminder never seen in such an obvious way at Ceardlann that he was an acquaintance of the ruler of the empire. They entered the Inner Office and Kenton rose and bowed.

Tain glanced around. "Where's Richardson, Kenton?"

"With His Majesty, Your Highness."

"Oh. Is anyone else there?"

"Only Judge Tancred, sir. May I announce you?"

"Yes, please, if you think it's all right."

"I'm sure it is, sir. Might I ask your companion's name?"

"I forgot you didn't know. Master Calumiel Galdwin, Secretary Kenton."

Adeone dismissed Richardson with a glance as Kenton left after announcing the boys. "Nothing but trouble, are you, Tain? Three interruptions in one day. How will I cope?"

Tain grinned. "I'm sure you'll find a way, sir. I'm showing Cal around."

"So I see. Come on in properly, young Cal. Welcome to the Inner Office – my cell of a working day. The views are agreeable when I get chance to peruse them."

"Thank you, Your Majesty. It's a pleasant room," replied Cal, looking around the large room with its polished woods and marbles, the touches of gilding and scarlet velvets and silks.

"I suppose it is, but I've seen it too often to fully appreciate it."

Tancred said softly, "Over time the most beautiful things can become commonplace, Your Majesty. I have always thought this room is made by the king of the day."

"Thank you, Judge, but I can see the lawyer in your ambiguity," replied Adeone wryly.

Tancred chuckled. "It appears occasionally, Sire. May I leave you to your other guests?"

"I suppose you realise with both of them I've lost any chance of being declared sane by the time they leave?"

"I am sure His Highness will consider the good of the empire and leave Your Majesty's sanity as intact as ever."

Once the judge had gone, Adeone smiled to himself. "That was a good lesson in informal formality. He never said I *am* sane, did he?"

Tain grinned. "No, but he got out of it neatly. Father, can I show Cal the King's Hall? Technically, it is within the Court."

"I'll write a note for if anyone becomes officious. So, young Cal, what do you think of the Palace?"

Cal considered for a moment. "It's very large and ornate, but it's nice. Completely different to Ceardlann, Your Majesty."

"Yes, isn't it? It runs on different rules as well, but then it needs to. I'm sure, when you're at Ceardlann, Tain will explain them at length, but it's not as daunting as it appears; you just have to remember to be careful what you talk about in the public areas."

* * *

By the time they reached the King's Hall, both Cal and Tain had lost track of time but were certain it couldn't be close to the three hours Maria had stipulated. The guards on the doors eyed Tain approaching and looked sideways at each other.

"I'm showing my friend around. We won't go further than the hall," explained Tain.

The senior said, "Please don't, Your Highness. We'll get into awful trouble if you do."

The door thudded shut behind them as Cal took in the sight that met their eyes. They'd entered the hall on the dais and the long trestle table was already being laid for the Court Supper. The servers turned on hearing the dais doors open and, surprised, made an obeisance.

Tain grinned at them. "Carry on, we'll try not to get in your way."

Cal hardly heard him; he was turning on the spot intrigued by the vast space and marvelling at the carvings on the rafters: faces and creatures snaked around the arches. The more he saw, the more he could see. Hidden imagery was within the spaces between the carvings. There were owls and wolves, suns and stars, foxes and snakes, oak leaves and acorns, bluebells and roses. As his eyes adjusted, he began to see other, less natural shapes: keys and scales, arrows and vials. He tore his eyes away from the rafter closest to him and took in the wider hall. Like many other buildings, the floor was flagged but the stones were whitened and the cracks filled with clean sand. The long tables at each side of the room were laden with platters and candelabras, gold and silver glinted amongst the serving dishes already being filled with fruits. Doors led from the room and fireplaces spaced between them were being cleaned. People were coming and going. Neither boy noticed one server leave purposefully.

Tain grinned at his friend's astonishment. "What do you think?"

"I can't think, Your Highness..."

"Perfect, I've been waiting *ages* for you to say that." He laughed. "It's rather good, isn't it?"

Cal swallowed. "Yes, sir, it is. It's amazing."

A door at the far end opened and a set of dancers and musicians entered.

Tain glanced over. "They must be practising for tonight and not realised I'm here. Shall we stay and watch?"

Cal nodded distractedly; he was still gazing at the rafters.

Tain nudged him. "We'll sit on the end dais steps. That way, you won't get too giddy."

Cal tore his eyes away from the carvings. A few minutes later he asked, "Sir, the musicians are in their gallery, but what's the other one for?"

Tain glanced up. "That's the Viewing Gallery; no-one's got into it for a few hundred years. The entrance was lost during the Age of Tyranny. There's some history to it. I think it involves the murder of King Alvern."

"Surely, though, someone's climbed into from this side, Your Highness?"

Tain shook his head. "No, there's a sort of taboo on mentioning anything to do with it. It's like it doesn't exist and if you look carefully, you'll see you couldn't climb into it from this side. It's got an overhang and the carved screen has no opening wide enough. Rumour says it's protected by magic. It used to be where the Cearcall sat, from something I've read."

* * *

A voice behind them said, "Your Highness shouldn't be in here, sir."

Tain got up and turned around. "Master Calumiel Galdwin, might I introduce the Steward of the Palace of Oedran to you?"

Cal made the usual reply that it was nice to meet him.

The Steward gave a brief nod before repeating himself. "Sir, you shouldn't be in here." Had the Prince meant to insult him? He was surely of a higher status than a boy. Calumiel should have been introduced to him, not the other way around.

"We've not gone any further, Steward."

"Nevertheless, this is part of the Court and Your Highness is not yet fifteen. There are things that need to be done."

"We're not stopping anyone working, we're sitting out of the way, Steward, and no-one but yourself has raised a murmur of protest."

"No-one else is in a position to, sir. I must ask you to leave here."

Tain handed over his father's note. "I was hoping to avoid this."

The Steward read the note before returning it. "Very well, Your Highness." He looked galled and Tain didn't miss the fact that he didn't leave the hall but busied himself further along the dais.

Sitting back down, Tain murmured, "He never learns."

"Should he have done any of that, sir?" whispered Cal.

"He can point out if I'm in places that I shouldn't be, but he shouldn't ask me to leave so pointedly."

"Oh, what will you do?"

"Nothing, there's nothing I can do. I'm not yet fifteen. That's why father wrote the note. I wonder what's on it?"

"Won't you read it?"

"Not yet. I might when we get to Ceardlann, but I shouldn't be seen to read it here."

* * *

About half an hour later, Adeone entered the hall in a small flurry. He spotted the boys. "You do realise the time, Prince Tain? Maria's been hunting for you."

The Steward walked over to greet the King. "Your Majesty, I did try to tell His Highness he should be elsewhere."

Adeone held up a hand. "Prince Tain, the truth, please? Steward, stay where you are."

Tain took a breath, still biting his lip. "The Steward merely told us that we shouldn't be here and asked us to leave, Sire. I honestly didn't realise what the time was. I'll apologise to Maria as soon as I see her. We were watching the dancers for this evening and lost track of time."

"It's true, sir," added Cal. "I should take some of the blame. I've been fascinated by the hall and not wanted to leave."

215

Adeone eyed them both. "Hmm. Prince Tain, did you have cause to give the Steward the note I wrote?"

"Yes, sir."

"Wait by the doors for me."

From where they stood the two friends couldn't hear the whole of the *discussion* between King Adeone and the Steward, they heard the word 'son' and 'Prince' along with 'berate', 'conscience' and a tone suggesting the Steward was getting a dressing down to remember. When Adeone walked towards them, Cal bowed but Tain eyed his father uncertainly.

Adeone said, "We're expected at the stables."

Tain sighed. "Sir, I'm not dressed for riding."

"Then make sure you keep an eye on the time in the future."

"I really am sorry, Your Majesty," whispered Cal.

Adeone studied him for a moment. "I know that, Master Calumiel. Thank you for the apology. Come on. Ceardlann and mayhem await us."

Chapter 42

LESSONS

Evening

Ceardlann

THEY WALKED to the stables in silence, thereby avoiding adding any more gossip to the rumours that would abound after the Steward's dressing down. Cal's eyes roamed as they walked down each corridor. They passed from the gilded passages near the Court to more utilitarian ones as they neared the stables. Runners, couriers, pages and ushers, clerks, scriveners and officials, maids and footmen all stood swiftly aside as they passed. The guards saluted. Cal noticed that none of them looked at the small party as they passed. At the stables, the bustle stopped with a warning whistle. A man crossed to them as Adeone motioned for everyone to continue. A few moments later, everyone was in the saddle.

As they left the Palace, Tain and Cal shared an anxious glance. It wasn't that Adeone had been short with them. His silence was probably worse. With the multitude of people around them, though, Tain knew better than to talk about it. They rode all the way to Ceardlann without exchanging a word.

The Comptroller greeted them and noted the two boys were subdued. He looked questioningly at the King, who said softly,

"I'll come and find you in a few minutes, Comptroller. Boys, come with me, please."

They followed him with trepidation and, once ensconced in the King's study, Adeone sat facing them both.

"The Steward is a fool and other than not noticing the time, *nothing* is your fault, I hope you both realise that. Cal, did you feel you didn't know what you should be doing in the Palace – how to behave and so forth?"

Cal hesitated. "A bit, sir, it's some years since I read all the protocols the Steward originally sent me and I've realised how different Ceardlann is."

Adeone nodded. "Yes, it is different. Would you mind if I asked Spellen to run through everything with you? I don't want you to feel it's a criticism."

Cal dropped his gaze. "Thank you, sir. It might help."

"Good, and there's no need to feel like it's an imposition. I want you to feel easy when you visit us there. I'll get some plans of the Palace drawn up for you both to examine and, that way, next time, you can plan your mischief with slightly more precision. The cooks mentioned that you might not need any dinner—"

"Father, you never go down to the kitchens!" exclaimed Tain.

Adeone winked. "Doesn't mean someone else didn't go there for me to hunt for you, does it?" (Tain sagged.) "However, it was a guess. Had they got anything nice?"

Tain grinned. "Bakerson gave us some fresh bread and dripping and there were a couple of pasties—"

"Don't forget that lemon cake, sir," said Cal.

"Oh, yes, and then there was—"

Adeone chuckled. "I get the picture. Lemon cake? The Visir must have been in contact then. I hope there's some left for me."

"Some, father; we might have missed a sliver."

Once they'd gone, Adeone rang the bell and dispatched a footman in search of Advisor Spellen. When the gentleman entered, he appeared unconcerned.

"Spellen, how is Master Calumiel progressing?"

"Er, very well, sir," said Spellen, disconcerted. Was the King more interested in a merchant's son than the Prince?

"What was the last lesson you had with him?"

What had it been? After a moment, Spellen remembered. "The cultural differences within the empire, Sire. In particular the Macian Isles."

Adeone frowned. "It has its place, but surely Ewall covered that a couple of years ago. There's no need to repeat the early lessons."

"I can't give him the same lessons as His Highness, sir."

"Not for the in-depth law, though some, like the treason laws, might be worthwhile. With the protocols and traditions, it would be wise to mirror the lessons. He visited the Palace earlier and was rather fazed by the difference from here; I'd rather that didn't occur again. Give him the same lessons you'd give a Lord of Oedran, please."

"He's going to become a cloth merchant, sir," replied Spellen, perplexed.

"The future is by no means certain; no matter whom you are."

"If that's Your Majesty's wish, of course I'll teach him protocols, sir."

Adeone nodded. "Don't leave it at protocols though, Advisor. I suppose you could give him the lessons you yourself had in training. He has good judgment and, unofficially, I can see my sons asking him for his opinions."

"Very good, Sire. I'm to make him fit as an advisor and a lord even though he's to be a cloth merchant?"

Adeone took a deep breath. "He's a friend of princes, Spellen. I don't plan to outline it further. You have your instructions."

* * *

Adeone entered the Comptroller's office still fuming. He caught the Comptroller's worried eye. "Oh, it's nothing really. Tain and Cal forgot the time earlier, and I've realised Cal isn't being taught about the Palace and protocols, which he should be. In pointing that out to Spellen all the advisor did was berate my conscience with Cal's birth rank. The Steward's also been a fool today; I've had to give him a dressing down. There must be something in the wind."

"Let me change the wind, sir. Have a whiskey and tell me how everything else is."

Adeone took the proffered drink and sank onto a chair. "It would be better if Arkyn was here, but the review is concluding. There'll be a new Domini by the end of it. Captain Jones has been murdered in the keep of Paras Castle, but no-one saw anything or heard anything; it happened at night. It means we can't catch the killer. The motive was obvious. The Major's got a list of potential captains. I'll send one of them north and let the sergeant do the spying instead."

Less concerned by events than people, the Comptroller asked, "How is Prince Arkyn? It'll be nice to have him home."

"He's overworking again. When he arrives in a few weeks, don't deluge him with work, please." Adeone rolled the empty glass in his hand. "I wish there was more I could do for him, for them. I watch Tain and I can see the changes sweeping over him as he realises everything he has to do. I curse those changes and duties. They make us grow up too quickly."

"Aye, they do, sir, but, if you'll forgive me, the fact that you realise it as you do means a lot to the Princes. It's why they never seriously play you around."

"Thank you. What would I do without Ceardlann?" asked Adeone rhetorically.

"You'd invent it. Let me top up your glass and settle down to a couple of hours of relaxing talk – if Your Majesty can stand that?"

"I don't know about standing it, Comptroller, but I'll certainly take it sitting down. Is there any cake on the horizon? My son mentioned a lemon one at Oedran and it got my mouth watering."

The Comptroller laughed. "I'm sure we can find some, sir. It might not be lemon though."

"I'll cope," said Adeone with a smile. "Tell Cook he appreciates a challenge." He glanced around as a purring cat crept into the room. Bending down, he picked her up and fussed her. "You always know when I need you, don't you, Speckles?"

"That cat just knows how to get treats," muttered the Comptroller. "She'll fuss anyone she thinks is a soft touch."

"Are you saying your King's gullible?" asked Adeone wryly.

"Yes, when it comes to that cat." He chuckled. "I'll see if Cook's got a saucer of milk for her, shall I?"

"Who's the soft touch now, Speckles?" replied Adeone with a wink as the purring cat curled up on his lap.

Chapter 43
PROFESSING ALL

A FEW DAYS LATER, Tancred dismounted and left his horse at the street stables. He glanced at Smithers.

"Thank you, Sergeant. I will see myself from here."

"It's all right, sir. I've got to go your way anyway. It's no trouble."

"Sometimes a guard highlights the target." He sobered. "Thank you, Smithers, you can go."

Recognising a real dismissal, Smithers saluted and remounted his horse, but a conversation with a groom of the stables lasted long enough for him to see the judge safely inside his door.

Removing his riding cloak and gloves, Tancred passed them to his footman with a small smile. "Evening, John. Are there any messages for me?"

"No, Judge, not one."

"Thank you." He turned and spotted the maid. "Maisie, where is your mistress?"

She smiled. "In the drawing room, Your Honour, with the professor. I'll fetch more tea."

"Unless your mistress has requested it, could you bring me something cold instead?"

Tancred entered the drawing room, bent down and kissed his wife's cheek as always.

She smiled. "I wondered if it was you."

Tancred eased himself into his chair. "I am glad to be home. Sergeant Smithers saw me in the door; he is too efficient by half that lad." He looked at his son. "What brings you here then, Thomas?"

"I thought I'd keep mother company. How is Prince Tain?"

"Well. I shall tell him you were asking. Bets, I wondered if I might invite His Highness to dinner one night."

"Why do you entertain them?" grumbled Professor Tancred. "It's a little hypocritical, surely?"

His father stilled. "No, it is not. I have nothing but respect for King Adeone and his sons. I entertain them because I wish to have good conversation and think it is polite to. I am surprised that you have not learned how crucial both aspects are whilst teaching. A lawyer soon learns the lesson."

"As I can never emulate my father's achievements, I have chosen a different path," said Thomas.

"Then I am, as always, intrigued you did not deviate altogether and try as an advisor."

Thomas inwardly grouched. Would his father ever accept his choice? He'd become a *professor*, a man whose knowledge and skill the Law School celebrated, but his father still thought he should have done something different. "I prefer to teach than to compensate for people with no common sense."

Tancred pursed his lips. "That is a sweeping statement. Advisors have many duties."

"I'm sure they do, father, but look at Prince Arkyn; if he's as astute as we're led to believe, why does he need six advisors?"

"It is traditional and there are many reasons for it."

"I don't believe the FitzAlcis hold all too much with tradition though. Look at the King. Before he *was* King, he didn't care a jot about it all. Are we meant to believe that it all changed because his father died? I don't hold with that."

"Thomas, you will not talk of His Majesty in that manner again under my roof! He is not, and never has been, as flippant as you make out. He is a good man and a good ruler. We could do far worse."

"After all they've done, you *still* defend them; that's what astonishes me. In your lifetime, they've wrecked our family, forced your conscience and you'll *still* work for them!"

Keeping his temper, Tancred said, "Many families lost people in the Bayan Rebellion and time would have claimed them anyway – time or poverty. As to forcing my conscience, I have never disagreed with the ideals of the empire and I will not start dredging up the past for the gratification of the present. I will not listen to your half-informed prejudices. If you wish to continue spouting them, go elsewhere but be careful, Thomas, for sometimes you get too close to talking treason. His Majesty is our King and to talk of others is suicidal."

"So, you don't question because of fear?"

"I do not question because I find nothing to question that is my place to do so. Now, either modify your behaviour or go home."

Tancred watched him leave before whispering, "Sorry, Bets."

"Don't apologise; you've had a long day and you have your standards and opinions. He's not exactly endearing himself."

He smiled and held out his hand. Still sitting, she leaned over and took it.

"Am I doing the right thing, Bets? Sometimes I feel he is right and I am hypocritical, but they are not responsible for what happened and they are fighting far worse than rebels now. Do you see it as hypocritical?"

"No, my dear, I think you're doing everything you can for the right reasons. You care about the future. If you think that by being involved with the FitzAlcis you can improve that future, then be involved."

There was a brief knock and John entered. "Lawyer Jenkins wonders if you have a moment, Your Honour."

Tancred sighed. "Show him to my study please, John."

His wife looked at him compassionately. "Don't be too long. You don't need anything else tiring you tonight."

Chapter 44

AMARA

Septadai, Week 13 – 7th Macial, 7th Macis 1212
Palace – Court

THAT SEPTADAI, Landis introduced Julia to Lady Rhian and continued his saunter around Court, purposefully avoiding further contact with the two ladies. Rhian's company would be educational for his daughter. What he hadn't anticipated was Lady Amara attending Court. As the presiding lord, he walked over to greet the King's aunt.

"Oh, it's you, young Festus. Well, there's probably nothing happening I've not seen or heard before and you needn't bother introducing a lot of ladies to me who are far too busy trying to find likeminded souls because I certainly won't be one of them. I'm hunting for my daughter; I have a small bone to pick with her."

Landis smiled. "Your Ladyship, I wasn't planning on introducing any lady. There are none here that you don't know already. As for the predictability of the Court, you're right—"

"Stop the flannelling. I can tell when I'm being sweet-talked. Is His Majesty here?"

"No, my lady. Should I advise His Majesty you are asking?"

Amara eyed him. "No-one interferes in the King's choices. Where's my daughter?"

"Which one, my lady?" enquired Landis, trying to keep a straight face.

"Rhian; Neassa has her limp rag of a son to concern her. She's here? Good. You'd better come to make sure no-one else tries to talk to me."

Landis' lips twitched. Lady Amara's act was always worth it. He offered her his arm. Linking hers through it, they companionably traversed the Court with most people moving swiftly aside.

Rhian spotted her mother and Landis. Seeing her attention had been caught, Julia glanced around and would have moved off.

Amara said, "Stay there, young lady, and lend me your arm. Your father's got some highly important things to see to no doubt, and, if he hasn't, I'll find him something."

Lord Landis relinquished Amara to his daughter's care. He considered rescuing Julia, but she had wanted more meaningful conversations at Court and education came in many forms.

* * *

Rhian greeted her mother with a slight reserve.

Amara's beady eyes watched her carefully. "You don't want to trust young Julia, Rhian, not only is she Festus' daughter, but anyone who is this composed when I'm here has to be hiding something."

Rhian smiled. "Lady Julia, you must forgive my mother; she has taken years to perfect this act, an appreciation of it is all that is required."

Julia chuckled. "I have nothing but respect for Lady Amara. All the men of my family and nearfamily have carefully instilled it in me."

"I can imagine they have," observed Rhian.

Lady Amara laughed, appreciating the wry humour. "So can I. Come on, let's find somewhere to sit companionably."

"The private rooms all had people in them when we looked, mother."

Amara eyed her. "Did they? Oh dear. Lady Julia, you'll join us." Once ensconced in a briefly vacant room she continued, "Yes, you've got Festus' eyes… I remember someone else who had them, but you're far too young to remember him; so, we won't go into that. I might blush. Do you like Court, young lady?"

"At times, my lady." replied Julia. Would Lady Amara ever blush? "Today has been one of the few recently I've truly enjoyed. For one thing, I've not been treated like a child or someone out to find a husband."

"Yes, that can be annoying. I remember when I was your age, Alcis the lords were vying for attention. Never did them any good. You stick to what you want in life, young Julia, and if you come by information that can be of help to your nearfather in the meantime you pass it on."

"My lady?"

"Don't come the innocent with me. You know what I mean. Use your brains, that's what you have them for. I've been more frustrated watching you than any other young lady here. Don't let the world see you're laughing, but Rhian will tell you it's rewarding."

* * *

Half an hour later, Adeone entered. "Here you are, aunt."

All three ladies rose and curtsied with differing emphasis and depth.

Amara said, "Surely I wasn't that hard to find, Sire."

Adeone walked over and gave her a peck on the cheek. "No, but asking you what you're up to with an open door isn't a wise move. Rhian, Julia, has Aunt Amara been behaving herself?"

Rhian smiled. "Mother has been her normal self, Your Majesty."

Adeone sighed. "Oh dear. May I join you all or is this the sort of conversation where a man gets in the way?"

"I'm sure if it is, we can change it, Sire," admitted Julia.

Adeone laughed, pouring himself a goblet of wine from the sideboard jugs. "I'm not sure which would worry me more. What brings you to Court, Aunt Amara?"

"Checking that you're all behaving yourselves."

"I could believe that but, after a little persuasion, Landis told me the whole of your conversation."

"Never trust a lord who is friends with a king. I fancied seeing my daughter, Sire. What else would bring me here?"

"A lifetime of cunning endeavours?" enquired Adeone, settling himself onto the corner seat of a sofa.

"You're not too old to be shown what I think of such cheekiness, nephew!" she said, sitting opposite him.

Adeone's eyes glinted, watching her. "I'm sure I'm not, but you'd never so forget yourself at Court."

With the quickness of a spring breeze, she changed direction. "I would never dream of it, Sire. I came for a change of scene and thought I might worry the ladies by staying for the Court Supper. If that's no inconvenience?"

"Aunt, it would be a pleasure to have you beside me. I might get supper in peace then. Julia, stay where you are. If I didn't trust you, I wouldn't be talking like I am."

Amara smiled. "How are things?"

"Busy as ever. Arkyn's having an interesting time in Paras but will be home soon. Tain is absorbing Tancred's lessons. Elantha's becoming quite a lady—"

Amara's face softened. "You still miss Ira though."

He swallowed. "Don't you miss Uncle Ewart?"

She nodded. "Yes, but I don't wear his ring and play with it constantly when I talk of my family."

Adeone didn't stop running his thumb and fingers over the ring. "The Queen's Ring is safer on my finger than in a locked box, aunt."

"It is. Can't have that falling into the wrong hands. I remember it on four ladies' fingers. I wonder if I'll see it on a fifth."

Adeone crooked an eyebrow. "You've heard the rumours." He laughed. "And engineered this!"

"I can't imagine what you mean, nephew."

"Well, I'm not about to make another queen. So, that's the end of that. Agreed?"

Amara smiled. "Agreed – until I get bored. Now, when you say Prince Arkyn is having an interesting time of it in Paras, what exactly did you mean? Oh, and whilst we're on the subject of the youngsters…"

By the time Landis informed them the Court Supper was to be served, Adeone had exhausted his small talk, family talk and empire talk. Julia had learnt a lot about manipulating conversations, and Rhian had watched with a small smile and incisive comments. Supper, by contrast, was a hushed affair, after which Adeone escorted his aunt to her chambers and left. Sleep would be a blessing.

Chapter 45

BANTLING BOUND
Alunadai, Week 14 – 8th Macial, 8th Macis 1212
Black Hills House

BANTLING STUDIED SCANLON for hints as to his mood, wondering how he would receive the news. "Greatness, we've found out who Prince Lachlan spoke to in his final hours. We had a hard time persuading certain servants to talk."

"Before I decide what to do about your tardiness, tell me who it was."

"There were two visitors, sir. Firstly, His Majesty and then, when he was called away, Judge Tancred."

Scanlon paused. "Ah. Did they reveal anything else?"

Bantling hesitated. "I don't know what credence to give it, sir, but one man mentioned that the old judge has secrets he wouldn't want revealed. He said it's the sort of secret that no-one has talked of for years – a family secret. There was a time when Madam Tancred left her husband."

"Hardly enough to discredit such an eminent man. You're scarcely worth your keep." Scanlon sneered as his advisor dropped to one knee. "Are you scared of me?"

"No, sir."

Scanlon walked behind him. "You lie! I will not have any member of my retinue lying to me. The going rate is twenty lashes. Should I waste them on such a trivial lie? Or should I check my records, count every lie and add up your debt?" The sneer played about his lips. "Or maybe I should leave you to my cellarer. What say you? What do you *advise* now?"

"I am unable to advise you on this matter, Greatness." If Scanlon had deduced half of the lies, even a quarter, he wouldn't survive the whipping.

"A coward's reply. Take your tunic off."

Unseen, Scanlon turned a brand in the fire. Twitching the tunic from Bantling's fingers, he threw it to the other side of the room before retrieving a horse whip and flicking it so that Bantling winced. Using the whip, he prodded Bantling, forcing the advisor against the far wall, where restraints would hold him in place. Taking care to make them tight, he secured the advisor facing the wall. There was no pleading. That was upsetting. He liked it when men pleaded. Enjoyed disappointing them and hearing them scream. He stepped back and stripped. Blood was difficult to get out of silk. Bantling's physique wasn't worth saving. He swung the whip. Bantling winced at the crack alone. He smiled. Anticipation would help as much as pain. He swung it again, letting the tip caress Bantling's back. The advisor flinched. He stepped forward and leant all his weight behind the next stroke. Flesh parted. Blood sprayed. He tasted it on the air. The power in the stroke hardened him. Again. Arm back. Muscles taut. Transfer of weight. Blood spraying. And again. No need to be kind. Again and again. Every one more gratifying than the last. Bantling bit back all sound. He wouldn't give Scanlon any satisfaction.

After the tenth stroke, Scanlon examined his work. His fingers traced the parting flesh. These would scar. He smiled to himself. That was good. He didn't want his advisor forgetting the lesson. Stepping back again, he hefted the whip in his hand.

"If I were to clear your debt of lies this way, you know as well as I do that you'd die, do you not?"

"Yes, Greatness, though no lie ever hindered your wishes... Ah." Two more strokes landed.

"Another debt of twenty lashes. So, you acknowledge that if I stop before you're dead, I have saved your life? You will swear to it."

There was no escape. His voice barely audible, Bantling said, "I swear you have, through mercy, saved my life, Greatness." Two more strokes landed. Blood ran down his back. The room began to spin.

"Good. Then it is mine." Scanlon retrieved the red-hot brand, burning Bantling in the one place no-one but a doctor would ever look. Bantling screamed.

Still sneering, Scanlon snapped, "You were doing so well." He tossed the brand back into the fire. "Now, I've found this the most effective..." He stood directly behind Bantling, his arms encircling his advisor. Pressed close for emphasis, his hand in an indelicate place, he squeezed lightly. "Do you swear to never lie by any method to me again?"

"Ah. I do so swear, Greatness."

His grip tightened. "Do you swear that your speech is bound to my wishes?"

"I do so swear."

"Do you swear to always do my bidding?"

"I do so swear."

"Do you swear to answer all questions put to you in my name?"

"I do so swear."

Scanlon tightened his grip. "Do you swear to bind your blood to my cause and never betray it by any word?"

"I do so swear."

"And bind!"

"And bind, to your cause, Greatness," whispered Bantling, tears streaming down his face.

"May your binding never wane," sneered Scanlon. He crossed to a small washstand and washed the blood off before resuming his tunic. Once more, he stood admiring his work. Each back was unique. This one had a pleasing symmetry about it, or it would have if the advisor wasn't slumped in the restraints. Disgusted by the weakness, he released the advisor, who fell to the floor.

Scanlon kicked him in the ribs. "It was only a matter of time, runt! As long as you follow my wishes precisely in all matters, your family shall come to no harm. Resume your tunic and leave. Locate a man for the next job within a week, or I'll have your son fed slowly to the dogs."

The room spinning, Bantling carefully resumed his tunic, still on the floor. "I could undertake the task myself, Greatness…"

Scanlon pointed to a spot in front of him and Bantling found himself moving there before conscious thought happened.

"Did you really study for so long to stoop so low?"

"No, Greatness."

Scanlon eyed him. "I will decide when I have no further use for you. Get out."

* * *

Once alone, Bantling found a closet and threw up several times.

A voice said, "Dear, dear, bantam cock, was it really that bad?"

Bantling turned as quickly as the congealing blood would let him. "My lord?"

"I asked you a question, which I believe Lord Scanlon would want you to answer."

Before Bantling could consider his answer, he'd said, "It was."

"Stand still, in Lord Scanlon's name."

Bantling was rooted to the spot.

"Dear, dear, he did do a good job. Bend over, in Lord Scanlon's name."

Bantling bent over and felt his tunic rise.

"Oh dear. Branded too, I see. You're nothing more than Lord Scanlon's slave now. He has ordered I'm to make myself at home. In his name, come to my rooms."

Bantling fought against the wish to go but every time he moved away from where the lord was, his body burned up. Eventually, he was in the room, shaking and exhausted.

Reclining on the bed, the lord smiled. "Good. Lord Scanlon wanted me to ask you about the information you gleaned on old Judge Tancred. He wanted you to tell me tonight."

Bantling told everything he knew.

"Is that right? Well, that's interesting. Lord Scanlon did say that he didn't want you to mention the fact that you'd told me. He wants me to feel at home and to ask for anything I need. So, I suppose, in his name, I'm requesting you attend to my whims this evening. Step this way." The lord smiled as the advisor walked towards him. "Strip and lie on your front, bantam cock." As the advisor did so, the lord pulled out a rope tied to the far side of the bedframe and slipped the noose over the advisor's hands, pulling it tight. Ignoring Bantling's unease, he straddled the advisor, a bag of salt beside them. Carefully and methodically, he questioned the advisor as he rubbed salt in each wound. When Bantling screamed, he gagged him and waited, prolonging the ordeal. When he had discovered everything he could, he removed his belt. This work had its compensations.

The door opened and Scanlon entered. He took in the sight of his advisor, naked, prone and restrained, his guest straddled over him, removing his belt. He crooked an eyebrow. His guest shrugged and motioned that Bantling was Scanlon's if he wished.

"Release him!"

His guest did so, whispering in Bantling's ear, "Another day, bantam cock."

Bantling slipped off the bed. Using the bedpost he hauled himself to his feet and bowed to Scanlon.

"I'm now your liege," snapped Scanlon. "You kneel." He sneered as Bantling knelt. "Why are you here?" On hearing the explanation, he said, "In future, I will tell you personally if I want you to enlighten His Lordship. Get out." After Bantling left, Scanlon turned to his recumbent guest. "You worm. I don't pay you to double-cross me! How did you know I'd bound him?"

"Intuition. I was collecting information for you. Judge Tancred's secrets are linked to the rebellion of 1169. Bantling must have forgotten to mention it."

Scanlon eyed him. "That's not the reason you made him come here. Mark me well, if you attempt to force members of *my staff* again, I'll have you in court."

"Where I'll tell all I know. Face it, *Greatness*, there's nothing you can do if I were to rape any wife of yours. I know too much. Especially after this evening. How soon would you like Tancred to meet *his* end?"

"I never said I wanted that!"

The lord's lips twitched as he cleaned blood and salt out of his nails with his dagger. "Of course, sir. How I forget myself in this game. When would you like to punish me?"

"Make no mistake, I shall pick my time."

"Oh, I make no mistake, Greatness; it's why you pay me what you do."

* * *

Scanlon stormed through Black Hills to his study. His guest would have to leave before he did more damage. Or would he? Maybe he could get rid of two problems at once? He told his manservant to take warm water to Bantling's room and, several minutes later, entered it with his administrator to find the advisor writhing in pain, trying to wash his own back.

He dismissed his manservant. Bantling's terrified eyes dropped. Terror was good. Terror made men obedient. He pulled Bantling up by his hair. This was a necessity, nothing more. He threw the advisor face down on the bed and dealt with the wounds. As the pain eased, relief flooded into Bantling's mind. Fear also. Why was Scanlon doing this?

"Have you persuaded FitzRyson?"

"He is amenable, Greatness. Your reassurances were well received."

"Good." He slipped a hand around his advisor once more. His guest would not be able to manipulate this oath. When he'd squeezed the binding and information from his administrator, he said, "You're of no further use to me. Forget your past. You are nothing."

As Scanlon left, Bantling's mind briefly registered freedom before everything went dark.

Chapter 46
ARRIVAL
Tretaldai, Week 17 – 3rd Meithal, 10th Easis 1212
Palace – Stables

ARKYN ENTERED THE STABLES of the Palace, glad to do so. He jumped down from Ponder and handed the reins to his groom.

"See he's settled, Simon. I shouldn't need him again today. Edward, you'd better bring the report for His Majesty. Kadeem, can you see to my rooms, please? I don't know how long I'll be."

Kadeem gave the Prince an evaluating glance, which Arkyn ignored as he walked towards the Palace. Making his way through the building, he acknowledged the guards' salutes and greeted others in passing but aiming for his father's chambers first. The guards on the Audience Chamber saluted. Arkyn didn't recognise the sergeant.

"You are?"

"Sergeant Kilbride, Your Highness."

"Thank you. How long have you been in the King's Guard?"

"Cisluna-month, sir."

"I hope you're enjoying it." Arkyn entered the Audience Chamber. How many new guards had his father acquired during his absence? He passed into the Outer Office and Richardson rose.

"Welcome home, Your Highness."

"Thank you, Richardson. Is His Majesty free?"

"I'm sure he will be in one moment, sir. Merchant Chapa is currently there."

"His Majesty asked him not to shun the Palace, as I recall."

Richardson murmured, "Was he in his right mind at the time, Your Highness?"

Arkyn chuckled. "I ought to rebuke you for that, but, after riding from Paras, I don't have the energy. I'll disturb the King instead. Can you find Edward a chair and some refreshments, please? Thank you."

Arkyn knocked on the Inner Office door and entered, smiling. Adeone glanced over and got up.

"Thank Alcis, you're home!"

"So I am, Sire. I'm sorry to disturb your conversation."

Merchant Chapa, who'd risen, said, "It's no matter, Your Highness, I wouldn't interrupt a family reunion."

Arkyn stated quietly, "As you're part of the family, Merchant Chapa, I don't think that is an issue but thank you for the consideration."

Merchant Chapa smiled. "Thank you, sir, but I really should go. Sire?"

"Give my best to your family," said Adeone, privately glad he didn't have to ask his mother's cousin to leave. As soon as the door closed, he hugged Arkyn. "How are you?"

Arkyn wanted to lie but couldn't. "Tired but glad to be here, father. You've some new guards."

"I've also a new secretary. Come and sit down." He rang the bell and when Simkins entered so did a tray containing tea and fruitcake.

Adeone smiled at him. "You read my mind, Simkins."

"I'm sure that's not possible, Sire, but thank you. Welcome home, Your Highness. Can I take your cloak?"

Arkyn, who'd forgotten he was wearing it, handed it over with a word of thanks.

Adeone studied his son. "Simkins, tell Edward to leave the report with Richardson and book a time for myself and His Highness to discuss it after I've read it, please."

"I could have coped, sir," said Arkyn when Simkins had gone.

"I know, but I'd rather not have to face it all. Thank you for everything you've done in Paras. How's our new Domini?"

"More focused than Synclare, who wasn't too happy."

"Then he shouldn't have been an idiot. How did Lord Irvin cope?"

"I don't know, sir. I think well enough, but he was quiet. I don't mean reserved, I mean quiet. Without wishing to disparage him or his abilities, I think it would be better if he doesn't accompany me next year. I think his confidence would be better for it."

"Really? The libraries of Lufia are very fine. I'd have thought you'd have liked someone to go with you."

Arkyn chuckled. "I would. I've found I need to relax of an evening with congenial company, but I think Irvin needs to become confident with his own abilities first before being thrown into official meetings."

Adeone nodded. "I think the Dean of the Advisors' School would agree; he was most reluctant to let both Julius and Irvin be absent. Did you find everything you were looking for in Paras?"

Arkyn grinned. "Yes, I think so. I've found a present for both Tain and Elantha. I was thinking of giving Cal one as well, if that's all right?"

Adeone raised an eyebrow. "Why on Erinna shouldn't it be? He's living with us as part of the family, for want of a better term. I think he's grown up quite a bit. He's certainly losing the child; I feel guilty that his parents aren't seeing it."

"They agreed to Cal being at Ceardlann and they have permission to enter the valley to see him. It's their choice if they've not gone."

"Maybe. I don't know if I made them feel they really could visit. There's much that people assume you're saying to be polite. I felt so guilty when Master Galdwin pointed out that they couldn't enter the valley."

"I understand that." Arkyn considered for a moment. "Take them with you one day. Or trick them into going with you. Maybe they need to go once to go again, if that makes sense."

"It does. I'll speak to Landis about it. He'll manage something. He always does. How did you find Paras in the end?"

"An interesting city. Lord Kensal showed me round it unofficially. I've invited him down to Oedran for a time – if you don't mind? He's copying out some texts for me, ones that Synclare wouldn't let him read, so I did a bit of devious dealing. He couldn't object to me reading them and then, with the change of Domini, the new one held no objection."

Adeone laughed. "You're certainly learning manipulation, son. Good. I'm pleased. Lord Kensal, I'm sure, appreciates the touch also. His father was unassuming; is he?"

"I wouldn't say unassuming, sir; he has a quiet confidence in his abilities. I spoke to several other historians in Paras who said that he had already achieved the reputation of a man to watch and to listen to. He knows his subject. I don't know how long he'll stay."

"Make him a Guest of Court and then it won't matter. Just inform the Steward and Lord Kensal. It'll save him some expense."

"Thank you, Sire. I'm sure he'll appreciate it. Talking of guests, is Cousin Rhian here?"

"Yes. I'm surprised no-one's informed you of the rumours…"

"What rumours?" enquired Arkyn, eyes narrowing.

"Oh, it was nothing, but I asked her for a dance on her first evening here and the Court is *still* talking about it!"

Arkyn chuckled. "What would the world do without conjecture? She's your cousin; it's hardly a suspicious circumstance. From all I've ever understood, she's happily unmarried."

"Yes. She is. Talking of which, did anyone catch your eye in Paras?" enquired Adeone mischievously.

Arkyn blushed. "No, father, no-one. I don't think I'll be marrying for a couple of years at least. If that's all right?"

"I'm not going to force you into marriage. I've been advised to remarry and won't, because I don't want to endanger anyone else, so insisting on you getting married would be rather hypocritical. Don't worry, the person who advised it was saying it in my best interests at the time. Would it disquiet you?"

Arkyn sighed. "I don't know, father, I suppose it would depend on who it was. I know you loved mother and so I know it wouldn't be in detriment to her memory but it would be rather strange."

"Yes, for me also. As Percival would say, though, I'd like to see people's reactions."

Arkyn laughed. "Yes. Do we know how Kristina is? She must be nearing her time."

"Yes. It looks like the child will be premature for she's large already."

"Father, are you practising that for Court?" asked Arkyn with a snort. "Because it's not convincing, but then, I suppose, I know she was pregnant before she was married. What does one get as a blessing gift? I'd like to send them something."

"It has to be personal choice. It normally depends on the sex of the child and how close you're to be to it; so, a blessing gift from a nearparent is different to that from a friend of the family and from an acquaintance. Waiting until the child is born is probably best. Do you want a top up?"

"Please. Then I ought to leave you to get on."

"No, you don't… Richardson will hand me reports to read and I'd rather talk to you – unless, of course, you want to unwind away from my almighty presence?"

"I can't say I've noticed the almighty part, father. I was thinking of getting a massage. I can feel myself seizing up after the ride."

Adeone smiled. "How is your masseur?"

"Good but not as good as the Terasian one. He doesn't know his oils so well."

"He'll learn. If you're awake later, come and dine with me."

"Thank you, father, I'd like to."

Chapter 47
REACHING CEARDLANN
Imperadai, Week 17 – 4th Meithal, 11th Easis 1212
Ceardlann

AFTER AN EVENING in Oedran, Arkyn returned to the Rex Dallin. He dismounted in the stableyard and greeted the Comptroller with a smile.

The elderly man wasn't fooled; the Prince was exhausted. After the normal pleasantries concluded, the Comptroller said, "Prince Tain and Lady Elantha have gone to visit Laioril, sir, and your nearcousins left for Oedran yesterday."

"Yes, I saw them. If I didn't know better, I'd think father and Uncle Festus have been scheming."

The Comptroller crooked an eyebrow. "I'm sure His Lordship simply wished to show them progress on the house, sir."

Arkyn sighed. "How has it been with them here?"

"Busy, sir, but they're no trouble. I think Lady Elantha has enjoyed their company."

Taking his cloak off, Arkyn said, "Her letters certainly suggest it. If she and Tain are listening to the Chief, where's Cal?"

"Here, sir. I believe he's writing to his parents."

"I'll go and see him. Can you bring us some refreshments, please?"

* * *

Noticing Cal was engrossed in his letter and hadn't heard the door, Arkyn sank into a chair and waited for him to finish. It was relief to his aching muscles. He glanced at the occasional table beside him: a pack of playing cards, a toy squirrel and a sketch of the room. Elantha had captured the disordered mayhem of the day perfectly. Tain and Cal building a card tower that was just beginning to topple, Marcelea reading, Antonia writing something, Lucius playing with a carved horse below the window seat and young Ira toddling about. He turned it around with a smile. He'd missed them all. Marcie for her quiet humour, Antonia's gentleness, Lucius' polite curiosity, Ira's directness, Tain's bounce and Cal's careful mischief. A lump rose in his throat. Home had many meanings. His manservant disturbed his contemplation bringing refreshments.

"Thank you, Kadeem. Cal hadn't realised I was here."

Cal grinned. "Oh, I had, Your Highness, I wondered how long you'd sit there silently for…"

"You had your back to me!"

Kadeem motioned for Joe to set the tray down and leave. He poured two goblets of juice and putting them on a platter handed them silently to the Prince and Cal.

Cal grinned. "Yes, sir, but you see anyone else would have said something. Prince Tain and Lady Elantha for certain, the servants would have knocked and the Comptroller wouldn't have sat there silently. His Majesty would have greeted me, and anyway if he'd come with Your Highness there would have been conversation occurring; therefore, I surmised it was you, sir."

Arkyn sighed. "I've been outwitted, Kadeem."

"Wit is but a fool's toy, Your Highness."

"There you go, Cal, Kadeem is calling you a fool."

Kadeem stilled and turned to apologise.

Cal shrugged. "I'd have said a clown."

Arkyn laughed. "A more forgiving and self-deprecating comment than I've heard in a long time. Thank you, Kadeem, that's all for now."

Kadeem left; Master Calumiel had grown in confidence since they'd departed for Paras.

As the door shut, Arkyn asked, "A clown? Surely—"

"I leave the higher echelons of fooldom to Prince Tain, sir."

Laughing, Arkyn nodded. "Probably wise, Cal, probably wise. How have things been here? How's the weapons training?"

"Going well apparently… and I'm beating His Highness at archery most bouts."

Arkyn snorted. "If we're being honest, he's quite useless at it. A prince should excel. We've our work cut out, haven't we?"

"Can't we leave him being useless at it, Your Highness? It's nice not to be beaten at *everything*."

"I know what you mean. I suppose we could," pondered Arkyn, "but let's give him a challenge. We can watch and laugh."

"Sounds good, sir. How was your journey?"

"Tiring. I'm glad to be home. I can escape from officialdom for a couple of days. I'm sure given that long something will occur that I must think about. What's the smile for?"

"When you return from a review, Your Highness, there is a different edge to you. It's not a bad one but just a reminder that you have an official position to maintain."

"I'll try to remember to leave it at the Pillars of Alcis then, I don't want it to invade the Rex Dallin."

Cal smiled. "It wouldn't suit the valley at all, would it?"

"No, it wouldn't. I miss Ceardlann when I'm away. Miss the feeling that no-one can get to me. I understand now, I think, how father feels. So, we'll have to find something to do. Is Tain meant to be seeing the judge tomorrow?"

"No, sir, but I'm not convinced you'll persuade him to skip the work Judge Tancred has given him. He's become studious."

Arkyn rolled his eyes. "It won't last. I'm convinced of that. Oh well, if I can't stop his lessons, I'm sure I can stop yours and Elantha's for a couple of days. We could go for a ride or—"

Cal smiled to himself. "Or we can relax here and not tire ourselves out."

"Is it that obvious?" enquired Arkyn, defeated.

"I'm sure Kadeem would say 'Only to those who know you', sir."

"I'm sure he would, Cal. The problem is that I never believe him when he says it. It generally means I look ghastly and ought to stop working for a couple of days."

Cal regarded Arkyn with a critical expression. "I wouldn't say *ghastly*, Your Highness, just not your normal bright self."

"If that's meant to reassure me, it failed." He yawned. "I oughtn't to stop you writing."

Cal said, "Thank you, sir. There's a comfortable cushion on that couch if you want a nap."

By way of a retort, Arkyn located a different one and tossed it at Cal. Six minutes later he was dozing.

* * *

Two hours later, Tain breezed into the room, but some instinct had stopped him causing too much noise. He spotted his sleeping brother and stood gazing at him, an inscrutable expression on his face.

Cal looked over and smiled conspiratorially.

Tain raised an eyebrow. He mouthed the question of how long had his brother been asleep, on hearing the answer he found a quill. With the feather he tickled his brother's ear until Arkyn's hand brushed it away. He carried on. It was whipped from his fingers.

"Sleepy head!"

"Not for long with you around. Still causing trouble?"

"No, it's all Cal. I don't do anything. I'm a model prince."

"Right, now I know you're lying," scoffed Arkyn. "Apparently, you're still atrocious at archery, and, so, all else aside, you're *not* a model prince."

"Who said I'm useless at archery?"

Elantha ran into the room. "Everyone! Arkyn, you're back!"

235

"I am. You're looking remarkably well, little flower. These two haven't driven you to distraction?"

"Every day. I've missed you! I wish I'd been here when you arrived."

"I don't mind. I was looking at your sketch."

She saw it by his hand. "I don't think I got Antonia right."

Tain scrutinised the picture and couldn't find a snide comment in him. "You're getting good, aren't you?"

Elantha beamed. "Really and honestly?"

"Really and honestly, El. I'll have to stay out of your way."

She grinned. "I've got enough sketches of you. I need someone else…"

"Count me out," said Cal. "I've got a nice regard for ignorance; artists are meant to show your soul and I'm happy not seeing mine."

Arkyn laughed. "The Comptroller might humour you."

Elantha frowned. "I don't want to be humoured."

"All right, I phrased that badly. I'll get him talking one day and give you an opportunity; how about that?"

"Would you?"

Arkyn watched his young cousin affectionately. "Of course I will. Cal, you're closest to the bell. Will you ring it for me?"

Two minutes later, Arkyn asked Kadeem to bring in a chest. Tain regarded his brother with another inscrutable expression.

"Chest?"

"You'll see. If you were an animal, you'd be a cat!"

"Most would say a monkey."

"Yes, but curiosity doesn't kill those."

Cal grinned. "My lady, what would you say, monkey or cat?"

"Monkey!"

Arkyn's eyes narrowed. "What are you up to, Cal?"

"I was just thinking cats turn somnolent in the heat of day…"

Arkyn tossed another cushion at him. "Very funny. All right then, if Tain's a monkey and I'm a cat, what are you?"

"I'm not sure I'm anything—"

Kadeem and two footmen entered with a locked trunk. Arkyn nodded for them to bring it closer and set it down. He took the key from Kadeem with a word of thanks and dismissal.

Chuckling at Tain's puzzlement, he said, "I found a couple of things in Paras I thought you'd be interested in or would like. Elantha, this is for you…"

They watched as Elantha unwrapped an inlaid artist's case containing a delicate glass water pot, sable brushes, finely ground paints, good quality paper and graphite pencils. She gave Arkyn the strongest hug she could.

He grinned at her excitement. "There's a small slope that lets down from the lid, if you want to take it and paint elsewhere in the valley."

She just thanked him again, and he delved back into the chest.

"Tain, you've apparently become studious, but we can't have that, so there's this: an ancient game based on the Cearcall. We'll have to give it a go; it takes either two, three, four, six or twelve people to play, so we should manage it quite easily. The rules are all enclosed, as is a history of the game. The board is *old*; it even reads Iridian for the Low Plains. The pieces, I'm reliably informed, are original, but the instructions aren't. We'll have to find some that are, if there are any."

Intrigued, Tain took his present and placed it on the table to examine it in detail. Cal's eyes followed him but returned to Elantha, who was already sketching.

Arkyn said, "I hadn't forgotten you, Cal..." He passed over another beautifully inlaid box.

Cal took it gingerly. "Sir, there's no need."

"It's a present. Please accept it. I had fun choosing it. Have a look."

Cal opened the lid to find, as Elantha had, a careful arrangement of pieces: an inkwell and writing slope, two beautifully inlaid drawers opened to reveal paper, scroll settings, solid inks and, to Cal's incredulity, proper pen-nibs, the sort that cost a couple of darl a piece. The holders for them were all turned from burr walnut.

Cal swallowed. "Sir, I can't—"

"Yes, you can accept it; it's got your name all over it – literally, if you look at the lid. The inkwell and nib case are etched with your initials. There's no refusing it, Cal, just enjoy it."

Cal grinned. "I've been caught out then?"

"Possibly so. *Do* you like it?"

"Yes, sir, *very* much. Thank you. I hope you found something to remember Paras by yourself."

"I did, but it's rather large for this room. They made me a gift of a desk, rumoured to be the Bard's. I'm going to have it brought here. I'll not need it in Oedran. The palace carpenter is running his professional eye over it. I'm thinking it can go in the Cearcall Chamber to display the Memini's Manuscript and other Cearcallian relics. We'll see. Even if it's not the Bard's desk, I obtained a couple of rather nice books that are contemporary to the Fall of the Cearcall."

Cal smiled. "I bet they've made an interesting read."

"I'm having them copied. Then I'll read the copy and return to the original only as needed. Kensal nearly fell over himself when I mentioned

I wanted them copied. He'll be coming to Oedran to deliver them."

Tain looked over. "He's the historian, isn't he? Can I meet him?"

Arkyn raised an eyebrow. "Whatever for?"

"Curiosity's sake… Never mind. Father probably won't let me out of the valley."

Arkyn caught his brother's frustration. "Tain, it's for our safety that father is, well, father."

"Yes, but you—"

"I'm older and must be seen. I wish, I truly do, that it wasn't the case, but it is. I'm sure father will agree to you being in Oedran soon."

"Only because you'll tell him I'm pining."

"All right, be morose," retorted Arkyn, "but I promise I won't tell father."

"But you will," mumbled Tain.

"I said a *promise* and I meant it! Can't you trust me?"

Elantha and Cal were silently watching the brothers. Arkyn was eyeing Tain with an injured honour. Tain wouldn't meet the gaze and so Arkyn left the room.

To his and Elantha's surprise, Cal said, "That was unfair, sir."

"What do you know?" Tain threw back harshly.

Cal left, reasoning he had three good friends at Ceardlann. If one couldn't see his foolishness, he'd support the one with injured pride. He found Arkyn in the snug, staring into an empty fireplace as though flames burnt brightly there.

"He's frustrated…" murmured Cal.

Arkyn swallowed. "Aren't we all? Alcis knows I am on his behalf but to blank me…"

"Was ungracious and unforgivable?"

"No, I'll forgive him. I always will; he's my brother. I know his frustration as I know myself and I understand how it can alter someone. I just don't know what I can do."

"Could you not… I'm sorry, but could you not speak to the King?"

"I promised I wouldn't, Cal. It was still a promise, even though he rejected it."

Cal watched him for a few moments. Arkyn was deep in thought. "I ought to finish my letters."

Arkyn smiled. "To whom do you write?"

"Family, friends and acquaintances, Your Highness. Might I suggest something?"

"Why ask? Between *friends*, you should just suggest."

Cal smiled. "Then I'll be franker than I planned to be and say my Prince did order it so…"

"Stop taking courtier lessons and get on with it."

"Go and lie down, sir, you're *now* looking ghastly."

"Certainly not courteous at all there, Cal. Don't tell Tain. He'll worry when he's calmed down."

* * *

The following day, Adeone received Cal's letter. It told him more than Cal could ever put into words. He made quiet arrangements and rode for Ceardlann. Tain received him with a welcome that told Adeone Cal been right, and Tain was entering a difficult age. He suspected at once that his brother had betrayed his promise. Cal admitted he'd written to the King without any other's instigation. Adeone and Arkyn, not to mention Cal, all watched Tain's reaction to this news with apprehension. Was it the first fracture in a firm friendship?

Tain bit his lip, glaring at Cal before running off.

Adeone glanced at Arkyn and Cal. "At least it wasn't worse. Thank you, Cal. I enjoyed your letter; you should write more often, if not to tell me I've been too long absent simply to send other news."

Cal blanched, aghast. "Your Majesty, if I had ever dreamt the letter might be a criticism, I should never have written it."

Adeone ruffled his hair. "I never took it as such. I have been in Oedran too long. I ought to find my younger son. Arkyn, make Cal believe me; he's still a little pale."

He was gone and Arkyn said, "I didn't think you'd *write*."

"I haven't a messenger, sir, have no intention of trying to call one, and I didn't know when he'd next come. The Comptroller was most obliging when I gave him the letter."

Arkyn laughed. "I'm sure he was. Come on, let's raid the kitchens. Then you can explain why you'll not call a messenger."

"Both Your Highness and Prince Tain have one and knowing I can't contact you by messenger keeps my father hoping the friendship will vanish when Prince Tain returns more permanently to Oedran."

"Do you mean to say that you wouldn't want to contact us?"

"Your Highness gave me a writing desk; therefore, I can write to you," replied Cal with a grin.

"Exceptionally long letters to my memory."

"There's so much I need to tell you to stop me getting *all* the blame."

"Yes, between yours and Tain's accounts, it is always the other who's to blame. How am I to reconcile the two accounts? How am I to know with whom an idea originally lodged?"

Elantha's voice said, "Normally it's half and half. Is Uncle Adeone here?"

Arkyn put his arm around his cousin's shoulders. "Elantha, whose *are*

239

the madcap schemes?"

"As I said, both of theirs. You didn't answer my question."

"Yes, father is here somewhere. Tain's disgruntled with us. Me for not breaking my promise and Cal for writing to father to tell him that Tain was missing Oedran."

"Well, I said I thought the Prince was feeling trapped," clarified Cal.

"Good. He's being a right misery guts," stated Elantha.

Arkyn smiled. "So thought I, little flower, but I'd made a promise."

"That's your heart and honour, sir, unfortunately I am the fool who never stops to think. I have betrayed a friend." Cal blinked hard.

"No, you tried to *help* your friends. There's no shame or blame in that. It's just a pity that all friendships cannot always agree. Elantha, make him see he is not to blame for Tain feeling aggrieved."

"But I am, sir, that's the point. If I hadn't written…"

Arkyn lost patience. "No, Cal, you should have written, just maybe not have admitted to writing quite so soon."

Cal nodded as they entered the kitchens to be greeted by Cook.

"We're very busy, sirs."

"We're feeling morose, Cook," said Arkyn.

"If I give you some food, will you leave us alone?"

"All right, we will make ourselves scarce. Make sure dinner's a good one and we might even forgive you."

"It'll be a good one, Your Highness. Now…"

"We're going, we're going. I don't know, bullied by our own staff."

"Only with practice, sir."

Two hours later, Tain said to Cal, "I'm sorry…"

"No, sir, I am…"

"Don't be a clown…"

"Then don't be a fool…"

Chapter 48
GENERAL BANDITRY
Tretaldai, Week 18 – 10th Meithal, 17th Easis 1212
Inner Office

THE FOLLOWING WEEK whilst reading Arkyn's report on the review, Adeone looked up as Richardson asked if he'd got time to see General Paturn and Major Wynfeld. Half distracted, he enquired if it was important.

"I'm afraid the General wouldn't say, Your Majesty."

That had Adeone's attention. The General might hold a King's Token but it was rare for him to fail to declare his reasons for needing to see the King. Adeone put the report to one side. Gravely he asked Richardson to close the door.

"Is there anything on my desk that needs to be sorted as a matter of extreme urgency?"

"There shouldn't be, Sire. We cleared most of it so that you could concentrate on His Highness' report. His Highness was meant to be reporting to you in person tomorrow, to answer any queries."

Adeone got up. "He's meant to arrive in the next couple of hours – when he does, ask him to come in. I don't know what the General will discuss but, whatever it is, it's important and I think it may be valuable if Prince Arkyn was included."

Richardson nodded. "Shall I clear your desk of paperwork?"

Adeone's lips twitched. "No, thank you. If Paturn sees it's empty, he might well fill it up. As it's coming up to lunchtime, ask Simkins to see we get some refreshment."

Adeone glanced at the General and Major as they saluted. Something in Wynfeld's posture suggested the Major wasn't quite sure why the meeting had been called.

Adeone waved them to chairs. The General sat with a word of thanks but the Major moved back a couple of steps and, as Paturn didn't make a move to object, Adeone let it pass. The Major technically answered to the General before the King.

Sitting down, Adeone steepled his fingers against his mouth. "How concerned should I be?"

"It's not rebellion, Sire," replied Paturn. "I fear we have a situation developing with the malcontents of the empire – the bandits, outlaws and outcasts. I've been speaking to the Major of the Northern Empire. He's hearing increased reports of incidents on the main highways. He's at Garth, currently, but I didn't like to approach the Exarch without first alerting Your Majesty. We thought we'd cleared the ridge a couple of years ago but we might not have managed it as successfully as we believed."

Adeone made a couple of notes. "I'll speak to the Exarch myself. Thank you for not doing so. Do we know the geographical spread of the problem?"

"Not yet, sir. I've told the Northern Major and Wynfeld to start taking detailed reports. I think it's in Anapara and Bayan, but Bayan has always been more volatile and I believe we receive more reports because of it. Major Axton understands what's at stake."

Adeone nodded. "Good. I don't need someone half blind—"

A knock at the door preceded Richardson announcing Arkyn without preliminaries. Wynfeld, standing by the door, saluted as both Adeone and Paturn got to their feet. Moving out of the line of sight between the King and Prince, the General also saluted.

Arkyn's acknowledged the salutes with a quick nod, met his father's gaze and bowed. "Sire."

Adeone smiled. "You're even earlier than I expected."

Arkyn grinned. "I thought a couple of hours wouldn't matter, Your Majesty, and I rather gathered that Prince Tain and Master Calumiel wouldn't need my assistance with their current endeavour."

Aware the General and Major were amongst the men closest to him, Adeone allowed himself to groan. "I shan't ask what that endeavour was."

"Probably wise, Your Majesty. Richardson mentioned you wished for a word, if I'm not interrupting?"

"The General was outlining a developing problem with bandits."

"Right, Sire. Where have the reports come from, General?"

As Paturn reached the end of a swift explanation, Adeone said, "I believe we should resume the discussion."

He crossed to the table putting down his notes. Well used to the procedure, he hardly realised the General pulled out his chair and seated him but he noticed the Major did the same for Arkyn and it made him smile. Here was proof that his son had become the official he had to be.

"Please take a seat, General, and with your permission I have no objection to Wynfeld being seated also." Moments later, with writing materials from the centre of the table at everyone's hand, Adeone continued, "I want to know the geographical spread of this problem."

Arkyn dipped a pen, noting the request. "It's empire wide, Sire."

That made them all stop.

Adeone said, "Go on."

"There were reports in 1209 and 1210 about Bayan; there were reports last year in Areal, not to mention the bandits captured during our journey north. The Chief Merchant of Paras mentioned a couple to me in passing over a banquet and, having once talked with Secretary Thomkins in Tera about the troubles of long journeys, he mentioned that there had been reports in Gerymor, which was why he was reluctant for Karl and Elsa to travel there alone—"

The General paused, "I'm sorry to interrupt, sir, but there were several names there that I don't recognise."

Arkyn smiled. "Of course, my apologies, General. Secretary Thomkins is, or was, Chief Secretary to the Margrave, Karl and Elsa are his children – their mother, who has now forsaken them, lives in Gerymor. Your

Majesty, I wouldn't be surprised that if you made careful enquiries in Lufian, Denshire and Tradere that you would find reports there. I might suggest, Major Wynfeld, that getting men into the yearly Frander at Byfa might well prove evidential of the spread of trouble. That trade fair has people from all over the empire attending it…" Arkyn caught his father's eye. "My apologies, Sire. I've started rambling again."

Adeone nodded. "Thank you, Prince Arkyn, but I wouldn't call your conclusions rambling. Are we sure it's just banditry?"

The General never hesitated. "That's all that's reached my ears, sir. Wynfeld?"

"I've not had anything brought to my attention, Sire, but I shall pursue the issue closely. Might I make enquires of the Guardian of the Isles?"

Adeone said, "Please do, Major. He should know if there are any pirates plying their trade. Is there anything we can do as an immediate step to curtail this?"

Arkyn, who'd been thinking, was surprised when the General replied neutrally with,

"I think we need to see how wide the spread is, sir."

"If you think that's best, General," said Adeone.

Arkyn interrupted, "Sire, didn't King Altarius have yardage cleared either side of the major highways of trees and shrubs? Anything that could act as a cover for malcontents and rebels?"

Paturn replied, "Yes, Your Highness, as a response to the 1169 rebellion. It kept the army occupied for quite a while."

"Yet it hasn't been maintained, General. On my ride from Paras, it intrigued me how much growth had occurred. Sire, might I suggest the policy is reintroduced? Especially on the military roads and the main highways. It might also be time to replace some of the mile markers."

"Prince Arkyn, you realise you've just requested an overhaul of the entire network of maintained roads?" queried Adeone, privately impressed.

"Yes, Sire; well, I missed off undertaking the repairs needed to some; however, if everything else is being done, couldn't we get that done as well?"

Adeone refused to look at the General, but a smile played around his lips as he asked for justification.

"The army is reliant on decent highways and it discourages banditry, Your Majesty," stated Arkyn. "I am aware, however, of the financial implications such a scheme would place on the empire's funds. It might be worth working province by province with the reviews as the mechanism for it. The Terasian Review already allowed for the roads to be improved. I'm not sure how far Your Majesty has read the Anaparian one, but I have recommended that the roads to Oedran are kept repaired and maintained with regular checks. The Chief Merchant there proved to me the loss caused by bad roads to our economy. I'm not sure what I'll find in Lufian next year; that is, Sire, if you wish me to do another review."

Adeone avoided the Major's eye. "The money isn't limitless."

"I am aware of that, sir, but surely it is cheaper to send one team of people out to work on the complete road and its environs the first time than to send two or three teams out, each to do a different job at different times. Major Wynfeld, how many men are allocated in Anapara for road maintenance?"

"Half a unit per regiment, sir."

Arkyn did a bit of quick arithmetic. "That's about five per cent of a regiment undertaking maintenance to the roads full time."

The General said, "Your Highness, they're not maintaining the roads full time. They maintain them when there is cause to do so."

"Thank you, General. I think we've found the reason the roads are in the state that they are. Your Majesty, as I understand it, each town or city in Anapara handles the roads within its bounds, using men employed for that purpose."

"That is correct, Prince Arkyn."

"Yet the maintenance of the roads outside of those bounds is done by very few men and only when there '*is cause to do so*'. Who determines that cause, Sire?"

Adeone, trying not to show his amusement, raised an eyebrow at the General. "I think that's one for you, General."

The General deferred to Wynfeld. "Major?"

Wynfeld glanced at the General. "Very well, sir." He turned to his Prince, knowing how little he liked prevarication. "Your Highness, the maintenance of the roads is started when someone the captain or commander of a fort can't ignore complains."

The General gave a small cough.

"I thought that might be the case," observed Adeone mildly.

Prince Arkyn smiled. "Yes. If we're to deal with this growing problem of banditry, then we need to clear the roads. Sire, might I ask a blunt question of the General?"

Adeone said, "Of course."

"Thank you, sir. General, would you consider my concerns ignorable?"

Paturn weighed up his answer. "No, Your Highness, but I think they would have to be substantiated."

"Do you count the Review Report of Anapara as substantiation?"

Adeone was watching proceedings with what Percival Wealsman might have called an ironic eye.

"I would say it is a valuable document, sir, that might well help," replied

Paturn, "but I cannot allocate the men and resources for such a complete overhaul as Your Highness thinks is necessary. I have only a limited number of men in Anapara."

Adeone gave his son a hand. "You have nearly thirty legions in the province, Paturn."

"Yes, Sire, many of them still training."

Arkyn's lips twitched. "Then what better time for them to learn all the skills they need? It's in excess of thirty thousand men, General. Are you telling me that there is no way you could spare a regiment for a cisluna-month each on a rota basis, working from each fort, to maintain the roads which they march over regularly?"

The General eyed the young Prince. "I would have to examine the figures, Your Highness, but we might manage that for a short time."

Adeone said, "Maybe you could work together on those figures? Thank you. Returning to the problem of the bandits. Make acting on reports of banditry the primary objective of the fifteen legions on the Gardian Ridge. We'll discover what's happening elsewhere in the empire and determine if there is a common strategy that we can apply." He smiled slightly. "For now, that's all we can achieve. Thank you, General, Major. I look forward to your reports on the matter." Once the officers had left, Adeone said, "You realise you take over proceedings with a simple air, don't you?"

Arkyn hesitated. "I'm sorry, Your Majesty, I never meant to do any such thing."

"Had I objected, you'd have known about it."

"Would I, sir? With the General and Major there?"

"In that sort of meeting, yes. Your questions were the type that my greater knowledge of the mechanisms at work would have rendered laughable. There is much they will assume you know as a king but as a prince you have more licence to ask the simple but revealing questions – take advantage of it. When people have to explain what is well known to them, and considered by them as obvious, they will start to question that knowledge and sometimes the practices as well. Continue asking the questions and coming up with the compromises but remember that you won't get universal support."

"I know that, Sire. I just hope I didn't alienate the General."

"I don't think you did. I think you merely discomforted him. Remember, he's had a long career in the army. Listen to him, you'll learn a lot, but also remember you *can* request him to do things. You are a higher officer of my army than he is; many people forget that, including yourself."

"It's not that I forget it, sir, but I don't feel like I should give orders during peacetime."

Adeone put an arm around his son's shoulders. "Thank you for the consideration, but I'm sure no-one will mind as long as they're sensible ones. Now, I hesitate to ask this, but what *was* Tain up to when you left?"

Chapter 49

COURT TALK

Evening

Court

THAT EVENING, in a corner of the Court, three Lords of Oedran were talking quietly. Nervous their conversation might be overheard they were standing so they could see if anyone approached from any direction, which in itself raised suspicions and eyebrows.

"Tyron, you need to be careful; he's noticed your daughter," warned Para.

Lord Teran shrugged. "My daughter will be married soon enough. He knows he has my loyalty but my family is not for his delectation..."

Lord Cearis laughed. "Do you believe that? You're a fool. If he came asking, you wouldn't dare refuse. He could destroy us all—"

"Not without destroying himself, and he knows that."

"There's means of destroying men without them talking," pointed out Para. "Or have you made depositions we should know about, Tyron?"

"Do you think I'd tell anyone if I had?" scoffed Teran. "Have you?"

"With spies around every corner, no – there's no-one I can trust."

"Not even us?" enquired Cearis with a grin.

"Not even you, Ris."

Teran frowned. "Surely you don't believe there are spies around every corner, Joren? I thought I was paranoid."

"Everyone is a spy for someone, or have you forgotten we ourselves hand information back? Can you trust your entire household? Can you even trust your family? Every year it gets more dangerous for we who are loyal to the traditional ideals of the empire. The so-called Major of Oedran isn't easily fooled and no-one I know has found his price yet."

Teran cursed. "I want to deal with him—"

"Then you're a fool. We'll get no thanks for it; it would have the King turning over every stone. Whoever murdered Jones was foolish enough. No, we need to continue to buy people lower down. It's ridiculously easy."

Cearis murmured, "Isn't it? I don't think the Major is our problem though, not at the moment. It looks like we've bigger fish to catch, or have both of you been deaf to his requests?"

Para sighed. "No, but it's going to take some figuring out for them both.

How does one discredit such close friends of the King without being on the receiving end of His Majesty's fury? I don't know about you but I quite like being a Lord of Oedran and being in Oedran is where I want to be."

"You'll have to show your allegiance sooner or later," observed Teran, "and I don't think the King is fooled by your seemingly neutral stance."

"I know he's not but equally he knows I'm not going to risk everything."

"Oh dear, of course, you've only one son… Marry again. I'm sure we can find you a bride."

"Keep your nose out of my family affairs, Tyron, lest I invite someone to a family dinner of yours. "

A server approached them and they broke off their conversation until he had passed.

When he was out of earshot, Teran commented, "Feel free, Joren, but I'm not the only one with a beautiful daughter, am I? You ought to be more careful, Julius Landis has been eyeing her up recently."

Para grimaced. "He can eye all he likes. Neither I nor his father will agree to the match and that's all that matters. Anyway, the young man has been eyeing up every unmarried lady at Court. He's also a drunkard. It's only because the Steward's too afraid of the King and Lord Landis that something hasn't been said."

"He reminds me of Festus years ago…" observed Tyron.

"Yes, but without the saving graces. I might tell my daughter to cultivate his company. Through Julius there's a link to the Princes and from there…"

Eyes darting to the edges of the room, Cearis murmured, "You'd be a fool to do that. Prince Arkyn isn't at all gullible, and he will spot ulterior motives quickly."

"Is he really as astute as that?" scoffed Teran. "I'm surprised."

"He's not a fool, trust me. I had to answer some questions recently and just hope you never have to. He saw through my answers and—"

"He never commented?"

Cearis shook his head. "No, but both of us knew he had seen my answers for what they were."

Para shrugged. "I've heard he takes over the King's meetings when His Majesty is there."

"I doubt that. I expect His Majesty is just being too tolerant of his son. Allowing him to learn through methods unthinkable to us. I'm not saying I agree," added Teran hastily, "but you've got to admit that he's not insisted on Prince Arkyn being at his books since he turned cisan-age."

"How do we know? He's at Ceardlann a lot and his former tutor is also teaching Prince Tain. I can't believe that His Majesty wanted an advisor to teach Prince Tain; if that's so, one has to ask oneself why Spellen's there. What went off in Tera, I wonder? After all, Spellen was reappointed shortly after their return.”

“All that occurred there is a review and controversial appointments,” grumbled Teran.

“Yes, those appointments were the reason I expect,” stated Cearis.

Para hesitated. “No, I don’t think the King saw them as controversial and therein lies our whole point. A minor lord and a man of no rank in charge of an entire province, it’s unthinkable, unbelievable and untenable.”

“Isn’t it just but a slight correction is needed, Lord Wealsman is now an overlord,” pointed out Cearis.

Teran crooked an eyebrow. “Supposedly. Come on, if a man born cisan can never be considered of the alunan, no matter how much money he earns to give his children that rank, what makes you think Terasians view Wealsman as anything but a minor lord?”

Cearis said, “I’ve heard he’s well liked.”

“Every man who is a friend of kings is well liked, which is why so much energy is expended in discrediting them, which brings us neatly to our task. Do either of you know *anything* that might help?”

Para shook his head. “No, and that’s worrying me. Everyone has skeletons to discover, don’t they?”

Cearis considered. “I thought father said yours had crossed swords with him in the past. There was something to do with your grandfather, I think. Something hushed up. Something your father couldn’t seek revenge for given his standing in the eyes of the FitzAlcis. We’re not going to find anything recent, are we?”

Tyron muttered, “Kenelm might help, Joren. Watch out, Lux is coming.”

Para turned. “Evening, Lux.”

“Evening, Para. You realise you’ve all been spotted?”

“What’s wrong with three Lords of Oedran talking to each other?”

“Nothing, but it’s more your hushed voices and general bearing. Teran, I’m to give you this and, before you read it, maybe we should take a walk.”

Once they’d gone, Para said, “So who do you think is most in favour at the moment?”

Cearis smirked. “Do we discuss such things? Here? Now? How very foolish. I’d say Tyron. You?”

“Lux. That letter was an invitation and one’s never invited to dinner with Lord Scanlon for a congenial evening.”

“I wonder if he’ll go.”

“I wouldn’t like to see the reaction if he didn’t. I had a request. It wasn’t pleasant; the fact I’m a Lord of Oedran was the only thing that saved me,” admitted Para. ·

"He would never physically discipline any but a servant," mused Cearis. "Have you seen him when he does? And have you forgotten Finn?"

"No. I don't think we're meant to. His aims are just though."

Para nodded. "Yes, but care is needed. Once he's where he wants to be, his methods will change. Server! Are we invisible or are you blind? Our glasses are empty."

PART 4

Chapter 50
PROGRESS

Alunadai, Week 22 – 8th Seral, 1st Seris 1212
Landis House

LORD LANDIS EXAMINED the evidence in front of him, disbelievingly. He walked along hallways and landings, ran his hand over familiar furniture. An hour later, he mounted Skit and left for the Palace.

As he entered the Inner Office, he saw Adeone's lips twitching whilst he read a report. Eyes narrowing, he asked, "What's making you smile, Sire?"

"Oh, nothing. How was your *ride*?"

"You know, don't you? You've known for weeks, and you've kept me so busy here that I've left everything in Cornelia's hands and she, she's… Did you tell her not to tell me?"

"No. Of course not. I wouldn't interfere in your life that much."

"Just this much," muttered Landis.

"How's your new house?"

"Rather more completed than I expected, sir."

Adeone laughed. "I'm glad."

"Have we been that bad as guests?"

"Were you guests? I never noticed. Sit down, stop grouching and tell me."

Landis rested his hand on the back of a chair. "Oh no, Sire. You're not avoiding everything. Richardson says you've nothing on for a couple of hours. Come and see."

"You want me to?" As Landis crooked an eyebrow, he pulled a wry. "How many guards do I need?"

Landis finally cracked a smile. "None. Your Defender will be there."

"See the stables and my guards alerted then."

"Everyone is waiting for us, Your Majesty."

"Revenge comes in many forms," said Adeone, amused.

Cornelia was in the Audience Chamber. She curtsied swiftly as Adeone entered, caught his grin and returned a smile.

"We're in trouble, Lady Landis. Or, at least, I am."

She chuckled, slipping her arm through her husband's. "I'm sure that's not possible, Your Majesty."

* * *

They rode in at the main gates. The front of Landis House looked much the same as it always had but the new wing, where the old house had been, now appeared seamless. Once the stone had weathered, it would be difficult to tell they were built a hundred years apart. Grooms ran forward to take their horses. Dismounting lithely, Adeone handed Pursuit's bridle to Clodach and caught Landis' eye.

An unspoken conversation later, they both understood the other was impressed. Landis led the way into the house where Backery held the main doors open for them. Adeone entered the hallway for the first time in months and whistled under his breath. A broad sweeping staircase with polished handrails led up, through the door at the top were glimpses of marble-topped tables and carved doors.

The passage that had led to the old house was still there. Landis led the way along it, saying, "We kept the ground floor on this wing much the same, sir. After all, it's easiest with the stable and kitchen yard being in front. My steward's and warden's offices have been expanded to give them more room and the kitchens are more spacious, for which, I believe my cook is grateful."

As they entered the kitchens, the reply reached their ears, "Aye, as long as Your Lordship watches where you're going."

Adeone chuckled. "How are you, Cookie?"

"Glad to have a kitchen again, Sire. When do I need to expect the mayhem to commence?"

Adeone's lips twitched. "What do you think, Landis?"

"I'll let you know, Cookie, or Lady Landis will."

They left the kitchen by a far door and walked up the backstairs, coming out in a long hallway with several doors leading off it.

Landis explained. "We've tried to use this area for our trusted servants to give them a bit of space. So, the Kadeems have a sitting room, and our other senior servants have one too. We've got the nursery and schoolroom here. It felt odd to move them. A couple of guest rooms…" They turned the corner and were back where the stairs led from the entrance hall. "Family rooms here. I've created a few extra so the girls can all have their own. They're smaller than the old ones, but I don't think they'll mind. Bathrooms and dressing rooms between each set of two, so they'll still have to share. Which is why mine and Cornelia's rooms are down the far end."

Adeone chuckled. "You're a coward."

"Yes. I am." Landis continued leading the way. "We've a linen cupboard and storage room – Cornelia's sensible suggestion…" He turned left down the final landing. "Mine and Cornelia's domain, and also…" He opened a door directly ahead of them. "Your Majesty's room."

Adeone gaped. The room was large, with windows overlooking the gardens. A fourposter bed had brocade curtains in scarlet and gold. A comfortable chair invited him to sink into it and a small desk already had writing impedimenta laid out. To one side, a door stood ajar, the edge of a bath visible. Mirrored sconces already held four-hour wax candles and, under his feet, a woollen carpet begged him to take his shoes off.

Landis beside him waited.

After a minute, Adeone said, "Why?"

"You have stayed before. We thought it would be nice if you knew you weren't an inconvenience when you did."

Adeone blinked. "I… didn't expect… Cornelia, can't you do anything about him?"

She chuckled and gave him a hug, whispering, "What makes you think it is only him?"

He caught her eye. "Thank you."

"You've done so much for us, for the children. This is nothing."

Adeone shook his head. "I overwork Festus regularly. Maybe I'll have to do it more often if this is the thanks."

Landis laughed. "Revenge comes in many forms, was it, sir?"

"Oh, shut up."

Chuckling, they left the room. Walking down a flight of stairs, they returned to the ground floor by a door to the new terrace overlooking redesigned gardens. Landis, though, turned back to the house. He motioned to rooms on his left. "Extra sitting rooms for when the children get older and married. At the moment, being used to store things I need to sort out." He opened another carved panelled door, this time with a motif of scrolls and books. "The library, Sire. They managed to save the entirety of the old one, for which I am exceedingly grateful, given the rarity of some of the texts."

Adeone entered. Where most houses of great lords had a few shelves in a room kept for the sake of it, Landis had floor to ceiling shelves in alcoves by the fireplace opposite the door. There was shelving on every other wall, each side of the three doors. Getting his bearings, Adeone realised a new door had been created into the drawing room on his left and the one on his right must lead to Landis' study. Their panelled doors weren't carved but rather painted with scenes from history or landscapes.

"Are you sure you've got enough shelves?"

Landis shrugged. "Never, sir. Come through to my study…"

"I'll leave you to it. If you'll excuse me, Sire?" said Cornelia.

Adeone smiled. "You're welcome to join us."

"I realise that, sir, but I do need to see everyone is happy. I'm sure Festus doesn't need my sobering presence."

Adeone entered the study. The last time he'd seen it, it had been open to the elements. Now square-paned windows overlooked the gardens on two walls, a fire was blazing in the grate and two old sagging couches upholstered in worn green leather were placed strategically in front of it. Behind them, in front of the windows, Landis' new desk looked too tidy, too unused, but Adeone recognised the comfortable chair. Sideboards were by a door that must lead into the hallway near where the stairs led up to the first floor.

Landis waved to the couches and poured his friend a whiskey from a glass decanter. "Welcome to Landis House, Sire. It's been completed in remarkably quick time."

Adeone laughed, taking his drink. "Your thanks are appreciated."

"I'm in shock. I was honestly expecting it to take a year. Two seasons wasn't even a dream. You must have supplied an army to get it done."

"Now you mention it, they needed something to do."

"You can't mean—"

"I do. They did a lot of the heavy lifting and logistics. It built strength and resilience and taught some recruits new skills that they can put into practice as they tour the empire. Buildings always need repairs. All I'm bothered about is whether the work meets your expectations.

"It surpasses it, Sire," said Landis. "When Cornelia asked me earlier if I wanted to inspect progress, I wasn't expecting a completed house, let alone such a pristine one. Even the servants' areas have been completed with perfection instead of pragmatism. That was pleasing. Thank you. In all seriousness, when would you like us to move out of Ceardlann and the Palace?"

"Whenever you're ready. The company has been enjoyable for all of us, but this is your home. It's a couple of weeks until the Mundimri. I won't be offended if you wish to spend it here, or if you want to leave it until after, so the nearcousins can run riot at Ceardlann and your new house doesn't get destroyed."

Landis chuckled. "I'll ask Cornelia. Thank you. With Emrys arriving, it may be best to not complicate matters."

After a pause, Adeone said, "You didn't have to do that room for me."

"We did. It doesn't need to be general knowledge. Only the Kadeems will be allowed in to clean and tidy, so it should remain safe."

Adeone tilted his head. "Do you ever doubt them?"

"No. Our families have an intertwined history going back generations. I don't expect or require gratitude from them. They're free to leave if they wish. In fact, Kadeem did – to work for you—"

"And I'm sure the fact you realised Arkyn would need a manservant had nothing to do with that!"

Landis' lips twitched. "Why did it have to be me? William and Simkins are both more than capable of plotting in our best interests."

Adeone snorted. "The three of you conspire regularly in mine. Well, maybe not William so much. I don't suppose any of his remaining sons want to be Tain's manservant?"

Landis shook his head. "Adam is settled with Julius, and Harold isn't old enough yet. Are you having trouble? What about Joe from Ceardlann?"

"I've asked. He prefers to remain in the valley. Same with David. Though they will look after Tain and Cal at Ceardlann once they leave the nursery. They're happy to do that. If Simkins can't find someone, I'll leave it all in the Steward's hands, I think. There are enough footmen in the Palace for him to recommend someone for promotion. There's a bit of time left. Though I'm hoping by the end of summer next year, it'll be settled."

"They're all growing so quickly. I can't believe Ira's two, Lucius five and Antonia nine. Let alone Marcelea turning thirteen in a couple of weeks and the twins are sixteen. Where's it all gone?"

Adeone smiled. "Into history, as Wynfeld once said to me. How's Julius? I've not seen much of him lately."

Landis sighed. "Truth be told, I don't know what to do with him these days. He's forgetting himself. I thought the Macia trip might help but he's still being rash. He'll get himself into more trouble than even we did."

Adeone crooked an eyebrow. "If I hadn't been FitzAlcis, I'd have been in far more trouble, Festus. Maybe being at home will help him. It can't have been easy studying in Oedran with most of his family at Ceardlann. You and Cornelia have been busy too."

"True," said Landis. "Were you drawing my mind away from this house?"

"Actually no. I am worried about what Scanlon's up to. Your presence at Court and counsel has been invaluable. It's amazing how having a Defender around concentrates people's minds."

"I'm glad I'm useful. I realise my brood is at Ceardlann but I don't think I've actually seen Tain or El for weeks."

"They're fine. I think having had her cousins around has helped El. Tain is still Tain and plotting who-knows-what with Cal.

Landis chuckled. "How's young Cal coping these days?"

"I don't know. Did we do the right thing in taking him to Ceardlann? His parents still haven't visited and I think he's missing his family more than he'll ever admit. I would hate to think that our actions have resulted in misery for him."

"Don't doubt your decisions, sir. I don't think, however homesick he might get, he wants to leave. As long as he gets to see his family, he'll be happy. Tain is far better for the company and Arkyn also. Have you forgotten how frustrated they used to get with each other? Cal's become a friend to them both and they couldn't have a better one."

"I begin to wonder if it fractures."

"No. I don't think it does. They are growing up and not at the easiest age."

Adeone nodded. "You can say that again. Spellen thinks I'm a fool having Cal trained as I am, but I can't believe that he'll simply mind the shop once Arkyn is king. Can you?"

Landis gave a snort. "No. Whatever his father wishes, he'll be a friend of kings and that never ends in running a shop. He's a good head on his shoulders. Top up?"

"Might as well. Then I ought to get back to the Palace before Court this evening. I wonder if Rhian will be there."

"I'm sure she could be, Adeone. Why?"

Adeone saw his friend's grin. "She's my cousin and, so far, I've had very little chance to talk to her. What else?"

"Far be it from me to speculate, Your Majesty."

"Oh, shut up. Stop teasing me," grouched Adeone. "You know it's nothing more."

"I am yours to command." (Adeone glared at him.) "It's only what they'll all be saying."

"That annoys me more than anything else. I can't have a life that doesn't become the gossip of the day. Why can't I talk with the female members of my family as well as the male? Why must there be speculation?"

"I've not seen anyone speculating if you talk to Lady Amara, Sire."

"Maybe there could be a good reason for that – she's my aunt is the start of it."

"I wonder if anyone ever would mention the end of it, sir?"

Adeone laughed. "Probably not. Are you up for Court?"

"It would be my greatest pleasure to accompany Your Majesty there."

The King once more glared at him. "There's one thing missing in this study, Festus: something I can throw at you."

Chapter 51

OBSESSION?

Pentadai, Week 22 – 12th Seral, 5th Seris 1212
Inner Office

HAVING DINED PRIVATELY with Arkyn the night before, Adeone sat considering everything his son had told him. He'd have to do something. He sent for the judge and an hour later Tancred entered the Inner Office and knelt with a trace of anxiety in his manner.

"Get up, James."

"Sire, I think I should stay here."

Adeone considered for the briefest of moments. He'd known Tancred all his life, and Tancred had known him. He knew the foibles of the judge as the judge knew his. "Why?"

"I might have caused unintentional harm to His Highness, sir."

Adeone regarded Tancred thoughtfully. "You mean you're the one responsible for getting my son to enjoy the law?"

"Sire, I have caused His Highness to be obsessed by it."

Adeone walked over to Tancred; he offered his hand to the elderly judge. "Please get up. I detest seeing friends kneel." He waved to the chairs by the fireplace. "I did want to talk to you about Tain and his current enthusiasm. You've used the word obsessed; do you truly believe it has become an unhealthy zeal?"

Tancred seated himself. "I am becoming worried, Your Majesty. His Highness is a passionate boy; it can be hard to tell when he has become too immersed in a subject. With my not being at Ceardlann it is sometimes doubly hard."

"I understand that. Arkyn has also become concerned. What can I do without crushing all the enthusiasm out of him?"

Tancred paused. "Sire, I would rather not encroach on this area."

Adeone regarded him; the old man's eyes were still kind but had become reserved. "James, please. Do you think Tain would benefit from a couple of weeks where I lock his books away and make him take time for a breath?"

"If you are determined to have an answer, Sire, I would say that it is probably a wise move, but a week might suffice."

Adeone nodded. "Then I'll give him and young Cal a week without any lessons. They've not had a true break since the beginning of the year. I do not mean to interfere in the law, but what exactly are you teaching my younger son?"

"It is no interference, Your Majesty…" replied Tancred as he explained.

A couple of minutes later, Adeone asked, "Have you examined his responsibilities as Justiciar?"

"Yes, Sire, but I am introducing them alongside his other studies. I do not want, or wish, to frighten him at this stage. Come the summer, I shall increase the regularity I speak of such things but I would rather he understood to what his responsibilities will pertain before I explain in full those responsibilities. I am hoping, with your permission, sir, when he is thirteen or fourteen, to have him sit with me in the courtroom and to learn by observation other aspects."

Adeone nodded. "Sometimes observation is best. It's a shame that not all life's lessons can be taught that way. Yet one can learn much from listening to those whose lives have provided them with many an experience." He caught Tancred's eye. "I speak from familiarity, James. Don't make all your lessons about the law. Leave some of that to Spellen. I'd like it if you could guide my son as well. I learned much from you and Uncle Lachlan; I'd like my son to as well."

Tancred heard the sincerity. "Your Majesty, you flatter me unfoundedly. If, however, it is your wish that I vary my teaching, I will be more than willing to do so."

Adeone shook his head slightly. "James, your modesty is sometimes the most surprising part of your personality. I think, as you're a mentor to the Prince, I would like him to learn more than the law from you."

Tancred studied Adeone's face. "I cannot promise to be all you wish, sir, but I can do my best to show His Highness that there is more than one type of life to live."

Adeone nodded. "He might have need of the knowledge over the coming years and, even if not, I believe it will make him a better justiciar. Judge Fairson was rather narrow-minded when teaching Lord Scanlon and although my brother's personality led him down one route his mentor's teaching would have had an effect."

"Yes, sir, I suppose it would have done, but Judge Fairson is not a particularly harsh man."

"No, he isn't; he is just of the aristocracy and being from a large family had to make his mark."

"It is the wish of most men to do that, sir," replied Tancred.

Adeone eyed him. "I don't believe it is *your* wish, James."

"No, Sire, but then I have preferred to live my life quietly."

"I wish I too could have had a quiet life, or at least a quiet*er* life. When were you next meant to be seeing my troublesome son?"

Tancred smiled. "Imperadai, Sire."

"Make it the following week. I'll go over to Ceardlann tomorrow and let him know."

"Very good, sir. Might I invite His Highness to dinner one evening soon? I have some items in my library that I believe he'd be interested in, but I shall be careful when I show them to him."

Adeone chuckled. "I'm sure he'd be honoured to accept. Now, if I'm to take tomorrow off I ought to clear my desk. Could you ask Richardson to join me, please?"

* * *

Six minutes later, in the Outer Office, Richardson eyed the new secretary. "Marcle, why have documents from a week ago only landed on the King's desk today?"

"They weren't urgent, sir, and others took priority."

"However, His Majesty now has a protracted day because you can't prioritise. If it is three days before it's needed, it arrives on the King's desk. I made that plain when you arrived in the office."

"You did, sir, but it perhaps didn't sink in amongst everything else."

Kenton winced and, hearing a soft footfall, glanced up; he stayed seated at a shake of the entrant's head.

Richardson was saying. "Let's hope that your ship doesn't founder because of it. If I find your ineptitude has resulted in causing any ill to His Majesty, I'll take steps. Smarten up your act. Kenton, have you got nothing to do?"

Kenton motioned with his eyes and Richardson turned. He bowed.

"Trouble, Richardson?" enquired Arkyn.

"Not any more, sir."

They exchanged a glance.

"I can see where Edward gets his efficiency. Marcle, I'm *told* Richardson's bark is worse than his bite." He turned to the King's Administrator. "I'm about to leave for the Rex Dallin. I shan't interrupt His Majesty for long."

"I'll announce you, sir."

Arkyn nodded, smiled at Kenton and entered the Inner Office.

Once the door closed, Richardson said to Marcle, "What His Highness forbore from saying was that it's universally recognised as being rather difficult to distinguish my bark from my bite."

Marcle simply said, "Sir."

Chapter 52

DISCONTENT

Hexadai, Week 22 – 13th Seral, 6th Seris 1212
Ceardlann

Tᴀɪɴ STARED AT THE BOOK. A piece of paper by his hand was scrawled with his notes. He distantly heard the sounds of the house around him. The breeze from the open window carried the chill and scents of autumn – damp earth and bonfires – the snorting of horses and clop of hooves crossing the stableyard, the jingle of harness and the banter of grooms. He'd close the window soon. Someone walked along the passage and into a nearby room. Was that Cal laughing, talking to someone? It must be Elantha or Arkyn.

Had he read that sentence already? He cursed trying to refocus his mind.

The door opened. Exasperated, Tain threw down his pen. He whipped around to tell the entrant to leave him alone and faced his resolute father, still cloaked from his ride. Tain rose, inclined his head and grinned. His father returned the smile and crossed to give him a hug. Tain tried to return it but couldn't relax.

Adeone said, "Close your books and come for a breath of fresh air, son."

Tain shook his head. "I need to learn this."

"It wasn't a request. Close your books."

Half-heartedly, Tain put a page marker in the volume of law. Why was his father annoyed with him?

Shepherded into the fresh air, Tain turned his face to the breeze. His father's arm went around his shoulders. They were getting closer in height every year.

As they walked through the herb garden with its calming fragrances, Adeone said, "I've told Spellen you're having a week off and, to make sure of it, he is returning to Oedran to see his family." Sitting on a bench, he motioned for Tain to join him and kept his arm around his son. "You're working far too hard. I know why and I respect the reasons for it, but the judge is worried. Not only is he worried enough to admit he's concerned, but so is your brother – Cal also thinks you need to take it easier, though he was diplomatic enough not to say it to me. You've still got two and a half years before you take over the Oedranian courts. That's when you should start truly learning all the in-depth law. All that's required, when you begin in 1215, is that you can handle a court and assimilate information. Your lawyers will advise you on the law. You don't need to know it all."

"No, but I…" He bit at his lip; how could he explain it to his father? He had to try. "How will I know that Uncle Scanlon isn't telling them to mislead me? He'll still be the Justiciar for most of the empire."

"You can never be certain. I can never be certain that what people tell me is the truth. Get multiple opinions, if you are ever in doubt. What's more, simply do it as a habit from the moment you start. People might think it odd, but they'll accept that is how you like to work. If people know you'll check what they tell you, they tend to tell you a lot fewer lies. It's hard to show what can be construed as distrust but, sometimes you must. You're right, your Uncle Scanlon's influence will still continue but – and this is a big 'but', Tain – if your decisions are fair and just, few will ever consider it. Be better than him and people will accept you. You'll be a fantastic justiciar but being a justiciar doesn't simply mean knowing the law like you know yourself. It helps, but it should be knowledge built up slowly and carefully crafted over time. I didn't become a king in a day, whatever popular belief has it. I had to work hard. You have to break habits formed over years if you don't like them and if they don't work for you. For example, I hate to see people kneeling to me. That is why I have insisted it is only the first time they meet me that they kneel. There are exceptions; bad news is one. The point is, however, it took me a year to get that over to people. If he wished, Arkyn could reverse it to the way my father worked which was unless you were family or household, you knelt when he entered a room and waited to be told to rise. Even if you were family you knelt to him at Court. Now, I use kneeling for oaths and to indicate displeasure. For you, there won't be that protocol. You'll have to find something else. We have strayed from the point of this conversation though."

"I don't mind, father."

"No, I expect you don't. Anything is a worthwhile distraction?"

"Normally," admitted Tain with a shrug.

"Yes, well, this isn't a normal conversation, young Tain. You're going to take things easy this week. So easy that you are not going to be opening anything that might be construed as a textbook. I've cancelled your lessons with the judge as well. Though he did invite you to dinner one evening if you'd like to go? You'll stay overnight at the Palace."

Tain nodded. "I think I would, father, and it would be rude to refuse."

"How are you feeling?"

Tain bit his lip again and looked away from his father's face. "Tired. I can't concentrate."

"I'm not surprised. You're trying to absorb too much information at once. I have the same problem occasionally."

Tain tilted his head. "What do you do to stop it?"

"Tell everyone I'm taking the evening off and normally annoy your Uncle Festus or come here. I much prefer coming here though."

Tain smiled. "You should do it more often, father."

"That's me rebuked then. No, don't apologise… I don't know, cheeked by my own son."

Tain laughed. "But I love you."

Adeone gave his son a hug. "I you. I'm just worried when you overdo things. You get so passionate about life. Shall we go inside?"

"I like it here."

Adeone watched his son. "What's troubling you?"

"I don't want you to leave for Oedran," admitted Tain, kicking at a stone.

"Then we'll hide out here for as long as possible. I don't want to leave for Oedran either – though I have to return tomorrow morning straight after breakfast."

Tain chewed at his lip. He always missed his father's company but he had to be stoical. His father ruffled his hair. Instead of smoothing it back down, Tain ruffled his father's. By the time his father stopped tickling him, he was limp. Tears welled, spilling over, flowing faster; he curled into himself sobbing. It was so unfair. He'd done everything he thought was right. Was everyone disappointed in him? His father lifted him, and he snuggled into the comforting embrace. His father's cloak enveloping him reassuringly. Closing his eyes, he hugged his father.

* * *

As Tain fell to sleep, Adeone rose, carrying his son into the house.

Seeing the Prince asleep in the King's arms, Joe simply held the doors open for him. Adeone smiled in thanks as the footman drew back the covers on Tain's bed and left the King to tuck him in. Adeone tenderly brushed the hair away from his son's forehead and bending down placed a kiss on it. What would Ira have made of Tain now? She'd always said he was worth all the trouble in the world.

* * *

As Adeone entered the sitting room the children used, they all rose. He said, "Do you have to? Oh, yes, you do. I wish, though, tonight that you could forget that you have to, including titles – even you, young Cal!"

Cal grinned. "I'll try, Sire."

"Failed – at the first attempt. Do you mind if I join you?"

Arkyn shook his head. "How is he?"

"Asleep. I think he'll be more sensible from now on."

Elantha giggled. "Tain's never sensible."

"Too true. I can't imagine where he gets it from!"

"I can, father," remarked Arkyn.

"Thank you for that startling honesty."

"I was going to say Uncle Festus, sir," replied Arkyn, innocently.

"Yes. Right. Very quick. I'll inform him that you think he's responsible for your brother's ways. Then I'll call Doctor Chapa to him as he nearly dies of laughter. What have you all been up to?"

Arkyn said, "Cal's been looking at the Skifta's Sword in the hall again. Though he's not tried to take it down."

Adeone smiled. "It is intriguing. I got it down when I was twenty, but it's not balanced right for me. In a few years, we'll have to see if it is for you. It's been undisturbed for far too long."

"Thank you, sir," replied Cal, "but it's the patterns that take my eye. It's like there's fire in the blade."

"I know what you mean. Have you ever been told the story that surrounds it?" (Cal shook his head.) "During the Age of the Cearcall, this house was the home of the Skifta: a shifter, a man or woman who could move between places in the blink of an eye. On rare occasions, they would host the Kings of Anapara, or, as we have later become known, the Kings of Oedran. The FitzAlcis had their retreat, Arilla, a palatial house. Here, though, they found something else, something quieter, something that spoke within their souls and called them home. The Cearcall was too powerful to challenge but my ancestors often suggested they could provide the Skifta with another home if they would relinquish the valley. They were met with laughter. Having something kings covet is a form of power in itself; as is the protection and inviolable sanctity and privacy of the valley. The kings couldn't enter without an invitation and only then, it is said, if they obeyed strict rules, keeping what they knew of the valley to themselves. There are mentions, or speculations, that the Skiftas extracted oaths from my ancestors. During one visit, the last Skifta, a man called Ennor Salway – Lufian born, but classed as Anaparian as soon as he accepted the star stone, as the Skifta's home was here – joked that if the Cearcall ever fell then the King of Anapara could inherit the house. King Adelard Almeric made him put it in writing. It's said he even had the Skifta seal it with a Cearcall seal handed down through the generations so that the next couldn't renege on the promise. They apparently laughed about it. Hindsight is a lesson Ennor Salway never profited from. In 600, he travelled to Cearcallead, to the Cearcall Tower, to the fate that awaited them all. Being the Skifta, he hadn't taken the sword, simply appearing for the meeting and intending to come home straight afterwards. When he didn't return, when news of the catastrophe arrived, the then Comptroller placed the sword above the door and it's remained there ever since." Adeone watched Cal's face; he wasn't satisfied. "The sword, though, has more of a story than that. Myths and legends surround it. When Ull brought the first Cearcall together, the first Wright had forged a sword with which he avenged his father and killed his patricidal brother. Was this sword that ancient one?

Some stories say it was. Some histories, written by historians who had mostly never seen it, wove tales of it being passed from guardian to guardian, from hand to hand, drawn in defence, slaying enemies, held not for show but for defence. Others are more practical saying it is merely a sword made by a Wright at some point for the Skifta of the time. Even men who can disappear may benefit from carrying weapons, if only as a deterrent. No-one knows the truth. The blade could have been re-hafted. It might even have been reforged. Is a reforged blade the same weapon as the original? That is a question for others, but all we know for certain of the Skifta's Sword is that the truth is lost in the mists and myths of our history. The one thing that all stories agree on is that, one day, someone will claim it as theirs. That until that day, it will never be balanced right for anyone else."

"I've had the feeling it's been here for years and that it should always be here," remarked Cal.

Adeone smiled. "I know what you mean. You get a sense of age when you look at it. Like it could tell you a hundred tales if it could speak."

Cal nodded. "Yes. A hundred tales that even the Chief wouldn't know."

"Are there a hundred tales Laioril wouldn't know?" queried Adeone satirically.

Arkyn laughed. "Not that he'll ever admit to. I get the same feeling with some buildings – as if you can feel the past contained within them. Irvin certainly thinks you can. He's still convinced he found the Palace of Tera."

"From what Percival told me I think it is likely he did. It does seem a waste if he is such a good historian to have him train as an advisor simply because it is family tradition."

"He has to train in that, law or the military and he didn't want to disappoint Lord Iris. I persuaded him, if he trained as an advisor, more doors might open for him and he could pursue his interests with a clearer conscience after graduating."

"I know, but I'm wondering whether to persuade Lord Iris to remove him from the school. I could make an exception and accept a different form of education if he petitioned me to."

Arkyn shook his head. "It would appear as though we thought him unsuitable to train as an advisor; especially after he has returned from Paras with me. Is it a wise idea to sow the seed of doubt about a future Lord of Oedran?"

Adeone regarded his son with a strange expression. "When did you become so authoritative in expressing your opinions? I've noticed it a lot recently."

Arkyn laughed. "Since you sent me to do the reviews."

"He's also full of them!" chipped in Elantha.

Adeone said, "I can imagine. I don't know, I keep finding I'm responsible for things."

"Yes, father, but as you keep telling me – it's part of the job," remarked Arkyn.

"There you see, Cal, something else I'm responsible for. All I wanted was a quiet life."

"That's a pity then, isn't it, sir?" replied Cal, amused.

Adeone gave a mock injured sigh. "You're all ganging up on me now. I'd have thought you, young Cal, would have stood up for me."

Grinning, Cal got up with a flourish. "My apologies, Sire. I am, as always, yours to command."

"Quite the courtier, young Cal. Who's been teaching you those manners?"

"Advisor Spellen, sir."

Adeone groaned. "Something else I'm responsible for. Well, you'll be pleased to know, Cal, that I've cancelled yours and Tain's lessons for a week. I'm sure you'll cope."

Cal grinned. "I'm sure I shall, sir. Thank you."

Adeone nodded. "That's all right. It was a sensible idea, even before Tain collapsed." He saw their faces. "He should be fine in the morning. Overwork happens to us all. Though you might escape it, El."

After a knock at the door, Kadeem entered and the King raised a querying eyebrow.

Calm as ever, the manservant asked, "I wondered if you needed anything, Your Majesty?"

Adeone smiled. "Actually, now you mention it – wine all round, please, Kadeem; watered down for the children. I've also decided to stay the night. Could you inform the Comptroller and let Simkins know he can have the evening off? I'll fend for myself."

"With pleasure, Sire."

Arkyn smiled. "Kadeem, I think it would be wiser if you attended on His Majesty this evening."

Adeone said, "Anyone would think I'm hopeless."

"Not *anyone*, father."

"Is that meant to reassure me?"

Arkyn chuckled. "It's what families are for."

Chapter 53
PAST AND PRESENT
Evening
Ceardlann – Snug

ONCE THE YOUNGER CHILDREN were in bed, Adeone went in search of Arkyn and passed him a drink. His son had been reading and Adeone idly looked to see what.

"What's so fascinating about the Cearcall?"

"I don't know. I suppose it's not them in themselves but the world they created. We live in such a different one, after all. I cannot imagine what it must have been like to ask for advice from people who could communicate between themselves without talking. It's not just the magic, father, but the way the spirits worked together to produce something much stronger and more resilient. They must have been formidable at their height of power, but there's no account of rebellions against them."

"When they could see what was happening many miles away, is it surprising?" enquired Adeone, hooking a footstool towards him. "There was a rebellion in the end, and it proved their downfall. There's a lesson in that somewhere, I'm sure."

"Yes, but if the Darkal hadn't found the Tribility first then surely that rebellion would never have happened."

"Maybe not and in *that* there are several lessons: not least, never let seemingly 'safe' shadowy organisations find their weapons first, be they sharp edged or of the human variety. Magic is temperamental, it doesn't do to rely on it."

"No, sir, but why are you so against it?" asked Arkyn. "Even when it's proved useful."

Adeone regarded him. "I have my reasons. Take Butterworth: he's rather like a weather-vane: only if the wind is strong enough does it move. He doesn't actually know what he's telling us."

"Maybe he doubts what his instincts are telling him and doesn't want to mislead anyone. He thinks he's a medium, not a Sensor. If he knows the entirety of his skills, he might lose his uncertainty and be more reliable. He could also protect himself far better. All he knows is that Wynfeld thinks he's useful."

"I shall think about it. So, what exactly are you reading about tonight?"

Arkyn grinned. "This house. I didn't realise there was so much mystery surrounding it. Your story about the sword got me thinking, and I wondered what else is here, but I can't find any definitive account of our treasures."

"Maybe you should try and write one. There are inventories somewhere, probably in the tower. A little innocent detective work can't harm. I'm sure the Comptroller will be pleased to help."

Arkyn nodded and changed the subject. "What prompted you to make Lord Iris King's Counsellor?"

Adeone put his drink down. "He tried to resign and looked so stricken when he did that I couldn't accept it. It was a compromise we reached. I wanted to talk to you about it though. I'm in need of a new Deputy Chief Advisor. I know who I'd like and your nearfather has agreed. Would you mind losing Rayburn now?"

Arkyn paused. "Of course not, sir. I'll miss his help, but I knew he'd be returning to your staff at some point. I'll have to think about whom to promote and see about getting another advisor."

Adeone topped up his son's glass. "That reminds me, your Uncle Festus should be attending the finals of the Advisors' School to do just that for you. Unless you've changed your mind."

"No, I haven't, but should we really do that to Lord Landis?"

Adeone chuckled. "Yes, it'll do him good... Can you keep an eye on Tain? He's been overdoing it more than either of us realised."

"Of course. I'm not sure he'll listen to me though."

"Brothers never listen to each other, but you two are closer than you'll admit, or, at least, I like to think so."

Arkyn smiled. "Surely the enigma is part of parenthood, father."

Adeone eyed him. "Very funny and uninformative. How are you, in yourself?"

"Ceardlann is the best restorative I know."

"Yes, it is. How's your household?" enquired Adeone, adding a log to the fire.

Arkyn watched him. "They're their normal efficient selves. Have you got any further with the hunt for a manservant for Tain?"

"No, I've not had chance to pursue it. I don't suppose Thomas or Alan would be right?"

Arkyn shook his head. "Not for Tain, father. They're both rather too exact to cope comfortably with his foibles. He needs someone with an edge of spontaneity about them. Anyway, being selfish, I'd rather not lose either of them."

"I don't blame you; good servants are worth their weight in gold. It's just a pity we can't pay them that."

"If we could, we'd lose them, as they'd have no reason to work."

Adeone was still chuckling when the door opened. He glanced over. "You should be in bed, Tain."

"I couldn't get back to sleep, father. Can I... May I join you?"

Adeone held out his hand and Tain walked over to be enveloped in a one-armed hug. "Of course you can. Would you like a drink?" (Tain nodded.) "As I'm feeling lazy and irresponsible, you'll have to have a well-watered whiskey."

Tain poured himself a drink and his father eyed it.

"A bit more water, Tain, I'm not feeling *that* irresponsible. Now, come and tell me why you're a fool. You've had me worried."

His son became subdued. "I'm sorry, sir."

"No need to be, but I'd rather you didn't collapse again."

Tain swallowed. "Me too. I'll leave that to Arkyn."

His brother threw a cushion at him. "I sleep; I don't collapse… often. We'll have to give that Cearcall game a go tomorrow, if we can work out the rules."

Adeone hesitated. "Wish I could join you. If it's the game I'm thinking of it should be good. It's more involved than chess but equally as enjoyable."

"More involved than chess? Is that possible?" asked Tain.

"Yes. With this game it isn't capturing the king that matters. This one is based on pairing up the Cearcall and knowing what their strengths and weaknesses are. You have to capture both of a pair before you can add them into the tower. Whoever has the majority in the tower wins the game. So, for example, the Beran and Rheol are paired up and to add them into the Cearcall you need to have both your opponent's pieces for them. Then there's the slight issue that if you allow a Skifta to get on the same square as another spirit, on their side, they can release any member of the forming Cearcall from the tower, necessitating the handing over of the twin piece also."

"It could take hours!" exclaimed Tain.

"Or even days but, once you've grasped the game, it's good fun, if frustrating. Capture the Skifta first. That's always a good move. The more people playing, the more difficult it becomes and you need teamwork."

"We're going to have fun working it out," said Arkyn. "Will you excuse me, father, if I go to bed now?"

Once Arkyn had gone, Tain said, "Father, I'm sorry for earlier."

"Don't feel guilty about it. We all have such moments," admitted Adeone reassuringly. "You need to learn to recognise the signs before you collapse. I admit, I didn't expect you to work too hard for a couple of years." As Tain pouted, Adeone ruffled his hair. "It's not a bad thing. Be a child. Run around the Rex Dallin, annoy Laioril often and the Comptroller rarely."

"Well, as the Chief's here, I can manage that."

"Is he? I ought to greet him before returning to Oedran. Maybe you'd like to get up early and come with me?"

Twelve minutes later, Kadeem entered. "My apologies for disturbing you, Sire. Maria has realised that His Highness isn't in bed and I wondered if he was with Your Majesty."

Adeone smiled. "Yes, he's here. Tell Maria I'll see him settled, but he's to be up at six to come and see Laioril with me. She can get to bed."

* * *

Adeone and Tain walked to the Wanda camp before anyone else but the servants at Ceardlann were awake. The early autumn frost crunched under their shoes. The wise woman of the tribe greeted them with a smile, her arms full of scavenged wood.

"Miranda! You're looking well."

"Thank you, Sire. I'm glad I can say the same of Your Majesty and Highness. Are you as well as you appear?"

"We have our moments, don't we, Tain? I thought I ought to come and greet the Chief before I return to Oedran. Is he about, or do I have the opportunity of catching him unawares for once?"

A voice behind them said, "I heard that, lad!"

Miranda chuckled. "I believe the Chief is behind you, sir. I'll leave you to his care, but I've a couple of bottles of elderberry wine for you."

Adeone sighed. "You know how to take care of a man, Miranda."

"Thank you, sir. One's intended for Lord Landis, but I wouldn't be surprised if he lost his bottle—"

"He always does," murmured Tain.

Laughing, they parted company.

Laioril studied them critically. "Hmm, you're both strained. First time I've seen Tain looking it but it had to happen at some point. Come and get a hot drink whilst you try to get some sense out of me."

Adeone laughed. "I thought sleep would help. You're too perceptive."

"So I've been told, lad. Come on, I've a nice bit of bacon put by as well."

Tain grinned. "Where from, Chief?"

"Ask me no questions, lad, and I'll tell you less lies."

"Looking after you well at the house, are they?" enquired Adeone.

"If unknowingly sometimes." He saw the perplexed expression on Tain's face. "We have to eat, lad."

"Yes, Chief, but Cook throws us out of his kitchen; so, I'm just wondering how you get around him. I could do with some pointers."

Laioril laughed. "I tell him that, if I feed you, he gets peace and quiet."

Adeone hadn't stopped smiling since the Chief had first appeared. "Haven't you been using that line since I was raiding the kitchens?"

"The old ones are the best, lad."

Tain grinned. "That must make you the very best, Chief."

"Tain," warned Adeone reprovingly under his breath.

Laioril chuckled. "So it must. What can I do for you this fine morning?"

Adeone shrugged. "I wanted to drop by before returning to Oedran. I came to sort this terror out. He's been working far too hard."

Laioril's eyes twinkled at Tain. "I can't believe that but then I always avoid work. I had noticed I've not seen him much… It's a shame. I've still a fund of stories to explore with him."

Tain grinned, taking a beaker of warm apple tea. "Father's making me take time off so you'll probably see too much of me, Chief."

"That could be both good and bad. You couldn't have timed it differently, I suppose, Adeone?"

The King shook his head. "Sorry, Chief. I know you'll cope though. How's life on the road?"

"Troublesome. A few *problems* are developing. Chief Darshan knows and he's in Tradere."

"Who's he?" enquired Tain.

"I suppose you'd call him the Wanda King," explained Laioril. "He's head of all the tribes. Not many in Anapara have heard of him though. His tribe wanders the roads of Tradere and Areal."

Adeone sipped at his tea. Was he imagining the slight hint of star anise? Had Laioril pinched more than bacon from Ceardlann? "Let Chief Darshan know I'm looking into the reports. He'll be worried if I messenger him."

"Right you are, lad. Might I ask you a favour?"

"Chief Laioril of the Wanda requests a favour of mere mortals? Wonders will never cease. What is it?"

Laioril's eyes sparkled. "If a king is a mere mortal, I've missed something. I'd like to winter here this year. Would that be inconvenient?"

"Not at all, Chief. It would be a pleasure to have you here; just go easy on my kitchens."

Laioril laughed. "Of course, Sire. If we catch too much to eat at any point, we'll add it to your larder."

"Would that be poaching?" asked Adeone, eyes glinting.

"Not at all, lad, we'll roast or stew most."

Tain laughed. "I'll remember that one."

Adeone ruffled his hair. He put his empty beaker down. "I'm sure you will. Well, Chief, we must return to Ceardlann for breakfast. Come on, Tain, let's get you causing trouble at Ceardlann so I can cause it in Oedran."

Tain smiled half-heartedly. "I'd rather we both caused trouble in the same place."

Laioril said, "I'm not sure many people would though, lad. Anyway, your father's heard all my stories many times over; he'll not want to hear them again.”

Tain looked between his father and the Chief. “Are you sure? Because, father’s face says he isn’t.”

Adeone glanced with good humour at Laioril. “I know intentional temptation, Chief, no matter how well you wrap it up. I’ll come and stay later in the winter and you can tell tales to us all around the fires at Ceardlann. I’ll even ask Wealsman for some Terasian whiskey.”

Laioril winked. “I might manage that. Now, go on before one of ‘em comes to fetch you.”

* * *

They entered Ceardlann by the kitchen door. Not because it was closest to Encampment Field and the Wanda camp but simply because they wanted to. They were teasing each other, banter rolling around them as though they sailed in a sea swell.

Cook groaned. “Cover the food.”

Adeone chuckled. “Morning, Cook. I understand you might be missing a side of bacon and some spices.”

“Aye. We gained a haunch of venison though. The gamekeeper was much perplexed. How long are you here for, Sire?”

“I leave after breakfast.”

Tain grinned. “Don’t give him breakfast, Cook. Please.”

Adeone ruffled his son’s hair. “Any meal after a fast is a breakfast.”

Tain’s face fell. “Please stay for today. We can play that game and you can annoy Cook.”

“What did I do to get dragged into this?” asked Cook indignantly as everyone else laughed.

Adeone glanced at Cook and then back at Tain. If he was honest with himself, a day spent with his children and Elantha, without worry, without meetings, without anything but good food, good company and friendship was the most tempting proposition he’d had in months. He shouldn’t stay. He should return to Oedran, to his desk, to those duties, those meetings, those decisions, that whirlwind that was the Court. Torn, he said, “Let me decide over breakfast.”

Tain shook his head. “No. You said you’d return after breakfast.”

Innocently, Cook said, “Lucy, what did I plan for dinner tonight?”

The young kitchen maid hesitated. “I thought we were having stew, with herby dumplings and an apple and cinnamon pie for afters, Cook. Why? Do I need to change anything?”

Adeone caught Cook’s eye. “Stop *helping*.”

Cook nodded. “Of course, Sire. I’ve just made a batch of lemon curd and I ought to check that the meringues finished overnight.”

273

Susan's lips twitched. "I'd say they did, Cook. I checked one early. All crispy outer and gooey centre. The King won't want any at all."

"I sense a conspiracy," muttered Adeone.

Tain laughed. "Please stay, father."

"If I stay, it's only for today." He glanced again at Cook. "Would it put you out?"

Cook laughed. "Sire, since when has warning been necessary?"

Adeone grinned. "Always. I just don't give you any, which is a completely different matter. All right, Tain, I'll stay, *for today*. Run and tell Arkyn, Cal and Elantha that we'll breakfast together. Susan, can you sort out the Great Hall?" As the housekeeper and his son left, Adeone looked at Cook. "What about lunch? Any temptations there?"

"Plenty, if you'll let us have space to think them up."

Adeone chuckled. "I'm going. Biscuits would be nice. Shortbread or ginger…"

Chapter 54
COMPETITION
Septadai, Week 22 – 14th Seral, 7th Seris 1212
Snug

LEAVING THE KITCHEN, Adeone wandered through the house to the Comptroller's office. He sat waiting for the messenger link the Comptroller was in to end.

Exiting the link, the Comptroller took in Adeone's placid but harassed air. "Morning, Sire. You have the look of a man who's just had his arm twisted."

"Tain and Cook conspired, then Susan joined in."

"They are getting very adept at that. Richardson has said nothing will disturb you here."

Adeone nodded. "Is there anything you need from me, or am I to be left to the merciless attentions of my sons?"

"I would not come between family, Your Majesty."

"You are kindness itself, Comptroller." He watched the stableyard for a few moments. "I'll take the terrors on a ride after breakfast. Probably go up to the pools. It looks like it'll be a nice day. Cook did say warning wasn't expected, so we'll take a mid-morning picnic with us and then return for lunch."

"I'm sure Cook will appreciate the challenge, sir."

"I hope not," said Adeone with a grin. "That would rather spoil things."

The Comptroller's chuckle followed him out of the room.

Breakfast was lively. Tain's light-hearted mood and banter from the morning continued at every possible chance. Adeone let it. After his son's collapse the day before, it was heart-warming to see him happy. Adeone suggested the ride, but it was met with little enthusiasm, which perplexed him.

"Can't you teach me the Cearcall game, father?"

"Of course I can. Do you want to bring it to the snug and we can hide there? Cook should be making us some biscuits."

Arkyn said, "Do you mind if I watch?"

"Not at all. El, Cal, are you joining us?"

Cal hesitated. "I hoped to write to my parents today, sir."

"Then do, but you're welcome to join us when you've finished."

"Thank you, sir."

El hesitated. "I've a painting I want to finish, Uncle Adeone, and I don't like to paint in the snug. There's no table I can use."

* * *

Tain collected the game with its pieces and wandered down to the snug. The cosy room's fireplace took up a third of one wall. Its clean, swept hearth held a basket of logs, the fire irons, a small tripod for a kettle, and a toasting fork leaning against the stonework. Its twisted brass handle ended with a tiny model of Ceardlann, without the tower or the south wing, now so integral to the house no-one considered it a wing. On the mantlepiece were other small ornaments. A gilt model of the Wishing Tree in gold, its leaves delicately hung from the branches, a tiny face carved into its trunk. There was a carved model of a figure playing a small Iridian harp, a trinket box painted with a scene of the Pillars of Alcis, and three silver candlesticks. One narrow window looked out towards the forest. Carved wainscotting lined the walls, as it did for most of Ceardlann. The ceiling was lower than most in the house and the enveloping feel was why it had become known as the snug. Opposite the fire was a comfortable couch, long enough for five people. At either end were single well-padded chairs, perfect to curl up with a book, which was what Arkyn immediately did whilst his father and brother sprawled in front of the fire, laying out the game.

Tain tried to figure out the board. It had a map painted on it. Though the lands weren't as he would recognise them on a cartographer's map. They were twisted, distorted. Various of them were too large or too small and they curved unnaturally to fit the circular board. Around the edges of the map were small dots, alternating in purple and gold, twenty-four in total. Each had a small symbol next to it. Tain smiled. They were the same symbols as the provinces still used. A bear's paw for Terasia, a coiled snake

275

for Serpent Isle, scales for Gerymor, the eye for the Low Plains and so on. He carefully unpacked the pieces. Each represented one symbol. Two sets, one in amethyst and one in gold. Adeone picked up the gold arrow, designed to stand on its fletchings and represent the Skifta. The weight told him it wasn't gilt. He glanced at Arkyn, who, sensing the look, winked.

"Where did you find this set?"

"Kensal pointed me in the direction of a trader who deals in ancient and beautiful pieces, father. He said he had it from a manor whose lord wasn't bothered by 'idle pursuits'. I was tempted to enquire what pursuits the lord was bothered by, but I behaved myself."

Adeone chuckled and helped Tain set out the pieces. At the centre of the board was 'The Tower' and as Tain was to discover, it wasn't easy to add his opponents' pieces. Each token had different moves, rather like in chess. The Skifta could move wherever he wished, the Espier and Sensor could move more swiftly than the Beran and Rheol who had to move together even if they were on opposite sides of the board. So if Tain rolled a two and moved the Beran, the Rheol would also have to move, which often meant undoing a strategy. The dice – two amethyst and two gold – were dodecahedrons. One for the token, one for the spaces to move. The spaces on the board were haphazard and all different sizes; those that could be moved between were marked by a gap in their outline. Other spaces were coloured purple or gold and blocked the opposite player using them. Some pieces could only capture their opposites. A Jeci could only capture a Jeci but the Espier could capture all but the Jeci. It wove the game into a mixture of luck and chance that had Tain frustrated and laughing in equal measure to his father's annoyance and pleasure. By the time Cal joined them, the gloves were off and Arkyn was throwing in helpful comments. Kadeem and Joe entered with refreshments, tea, biscuits and meringues. Tain and Adeone almost completely ignored them. Tain had just captured his father's Skifta with a net of pieces including his Beran and Rheol when a black griffin appeared.

Adeone eyed it balefully. "You pick your moments, Magucan."

"I didn't pick it. Lord Wealsman wonders if he could have a word, Sire."

Adeone shared a glance with Arkyn and then nodded to the messenger. Wealsman wasn't normally one to interrupt him during the day.

Tain frowned as the link formed. "Father promised we could have today."

Arkyn said quietly. "At least this can't take him back to Oedran. It's not going to be to do with any disaster there."

Tain bit his lip, looking at the game board. "I'll put this away."

"No, you don't. Wait and see what's happened first!"

* * *

276

In the messenger link, Adeone exclaimed, "You look like death warmed up!"

"Ah, that would be the King's compliments! I'm fine, Adeone, it's just been a long day, night, whatever it was. Kristina's been delivered of the child. I've… We've a daughter."

Adeone smiled warmly. "Congratulations to you both. I'm pleased. I really am. They're both well?"

"Yes. Thank you. I wanted to ask you something, well, two things actually. I… *We*, definitely we, would like to name her Adeona… Would you…? Do you mind?"

"Why on Erinna would I mind? I'm quite honoured, but I guess you'll tell me it's nothing to do with me."

Wealsman sighed. "Sometimes, I despair of you. It's everything to do with you. You're the best friend I've ever had and both I and Kristina owe our happiness to you. The other thing I wanted to ask you is slightly more awkward… Kristina and I were talking before Adeona was born. We were trying to decide on the babe's nearparents. We'd like to ask Prince Arkyn to stand as her nearfather, but I'm aware that—"

"You think that I'd assume you'd ask me? Percival, I know Arkyn has a far better likelihood of being here in future years. If I were to be totally selfish, I might point out that I already have far too many young people on my conscience either as wards or nearchildren. So, without feeling it is a betrayal of our friendship, because it isn't, just ask him. Then I'll pick him up when he gets over the shock."

Wealsman ran his hand tiredly through his hair. "Thank you. I did feel it was a kind of betrayal. How is he? I hear he did good work in Paras."

"Did you ever truly think that he wouldn't?"

"No, but I think others suspected it."

"Probably." Adeone studied Wealsman's face. "Is Kristina asleep?"

"She was."

"Then go to bed yourself. Go on. I'll contact your Deputy Governor and tell him you're taking a few days for yourself and he's to tell me if you appear at your desk. Talk to Arkyn later. I'll let him know that Adeona's been born. The rest can wait until you look like you're once more in the land of the living."

Wealsman yawned. "Thank you. Do I have a choice on the days off?"

"No. Sleep, Percival. I'll speak to you soon."

The link broke and Adeone shook his head at the fact Percival had been too tired to even register any serious protest at being forced to rest.

* * *

As the snug reappeared, Adeone ruffled Tain's hair. "I'll be back with you momentarily, and no cheating."

"I don't cheat!" protested Tain.

Adeone winked, called his own messenger, and obtained a link with the Deputy Governor of Terasia.

Arkyn watched Tain's morose face. "Who's winning?"

"No-one. We're all losing. Why can't we have just one day, Arkyn?"

"The empire is too large to let us. Anyway, this might be good news."

"Not if he's talking to the Deputy Governor as well."

"I'm not so sure. Let's see what happens."

When Adeone came out of the link, he ruffled Tain's hair, re-rolled his move and captured his son's Meithrin.

"That's not fair. You had time to think about that!"

Adeone chuckled. "It was luck. I didn't have any time to think about it. Kristina's just been delivered of a baby daughter."

"How is she? How are they?" asked Arkyn, concerned.

"All doing well. I've sent Percival to bed. He looks atrocious. Ernst's taking over for a few days."

"Good. Do you know what they've named the babe?" (Blushing, Adeone told him.) "I'm pleased, father. Tain, what are you—?"

Adeone looked at his younger son, who was beginning to put the pieces away.

"Ah. No, you don't, son. Put them back. I've got to catch your Skifta."

Tain bit his lip and caught his father's eye, a tear in his own.

Adeone squeezed his shoulder. "I can't help it if one of our closest friends just became a father for the first time. You have my undivided attention."

Still sprawled in front of the fire, they continued their match. Even when Elantha joined them, Adeone did little but wink at her. By the time the Comptroller appeared to ask them if they wanted lunch, Tain had regained lost ground and Adeone was assessing his possibilities.

"Cook's done you a chicken pie, Sire, with roast potatoes and batter puddings…"

Adeone looked at Tain, who grinned.

"I'll eat them if you won't, father."

Laughing, Adeone looked at the Comptroller. "Can we be indulgent and picnic in here?"

"We'll bring the trays through, Sire."

* * *

Three hours later, Magucan appeared and asked for a link with Arkyn. Adeone was intrigued. He'd expected it to be evening before Percival woke. The link closed on Arkyn's astounded face.

"Father, you might have warned me!"

"Why? Your emotions are revealing. Are you pleased?"

"I'm stunned. I'm seventeen. What kind of nearfather will I make?"

Adeone's lips twitched. "Arkyn, I was eighteen when you were born and I'd hope I haven't been a bad father…"

"Of course you haven't but there's still a year's difference."

"Maybe in numeracy, but not in mental age. Arkyn, you'll be fine. I take it you have accepted?"

"Yes. I don't think I could ever have refused. I think Percival wanted to see my face; he was certainly smiling at the effect. He also said something about having been bullied whilst the balance of his mind was disturbed and he hoped you'd excuse him not obeying you. I think he was registering his protest that you had caught him at his weakest moment."

"Damn right. Only chance I ever get. If he tries to wriggle out of it, I'll think of a just reward," growled Adeone, "and he'll need more than a few days off at the end of it. So, what are you sending as a blessing gift?"

"I have absolutely *no* idea. I'd welcome any suggestion."

Adeone nodded. "As it's a girl, maybe some small piece of jewellery that can be adapted as she gets older."

Arkyn paused. "I like that idea, father. It's certainly got a practicality about it, which appeals to me. I shall have a good think."

"So will I; I want to send them something." Seeing Tain's face, he chuckled. "Your brother has accepted a lifetime of responsibility."

"Another?" asked Tain blithely. "Father, I don't think we're going to finish this game today."

Adeone looked at him. He had lost the competitive joy from earlier, and it wasn't due to Magucan's second interruption.

"Well, we can create a plan of where the pieces are and continue it another day, or we can start again then."

Tain bit his lip. "Let's start again and consider this a draw."

Adeone ruffled his hair. "Sounds perfect."

He pushed himself up, and groaned. Sprawling on the floor was all very well but it didn't help his back. He looked at the two individual chairs. Elantha giggled as he tickled her feet. She wriggled round and, recognising defeat, got up. Adeone took her place and sat her on his lap. Tain glanced up, appeared perplexed before continuing to clear the game away.

"I'm ready for a drink," said Adeone with a sigh.

Arkyn leaned over and rang the bell. "Well, you've been doing a lot of talking, father."

"Very amusing. What are you reading?"

"Inventories. I've started on the research we talked about. There's a lot hidden in these cabinets. Though a few items have been moved around."

"Your brother destroyed one cabinet."

"I didn't mean to, father," grumbled Tain.

Adeone's eyes twinkled. "No, but it's why a few things found new homes."

A few moments later, Kadeem entered and left with a request for tea and cake. Arkyn rolled up the scroll he was perusing, Tain finished putting the game away. Cal, who'd been intermittently reading and listening, closed his book, putting it on the occasional table. Tain scrambled inelegantly to his feet and curled up at the other end of the couch.

"We could go for that ride now."

Adeone shook his head. "Save it for tomorrow. My back is aching."

"But you won't be here."

"No." He saw Tain's face. "It doesn't mean I don't wish I could be."

Tain nodded. "Could I go for a ride, father?"

"Of course. Just return for dinner."

Tain looked at Cal and Arkyn. "Coming?"

Arkyn shook his head, Cal accepted and the boys left.

When Kadeem re-entered with the tea and cake, Adeone persuaded El to sit on the couch and eased himself in the chair in such a way that, when he had served refreshments, Kadeem moved a footstool close to the King and enquired if there was anything else he needed.

"No, thank you, Kadeem." Half an hour later, he was napping.

Watching him, Arkyn whispered. "Let's leave him be, El."

They crept out of the room.

Chapter 55

TANCRED'S MORNING

Alunadai, Week 23 – 15th Seral, 8th Seris 1212

Courthouse

FOR TANCRED, watching the Prince go from indifference to engagement had been gratifying but watching him overwork was quite the opposite. Tain had to learn the fundamentals, but Tancred blamed himself for Tain's burgeoning preoccupation. Relieved the King had taken action, he readied himself for his day with practicality. There was no need to contact Spellen, no need to prepare a lesson for Imperadai, no need to be anything other than a judge. After a modest breakfast of porridge and fruit, he walked to the Courthouse. The air was chilly but the light city frost had already dispersed by the time he reached his destination. The Keeper's office was its normal cluttered self with its owner apparently as scatterbrained as the paper dust dancing in the air.

"James, you're looking well! Can you see the latest list of trials?"

Tancred chuckled and started looking through the piles. "Where is your scribe?"

"Somewhere hunting out the list of jurors. I'm sure there's several people hanging around outside the Courthouse being picked far too regularly. Ah, thank you," he took the list Tancred passed him and brushed it off automatically. "I ought to get a system sorted."

Tancred crooked an eyebrow. "I hesitate to mention this, but you have been saying the same for years."

"Yes, yes, I know. Problem is the job gets in the way. Judges keep disturbing me."

Tancred chuckled, moved a box of scrolls off a chair and sat down with deliberation. "I am sure you would not have it any other way. I came to see if you have anything for me this week."

"I'm sure there's something." He rifled through the list in his hand. "Ah yes, we've a young lad up for pick-pocketing. The yeomen caught him. He's about twelve from what we can work out and probably needs someone to be understanding. The yeoman who brought us his case was rather sorry to do so, from what I can gather. He's been here before, but I'm not sure that means much given his circumstances."

"Right, I shall see what I can do with it. I cannot blame some of these boys. They have a hard life. I was fortunate my parents were alive and my father worked hard for us…" He paused. "I will take the case, Keeper, and leave the past where it is. I shall be free all this week – His Highness will not require my services – so, if there is anything else, do ask."

The Keeper smiled. "Thank you. How is Prince Tain?"

"Very well. The King thought His Highness would like a week without lessons whilst the weather is still pleasant. Have you heard from Lord Scanlon recently?"

"I don't expect to, Judge. He's in Lufia, I believe. Long may he stay there."

Tancred gave a non-committal nod. He pushed himself to his feet and replaced the box of scrolls. "Let us hope the Deemster thinks the same. I shall leave you to continue. I will be in my office here all day."

"Right you are, James. Oh, it's none of my business, but Selth hasn't been looking too good recently."

Tancred made his way through the Courthouse feeling scrutinised more than normal. He tried to ignore it, but someone was definitely watching him. Reaching his office, he closed the door on the corridor. He glanced at his scribe, who'd risen, intrigued.

"Morning, Judge."

"Morning, Selth. Any messages for me?"

"There are a couple on your desk, sir—"

Tancred whipped open the door and grabbed the tunic of the young runner who was listening at it. He pulled the boy into the office and shut the door with his foot.

"Well?" he asked with an authoritative lilt he normally saved for courts.

The lad swallowed. "I was just to follow you, sir."

"On whose instructions?"

"I don't know, sir. I was given a darl and told to keep watch on Your Honour. Sorry, sir."

"Who gave you the darl?"

"I don't know his name—"

"When were you to report to him?"

"He said... he said he'd find me, sir. I'm sorry, sir."

The judge eyed him. "The time for apologies is past. Do you know how much trouble you could be in for following a member of the King's staff?"

The lad blanched, shuffling his feet. "I'm really sorry, sir..."

"Yes, well, you will not be following me again, I expect."

"No, sir, I won't that."

"Then you had better go before I decide to take your name and inform the Keeper. I presume you still want your job."

"Yes, sir. Thank you, sir."

When the boy had gone, Tancred raised an amused eyebrow at Selth. "An interesting interlude to my morning."

"Should you have let him go?"

"What can he report but that I went to see the Keeper and then came here? There is nothing nefarious or unusual in that. He is harmless. I am intrigued by his actions though. It seems that someone is trying to discredit me. Now, I have been informed that you have not been well recently. Is this correct?"

"Yes, sir, but I'm fine."

Tancred eyed him. "I hope so. If you are unwell, you must tell me. I am sure I could manage for a few days without your excellent help, invaluable though you are. How is your family?"

"Mary's the same as ever. The youngsters are tripping me up but our eldest seems to be doing well. You were right to persuade him to train."

Tancred smiled. "I did nothing, Selth. Peter is bright; I am glad his studies are progressing. I had better see what you have kindly put on my desk."

It was lunchtime before he left his office and caught Selth unawares. The scribe appeared dazed and distant.

"Selth, go home. Take a week off."

"No, sir, I'll be fine. I can't afford to take the time off."

Tancred shook his head. "If that is what concerns you, be easy; after so long you deserve some paid leave. You are not well. Go home and let your wife take care of you. I shall find another scribe for the meantime. There must be one I can borrow. They will not be your replacement. I do not count illness as incompetence, you should know that."

Selth got up. "Thank you, sir."

Tancred watched him leave and locked his office behind him before calling once more on the Keeper who provided him with the name of a scribe he could use during Selth's incapacitation. He went in search of lunch, pondering on all the morning's happenings. What he had told Selth was true: he was not worried about the runner. He was unsurprised by such tactics. There would be many people interested in his movements. He merely hoped it was the future they were concerned with, not the past.

Chapter 56

WRITING ON THE WALL

Cisadai, Week 23 – 16th Seral, 9th Seris 1212

Ceardlann

THREE WEEKS LATER, Cal tried to focus his wandering thoughts, tried to concentrate. A letter shouldn't be haphazard, it should be ordered and logical moving seamlessly from one subject to another. The aromas of home stole into his senses, kitchen herbs, vegetable soup, tallow candles burnt down. The racket of his siblings arguing, the jangle of the shop bell and the thud of cloth being moved around rang in his ears. He reached out, as though he could see and touch everything that was familiar in the memories. Sick and dizzy; he grasped at the edge of the desk, anchoring himself to reality, but the churning sensation didn't leave him all day.

The following morning, he picked up his pen again to write to his siblings. Was that Louisa's laughter? Was Hal sulking and Crispin hiding? The room blurred around him; dizzy, he laid his pen down. It would pass. He poured himself a glass of water and watched the herb garden, trying to convince himself it was nothing to worry anyone else over; they'd laugh at him; he'd be bothering them unnecessarily. Wouldn't he? Eventually, he went to find Maria.

"Can I... can I talk to you privately, please, Maria?" (She closed the door with an encouraging smile.) "I... I keep feeling dizzy and distant."

"Well, you're growing it might be that when you stand up..."

"It's when I'm sitting down, mostly, and it's not the sort of dizzy you get when you stand up too quickly."

"Right… I think it might be an idea to talk to Doctor Chapa then. It's a bit outside my expertise, but I'm sure it's nothing to worry about."

"I feel a fool," admitted Cal.

"Don't. Everyone gets ill at some point and if nothing else, he can explain what you're likely to feel as you grow up and eliminate those aspects as normal. Shall I ask him to come?"

"I don't know him."

"Does anyone? He's very… caring. Eccentric but caring. He was Queen Eliza's cousin, so he's got good reasons for seeing the FitzAlcis and their friends stay alive. More than most doctors would have. If you're worried about what His Highness will say, I'll ask Doctor Chapa to give him a check over for excess of mischief at the same time."

Cal smiled. "I hope there's no cure for that. Thank you."

"Not at all. Now, I think there's just one thing left to do…" She pulled him into a hug before saying, "Go on with you. Get some fresh air."

* * *

The following day, Chapa entered Ceardlann and grinned at the footman who greeted him. "Where's Maria, Joe?"

"She's up in the nursery, sir. Is there anything I can do?"

"I'd hope quite a lot, but there's nothing for me. Thank you." He made his way up to the Princes' sitting room.

Cal glanced over as the door opened and frowned, momentarily puzzled, before enquiring, "Are you Doctor Chapa, sir?"

"So I've been led to believe. I take it you are Master Calumiel Galdwin?"

"Yes, doc… Doctor. Sorry, sir."

"Doc is fine, lad. I prefer it. Maria told me you've not been feeling your best."

Cal swallowed. "I'm having dizzy spells but it's when I'm sitting down and they're getting more frequent."

Chapa sat opposite him. "Are you doing anything in particular when these attacks happen?"

"Normally I'm writing letters."

"All right. Watch my finger… Hmm. Look at me directly… Well, I can't see anything wrong with your eyes. How often do you write letters?"

"Every day, sir. I like to write home…"

"I can imagine. Do you get homesick?"

"Occasionally, doc… I shouldn't but I do, I think. Or, at least, I wish I could see my parents more… What's the matter with me?"

"You know how to unsettle a doctor, don't you?" replied Chapa. "Well,

284

it's not your eyes, I rather think it's psychological and I don't mean that you're imagining it. I think, when you concentrate on what you miss, your mind over reacts and blurs your vision. Might I recommend you write every other day for a time and see if that helps? If it doesn't, we'll start looking at much more mundane matters like your diet… That, however, would be tedious for a growing lad with mischief still to do."

Cal nodded. "Yes, it would. Thank you…"

The door opened and Tain entered. Doctor Chapa rose and bowed with an overstated emphasis.

"Doc! What are you doing here?"

"Right now, talking to Your Highness." Chapa chuckled at Tain's unamused face. "Introducing myself to Master Calumiel, but I came to see Maria."

Tain paused. "She's not unwell, is she?"

"Not that I'm aware of, sir. I think she might have thought the time was right for me to explain some of the facts of life to you both."

Tain squirmed. "We're not naïve."

"No, but myths abound. Then there are other facts; for example, despite my best efforts, I failed to find a cure for mischief."

"You'd be one of its first victims, according to father."

"His Majesty must never be doubted. Will you excuse me if I find Maria?"

Tain nodded and when the door had closed said to Cal, "So you've finally told Maria you're not well?"

Cal swallowed. "Your Highness?"

"Oh, for heaven's sake, cut out the honorifics once and for all! I'm sick of hearing you use them. You're living here with us and this isn't Oedran."

Cal eyed him uncertainly. "It's only words, Tain, not a comment on friendship, I thought. It's like another name, I suppose, and… well… you're still… that is…"

"Do you think there are not enough people reminding me I'm different? Can't you treat me normally?"

"That's it though, isn't it? I *am* treating you normally, if normality is set by the majority."

"Then treat me differently! I don't care, just stop using honorifics. I can't stand them."

A voice behind them said, "Like them or not, Your Highness, you should get used to them. They exist as a mark of respect, sir."

Tain turned. "I know *why* they exist, Advisor; that's not my argument with Cal and I suppose that's also a point, it's *my* argument. Were you here for a reason?" As soon as the words left his mouth, Tain knew the tone had been wrong. He watched the Advisor's face. "I'm sorry, Advisor

Spellen, that was very rude of me. I apologise."

Spellen hesitated; he hadn't expected an apology. "Thank you, sir; you had every right to be annoyed. I was obviously getting involved in personal matters that I shouldn't have been. I simply came to make sure Your Highness wasn't having difficulty with work that Judge Tancred has asked of you."

"I've not had any problems yet, Advisor, thank you," replied Tain.

Spellen bowed and left.

Cal and Tain eyed each other.

Tain grinned. "I've not had any problems because I've not done any of it. I suppose we'd better make a start."

Cal smiled. "Probably, but why break the habit of a lifetime?"

"I've got better…"

"I meant me, sir… Tain."

"Thank you. I'm sorry I got so wound up."

"Yes, so am I." Cal laughed. "Oh, what does it matter? Come on, sooner we've finished the better."

Tain nodded. "So, did you tell Maria you weren't feeling well?"

"I… Yes. I didn't think you knew."

"I didn't for sure. What did the doc say?"

"Just that I should give writing letters a miss occasionally. I keep getting dizzy, you see. Well, I get dizzy when I'm writing home. It'll clear itself."

"Hopefully, otherwise you'll be going round and round in circles. Mind you, I think you do anyway."

"I follow your example. What are you meant to be reading?"

"Some minor laws and theories relating to thievery. I'm getting quite fed up of the minor laws, if the truth's told."

Cal grinned. "I thought telling the truth was the point of law."

"If only. It seems to hang together on what's not told."

Half an hour later, Doctor Chapa re-entered the sitting room to find both boys had disappeared. He went to find someone else to annoy until they reappeared. A minute later, Cook was waving a spoon at him.

* * *

When he returned to Oedran later that day, Chapa made his ambling way to the Inner Office. Richardson didn't try to stop him from entering, and the King greeted him with a quiet smile.

"All well, doc?"

"Mostly, sir. Prince Tain's a bundle of energy again. Lady Elantha's wry humour is becoming endearing. Young Calumiel, though, is getting dizzy spells. I'm not sure why, so I'll do some reading, but he says he's writing to his family daily. I wondered if a few days at home might help him."

Adeone considered. "I can't see why not. The Mundimri seems like a good time. He can come home for a couple of weeks and Tain can come and stay in Oedran and have a few more lessons at the Courthouse. I'll ask El if she'd prefer peace or to stay with her cousins."

"I'm sure His Highness won't know how to thank you, Sire."

Chapter 57
EMRYS

Tretaldai, Week 23 – 17th Seral, 10th Seris 1212
Oedran – Carnford Gate

LORD EMRYS DAIOCH rode through the gates of Oedran and asked the way to Landis House.

"Why'd you want to know, lad?" enquired the yeoman.

"Because he's my uncle."

"Ah. Right you are. Can't be too careful. Go along The Strait. First major turning on the left is the Maclan. You won't miss Landis House on your left. Big wrought iron gates, normally standing open."

Emrys rode along The Strait. Oedran's stone-built grandeur was a contrast to his home province where stone could not exist. The weight of it pressed on him. The noise of wheels and hooves clattering on stone was alien and strange, clanging in his consciousness with brutal suddenness. Even the sound of metal was foreign to him. The Low Plains' earth would swallow any metal, dragging it down from one's hand with a weight far beyond typical endurance. Only the strong could carry metal there, but here everyone held metal in their hand, or on their waist, in their clothing or on their shoes.

Normal city odours, the bouquets of decay and decomposition, passed him by. They were no different from the scents of Eyllyn. The vying scents of empire foods, which spoke of home to some, turned his stomach.

The yeoman had been right. He couldn't miss Landis House. On a street of bow fronted shops that opened directly onto the pavement, the gates standing wide leading to a house set back from the road were noticeable. Had his mother really grown up here? In this city chaos. Were these streets her memory? He tried to imagine her here. She'd spoken of Oedran but in a way that was hard to reconcile with the assault on his senses.

He rode towards the house. A groom, who'd been standing near the front door, ran forward but not before he'd jangled the bell.

Emrys dismounted. "Is Lord Landis at home?"

The groom could only nod before Landis was striding out of the house.

287

"I certainly am, Emrys. Come in and we can greet each other properly."

Emrys shared features with his uncle, but Landis was far more laid-back than he expected. "Sir."

Landis laughed. "You can cut that out today. I'm Uncle Festus to you."

A female voice said, "His Majesty has other names for you, father."

"Julia, was that really necessary?"

Emrys took in the hourglass figure of his cousin. She was watching him with bright eyes, unconcerned by the reprimand. She had the same eye shape as his mother, but with a more mischievous glint.

"Probably not, father. Cousin Emrys, come on in. I'm Julia. Julius is probably avoiding lectures..."

Landis sighed. "He better not be. Emrys, have I said welcome to Oedran?"

Emrys chuckled. "No, uncle, but then mother did warn me it might take you some time."

Landis put his arm around his nephew as he led him inside. "Yes, well, your mother and I have many similarities that we won't go into. Come and get refreshed whilst everyone sorts out your things. Are you ready for the mad house that we live in?"

"I'm sure it can't be worse than home, Uncle Festus, not with father being Deputy Governor."

Julia grinned. "Father's important as well. I'm not sure anyone's told Uncle Adeone though."

Landis said, "Letting you spend time with Lady Rhian and Lady Amara was a foolish idea. Haven't you got an embroidery lesson or something?"

"Why needle fabric? Sorry, father, I'm going, I'm going. Come and find us later, Emrys."

Emrys followed his uncle to the study. He understood it was new, had listened as his mother read out his uncle's letters following the fire, but it felt well used. There was a fire chasing away the chills of approaching winter. An embroidered fire screen was set to one side. He idly wondered who had stitched it. The geometric shapes were very different from the other more fluid carvings in the room.

Landis saw him looking. "Your mother's work. She hated it. I've always loved the simplicity of it. She took to embroidery far more diligently than your Cousin Julia."

Emrys didn't know what to say to that.

Landis saw it and ruffled his hair. "You've got both your parents in your features and, I rather suspect, in your personality as well. How are they?"

"Very well, uncle. They've both written long letters for you and Aunt Cornelia. They're in my luggage. I'll find them, eventually. Father's busy.

Mother's, well, mother. I don't think she wanted me to come to Oedran, though she'd never say it."

"I wish she'd visit, but there're many reasons why she hasn't."

Emrys asked, "Is it true that she wanted to marry His Majesty?"

"How do you know that?"

"Conversations carry. I didn't mean to overhear."

They exchanged a glance. Emrys realised that his uncle wasn't quite as carefree as he portrayed.

"I suppose you'll have to know; people at Court may remember. Your mother and His Majesty were roughly of an age. Closer than I am to him anyway. When His Majesty and I became acquainted, he spent time here and obviously came to know Nia well. When she started attending Court there was speculation that they might marry. Your mother came to half believe it, but His Majesty married our cousin Ira. That's all there is to it."

"So, he effectively jilted her?"

Landis shook his head and his answer was emphatic. "No. There had been no formal agreement, no understanding either. Your mother was upset for many months but, whatever anyone else has it, it was His Majesty who coaxed her back to Court, where she knew your father and they fell for each other."

Emrys absorbed the family history. His mother's broken heart was something he wished she'd told him about.

Landis continued. "The King's expressed a wish to meet you early in your stay."

"Father said I wasn't to be surprised if he didn't."

"Contrary to popular scepticism, His Majesty has many calls on his time."

"Then I shouldn't add to them…" said Emrys uncertainly.

"Emrys, most of the Oedranian Court think you are a minor provincial lord with little standing, but you're my nephew and the son of a deputy governor. Whatever the Court supposes, you do have status, and I am going to make damned sure they recognise it. His Majesty wants to meet you, and, busy or not, you will be presented to him the first time you're at Court together."

"Thank you, uncle," whispered Emrys uncertainly.

"It won't be daunting, I promise. As for Court, you'll know Julius and I've asked Irvin Iris to come and meet you tomorrow, before you go. He's your second cousin—"

"I know, or at least I knew he was some sort of relation. Uncle Festus, will I… that is, I don't know what to expect of Court and I'm not sure I want to attend."

Landis eyed him. "Court is a mixture of disparate elements all trying to gain ascendancy; you can either join that game or simply visit it for companionship. Just remember to be aware of who's around you and never discuss anything you hear in this house or about the FitzAlcis – even if people tell you that it's normal. My positions mean that you may see strange visitors at strange times, or normal visitors at normal times, but never talk about them. It's certain that, during your stay with us, you will be here when His Majesty and Their Highnesses visit. When they're here, we try to be as easy and informal as our individual consciences will allow. Which normally means mayhem ensues, but I try to make sure that they can relax."

Emrys nodded. "I'll try to remember, Uncle Festus, but I find the idea of being that close to the FitzAlcis daunting. Men at home talk about them as distant figures, not real."

"What do they say then?" enquired Landis, trying to make it appear a normal pleasantry.

"That the King's decisions are troublesome to us and that Prince Arkyn must have brilliant advisors, for it can't be his own work. That Lord Scanlon is hard, but his methods work, and that Prince Tain must be unstable as he's never in Oedran…"

Landis snorted. "The only thing true in that is that Lord Scanlon is a hard man. It's all nonsense, for all I might be said to be biased. The King's decisions are a matter for him and his advisors; they might not benefit all men, but they've so far stopped rebellions. Prince Arkyn's advisors are good, but it was his work and vision that produced both reviews. Prince Tain's no more unstable than I am—"

A female voice said, "Is that meant to be reassuring, Festus? Welcome to our home, Emrys. I'm sorry I wasn't here to greet you; I was visiting Lady Rhian. You've been provided with a drink; I don't suppose Festus even considered food?"

Landis muttered, "Your aunt likes to keep me in my place."

Chuckling, Emrys got up and accepted a kiss from his wed-aunt. "I'm not sure, Aunt Cornelia. Thank you for the welcome."

She smiled. "That's all right. Have you been told not to talk about what you see and hear in the house?"

Emrys swallowed. "Yes."

Cornelia glared at her husband. "You promised you wouldn't scare him yet. Emrys, I'm going to take you away from your uncle's care and introduce you to your cousins so that you might have some sanity left by dinner time. Come in, William. Lord Landis will also need sustenance."

As they left, Landis sighed. "Anyone would think I've no sense or feeling."

A quiet voice said, "I'm sure that's not true, my lord, you simply have a different perspective on life."

Landis shot a withering glance at his manservant. "Aren't you meant to reassure me?"

"Reassurance is merely transitory when one constantly questions oneself."

Taking a cup of tea, Landis sighed, exasperated. "I can tell Kadeem is your son. That's the sort of thing he'd say to Prince Arkyn. Is Lord Emrys' manservant provided for?"

"Yes, my lord, and his groom. Apparently, the horse needs special attention, as it can't be shod in metal."

"Yes. Though, whilst here, it might be an idea to try. Wood or leather will wear down too much on our roads. If the horse can't tolerate it, then we'll think again. Oh, make sure Emrys' groom doesn't find out too much about mine."

William nodded. "Of course, my lord. They discovered another man watching the house last night."

"I suppose after all this time it's horseplay to them. Thank you, William, I'll just hide from Her Ladyship."

When she returned, he said, "He had to know and as soon as possible."

"Julia's taking care of him."

"Let's hope he survives. She's become *very* single-minded."

Cornelia smiled and walked over to her husband. Stooping, she whispered, "Not at all like her father then?"

Catching her with an arm around her waist Landis said, "You must have married me for a reason."

"Yes, I knew I'd get peace and quiet but I didn't expect so much. How's Adeone?"

"Busy. What are we doing this evening?"

"Court with Emrys; he's just asked to get it over with."

"There was me thinking that I need an early night."

She kissed him. "Maybe tomorrow, and by then so will I."

Chapter 58

INTRODUCTIONS

Evening
Palace – Court

As the evening light dimmed and darkness took hold outside, candles were lit to brighten and warm the Court. Candle wardens appeared every couple of hours to trim wicks and replace burned down tapers. Their presence ignored by those around them, as most of the Court servants were.

Adeone walked around Court talking with Lord Iris. His eyes roaming over the attendees. His cousins, Rhian and Neassa, were talking together. He wondered if he was imagining the distress on Neassa's face. It wasn't the moment to enquire; Rhian's protective stance told him that.

Entering the FitzAlcis Chamber, the usher announced him. Every man and woman in the room made an obeisance. Adeone's gaze swept over them all. He smiled at the ladies to rise from their curtsies, as the men were already straightening up.

Emrys stayed kneeling. Adeone studied him for a moment. He glanced at the young lord's companions and smiled warmly, giving a brief nod.

Lord Landis murmured, "Get up. The King wants to meet you."

The room watched as they made their way over to the King. Once in front of him, Emrys knelt once more.

In a sonorous voice, Landis said, "Your Majesty, may I present my nephew, Lord Emrys Daioch, to you: son of Lord Daioch of the Low Plains and my sister, formerly Lady Feronia Landis."

A smile lit Adeone's voice as he held out his hand. "Of course you may, Lord Landis. Lord Emrys, welcome to my Court. I'm very pleased to meet you at last."

"I you, Sire," replied Lord Emrys kissing the King's signet ring.

"I hope your parents were both well when you left the Low Plains."

"Very well, thank you, Sire. They each asked me to give you their regards and loyalty."

"Which are never in doubt. Please rise, my lord, that floor isn't the warmest, and walk with me for a time."

Emrys rose, discomfited by the way his uncle and great-uncle bowed and left.

Adeone saw the look. "When did you arrive in Oedran, Lord Emrys?"

"Earlier today, Sire."

"Then I'm surprised you didn't wish to rest this evening."

"I hadn't come far, Sire. It's only a couple of days travelling from my father's manor."

Adeone's eyes swept around the room and his courtiers decided that they preferred talking to their companions to watching him.

"I suppose that's true. I ought to insist he visits Oedran more often because of it. Do you think you could help me persuade him? It is some years since I've seen him outside of a messenger link. I really can't get the same level of conversation with him in that situation. For one thing I can't strangle him for being too, well… florid isn't quite right but it will do."

Emrys smiled. "He does have a certain style, Your Majesty."

"Yes, I had noticed. How are the rest of your family?"

"Well, thank you, sir. My mother's in the peak of health and my sisters, although I'm biased, are very well."

"I can't believe that a future advisor would ever be biased against anyone, my lord; for he should be impartial at all times."

"I never said I was biased *against* them, Sire," replied Emrys, nerves getting the better of him. He stilled.

Adeone looked him full in the face and paused for a long moment. "Yes, you're definitely Ifor's son but without the experience of being at Court. All I can say is, you'll learn, Lord Emrys."

"I'm sorry if I gave offence, Your Majesty."

"You have merely shown that you haven't attended Court before. Have you met any of the young lords and ladies here yet?"

"Only my cousins, Your Majesty."

"Oh dear. If you're left to Lord Julius' care I wouldn't have much hope for your father's continuing sanity, and that is one thing I need to be certain of." The King glanced around the room. "Lord Irvin, would you join me, please."

The room fell silent. Eyes followed Irvin as he broke off his conversation and crossed to where the King was waiting. He bowed, lower than many of the Court did.

The King said, "Lord Irvin Iris, might I introduce Lord Emrys Daioch? I believe he's your second cousin, at the closest relationship. Lord Irvin is Lord Iris' grandson, Lord Emrys, as his bow suggested. You'll be fellow students."

"Thank you, Sire," replied Irvin. "I'm glad to meet you, Lord Emrys."

"I you, Lord Irvin."

Adeone smiled. "Then I shan't stand in the way of you both becoming better acquainted." He winked at them and walked off.

Emrys let out a breath. "That was unexpected."

"Welcome to the Court of Oedran."

"Thank you. I have a lot to learn."

Lord Irvin smiled. "Then let me start by introducing you to a few people."

* * *

Half an hour later, Arkyn entered Court and asked an usher where Irvin was. As he entered the FitzAlcis Chamber, the usher announced him and the room again stopped, but this time only half bows and short curtsies were given. Arkyn acknowledged them and caught Irvin's eye, crossing to him. As Irvin inclined his head, the Prince's gaze took in Emrys.

"I'm sorry, I'm interrupting your conversation."

Irvin smiled. "Not at all, sir. Might I present Lord Emrys Daioch to

Your Highness?"

"Of course you may. Welcome to Oedran, Lord Emrys. Aren't you staying with Uncle Festus?"

"Yes, Your Highness."

Noticing Emrys' hesitation, Arkyn said, "Then you should dine with me one evening soon. I'll ask Kadeem to sort something out and send an invitation. Will you excuse me? I ought to find His Majesty."

Once with his father, Arkyn said quietly, "So, Lord Emrys is here."

"Yes. He's got a lot to learn. Have you invited him for dinner yet?"

Arkyn took a drink from Kadeem. "Yes, Sire. Were those thoughts connected, Your Majesty?"

"Whatever gave you that idea, Prince Arkyn?" enquired Adeone rhetorically. "Talking about dinner, I'm getting meaningful glances from the Steward; I think he's trying to tell us that the Court Supper is ready to be served."

"As the Margrave would say, Sire, until you're ready to eat, it is immaterial."

"I think letting you go to Terasia was a mistake. Or at least letting you meet Percival was," grumbled the King.

"Hindsight, Sire, is often all the more poignant when viewed from another's perspective."

"Is that unintelligible through your choice, or is it one of Kadeem's?"

"Does both count, Sire? Apparently, it means I might agree, sir."

Adeone laughed. "Does Kadeem ever say what he means?"

"On rare occasions, Sire. Are we to hall?" asked Arkyn, his stomach rumbling.

"Yes. After the supper, are you planning on staying at Court?"

"As I've just noticed Chapa, probably not, Sire. Is Your Majesty?"

Entering the King's Hall, Adeone muttered, "No, and for the same reason. He's watching us *both* appraisingly."

"He's good at it, Your Majesty."

Chapter 59

SMALL CRIMES

Imperadai, Week 23 – 18th Seral, 11th Seris 1212
Fitz's Inn

AFTER A CHILLY RIDE, Fitz's schoolroom was warm and inviting. Its fire danced merrily in the grate and Tancred was warming his hands at it when his pupil entered. He turned, noted something close to discontent and bowed.

After Tain was settled in his normal chair, Tancred said, "So, Your Highness, have you finished reading the texts I recommended?"

"Yes, Judge, but why am I still looking at the smaller crimes?"

Tancred regarded his charge. "Could you give me an example, Your Highness?"

"Yes. You asked me to read the laws regarding thieving articles of less than a talence in value."

"Which would include?"

"Well, loaves of bread for a start…" Tain's tone was disparaging.

Tancred was still grave. "May I tell you a story, Your Highness? One that could answer your question." (Tain nodded.) "Thank you. When I was young, there was a bad harvest. I am talking about the harvest that set taxes rising and led ultimately, years later, to the rebellion of 1169. As I said, I was young. Food was scarce. The yeomen were in the future and each lordship in Oedran administered local law. The Courthouse existed, but it was for what Your Highness might term the larger crimes. The street I lived on, along with many others, was starving. Hunger was ripping through the city. Everyone had to protect their stocks of food. Then one day a man was caught stealing a loaf of bread. A small thing, but it was not small at the time. It was life itself. If that man had succeeded, someone on our street might have died of starvation. It would have been as though they had been murdered. That was how the people on our street saw it. It was how I saw it, and I still believe that we were right. Whether the consequences were correct, I shall leave to Your Highness to decide. There was an impromptu court. The man was sentenced to death by his peers."

Tain was quiet. "How?"

"Does it matter, sir?"

"Yes."

Tancred was grave. "He was sentenced to be starved to death. At the time, it would not have taken many days." Tancred looked at the Prince's quiet face. "Then mercy won, sir. He was saved by a young lady who pointed out that since when did we, the hard-pressed, turn our backs on our own. That we would get through by helping each other, not instilling fear. She was right. She was always right. The man was reprieved. A few weeks later, the woman who had saved his life died when she caught a fever. She did not have the strength left to survive it. The winter ended an aluna-month later and the famine began to lift."

Tain was quiet, absorbing the story. Tancred studied the Prince's face: a boy having to evaluate a man's world.

It was several minutes before Tain said, "The lady, who was she?"

"A woman of our streets. She would have made a good lawyer, if she could have become one. Instead, within weeks of saving us all, she had died."

Tain's brain raced. He'd hardly heard the judge reply. "It still seems a harsh sentence for such a small crime."

Tancred said, "Then let us take a hypothetical situation, Your Highness. That was a situation taken at the worst of times. Will you pick a scenario for us to discuss?"

Tain thought. "The stealing of two talence from a rich man."

"Who is carrying them and for what purpose, sir? Is the rich man? Or maybe it is his servant?"

"His servant, going to pay his master's bills."

Tancred smiled. "Very well, Your Highness. We have a servant relieved of two talence when he is on his way to pay the bills. I think he has been in service all his life, not the most trusted servant but not the least either. Does that seem fair to you, Your Highness? A perfectly ordinary servant, you might say." (Tain nodded.) "Then I would say he has money to pay three people – one a bookseller, one a leatherworker and one a pin-lady. Again, do you agree with that, sir? Thank you. Now, tradition dictates the man would pay the one to whom the most is owed first; however, on his way there, we have decided he is relieved of some of his money. He does not notice. It was a slick pickpocket who took the coins. He pays the bookseller; to whom his master owes several darl. Then he calls on the leather worker. It is now he realises he is short by two talence; however, he has enough to pay the merchant. He clears his master's debt. He leaves the shop and wonders what to do. He cannot pay the pin-lady. He salves his conscience with the fact it is only a few crescents – or to use the street term, res – that are owing. It is nothing. Less than a day's wages for him. He 'forgets' to mention the issue on returning to his master's house. Is this a small crime, Your Highness?"

"Yes, Judge, by our laws it is."

"Very good, sir. Will you allow me to carry the story on?"

"Yes, but you'll not change my mind."

Tancred smiled and added a log to the fire. "I have always appreciated a challenge, but I shall tell the story. The man says nothing and then a few days later the pin-lady knocks and asks to be paid. She is obviously nervous. The man lies. He does not want to lose his job and admitting that he had not kept his master's money more secure would result in that. So, as I said, he lies. The lady is turned away. She returns a day later and this time they have the yeomen arrest her for being a nuisance and for trying to swindle money out of their master, a member of the alunan and a man of standing. The woman is thrashed and sent on her way. She knows she has no hope of anything else and so returns home. She had been relying on that money for food and warmth. Spending her last res on food, she just manages to last until someone else pays her for her work."

"What's your point, Judge?" enquired Tain, intrigued.

"Well, sir, you asked what was the point of studying the small crimes. What does that story, hypothetical though it may be, tell you? It must tell you at least one thing."

Tain thought. "That small crimes still matter to someone."

"Good, a valuable lesson by anyone's reckoning. You will make a lawyer; however, that story might have other messages hidden in it."

Again, Tain thought hard. "That money is relative to your income. Like the loaf of bread. If you have nothing, everything matters."

Now Tancred sounded happier. "Good, Your Highness. That is the lesson of life for many ordinary people. Carry on."

Relaxing into the lesson, Tain said, "That every action has consequences beyond that action. Consequences that might be unseen. There is more to crime than the initial action."

"Good. Now you might make a better lawyer, possibly even a judge."

Encouraged, Tain continued, "That, maybe, there are as many crimes not found out as there are discovered, and that they have as great an impact on lives as those which are identified."

"Carry on with that thought, Your Highness."

The answer came to Tain in a flash of inspiration. "Small crimes are large to their victims. There are no *small* crimes except in our law books. A crime is a crime."

Tancred relaxed. "You will make a justiciar yet, sir. Prince Lachlan would have been proud."

"Yet, if there are no small crimes, why aren't all laws given the same sentence? By the two stories you have yourself told, more than murder can end in death – that ultimate crime of taking another's life."

"There are many reasons, Your Highness," replied Tancred gravely. "Think on this: what does the word 'justice' imply?"

"The righting of a wrong."

"Good and now what does 'mercy' imply? In one word."

Tain thought hard. "Humanity."

"Close but not close enough. We go to war. We kill each other. What does 'mercy' imply?"

"Kindness."

"Does mercy overrule justice?"

"No."

Tancred nodded. "Good. Now, why do all laws not have the same sentence?"

Tain thought hard. It took several minutes until he said hesitantly, "Because then justice would be seen to be disproportionate to the perceived crime and mercy could have little place."

Tancred smiled. "As I said earlier, sir, Prince Lachlan would be proud. Now, should mercy be part of our justice system at all?"

"Yes."

"A reason helps me to understand your answers, sir."

Tain grinned. "I don't know why; I just know it should."

"Do you expect your lawyers and judges to accept that as a reason, sir? Would you accept it from them as an answer?"

Tain frowned. "No, Judge, but I am going to be the *Justiciar*."

Tancred nodded. "Yes, sir, you are. No-one would openly question your acts but beware of the dagger in the back. It is always better to see your enemy. Be ready to give your reasons for actions. If you do not, it could be seen as a wish for absolute power. Do not give people an excuse to make that dagger, sir. Always have your reasons ready."

"Spellen says that princes shouldn't always give their reasons."

"Advisor Spellen is an erudite man but, although you do not always have to give them, it does not mean that you yourself should be ignorant of your reasons. Always have them ready to give. It gains more respect and when people respect Your Highness there are more benefits to reap."

Tain eyed him and Tancred knew he had annoyed his charge, but that the Prince also recognised the truth. Tancred looked steadily back and, in that gaze, Tain saw the kindness of an old man who had a hard job to do. The anger in his eyes melted away.

"I'm sorry, Judge."

"So am I, sir. It seems I have become too impatient or too zealous. Maybe it is time to take a break."

Tain shook his head. "You haven't, Judge. I can carry on, if you can."

"Then, sir, we shall continue... whilst Your Highness is in the mood. Can you tell me your reasons for why mercy should be part of our justice?"

"It should be there, that's all I know. We should temper justice with mercy and let the truth decide."

"A good mantra, sir. Let me advise you. What is the definition of tyranny?"

"An absolute power which is used to subjugate peoples," recited Tain.

"A concise description, sir. In the justice system who or what would be the tyrant?"

"The judges."

"Or?"

"The Justiciar."

"Think of the 'what', sir," hinted Tancred.

"Then it would be the law, Judge."

"Good. Now do you have enough information to tell me your reasons for why mercy should temper our justice?"

Tain grinned, alive with the answer. "Because… that is… The reason is that the tyrannised will always rebel against the tyrant given time. That is why the Age of Tyranny was doomed, even without the Cearcall. People would overthrow those who tried to implement the law if we didn't have mercy. It, the empire, would descend into factions and fighting. It would crumble and, therefore… therefore, we must show some kindness in our decisions so we cannot be described as tyrants."

"I am impressed, Your Highness. Is there anything else?"

"Yes. Mercy is more than simply a part of our justice system, to be added at the discretion of the judge; it is already interwoven into our laws. The mitigating circumstances surrounding each sentence are just that."

"Does that mean we should not effect our own mercy on proceedings?"

"No, Judge. Mercy buys respect, respect buys loyalty, loyalty keeps the empire safe, which means people can live their lives unmolested."

"Of where should mercy stop short?"

"It shouldn't undermine justice. A wrong should be seen to be righted."

Tancred decided to push Tain further. "Should any section of society be excluded from our justice, sir?"

"No."

Tancred nodded a slow appreciative nod. "Your Highness, I wish some of the lawyers of Oedran could be here to hear you speak today. You are going to be a force to be reckoned with. It is only fair to give them some warning."

Tain laughed. "I take it I've passed then, Judge?"

"I think you have passed this lesson, sir. What do you think is the most important thing you have come to realise today?"

Tain chewed his lip. "That there is no such thing as a small crime. A crime is a crime – there should be no barriers in my mind as to the severity of the action. Yet to treat each as the law dictates but to never forget that a bit of mercy can go a long way; however, too much mercy can destroy instead of protect."

Tancred nodded. "A swift summation."

Tain bit his lip. Other aspects of the judge's story coming to mind. "Why would the pin lady have been thrashed, Judge? She wasn't charged with a crime."

"The yeomen have received orders that for misdemeanours that have not resulted in loss of property or physical harm, where there are witnesses *of good character*, then the yeomen can take *appropriate* action. The appropriateness of their action is their decision."

"But they inflicted *physical harm*. That's not right, is it?"

"I do not believe it is, sir, but that is the instruction the yeomen have received."

Tain shook his head. "It's not right. We shouldn't be above the laws we create for others. What can I do?"

Tancred smiled. "Remember the lesson, Your Highness. Until you are fifteen, there is nothing else. Your father has not changed your uncle's mind and he will not risk being seen to undermine his Justiciar. Now, we both deserve a drink. I will ring for Fitz…"

"I can do that, Judge."

"Your Highness…" said Tancred, pointedly.

Tain grinned. "Rest yourself, Judge. Take advantage of the young."

Tancred smiled. "If you promise to listen to the wisdom of age."

"I think I can stand that. Can you listen to the prattling of youth?"

"As well as any, sir."

They looked at each other and smiled. Tancred realised that somehow Tain had captured his aged heart. He would go to the end of Erinna for him.

Both of them felt that in the morning's work they had reached a turning point.

"Sir, would you think me presumptuous if I said my name is James and that at times it might be more appropriate than 'Judge' or 'sir'."

"Why is that presumptuous?" enquired Tain.

"It is against our social code…"

"Then shall we level the score? Mine is Tain as you well know and I prefer it to be used also."

Tancred said, "I'm not sure…"

"Did you call my Great-uncle Lachlan by his given name at all?"

Tancred smiled. "Very rarely, sir, but I suppose I did."

"You call the King by his name, on occasion; I have heard you…"

"That is at his request, Your Highness."

Tain grinned, triumphantly. "This is at mine. It doesn't have to be often, does it?"

"I suppose not, sir. Maybe, as we've been speaking of Prince Lachlan…

there was a name he used to call you by. Do you remember it?" (Tain shook his head.) "He used to call you 'Tailan'."

"Actually, I do remember something now… A joining of both my given names. Young Tailan… I do remember it. I remember him taking me round the Courthouse. Then maybe 'Tailan' would be better."

"Maybe, sir. Are we going to let Fitz in?"

Tain jumped. His journey into nostalgia had made him deaf to the knock of the old guard. He ran and opened the door. Fitz carried in a loaded tray.

"No need to ask what you both needed – was there, Your Highness? Growing boys need to be fed."

Tancred smiled. "What is my excuse then, Fitz?"

The old-guard-come-landlord observed, "The wanderings and peculiarities of age need none, Judge. Trust me on that."

Tancred laughed. "I certainly shall. It saves me thinking of reasons."

"Always have your reasons ready, Judge," said Tain innocently.

Tancred groaned and caught Fitz's eye. "I would blame his tutor."

Fitz laughed and, inclining his head, left.

Amused, Tancred turned to Prince Tain. "At least I know that one thing from this morning has stuck, sir."

"Sorry, Judge, I couldn't resist."

"I can believe that. I can see Prince Lachlan in you."

"What was he like?"

Tancred sat for most of the afternoon talking about the past. There were lessons and pointers in the talk but mostly it was just talk.

Chapter 60
GIFTS AND GARLANDS
Hexadai, Week 24 – 27th Seral, 20th Seris 1212
Ceardlann

A DAY BEFORE the Mundimri celebrations started, Kadeem entered the Prince's chambers and found his master reading in the window seat. He had obviously been after solitude and Kadeem couldn't blame him; the rest of the house was in unmitigating uproar as Tain and Cal decorated it.

Seeing understanding in Kadeem's features, Arkyn raised an amused eyebrow. "I'm waiting for normality to resume."

Kadeem smiled. "As Doctor Chapa has said to me, sir, what is normality?"

"Very true," Arkyn paused, hearing the clop of horses' hooves. "I do hope that's not father looking for a peaceful evening."

301

"Shall I find out for you, sir?"

Arkyn nodded. "If you're brave enough."

Twelve minutes later, which was far longer than Arkyn imagined Kadeem would be, his manservant returned, looking thoughtful.

"There was correspondence forwarded from Oedran, sir. Joe and David are bringing it along."

Arkyn frowned. "I can't believe I've as many correspondents as that, Kadeem. What's the mystery?"

Before his manservant could reply, the two senior footmen entered, carrying a fair-sized trunk. Arkyn frowned, puzzled. He nodded in thanks and dismissal at the two men.

"This, I think, has Percival written all over it."

Kadeem smiled. "I'm not sure, sir, but then the letter which came with the trunk wasn't sealed with His Excellency's seal."

"Well, let's have a read." He took the proffered letter, noted the seal with a raised eyebrow. It was intriguing for it was triangular and therefore a woman's and yet it wasn't Lady Wealsman's or Lady Daia Sansky's. Now more fascinated than ever, he broke the seal, read the signature and raised another eyebrow. "It's from the Visir's wife. Lady Terasina Silvano as was." He read the letter in more detail. "Apparently the trunk is Her Ladyship's thank you for my work in Terasia and for the fact she's happily married. It also seems that Lady Roth has become reconciled with her father, the Visir; I'm glad about that. Now, shall we take a look?"

Kadeem smiled. "Certainly, sir."

Arkyn got up and walked over to the trunk. "I can't quite believe she's sent this, Kadeem."

"It's not unusual for the FitzAlcis to receive gifts, sir."

"Then tell me, Kadeem, in the three years since you began working for me, other than at official times when have *I* ever received gifts?"

"The King does regularly, sir, and Your Highness has begun your official duties, so surely it can't be too perplexing, especially with the Mundimri so close."

Arkyn said mildly, "Nevertheless, I am surprised. Is there a key?"

Kadeem handed it over, saying, "Surprise reminds us we're alive, sir."

Arkyn glared at him. "Very amusing, Kadeem. Has it been checked?"

"Yes, sir, in Oedran."

"Good. It's not that I distrust Her Ladyship but her brother did try to kill me and she might, just might, be feeling aggrieved at his execution."

"Possibly, sir."

"Very noncommittal, Kadeem. Your mastery of the ambiguous is improving." He pushed open the lid of the trunk and whistled slightly, "Her Ladyship doesn't do anything by halves, does she?"

Kadeem smiled. "Apparently not, sir."

Arkyn answered a knock at the door. "Yes. What is it, David?"

"His Majesty has arrived, sir, and wonders if you have a moment?"

Arkyn got to his feet. "Where is the King?"

Adeone entered the room, beaming. "Here. Thank you, Kadeem, David."

The servants left, catching each other's eye meaningfully.

As the door closed, Arkyn said, "I'd have come downstairs, sir."

"I wouldn't put you through it. Your brother can make more noise on his own than a regiment."

"I'd noticed. You didn't need to get David to herald you though."

Adeone sat on Arkyn's bed, running his hands across the candlewick throw. "I didn't know what you were up to. After all, that trunk might have been from a so-called conquest in Tera. I was courting your mother when I was your age and the thought simply occurred to me that you might have your eye on someone."

"No, sir, I'm afraid not," replied Arkyn, without emphasis. "As I said before, I'm not looking for a wife yet."

"So, who *is* the chest from? I'm as curious as the next man."

Arkyn smiled. "It is from a lady, as it happens: one whom I met briefly—"

"Brief encounters rarely result in such gifts. It must have been memorable."

"Father, stop it!"

"All right, I'm sorry. Who is the lady?"

"The Visir's wife, Lady Raheem – Lady Terasina Silvano, as she was. Yes, that was my reaction. Have a read of her letter."

Adeone said, "If you're sure there's nothing confidential in it I certainly will." By the time he reached the end of the letter, he nodded. "I always thought there was sense somewhere in that family. Pity it wasn't in the elder son. What is in the trunk?"

"I'm not sure. It's full of bits and bobs and lined in silk; that's as far as I'd got."

"Then let's explore."

Arkyn once more opened the lid. Seeing the arrangement, Adeone knew it had been a well thought out gift. Even if Lady Raheem was trying to gain favour, she was doing so with practical gifts.

"This, my son, is a Denshirian Travelling Trunk; trust me they *are* worth their weight in gold. No other province has ever mastered their production to the same standard. It will hold everything from a handful of tunics and shoes to correspondence, food and drink."

"That's not possible, father."

"Then explore it. I'd be curious to see myself. I've never actually got around to getting one and now have little need of one."

Arkyn grinned. "Then this should be interesting. Maybe we should get Kadeem here; he'll be dealing with the trunk."

"A wise precaution."

* * *

Three minutes later, Kadeem said, "Allow me, sir. These chests, I believe, have many secrets, like the Denshirian people…"

"Very poetic, Kadeem."

"Thank you, Sire. The trick, I'm told, is to remove the securing rods. One acts as part of the hinge and there is one at each corner. It means that the trunk unfolds at each side to allow easier access and to pack flat when the trunk is empty. I suppose it slots together as a jigsaw puzzle with inner divisions and straps. Each piece is made for this particular trunk…"

Arkyn murmured to his father, "Have I ever mentioned that Kadeem is a fund of information?"

"Ssh, he's got more."

Having paused, Kadeem continued blithely, "It's a masterpiece of craftsmanship. It even contains a chair, but no table, as such, which is very remiss of them."

Arkyn said, "I suppose, we shouldn't breathe down Kadeem's neck whilst he unpacks it, sir."

Adeone smiled. "I'm sure Kadeem won't mind if we stay. I'm curious and I suspect you are."

Kadeem said, "I have no objection, sir."

"Then come on, let's explore."

By the time the trunk had been unpacked all three of them had had a hand in it. There was a tunic case, shoe box, male toilet set, writing desk – with all accoutrements – medical kit, aromatherapy kit, decanters, glass goblets, a games box, small book chest and a document holder.

Arkyn looked at it all then looked back at the trunk. "How?"

Adeone shrugged. "Such is the myth. It is more impressive than I thought it would be."

Arkyn nodded. "It certainly is, sir, and a lot of thought has gone into the gift. How do I reply to it?"

"With a carefully worded letter to Her Ladyship and possibly His Excellency," replied Adeone. "He must have had a hand because it's all marked with your seal. I'm sure you'll cope."

"Thank you for the confidence, Sire. I'm still dumbfounded. Kadeem, are you sure you can pack all this away again?"

Kadeem smiled. "Yes, Your Highness. For the maker sent me an instruction sheet."

"No wonder you know such a lot," observed Adeone. "We shall leave you to it. Arkyn, let's find somewhere out of the way to sit."

"Why? Don't you appreciate Tain's boisterous nature?"

"Not at the moment. I have a headache."

Twenty-four minutes later, Kadeem entered the snug on soft feet bearing a tray of refreshments and a headache remedy.

* * *

Adeone and Arkyn were talking when Tain and Cal breezed in with garlands made from evergreens to hang around the room. Adeone held out his hand to his younger son.

"Can you do it quietly?"

Tain bit his lip but nodded. Once the garlands were hung across the fireplace and window, Tain sat by his father.

Adeone gave him a one-armed hug. "Would you be very upset with me if I said I'd planned for you to visit Oedran this Mundimri?"

Tain's eyes lit up. "Can I come to the feast?"

"Not that bit, no. You don't need to watch the Court make fools of themselves yet."

"No, you can do that anytime," muttered Arkyn mischievously.

Adeone's lips twitched. "Don't look so disappointed, Tain. You can still run riot around the Palace, visit your nearcousins and cause absolute mayhem. Cal could visit his family as well."

Tain looked at Cal. "What do you think?"

"I'd like to see everyone, sir," said Cal, "but it would be a shame to miss all of this."

"This?" asked Adeone suspiciously.

Tain chuckled. "We've planned our own feast here, with the Comptroller and everyone, in the Great Hall. Well, everyone who doesn't want to spend it with their family. There's enough. That's why we've been decorating. We asked Laioril, but he's not bothered. Some of the rest of the tribe accepted."

"It would seem a shame to spoil that. Why didn't you tell me?"

"Because you're always at the feast in Oedran," replied Tain with a shrug. "Arkyn thought it would be all right."

"It's very tempting for me to give Oedran a miss this year," said Adeone.

Arkyn chuckled. "Who is due to preside at Court?"

"Ryson, it's always Ryson for Alcis Day feasts. He enjoys organising it with the Steward. I will see if he would be offended if I spent it here. Unless, of course, you've got more planned that I shouldn't know about," he added shrewdly.

305

Tain chuckled. "Nothing, Sire. Not yet. We've still got time."

* * *

The following evening, Ceardlann's Great Hall was packed with the residents of the valley who lived nearby, the servants, the Wanda and the FitzAlcis. Those who could play instruments provided music bringing the usually silent magnificence of the hall to life. Out on the lawn torches marked out paths, their flames giving warmth and light into the night. The full moons shone in a cloudless sky, bathing the valley in a bright silver light. Laughter spilled into every corner, Adeone's amongst it. His heart was light with good food and good company. He half wished the Landises hadn't moved back home. His nearchildren would have loved the experience. Arkyn sat beside him, watching the melee. The feast had started early enough for some of the children of the tenants to be there. Tain and Cal were running around with them, completely oblivious to the parents exchanging glances.

Adeone chuckled. "I think our tenants are wary of Tain's influence."

"Or of their children being too close to us."

"That too. You know, Tain and Cal have put the Palace feast to shame. This is better than I ever expected. I can feel the valley enjoying it."

Arkyn smiled. "You always speak of it as though it is a person."

"Have you never heard the story that the Cearcall personified it? They created two deities, personifications. The Lord and Lady of Encilla. Bringing peace and strength to its inhabitants."

"I've heard the stories, sir, but I've never seen evidence they're true."

"Sometimes belief or faith are all we have." He smiled as a lady passed in front of the dais. "Miranda, come and talk. Bring Sayre as well, wherever he's hiding."

The wise woman of the Wanda smiled. "I'm not sure he's in a fit state, sir. He found one of Cook's barrels and Cook."

"Oh dear. How's the barrel?"

"Empty, I believe." Miranda walked to the end of the trestle table and then back along it until she could sit near the King. "Are you out of elderberry wine, Sire?"

"I'm out of that the evening after you give me a bottle," admitted Adeone. "Why's the old rogue avoiding this feast?"

Miranda shrugged. "I think he prefers the peace of his tent, sir. I can't imagine why."

Adeone eyed the crowded hall. "Do you think they'd notice if we also hid elsewhere?"

Miranda chuckled. "Probably more if you did than if I did, Sire." She watched the children running around. "They're all growing so quickly. Lady Elantha has lost the infant."

"Yes. She's certainly now a child. She's going to grow into a beautiful lady. She has her mother's delicate features."

"I hope the future is kind to her. It isn't always for ladies."

Arkyn said, "We'll do our best, Miranda."

"I didn't mean to imply you wouldn't, Your Highness. It's everyone else I'm worried about."

Adeone snorted. "Yes. We all worry about them. Personally, I'm going to enjoy seeing what everyone makes of Tain. As you can see, Arkyn is very sensible. He keeps himself out of harm's way. Tain on the other hand…"

Miranda laughed. "Isn't that what you have guards for, sir?"

"It might well be. I'm keeping them exceptionally fit just for Tain."

Arkyn snorted. "They won't know what's hit them. Do you think Tain and Cal should be going to bed if they're visiting Oedran in the morning?"

"Do you think they would go quietly?" asked Adeone.

Miranda watched the boys. "I'd say not, sir. Would you like me to dose their juice?"

Adeone laughed. "No, thank you, Miranda. We better not start with that. You might be in demand for remedies in the morning though."

"I'll go and prepare some, Sire."

Once she'd gone, Adeone relaxed back in his chair. "I honestly don't know when this hall last hosted a feast."

"I think it's been good for us all, father."

"Yes. It reminds me what feasts should be. No worry, no concern, no fear. Your rascal of a brother has always had a lot to answer for. This not least of all."

Chapter 61

DUNIUS?

Cisadai, Week 25 – 2nd Ralal, 2nd Ralis 1212
Diary Archives

Tain SAT READING his great-uncle's diary from the early years of Prince Lachlan's life; they were a fascinating insight into a lost world and the mind of a man that all, or nearly all, had respected. Reassuringly, the pages contained the same fears for the future Tain had. Gradually change suffused the page and Lachlan had become reconciled to his future.

Tain read about his own grandfather from a brother's perspective. Would he and Arkyn ever become so frustrated with each other? King Altarius, it transpired, had been too sombre for Lachlan and yet, when Tain read

Altarius' diaries, it appeared it wasn't his grandfather's fault.

Their father, King Apolinar, had held definite views on how his elder son should behave. Altarius' and Lachlan's childhoods had, therefore, been very different. To Altarius had fallen the responsibility and Court facing duties. If he went beyond what Apolinar directed, it wasn't only a dressing down he received. There were early accounts of beatings and hours of relaxation rescinded for being seen to laugh at the wrong time, for not knowing his lessons and for not being as staid as Apolinar thought proper.

In contrast, Lachlan had been left to himself; to grow up without his father's scrutiny, and where sympathy for an older brother might have appeared, there was only frustration.

One name occurred in both diaries without explanation, and it was one Tain had never heard before; yet the regularity of its appearance suggested a close connection with the FitzAlcis. Trying to solve the mystery, Tain continued reading. He reached the death of Apolinar and the brief, all too brief, feeling of release Lachlan and Altarius shared.

He read of the Bayan rebellion from Lachlan's diary only. Altarius had been far too busy to keep one. The pace of the rebellion had been quick and Altarius' reaction just as speedy.

Lachlan had fought alongside him, all frustration forgotten. There was the mention of traitors in the Anaparian camp, executions, battles won, rebels turned, the Citadel of Garth stormed and the rebels executed. In a brief sentence Lachlan wrote that Queen Orphelia and Prince Adlai had caught a fever. Lachlan thought Altarius should return to them, leaving him to secure the forts. Altarius had ignored him. Knowing what was coming, Tain read on with an insatiable appetite. Altarius discovered Orphelia and Adlai had died and the news had been kept from him. Tain read the next passage.

Dunius was a fool but he shouldn't have kept the news from Alt. I don't know if I'll ever forgive Alt for executing him - exile might have been better, worse for a time but, when rage cooled, Alt might have relented. Now we'll never see Dunius again. Exile would have been a greater shame than dying. I wonder how his family is taking it. I'll have to stop talk at Court; I owe him that much...'

The extract puzzled Tain more than any other that had mentioned Dunius. Here was incontrovertible proof he had been close to them. From other accounts, Tain knew there had been one execution on his grandfather's return from Bayan: Altarius' nearfather. Dunius must have been that nearfather and yet why had Tain never heard the actual name? He closed his great-uncle's diary and, putting it back, looked at Thomkins.

"Might I ask a question?"

The archivist smiled. "Of course, sir."

"Were you in Oedran in 1169?"

"For some of it, sir. I went to Bayan with His late Majesty."

Tain hadn't expected a clerk in a position like Thomkins' to be in battles. "Oh, so do you know exactly who Dunius was? I keep finding his name. I think he was my grandfather's nearfather, but it's not stated anywhere."

"I'd say that is one mystery better left to the past, Your Highness."

"Why?"

"Because sometimes the mud of memory is better unstirred. It's like a swamp: you never know what you'll bring to the surface."

Tain sensed the old archivist wouldn't divulge anything else. "Right. I'd better go…"

Thomkins smiled. "I hope I'll see you soon, Your Highness."

Tain ran up the stairs. His guards, waiting at the top, saluted, then hurried after him. The Prince half ran through the Privy Wing and, once in the King's Corridor, turned round and grinned. Only Smithers had kept up.

"You're all getting slow."

Smithers chuckled. "Or Your Highness is getting quicker, sir. Shall I wait in the guardroom?"

"Please." He ran into the Outer Office, where Richardson caught his eye. Tain stopped. "Don't tell me, father's in a meeting?"

"His Majesty has a meeting in six minutes, sir, but is currently free. Would you like me to announce you?"

Tain grinned. "No. I'm sure I can do it myself." In a fit of mischief, he managed a passable imitation of Richardson as he announced himself.

When the door closed, Adeone said, "Stop teasing my administrator, you young rascal. What can I do for you?"

Tain grinned. "I've just been reading Great-uncle Lachlan's diaries and I want to ask you something."

"This sounds dangerous."

"Who was Dunius? I mean, I *think* he was grandfather's nearfather, as the diary refers to him being executed, but I can't find out for certain. Thomkins won't tell me, and I don't know who else to ask."

"How about Aunt Amara?" suggested Adeone, intrigued.

"I don't think she'd tell me."

"Why not?"

Tain tried to formulate a reply. "Because if he was grandfather's nearfather surely he'd have been hers… I also feel a bit odd admitting I've read the diaries, so know about her childhood."

"Understandable. I'll see if I have any more luck. You'd better run along. Give the judge my greetings when you see him."

* * *

Two hours later, the King had a meeting with Wynfeld at the end of which Adeone said mildly, "I'd like you to find out something for me, well, for Prince Tain. He's been reading my uncle's diaries and has come across a reference to one Dunius. Can you see what you can discover, please?"

"Certainly, sir. How far in the past is this?"

"Before my father became King, but I'm sure you'll meet the challenge with your normal competence."

Wynfeld smiled. "I enjoy mysteries, Your Majesty; however, I'm not sure how long this one will take me."

"Patience, I've always been told, is a virtue. Thank you, Major."

* * *

Wynfeld left the Inner Office considering the request. There were several people who might help, but none he could approach without speculation. He walked to the barracks and entered the vast intelligence archive. A corporal he didn't know rose and saluted smartly. The Major nodded to him and went to search through the drawers.

The corporal hesitated. "Sir, no-one is meant to personally look through this lot without a chitty."

Wynfeld continued. "Check the last ten and check who signed them."

The corporal did so. "Sorry, sir. Can I help?"

"Thank you, but I know my way around this archive, Corporal...?"

"Garron, sir."

"It's chilly in here, Garron. Go and warm up for twelve minutes. That's an order."

The corporal saluted and left. The new Captain of Intelligence spotted him and gave him a dressing down; to which the corporal replied that he was following Wynfeld's orders, savouring the moment.

Fysher rallied well. "I hope he's still there. Dismissed." He arrived at the archives in time to see the Major replacing a box thoughtfully.

"Sir?"

Wynfeld turned round. "Captain, is there something I can do for you?"

"My understanding was that these archives weren't to be unmanned, sir."

"There're not unmanned. I'm here."

"Yes, sir, as I see, but if anything comes in?"

"I'll record and file it. You have forgotten that I am responsible for many of the practices under which you work. Now, you've got much to

310

do, I suspect and, if you haven't, I'll find you some more."

The Major spent the time before Garron returned checking the records of who used the archives before leaving for his office. Once there, he cursed. The archive had contained nothing useful. It wasn't surprising – the intelligence regiment had been set up by Altarius. He answered a knock at the door absentmindedly and then rose hurriedly and saluted.

"General?"

"Major, I've had Fysher in my office with a complaint… Seems you were in the archives and dismissed Garron."

"Yes, sir. I wanted to be alone. Are you taking any action?"

Paturn sat down, smiling. "Not on you. Fysher is discovering the joys of trying to undermine his superior officer do not include my approbation. What were you hunting for?"

Wynfeld weighed up his answer. There could be little harm in telling the General. "Information on one Dunius, sir, alive during King Apolinar's reign."

"Leave it to the past, or I must take action against you."

Rather perplexed by Paturn's attitude, Wynfeld explained further.

The General's astonishment was obvious. "Alcis! But, surely, His Majesty knows already? He must… I'll go and see the King. You forget about it, that's an order, and I don't bloody care who tries to override it. Do you understand?"

"Yes, sir."

"Good. Had you mentioned it to anyone else?"

"No, sir."

"Even better!"

* * *

Adeone smiled warmly as the General was announced but something in Paturn's bearing made him pause.

"What can I do for you, General?"

"Your Majesty, I understand you've been asking about Lord Dunius."

"I have – although I didn't know he was a lord. What of it?"

Paturn hesitated. "Might I suggest it is left to the past, sir? I'm not sure Your Majesty actually wishes to know about him."

Adeone got up, poured two drinks and pointed to a chair before replying. "I am getting more intrigued the more people refuse to explain. Prince Tain asked me about him because Thomkins, the Diary Archivist, refused to enlighten him. What is the secret? His Highness says he thinks Dunius was my father's nearfather."

"He was, Sire, and he was executed as a traitor in 1169. Subsequently,

311

your father, or rather Prince Lachlan, ordered that there was never to be a mention of his name. He was expunged from history; I suspect it is only in their diaries that he still lives. His family was influential, *is* influential, and no good will come of raking up that past."

Adeone took a sip of whiskey. "You'll have to tell me, General, or I'll continue digging by other means, which might well prove more damaging."

To Adeone's astonishment, Paturn knelt.

"Sire, I think it's best not. Please believe me, there is more damage to be done, even now."

Adeone regarded him for several long moments. The General had always answered his questions since he had become King, irrespective of his father's orders. For Paturn to refuse so resolutely meant the orders had existed for a *very* good reason; one that, on reflection, Adeone probably *didn't* want to know.

After a couple of minutes of silence, Adeone said, "Just promise me, I will be told, if I need to know."

Paturn held both hands out, palm upward, as though about to salute. "I swear it, Sire."

Adeone put his hands palm down. "I accept your oath."

There was no escape from his promise now and, knowing it, Paturn sealed the matter by kissing the King's signet ring.

Adeone regarded him. "I hope you're not planning on being on your knees all day, General."

Paturn got up. "Your Majesty; I should not wish to inconvenience you any longer."

Adeone smiled. "I thought I had troubled you. As you're here, how is the bandit situation?"

"We've captured three groups, Sire: in Areal, Gerymor and on the Anaparian-Bayan Ridge."

"Good. Keep it up."

Chapter 62
GUEST
Tretaldai, Week 25 – 3rd Ralal, 3rd Ralis 1212
Palace – Prince Arkyn's Office

THE FOLLOWING DAY, having spent time at Ceardlann on his own, Arkyn arrived in Oedran to a pile of letters from friends, invitations from various lords in Oedran and updates from his advisors on the petitions and the road network. He glanced at the titles and put them to one side.

He'd talk with his chief advisor another day. He couldn't completely warm to Caple. Was he missing Rayburn's more experienced, less wary attitude? Caple hadn't worked directly for the FitzAlcis before, whereas Rayburn had years of experience with their conflicting priorities and requirements.

Having put off reading the reports, Arkyn turned to the correspondence. Edward had noted on the invitations which could be accepted without issue. Two clashed; Arkyn wrote a reply declining both before asking Edward to find opportunities for him to dine with Lords Iris and Fairson when he wouldn't be seen to be favouring one over the other.

By the time he broke Kensal's seal, he'd read and replied to letters from Wealsman, Lady Daia and Lord Roth in Terasia, and Lord Ogilvie in Gerymor, who wanted to ingratiate himself. After that sycophantic and obsequious missive, he was more than happy to find Kensal's practical and friendly letter informing him the weather for his journey had stayed reasonable and, all being well, he hoped to be in Oedran by the end of the week. Arkyn smiled. Most lords avoided travelling between mid-autumn and early spring, only venturing forth if there was real need to do so. Kensal obviously didn't worry about such trifling things as snow and ice.

Half an hour later, the Prince watched as the Steward entered his office. He was in his late thirties, which suggested that someone had pulled strings to get him the position. Dark red hair showed flecks of grey. His serviceable and crisp linen tunic, tailored to perfection, hid woollen and cotton under-tunics. A wide leather belt was tightened over an expanding paunch with a buckle showing an elaborate gold S over a deep red enamel. He wore the mark of his position with pride, making sure it stood out against the natural cream of his tunic. Arkyn's skin crawled for no obvious reason.

"Thank you for coming, Steward. Lord Kensal Parchi is due to arrive later this week. I presume everything's in order?"

"Yes, Your Highness. A suite of rooms on the east side of the Court Wing is being prepared."

Arkyn hesitated. "As His Lordship is here as my guest, it seems unfair to make him cross the entire Palace. The Court does not, I believe, have enough guests to warrant the rooms suggested."

"It might be easier if we knew the length of His Lordship's stay, sir."

"As long as he wishes, Steward, at my invitation. Please move His Lordship's accommodation to the third floor – off the square – east facing."

"Your Highness, those rooms are some of the best in the Palace. Perspective alone suggests that His Lordship will feel out of place. They are kept for—"

"Ambassadors, Embassadors, visiting Provincial Lords and – certainly relevant here – friends of the FitzAlcis not accommodated in the Privy Wing. *I* invited Lord Kensal here; his rooms will befit that."

"Your Highness, forgive me, but you're not yet of alunan-age—"

"Being over cisan-age, I can request anything which does not alter, or interfere in, Palace procedures and protocols. I consider my requests fall within that remit. You may, of course, appeal to His Majesty outlining in full all matters and ramifications of following my wishes. I had hoped to save His Majesty's valuable time by dealing with this visit myself but should you wish to involve His Majesty and, in pursuing this matter, use up such time as the King can spare then I can but urge you to do so. You must, of course, follow your conscience."

The Steward swallowed. "Thank you, Your Highness, you are, of course, correct: His Majesty need not be troubled; I shall see the chamberlain immediately."

Arkyn gave a brief nod. "Thank you, but I never said His Majesty need not be troubled, I said I did not wish to. If I am unable to greet Lord Kensal personally, I shall let you know; however, for now, that's all."

The Steward bowed and left, several comments he wished to make unsaid. The Prince watched him go and half knew what he was thinking. In Oedran, Arkyn had limited authority because he wasn't yet in his majority. When he travelled within the empire, his authority came from the fact that he was proclaimed a King's Representative so he could undertake the reviews. Without that proclamation he was effectively a figurehead and no more. It had worried and concerned many men of influence all over the empire when Adeone had made Arkyn a King's Representative whilst he was still an adolescent. His subsequent decisions had only heightened their anxiety instead of proving it well founded. After two reviews, which had cut swathes through the political dealings normally integral to them, some governors were wondering if they'd survive their next review, whatever the King apparently thought of their stewardship.

Chapter 63

IMPERIAL GARDEN SECRETS

Hexadai, Week 25 – 6th Ralal, 6th Ralis 1212
Palace – Imperial Garden

THREE DAYS LATER, Tain mooched into the centre of the Imperial Garden and sat on one of the twelve stone thrones that circled it. He wanted to be outside but didn't know what he wanted to do. Used to having Cal around, he was finding his own company hard to bear and

Arkyn hadn't been there to disturb. Smithers was being an unobtrusive presence in the background, letting him wander wherever he wanted.

A voice said, "The sun's shining, it's a day for smiling."

Tain saw a young man, still cloaked and booted from riding. Tousled brown hair suggested someone who didn't spend hours worried about his appearance and bright amber eyes were watching him kindly.

Tain gave a wan smile. "I'm wondering what to do."

Smithers stiffened, as though about to intervene. Tain shook his head at the sergeant to stop him. Any distraction suited his mood.

"Well then, we'll have to find something. I've been looking around this garden, but I don't know much about it."

Tain sighed. "It's the Imperial Garden. It celebrates the empire. That's why there are twelve thrones set here."

The young lord turned on the spot, taking in the stone pillars and open roof structure. "I'm not sure it does, I think it celebrates the Cearcall. I don't suppose you know when the thrones were set here, do you? They seem older than the empire."

"Oh. I wouldn't know. Why do you say it celebrates the Cearcall?"

"Each throne has the symbol of a member of the Cearcall."

"They're also the symbols of the empire."

"That's true, but surely then they'd be carved with scenes that are related to the provinces when actually they seem to portray magical actions. For example, you were sitting on the throne I suspect is thought of for Gerymor, yet it doesn't show gems or mines or mountains. It shows a pair of scales and a figure weighing something on them. The figure is androgynous as they all are but I think it's meant to be a woman; I think this is meant to be the first Rheol. If you look carefully, you'll see that there are hints of lines coming in and out of her hands, like someone winding wool and, if you follow those lines around, they move onto the next throne, where another figure is holding out his hand to receive them, whilst in the background a rock is metamorphosing into an ingot. On and on this goes around and around these thrones. I can't think that these represent the empire."

Tain paused. He'd jumped up when the lord had mentioned the threads appearing on the next throne and he saw that he was indeed right. He paused chewing on his lip. "The lady could be weighing gems, couldn't she?"

"Of course, but what of the threads? Can you explain those and Gerymor? Or could anyone? I'm not sure how much you know about the province."

Tain grinned. "Enough. All right, if this garden is meant to represent the Cearcall and not the empire, convince me..."

A voice behind them said, "There's a challenge for you."

Tain whipped round. "Go away, Arkyn. This is getting interesting."

Arkyn laughed. "All right, I'll go. Welcome to Oedran, Lord Kensal. When my brother deigns to let you leave, get someone to show you the way to my office." Arkyn winked at him and left.

Rising from his bow, Kensal realised the boy he'd been talking to was Prince Tain. "I'm sorry, sir. I didn't recognise you."

Tain shrugged. "I enjoyed the sensation. Arkyn says you're a historian."

"I try to be one, sir, but I'm not sure I've managed it yet."

"Convince me then. I'm certainly not a historian, but I am interested in the Cearcall."

Kensal grinned. "It's a fascinating garden, or at least here in the centre it's fascinating. Let's examine the thrones. I've heard about them for years and seen drawings of most, but there's always something missing on a drawing. Things seem to change in real life as though magic was at work here. The one thing I noticed immediately, other than that magnificent fountain, was the fact that all the thrones but one had a figure on."

Tain frowned. "They all have one."

"No, sir, they don't. I'll stand here so you know where you've started; now hunt."

Tain eyed him and did so. He reached Kensal again. "It's odd, you're right but I'm sure you're wrong. I know that the Anaparian throne had a figure on, I remember it distinctly."

"Do you, sir? It's not there now."

"No, but… All right, I accept that there isn't a figure of a man or woman on that throne, but then how can my memory be so vivid? It was holding out a hand as though about to lay it on a sword."

"Really?" asked Kensal becoming animated. "That's interesting. There is a tale that there was once a sword owned by the last Skifta that survives."

Tain grinned. "It's meant to be one at Ceardlann. Do you believe me though?"

"I think I might. The question is, where has that figure gone?"

"Where could it go? It's carved out of stone! It can't walk away."

Kensal considered. "Are we sure? This garden could be magical, there're meant to be globes of power still at the Palace."

Tain's eyes sparkled. "Well, if it's stone, let's hunt for it. How about one of the pillars?"

Kensal turned on the spot, muttering to himself. "Twelve pillars, each supporting an arched roof strut. We can't check the struts but the pillars…?" Eighteen minutes later, he added, "So, he's not gone there. The ivy might be covering him…"

"I could try to get them to cut it back."

"No, I like it and who would hide inside ivy, sir?"

"Other than a stone carving that doesn't want to be found? I can't think of anyone. It's not thick enough. I didn't see an extra figure on any throne and I looked for one. People hide with other people, so carvings hide with other carvings."

Kensal began to think the conversation would get people wondering if either of them was sane. "Just out of interest, sir, why the roof struts? There is no roof."

Tain shrugged. "I don't know. I thought that was how it was meant to be."

"I wonder. I don't think anything here is what it's meant to be. I can't help feeling this garden is ancient. Was there meant to be a roof? Was this actually a meeting place? Did you know that at the top of the Cearcall Tower was meant to be a room where none but the Cearcall went?"

"Yes, I did."

"Did you also know, sir, that there was meant to be a font there? I wonder if this place is meant to mimic that room. Twelve seats that we believe – I hope it's now we – represent the Cearcall and also the fountain…"

Tain grinned. "Well, you're convincing me, but where is that Shifter, if he's gone from his throne?"

"That is the question, Your Highness. Well, he's not on any throne or on any pillar that we can see. I think he's playing with us. Where's left?"

"Under our feet?"

"No, the flagstones aren't carved…"

"How about the fountain?"

"No self-respecting Shifter would want to drown, sir."

Tain, feeling slightly unreal at the lunacy of their talk, said, "What about the pedestal, he wouldn't drown there and he'd be out of sight."

Kensal nodded. "A good idea, sir, but we'll have to lie on the ground."

"So?"

They lay examining the underside of the bowl. Then Tain glanced at the pillar.

"I have him! He's here… Have you got his sword?"

Lord Kensal said, "This is interesting, sir. Have you looked at the underside of this bowl? This symbol, I've seen it before. Where have I seen it? It's simple, but I'm sure there's something familiar about it… Your Highness, have you seen it before? Sir?"

Tain giggled. "Sorry, Lord Kensal, it's a bit hard to concentrate when the King's tickling your feet…"

Before Tain could draw breath, Lord Kensal rolled over and was in the clear garden. King Adeone was indeed tickling the Prince's feet. He knelt, but all Adeone did was wink and continue. Tain rolled out of reach and rubbed at his feet.

"Sire! We'd just found the Shifter."

"I've been looking for one for years," said Adeone. "Thank you, Lord Kensal, you can rise. Tain, what do you mean that you've found the Shifter?"

Tain started to explain and Adeone raised an amused eyebrow as the end of the story was reached.

"I'm impressed. Your imagination is unbounded. Now, run and tell Maria that you're dining with me tonight."

Tain sighed. "You don't believe me but it's true."

Adeone crooked an eyebrow. "This takes a little more conviction than normal. Go on, I'm not annoyed but I passed Judge Tancred on my way here."

Tain grinned. "I'd completely forgotten, Sire. I'll find him. Thank you, Lord Kensal. I hope to see you soon." With that and a quick bow to his father, Tain hared off.

Adeone watched Lord Kensal shrewdly. "Prince Tain's imagination is sometimes the most surprising facet of his personality."

"It certainly would be impressive if he had been inventing that," remarked Kensal, "but I ought to say, Your Majesty, that it was all perfectly true."

Adeone paused. "Are you truly expecting me to believe that a carving disappeared from one of these thrones and appeared on the pedestal of the fountain, Lord Kensal?"

"Let's see if he's still there, Sire." He knelt and pointed. "There you are, sir, and his sword is just out of his reach again."

Adeone knelt and saw the carving. "All right, that's strange, but that carving could have been there for years."

"I don't think it has been, Sire. There are twelve stone figures in this garden. I think that's significant."

Adeone pushed himself to his feet, turning on the spot to take in the garden. "How old do you think this place is, Lord Kensal?"

Feeling self-conscious, Kensal hesitated. "I'm honestly not sure, Sire, but I think over eight hundred years. The amount of lichen on the stones, suggests it's old; it grows extremely slowly. I also think it was roofed at some point."

"It would have been dark, if it had been, don't you think?"

"Not if it was in glass and I wouldn't be surprised if each section was a different colour, one for each star stone, maybe?" He stepped back and inclined his head. "I'm sorry, Sire. I'm presuming far too much."

Adeone watched the young lord; he had a real passion for his subject. "Maybe not. What would you suggest went above the fountain, where the struts meet in that circle?"

"I don't know, Sire, but I would suggest a prism. The sun would send rainbows all around here and the light might well bounce off the fountain."

Adeone smiled. "I can almost see it. You're a convincing fellow, Lord Kensal, but both mine and my son's questions have kept you from relaxing after your journey."

"I'm not at all bothered, Your Majesty. I've enjoyed the last hour. I ought to find Prince Arkyn though. He asked me to go to his office."

"I'm on my way back to mine," admitted Adeone. "If you'll walk with me, I'll show you the way."

"Thank you, Sire; I hear the Palace can be a bit of a maze."

"If it's only 'can be' I'll have to do a bit of building work. I don't want my officials to escape too easily," said Adeone, tongue-in-cheek.

Lord Kensal chuckled. "Really, Sire?"

Adeone raised an amused eyebrow but that was all the comment he made. On the way to the offices, though, he did say, "Lord Kensal, I'd be grateful if you'd keep your observations regarding the Imperial Garden to yourself, or at least talk only to the Princes of them. They are interesting, but I'd like to see if anyone else notices what you did."

"Of course, Sire, if that is your wish," replied Kensal, intrigued.

A few minutes later, Adeone nodded to a couple of guards to open the door at the end of a corridor. He walked in and Edward rose and bowed.

"Edward, Lord Kensal is here to see His Highness. Is he here?"

"Yes, Your Majesty."

"Then I'll have a word; maybe you could make Lord Kensal feel welcome." Adeone knocked and entered his son's office.

Arkyn smiled as he got to his feet. "Sire."

"Arkyn. You have some interesting friends, but I'll let Lord Kensal explain what he and Tain discovered in the Imperial Garden. Don't tire yourself out entertaining…"

"I'll be fine, father."

"Yes, well, I came to ask you to join me at dinner."

"Would you mind too much if I didn't, Sire? I'd organised a dinner with Lord Kensal and Lord Irvin."

Adeone shook his head. "I don't know, throwing away the chance of annoying your father and deserting me for your friends; how will I cope?"

"Probably by inviting Uncle Festus. I'm sorry, father."

"That's all right, I should have realised you'd have other plans this evening. I'll leave you to chat the afternoon away."

Adeone lingered to say a couple of words to Lord Kensal and, after the door had shut on his son and the young lord, turned to Edward,

"Keep tomorrow free for His Highness. He should spend time with his friends. Just give me chance to be ensconced safely in my office before you tell him."

Adeone walked thoughtfully to the Inner Office. Kensal's discoveries in the Imperial Garden were already drifting into memory and disbelief, but Adeone knew in his bones the young lord had been right. He walked into the Outer Office and nodded at Richardson but didn't say anything. Tain had taken it all on board as though finding a carving moving around a garden was the most normal thing possible, but was that simply a childish abandon, or was it something deeper? Was Tain beginning to truly believe in the ancient magic instead of just dreaming about it? Somehow, he had to turn his son's mind away from the subject. Magic was dangerous. He knew it even though he utilised it as a medium. He knew its uncertainties and consequences as he knew himself, but he couldn't explain what it was he understood. Had he discussed his thoughts with Landis or Wealsman they would probably have told him that he wasn't afraid of magic but of someone discovering that he could wield it, which was perfectly true, but he convinced himself it wasn't the whole of the matter.

Chapter 64
HISTORIANS
Late Morning
Prince Arkyn's Office

ARKYN MOTIONED TO A CHAIR as Lord Kensal entered and bowed. Noting his friend was booted and cloaked, he rang the bell before saying,

"How was your trip?"

Kensal sat. "For me, uneventful, sir."

Arkyn's ears pricked up. "For someone else?"

"Two merchants I ran into said they'd been accosted. They were in a sorry state. I gave them enough to get them safely home but I was worried. The local fort had already had another couple of reports."

Arkyn sat considering for a long moment. When his manservant entered, he asked for refreshments and sent for Wynfeld. When Kadeem left, taking Kensal's cloak, Arkyn enquired, "What did you give the couple you mentioned?"

"I can't remember exactly, Your Highness."

Arkyn smiled. "Good try. Just tell me. I can be discreet."

Kensal told him, adding, "…They were merchants without much anyway. I hope it helped."

"It probably did. I'll have the Treasurer make it good."

Kensal eyed him. "Your Highness, that is unnecessary, I assure you. If

I hadn't been happy with the situation I would never have acted as I did. Being a lord doesn't mean I'm completely heartless; I just keep the heart in another library for reference purposes."

Arkyn chuckled. "It's always a problem finding the right page though. So, what did the King mean when he said I should ask you about the Imperial Garden?"

Kensal was nearing the end of the recitation when Edward announced Major Wynfeld.

A swift introduction later, Wynfeld said, "I hope your journey was uneventful after you met the merchants, my lord."

Arkyn chuckled at his friend's expression. "I wondered if you'd heard about that. Lord Kensal, tell Major Wynfeld everything you can recall."

Kensal nodded. "I'll do my best, sir, but my memory might also be in another library."

"I'm sure you still know your way there though, sir," remarked Wynfeld. "You met them at the Manger Inn, if my information is correct."

"Yes. They were eating, looked shaken, their talk was hushed and worried. It took them some time to confide in me. They'd felt like they were being followed for a couple of days but knew, if you're travelling at a similar pace, you can end up dining with the same people every day so thought they were being paranoid. Their description left the impression of non-descript men apart from one man who had a scar running from the corner of his eye to his lip. I wondered if some half-formed prejudices in their minds had triggered the feeling of paranoia. They must have seen it because they went on in a very determined manner. One day there was no-one else close by. A group of men harried them off the road, tied and beat them – it seems for fun – and searched their belongings. Everything that could be of value was stolen. Including their food, spare clothes and woollen cloaks. All that remained were some documents, which the bandits burned. After we finished eating, I invited them to my room and was shown proof of the beating. I carry some medical kit and, between myself and the innkeeper, we got them patched up. They told me they were from Paras and I asked them how much they had been carrying to get them home. They told me and I saw they were trying not to tell me but were in need of something, so I doubled it. I also told the two men I had with me, as protection, to escort the merchants home—"

Arkyn said, "That'll be your foolish heart then, Kensal."

Kensal shrugged. "That or I decided that history could well manage without me, but the merchants are the lifeblood of the empire. Anyway, after they left, I contacted the fort. The captain admitted he'd had other reports about the same group. I tried to lean on him to get it sorted, but

I'm not sure he took me seriously."

Arkyn looked at Wynfeld. "He will now." It wasn't a suggestion.

Wynfeld nodded. "He will, sir."

"Then, Major, that's all for now," said Arkyn. "I'd like to know of any progress." Once they were alone, Arkyn topped up Kensal's glass saying, "See, your memory was there."

"Like one of the dustier pages of history to be discovered just when it's needed?"

"Have you found any others recently?"

"A couple but nothing that blows our conceptions to pieces, sir."

Arkyn raised an eyebrow. "Maybe it's not the evidence that needs changing but the interpretation?"

"Our lives and preconceptions affect our interpretations, don't they?" enquired Kensal.

"True but surely a mind that constantly questions doesn't root itself in preconceptions unless in trying to find the way out of a maze."

"When one is lost preconceptions rarely help, Your Highness."

Arkyn nodded. "Yet in being lost, surely one clings onto what one knows."

"Sometimes one needs to let go to make the leap that proves others mistaken."

"Can proof overrule preconceptions? I have always observed rather the opposite."

"Surely the point of proof is that it *is* proof?"

Arkyn sighed. "It can always be contested, can't it?"

"I suppose it can, sir, but, if proof is so transitory, why do we bother?"

"Because, without it, there would be no leap of faith into the unknown."

Kensal said musingly, "Haven't you just turned that round on me?"

Arkyn laughed. "Yes, sorry. It took a while though. So how has the new Domini been?"

"Oh, far better than the last, Your Highness," admitted Kensal. "No library is safe forever."

Arkyn muffled a smile. "I can imagine. Alcis, save the archives from an unprincipled historian."

"Principles aren't always based on morality but sometimes on genuine belief. I believe history is important to every one of us and will try to uncover everything I can. Whether that matches what others wish me to say or not."

"I hope academia is ready for you."

Kensal grinned. "I hope the empire is for Your Highness, sir."

"I'm not as formidable as that, whatever rumour and speculation may have it. Alcis, I'm not even in Oedran that often."

"Yet often enough for information to escape, sir. Luckily, some of us have met you so can distinguish between probable and improbable rumours."

"You mean you believe the improbable ones?"

Kensal hesitated. "Of course not, sir, I'm a historian – belief isn't as much fun as conjecture."

Arkyn laughed and turned the talk towards Kensal's visit. Half an hour later, Kadeem discreetly passed Kensal a note whilst he cleared the remains of the refreshments.

Two moments later, Kensal said, "Might I ask Kadeem to bring in the chest which this note regards, Your Highness."

Arkyn nodded at Kadeem, who left. Two moments later, the manservant carried a small book chest into the office. The hinged lid lifted halfway to allow the front to be let down or removed, revealing the books. Usually, a drawer at the bottom would contain page markers and writing impedimenta. This chest was brass bound and lockable, its polished wood uncarved but a rich red cedar. Kensal didn't unlock it but simply handed the key over.

Arkyn smiled. "That seems quite heavy."

Kensal chuckled. "Of course, Your Highness. I have the texts you wished copied. I have been so forward as to make you a list of interesting snippets that I noticed. The originals I've put carefully in their own box and I hope they've survived the journey."

"Thank you. I'm sure they will have done. Yet two books and their copies couldn't fill such a chest."

"I thought you might be interested in the other books also, sir," replied Kensal. "They are a diverse look at our history by some of the most controversial historians in that history. I'm sure your conclusions reading them will be different from my own."

"Possibly. I'll make sure I finish them before your return home."

"Your Highness, these aren't on loan but a gift, the chest also."

"I hope this may go some way towards repaying it." Arkyn passed Lord Kensal a sealed letter and nodded for him to open it.

Kensal read it swiftly. "But… I was denied entry to the archives in Paras for five years and you've just tamely handed me entry to the Oedranian ones?"

Arkyn continued to smile. "Yes. I hope you find it of some use."

"Some use? Sir, you can't imagine what this means."

"Oh, I think I've a fair idea."

Half an hour later, Kadeem informed them Lord Kensal's rooms were prepared and was amused when Kensal, far from going and relaxing, carried on debating Oedranian history with Prince Arkyn until Lord Irvin arrived for dinner.

Chapter 65

FUTURE TRAVEL PLANS
Cisadai, Week 31 – 16th Anapal, 2nd Anapcis 1212
Palace

BY THE MIDDLE OF WINTER, Lord Kensal had spent several enjoyable and productive weeks in the Palace Archive and, much to the consternation of the archivist, enjoyed himself – such a thing was unheard of. Having offered to help file and catalogue the older papers, the archivist couldn't complain at the way Kensal bent his mind to the task, nor the end result. They got to know each other well and, although the archivist still held prejudices about lords in general, he found Kensal to be an interesting gentleman whose companionship he valued. Kensal hardly noticed as he worked his way through the early empire papers. He even found plans for the building of the Palace around the King's Hall, which showed rooms never completed and others which now had far different functions from those intended.

Arkyn had spent the time between Ceardlann and Oedran. The evenings in Oedran were spent, if not at Court, with both Kensal and Irvin.

One evening Irvin asked in his normal quiet way how long Kensal would be in Oedran for, mentioning that he would be sorely missed if he returned too soon to Paras.

Kensal laughed. "Why would I wish to go when I'm finding out so much here? I'm working on several theories about the effects the Fall of the Cearcall had on Oedran; I can't leave until they're completed. Can I?"

Arkyn said, "I didn't think the Cearcallian demise affected Oedran in any way but a positive one."

"You'd be surprised. For example, at that time, a lot of Oedranian trade was done with Areal but their descent into civil war, and the piracy that resulted out of Amphi, meant that trade with Amphi in particular was almost impossible. In fact, the capital of the country moved for a time to Amista. Oedran lost almost half of its trading rights. Obviously, as a province, we exported something much more durable in the end, but, for a time at least, the country was affected."

Irvin frowned. "What did we export?"

"The army," said Arkyn dryly. "Areal was the first country we 'helped'." The inverted commas clanged around the word like a gong.

Kensal looked at him. "We exported peace in the end, sir."

"After having massacred and destroyed several towns. King Mushin stood no chance."

"In the end, he couldn't control his own army or court."

Arkyn grimaced. "Yet he surrendered far too easily. He gave his country up as though it didn't matter."

"Maybe it didn't to him, sir. Or maybe," said Lord Kensal, "He knew that, sooner or later, he'd have to capitulate. He saved his people from the worst. There was no doubt he'd be assassinated and his General would wrest power. His sons had already died in mysterious circumstances, his daughters were very young and he saw a way out for them all."

Irvin asked, "Didn't he kill himself the night that the Oedranian army entered Amista?"

Kensal nodded. "So it's said. His daughters were cared for by our king and brought up as his own. He did them the honour of letting them keep their identity."

Arkyn sighed. "Yes, but I wonder if that means he was a good man."

"He was a man of his time, sir. It is never right to judge a man of the past by modern conceptions and standards."

Arkyn grimaced. "When modern men are judged by past ones, why not past by modern? Anyway, Kensal, how long *are* you staying for?"

"Trying to get rid of me, Your Highness?"

"Why would I want to do that? I just wondered. Come the summer, I'll be travelling again myself; this time to Lufia."

"It's a pity I'm at the Advisors' School," commented Irvin. "I'd like to see Lufia; that is, if you wished for my company again, sir."

Arkyn smiled at him. "I think I could stand it, Irvin, but you're right. I doubt the school would look favourably on the idea. I'll have to find other companions this year."

"Do they have to be Oedranian?" enquired Kensal.

Arkyn laughed. "Are you offering to put up with the miseries of the road to lighten my lonely evenings or because you know the libraries of Lufia are well renowned?"

"Well, travelling to Lufia as the companion of our future king can, of course, have no benefit to a lowly lord of Anapara."

Irvin smiled. "I think he might be partial to the experience, sir."

"I rather thought that as well," replied Arkyn. "I didn't, however, have an answer to my question…"

Kensal's lips twitched. "Lufia, I suspect, will hold many delights for both of us, Your Highness, but there is room in a day for both research and companionship."

Arkyn eyed him. "I don't think exposing you to the Court of Oedran was a good thing. Your replies are becoming annoyingly refined."

Irvin said quietly, "I'm sure his other self is still there."

Kensal grinned. "Aye, in another library."

"Where else?" queried Arkyn dryly.

* * *

Several days later, Arkyn was dining with his father and brother when Adeone said,

"I've had a letter from Lord Faran. He's invited you to stay on your way to Lufia."

"That was kind of him," stated Arkyn.

"Very noncommittal. What shall I reply?"

Arkyn smiled. "I'd be happy to accept the invitation, father. At least this time I'll know he's a friend of yours."

"Father, can I go with Arkyn this year?" asked Tain.

Adeone shook his head. "You're still a bit young. One year I promise you can go, but it won't be for a couple yet. Are you so adamant to see the rest of the empire?"

Tain gave an emphatic nod. "How can we rule it if we don't know it?"

"Quite. I was fortunate. I spent eleven years on the reviews; the only province I've never visited is the Pale Lands. I regret that, but life's journey brought me here."

"I hope I get to see all the provinces," said Arkyn, "but I can bear seeing them at the rate of one a year."

His father smiled. "I bet you can. I'll let Faran know. I know he'll be genuinely pleased to have you visit. Have you thought any more about taking a companion?"

"Quite a lot, Sire," admitted Arkyn. "I wondered if there'd be any objection to Kensal accompanying me. He's not restricted by studies as Irvin is and he'd appreciate the libraries just as much."

Adeone chuckled. "I can't see any problems with that, Arkyn. I'll inform the Sagamore and let him know that Lord Kensal *will* be using the libraries and archives."

"Has he actually seen anything of Oedran other than the inside of the archives?" asked Tain.

Arkyn frowned. "I don't think he has, now you mention it. I'll have to drag him out for a ride at some point. Do you want to join us?"

As the talk turned away from Arkyn's travels, Tain became happier.

* * *

The following morning Adeone sent for Arkyn and, as his son entered the Inner Office, smiled warmly.

"I wanted to mention an idea I had last night after you'd gone to bed. Laioril has promised us an evening of stories around the fires at Ceardlann. It occurred to me that there are two other people who would

326

really appreciate hearing them. I believe you once promised Lord Irvin that you'd introduce him to the Chief?"

Arkyn's face showed his astonishment. "I did, sir, but Your Majesty can't mean…"

"Arkyn, get rid of the formality. I can't see one evening doing much harm. Would you care to extend my invitation to Irvin and Kensal to spend an evening listening to Laioril's stories?"

Arkyn shook his head to clear it of disbelief. "Of course, father, but I'm rather surprised and if I am—"

"Their reaction will be all the more understandable to you. Thank you. I'd like to know what they think of the old rogue's telling."

Arkyn grinned. "I'm sure they'll have ample opinions, sir."

* * *

The Prince was pensive over dinner and his friends, noticing his mood, talked about the day's happenings and Court whilst he listened. At the end of the meal, he dismissed his household. Once seated comfortably, Kensal asked the question that Irvin would never have done:

"So, what's got you thinking, sir?"

Arkyn smiled. "Something or nothing." He put his drink down on the table and got to his feet. Crossing to the window, he saw in the reflection that both his friends had got up also. With laughing eyes, he said, "You might as well sit back down. You'll need to be seated, trust me. First though, Kensal, I'd like to invite you to go to Lufia with me."

"I'd like that very much, Your Highness, thank you," answered Kensal.

Arkyn turned back to the room. "Good. The Sagamore is being told that you *will* be exploring the libraries and archives. Also, we'll be stopping for a time with Lord Faran."

"I don't think I've heard of him, sir."

"He's a Lord of Lufian, but he was our ward, so became well acquainted with father. His invitation means we'll get a good break from travelling. The other thing concerns both of you. You've heard me talk of Laioril and his tales. His Majesty has organised an evening of storytelling and has extended an invitation to both of you to attend it."

Kensal said, "That would be fantastic, sir. Can you thank His Majesty?"

"Your Highness, Chief Laioril never comes into Oedran…" remarked Irvin, confused.

Arkyn smiled. "He has been known to, but, you're right, he comes here very seldom. No, the invitation is for an evening at Ceardlann."

Both faces drained of colour before Kensal enquired, "Ceardlann?"

"Yes. I told you you'd need to be sitting down. Getting the old rogue here is impossible. His Majesty thought both of you would appreciate his stories."

Irvin said, "Sir, we can't accept. Ceardlann is, well, it would be wrong."

"Not at all, Lord Irvin. His Majesty broached the idea to me this morning. I've not had a hand in it. Anyway, Lord Iris has visited Ceardlann before."

"Yes, Your Highness, but grandfather was a close acquaintance of King Altarius."

"As you are of me, Lord Irvin. If you feel so uncomfortable then you must follow your conscience but I can't imagine you'd disdain listening to the Chief."

Irvin swallowed. "I wouldn't, sir, but I have to get used to the idea."

Arkyn nodded. "I can understand that. Kensal?"

"I would be pleased to accept, Your Highness – pleased but stunned!"

Arkyn laughed. "There's a condition from me. You talk to no-one but each other about the visit. I can't imagine what the Court would think if it knew. Obviously, Irvin, you may have to tell Lord Iris as you're to be absent from home, but I'd prefer it to be only your grandfather and not the rest of your family."

Irvin swallowed. "I can make you that promise, sir. Thank you. I'd be a fool not to go because of preconceptions. I'll gratefully accept the invitation."

Chapter 66
DINNER AND DOCUMENTS
Tretaldai, Week 32 – 24th Anapal, 10th Anapcis 1212
Inner Office

DRAWING HIS DOCUMENTS TOGETHER, Landis glanced at the King's set face. Justice Counsel had been its normal mixture. Scanlon's tenure as Justiciar was becoming increasingly harsh and there was little Adeone could do about it without being seen to interfere.

The glum and pensive expression on Adeone's face had been there before counsel, though, so that wasn't the whole of what was bothering his friend.

"Is there anything I can help with, Sire? You're not your normal self."

Adeone hesitated. "I'll be fine. You'll only speculate if I tell you why."

Landis eyed him. "Rhian's said she's returning home, hasn't she?"

"Yes. It's hardly weighty, but I'd like her to stay for longer, yet I can't ask her without it raising conjectures," grumbled Adeone.

"Leave it with me, Sire. I'll see what I can do."

"I'm not sure that is reassuring but thank you. There was a matter I needed to see you about: Arkyn's advisors. There is a post vacant."

Accepting the change of subject, Landis nodded. "Yes, Sire. The finals for the Advisors' School are taken at the beginning of spring with any retakes near to the end."

"There is no recent graduate then?"

Landis paused. "Not that I feel meets His Highness' strict criteria. I've had the current final year students' records sent to me and am going through them. There are some promising students whose final exams I'll attend and see if they match their paper potential."

Adeone nodded. "Good. Though, Landis, the post will need to be filled *very* soon as the advisor in question will need to know what he is doing before the Lufian Review."

"He'll know, Sire, I promise you that."

After he left the Inner Office, Landis' wanderings took him down to Court where he took a drink from a server and seemingly walked around without a purpose, but he was hunting for two people; however, a third caught his attention first.

"Advisor Rayburn, aren't you on duty today?"

"Yes, my lord, and His Majesty knows where to find me should he require my services. I thought I would see what the rumour front is making of my appointment."

Landis smiled. "Have you discovered anything?"

"No, my lord. They're all reticent whenever I'm near – rather unfortunate but not surprising."

"Quite, Advisor. Will you excuse me? I need a word with Lord Fairson. Come and see me soon I would value your opinion on a couple of matters."

"The pleasure would be mine, sir."

Landis gave a short nod and walked over to Lord Fairson who greeted him with a smile and the words,

"We don't often see you here during the day, Festus."

"I was visiting His Majesty, Gerens, and needed a drink."

"Then why is your glass empty? Server!"

Once the server had left, Festus smiled. "How are you?"

"Fine, thank you. I hope both you and Cornelia are well?"

Landis nodded. "Well enough. You and Malti will have to come to dinner soon."

"We'd be glad to. I'm curious to see your new study; His Majesty says tearing you out of there is a feat best left to others."

Landis laughed. "Only because he finds the chairs too comfortable to move himself. If you've not yet seen the house, you certainly will have to come. Are you busy on Septadai?"

"I don't believe we are. Thank you."

"I look forward to it. Oh, is Lady Rhian still staying with you?"

"Yes, why?"

Landis smiled. "I was just going to extend the invitation to her also. I hope she'll come."

"I'm sure she'll be glad to accept. Will His Majesty be joining us?"

"As I've only just thought of the dinner party, I haven't invited him," replied Landis. "Do you think I should?"

"Why not?" Fairson dropped his voice. "It would make an even number."

"So it would. If you hold no objection, I shall invite him."

"Why should I object? I've never fully defined the relationship, but we're some sort of cousins, if only wed-kin – through the marriage of Great-uncle Ewart to Lady Amara."

"True. I'll see you soon. I've just spotted Vanval and I need a word…"

* * *

Adeone arrived at Landis House at the same time as Lord Fairson and the other guests. Dismounting, he handed Pursuit's reins to Clodach, who inclined his head smartly whilst others ran forward to steady Lord Fairson's coach horses. With a small smile, Adeone handed Lady Fairson and Lady Rhian out of the coach himself, much to the surprise of Backery, who had moved forward to do the same job.

Lady Fairson thanked him quietly but Rhian caught his eye and silent humour passed between them.

Adeone winked and turned to Lord Fairson. "Good evening, my lord."

"Good evening, Your Majesty. I hope you had a pleasant ride."

"Very, thank you. The night may be cold but not at all unpleasant. I understand you've not yet seen the new house?"

Lord Fairson said, "Not yet, Sire. I am looking forward to being shown around. It is rare for a Lord of Oedran to have a new residence."

"Rarer for a King, I think. Do you think I should do some building work at the Palace?"

"Why risk spoiling perfection, Your Majesty?"

Adeone smiled. "Very quick, Gerens." He glanced towards the house. "Lord Landis, you're getting slow."

Landis, who'd just walked out to greet his guests, smiled. "Or Your Majesty is early, Sire?"

Adeone shook his head. "I preferred the one where you're slow. Fairson?"

Fairson smiled. "Definitely, Your Majesty."

Landis turned to Lady Rhian, "Am I slow, my lady?"

Rhian grinned. "How can I disagree with His Majesty, my lord?"

Adeone laughed. "Festus, are you proposing to keep the ladies in the cold simply to prove me wrong?"

Landis gave an emphatic bow. "My apologies, please come in."

Once within the warm hall, Adeone said, "I believe Lord and Lady Fairson are looking forward to being shown around. With your agreement, Lady Rhian and I will keep Lady Landis company whilst you give them a tour."

Landis nodded. "Of course, I'm sure Cornelia will be only too happy."

Lady Landis, walking to greet them, nodded. "Good evening, Sire."

"Good evening, Cornelia. How are you?"

"Very well, Your Majesty. Gerens, Malti, welcome to our rebuilt home. When Festus has finished showing you around, we'll be in the front drawing room. Rhian, you're looking well…"

As the party split, Adeone followed Cornelia and Rhian, smiling to himself. Once seated with a drink, he simply listened as the ladies talked. Eventually, Rhian looked over at him and caught his amusement.

"What?"

"I thought Tain was bad for talking."

Rhian laughed. "Maybe it's something to do with the FitzAlcis streak, Sire. Anyway, it does you good to listen for once."

Adeone stretched his feet out in front of him. "It certainly does my throat good. As does this wine; what is it, Cornelia?"

Lady Landis smiled. "Can't you guess, sir?"

Adeone took another sip. "I didn't think it would have lasted this long."

Cornelia laughed. "The bottle you passed on didn't but Festus asked the Comptroller to try and get another."

Adeone shook his head. "Save Miranda's wine from unprincipled lords. She only ever gives me one bottle a year."

Rhian smiled. "Maybe this is your second, or didn't you notice we were given different drinks?"

Adeone frowned. "No, I didn't. What's Festus playing at, Cornelia?"

"I wish I knew, sir. Why don't you just ask him?"

The King sighed. "Whenever he has a scheme, getting answers out of him before he wants to tell me is impossible."

Rhian laughed. "I'm sure if you really wanted to know, Adeone, you'd get the answers from him."

Adeone caught her eye, his gaze softening. "Probably."

Twelve minutes later, Landis and the Fairsons joined them.

After dinner Adeone found himself talking quietly to Rhian about family.

"How's Prince Arkyn?" she asked quietly.

"He's getting there. Having Lord Kensal here has done him the world of good."

Rhian nodded. "I'd noticed. How long is His Lordship staying for?"

"I don't know. He's going to Lufia with Arkyn next year, so probably until they return from there. I hope so anyway. More importantly though, you're not going to desert us so soon, are you?"

Rhian smiled. "I do have matters that require my attention in Tradere."

"Then go, settle them and return, Rhian. I'm not the only one who enjoys your company here."

She smiled. "Yet I hardly see you when I am here. You're always closeted in meetings…"

He sighed. "Don't remind me. Will you stay?"

"Is the King requiring my presence in Oedran?"

He took her hand without realising. "No. I'm asking you, as a cousin, to prolong your visit."

Landis glancing over smiled to himself. He hoped Rhian would say yes. His friend was easy in her company and it took a lot for him to relax around others.

Rhian took her hand back. "I can't stay forever, Adeone."

He sighed. "I know but at least stay another couple of seasons. Please."

"Promise we can have more evenings like this and I might manage it."

He nodded. "Gladly."

* * *

Later, when she and the Fairsons had left, Landis said, "So?"

"She's staying for longer. Thank you, Festus."

Landis nodded. "Good, and there's no need to thank me. I quite enjoy watching her put you in your place."

Adeone laughed. "With friends like you, Festus, I'm surprised I have any enemies."

Landis raised an eyebrow. "Can't imagine what you mean, Sire. Now, I wanted to show you something that has me puzzled."

"What's that then?"

Landis passed over a sheet of parchment, yellowing with the passage of time.

Adeone took it. He looked with interest and surprise at the drawing of an ornate, enamelled and jewelled circular box. Its garish opulence and size was immediately recognisable.

Landis was saying, "I found it in some papers that survived the fire. I have got it right, haven't I? That was a blessing gift given to King Altarius?"

Adeone swallowed. "Yes, it holds his ashes, at his request. I… How does it come to be here?"

Landis sighed. "I don't know. I don't recognise the name on the bottom of the order. I'm as puzzled as you are, sir."

Adeone read the whole of the order instead of just looking at the artist's sketch. He glanced at the signature and seal that adorned the page and blanched.

"I'll take this with me. There're a couple of things I need to check."

Perplexed, Landis watched his friend. "Of course, sir. Are you all right?"

"I need to check something, that's all! I'll see you tomorrow."

Part 5

Chapter 67
PUZZLES
Septadai, Week 32 – 28th Anapal, 14th Anapcis 1212
Landis House

ADEONE RODE TOWARDS THE PALACE in turmoil. Instead of passing the gates to the City Alcium, he rode through them. His father's ashes were in a crypt, along with the ashes of many other kings and their burial tokens. Reining in, he dismounted. The Alcium never closed. As he entered, a white-clad alcia stepped forward to greet him.

Adeone murmured, "Is the Moonshi still awake?"

"I will check, my king," whispered the alcia.

"Thank you." Adeone walked forward until he was under the centre of the domed room. He sat cross-legged and let his mind fill the space until he could hear everything, every breath and movement. The muffled tread of a heavy-set man came closer. He pushed himself to his feet as the Moonshi walked towards him.

"I would like to visit my ancestors, Your Benevolence."

Clad in silvery robes, the Moonshi motioned with his hand and Adeone walked with him in silence. On the palace-side of the City Alcium was a small private alcium to which only two people ever held a key, and Adeone had left his at the Palace.

The Moonshi unlocked the door and lit the candles before bowing out. Adeone again sat cross-legged and waited as his mind filled the room. No-one would *ever* disturb him here. Once truly content, he closed his eyes, trying to hold fast the feeling. A change in atmosphere made him open them. Ira was standing before him.

"You are worried, Adeone. Why?"

"I fear what the past is revealing."

"The past is past; it is the future that matters. How are our sons?"

He smiled. "Worth every moment of heartache. Arkyn's quite a man now and Tain is growing too quickly. They'll be everything we could ever hope for."

"Good. Ella's here."

Adeone fought back tears as his daughter smiled at him. He wanted to wrap both of them in his arms but couldn't. They weren't truly there. Ira smiled as she and Ella shimmered out of existence. He was left watching the blank spot. He closed his eyes, fighting his emotions. When he finally opened them, his father and mother stood in front of him.

Queen Eliza said, "Emotions do not make you less of a man, son."

Adeone smiled sadly at her. "No but they reveal too much sometimes, mother. I miss you all…"

"Your heart always overruled your mind," observed King Altarius.

"No, father, not always."

"So why are you here tonight?"

Adeone brought out the parchment. "Festus found this, and I needed somewhere to think."

Altarius seemed to focus on the parchment, "I should never have had him executed in the manner I did. Make it right for me. It was the worst decision of my life."

Eliza took her husband's arm. "You were traumatised, Alt. He would never have blamed you."

Obviously guilt ridden, Altarius said, "I wrecked his family as I'd wrecked others that year. I had simply lost mine; their memory wasn't besmirched. Make it right for me, Adeone. Make it right, my son."

They faded as Adeone was asking, "Who was Dunius?"

He was left with the echo of 'Make it right…'

Adeone closed his eyes and let the room enter his senses once again, but when he opened them there was no-one there. He pushed himself to his feet, noticing half-distractedly the candles had burnt down. He left the King's Alcium and nodded to the Moonshi. As he walked out to his horse, he stopped surprised, blinking in the morning light. He must have fallen to sleep at some point for it was daylight and his guards were decidedly worried.

On hearing it was eight o'clock, Adeone turned to his sergeant. "We'll go to the barracks before we return to the Palace, Kilbride, but you'd better tell one of the lads to go and stop Simkins and Richardson getting too concerned."

* * *

At the barracks, Adeone made his way straight to the General's office. Once the door closed, Adeone faced Paturn.

"I *need* to know who Dunius was, General."

The General stilled. "Sire, I thought—"

"You swore that you'd tell me. You can't have forgotten so soon. What was his full name?"

Paturn blanched. "Your Majesty, can I first ask that you won't blame me for the consequences?"

"Of course I won't, General!"

"Thank you, Sire. His full name was Lord Dunius Feste Landis."

Adeone froze for several long moments before getting to his feet. "Thank you, Paturn. I will see you soon, I hope."

Once he was in the Inner Office, the King put his head in his hands. How had it been kept from him that his best friend had a convicted traitor in the family? How had it never come to light? Landis must have been ignorant of it himself. What was the relationship between Festus and Dunius? It couldn't be a direct line because someone would certainly have mentioned it; if only to discredit Landis. Was this a trap, a scheme of Scanlon's to strip him of support? If so, he'd managed to involve several men whom Adeone would bet his life were loyal, but maybe that was the point: put your trust in the wrong men and your life was the price you paid. He asked Richardson to send for Landis.

When Landis arrived, Adeone was irrationally furious. Trying to control the anger, he snapped, "Does the name Dunius truly mean nothing to you, Landis?"

"No, Sire, should it?"

Adeone heard Rhian saying, *'I'm sure if you really wanted to know, Adeone, you'd get the answers from him.'* The King in him said, "Kneel and pass me your hands."

Landis knelt. "Sire, might I know what's happening?"

"No." Adeone took his friend's hands and, swallowing the feeling of nausea, asked, "In truth, do you know *anything* of Lord Dunius Landis?"

"In truth, my liege, I do not."

"In truth, are you aware of any traitorous actions in your family's history?"

"In truth, my liege, I am not."

Adeone's hands shook. He couldn't say the words to make Landis forget the interrogation. He broke away, stumbling to a comfortable chair, his head in his hands, his stomach churning. Part of him didn't care what his friend did.

Landis got up, angry at his friend for putting him through another fealty test with no apparent provocation, but anger wouldn't help and Adeone must have had a reason. He poured two glasses of water and sat opposite his friend.

"You've got to tell someone."

Adeone looked at him. "He was the traitor executed by my father in 1169, the one who kept the news of Queen Orphelia's and Prince Adlai's death private. He was my father's nearfather and, I think, working out the generations, your great-uncle."

Landis blanched. "Sicla! How did you find out?"

Adeone explained everything that had happened since Tain had found the diary entry to the point of Landis passing him the parchment the evening before.

"Your family kept your lordship; therefore, I can't suppose my father blamed anyone else, for once. Yet this has wounded me. How far can I now trust you? Will history repeat? Such conjectures may be unfair, but they're being made with a startling rapidity. And I wish they weren't. I finally understand why my father didn't want nearfathers in our family. Maybe he was right. I don't know. But I do know I hate what this knowledge is making me do."

Landis sighed. "It is making me question if this is why my father wasn't happy when we became close friends, if it's why I keep feeling history closing in around me and if it's why I find it difficult to disassociate the different aspects of my many roles. Maybe there's something in my family's blood that says we shouldn't be close to kings, but my life would have been dismal without your friendship, Adeone."

"Father always warned me away from trusting people," admitted Adeone, "but without trusting you I'd have been isolated. Your ancestor's actions are in the past; they can't have known that the order for the blessing gift still existed or they would have destroyed it, I'm sure of that. I can only think that my father regretted his actions as he asked for his ashes to be stored in the gift. If he had continued to blame Lord Dunius, he would never have asked for that. I think he wanted to make it right but didn't know how. I, like you, rather suspect that the odd constraint between our fathers was as a result of this. Maybe father saw a way of easing his guilt when we became friends. Festus, I think it's time I told you the truth about Nia."

Landis hesitated. "I rather think I know it now."

"Let me say it, please. Father knew we were close. He advised me that friendships can only be muddied if marriages get involved. At the time I put that down to personal experience with his and Uncle Ewart's but it can't have been. They were the closest of friends to the day Uncle Ewart died. I think he knew that, if I proposed to Nia, the past would be picked over and he wanted to leave it undisturbed."

"Thank you."

Adeone swallowed. "It wasn't my doing, Festus. I want to make this right, somehow, I want to stop this becoming a tool of Scanlon's for, if he knows our family history, he'll use it and I think he's trying to discredit you at the moment, rather than kill you. Death is immediate; disgrace is for life and is harder to bear. We need to make a decision.

Shall we use this before he does?"

Landis eyed Adeone. "It's not what others think that bothers me, it's what you think; so, yes, if you're unconcerned, let's use it. Or we can start the rumours ourselves and wait for someone stupid to think you'd care enough to be told."

Adeone laughed. "I'm sure, however, it wouldn't be one of his supporters to inform me, and my resulting rage would destroy a good man. No, I think I'll put magic amongst the mundane myself this time; however, first we should tell your nearsons. They at least must understand why we're acting as we are."

Chapter 68
WELCOME WORDS
Cisadai, Week 33 – 2nd Bayal, 16th Anapcis 1212
Road between Oedran and the Rex Dallin

THE FOLLOWING DAY, a small cavalcade passed through Dellwood on its way to the Rex Dallin. Adeone and Landis were riding, but Arkyn, Irvin and Kensal were travelling companionably in a coach. At the Pillars of Alcis, a groom from Ceardlann was waiting. During the change of driver, Adeone said through the coach window,

"I'd be grateful if you would close your eyes from here until Ceardlann, my lords. It is a precaution only; no comment on your trustworthiness."

Arkyn smiled as his friends did as requested. He glanced at his father, who winked and moved his horse to the head of the cavalcade. Arkyn spent the time it took them to reach Ceardlann thinking about his father's request. When someone was granted entry in the normal course of things such precautions weren't necessary, but he supposed as Kensal and Irvin were only visiting this once, that anyone could foretell, they shouldn't remember the way to Ceardlann. They were there to hear the stories, not to visit the house and valley.

On reaching Ceardlann, Arkyn said quietly, "I think you can open your eyes now – that is, if you've not fallen to sleep."

As they alighted from the coach, the Comptroller was waiting to greet them and the King had already entered the house.

"Comptroller, might I introduce Lord Irvin Iris and Lord Kensal Parchi to you?"

"Certainly, Your Highness. Welcome to Ceardlann, my lords. Lord Irvin, it is a while since we welcomed an Iris here but you *are* most welcome. Lord Kensal, I hope you find as much to interest you here as in the archives at Oedran."

Irvin smiled. "Thank you, Comptroller. My grandfather sends his greetings to you."

The Comptroller nodded. "I hope you will return mine, my lord. Now, if you'd just like to follow me, I will show you to your rooms."

Arkyn said, "Treat them gently, Comptroller, they're still a bit fazed."

"As gently as I can, sir. Prince Tain, Lady Elantha and Master Calumiel are in their sitting room."

"Thank you for the warning. I shall see you when you've settled in, Irvin, Kensal."

Irvin gave a short bow. "Of course, Your Highness."

As Arkyn walked away, he remarked, "The Comptroller will explain to you how this valley works… including the issues around formality, I hope."

The Comptroller chuckled. "I think that means His Highness would prefer you to call him Arkyn whilst you're here."

"We can't, Comptroller," replied Irvin.

"Far be it from me to offer Your Lordship advice, but it might be wise. Ceardlann is the FitzAlcis' retreat. They find it hard to relax with Oedranian formality here – especially from their friends. The honorifics you will hear some use are, shall we say, tolerated but not appreciated. As guests of His Majesty, please ask if you need anything."

"We're only here for one evening, Comptroller," said Kensal surprised.

"One evening or one year, it makes no difference to our hospitality, I hope. As your servants couldn't accompany you, I've asked Joe and David to attend on you. Dinner will be in the Great Hall, but, until then, I hope you can feel easy enough to explore. The first floor comprises of private accommodation but the ground floor has many different rooms – the only one I would ask you not to enter is the King's study and I might advise you to give the kitchen a wide berth: Cook's not in the best temper today."

Perplexed, Irvin hesitated. "We'd never have entered the kitchens."

"Why not? Everyone else does. Cook regularly throws people out. We all need to eat, and he makes some delicious pasties. Anyway, this is your room, Lord Irvin. It was a favourite of your grandfather's. Lord Kensal, yours is next door. I hope they're satisfactory. Ask someone to show you the way to my office should you wish or need to ask me anything."

* * *

A couple of minutes later, in the Comptroller's office, the King grinned. "Are they settled?"

"I think so, sir. Slightly disorientated, but they'll be fine by this evening."

"Good. Landis and I need to see the Princes without speculation arising…"

342

The Comptroller chuckled. "What are you planning, sir?"

"For once, it has a serious purpose. We'll be in my study."

Half an hour later, Arkyn and Tain had heard the whole of the explanation about Lord Dunius.

Arkyn said mildly, "I don't think it's Uncle Festus' fault that he didn't know, father. Surely, it's his actions and not his ancestor's that matter to us?"

Adeone smiled. "Yes, but secrets such as this can be devastating."

Tain chewed at his lip. "Only if one lets them be, father. Uncle Festus, I'm sorry I ever asked."

Landis slipped an arm around his nearson's shoulder. "I'm not. It's helped me to understand an awful lot."

"Oh, good. So, we can leave it all in the past?"

Adeone glanced at Landis. "No. We're going to let this get out into Court gossip. That way no-one can ever use it against your Uncle Festus or against me. We just need to know that both of you agree with our decision to do that."

Arkyn and Tain looked at each other.

"Surely, if we don't mind, that's all that matters, father," pointed out Arkyn. "Why rake it up for the disgrace of the Landis family? Have you consulted our nearcousins?"

Landis and Adeone looked at each other.

Landis said, "He's got a point, sir, we haven't."

Arkyn continued, "There are more reputations at stake than Lord Landis'. Julius is already..."

Landis frowned as Arkyn tailed off. "Already what, Your Highness?"

"Already getting a reputation that isn't beneficial, Uncle Festus. Or am I the only one who's noticed how bored he is at the moment?"

Landis sighed. "No, I'd seen it, but I didn't know it had got so bad. I'll talk with him."

Arkyn glanced at his father. "It might be better if you did, father. He's messed up and I think it's the type of situation where I'd talk to Uncle Festus rather than you, sir."

Adeone looked at him, then at Festus, who gave a slight shrug.

Adeone said, "We'll think about it, Arkyn, but thank you for being so candid."

"So, are you going to tell everyone about Lord Dunius?" asked Tain.

Had Tain known the time was right for a change of subject? Or had he simply got bored as everyone talked over his head again? Adeone didn't know, but he appreciated the interruption.

Glancing at Festus, he said, "We'll leave it for now."

Landis nodded. "Yes, I think so."

When the Princes had left, Adeone said, "Shall we find ourselves a drink and a quiet corner?"

They tucked themselves away in the snug and managed to remain undisturbed for some time.

* * *

Peace shattered when the door opened and Laioril entered.

Adeone grinned. "Chief, you're looking far too well for a man your age."

"There's a compliment for you. You're looking far too relaxed for a king, lad."

"It's this place. What more can I say? Come on in. Can I get you a drink?"

"Nay, lad. Young Festus can. Wouldn't want to disturb your contentment."

Adeone laughed as Festus got up, saying, "Surely that's a bit late, Chief."

"Better late than never. Now, how many stories do you insist I tell you all tonight?"

Adeone smiled. "I would hope I never insist on any such thing, Chief. As many as you wish to. If, however, you wish to simply warm your bones by the fire, that's fine by me."

"Everyone else would be disappointed, I suspect. I noticed more arrivals than normal. Who were the two youngsters with Arkyn?"

Festus passed the Chief a whiskey as Adeone said,

"Lord Irvin Iris and Lord Kensal Parchi. Both of whom have spent many hours in libraries across the empire reading every historical text they can get their hands on. I thought they might like a change of scene and the opportunity to hear a master storyteller at work."

"Flattery, lad, gets you nowhere."

"I'm glad because that was simply the truth. Jesting aside, how are you, Chief?"

Laioril eased himself into a chair. "Very well. Wintering here is very pleasant. I might not want to leave."

"Surely the point of the Wanda is that you are nomadic," stated Landis, amused.

"Oh, I'll let the others leave, but I'll root myself here. Anyway, the Wanda are nomadic because they have never been given a home here. If the Wandarin Ocean was navigable, then they'd never be here. Or did you miss that bit of history, young Festus?"

"I can't say I lived through it, Chief, but I certainly recall your stories."

Laioril chuckled. "Glad something stayed with you. Now, lad," he turned to Adeone. "How many people am I entertaining tonight?"

Adeone smiled. "Chief, you're here as my guest, not as *the entertainment*. If you chose to honour your promise, though, there will be eight of us."

"I always honour my promises, lad."

"I know. That's why I try to get you to promise to stop poaching."

Laioril laughed. "Carry on trying, lad, there's no harm in trying."

* * *

Once dinner was over, they were all happily ensconced in the drawing room. After a few minutes of talk, Laioril said lightly,

"I believe, I promised you stories, in a moment of frailty. So where shall we start?"

Tain grinned. "Ull's story?"

Elantha shook her head. "Fall of the Cearcall."

Adeone glanced at them. "How about something more recent?"

"But not too recent," said Landis.

Arkyn glanced at Kensal. "Chief, what do you know of the Early Empire?"

"I've been told I can tell it like I was there, lad," answered Laioril.

Adeone grinned. "That's been said of every story you tell, and yet that would make you well over a thousand years old, which certainly isn't possible. It's been a while since I heard the Early Empire stories though."

Laioril nodded. "Then I shall tell the stories of that time to the Age of Tyranny…"

Chapter 69

INSIGHTS AND PROPHECIES

Mid-evening

Drawing Room

LAIORIL WOVE A TALE of kings and princes, of halls of power and dead men, of provinces fighting and surrendering. Pirates sailed the seas and outlaws killed kings. Generals turned traitor and loyalty fled. The Oedranian Empire was forged from destruction and diplomacy. The end of the Age of Battles came with an arrow, bringing death to King Alvern Abadin as he sat in the King's Hall of Oedran and the Age of Tyranny was born.

As he finished, Laioril watched his audience with bright, piercing eyes. Everyone was enthralled; everyone but Lord Kensal, who scrutinised him with a perceptive eye. Laioril winked but the expression didn't dissolve, and, for the briefest of moments, the Chief felt uncertain.

Kensal said, "Like you were there, Chief?"

Laioril smiled. "So I've been told, lad. Do you agree?"

"Your telling is certainly one I've never read."

345

Adeone smiled. "Come now, my lord, such was the point of me inviting you. Where did the Chief go wrong?"

Kensal turned. "Sire, I didn't mean it as a criticism. In facts it was the same as every other account, but the pictures in my mind were far, far more vivid than those conjured up by even contemporary commentators. I could almost see the halls full of dead men and feel the fears and triumphs, but I rather suspect that if you were to write the story down, it would lose all those images. It was rather remarkable."

Cal, who'd been quiet with two lords he didn't know, said, "That's why we listen to the Chief, Lord Kensal."

Adeone nodded. "It's why most men listen to the Chief."

"And women, Uncle Adeone."

"And women, little flower," Adeone corrected himself, smiling at his niece.

Laioril sighed. "What it is to be wanted."

Tain grinned. "You know you enjoy telling the stories as much as we enjoy listening to them."

"He'll never admit it though," observed Landis. "Top up, Chief?"

"Please, lad. It's a thirsty business this. Now then, we've a thousand years of history to tell of. What would you like to hear of next?"

Kensal was leaning forward. "Maybe your own story, Chief?"

Laioril caught his eye. "My story is nothing spectacular, lad. I'm a Chief of the Wanda, nothing more."

"But surely every story of great note is full of small personal stories which weren't considered important by the owners of them. Isn't history full of ordinary men doing ordinary things that change the course of events?"

Laioril eyed Adeone. "I'm not used to such intellectual probing, lad."

Adeone laughed. "He's got a point though, Chief."

"Aye but so's a dagger." The Chief faced Kensal. "So, you wish to hear of the doings of ordinary men?"

Kensal hesitated. Had he inadvertently overstepped a line? Should he apologise? How could he without raising suspicions? He said lightly, "Surely any story involves ordinary men, Chief?"

"Was Ull ordinary, lad?"

Kensal smiled. "As far as majistars from another world go, yes."

Laioril laughed. "Ah, but I remember stories that said that Annire never existed and that Ull was merely the son of a serf. That his father saw great troubles and made him leave to find his own fortunes. That Ull himself was not the bringer of magic but the first wielder. That he found a unique, egg-like star stone of many colours in the Takarin Mountains, that gifted him immense power, that that stone is the source of magic from which the others draw their spirits. It was written on the winds of night, so the ancient legends said.”

Everyone fell silent. In one short statement Laioril had called into question all they knew about the beginning of their history and reckoning of the years.

Tain leaned forward. “What do you mean, Chief?”

“An old man’s folly, lad. When something is known some historian will always question that knowledge trying to make his mark.”

Kensal swallowed. The comment had been directed at him and as a warning. Why? The Chief didn’t seem to be the kind of man to go for a reprisal because someone had called into question his knowledge.

Lord Irvin asked, “Do historians do that? Or do they merely give their opinion?”

Adeone shrugged. “Historians can alter the present by changing our perception of the past; therefore, some do try to make their mark in that way. The result might be small, but it’s the men they influence we remember. Men who searched for an ideal or—”

“Or killed far too many men in pursuit of their goals,” said Laioril.

“War is nothing more than manifestation of greed,” stated Arkyn. “It is rarely waged for intellectual belief. To force men to fight because you want more is one of the most despicable facets of power.”

Adeone looked at him. “What if it is for protection?”

“Then there may be justification in defence but never in offence. I meant my remarks for the taking of offensive action rather than defending the defenceless. Even in that case, men should fight freely and not be conscripted. If you are to ask a man to kill another, then at least let it be by free will; for if none will fight for you, there must be good reason.”

Adeone nodded. “Privately, I tend to agree but we are not private now.”

Arkyn blushed. “I’m sure neither Lord Irvin nor Lord Kensal will mention our words elsewhere.”

Cal said quietly, “And neither will I, Your Highness.”

Arkyn smiled. “Thanks, Cal.”

“That’s all right. Chief, will you tell us about the Fall of the Cearcall?”

Stories filled the rest of the evening and the more that Kensal and Irvin listened, the more entranced they became. They were lost to different times. Adeone watched their faces and those of his children and knew if this group of youngsters had their way, fascinating though they found the stories, war would never be part of the empire. Deep down, he was pleased they could disassociate valour and violence.

* * *

When the younger children had been sent to bed, and everyone's glasses were topped up, Adeone settled into his chair and smiled at Laioril.

"Magic put truly amongst the mundane, Chief."

"It's my trademark, lad. It's nice to see you all so relaxed."

"Glad you notice when we're not. How's the whiskey?"

Laioril took a sip. "Very nice. Tell the Margrave it's lucky I don't get chance to travel to Terasia, his stocks wouldn't be safe."

Adeone chuckled. "I'm sure he'll appreciate it. Will you stay here?"

"Nay, lad. I like my pallet. Will you walk back with me?"

Kensal and Irvin were intrigued by that and even more perplexed when the King said,

"Thank you, Chief, I'd like to very much."

Landis murmured, "Adeone, far be it from me—"

"If it's far from you, Festus, I'm glad it's not close enough to matter. Shall we, Chief?"

* * *

When they were outside, Adeone said lightly, "You could have stayed."

"Aye, lad, I know, but I like the fresh air. Houses are not for me, no matter how nice they are. I've have lived too much of my life on the road to settle elsewhere. Now that we're clear of big and little ears, how are your dreams?"

Adeone was glad of the night's shadows. "Getting worse. I've seen things I hope never to witness in real life."

"What things, lad?"

"A time with Tain gone and Arkyn poisoned. I know it's my subconscious fears manifested, but they're so vivid, Chief, so very vivid, and every time I see my sons, I feel the fear of it. I've seen travels and tears, tribulations and terror, but I've rarely seen smiles and I fear that they'll never come to my dreams."

Laioril put a hand on his arm. "Dreams are uncertain things and the memory will recall terror more easily than pleasure. The smiles are there, but not recalled. Or how else could you ever awaken?"

"I sometimes think I wake because I must, Chief. I've just found out about Dunius as well…"

"Ah. I wondered whether you'd ever discover that truth."

"Yes, and I saw my father in the King's Alcium. He asked me to make it right, but I don't know how. I let him down enough when I was a prince. How can I let him down now as King?"

"Does young Festus know that you know?"

Adeone nodded. "Yes, and we've told Arkyn and Tain."

"What did the youngsters say?"

348

"They weren't bothered."

Laioril smiled. "Then maybe in making it known and knowing it yourself, you have made it right by not being bothered. Your father never forgave himself for his rage. I know it. Your mother helped him come to terms with it, but he never stopped feeling guilty. There were other lives his actions affected that year and he never faced up to that either for years but, when he did, he made ample reparation. It is often a trick of the mind to think we never can do enough to make up for a wrong. Dunna fall into that trap, lad."

Adeone hesitated. "I'll try hard not to."

"Hmm. Well, you're a king – it's difficult to give over-generously of anything, isn't it?"

Adeone chuckled. "You'll give me a bad name, Chief."

"Only with a bit more practice, lad. We know you're a man at heart but never forget, for the safety of everything you hold dear, you have to be a king in mind."

"I hope I am that at least."

"Mm. Now, young Lord Kensal…"

"I'm sorry for his manner," whispered Adeone, watching the stars.

"Nay, lad, dunna be. I find him rather intriguing. I'd listen carefully to his summations of history and if he ever mentions how a place looked or how it was used in history, believe him."

Adeone stopped walking. "Why, Chief?"

"Because he's no more a historian than I am, lad. He's a timer, an Amser if he could find the star stone. He can see through time and, if that's not enough, you've got him in the most historically emotional city in the empire. He won't want to leave."

"Does he know it?"

"Not exactly. He simply thinks he has an exceptional imagination." Laioril squinted at Adeone. "He is not to be feared, lad. He cannot know magic as a sensor or espien can. He will not know you are affected by it. Do not force him to leave Oedran. Oh, dunna look like that. I've heard of Butterworth. Not all who wield Ull's Legacy are a danger to you."

Adeone sighed. "Chief, I'm lost without a map at the moment."

Laioril laughed. "Then accept the advice of a seasoned traveller. Do not fear the future for the future will come and men can change it, do not cast from you all that can help for fear of being discovered for discovery is the end of fear, and remember that dreams are the artist of your imagination painting pictures in your mind."

"I'll try to believe all that, Chief."

"Hmm. You always were very trying, lad. Now, I'll see myself from here, but I think I should give you one last word of warning… Magic is coming, whether you wish it or not. It may take years, but it's coming. The winds of the world are swirling it around us even here. Soon there will be more claiming it but do not fear it for in fear is danger. Accept it and it will accept you and help your cause."

"Does it know consciously what it does? Does it have a mind?" enquired Adeone semi-sarcastically.

Laioril chuckled. "Nay, lad, but the people it finds have. If you reject all that can use magic, Scanlon will welcome them, and blades and armies cannot fight it. Work with what you discover and let it work for you."

Adeone nodded. "Thank you for the advice, Chief. I hope I see you again soon."

"I'd bet on tomorrow morning. We're out of bacon. Sleep well."

Adeone was still chuckling to himself as he returned to Ceardlann.

* * *

He went to find Festus and discovered him sitting alone, sipping whiskey and watching the flames of the fire.

"The boys all gone to bed?"

"Yes. What did the Chief want to see you about?"

"Dire warnings of consequences. What else? Apparently, magic is coming to be claimed again."

"I never truly thought it had left. The Chief's just trying to unsettle you, Adeone."

"I don't think he is. That's what worries me. Do you think Irvin and Kensal enjoyed themselves?"

"I think so. I think everyone did, to be frank. Even the Chief. You were more relaxed than I've seen you for weeks outside of Rhian's company."

"What does that mean?" asked Adeone.

"That when you're with her, you're obviously easier. Just as when you're with your sons and no-one else is around you let yourself unwind. It's a good thing."

"I'm sure it is. I think I'm going up to bed. Don't stay up too long."

Landis pushed himself to his feet as Adeone did. "I think I'll go up as well. Otherwise, I'm likely to fall asleep here. Thank you for the evening. I've really enjoyed it."

Adeone nodded. "We'll have to do it again, if the Chief's amenable."

"I'm sure, with a bit of persuasion and a lot of flattery, he would be. Night, Adeone."

"Night, Festus."

Chapter 70
PREPARATIONS
Tretaldai, Week 36 – 24th Bayal, 17th Bayis 1212
Low Plains – Eyllyn

THE TUCHLIN, governor of the Low Plains, entered Lord Daioch's office as the gift Daioch was sending to Adeone was being delivered for his final inspection. Lord Aldwy eyed it with interest when it was unwrapped and just managed not to whistle.

"Are you trying to outdo every other province, my lord?"

Daioch looked over. "Not at all, Your Excellency, not at all. I thought, simply thought, His Majesty might appreciate this small trifle."

"I rather suspect he will. It's exquisite but rather disloyal to this province. What are all the gems for?"

"They represent water or woods, sir. I thought it showed more how much trouble we have to go to, to produce something like this. It shows time and effort, does it not?"

"I suppose you have also many fine woods and marquetry displayed. Do you honestly think it's in His Majesty's taste, Ifor?"

"I hope so, Your Excellency, I do hope so. I think he'll certainly appreciate it. He is not all controlled and practical. He does like a show of ostentation occasionally, certainly he does. More so, I suspect, when he's not responsible for it. Would you like to add your name to the gift?"

Aldwy eyed him. "I think not. It has all been your doing, in your imitable way. How's your son coping with Oedranian life?"

Ifor smiled. "Very well, I think, yes, very well indeed. He writes to us of his doings, though with my wife's family it's often mirthful."

The Tuchlin smiled tolerantly. "With Lord Landis as their father I imagine his cousins are mischievous."

"Only at appropriate times, sir, only at appropriate times."

"I see. I'll leave you to continue."

When he'd gone, Ifor examined the gift again. It was exquisite; the craftsman had done a superb job – it was flawless, totally flawless. He packed it into a case and sealed it shut; half wishing he could see Adeone's face when he unpacked it.

Chapter 71

UNWRAPPING

Alunadai, Week 37 – 1st Teral, 1st Teris 1212
King's Bedchamber

THE MUNLUMEN saw the King rise early, with two full moons it was often hard to sleep but he woke refreshed, and rather surprised Simkins by ringing for him earlier than expected, not that the manservant let it show.

"Sorry, Simkins, but I won't get back to sleep. For some unknown reason I'm feeling particularly mellow. Don't warn Richardson I'm about earlier than expected, I'll see if I can sort some things, before he puts more on my desk."

Simkins smiled. "Of course, Your Majesty. Richardson, I'm sure, will live through the shock. Out of interest, if you're in such a mellow mood, with regards to this afternoon, should I perhaps warn Richardson that he won't be needed?"

Adeone rolled his eyes. "Why, you anticipate my every request. Disasters aside you might as well take the afternoon off yourself, I'm sure I'll cope."

"Thank you, Sire, but if you're not to be working, I'd rather be here. I don't know what I'd return to, you see."

Adeone eyed him. "With a sense of humour like that I'm surprised I keep you around. Is my bath ready?"

"It will be in six minutes, sir. I'm sorry to say I didn't anticipate Your Majesty waking so soon."

"How will you live with yourself? All right, thank you."

Simkins bowed and left smiling. The King *was* in a mellow mood to have continued the banter so long.

As his manservant left, Adeone took a drink of water, pushed the heavy covers off his bed, got up and padded over to the window, looking out over the Palace grounds and what was visible of the city beyond. The view always inspired and depressed him, reminding him what he ruled over and what he had to do. He didn't know how long he stood watching the sky lighten but, when Simkins disturbed him to say his bath was ready, he was as content as he had been on waking.

* * *

When Richardson knocked and entered the Inner Office, he bowed and waited; a sheaf of documents in his hand.

"Did you oversleep?" enquired Adeone amused.

Richardson smiled. "I must have, Sire. I'll get my timepiece fixed. I

352

understand Your Majesty won't be working this afternoon."

"That is the plan. If those documents in your hand don't wreck it?"

"They shouldn't, Sire. Standard reports, one or two letters also and there is, I regret to say, what looks like a chest from Lord Daioch. There's a letter from His Lordship also."

Adeone nodded. "I'll read his letter first."

The letter was a normal piece of correspondence between two friends. It didn't hint at what the chest contained and Adeone finished it, rather puzzled by the secrecy, as Landis entered. Adeone half smiled in welcome as he put the letter on his desk.

"Landis, your wed-brother gets more cryptic. He's sent a chest and made no reference to it in his letter. I have a feeling he's trying to surprise me and I'm not sure I appreciate it."

"Ifor would never have malicious intentions, sir. If he has said nothing it will be for good reason. Why don't you see what's in the chest."

Two minutes later, Adeone checked the seals and, concluding they hadn't been tampered with, took his dagger out and cut the cords that secured the chest.

Landis said conversationally, "Using your dagger like that won't do it any good, Sire."

Adeone ignored him and lifted the lid. Beneath it were sweet aromatic wood shavings. He smiled. Ifor had even planned the packing material. "I don't think it's a wise idea for me to put my hands blindly into that."

Landis chuckled. "Probably wise, sir. Ifor was involved in several of our schemes when we were younger."

"I'll get Sergeant Kilbride, Your Majesty," said Richardson.

A few minutes later, Adeone was looking at what would be described as a sculpture. It was more map-like than anything else: a perfect miniature of the Low Plains in three dimensions under a glass dome. Different woods showed roads and rivers, but the forests were crushed emeralds and Lake Drenga crushed blue sapphires, with Ull's Watchtower being a single polished column of obsidian. Adeone inspected it with delight.

"Kilbride, put that back in the chest and remove it from this office," ordered Landis, his blood running cold. "Your Majesty, I shall explain once that device is out of this room."

Kilbride hesitated but, at a nod from Adeone, did as requested. Once he and the chest had gone, Adeone glared at his Defender.

Landis read more than a request in his face; it was an order. "Sire, this will be as difficult for me to say as it is for you to hear. That gift – it is not as innocent as it seems."

Adeone froze. "That is hardly an explanation, Landis!"

"Can I speak to you privately, Sire?"

"Richardson, you'll know when I need you. Postpone counsel. I rather think His Lordship decided my day didn't have enough upset." Once Richardson had gone, Adeone snapped, "So?"

"Obsidian is a scryer's tool, Sire. Have you forgotten? That fine sculpture, and I admit it is exquisite, has a polished obsidian surface. It could be used to scry on Your Majesty, to discover what your decisions are, what Your Majesty is currently working on—"

"Thank you. I get the picture," snapped Adeone. "Sicla! Why did you have to tell me?"

Landis said, "Do you think it gives me pleasure to incriminate my wed-brother, sir?"

Adeone walked away. He had to – had to collect his thoughts.

Landis, standing foursquare, waited. Adeone never liked distrusting his friends, and it wasn't that long since the revelations about Dunius had shaken his faith, their faith in long held certainties.

"There's no doubt that came from Daioch?" demanded Adeone.

"None, sir. You inspected the seals yourself."

Adeone frowned. "How could he have been so foolish? Made such a potentially devastating mistake? How?"

Evasion wouldn't save his wed-brother. However much he, Landis, wanted to help, Adeone wasn't daft. "Ifor is an expert in the commodities of the Low Plains, sir. He cannot be ignorant of the uses for obsidian."

"That didn't answer my question."

Landis gritted his teeth for a moment, trying to deny what he thought and not succeeding. "We have no evidence that it was a mistake, Sire. It could just as easily be intended."

Adeone glared at him. "Are you trying to push me into this action?"

"No, sir, I am, I hope, merely stating facts. I am too involved privately with Lord Daioch to make any sort of informed decision."

"So, this is entirely left to me?" scoffed Adeone. "How supportive."

Landis sighed. "I can tell you what I think is the right action, but I don't think my sister would thank me for it."

Adeone nodded. "Then you'd better leave. Tell Richardson I'll need him in two minutes."

Landis bowed, relieved but guilt-ridden. "Thank you, Sire."

* * *

Once alone, Adeone summoned Dragoris. His small red dragon messenger appeared on his outstretched palm. Two moments later, a hazy link formed, totally opaque to an outsider's view. "Tuchlin, I am about to order the arrest of Lord Daioch. I am sorry for the inconvenience."

The Tuchlin stared. "Arrest? Ifor? Why? Sire?"

Adeone said grimly, "There is a matter on which he needs questioning. Please do not warn him. Just see the commander gets all help he requires."

"Of course, Your Majesty, but I think I am entitled to an explanation if you are arresting my Deputy Governor, Sire."

Adeone eyed him. "Obsidian is the reason, Aldwy."

The Tuchlin frowned. "We trade it for many things. Mostly it is considered a sort of gemstone. Luckily, it's good for knives—"

"Also, it is used for scrying."

The Tuchlin's face became a picture of realisation. "Ah. That had slipped my mind, sir. I'll certainly have some questions for him."

"No, Aldwy, my commander will have," stated Adeone.

"Surely, sir, that's a bit forceful—"

Adeone's face set. "It was not a suggestion, Your Excellency. To endanger the security of my office is treason. I presume you understand all implications and actions. I shall contact the commander, expect him to be with you shortly. Do *not* alert Lord Daioch, unless you also wish to be under arrest."

"Very well, Sire. Thank you for the warning. I still think there's some mistake though."

"If there is, I doubt you will be the only one celebrating."

Adeone contacted the commander stationed at Eyllyn Fort, the conversation was one he'd never dreamt he'd be having and almost resented Landis for having recognised the issue. He'd not say Landis had forced his hand; he'd done what his duties demanded of him and no more. If Daioch hadn't been his wed-brother, Landis would have taken on far more, but this was, for once, solely the King's decision and doing.

The Eyllyn Commander couldn't have been more shocked had it been himself under arrest; ironically, it went some way to ameliorate Adeone's feelings. It wasn't just he who couldn't believe it. The conversation was short, bare essentials only, nothing to betray Adeone's feelings: either the incredulity or the nagging doubt it could be true that Lord Ifor Daioch was a traitor.

Chapter 72

ARREST
Morning
Low Plains – Eyllyn

LORD ALDWY exited from the link with the King in a grim mood. Why hadn't he thought about the present when he'd seen it? He might have been busy, but he should have considered what was being sent to the King with more diligence. The Low Plains had no scryers, the concentration of obsidian distorted what they could observe. A seer of legend was meant to be the only person who could use magic to observe the province.

Quarter of an hour later, his secretary announced the commander.

"Come in, Commander. Lord Daioch is in a meeting and I'm—"

"Not for much longer," interrupted the commander. "I am not here to receive orders, Your Excellency. I understand you wish to be present at the arrest and interrogation. Your Excellency may be present at the arrest but *not* at the interrogation. Those are the King's orders."

"We'll see. Let's go."

Holding open the door, the commander bit back his annoyance. The last thing he needed was a lord hindering his investigation.

Ignoring Daioch's secretary, the Tuchlin entered the Deputy Governor's modest office. His eyes swept over the other attendees. "This meeting may be finished at a later date."

As the perplexed attendees left, Daioch's eyes flicked to the commander and four guards. He opened his mouth, but Aldwy said,

"Do not resume your seat, Daioch. There are many questions you must answer—"

The commander cleared his throat.

Daioch looked between them. "Might I ask, just ask, what this is about?"

The commander replied before the Tuchlin could. "Lord Ifor Daioch, you are under arrest for treason…"

Ifor blanched. "What—? I've not— I'd never— I—"

"That is not the opinion of the King after the little gift that was sent—" remarked Aldwy.

The commander snapped, "Sir, would you please mind if I conducted this interview in accordance with His Majesty's instructions? No? Good! Lord Daioch, what was the gift?"

Confused, hands shaking, Daioch said, "A map of the Low Plains in woods and gems. What's—? Why—? Commander, of *what* exactly am I accused?"

"I have already said. Why did you send *that* gift in particular?"

"It seemed fitting and it was beautiful workmanship, very beautiful. The King is an admirer of such things. How on Erinna is it treason to wish to please your King?"

The commander was still grave. "Who made the piece?"

"A craftsman of Eyllyn. I had him supplied with the materials. What is the problem, Tuchlin?"

The commander shot Aldwy a glance to keep him silent and the Tuchlin bit his tongue; he didn't need the commander informing the King that he'd interfered beyond his remit.

The commander said, "We'll need the name of the craftsman, so we can pay him a visit. Did you see the piece before sending it to Oedran?"

"Yes, yes, of course…"

"Did you, Tuchlin?"

"Briefly. It was from Lord Daioch personally, and I would point out, Commander, that you are meant to be questioning His Lordship, not me."

The commander grimaced. Just because the King trusted the governor didn't mean he would, but *he* didn't need *the Tuchlin* making a complaint about his manner. "My apologies, sir, anything that threatens the King gets me annoyed. Lord Daioch, you say you saw the finished piece, you acquired the materials in fact… not surprisingly; that much obsidian must have been hard to obtain – especially as *scryers* the empire over require the stone. Ah, I see you've realised what you sent to Oedran." His voice changed from polite enquiry to a harsher, more determined tone. "You have endangered the safety and security of the King's office. You *were* responsible for the gift. We will investigate, but you had better hope the King is feeling merciful. I shall return after we have spoken to the craftsman. For now, my men will escort you home and you will remain under house arrest until we have contacted the King to see what he wishes to do on the matter. You are to talk to no-one about what is happening, not even your family. You will contact nobody. What is the craftsman's name?"

Daioch gave it, sick at heart. It was surely a mistake. Even then, the consequences would be far-reaching. How could he convince them he hadn't ever considered the use of obsidian? He couldn't. He had merely seen a gift, something to send to the King, and now he'd pay the price for someone else's plans. Had Scanlon been the architect of the situation? Had he fallen into a trap? Had he implicated Aldwy as well? Had his stupidity opened up the Low Plains to Scanlon's schemes? Then, from the depths of his memory, from a conversation in the past, a thought surfaced, an ancient law – one that could work for him, probably the only one that would. He drew in the deepest breath of his life.

"As the Alcis will bear me witness, I knew not what I sent. I would ask that I am taken before the King, to prove my loyalty to him. I will swear it on my fealty." As the words left him, bile rose. Adeone wouldn't thank him, but he had to hope that the King would understand why he had made the request.

Aldwy blanched. "You would be tried by the fealty you have sworn, and are yet to swear?"

Daioch held his gaze. "I would. I most certainly would. May truth spare my liege and my life."

The commander glanced between them. Amongst lords, the phrase *to swear on one's fealty* was common enough and wouldn't impress him into believing someone's innocence. Had he missed something? The Tuchlin and Lord Daioch were eyeing each other in an odd way.

Aldwy said, "I cannot read the proof, for having seen the gift, I am also under suspicion. You will have to undergo a full trial—"

"If the King will see me, I will travel to Oedran."

The commander interrupted, "Maybe I wasn't clear; you're not going anywhere, Lord Daioch."

"Be quiet!" snapped Aldwy. "If you have such little knowledge of the ancient laws, be good enough not to share your ignorance with us. Lord Daioch, I shall contact His Majesty, but what will you do if he doesn't accept the trial?"

"Put myself in the hands of the commander and resign my post. I cannot continue in it without both yours and the King's trust and I know of no other way of proving my innocence."

Aldwy nodded. "So be it. Commander, Lord Daioch *must* be given access to an alcium to come to terms with what he's decided. I shall speak to the King."

The commander said, "Might *I know* what he's just decided?"

"To travel to Oedran, barefoot, and to swear a life-binding fealty, then to be asked questions on this treachery – if he lies or admits he ever considered the uses the gift could be put to he will die where he stands."

The commander let out a curse. "You would do this even though we might prove your innocence another way, Lord Daioch?"

Daioch nodded. "Yes, of course, yes. You might prove it was not my idea but this is the only way to clear my name completely."

The commander let out a long breath, genuinely impressed. "You're braver than me. You'll have to live with that life-bind all your years."

"I am aware of that, very much aware of that," replied Daioch, his stomach roiling. He had a few days to come to terms with his decision, but he knew how risky it was, as well as how necessary. If Adeone's rage at the situation was such to instigate his arrest, if it hadn't cooled by the time the life-bind happened, that rage itself would cause him untold pain.

"I shall speak to His Majesty." Aldwy left the office. If their places had been reversed, would he ever have considered what Lord Daioch just had done? No. The trial would last his lifetime. Was there any way he could talk his Deputy Governor out of the action? Probably not. Daioch was astute and erudite. He understood everything he had requested.

He contacted the King, his mind still in turmoil. Daioch's request wouldn't just affect him. He had asked more of the King than any man in a hundred years, and the King didn't have to agree. As the link formed, he tried to compose himself.

"Well, Your Excellency?"

"Lord Daioch was at a loss to understand why he was being questioned until the issue of scryers came up, Sire. I would think he is innocent. His actions certainly suggested it. He wishes for trial by fealty, sir."

"Pardon?" exclaimed Adeone.

"He wishes to prove his innocence to you by a life-bind," replied Aldwy, examining the King's face as closely as he dared for any sign of acceptance or rejection.

"That certainly suggests he's innocent," replied Adeone, gravely. "He is determined?"

"Yes, sir. He says it is the only way to prove his innocence. I'm not convinced—"

The King cut across him. "If I refuse to permit it?" Ifor was right, but the consequences of a trial by fealty might be further reaching than Daioch had considered. The law was ancient, older than the Oedranian Empire, but, over the last couple of hundred years, it had been forgotten or regarded as obsolete. To resurrect it might be dangerous, but it might also be fortunate. It would certainly put people off conspiring if they knew the King was willing to shed his own blood to hunt down traitors.

Aldwy replied without hesitation. "He'll resign and I suspect will do himself some harm. He said he'll leave himself in the commander's hands, but I think he knows there is no coming back from this, not unless he proves his innocence to Your Majesty."

With those words, Adeone also began to wonder if someone wanted to undermine Daioch. Aldwy was perfectly capable, but he would retire from his post within the next few years. Daioch would have been the natural choice. As soon as Adeone considered it, it made more and more sense. Someone was again undermining the reputation of his loyal officials. Daioch had never shown the slightest sign of treachery. Had Adeone, for once, let paranoia get the better of him? Had his father influenced him so much, in instilling in him that he could trust no-one, that he questioned even his most loyal officials and friends? He despised himself. First Landis, now Daioch. Aldwy was right: Lord Daioch was likely to do something even more foolish if he refused to permit the trial. He would have to travel to Oedran. History would have to take its course.

Adeone finally said, "Very well, let him come. Just one thing, Aldwy… No, a few, actually. One, make sure he has a loyal guard with him. Two, the post of Deputy Governor is his. If he's proven innocent, I'm not having him thrown out of office for a mistake. Three, make sure the bloody commander clears up the rest of the mess. I have the sudden feeling this will trace back to… Never mind. It might take time, but I now have a feeling that this didn't originate in Eyllyn."

Aldwy looked at the King. What had changed his mind? "Very good, Your Majesty. When shall I tell Lord Daioch to set off? It might take him a while to reach Oedran."

"As soon as possible. Just make sure he has a guard. I'm not having him die en route to a life-bind."

Lord Aldwy nodded. "I understand, sir. Must he walk?"

"Yes. It's all part of it. It is, you might say, symbolic." He was thinking, *'When Scanlon gets to hear of how he's being thwarted, he'll hopefully die of apoplexy and save me some trouble!'*

Chapter 73
DISTRESS AND DECISIONS
Tretaldai, Week 37 – 3rd Teral, 3rd Teris 1212
Messenger Link

SOME PEOPLE believed there were few preparations for Lord Daioch's arrival in Oedran. They were wrong. Adeone postponed many meetings, devoting the time to the occurring events. Landis supported and advised whenever asked but in the back of his mind was the conversation he'd had with his sister, Daioch's wife. She had been distraught. Ifor wasn't a traitor; she knew it in her bones. Landis privately agreed and knew Adeone did as well; however, there had had to be action. In trying to explain, all that had happened was apportioning of blame.

Landis eventually said, "Come to Oedran, be here…"

"No. Ifor doesn't want me to see what happens. You've got to stop this, Festus."

"Nia, I can't, I truly can't. It's not in my power to—"

"You're—"

"Whatever I am, I can't stop this. Ifor wants a trial by fealty; he didn't have to do this. It *is* the only way to clear his name completely."

"I know he's innocent, Fes. I know it. Surely Adeone does..."

Landis sighed. "You know he can't treat his friends any differently to others. Nia, Ifor's innocence will be proved."

"Not if he dies en route or from exhaustion, it won't," pointed out his sister. "Alcis only knows what stupidity he'll get up to."

Landis eyed her. "You've got to pull yourself together for his sake. Things will take their course. There's nothing else we can do. Everything possible is being done that can be done."

Feronia struggled with her emotions. "Fes, I love Ifor deeply, as deeply as I loved Adeone... I wish I could do more."

"I know, and so do I but this is now a waiting game. I promise I'll let you know what's happened as soon as I can. You have my word, sis."

"Can you give my love to Emrys?"

Landis smiled. "Of course I can and will. Try not to worry yourself too much."

* * *

Entering the Inner Office the following Alunadai, Landis found the King deep in discussion with Advisor Rayburn and Judge Tancred.

"Rayburn, you're sure about that?"

Advisor Rayburn nodded. "No doubt, Sire, and people might expect His Highness to be there."

"I do not think it is what people expect that matters, Your Majesty," observed Tancred. "Prince Arkyn is old enough to cope with the experience. Indeed, there are many more reasons for his presence than because people might expect him there. It will not be for many years but, one day, His Highness will be king and may well find himself in a similar position."

Landis guessed what was being discussed and caught the King's eye. "Prince Arkyn should be present, Sire. Daioch will be bound not just to Your Majesty but your heirs. They should at least be able to recognise each other."

Judge Tancred said, "My understanding of the situation, Lord Landis, is that, with a life-bind, there is more to the recognition than simple physical characteristics." Seeing puzzlement, he continued, "The law came about during the Age of the Cearcall, Sire. Some of the ancient documents suggest that a vassal under a life-bind will feel the presence of his liege or his liege's heir. It is unclear exactly what this means, but it is believed that a form of intuitive and instant recognition occurs."

Landis said, "So, even if blind, the vassal could recognise the liege?"

"Yes, my lord. With the sharing of their blood, they are part of each other."

"Judge, what else would the vassal feel?" asked Adeone.

Tancred watched him carefully. "Everything you do, Sire, with relation to themselves. In the old texts, it says that should a liege get annoyed with a vassal then the liege's displeasure or pain is amplified for the vassal. The binding process is potent and profound. Some texts spoke of a sort of slavery with relation to the vassal. Bound to every whim, you see. It is not a pleasant thought, but all fealties are that – life-binding is merely a stronger form of it."

Adeone got up and turned away. "I don't like the thought of that."

Having stood, Judge Tancred said, "Sire, as a man, that is understandable but, as a king, it is rare in this situation."

Landis dismissed Rayburn with a glance.

Adeone cursed. "What you mean, James, is that I have no choice?"

"I rather fear that is what I mean, Your Majesty," replied Tancred inclining his head slightly. "These happenings are in motion. History is moving; there is no way to resist it."

Landis murmured, "Judge, maybe there's a time and a place."

"Maybe so, my lord, but surely it is better to be honest than hide what is true simply because it might be unpleasant," replied Tancred, still watching the King.

Adeone smiled wryly. "You're right, but everyone is always keen to prevent me knowing anything unpleasant."

As the understanding of the years flashed between them, the elderly judge said sadly, "Then they are fools, Sire. Unpleasantness is part of life and there is no doubt life is richer for it."

Adeone chuckled. "Quite. Landis, why did you dismiss Rayburn?"

"I thought it would be better for him not to hear the honesty of Your Majesty's discussion," replied Landis dryly. His friend tended to forget others when he was debating with Judge Tancred. It was a depth of friendship he had with few others but it didn't mean it was wise.

"Get him back, please. Judge, what about Prince Tain?"

"Sire, he's only twelve!" exclaimed Landis.

Tancred resumed his seat as Adeone did. "Although I appreciate His Lordship's concern, I have to say that my thoughts are contrary to his. I expect His Highness will cope with the ceremony and have far more understanding of its implications than we can appreciate. In 1215, he will dispense justice in this city. He can cope with observing an unconventional trial, Sire. Especially one that is so rare. The opportunity is unprecedented in living memory."

Sitting down, Rayburn said, "Sire, His Honour has made some good points. Prince Tain will benefit from the experience, I have no doubt."

"Your Majesty, I can appreciate the importance of the event but surely

His Highness is still too young," observed Landis, half incredulous

Adeone's lips twitched. "Maybe not. He might surprise us all – other than Judge Tancred who has absolute faith in him."

"Sire, what if His Highness does not cope well with the experience? Your Majesty will be unable to act. Prince Arkyn shouldn't move from your side being your heir and I won't be able to do anything as I'm there as your Defender."

"That *is* a good point, Sire," observed Rayburn.

Adeone said briskly, "Judge Tancred, as this is a trial, we should have a judge present. Would you please attend?"

Bright eyes glinting, Tancred inclined his head. "Certainly, Sire."

Chapter 74
LIFE-BIND
Alunadai, Week 39 – 15th Teral, 15th Teris 1212
King's Chambers – Audience Chamber

A WEEK LATER, Adeone made sure the route from the Carnford Gate to the Palace was as clear as possible when Daioch entered Oedran. He, his sons, the Lords of Oedran and Judge Tancred were waiting in the Audience Chamber, as soon as they had word Daioch was through the King's Gate and making his way along The Pike.

Tancred had told Adeone much about the law. How it had originated in Areal during the time of the first Memini and had spread during the Age of the Cearcall. How it had been used by kings when the empire was forming or in grave danger. Adeone wondered how this trial would sit amongst those others in the history books. What would history make of it? Would it be blown out of proportion? Or would it show the lengths men would go to, to prove to him they were loyal? Would it be remembered as an act of tyranny or loyalty?

As Daioch entered the Audience Chamber, Adeone's eyes swept over the Deputy Governor: bloody feet, pale skin, unfocused eyes and travel-stained clothes. Landis standing behind Adeone drew breath sharply, glad his sister *wasn't* present. Ignoring carefully devised protocol, Adeone rose from the throne and descended the dais steps to meet Daioch, who tried to kneel, falling forward. Adeone caught him. Slowly he lowered both himself and Lord Daioch until he was sitting cradling the Deputy Governor.

"Get Doctor Chapa, now! Landis, get some water from my office." He glanced at the guard with Lord Daioch. "What's happened?"

"I don't know, sir…" Disbelief blazed across Adeone's face and the fact that every man in the room was kneeling as the King wasn't standing, or enthroned at an official audience, reinforced the concept it was *the King* he was lying to. He amended his statement hurriedly. "That is… His Lordship has been refusing food and water for two days. Since Carnford, to be precise, Your Majesty."

Adeone swore and, still supporting him, looked at Daioch. A hundred messages were in his eyes.

Daioch's unfocused eyes roamed over Adeone's face. "My liege…"

"No, my lord, not now. You need to rest and I'm taking no more blood from you today."

"I will prove my innocence. I will." The voice was cracked, faint and dry but determined.

Adeone sighed; history would take its course. "Very well." Grasping one of Daioch's hands, he held his gaze as best he could. "In truth did you consider what use the gift could be put to?"

"In truth, my liege, I did not."

Adeone said, "The rest can wait." A shadow fell across them. "Thank Alcis. Doc, can you…"

Doctor Chapa nodded. "He needs to be in a private room…"

Landis returned and passed the King a glass of water. Adeone held it to Daioch's lips, but the Deputy Governor tried to refuse it.

Using power he knew he shouldn't, Adeone murmured, "Ifor, drink. I believe you're innocent, but if you don't drink, you'll never prove it to anyone else."

Compelled to do so, Daioch drank. Chapa asked for volunteers to help him to a room.

When all the lords eyed each other, Adeone snapped, "Do not make me angry today!" (Lord Iris got up.) "Thank you, my lord, but I was thinking of those who have the strength of youth, not the wisdom of age. Lord Teran, Lord Cearis, help Lord Daioch to his chambers, and then leave Doctor Chapa to his work." He turned to the guard with Daioch. "Go with them. Doctor Chapa will see you're given accommodation."

Not knowing what had come over him, the guard said, "I'll stay with Lord Daioch, if Your Majesty doesn't mind."

Adeone nodded. "Of course." He looked down to find Daioch had closed his eyes.

The guard took the Deputy Governor's weight. Stirring, Daioch opened his eyes and tried to stand. Slowly he managed it and, supported between Teran and Cearis, he made a painstaking exit from the Audience Chamber, Adeone's unwavering gaze watching him leave.

* * *

Two minutes later, Adeone seated himself in the Inner Office. Both his sons and Landis joining him.

"Why, Festus? Why did he force himself through so much?"

"To prove beyond doubt that he's innocent. For some odd reason you do command a lot of loyalty. I've never understood it myself…" Landis was obviously trying to make light of the situation.

Adeone sighed. "Yes, but you're an old reprobate. Do I take his life-bind? I know he's innocent."

Prince Arkyn said quietly, "I think you need to, Sire, to prove to the world that he is."

"Yes, but your grandfather, and my grandfather – to my belief – never took one life-bind and I will have taken two…" Finally, Adeone voiced his concern, "What will history say about that?"

Landis shrugged. "History may never find out about the first and, as for the second, it was at his instigation, not yours. Take it, Sire. If he ever makes Tuchlin, you will know he is to be trusted beyond doubt. If he betrays you, or your sons, he will forfeit his life—"

"That's the bit I dislike," admitted Adeone glumly, "the knowledge that it sentences men to a life where death sits at their shoulder."

"So it does in everyone's life, Sire," remarked Landis without emphasis.

"I suppose that is true. Tain, are you all right?"

Tain bit his lip. "Yes, father. I think Arkyn's right though, and Uncle Festus. The life-bind must happen and there will be security in the outcome."

Adeone hesitated. "I know. Look, I can't tell what's going to happen. Do you and Arkyn want to go and relax?"

Arkyn glanced at Tain. "Maybe it would be better if we did. Come on, father will be busy."

Tain nodded, and the brothers left for Arkyn's rooms.

Once the door closed, Adeone said, "Do you think he realises that was the first bit of advice on official matters he's ever given me?"

Landis smiled. "No, and I wouldn't point it out to him."

Two minutes later, Richardson knocked and entered. He passed the King a note. Breaking Chapa's seal, Adeone read the missive swiftly.

"Daioch says he'll not eat or drink until he's proved his innocence under a life-bind. Alcis! What do I do now, Festus?"

Landis said, "Take the binding, Sire. It's all you can do."

"It'll be a miracle if he survives it, even if innocent. According to Tancred it puts a strain on the body over and above the cutting of flesh."

365

"Have faith in determination, Sire. It's got him this far."

"No, *stupidity* got him this far – his and mine. Very well. Festus, you'd better come as principal witness. Richardson, get me Lords Ryson and Iris as well. Iris is responsible for the Low Plains and Ryson has taken an oath to justice as a lawyer. They're therefore more appropriate than any of the others. If he is still here, please request Judge Tancred to join us." Adeone turned back to Lord Landis, "What's more, Festus, if Ryson is still supplying Scanlon with information, I might just be giving my brother a heart attack so much sooner…"

* * *

Quarter of an hour later, Adeone, his sons and witnesses entered a bedchamber to find Lord Daioch half-delirious.

Adeone eyed Chapa. "If he's innocent, will he survive the trauma?"

Chapa shrugged. "There's no knowing, Sire. I would expect so. Part of this is due to the fact he wants to prove his innocence."

Adeone sat on the edge of the bed. Daioch tried to rise but Adeone simply place a hand on his shoulder to stop him.

He whispered, "My lord, if you truly wish to do this, I will honour that wish but I would ask you to regain some of your strength first."

Daioch said, "No, sir, I will do it now. I must."

Adeone sighed, defeated and out of options. "Very well. Lord Landis…"

His Defender knelt, offering his dagger. Adeone laid the cold steel across Daioch's palms and placed his on top. As he spoke the words of the life-bind, Daioch relaxed with each reply. When Landis withdrew the dagger, cutting their palms, neither flinched.

Bloody hands still pressed together, Adeone looked Lord Daioch in the eye. "Tell me about the gift."

Lord Daioch told him how a scribe had known he was looking for ideas and suggested a map of the Low Plains, about the craftsman, about how he'd wanted to use jet as it was easier to work but the scribe had convinced him obsidian was more apt. He had left the procurement to the scribe. He talked about the fashioning of the piece of seeing the beauty but not the danger.

Adeone asked for the names of the scribe and the craftsman and received them. "Lord Daioch, I hereby clear you of any involvement in the matter of the gift. You are innocent and that will be proclaimed. Now, take your rest." He leaned over and placed a kiss on Daioch's brow. He was drained so Daioch must be exhausted.

The lord's eyes closed as though he was under an overwhelming and undeniable obligation to sleep. Adeone moved his hands and when Chapa would have cleaned and bandaged them first, Adeone shook his head.

366

"See to Daioch; he is weaker; my hands will wait."

Ryson said, "Do you have a spare swab, Doctor Chapa?"

Chapa looked at the King, who simply nodded.

"Yes, my lord. In my bag. Thank you."

Adeone rested his elbows on the arms of the chair, whilst Ryson carefully tended his hands. The Lord of Oedran didn't say anything as he did so, and Adeone wasn't in the mood to make conversation. His eyes dismissed everyone else to the adjoining sitting room. Once they'd gone, he alternately watched Daioch and Ryson. In the former case, trying to work out if he appreciated the blind loyalty of others and in the latter, wondering what had motivated Ryson to take on the task. Doctor Chapa finished swiftly and moved over to Ryson.

"Thank you, my lord. Do you want a job?"

Ryson pushed himself to his feet. "I could never match your skill, Doctor Chapa."

Adeone rested his head on the back of the chair and eyed them both. "If you're getting too old to manage, Chapa..." it was said with a smile and a wry note.

Chapa caught his eye. "I'll let you know when I do, Your Majesty..."

Adeone winked. He looked at Ryson. "Please wait outside, my lord, but my thanks."

Ryson gave a precise bow and, on leaving, glanced at Daioch. A sad smile fleetingly passed over his face.

A couple of minutes later, hands bandaged, Adeone thanked Iris and Ryson for their presence and told them they could inform the other Lords of Oedran of events. Turning to Tancred, he said, "One for your history books, Your Honour."

"Maybe, Your Majesty. History, though, has more events unrecorded than any realise. It is often the consequences, rather than the event, which makes such times remembered."

Adeone nodded, half in thanks, half in dismissal. He waited until Tancred had left before turning to his sons. "I've arranged a private dinner for tonight..."

Arkyn smiled. "We're looking forward to it, father."

Adeone studied Tain closely. His son stood up to the scrutiny well and seemed perfectly at ease, as though he'd not just witnessed a momentous trial and his father's blood spilling. He gave them both a careful hug and watched them leave.

Once in private with Landis, Adeone said, "Lord Daioch's mention of the scribe was new. He obviously never thought about it in Eyllyn. I'll contact the Tuchlin. Can you reassure Nia? They both have to know he's innocent straight away. With regards to the scribe, it is, or it could be, a link to Scanlon. A king's clerk, a justice scribe. Such simple distinctions. Such a wealth of meaning. I wonder if he realises the significance—" There was the click of a door and Chapa joined them. "He will recover," it was a question, a statement and an order.

Chapa shrugged. "I'd hope so, Your Majesty. I'll do everything I can. His guard won't leave his side."

"No, I noticed that. Part of me is pleased for it. Though next time I speak to Lord Daioch, he *will* be elsewhere."

* * *

When Scanlon heard Syri's report on events, he not only swore but threw things as well. Another plan defeated. Daioch was now untouchable and destined to become Tuchlin. Another province would be lost to a leader loyal to the King. Was it too much to ask that he was given a chance to show the empire how much Adeone was destroying it?

Chapter 75
JULIUS
Imperadai, Week 39 – 18th Teral, 18th Teris 1212
Inner Office

THREE DAYS LATER, Adeone eyed his nearson. At sixteen, Julius was overcoming the gangly stage but still held the slim vigour of youth. He had the Landis good looks to go with it. Some of the young ladies of Court must have an eye on his nearson with his floppy dark blond hair, inherited from his mother, and his blue-grey eyes. He had a rakish sort of charm to go with them, but his behaviour currently didn't match his physical profile.

Adeone said, "The Steward has finally complained, my lord. You've done your reputation no good."

Julius reddened. "I'm sorry, Sire. I really am. I didn't realise how much I'd drunk—"

"You may need to apologise to Lord Emrys as well. He shouldn't have to look after you at such a time. Sit down. I've dealt with the Steward, but next time I *won't* be so tolerant. I am disappointed by your behaviour, especially given your Uncle Ifor's current troubles, but I'm not going to start yelling at you. Instead, we need to talk. Don't look so apprehensive; it certainly doesn't suit you. Tell *me* how you are."

"I'm all right, sir. Well, hungover."

"Even I, as distracted and beleaguered as I undoubtedly am, can tell you're not *all right*. And before you start with it, you can lose the formality. I'm still your nearfather. For both our sins."

A small smile escaped from Julius. "Sorry, Uncle Adeone. Julia thinks I'm frustrated and bored. Mother just thinks I've no sense and father is too busy to notice what I am half the time."

Adeone sighed. "Julia's right, I think. Your mother loves you very dearly and is merely concerned for you and, as for your father, blame me, not him. I'm responsible for the work he does."

"But not for the long hours he spends at it, sir, even before Uncle Ifor's recent troubles. He could delegate but he won't. I know it's hard, but I wish he'd… Oh, I don't know."

"You enjoyed being in Macia, just the two of you, didn't you?"

Julius gave a slight nod. "Yes, but since we returned, it's been worse than ever."

"I'll see what I can do…"

"No, sir, Uncle Adeone, I'd rather you didn't mention it. It'll only worry him."

"I never said I'd raise it with him, but I'll try to get him a bit more free time… That is, if he doesn't fill it with something else."

"That's the problem," muttered Julius, flicking his nails together.

"Why are you so bored?"

"It's the school. I'm fed up with it and well they can't forget I'm father's son. He's not helping. He hadn't been there for years and now he's there a lot and I know it's because of me…"

"Can you keep what I'm about to tell you private? Thank you. It's not because of you. Your nearcousin wished to give a recent or new graduate a place on his staff and so, as my Chief Advisor, I set your father the task of finding one. Much to his chagrin. He hated the school."

Julius blushed. "Oh. I… I've made a fool of myself, haven't I?"

"No. Misunderstandings exist for many reasons and few result in, or are due to, foolishness. Why are you so bored at the school?"

"I don't think I'm cut out to be an advisor, but I didn't think you'd like me going into law, and, truth be told, I wasn't enamoured of that either, or the army. What's worse is I haven't got a clue what I'd rather be doing, unlike Irvin."

"That's nothing out of the ordinary, to my understanding. I think you'll make a good advisor one day, but I think you learn more by doing something than by being lectured at. Until that opportunity arises, grit your teeth and try not to annoy your lecturers as your father did. At least, for a while. What are you meant to be learning at the moment?"

Julius shrugged. "Wish I knew. Something about the interplay of the different provinces." He grinned. "Thank you for getting me out of the lecture. I can't wait until they start with 'Formalities of the Empire'."

"That sounds dull. I suppose it covers modes of address and titles." (Julius nodded, glumly.) "Hmm. Just don't tell your lecturer you sit in the Inner Office with a whiskey, your feet up on the chair, calling the King 'Uncle Adeone'. I can't see you getting top marks."

Julius laughed. "Maybe not but I'd like to see his face."

"Then spare my reputation as a ruthless king, if you can."

"You mean I *can* tell him?"

"As I doubt he'd believe you, why not? What are your fellow students like?"

"They're a mixed bunch. I know those of the lordships quite well but others I'm only just getting to know. They seem all right though. There might be friends amongst them. Or could be if they'd see me as me."

"Give them time. I got to know a few people through your father being there. Some are now influential in their provinces because of it – including your Uncle Ifor. Julius, don't let boredom and frustration wreck who you are. It wouldn't be worth the heartache. Reputations are forged when young and can devastate and hold you back for years. It's not fair, but you won't be able to hide, or move cities."

Julius sighed. "I know, Uncle Adeone. I'm trying, but I'm not someone on whom boredom sits easily."

Adeone ruffled his hair. "No. As I know. To my cost. Start to laugh at the world but don't let it see you laughing. When you're not in lectures, do the work set and remember the school isn't your whole life and your time there *is* limited. They're worried whenever your father enters; one day it might be you getting them concerned. Enjoy the thought."

Julius' eyes were alight with fun. "Uncle Adeone... Should you be telling me to do any of this?"

Adeone grinned openly. "I'm your *near*father, not your father, and I have a rather different, sympathetic view of what you're going through. My years being tutored were harder than many realise. I know how that can destroy joy, how it can lead to overcompensating and how it can get you into trouble without realising. Your father and I... well, let's say we might have overcompensated on occasion." He chuckled to himself. "There was a time when I *accidentally* left the paddock gate open. Most of the horses were there as the vet checked them over. One crash later – planned, of course – and the horses bolted. I merrily walked inside and watched as the grooms tried to round them up. Took them hours. All the Palace gates had to be shut."

Julius laughed. "Did you get into trouble?"

"Father might have had a word with me, lips twitching. If you *ever* want to talk, moan or let your frustration out, I can listen with pleasure. It's not just the good times I'm here for."

"Uncle Adeone... I... Thank you. It's helped."

"Good, I'm glad. Now, have you tried..."

Six minutes later Julius left smiling; Adeone watched him go and nodded to himself. Arkyn had been right; Julius had needed to talk to someone outside his family.

Chapter 76
IFOR AND ADEONE
Pentadai, Week 39 – 19th Teral, 19th Teris 1212
Privy Wing – Daioch's Chambers

THE FOLLOWING DAY, Adeone entered Lord Daioch's rooms to be greeted by one of the Palace servants. Bemused by the King's unannounced visit, he informed Adeone that the doctor was with Daioch in the private rooms. Having ensured Daioch was decent, and the servant was taking a couple of hours off, Adeone entered Daioch's bedchamber again. His friend was sitting with his feet in a bowl of water and Chapa was bandaging up his left hand. Chapa pushed himself to his feet and bowed. Daioch would have risen, but Adeone crossed to him and touched his shoulder.

"Stay where you are. We wouldn't want the doc's handiwork undone."

Daioch watched Adeone and settled back down. "Thank you, Sire."

Adeone smiled, perching on the edge of his friend's abandoned bed. "Talking of your handiwork, doc, what's the verdict?"

Chapa said, "I don't think Lord Daioch's likely to suffer long-term damage from his journey, Sire... As you're here, would you like me to tend to your hands?"

Adeone nodded. "You might as well. Though finish seeing to Ifor."

Daioch tried to protest, but a glare from Chapa silenced him. A couple of minutes later, Chapa unwound the bandages on Adeone's hands. Cleaning them, he stopped, puzzled. There were scars suggesting Adeone had cut himself thus before.

"Who tended your other cuts, Sire?"

Adeone held his gaze. "Simkins, and that is as much as you need to know on the matter."

"Sire—"

"Doc, let me put this bluntly. You will not – in any way, shape or form, by any act – attempt to find out anything from anyone with regard to

371

those scars. What's more, you'll not speculate about them either. Have I made myself understood?"

"Yes, Your Majesty."

"Good and if you find a loophole in that list, as I'm sure you will, imagine I closed it."

"Sire."

Adeone simply waited until Chapa had risen once more and when the doctor excused himself, he looked over. "Thank you, cousin. We'd be truly lost without you."

"Thank you, sir, but there are other doctors," replied Chapa with an odd reticence in his eyes.

Adeone crossed to him, taking him gently by the shoulder. "I'm sorry. You know that all the other doctors in the empire would never replace you, don't you? Not just because you're a cousin but because you bully, cajole and keep us in line through deep-seated care. I'm not blind to it – frustrated occasionally, but I wouldn't change it, or you."

Chapa held his gaze. There was more to the sentiment and statements than the words could say. "Thank you, Sire, but about that frustration: I think you might benefit from an evening off, with good friends and mellow whiskey."

Adeone was amused. "That's put us both back in our place, hasn't it?"

Chapa laughed. "Seemingly so."

Wryly, Adeone said, "That evening off – nip and tell Richardson it'll be tonight and then come to dinner with me, if you can."

Chapa nodded. "I'd be glad to."

Once he'd gone, Adeone regarded Daioch and Daioch met the gaze tone for tone. The look lasted a couple of moments before the door opening interrupted it and the guard who had travelled with Daioch entered.

Adeone frowned. "Wait outside these chambers, please."

The guard said, "Sire, I'm—"

"Wait outside. I shall not ask again."

The guard saluted and left. Two moments later, Adeone checked he hadn't simply moved to the adjoining sitting room.

Sitting back down, Adeone said, "We need to talk, Ifor."

"I didn't think you were here to look at me, Sire. Certainly I didn't."

Adeone grinned. "Not lost that aspect of your personality then."

"I doubt, Sire, I do very much doubt, that I ever will. I'm sorry, very sorry for everything..."

Adeone smiled sadly. "You've done enough to prove how much you regret that small mistake. You don't need to say any more on the matter; however, I do. I'm sorry I ever had you questioned in such a manner. I let the knowledge that friends may betray me get the better of my judgement. I regret that more than you can imagine. It forced us both into actions that were out of proportion to the mistake that was made. I hope you can forgive me for it."

Daioch watched Adeone's face and realised why he'd ordered the guard well out of earshot. The *King* could never be heard to apologise for something that he had a duty to do.

"Sire, I chose the method of my trial."

"Yes, but I should never have put you in the position where you had to," admitted Adeone.

"Yes, you should, Sire, you really should. I could have knowingly sent that gift assuming because we correspond on a personal level that you'd never suspect it. You had to do what you did, as much as I had to do what I did..."

"Yet you've paid such a heavy price."

Ifor frowned slightly. "I'm sure your cousin, the former Chief Merchant, would tell you that the price paid for any goods is proportionate to what the purchaser is willing to pay to the vendor. I was willing, more than willing, to swear a life-binding fealty; I would have sworn one had you asked without provocation."

"I would *never* have asked," protested Adeone.

"No but I would have done it had you needed me to, most certainly I would. You are the King we need."

Adeone sighed. "I sometimes wonder."

"Then, my liege, might I say you needn't?"

"As you just have there isn't much I can do about it; however, let us end this discussion before I pour out any more of my heart. I have a couple of questions for you though. Why did you stop eating and drinking?"

Daioch shrugged. "My sentence to myself: I had a debt to pay – for even though I was innocent in whatever conspiracy there was, my name was linked to that gift..."

Adeone regarded him. "Ifor, you're a bloody fool at times for all you're a politician – thinking about it, they're the same thing."

"Thank you, Sire – your compliments never cease to amaze me."

Adeone laughed and his eyes met Lord Daioch's amused ones. "I get the hint. I will ask you no more of your journey here. Congratulations on making Chapa earn his money though. I've been trying to succeed at that for years."

Lord Daioch said, "He is certainly different, Your Majesty, very different."

Adeone nodded. "Yes. Has he patched you up?"

"Yes. Once he remembered he couldn't use balms that had been in contact with metal…”

“He’s meant to be clever!”

“He’s getting on a bit.”

Adeone snorted. “Yes, as he reminds everyone at every opportunity. Now, there are a couple of people I wish you to meet properly before you travel home… My sons. Come to Ceardlann for a day. One day Arkyn will be your king.”

“Not for many years, I hope.”

“I thought you were more erudite than that,” grumbled Adeone.

Ifor smoothed down the edge of his bandage. “I cannot consider your death now, sir. I cannot and would not even if I could. I chose to bear these scars and I will continue to bear them. I meant the words of the fealty.”

“I know, Ifor, it’s just the loyalty of others when given as you gave yours makes me uncomfortable. It’s nice to know you can’t betray me, but I don’t like having friends who can’t question me.”

“Maybe those friends don’t mind, sir. I took an oath as Deputy Governor. I’ve just reaffirmed it to my mind and Lord Scanlon, if you’ll pardon my bluntness, can go to Sicla’s Cavern! I’m your vassal and I am happy to be that, very happy.”

Adeone noted Ifor had realised who must have set him up. Without acknowledging it, he said, “Even if I’m unhappy that it’s to such an extent?”

“Then I feel concerned that I’ve caused you distress, my liege, but there’s not much I can do, not much at all. I’m made this way.”

Adeone laughed. “There are times, Ifor, I could quite cheerfully throw you to the wolves.”

“Please don’t, Sire. I happen to like my life and have been at some pains to extend it.”

Adeone sighed. “What can I do against such persuasion? How is life on the Low Plains…?”

* * *

When they were disturbed, it was by Landis. The Lord of Oedran entered the room smiling in an amused way, catching Ifor’s eye with a look that reminded Adeone more strongly than any words could have done that they were wed-brothers.

The King said mildly, “Planning some mischief?”

Ifor smiled. “Not at all, Sire, not at all. Festus is merely taking advantage of my presence in Oedran.”

“I dread to imagine what for. You’re not to be working whilst you’re recovering.”

Ifor shook his head. “I would never go against Your Majesty’s wishes. Your wish is my command.”

374

Festus chuckled. "He really means that as well, Adeone. I'd watch out if I were you."

Adeone said, "On the contrary, Festus: Ifor is one man I now don't have to watch, unlike my Lords of Oedran."

"Then I'm happy to disillusion Your Majesty by stating that I'm completely trustworthy, Sire," replied Landis with a laugh.

Ifor muttered, "*Never* believe an outright declaration such as that!"

Adeone winked. "I never do. Festus, did you disturb us for a reason?"

"Depends on your interpretation, sir. Ifor, are you up to seeing Emrys?"

Ifor hesitated. "I don't know. How is he?"

"The same as any adolescent who's not seen his father for a time."

"What's this about?" enquired Adeone concerned.

Ifor looked away, but was compelled to answer. "How can I face him, Sire? I have disgraced our name."

Adeone glanced at Landis, who raised an eyebrow eloquently.

"You must decide that for yourself, but I might suggest that you have to." He willed Ifor to meet his eye. When he did, Adeone said, "There is no disgrace in my mind."

Ifor blinked. "My liege, when I have my own head straight, I might try to sort his out."

Landis laughed. "Good luck."

Adeone chuckled. "I'll second that. Our sons' minds are their own, luckily."

Ifor smiled in spite of himself. "I'll see him before long, Festus, but not quite yet."

Landis sighed. "Nia's also said she's not heard from you…"

Adeone cursed inwardly. "Ifor, don't go through this alone. Let your family support you. Our families are the most important people in our lives, whether we acknowledge it openly or not. Don't shut them out."

Seeing Ifor deep in thought, Adeone changed the subject. "I'd better leave you two to talk. Keep Festus out of trouble, Ifor, whilst I cause some."

Ifor got up. "I can certainly try, Your Majesty."

"Certainly very trying," muttered Landis.

Chapter 77

DINNER AND DEBATE
Hexadai, Week 39 – 20th Teral, 20th Teris 1212
Inner Office

THE FOLLOWING EVENING, Lord Emrys arrived for dinner with Arkyn to discover a rare change of plan. He was to be dining with the King and, making their way to the King's Chambers, he asked Arkyn why.

Arkyn said mildly, "Because the King is the King."

The Prince wasn't given to enigmatic answers, so Emrys got the message to stop asking questions but his stomach turned. He liked the King. Had spent several enjoyable evenings at Landis House with him present, but the subterfuge spoke of something far deeper and more worrying. His father was life-bound. Where did that leave him?

They entered the Inner Office and bowed. The King was seated behind his imposing desk. Was he really still working?

Adeone rose. "Lord Emrys, I'm sorry for the ruse, but I thought if *I* sent the invitation you'd get concerned. Your father's next door and, I have to admit, doesn't realise you're going to be here. He said he had to get his head straight before seeing you, but I rather suspected that was going to take far too long."

Lord Emrys swallowed. "I…" then sagged. "I don't think he wants to see me, Sire."

Adeone said quietly, "He does, but he doesn't know what to say, that's all. Go on, just walk into the room and half the issue will resolve itself. As for the other half, ask your Uncle Festus to join me and that might well solve that."

Emrys took a deep breath, "Very well, Sire," he bowed and then hesitated momentarily before squaring his shoulders and entering the triniculum.

As Landis left, Emrys watched his father get up and hold out his arm. Emrys crossed to him. Wrapped in a hug, he fought back the flowing tears. Had he really been that tense without realising?

Daioch said, "I've let you down. I've let you all down so much."

Wiping his eyes, Emrys broke free. "No, you haven't, father."

Ifor turned away. "I've brought shame on our name, Emrys. Shame you'll bear as I do."

Emrys fought hard with himself. He'd always been taught never to question his father, but he had to; yet a lifetime's habit was hard to break. "I don't think there's shame in innocence, father, and I don't believe anyone else does. There's honour in what you've done, what you've endured.

You've given us all something to be proud of. You didn't accept a fate that was unjust; you fought it in your own way and proved yourself erudite. How many men knew of the existence of the law you invoked? How many men realised the power of what you've done? None, but now our name is known throughout the empire and history will remember it. How is that shame? History will record that you sacrificed freedom in the name of justice and truth."

"Maybe it was a selfish act, a purely selfish act," suggested his father.

"No, I can't believe it and you know it wasn't. I've heard you talk of the King behind closed doors. You admire and respect him. You would never have bound yourself thus unless you did. A selfish act means that you thought only of yourself. You didn't, you considered us all, I know it. The King needed to be given faith back in his officials. You've done that and you're here proving your support every day. Who cares what gossips say? I don't, mother and my sisters don't. I rather think His Majesty scoffs at them, the gossips that is, and the Princes both admire your resolve. Where is the disgrace for us in that?"

Ifor turned to face him and, for the first time, Emrys saw his father as a man who needed support.

"Father, whatever has happened, we still love you."

Ifor pulled his son towards him and held him in another hug; there was no reply he could make and part of him knew he'd never look at Emrys in the same way again. He'd grown up, no longer a child but a man to be proud of.

They sat down and, when the moment seemed right, Emrys said, "Have you spoken to mother?"

"No. I don't know what to say over messenger. I'm going to ask the King if I may return home. I am out of place in Oedran these days."

"Why doesn't mother come here for a time?"

Daioch sighed. "There is history there better unstirred, Emrys."

"At least ask her, father. She might get annoyed at an assumption."

"So she might. I know your Uncle Festus would like to see her."

Emrys smiled. "Yes, but then he could visit us also."

Ifor shook his head. "Not easily, Emrys, not easily at all. I don't think any of us, even His Majesty, truly realises how hard he works."

"Yet he's got a reputation that almost suggests the opposite. His post as Defender is ceremonial—"

"Not in the times we live in, Emrys, certainly not."

"As Chief Advisor, though, he doesn't seem to be in his office here much of the time."

Ifor chuckled. "It doesn't mean he's not working. He's just efficient, *annoyingly* efficient."

"I suppose so. It's very odd living with him. You know there's more to the house and possibly the household than meets the eye. My groom says his never let him get too close to them or their business. They'll talk to him, but then they'll suddenly look at each other and he can't get anything out of them."

Ifor chuckled again. "Oh dear. Hasn't he worked that one out yet? Keep this to yourself, Emrys, but your uncle's *grooms* are also his facilitators, for want of a better, polite word. They're the ones who make sure the house is secure, they sort out the people caught spying, pass on messages to certain city lowlife and collect information."

Emrys' face became a picture of realisation. "Oh, now it makes sense. As long as Drystan is giving them gossip, they'll listen, but as soon as he seems to be wanting information, they clam up. They're using him to find out… what?"

"Whatever they can."

"I'll be careful around them then."

Lord Daioch nodded. "It might be wise, very wise. Shall we tell His Majesty that we're talking once again before I reveal any more of your uncle's secrets accidentally?"

"That wasn't accidental, father, but we can certainly tell him we're talking."

* * *

At the end of the meal, Arkyn, Landis and Emrys left to spend what remained of the evening at Court. Daioch said he would get an early night and cursed himself when he saw a flash of emotion on Emrys' face. Adeone mildly pointed out it was probably the best idea, as Ifor's feet were still healing and to stand for hours at Court wouldn't do them any good.

Once the door closed Adeone looked steadily at Ifor, who said softly, "Thank you, Sire."

The King smiled. "It's what friends are for. We all do foolish things, trust me on that. Come and have a drink in more congenial surroundings, then, I promise, you can have an early night."

Daioch pushed himself to his feet. "Thank you, sir."

Once in the King's sitting room Adeone passed Daioch a drink and eased himself into a chair, nodding for Ifor to do likewise.

"How are your hands?"

"Healing beautifully, Sire, thank you. How are yours?"

"The same. Ifor, in here I am simply Adeone. I mean that."

"Just like before?"

Adeone smiled. "Just like before. Have I changed that much?"

"Not in essentials, never in essentials, but in the image you present to the world, I think maybe. You still watch the world with amused eyes, very amused eyes."

"How diplomatic, Ifor. Did you have lessons in it?" enquired Adeone, tongue-in-cheek.

"I believe I did but it was never my strength."

Adeone eyed him. "I think it is, because you know how not to be. How is Emrys?"

Ifor hesitated. "Conflicted but supportive. It is not easy for him and he will live with my foolishness longer than me. It will haunt his days, his position. I do not know how to make that right."

"I will do what I can, Ifor. I make you that promise. Julius and Finian will help too, and I wouldn't put it past my sons as well. Arkyn seems to be enjoying Emrys' company and Tain, well… I have faith in his character and so does Tancred."

"I was interested, very interested, that Judge Tancred is His Highness' mentor."

"Why?" enquired Adeone, puzzled.

"There are stories, rumours of his history on the Low Plains—"

Adeone sighed. "Which man in authority has not had rumours to contend with, Ifor? We both suffer regularly."

Daioch chuckled, but his heart constricted: the King didn't want to hear any rumours. He knew it as clearly as he knew his name. "Very true, sir, very true. If he has your trust, the past should be left alone where there is only rumour. It was pleasant to see His Honour again after so long."

Adeone tilted his head. "It has been too long. Tell me something, my friend: what would you do if I were to name you Tuchlin?"

Daioch stared. "I… don't know. Is it something Your Majesty is likely to do?"

Adeone frowned. "Ifor, can you try to get through this discussion without *any* formality?"

Ifor paled and nodded.

Adeone looked at him closely, "What's wrong?"

The words left Daioch involuntarily. "I have displeased you."

Adeone frowned. "But… That's never made you lose colour before."

"I wasn't under a life-bind before, si… Adeone."

Adeone swore to himself. "I… Ifor, I'm not displeased, just frustrated. It's forgotten, truly. We're both going to have to get used to this. Alcis, I'm sorry for what my overreaction has caused."

"Adeone, please believe me. I am not. Most certainly I am not. I did this in full understanding of the consequences. I respect you, and trust your judgements; if I hadn't, I wouldn't have bound myself so closely. I don't want to question you, don't want to annoy you. You're my liege, always will be. You and your sons can always count on my support, whatever happens; you always could, but now the empire knows it."

Adeone got up and detached the decanter. He refilled Daioch's glass and his own before walking over to the window but couldn't see out because of the reflection of the bright room behind him. He turned back to Daioch, who was watching him uncertainly.

"Ifor, I always thought that you gave your loyalty too easily. I am not as astute as you believe."

"I gave you my loyalty before you were King, Adeone, long before you were King. As I remember, astuteness was secondary to mischief at that time. Respect isn't always born out of tradition."

"You mean you respected my abilities to cause complete and utter havoc?"

Daioch rolled the whiskey around his glass, letting its amber brilliance catch the candlelight. "Very much so, but I also respected you for realising that as King maybe that wasn't the best idea. Adeone, please accept that this has happened. I'm life-bound to you and I don't care that I am. I don't care at all. I'm glad of it."

Adeone sank onto his chair. "I can't get my head around it, that's all, but I won't speak of it again. You mentioned my sons, but you've met only one of them properly. Come to Ceardlann for a couple of days and get to know Tain."

"I'd be glad to meet him, Adeone, very glad. Is he at all like Arkyn?"

Adeone laughed. "No. Arkyn mostly takes after his mother. Tain, I'm sorry to say, takes after me. Where Arkyn is reserved, Tain most certainly is not, but he's not wild. He targets his mischief with a precision that is worrying."

Ifor chuckled. "Certainly the son is like the father."

Adeone smiled ruefully. "Yes. I had to tell him about Scanlon and it's concentrated his mind. Even Cal can't distract him completely."

"Who?"

Adeone smiled slightly. "One Master Calumiel Galdwin. He's the son of a cloth merchant and made Tain's acquaintance shortly before Ira died. When I took Tain and Arkyn to Ceardlann, after Ira's death, I persuaded Master Galdwin, after quite a fraught discussion, to let Cal go also. The boys needed a confidant and friend and I recognised in Tain and Cal the right sort of friendship, rather like mine and Festus'. He's a good lad and I rather suspect will always be a good friend to both my sons."

"Arkyn also?"

"Yes, I think so. You know, I wonder what the future will bring for all those children under my care. Not just my sons and niece but my wards and nearchildren, and Cal, who is none of those. I shouldn't say it, but there are days when Cal almost feels like part of my family."

Ifor smiled. "If he has lived amongst you for three years, it is not surprising – family is many things, Adeone."

"I suppose it is. Master Galdwin, though, would be horrified if he heard me talk of Cal in such terms. He doesn't approve of his involvement with my family."

"Then how did you persuade him to let Cal live at Ceardlann?"

"I persuaded him in terms he understood, with a helping hand from your long-suffering wed-brother."

Seeing a pensive mood come over Adeone, Daioch asked, "So why is Master Galdwin so disapproving?"

Adeone sighed. "He had two cousins, both of whom went missing during my father's reign. One with the rebellion in 1169 and one later. When I was trying to persuade him to let Cal live with us Fitz did some digging but the conclusions couldn't set Master Galdwin's mind at rest when I gave them him."

"After all this time, that's not surprising. What do you think happened to them?"

Adeone shrugged. "I expect one died in the rebellion, the other was a maid here. I can only think she left of her own accord and didn't want her family to know why. Even here, a maid can't disappear without someone noticing."

"Contrary to popular belief," replied Daioch. "This Cal's happy though?"

"He seems to be. Has the same ups and downs as any lad his age but is generally happy. He writes to his family, close and extended, most days, but he hasn't asked to leave. I can see some interesting years ahead for them all. I hope I do see them as well."

"I'm sure you will."

Adeone swallowed. "I'm not, Ifor, I'm really not. The future is shortening for me every day."

"Every day, every man is a day closer to his death, Adeone."

The King glared at him. "I think you know what I meant, Ifor, but thank you for the cheery thought. I'll have it as my epitaph. I can imagine the stonemason's expression carving that as my memorial," Adeone looked at his friend steadily. "I've just remembered; I never had an answer to my question about what would you do if I named you Tuchlin?"

"Ah. I would have to accept, sir, but our governor is capable and astute, most certainly he is."

Adeone tilted his head, almost as though in agreement. "The time might be right for a change."

"I'm happy as Deputy Governor, Adeone. Truly I am. I'm very happy. I would not like to think I had pushed out Lord Aldwy."

"You wouldn't have done so. When's the next Low Plains Review?"

Ifor frowned. "Provincial, 1220. Law, 1219."

"It was the provincial I was interested in. I'd rather Arkyn didn't have to replace another governor…"

Ifor smiled. "He didn't replace the Sagamore, Sire… sorry."

Adeone eyed him. "I'll forgive you. You're right, but he's the first Arkyn's not replaced."

"Adeone, Portur was *murdered*! It wasn't as though Prince Arkyn had any choice than to replace him. He had no choice at all. The Domini was replaced on the recommendation of Lord Iris, who is now King's Counsellor, as well as your own feelings on the matter. His Highness isn't recommending the replacement of governors because he wants to abuse the power you grant him, most certainly he's not. He's replaced them because they need replacing for whatever reason. I can't believe he'd replace the Tuchlin, can't believe it at all."

"I think you've missed the underlying nuance. The Tuchlin has told me, in confidence, that he'll be retiring soon."

Daioch's heart plummeted. "He's not mentioned anything to me."

"I think the decision has been made quite recently."

"I just wanted to return to normality."

Adeone grimaced. "There is no such thing, Ifor. Aldwy was always going to retire; he knows my mind. I would like you as Tuchlin; as Deputy Governor you've more than proved yourself. I don't want to force you to it though."

As composed as he could manage, Ifor said, "Your wish is my command, Adeone, very much my command, but I do not wish aspersions to be cast against Lord Aldwy. It would be better, would it not, if His Excellency continued, at least for a time? If it is shown he has your confidence, speculation against us will lessen."

"See my earlier comments about having lessons in flattery and diplomacy. I will talk it over with him. Now, about Ceardlann, you will come?"

"I'd be glad to, sir. Then might I crave a favour and return home? Especially before the worst of winter sets in."

Adeone got up and walked over to the fireplace. He leaned on the mantelpiece, looking at the fire for several long seconds.

"Of course you can and should. I'll just miss your company, my friend."

Chapter 78

VISITING CEARDLANN

Septadai, Week 39 – 21st Teral, 21st Teris 1212
Rex Dallin

THE FOLLOWING MORNING, with the weather on their side, Adeone, Arkyn and Daioch rode to Ceardlann enjoying each other's company. They entered the Rex Dallin and Daioch recognised Adeone had relaxed. What was it that caused such an instant un-tensioning of muscles and the small smile to twitch at the King's lips? He looked around the valley and found himself smiling. Arkyn glanced at him amused.

"Welcome to the Rex Dallin, my lord."

"Thank you, Your Highness."

"Don't worry; it has this effect on everyone."

Adeone merely smiled and picked up the pace.

At Ceardlann the grooms hurried to meet them. Adeone nodded to Alfred, the chief groom, and then turned towards the house. He smiled as the Comptroller walked out to greet them.

"Comptroller, might I introduce Lord Ifor Daioch to you?"

The Comptroller nodded. "Of course you may, Sire. Welcome to Ceardlann, my lord. If you'd like to follow me, I'll show you to your room."

Daioch said, "Thank you, Comptroller, but I'm sure it can wait until His Majesty—"

Adeone crooked an eyebrow at the Comptroller. "Ifor, I can see to myself in my own home."

Ifor bowed and left. He missed Arkyn saying quietly,

"I'm sure the Comptroller will explain your thoughts on formality here, father."

Adeone glanced at him. "He'd better, otherwise I'm not going to be responsible for my actions. Where's Tain likely to be?"

"Alcis only knows. I'd wait for him to find you."

Tain bounced into the small antechamber six minutes later. Adeone reached out an arm and, when Tain was close enough, ruffled his son's hair.

"Father!"

So Adeone ruffled it some more.

Tain dodged aside and, when Adeone's attention was diverted, ruffled his father's in return. By the time Adeone had stopped wrestling with his son, Joe had entered, carrying refreshments.

Adeone glanced at him. "How's this terror behaving himself, Joe?"

Joe smiled. "Very well, Your Majesty."

"That'll change."

Joe's lips twitched. "I'm sure not, Sire. Was there anything else, sir?"

"No, thank you."

Once the footman left, Tain said, "Father, I do behave myself – mostly."

Adeone smiled. "I know, Tain, and they're hardly likely to tell me if you don't. It's only a pleasantry."

"At my expense."

The King glanced at his son; he wasn't happy. "All right. I'll stop asking and I'm sorry."

Tain swallowed. "Thank you, father. What's brought you here?"

"Why? Are you upset to see me?"

Tain grinned. "No. I just wondered. Arkyn was meant to be back a couple of days ago and then you arrive as well…"

Adeone looked at his son long-sufferingly. "Not only do you ask a lot of questions, you start piecing together the evidence for me as well. Who can I blame for that?"

"Judge Tancred; he's teaching me."

Adeone groaned. "So, what you're saying is that it is ultimately my fault."

"Court might condemn on evidence."

"Just come a bit closer and say that."

Tain dodged out of his way. "Sorry, father, but as I've said before, you must have approved of what I'm being taught."

"So you have. What would you say to a different tutor?" Seeing his son's terrified eyes, he continued, "I'd never do that to you. I thought you should meet Lord Daioch properly. He's just getting settled."

"Oh." Tain smiled. "Can I ask him what it was like?"

Adeone frowned. "We wouldn't want a guest to feel uncomfortable."

Tain shook his head. "I suppose not. I'll try to keep my inquisitiveness to a minimum, father, but Cal and I have been wondering."

* * *

An hour later, Adeone was discussing the valley's concerns when there was a knock at the Comptroller's office door and David announced Daioch.

Adeone smiled. "Come on in, Ifor. Is your room all right?"

"It's very pleasant, Sire, very pleasant indeed."

Adeone's only reply was, "Comptroller?" in a rather dangerous voice.

The Comptroller chuckled. "I did what I could, sir. His Lordship said he's still your vassal and will still be marking the respect he feels in the traditional way."

"They were Ifor's exact words, were they?"

Daioch said, "No, Sire, my words were more succinct, certainly more succinct… You're still my King."

"Here I'm no more than master of the valley; the Comptroller will tell you so. Don't ruin the illusion, please. I'm Adeone here to my guests."

"He means that, Lord Daioch," added the Comptroller.

"Then so be it, so be it."

Adeone held Ifor's gaze. "Good. Now, I'll just introduce you to the children… Comptroller, we'll finish later."

Adeone entered the children's sitting room half hoping to catch them out. Instead, he found quiet industry. Elantha was drawing, Cal was writing, Arkyn reading and Tain appeared to be studying. Adeone winked at his elder son and tiptoed over to Tain, closing the book with a swift movement. When Tain jumped and turned to protest, he said,

"Take a break and let me introduce Lord Daioch."

Tain relaxed and got up. "Lord Daioch, I'm pleased to meet you. I've heard a lot about you."

Ifor looked at the thirteen-year-old Prince, he saw someone black of hair and eye who bore the gangling marks of growing quickly. He recognised the late Queen in Tain's features but the King in his posture. He looked into bright eyes and bowed slightly saying,

"I'm pleased to meet Your Highness, sir, very pleased. I cannot but apologise for what you've probably heard."

Tain grinned. "But it's been good, my lord. Why apologise for the good?"

Adeone shook his head slightly. "Ifor, may I introduce my niece, Lady Elantha, and also Master Calumiel Galdwin?"

Once the pleasantries were concluded, Tain's curiosity got the better of him. "My lord, can I ask you what it was like?"

Adeone said quietly, "Don't feel you have to answer everything the terror asks."

Ifor smiled. "I don't, Adeone, but I'd like to answer what I can."

"Then I'll leave you to his, erm, care."

Once the King had gone, Daioch said, "It was rather overwhelming, Your Highness. It's not every day that you get accused of treason for sending a gift. I've known your father since I was in Oedran, studying at the Advisors' School. The last thing on my mind when I sent the gift was spying; in fact, it wasn't even on my mind. To then have the commander arrest me and the Tuchlin be involved was sickening, very sickening. I literally felt physically sick. It's amazing what goes through your head at such times. The question of whether you can prove your innocence is uppermost, after incredulity has waned. You start hunting in your head for ways and means, excuses and reasons are useless at such time; all you know is that you're innocent and that you have to prove it."

Tain frowned, thinking hard. "What if you know you can't prove it?"

"I knew I couldn't, sir. I had few options open to me. Then I recalled something that happened in Oedran years ago. I was dining with your father and nearfather. We were talking and laughing, planning Alcis only knows what mischief, but probably something dubious. Prince Lachlan dropped by for a word with your father. The upshot was that he was invited to dinner and to stay for the evening. He did so, and he was one man to whom age and generations didn't seem to matter in debate. Though I recall he always jokingly called Lord Landis '*young* Festus', no matter how old he was. There was laughter in his eyes. Anyway, this particular night he'd been working on something and had been looking at the ancient laws. Trial by fealty had appeared and he and your father debated on the merits of such a system and whether they'd ever use it. I don't remember what the conclusion was, but the fact of that conversation has lived with me for years. It was fascinating. The law is truly ancient; it seems to date from the first hundred years of our reckoning. So ancient that it had almost been completely forgotten. During the discussion, Prince Lachlan said it was the only way to prove innocence absolutely. I suppose I owe my life to him."

Tain had listened entranced. "Surely you'd have known about it anyway?"

"There are hints of its enormity in the everyday speech of Court – to swear on your fealty is one – but I don't think I'd ever have realised it was still extant, that trial by fealty was still a real possibility. It has another facet, one that is unique; it is the only trial which falls directly under the King's jurisdiction."

"How about a fealty reading, my lord?"

"That is part of the same law, my prince, but it tends to be invoked by the liege, not the vassal."

Cal asked, "Couldn't you just have requested a fealty reading?"

"No, Master Calumiel. That is, yes, I could, but it would never have proved anything. A fealty reading is a much weaker form of trial and when read from the hands can only give an indication of guilt or innocence. Oh, what is spoken is the truth as the supplicant understands it but a practised supplicant can change the truth to lies for the answer passes through the heart and if the heart has a different truth from the mind, then the heart can be taught to win."

Tain said, "So there is no way of knowing if someone tells the truth?"

Ifor smiled. "There are many, sir, many indeed, but a fealty reading is best left for extreme circumstances. Take one too many and the supplicant can lie in them if even part of them wishes to."

Cal said, "How many readings does it take, my lord?"

"There's no knowing, no knowing at all, Master Calumiel. For each man it is different. Never put your trust in them, my princes."

Arkyn broke his silence. "Lord Daioch, surely they are more reliable than you suggest."

"To start with, aye, sir, but if I may advise, only use them when you have no idea of the truth. To use them to get information can be very dangerous and very unwise."

Tain said, "My lord, did you actually think of the result of your request? Did you consider the walk, for example?"

Daioch hesitated. "Probably not in the initial action, sir, but I had enough time whilst walking to consider it. I reached Carnford and everything seemed to hit me. The fact that I was in a measure responsible even if I hadn't known anything about it; it was my name on the gift. I decided then and there that, whatever the outcome, I still had a debt to His Majesty. I stopped eating and drinking and I think that was the hardest decision of my life. I remember seeing the gates of Oedran swimming in front of me and then concentration got me to the Palace. On being shown through the building, I realised I was at the end of my strength, but I couldn't collapse. I must have entered the Audience Chamber without realising for suddenly His Majesty was moving towards me. You were there to see what happened."

Tain nodded. "Yes. You didn't look well, my lord. Did you consider that you might have killed yourself before reaching Oedran?"

"No. I should have done but I didn't. I knew I could do it. His Majesty made me drink and probably saved my life, according to Doctor Chapa. I have that debt to repay."

Arkyn said quietly, "I don't think he'll see it like that."

"I expect not, sir, but it doesn't mean it's not my own thought. I must have been a troublesome patient for Doctor Chapa. There was no way I was resting until I'd done what I set out to do, no way at all. When His Majesty reached the room, I didn't know which way up was – delirium was taking hold. It was only the King's presence that made me focus. The pain when the dagger cut into our hands brought my mind into sharp clarity and I felt the life-bind take hold."

Tain leaned forward. "How?"

"Oh, my prince, it should not be told."

Arkyn said quietly, "I'd like to know, my lord; one day I might have to take one."

Lord Daioch held his gaze. "Imagine your conscious existence can be felt like a net which covers your body. When the binding took hold, it gradually tightened over my heart, encasing it. As my blood flowed to

His Majesty, so did a thread of the net. I could feel it leaving me, gradually being drawn out, tightening all the time that web across my heart. I knew, if I veered from the truth, it would strangle and stop my heart. I can feel it still and around my mind is also growing a web. Every time I say or do something that displeases His Majesty it tightens. Once the displeasure has passed it relaxes, but, until it does, the pain is severe. I am truly bound to His Majesty."

Arkyn whispered, "Yet still you did it."

"I have always been loyal to His Majesty, sir, as I shall be to Your Highness when the time comes, if I'm still here; therefore, what I did only affirms that loyalty."

"Thank you…"

Tain looked between them and, for the first time, truly realised that Arkyn would one day be king, that he would hold the loyalty of others and command them. He could never say what it was that had made him understand it with such a blinding flash of realisation. He scrutinised Arkyn, as though his own understanding would have changed his brother. Daioch's loyalty was a more overt form of many others. If people would follow simply the title, there was a danger they would follow the bad as well as the good. The titles they held were dangerous. He finally understood why their father had said they had to be good men. Daioch was still talking and Tain realised he'd missed a portion of the conversation.

"No, Your Highness. Blind loyalty is as dangerous as treachery. If the King hadn't deserved my loyalty, I would never have bound myself to him. I cannot believe Your Highness is made in any other mould, nor Prince Tain. I have heard much of Your Highness' work over the last couple of years and nothing I have ever heard has given me concern. In fact, it has rather emphasised my view that His Majesty is worth the loyalty I have given."

Tain puzzled over that. Was it also true that other people could increase ones standing? An intriguing thought and one he needed to be alone to work out. Elantha smiled at him and he winked. Everyone had forgotten she was there, but she was sitting happily sketching. Would Lord Daioch ever get to see her sketch? Was it the sketch that mattered? Or was El as interested as they were?

Chapter 79

YOURS TO COMMAND
Septadai, Week 40 – 28th Teral, 7th Souis 1212
Court

ADEONE HAD WALKED AROUND COURT many times marvelling at the practised metaphorical dance of courtiers. They seemed to be unaware of his thoughts on them. As a collective body, they represented manipulation and avarice. Individually some were the opposite but, if they weren't trying to manipulate someone, someone was trying to manipulate them. Even with daily briefings, Adeone was never certain he knew what was happening. A week after Ifor had left, he nodded to the Steward and glanced around the room. Lord Lux walked over and bowed deeply, too deeply; the first thing Adeone wondered was what he was planning.

However, he said, "Lux, I hope the day has been quiet. Are there any new arrivals?"

"No, Your Majesty, and no guests wish to take their leave. The Court Supper is still on schedule—"

"It certainly has been a quiet day. There are no circumstances that require my attention?"

"None, Sire. Even the rumour front has been circumspect today."

Adeone smiled. "I'm sure it won't last. Thank you, my lord; I should keep you from your companions no longer."

Lux bowed once more. "I am yours to command, Your Majesty." He turned on his heel and left.

Adeone watched him go steadily. Under his breath, he said softly, "If only that were true." He raised his voice slightly, "Wynfeld?"

A few paces away, the Major melted out of the shadows, saluted and walked closer.

"What *are* the rumours?"

Wynfeld smiled. "I think it's best I tell you tomorrow, Sire."

"That bad? I'll expect you at half past eight then. Is Lady Rhian here?"

"In the Tradere Room, Sire, talking with Lady Julia."

With a nod to the Major, Adeone walked off smiling to himself. Advisor Rayburn was the first man to cross his path, and his bow said everything.

"Your Majesty, I hope you're as well as you look."

Adeone took a drink from his Court server. His hands were healing well, but he held the goblet with his fingers around the rim rather than gripping it. "Let's hope I don't look ill... No need to lose so much colour. I'm very well, thank you. Surprise me with the gossip as we walk."

Rayburn smiled. "I'm sure Your Majesty is beyond surprise when it comes to the machinations of your Court."

Adeone gave him a sideways look. "Try."

"There are a few rumours you might be interested in but they are not particularly devastating, Sire. People are getting wary of Captain Beaver, Lord Teran and Lord Anguis have been discussing Alcis-only-knows-what for some time, and some people are speculating about Lady Rhian's extended stay. Is there anything you would like me to discover more on?"

The King eyed him. "Not particularly, Rayburn. I'm just wondering what Wynfeld has heard that you haven't. Can you be at the Inner Office for half past eight tomorrow morning, please?"

Recognising the end of the conversation, Rayburn bowed. "I am yours to command, Sire."

"I know. That's what I pay you for. Thank you, Advisor Rayburn. Go and be obsequious somewhere else."

"May your evening be pleasant, Your Majesty."

Adeone was wondering how to repay the irony when a voice behind him said softly,

"I hope my new deputy is behaving himself, Sire."

"He's everything I expected, Lord Landis. Should I be worried your beguiling daughter is talking to my cousin?"

Landis smiled. "Do I have a beguiling daughter? And worried about whom, Lady Rhian or Julia?"

"Both, my lord. What are they up to, I wonder?"

"Why don't you ask them, Your Majesty?" He turned slightly. "Lady Rhian, Lady Julia, will you join us?"

Adeone threw him an inscrutable glance. As the ladies reached them, he said, "Cousin, Lady Julia, how are you both?"

Rhian curtsied. "All the better for seeing Your Majesty looking so well."

Adeone sighed. "I really will have to find a mirror; I distrust so many eulogies about my health."

Lady Julia reached into her Court reticule. "Borrow mine, Sire."

Adeone took the mirror, turning it in his hands. "I like the design."

Julia chuckled. "Blessing gifts may come in useful one day, Sire."

"Though rarely for showing the giver their own failings. Thank you, my lady. Now, what was Lady Rhian plotting?"

"Nothing that would concern Your Majesty, Sire. We were discussing the weather for a ride tomorrow."

"Then I hope you've consulted the Court Aeromancer."

Lady Rhian smiled. "Of course, Sire. We would be pleased if you could join us."

"I wish I could, my lady; however, another time. In recompense, I hope you will join me at the Court Supper tonight?"

"How can I refuse the King, Sire?"

"Traditions can be changed, my lady," murmured Landis.

Rhian glanced at him. "Yet why when there is no wish to do so, my lord?"

Landis's lips twitched. With exaggerated emphasis, he said, "I would never try to change anything if Your Ladyship was averse to the alteration."

She eyed him. "Does he *ever* get any better, Sire?"

Adeone laughed. "No, I try to keep him like that to confuse true courtiers. Lady Julia, how are you finding the Court these days?"

"I have found its diversions, Sire," replied his neardaughter.

"I'm pleased. And how is your twin?"

"Chastened and remarkably sober, sir. I told him it was his own fault."

Adeone shook his head. "That would be your sisterly affection, my lady. Your friends are giving us interested looks; shall we concern them a bit more?"

Julia grinned. "What had you in mind, Sire?"

Adeone winked. "Slip your arm through mine. Rhian, Festus, I'll see you at the Court Supper."

They walked around Court talking of nothing in particular. Glances followed them wherever they went, and it was all Julia could do to keep a straight face. Landis, however, watched them discreetly and eventually said to Lady Rhian,

"Sometimes I wonder if he does it to amuse himself or us."

Lady Rhian smiled. "Probably both, Festus. Can you do something for me? I must return to Tradere next year, yet I think His Majesty will use every endeavour to get me to stay. With so few confidants, I can't blame him, but I do need to go home for a time. Will you try to make him see reason? Please. I wouldn't ask if it wasn't important."

"He misses your company very much."

"We're family, Festus, nothing more, whatever speculation has it."

"I'll see what can be done."

Rhian smiled. "Thank you. Remind him that roads lead in two directions."

As she walked away, Landis chuckled to himself. As he made to walk off, a snippet of furtive conversation from two passing courtiers caught his attention.

"Missing, I've heard. I wonder what he's done or not done. Mind you, have you heard about…?"

Landis considered following them but decided it might be too obvious even for his practised manner.

Chapter 80

RUMOUR AND SPECULATION
Alunadai, Week 41 – 1st Geryal, 8th Souis 1212
Inner Office

ADEONE SAT WITH A DRINK for company, and fruit by his hand, in his favourite comfortable chair in the Inner Office. The early morning sun was shining, the day promised warmth and the blossom danced in the breeze, carried from the small orchard in the grounds. He glanced at the fireplace in front of him. How many of his ancestors had sat here through the seasons and years? How many had warmed themselves during colder months and sweltered during warmer days? The carved fire surround was intricate and oddly devoid of the normal symbols of empire and kingship. Instead, the masons had used vines and flowers to give structure. Were they trying to remind kings of the entangling nature of their work? Adeone wasn't sure he appreciated it.

He flicked open the daily report. Captain Beaver's work but with Wynfeld's sign off. That was interesting. Obviously, the Major had considered it important enough that his name was attached. Important, urgent, disquieting or just downright worrying. Any of those were possible. Adeone's eyes skipped over the daily list of lords in Oedran. Skipped over the minor intrigues of city officials. Raised an eyebrow at who had been caught in compromising situations in brothels, not that they realised they'd been caught but Lord Teran's brothers never did have much sense. He reached the Court gossip and began to frown. He reached the more specific details and the frown deepened. What was his little brother playing at? Arkyn's work in Terasia might have left him financially curtailed, but there was such a thing as tact. He corrected himself. There was such a thing as tact to most men. If Teran's brothers' profligacy was noticeable, so was Teran's absence. What was the lord up to? Para also had been noticeably absent. Adeone hadn't even taken heed. Neither lord was in his immediate circle, but he should have been paying more attention. Cursing, he continued reading. Lux was swaggering more than normal. Someone or something had given him confidence or greater standing amongst his peers. Adeone drank his tea and almost choked. Rumours were circulating that he was involved with Rhian, and that the fire at Landis House had been designed to destroy evidence of malfeasance. The intelligence regiment had evidence that the General, Lord Faran and Judge Tancred were also being targeted. Adeone had read enough, though he finished the report fuming. There were certain things he would tolerate and, so far, the day wasn't living up to the promise of the spring weather.

Trying to find something else to occupy his mind, he opened Wynfeld's second report. The investigation in Eyllyn had been thorough. On his return to the city, Lord Daioch's help had been invaluable, and all the cloaking persuasions had fallen away when faced with the man who had risen from the ashes of the scheme. The craftsman who had made the gift admitted the scribe had approached him before Lord Daioch and he had wondered if there was an agenda, but he had concluded that the scribe just wanted a promotion. The scribe, who'd been held at the prison of Eyllyn had been questioned before Daioch's return. The morning after Daioch arrived in Eyllyn, the guards went to collect him for further questioning. He was dead. The turnkey on his cell said a man claiming to be the scribe's brother had left him some food and a clean shirt. A day later the turnkey had been dragged out of Lake Drenga, strangled. Adeone fumed. The trail had gone cold again. There'd been no reason to suspect the turnkey of complicity. Prisoners were often supplied with food from relatives. Through his annoyance, he took a moment to acknowledge that Daioch's life-bind had at least saved his friend's reputation. No-one could cast aspersions on him for any of the events. He had no reason to cover anything up. He'd been proved innocent.

He'd barely put the report aside when Landis entered. Adeone caught his friend's eye.

"Presumably if I say 'good morning', Sire, you'll tell me it isn't one."

"Nor is it the moment for levity." Adeone threw both reports onto the seat next to him and motioned for Landis to read them. "The Eyllyn investigation is dead. As for the other, the Court rumours in particular."

Landis settled himself with an ease that belied his curiosity. Adeone watched him, watched his face as he read everything. His features darkened from thoughtful to furious and then acceptance, which surprised the King.

Eventually, the Lord of Oedran laid the report aside. "Daioch will be fine. I'll tell the commander to investigate the turnkey's death, but he'll find nothing. As for Court, at least no-one has found out about Dunius. It could be worse."

"Worse? They're suggesting you burnt down your house to hide illicit dealings."

Landis shrugged. "Better than them saying your son burnt down my house and that's why you helped with the rebuild."

"Who has said that?" demanded Adeone.

"No-one yet. Though, I admit, I'm surprised. Obviously, my dire warnings of consequence had some effect. The rumours about Rhian can't have reached Lady Amara's ears. It might be best that they don't. I admit I'm curious as to why they're targeting Faran."

Adeone's eyes narrowed but he answered a knock at the door. "Come in... Ah. Good morning, Rayburn." He pushed himself to his feet and crossed to his desk, fielding the daily report from Landis' hand. He passed it to Rayburn telling him to read the pertinent section.

As Rayburn settled himself into a chair in front of the desk and did so, Landis rang the bell for Simkins to clear the evidence of Adeone's early morning snack. Had his friend had a proper breakfast yet? A question he put quietly to the manservant a moment later, to receive the reassurance the King had been up early and had eaten a hearty meal.

Adeone crooked an expressive eyebrow as Simkins left. "Stop bullying my manservant."

"I can't stop something I've never managed, Sire."

"Someone is immune from Your Lordship's methods?" enquired Rayburn whilst still reading the report.

Adeone burst out laughing. Rayburn rarely teased Landis.

Landis snorted. "You've always seemed immune as well, Advisor. What do you make of that?"

Rayburn shrugged. "Nothing particularly unexpected, my lord. Rumourmongers always target recent events. Though I'm surprised they've taken so long to make capital out of your house fire. Maybe they had other—"

"Burning issues?" enquired Adeone, with a straight face.

"Flames to stoke," replied Rayburn.

"I'm not deigning that with a reply," said Landis airily. "Do you have anything to add that does not include being facetious?"

Rayburn sobered. "My apologies, my lord. Your Majesty, rumours at Court aren't my speciality. The fact Lord Scanlon seems to have changed tactics is not a matter for me to comment on. The fact he is targeting your General is unsurprising but extremely concerning. He is one man who cannot be disgraced."

Landis muttered, "So I can?"

Adeone's lips twitched. "I would be surprised if there is anything in the General's past I do not know about already. Disgracing him will be no easy feat. The same for Judge Tancred. Why do you think Faran's been targeted?"

Rayburn shrugged. "He's close to you, sir, and he's invited the Prince to stay. He's a notable voice in Lufian politics as well – for all he's not been in Lufia for a couple of years. Maybe someone there is trying to keep him out of the Sagamore's Court."

Landis leaned forward. "It's a good point, sir. Faran never had a wild youth to be used against him. He was annoyingly correct from recollection.

Rayburn, do you know of anything?"

"Nothing. Though it won't stop people inventing. Lord Para in particular. They have never had a comfortable relationship."

Adeone listened as his companions continued their talk. Rumours could be devastating. If his brother was using them, it would be a different type of fight. A guard could stop an assassin. Stopping rumours took overt use of power, which often caused more. He had to decide how to deal with the threat. When he said that, Landis stilled.

"You can ignore them, sir. You can force people to tell you if they're true. You can make people disclose their most private thoughts and feelings. You can't, however, control what people think. Once disgraced, it is often for life and—"

As Richardson entered, to announce Wynfeld and Captain Beaver, the King stayed Landis' monologue with a minute shake of the head. "Come in, Major. Captain Beaver, I've almost forgotten what you look like again. Advisor Rayburn will later explain why I dislike seeing a signature instead of the person signing the document, but don't let it concern you; your reports have been far better recently. You'd better both take a seat; obviously not the same one; it might get a bit crowded."

Amused, Landis caught his friend's eye, but Adeone resolutely kept a straight face as he said, "Major, please explain what didn't make the daily report."

Wynfeld started to recount how they'd come to focus on the rumours circulating around Court. How they'd realised Lord Scanlon had changed tactics. The lack of direct attacks was a factor that had disconcerted them until they realised it was what was happening. Then they turned their attention onto what was replacing that strategy, especially after the events with Lord Daioch had revealed Lord Scanlon's likely approach was to undermine those closest to their King. What they discovered was insidious and disquieting.

Beaver continued the explanation. They had people at Court listening to conversations. They had pieced together the targets Scanlon had set his sights on. Adeone's face hardened at the mention of his brother.

"Whatever Lord Scanlon might be, Beaver, he is still a member of my family. Please remember that and talk of him appropriately."

Beaver took a second to realise where he'd gone wrong. Maybe Wynfeld's constant reminders about titles had a reason. He blushed, apologised and continued. The fact Lord Scanlon was targeting Judge Tancred was incomprehensible to them.

"Judge Tancred is a token holder," explained Adeone. "I hope you're watching his back."

Wynfeld assured him they were, intrigued. When had the Judge been handed a fabled token? He concluded his recitation by saying, "Lord Scanlon has become interested in the events of the Bayan Rebellion, Sire, but we're not sure why."

Adeone glanced at Landis. "There's nothing there that can harm anyone is there, my lord?"

Landis smiled. "Obviously not, sir, if His Lordship is still searching."

Wynfeld's eyes flicked between them, wondering what the secret was. Advisor Rayburn asked himself the same question but knew they were unlikely to get an answer.

Wynfeld looked for permission to continue and received it from a slight nod.

"Thank you, Sire. The next thing to report is rather strange but also intriguing. Are you aware of the existence of one Advisor Bantling?"

"Isn't he what my brother terms his *private advisor*?" enquired Adeone.

Rayburn added, "Who's never permitted to leave Black Hills?"

Wynfeld nodded. "Yes. I don't wish to concern Your Majesty but he's gone missing. We don't know much about it, but it seems that the Justiciar has made changes. We don't have any further details and I didn't like to put it in the report."

Adeone considered him for several seconds before saying, "Beaver, that's all for now." He watched the captain salute and leave before crooking an eyebrow at Wynfeld. "Made changes? Don't know any further details? I expect more of you, Major."

Wynfeld exchanged a glance with Landis before replying. "We don't know if Advisor Bantling left willingly, Sire. We don't even know if he's still alive. We can surmise that Lord Scanlon became tired of him, or was annoyed by him, but we don't *know*."

Adeone pushed himself to his feet and went to examine the view from behind his desk. "Haven't you got someone inside Black Hills?"

Also on his feet, Wynfeld said, "No, sir. We've tried, but it's far too dangerous. Even men who aren't linked to us at all but have talked unwisely have wound up dead. Until I find an espien of legend, there's no way in."

"We need someone there. How about when His Lordship is elsewhere? Are his men loose tongued?"

"Not if they wish to keep their tongues, Your Majesty."

Rayburn said, "Then forgive me for asking, Major, but how do you know that Bantling has disappeared?"

Wynfeld flicked open a file. "A conversation between two men in a brothel."

"If you overheard them, are you sure you can trust their account?

Could they have been planted there to lead us astray?" enquired Landis.

"Yes, my lord, they could," admitted Wynfeld, "but until we can get anything else I think we have to assume that the Justiciar's advisor has disappeared and, in all likelihood, has been killed. I can't locate anyone who used to work for the Justiciar."

"There's nothing like a job for life," muttered Landis doodling.

Adeone raised an eyebrow. "Who is being facetious now, Landis? Do you mean to shock me with anything else today, Wynfeld? I certainly wasn't expecting to hear that my brother has, in all likelihood, murdered a member of his staff."

Wynfeld said, quite honestly, "No, Sire. They were the main rumours currently worrying me."

"Are you still happy with Beaver's command of the regiment?"

"I'm certainly happier, Sire. I will discuss several matters with him."

Landis nodded. "It may be a good idea, Wynfeld."

Adeone smiled. "Because, if not, I can see Landis paying him a visit."

Wynfeld chuckled. "I will try to prevent that becoming a necessity, Sire."

Landis said blithely, "I'd have thought you'd have welcomed my visits."

"I do now, my lord."

Adeone laughed. "I'm pleased you are appreciative of each other. What's the situation like with the bandits, Major?"

"We've taken five sets: three have been hanged, two await trial. The southern portion of the Gardian Ridge is clear, as is the Devoran Forest on the Terasian-Gerymorian border. The Margrave has been particularly helpful, if inventive in his use of invectives."

"That sounds like Wealsman. How about the Eyllyn situation?"

Wynfeld pursed his lips. "It's not ideal, Sire. I can't say I'm particularly impressed but given the prison is not solely under the jurisdiction of the Tuchlin, it is difficult."

Landis still doodling, said, "Do you have concerns about the Domesman?"

"Further than the fact he was appointed by Lord Scanlon to be chief judge, no, my lord."

"Very well. Investigate the turnkey's death."

Wynfeld nodded. "It's in hand, Defender. Though by all accounts he was a solitary soul. Lived outside the city in an isolated cottage."

Adeone cursed. "I'll say this for my brother, he knows how to find them. Thank you, Major. Give my regards to the General."

"With pleasure, Sire," said Wynfeld saluting.

The King turned to Rayburn. "Have a word with Beaver. I trust he's working hard, but we need to keep an eye on him as well. See if there's anything he needs. Whilst you're there, make sure that the clerks we supplied to the barracks are still working well. That's all for now."

Rayburn bowed and left, leaving Adeone and Landis simply looking at each other in silence for a long moment.

Chapter 81

PERSPECTIVE

Mid-morning
Barracks

LEAVING THE INNER OFFICE, Rayburn informed Richardson he would be at the barracks if he wasn't in his office. He retrieved the notes he had on Beaver: his background as a craftsman's son, his rise through the ranks and nothing more. Wynfeld had considered him skilled and trustworthy enough to take over as Captain of Intelligence, which was a good sign. The fact Beaver was not living up to all the King's expectations was unfortunate.

Arriving at the barracks, he gave the day's password, walked to the General's office, asking for a word with Paturn, who greeted him cordially.

"How can I help, Advisor?"

"Nothing disastrous, General. I'm here to exchange intelligence with Captain Beaver. I wouldn't want rumour to make too much of it."

Paturn crooked an eyebrow. "Should I read anything into the fact that he and Major Wynfeld were with His Majesty earlier, and now you're here?"

Rayburn smiled. "General, there is nothing His Majesty likes better than to keep me busy."

"Very well. Inform me if there is anything further you need. Thank you, Advisor."

Rayburn let out a breath once out of the office. He quite understood how Paturn had come to be feared. He made his way to Beaver's office, asked the soldier-clerk to tell Beaver he was there and in mere moments was waiting to hear the door close on the clerk's retreating back, whilst Beaver eyed him uncertainly.

"How badly did I mess up, Advisor? Have a seat."

"I've seen worse." Rayburn sat down carefully. The office had no luxuries. Everything was plain, serviceable and sturdy: a desk, chair and cabinet with drawers. There was no polish and no extravagance. Even in Wynfeld's day, there had been small personal touches.

"Let's start at the beginning, Captain. His Majesty has asked me to explain why he likes to see the people who pass him reports. This is not to polish anyone's ego. It is to endeavour to make sure the person signing the document is still alive, that their identity hasn't been stolen and that they can look him in the eye and swear to him that they have read and know the contents of the report. You cannot overexaggerate how important those factors are. His Majesty is, as you are more than aware, beset by issues. If he cannot trust the reports, they are worthless. No, do not interrupt. Major Wynfeld didn't rise to where he is now purely by chance. He did it through hard work, admitting to mistakes and by being seen. If His Majesty does not see you, does not come to know you, any mistake will cost you far more dearly. That also applies to Prince Arkyn. The Major's example is well worth following." Rayburn watched Beaver's dejected face. "You are hardworking. You've risen through the ranks as he did. It is unusual but admirable. Do not let your endeavours go to waste. As Captain of Intelligence, you have an unusual post that gives you direct access to the King. If His Majesty can't trust you, he will replace you."

Beaver hesitated. "Advisor, I have been trying to keep on top of everything, I thought His Majesty would be more upset if I failed in that."

Rayburn frowned. "Beaver, taking the report to the Palace is part of your responsibilities. There is no excuse. You have failed to keep on top of everything if you miss that vital part of your role. In fact, His Majesty is more likely to examine everything if he doesn't see you. I know Fitz was captain when you were posted to the regiment. His relationship with the FitzAlcis meant he could work by different rules. They know and trust him in a way that I've never seen since." (Beaver swallowed and nodded.) "Good. Next – yes, there is a next – no matter how much trouble Lord Scanlon causes, His Lordship is still the King's brother and will not be referred to as 'Scanlon' or 'he' in a disparaging tone by any officer of His Majesty's army. Is that understood?"

"Yes, Advisor."

"Good. I would not like to see such mistakes endanger your position. The information your men have been collecting and collating is good. Do not lose heart because of this. Every captain has bad patches. The King has not been attacked on your watch."

Beaver relaxed. "I still don't understand why Lord Scanlon has changed tactics, Advisor."

"Understanding the motives is secondary. Please do not get distracted by that, just be ready for when His Lordship changes again. I know you have been overworked but His Majesty has requested I check if you require any more clerks to help."

Beaver shook his head. "No. We seem to have enough for the meantime, Advisor. The addition of Stuart and Jacobs was welcome."

Rayburn pursed his lips. "Hmm. How have they behaved themselves?"

"Well enough. Jacobs had a definite grudge when he started but over time that has lessened. I'm not sure he'll ever be easy with his new role but he is less vocal than he was. Stuart has kept his head down. I think he realised far more swiftly than Jacobs that moaning wasn't going to get him anywhere."

"Good. Their private lives?"

"We've not had cause to watch them since late winter. Jacobs was drinking a bit, but he's not a loud drunk. Stuart keeps himself to himself. I don't have any concerns that they are so disgruntled that I need to take action."

"Good. Maybe you'd care to show me around your area, to dispel any rumours. I'm sure that my visit will have been noted. Let's make it visible."

"Won't that just be fuel to the fire, Advisor?"

"Not if you make it appear planned."

* * *

On finishing the tour, Rayburn walked to Wynfeld's office considering everything he'd seen. The corporal-clerk announced him to Wynfeld with an air of indifference.

"Come in and sit down, Advisor. How did your talk go?"

"There's nothing for you to emphasise, Major. I'm sure Beaver now understands the King's requirements much better."

"It's always a learning curve," admitted Wynfeld. "Your help was invaluable to me in 1209. I'll admit that much."

"You inherited a different situation. Beaver has had far more time to make his mark, and I wouldn't say he's been successful at that, even if he's been successful at his job. He's worried about Lord Scanlon's change of tactics."

"So are we all, Advisor. It's unusual for him to have not attempted something against our King and Princes, even against Lord Landis or another of our King's confidants. I can't shake off the preoccupation that something is coming."

"That's probably experience," observed Rayburn. "Jones was murdered."

"Yes, but, however useful he was, he wasn't a major threat. Not even with our Prince there. He was probably killed *because* His Highness was in Paras, but not, it seems, as a prelude to an attack on our Prince, or even the Domini. I think it was a warning that nowhere is safe."

Rayburn frowned. "Bit extreme."

"Not particularly. Not for a man like Lord Scanlon. Not from other reports I've had. Maybe Jones wouldn't do what he wanted. He didn't tell me he'd been approached but anything is possible."

Rayburn sighed. "The attack on Lord Daioch was well planned. If His Lordship hadn't known the true importance of trial by fealty, he would have been disgraced at the very least. Far be it from me to speculate on lords' motives, but the gossip might well then have extended to his family and wed-family. Through his wife is the link to Lord Landis. Young Lord Emrys' career would have been over before it began and he is a second cousin of our Princes through Queen Ira."

Wynfeld cursed softly. "I had forgotten that connection."

Rayburn pursed his lips. "Could Lord Scanlon now be playing a longer game? One where it's more difficult to prove who is behind his attacks?"

"Yes. That is becoming clearer, Advisor. I can protect my King from physical assault more easily than from this, and it isn't always easy to prevent physical attacks, as Gad proved."

"Then get more ears where rumours start. There is little point starting rumours to destroy men if the King will never hear and act on them, for they remain naught but rumours and will die after a time."

* * *

Rayburn returned to the Palace, wrote a quick note for his own files, before heading for lunch. Upper Hall was a boiling pot of gossip from men who couldn't normally show they were interested in it. He sank onto a comfortable chair, asked Denny for the simplest platter the chef could provide, then remembered the chef's sense of humour and added it should include bread, cheese and fruit. Denny took the order with a grin and delivered the request in double quick time, saying,

"You're thoughtful today, Advisor. Hope it's not 'cause we're in trouble."

"Not my business if you are, Denny." He glanced at the chief server's face. "I've not heard anything. Have you?"

"Well, thing is…"

As Denny started gossiping, Rayburn's worries ebbed from him. By the time he'd finished his lunch he'd learned a lot about Palace politics, how the Chamberlain was upset with the short-tempered Steward. How the gardeners were continuing as though there'd never been traitors amongst them. The footmen's network was as strong as ever with rumours about who was being moved where and bets were being taken on who might become Prince Tain's manservant. It was half an hour of scheming that had nothing to do with Lord Scanlon; Rayburn could stand aloof from it whilst also enjoying the anecdotes of staff craftily getting their own way. There was nothing he had to do anything about, and he accepted the tankard of beer that Denny passed him afterwards with a grin. The server certainly knew people's tastes.

Chapter 82

MAUDLIN
Alunadai, Week 46 – 8th Lufial, 1st Lufis 1212
Inner Office

Two weeks before the munewid, Adeone was about to stop working for the day when a knock at the door heralded Tancred's arrival. The King smiled warmly.

"Judge! It's an age since I last saw you. Richardson, that's all for the day. I'll finish this report off later, but any repercussions can wait. How are you, James?"

"Well, thank you, Your Majesty. I do not mean to interrupt you for long."

"Then I'll have to find a reason to keep you here for longer. What would you like to drink?"

"Whatever Your Majesty wishes, sir."

Adeone eyed him, amused. "I'll save the poison for later then. I'm not sure it can temporarily cure formality. Come and sit down. What brings you here?"

"I have a summary of His Highness' progress—"

Adeone smiled. "Is it necessary if you're happy? I probably wouldn't understand half of it."

Tancred said, "Sire, your grasp of law is far better than many imagine. As for the report in itself, it is a requirement of being a tutor to the FitzAlcis."

"Is it? That would explain why Ewall constantly provided them. I did wonder. I never reviewed the requirements after father died and before that he saw to the education of your Princes. Now, save my eyes. How is my troublesome son progressing?"

Tancred smiled. "He is an exceptionally quick learner with an enquiring mind. I think he is beginning to grasp the fundamentals of law..."

As Tancred talked, Adeone nodded appreciatively. He was pleased with what he was hearing, but he was almost as pleased just to be listening to Tancred. Years before, when Tancred had been trying to help after Queen Eliza had died, Adeone had spent hours listening to him talk. Although it might not always have seemed to help, it had made him respect the judge's knowledge and he learnt more than either of them realised.

Breaking into his own discourse, the judge enquired, "Sire, are you quite well?"

Adeone shook his head to clear it. "Yes, why?"

"No reason of any importance, Your Majesty."

Adeone sighed. "There's always a reason for you asking me that, James."

"You felt distant, sir, as though your mind was elsewhere. I do not mind, but I wondered."

Adeone smiled sadly. "I was remembering Ceardlann and listening to you talk there. I was considering how pleasant it is. Do you ever consider the past?"

"Every man does, Your Majesty. Why?"

"I sometimes feel there are more repercussions from the past than consequences of the present."

"There is more past to cause the repercussions, sir," explained Tancred.

"True. I should stop being maudlin."

Tancred shook his head. "Far be it from me, sir, but I do not think you should. The past has made us who we are. We should remember and honour the memory, however painful it may be."

Adeone studied him shrewdly. "You speak from experience, I think."

"I have lived many years, sir. Not all my life has been smooth, but the bad times helped mould me as much as the good. I have spent years judging other people; a bit of introspection is good for the soul. If you do not mind my asking, what repercussions have you been thinking on recently?"

"Nothing at all important. Do you remember Festus' sister?"

Taking back his glass, Tancred nodded. "Yes, sir, but I did not meet her."

"Her son arrived a few weeks ago. He's living with Landis. It's made me consider my decisions from when I was young."

"Everyone does eventually, sir. How is Lady Feronia?"

"In good health. I see both her and Ifor in Emrys and find the past haunting me, especially with recent events. I made sure I was absent when Ifor and Nia married. It was despicable and cowardly of me. I was pleased for them both, but I'd broken her heart. I sometimes think she settled for Ifor to get out of Oedran and away from the speculation. Landis knows she did but he'll never say it. He misses her."

"Lord Landis is one of the few people I know that will tell Your Majesty the truth. I think he would say it, sir, if it were true."

Adeone raised an eyebrow. "Yes, he tells me so much truth, I sometimes wish he'd stop."

Tancred smiled. "It would only take a word. How old is Lord Emrys?"

"Fifteen. He's starting at the Advisors' School. Talking of which, we've filled the last post on Arkyn's advisors. One Calderon Brackenhurst. Landis was in his exam. Apparently, young Brackenhurst demolished the examiner's 'fatuous and ill-thought-out scenario' without blinking. Landis' presence he took with a comment about it being irregular, which is more than most would dare, and then proceeded to give Landis perfect advice for 'a personage of importance' travelling when bandits are reported. Landis' telling had me in stitches. Especially when he said that the examiners looked like they'd swallowed whole lemons at his interference. He effectively ordered them to pass Brackenhurst and then left. I can only imagine their expressions. Still, I'm glad the post's filled…"

Neither of them noticed time passing and, by the time Simkins considered they really should eat, they'd covered a multitude of topics. As soon as the manservant announced dinner, Tancred said he should be going.

Simkins smiled. "Your Honour, I took the liberty of informing Madam Tancred where you are. She's not expecting you for dinner this evening."

Adeone laughed. "There you are, James, that's the efficiency of the King's Household for you. They reorganise your entire life without you knowing. I suffer from the affliction regularly."

"I am sure it is more out of concern for Your Majesty than myself," replied Tancred.

Adeone raised an eyebrow at Simkins who said diplomatically, "Concern is not a finite commodity, Your Honour."

Adeone sighed. "He said that to cheer you up. Come let's dine and we'll work out what to do about the rest of the evening afterwards."

Chapter 83
CHANGING YEAR, CHANGING TIMES
Septadai, Week 48 – 28th Lufial, 21st Lufis 1212
Palace of Oedran – Court

ADEONE ROSE on the last day of 1212 in a mellow mood. Tain would turn thirteen on the stroke of midnight, but Adeone wouldn't let him attend the feast. Irrationally, he wanted to keep Tain's birthday private again. It wouldn't last. In two years', Tain would be fifteen, Justiciar of Oedran and able to attend Court. His younger son would be one of his closest officials. His elder son, meanwhile, already was. He told Arkyn far more than his father had ever shared with him at the same age. Now, though, there were other threats in the wind and Arkyn couldn't be left tumbling along when change came.

Lord Ryson greeted him as he entered Court, but that evening the King wasn't bothered about what rumours abounded, if any problems had occurred and whether the lord had anything at all to relay of the doings of his Court. Ryson could deal with it. He ambled around Court looking for Landis or Rhian. Asking an usher to find his friend and cousin wouldn't give him the same chance to observe his courtiers. His son was talking with Irvin Iris, Julius Landis and Emrys Daioch. He smiled at Arkyn and continued his amble. He spotted Rayburn talking with another couple of his advisors and nodded to them. Before long, he'd noticed Lord and Lady Fairson talking with Ryson, and Teran talking to Lux and Rathgar but there was still no sign of Landis or Rhian. That unsettled him. Where were they? He was in the Denshire room when an usher announced his aunt. Smiling, he crossed to greet her.

"Court seems remarkably full, Your Majesty," she observed.

"Doesn't it, Lady Amara? You're looking well."

"Thank you, Sire. You look like you're missing something. I know what it is – where's Lord Landis? He's normally somewhere close being obsequious."

Adeone smiled wryly. "If only when he's at Court. I'm not sure, aunt. Did you have a bone to pick with him?"

"I can't imagine what you mean, Sire. Have you seen Neassa?"

"Not today," he replied carefully.

Amara eyed him. "She's your cousin."

"I know and I don't forget it, but she's married. I've not seen Lord Rufus either, so I assume they've not yet arrived. Rathgar's here, but he and his family don't always appear together."

"Quite. Let's find a private room, Sire."

Adeone nodded to an usher, who left to make sure the nearest private room was empty.

Once ensconced, Amara said, "Neassa's marriage is rocky, Adeone. I'm worried."

Adeone frowned; for his aunt to be telling him, she had to be more than worried. "Why? As far as I can ascertain it's been rocky since Peaga was born."

"True, but Neassa is rarely at home. She's either here or visiting friends. She's even borrowed Rhian's rooms and slept here on occasion. I don't know what's wrong, but she's distancing herself. I thought you knew."

Adeone shook his head. "No. What with everything else, it's escaped my notice. What do you think I should do?"

"You could start by talking to Neassa."

Opening his mouth to reply, Adeone closed it again when Landis entered, looking grave. He nodded to Lady Amara but for once forgot to make any obeisance to Adeone.

"Sir, Lord Rufus has just struck Lady Neassa. She might appreciate her mother's support."

Amara got to her feet. "Where is she, young Festus?"

Landis told her before holding the door open as she left.

Adeone took a deep breath to steady himself. "Witnesses?"

"Several. Myself, Cornelia, Rhian, William and my groom; not to mention some of the palace grooms."

Adeone swore. "I'm not going to stand by and see this happen."

* * *

In a room away from the Court, Neassa was shaking, trying to control herself. Adeone glanced around. There were only family or close friends present.

"I want anyone who witnessed it outside. Where's Lord Rufus?"

"Next door, sir. I've mentioned it would be better if he didn't leave."

"Mentioned?"

"Forcefully, sir."

"Good."

Neassa looked worried as everyone but her mother left. She became fearful when Adeone knelt by her and examined her reddened face.

He examined her arms where bruises were appearing. "What happened?"

She hesitated. "I can't..."

"You've got to tell Adeone, Neassa, or I will," said Amara gently.

Neassa tried to hug herself, but Adeone still had her hand. He released it, but she recollected herself and clasped her hands together instead.

"Rufus, well, he was saying how no good has ever come of him marrying me and how you seem to look right through us. I tried to explain that it's not who we are, but what we are inside that matters to you. Your Majesty is, at heart, a meritocrat and he's hardly likely to come to your attention if he doesn't excel. He didn't like that and the next thing I know is that we're in the stableyard here and he's taken me roughly by the arm. He was squeezing. I tried to pull away. He said something, I don't know what. Seeing I hadn't heard him, he slapped me to get my attention. I hadn't noticed Festus, nor Rhian, but suddenly Rufus was a couple of steps away from me and Rhian was wrapping me in a hug."

Adeone nodded. "I'm pleased someone was there. Neassa, you need to tell me something honestly. *Why* is your marriage failing?"

She glanced at her mother, tears in her eyes.

Amara patted her arm. "There's no harm in the truth."

"I don't like Scanlon," whispered Neassa, "and I can't hide the fact but the Rathgars are known to be... that is..."

"They support him." It wasn't a question. Adeone sighed. "I have to ask this, is there any true hope of reconciliation between you and Rufus?"

"Not now." Her eyes welled. "It's not the first time. I don't want to cause you more problems—"

"Fiddlesticks to the problems. If they come, they come. For me, your happiness and safety is more important; so, I'm going to break your binding. Do you object?"

406

Neassa shook her head. "I don't ever want to return to that house."

"You won't have to, but you will have to face him one last time. Aunt Amara, can you stay? I need to organise a few things."

Amara simply nodded.

* * *

Half an hour later, in the Inner Office, Adeone said, "Your uncle has struck my cousin in violence, Lord Rathgar. In front of several witnesses, and apparently not for the first time."

Rathgar stilled. "A minor marital dispute, Sire."

"No, this was pure anger born from not wanting to hear the truth. As for your paltry excuse, there is no reason that could ever justify Lord Rufus attacking his wife in such a way. You know as well as I do that the marriage has been rocky for years. All those years have not healed it, and tonight's events have made me conclude that it never will be whole."

"Your Majesty, I think they are married for life."

"Then you think wrong, my lord," stated Adeone. "The marriage agreement is quite clear on this. Only if both parties can agree that there is still chance of reconciliation does the binding hold true. Lady Neassa has mentioned to me that there is no chance in her mind; therefore, I am going to break the binding."

Lord Rathgar coloured. "Your Majesty, you cannot."

"I cannot? Lady Neassa is my cousin! I most certainly can."

"But Lord Fairson is her nearest male relation as dictated in law."

Adeone took a breath to control himself. "Where there is a close descent from the FitzAlcis to the third generation, that is the great-grandchild of a monarch, then the head of the family is the King. I am astounded that you are claiming ignorance. Would you prefer my lawyer to correct you?"

Lord Rathgar's colour was still high. "Your Majesty a King's Lawyer is not an expert in such matters."

"Where *did* you get your education, my lord? A King's Lawyer is an expert in matters relating to the FitzAlcis. How, therefore, can he be inexpert in this? I am informing Your Lordship that the marriage will be ended tonight. This does not require your agreement or presence. I'm sure our lawyers will conclude any formalities from tomorrow. That is all."

Lord Rathgar took a deep breath. "I'm sure they shall, Sire. Goodnight."

* * *

Moments later, the Moonshi – sworn to uphold the ancestors' memory, perform blessings, marriages and funerals – entered the Inner Office to find Adeone drumming his fingers on the desk. He listened as the King explained events and accepted the situation without demurral.

407

His agreement reassured Adeone he was right in procedure and action. As Guardian of the Heavens, Adeone didn't *need* his presence, but it was better for all that there was a reliable witness, especially given Rathgar's bluster. The King had little doubt that, by the time he reached Court again, Lord Rathgar would have started whispers labelling him a despot and Rufus a wronged party.

Once everyone was arrayed in the Inner Office, the Moonshi positioned himself between Lady Neassa and Lord Rufus; the latter looked recalcitrant. He'd obviously been told what was coming.

"Lord Rufus Rathgar, you have today dishonoured your family and caused pain and grief to mine. You have struck your wife in anger, proving, beyond all doubt, your true nature and the state of your marriage. Lady Neassa has told me that she cannot ever return to Rathgar House as your wife. You have failed to uphold your wedding vows and, as such, I am invoking my right, as head of Lady Neassa's family, and breaking your binding. From this moment forth you are no longer married to Lady Neassa, nor she to you. Will you both please surrender your wedding rings to the Moonshi?

Neassa took her ring off with shaking fingers. She looked at it one last time and then passed it to the Moonshi.

"What if I refuse, Sire?" demanded Rufus.

"Then you will bring your family far more shame as I have you arrested for treason. When you married Lady Neassa, you understood the terms of the marriage. Do you still wish to defy me?"

Rufus looked as though he was going to but then, with difficulty, removed his ring and passed it over.

Adeone said levelly, "Do either of you wish to reclaim the ring you gave to your previous partner?" (Both shook their heads.) "Then their worth will be given to you instead. Lord Rufus, not only have you outraged propriety, but you have also abused the hospitality of my Court and the modes of behaviour I require of my courtiers. Your actions have disgraced your ancestors' memory on a night when we should be honouring them. You will absent yourself from this Court and all others of the empire for a year. You can go." Adeone turned to the Moonshi. "Thank you for your time, Your Benevolence. I hope the events here have not caused too much issue for the induction of new alcias this evening."

In his gentle yet deep voice, the Moonshi said, "None I am aware of, Your Majesty. Lady Neassa, should you need time and solitude, do not forget the City Alcium is there for you and I can listen if you wish to talk."

Adeone smiled softly at that. The Moonshi had a soft heart underneath all his outward bearing. When he'd gone, Adeone walked out from behind his desk and wrapped his cousin in a strong hug.

"Can you face Court?"

Neassa said quietly, "Better tonight than tomorrow, Sire. I just need my family. I've…" She blanched. "What of Peaga?"

Adeone shrugged. "Being of age, he can make up his own mind."

Neassa sighed. "I was rather afraid of that."

* * *

Lord Peaga Rathgar was at Court. Seeing his mother, he crossed to her and bowed to Adeone.

"Your mother needs some understanding," murmured Adeone.

He grinned. "I understand perfectly, Sire, and I couldn't be better pleased."

That made them both pause.

Adeone nodded. "Lady Neassa, I'll hope you'll join the family for the banquet."

Neassa found a smile hiding and claimed it. "I can think of nowhere I would rather be."

Two moments later, Adeone found Rhian and Amara. Making sure no-one else could hear, he muttered, "It's done."

"I'll find her, if I may, Sire," replied Amara.

"Of course, aunt. Peaga was with her."

Rhian murmured, "Rathgar's already started the whispering campaign against her. Lux made the mistake of asking mother what was happening. I don't think he'll make that mistake again."

Scanning the room, he muttered, "Please tell me Lux hasn't died of apoplexy."

"I'm sure it could be arranged," replied Rhian innocently.

Adeone snorted involuntarily. "You shouldn't be able to make me laugh after what's just happened, Lady Rhian."

"Everyone has their faults, Sire."

* * *

Later, sitting watching the King's Hall, Adeone smiled gravely to himself. This hall – with its magnificent carvings, with its age – had seen more history than any one man ever could.

The raucous hubbub hid the whispers he knew would be speeding around Court. His cousin's divorce would be the subject for days, if not weeks. Stopping all the gossip would be impossible, but if it hadn't died down in a couple of days, he'd ask those close to him to hint to the people gossiping that bans from Court would result if they didn't stop. His cousin didn't need any more distress. Not that Court would be kind to her. She'd be the one at fault. Still, banning Rufus should have helped.

He glanced around. Julius, Irvin and Emrys were talking animatedly. Emrys had certainly settled into life at Landis House easily. Adeone was pleased. He'd be there for some years. The whispers about his father's life-bind had stopped and far from destroying his standing, the event seemed to have enhanced it; though Adeone had noticed several of his Court were wary around the youth, but that could happen with anyone seen to be in favour.

Landis saw his friend watching the group. "I don't know what they're planning, Sire. Should we ask?"

Adeone didn't reply. He didn't mind what they planned. What they did was something else. Julius had calmed down since their talk. He could plan away and take the consequences if he had to.

His gaze continued around the hall. From his place he could see the sons and daughters, brothers and sisters of the Lords of Oedran, the merchants and city officials, the ushers, pages, candle-wardens and servers. He couldn't easily see those who sat at the dais: the Lords of Oedran and even his own guests. Landis sat at his left hand, Arkyn at his right. As he looked around the hall, he said,

"Where's Lord Kensal, Your Highness?"

Arkyn groaned. "I've given up asking that, Sire. I expect he's still sorting out Your Majesty's archives. I tried digging him out of there earlier, but he said he just needed to finish something."

Adeone laughed. He turned. "Simkins, see where Lord Kensal's got to."

Arkyn waited until Simkins left before saying, "Why, sir?"

"Guests of Court should really be at the major feasts." Adeone lapsed into silence. Maybe he should have let Tain attend. His eyes traversed the hall again. Various servers were clearing empty platters and putting newly laden ones out. The meats and breads had mostly been cleared, now fruits and nuts lined the tables. Sugar sculptures stood tall on each table. No-one paid them much attention, but Adeone was always in wonder at their delicate artistry.

Kensal entered twelve minutes later, looking rushed but dressed formally. He caught the King's eye and bowed. Adeone merely inclined his head slightly with a smile, so Kensal joined Julius, Irvin and Emrys. They greeted him with knowing grins. Adeone chuckled.

"Do you want to join them, Arkyn?"

Arkyn glanced sideways at him. "It would be rather unusual, Sire."

"If you want to, do. It might worry your nearcousin for a start."

Arkyn laughed and, with a small bow to his father, made his way to his friends, who greeted him exuberantly.

From beside Adeone, Landis said, "Now I really want to know what they're planning."

"We're sure to find out. I doubt it's anything nefarious. Irvin and Emrys are too sensible. I expect they've just drunk wine, had good food and are enjoying life." He glanced at Simkins. "Ask Lady Rhian to join us, please."

Landis muttered, "Rumours?"

"Fiddlesticks to them." He paused. "Let them gossip. It'll take the pressure off Neassa. I doubt Rhian will mind that."

Rhian sat in Arkyn's abandoned place. "Is Festus behaving himself, sir?"

"Never," said Adeone. "Even if he seems to be, he's plotting something else. I wanted to ask you if you'd stay for the whole of the summer. Arkyn's leaving for Lufian soon and I need someone to keep me out of trouble. Festus doesn't. I'm sure Neassa would appreciate your support also."

"I'd be honoured, sir," said Rhian frustrated at being outmanoeuvred. "I won't be able to stay over autumn, however."

Adeone winked. "Do tell me if I ever use my rank unfairly, my lady."

Rhian carefully cut into an apple. "I'm Your Majesty's to command, Sire. My mother's made sure of it."

Landis choked on his drink. Adeone slapped him on the back, eyes glinting, lips twitching.

"I'm sure she has, cousin. Talking of which…"

Six minutes later, Rhian said, "Why are you watching the servers so intently, sir?"

Adeone paused. "Am I? Sorry. I'm hunting for a manservant for Tain. I can't seem to find anyone I'm happy with."

"Mother would say let the Steward earn his pay. He knows the footmen, servers and valets of the Palace and Court better. If there's no-one in yours or Prince Arkyn's household to promote, let him find someone from them."

He sighed. "I want it to be right."

"Perfect is the enemy of good, sir. Good can improve, perfect can never be found."

Adeone squeezed her hand. "Thank you for reminding me." He picked up his goblet and suddenly didn't want wine, didn't want anything but to sit quietly. The entertainments had finished an hour since. The feast was all but over. He glanced at Landis. "I'm retiring. Don't make a fuss."

Landis nodded and stayed seated as Adeone slipped out of his chair and left the hall. As he passed the end of the dais, a couple of furtive whispers from the servers reached his ears.

"His brother, that's what they said. Can you believe it? I can't."

"You'd 'ave thought the King'd know…"

Part of Adeone considered asking them what they were discussing, but the rest of him said that he probably did know; if he didn't, Wynfeld would soon tell him whatever it was, and, if neither of those things were true, he didn't need to draw attention to himself, or frighten his staff. That wouldn't be starting his year as he meant to go on.

Chapter 84
ARCHIVES
Cisadai, Week 3 – 16th Cearal, 16th Cearcis 1213
Barracks

BY THE TIME BEAVER informed Wynfeld of the rumours, the Major knew there wasn't much time to ascertain the facts. Three weeks had passed since the Munewid and those weeks had allowed the rumours to run unheeded amongst the Palace staff. Do what he could, he couldn't trace where they started, but they were beginning to leak into Court and if they flowed into the wider city, there would be issues. The Palace was its own village in many respects. A network of specialists that rarely needed outside help and most of the staff wouldn't gossip outside of the grounds knowing it risked their livelihoods. Courtiers were another matter entirely.

Wynfeld's files once more held nothing on the matter. Once more that wasn't surprising. 1169 troubles were too distant. He needed access to other records. Given the rumours, the archives might be best. They would hold papers and orders to do with the rebellion. Feeling as though time was running out, he went to the Palace. His King would be irate at the delay and any delay now would merely heighten the rage.

The archives' dim maze of small rooms, scroll shelving and desks was enveloping. Sound from outside was deadened and Wynfeld understood how Kensal could lose track of time. Rooms were stacked high with ledgers, scrolls and piles of paperwork.

Wynfeld had a quiet word with the archivist, ignored the raised eyebrow and was shown to where Kensal was diligently working his way through all the scrolls and documents in one room. The young lord looked up from his endeavours as though drunk on the history in front of him. Gradually his flushed face focused.

Wynfeld waited for the archivist to leave before saying, "My lord, I need you to do something for me and I need you to do it quickly. Can you search through all records relating to the 1169 offensive against Bayan looking for mention of traitors? I need you to list every single name you come across. Can you do it by tonight? I realise you're leaving for Lufian tomorrow with His Highness."

Kensal frowned. "I expect so, Major, but I don't have clearance to look at such recent documents."

"You do now but don't mention it to anyone. The archivist has seen the sense in taking the day off. Can you pass your scroll of names to Edward? He'll see that I get it. You might come across a couple of names that you hesitate about including. Put them *all* down. No-one other than myself will read the scroll and it will then be destroyed. I just need to know the names."

Kensal nodded. "What will you do with the names, Major?"

"Protect our King with more understanding about what's happening."

"Does His Majesty know what you've requested?"

Wynfeld eyed him. "If anyone questions what you're doing, I will explain to His Majesty or His Highness. That's not important. Those names are."

"If it wasn't for the fact I know the FitzAlcis trust you, Major, I'd be telling you I wouldn't do it."

Wynfeld smiled. "I'd hope so too. Thank you, my lord."

When Wynfeld read the list later, he frowned. How was it possible that those names didn't appear if the rumours were true? He swore. Could they be anywhere else? If not, then what had happened? Was Scanlon resorting to inventing slurs? It wouldn't be unusual, but in attacking such eminent men, he'd have wanted proof. Wouldn't he?

Where else could he look? Did he dare mention it to Paturn after the previous warning to avoid anything to do with Dunius? How long did he have? Should he just tell his King himself? He probably should but, again, he wanted to be sure of the evidence. Accusations – proved or not, rumour or not – would not be well received. Even seeding doubt in his King's mind about two of his closest confidants should be avoided. Was it worth asking Lady Amara? If anyone would know it was likely to be her.

The following afternoon, before he could decide, he received a summons from his King.

* * *

Wynfeld entered the Outer Office still puzzling over the problem. He saw Richardson's face and hope drained from him.

"He's really not in a good mood, Major. I hope you can reassure him this time."

Wynfeld paused. "Administrator?"

"It would be better coming from His Majesty."

Two minutes later, Wynfeld managed to say, "Sire, I had Lord Kensal check the records for 1169, there's nothing in the archives—"

"You bloody well knew and didn't tell me? Did you forget what is meant to go into the reports I read?"

Wynfeld said stolidly, "No, sir, I considered this was probably best not put down in writing and I didn't consider my job included destroying Your Majesty's friendships. I wanted to be absolutely sure of the truth before I informed Your Majesty of speculation. Unfortunately, my investigations have taken too long, for which I apologise. Might I ask if he knows?"

"I doubt he's in ignorance. I'd like to know why he didn't come to me himself if he knew people were whispering such things."

Wynfeld said, "Because he doesn't consider the gossip of the Court as particularly interesting, Sire. He didn't make his name there."

"No, and shortly he'll have no bloody name left. All right, Wynfeld, make it known at Court that if I hear they've been discussing this, my reaction won't be pleasant. There must be an excellent reason he's never mentioned it to me. As for Dunius, make it abundantly clear to everyone that there is nothing there to harm Lord Landis' standing, there is nothing that I and my sons do not know about that situation, and that undermining a Defender is treason. Oh, and next time, make sure I don't hear things such as this from a friend of Lord Scanlon's!"

Wynfeld nodded. "I do not mean to be trite, Sire, but I really hope there isn't a next time."

The King in Adeone said, "For your sake, so do I." As he left, Adeone cursed to himself. He didn't want to believe the gossip, but Daioch's hints came back to him. There were longstanding rumours on the Low Plains. He couldn't overreact as he had with Daioch, as his father had with Dunius. He needed the explanation before he took any action and he had to get it himself. Sending Wynfeld would destroy more than the rumours had.

Chapter 85

EXPLANATIONS

Tretaldai, Week 3 – 17th Cearal, 17th Cearcis 1213

Inner Office

RICHARDSON ANNOUNCED TANCRED with a sombre look on his face. The judge realised something had happened as soon as the King said,

"Don't sit down, Your Honour." Adeone regarded the judge silently for several moments. "Some interesting rumours have been brought to my attention, Tancred, regarding your family history. Is there anything you feel you need to tell me?"

Tancred stilled. He should have listened to Bets, should have realised Scanlon would discover the secret. He knelt. "Your Majesty, I…"

"Lost for words, Judge?" enquired Adeone acidly. Betrayal came in many forms; this was one he hadn't anticipated.

"No, Sire. I do not know what exactly you have been told and how history has twisted the truth, but on my life what I am about to tell you is that truth." He took a deep breath. "When Bayan rebelled in 1169, King Altarius raised a conscription. As my brother was of age, and not yet in any formal training, he was conscripted. He was young for fifteen. He did not have the maturity to deal with the… with what faced him. He was impressionable, always had been. Someone turned him from fighting for your father to fighting against him. We were told that he passed information to the Bayans. Not that he knew much, but he knew enough. He was caught and taken before King Altarius. I have never discovered what was said, but the outcome was that my brother was executed as a traitor. The crime was proclaimed daily for a year in Oedran. It killed my parents and almost destroyed my career. I have tried to put the memories behind me."

Still furious, Adeone said, "Yet you never told me you had a traitor for a brother. That, Judge, could be construed as treachery as you are employed by me to teach Prince Tain. You have had ample opportunity to."

Tancred whitened. "Sire, there is nothing I can say in my defence."

Adeone nodded. "Then I'd like to know how you got so close to my family with a traitorous brother in your past."

Tancred sighed. "By chance, Sire, by nothing more than chance. I was a young lawyer; my brother had been executed for treason; I was starved of cases. Two years later, I still had little work. My parents had passed on and I was trying to scrape a living. When I say scrape, I mean scrape. If I could afford a loaf, it was a good day. I took the defence of a woman who had killed her husband. No-one else would touch it. She had refused to speak to anyone about the incident. I had a meeting with her and still she said nothing. I talked instead; I told her something of my history. Where I had grown up; it was in the worst sector down near the wharf in the Ryson Lordship. I had grown up in two rooms. It was before the yeomen existed and it was not a pleasant place. There was violence everywhere – violence and poverty; the two worst killers in the world. I started to tell the woman I was defending how one day my father had hit my mother. Her eyes flicked to me as I explained how my mother, being the mouse she was, had taken it. It was not so very different to what was happening to every family around us. Then one day my father hit my mother once too often. She hit him back; unfortunately, she had a frying pan in her hand and he was unconscious for some minutes. It was only by chance that he had not been killed. My father never hit my mother again. When I finished that part of my story, the woman I was defending said, 'I couldn't take it anymore'. I had somehow got her talking. Her story was familiar to me. I knew I had to do my best for her. It did not matter that she had killed her husband. Her story was the story of many people in the city. It was the type of story that had made me decide to be a lawyer. I remember when I asked my father if I could train. What he said was true; we did not have the money to put me through the Law School. To start with I accepted that. Then I realised I had to fight for what I wanted in life. I started working harder than ever. I had been a dock runner since I was seven. I got other jobs as well. My father seeing how much I wanted it, scrimped and saved what he could. My brother also helped, my mother too. Together we found enough money to send me to Law School for the first year. There was no scholarship set up then; so, I would work every evening for whoever would give me work. Some nights I did not sleep. It took a lot of determination but I managed to pass all five years. Alcis only knows how. I graduated, as I said, and then my brother committed treason. My career was over before it began. Then came the case I mentioned. I took it in desperation. I had no hope of ever getting through it. The case was to be heard in Court Six – the then Keeper deemed it was perfectly acceptable – it is the smallest both in precedence and size. Two hours before the case was to be heard, the presiding judge was taken ill: terminally ill. The Keeper informed Prince Lachlan, who said he would preside, same time but in the Justice Hall. I was informed and, I must admit, I was terrified. I was a failing lawyer in threadbare robes whose brother had turned against the FitzAlcis. I stood in the Justice Hall, in those threadbare robes, and knew I could not sink any lower. Why, therefore, was I worrying? I had accepted the duty of representing a beaten woman; I would do my best by her. I talked for all I was worth. I told true stories. I even touched on my mother's story but I tried to show that the woman had reacted instinctively. That she had defended herself and that she had never meant to kill. Somehow, I managed to convince both the jury and Prince Lachlan. The woman was found not guilty of murder, though she was imprisoned for five years for the taking of her husband's life. I still remember the incredulity on her face that she would live, the tear in her eye as it caught the light. Moments later, when Prince Lachlan closed the court, he summoned me to his office. I entered that office in a daze. Prince Lachlan faced me; he congratulated me on my defence and then upbraided me for the state of my robes. I stood there, not knowing what to say. He saw that and asked me why I had become so tongue-tied after my eloquence in court. I, for want of something else to say, explained about my brother. Prince Lachlan said that they were my brother's actions not mine. He continued that my defence had been the best he had ever heard. I could not believe that and I said so. He simply told me to be quiet. So I was. He continued and asked me if I had ever thought about becoming a judge. I simply laughed. Then, seeing he did not realise how incredulous the suggestion had been, I explained: I had been born cisan, I was a lawyer on the brink of having to find another job and my brother had been a traitor. The last two alone showed the prospect unlikely; the first meant it was impossible. There had *never* been a judge from the cisan. Prince Lachlan asked me how precedents were set. I simply stared. My jaw even dropped, he told me later. He then passed me ten darl and told me to get myself some new robes. I had never seen ten actual darl together in my life. I held them for a moment and then returned them. I could not and would not accept charity from a man whose family mine had betrayed. I bowed and left, shaking. I do not know how Prince Lachlan reacted to my snub. I went back to the cupboard I was using as an office and sat and thought for all I was worth. I had insulted the Justiciar. He would never let me get away with it. A couple of days later, I was again summoned to his office. King Altarius was there. Alcis knows how I got through that; I still do not. King Altarius said to me that if I followed Prince Lachlan's wishes, he would do his best to see the memory of my brother's treason was forgotten. I did not know what to do but agree. I could not do anything but agree. King Altarius left. Prince Lachlan passed me a drink to calm my nerves. He then gave me what might have seemed strange advice but I followed it. He said to leave his office smiling. It was the best advice I ever received, Sire. Word spread and my caseload picked up. Within two seasons, I was no longer the struggling lawyer I had been. I even managed to buy myself some new robes. The whispers had stopped. Soon Prince Lachlan sent for me again and asked me to be one of his lawyers. I could not refuse and I am pleased I did not. I began to work for him, began to see beneath the general impression that he was a strict Justiciar. He was not. He was trying to make his brother's throne secure. I began to even like him. Something I thought, coming from where I did, I could never do. There are more prejudices in the slums than anywhere else on Erinna. Anyway, if you want the whole story, Sire, I began to even love him. Neither of us was heterosexual. Nothing ever really happened – I had a wife and child – but we became very close over the years. He persuaded me to become a judge, and I agreed to try. To my astonishment, the other judges accepted me. I became the first cisan judge of the empire. I still cannot believe it. The following years saw much change for the better. Prince Lachlan had listened to my 'stories'. He spoke to King Altarius and the yeomen were created. The area I had grown up in became altogether safer. We managed to create two scholarships at the Law School. I carried on working as a judge and I think, I hope, I have been a reasonable one over the years. King Altarius and Prince Lachlan were right; in the end, people forgot my brother's treason, though I knew it was a story that could haunt me for life."

Adeone nodded. "You have become something of a legend in your own time; you do know that, James?"

The judge relaxed. "Yes, Sire, but like all legends the truth is glorified."

"Yes, it is, isn't it?" Adeone rose and looked out of the window. After a couple of moments, he crossed to Tancred and helped him back to his feet. "I'm not going to take any action. I knew, deep down, that as the knowledge of your brother's treason had never surfaced before, Scanlon must have been digging hard. There was no reason other than you teaching His Highness why someone should try to tarnish your name after so long."

Tancred sagged. "Thank you, Sire."

"Nevertheless, *next time*, James, if you've got a secret, let me know before someone else does!"

"I could not find the words, Sire, especially after so long."

"No. I expect there's a lot of that going round at the moment. Lord Para, for one, might be finding them hard to locate."

Tancred stilled. "Why is that, sir?"

"I didn't appreciate the way he came and told me about the rumours. Tancred, what has made sense?"

"I am sorry, Sire. The lady I defended in front of Prince Lachlan was His Lordship's step-grandmother. I suppose it is another story that has been buried. His grandfather hit her once too often and she floored him with a paperweight. He never got back up."

"Why wasn't the case heard in the Justice Hall to start with then?"

"The Keeper set the case up for Court Six in the Justiciar's absence. I think he was trying to make sure that the lady was convicted and forgotten about. The family certainly wanted it so and the then Lord Para never liked his step-mother."

"Then why didn't he push for a more visible trial? Father would have made sure one happened after the killing of a lord."

"Yes, but Lord Para did not want everyone to remember what a beauty his step-mother was, and he certainly did not want his father's memory questioned by the knowledge he hit his wife. The whole situation was kept very private."

Adeone understood. "Then it was partly revenge that brought Lord Para here. Revenge for the fact the lady survived to bear witness that his grandfather wasn't quite as pristine as he seems to legend?"

"It is likely, Sire."

"That could be useful. He's hardly going to want people reminding that his grandfather wasn't perfect, is he? I wonder. Rumours can work in two directions… Well, James, do you want a drink?"

Tancred smiled. "I would not say no, Your Majesty."

"Good." Adeone poured him a brandy and himself a whiskey. Seating himself, he said, "I've never known your full story. It was interesting."

Tancred sat opposite Adeone. "Thank you, Sire. It was, at times, painful to tell. I have tried to forget some aspects."

"Then I'm sorry to have asked you to tell it; however, with your permission, I think some of it could be used to your advantage. Leave this office smiling."

Tancred laughed. "I always do, Sire. It has been the best piece of advice your uncle ever gave me."

"Yes… There was nothing about your brother in the archives. Scanlon must have had a hard time discovering all this."

Tancred blinked, then rubbed his hand through his hair. "Someone expunged it from history. There is only word of mouth to keep it alive."

"It will be forgotten. I promise you that."

"Thank you, Sire. I wonder who though…"

Adeone glanced at him, amused. "There are only two people who could have done it: my father and uncle."

Tancred sighed. "Of course, Your Majesty. Why though? If you can forgive me, your father was never tolerant of traitors' families."

"Yet he was of you. You said you grew close to Prince Lachlan? I think the only thing that would have convinced my father was the word of his brother. I think Uncle Lachlan vouched for you."

"He did not know me, Sire, not then."

Adeone smiled, saying, "You know, sometimes, by simply looking into someone's eyes, if they are for you. You and my uncle had a unique relationship. I believe you when you said nothing happened but it doesn't mean that, to start with, he didn't have ulterior motives, does it?"

"No, Sire, it does not. I just… Oh, Sicla."

Tancred rose and went to examine the view. Adeone left him for a couple of moments before crossing to him.

"Whatever the reasons behind it, James, your brother's treachery isn't down on any official scroll. There is only memory and memory is fallible. I'll see it's known that I can't find record of it. No record, no treason."

Tancred sagged onto the window seat. "Thank you, Sire. I do not deserve this."

Adeone laughed. "Of course you do." There was a knock at the door.

"Yes, Richardson?"

"Forgive me, Sire, but there is a lady here asking to see you. Something about Judge Tancred's past? She won't give her name."

Adeone nodded, and the lady was shown in. Tancred turning from the window stopped suddenly. "My lady, there was no need to come." Catching the King's glance, he continued, "My apologies, Sire, this is… well, she was once, technically still is, Dowager Lady Para."

"Thank you, Judge. I understand you wished to see me, my lady?"

The old lady said, "Yes, Sire. I heard that the judge had been summoned and I've heard the rumours that have spread. I just wanted to say that James Tancred is one of the best men I've ever met. I remember the events of the rebellion right enough. I remember the events of the following years and I remember that James Tancred suffered enough because of his brother then. He saved my life, Sire, and I'd swear on that life that he hasn't a traitorous bone in his body and never had."

Tancred swallowed.

Adeone was smiling. "A worthy speech, my lady, and one that I happen to agree with the sentiments of. I know His Honour is loyal. I just needed an explanation. Now I've been infernally rude to keep you standing. Won't you take a seat?"

"No, thank you, Sire. I should leave you."

"Before you go, my lady, might I just ask how you knew I'd sent for His Honour?" enquired Adeone, intrigued.

"I was visiting a longstanding friend here, Sire. It's all over the Palace."

"Yes, it doesn't take long, does it?" replied Adeone wryly. "Might I know the name of your friend?"

The lady smiled. "Certainly, Sire. I was visiting Lady Amara."

With that, she bobbed a curtsy and left, leaving the two men looking at each other, stunned.

"Looks like there might have been another reason my father and uncle took to you," remarked Adeone. "They were always protective of their sister. If she'd wanted something, she'd have got it."

"Yes, but I never…"

"Tancred, you saved the life of one of my aunt's friends. Did you truly not know?"

"No. I took the case without knowing anything but the alleged crime and victim. Court intrigues were well over my head at that time." He put his head in his hands. "Alcis! I feel a fool."

"You must have found out since?"

"On my life no, Sire. I have never cared for gossip." He laughed. "Well, Lord Scanlon, whether he knows it or not, has done me a favour. I know or have some inkling now why Lachlan tried to help me." He paused before saying, "I ought to let you continue, Sire."

Adeone groaned. "Thank you for the thought. Come to dinner with me this evening."

Tancred bowed and left. Had the audience happened quite how he remembered it?

Chapter 86
DINNER AND DELVING
Evening
Inner Office

EARLY THAT SAME EVENING, a young footman of the King's Household announced Judge Tancred and watched carefully the way the judge was greeted. Such a greeting in the current suspicious atmosphere was grist to the rumour and gossip mill.

Adeone smiled warmly, laying down his pen. "James, how was the court this afternoon?"

"Remarkably busy in the public gallery, Your Majesty, I have not had a trial so well attended in many a year. The defence gave the prosecution a good run and the defendant was acquitted. I hope the audience appreciated the show."

"Is the practice of law merely performed for the gratification of those watching, Your Honour?"

"Never in my court, Sire, but it sometimes helps if the atmosphere is more relaxed, it can lead to a fairer hearing."

The footman was taking his time leaving.

"Henry, if you've had your fill, you might ask Simkins to join me," ordered Adeone.

The young footman started and bowed out.

Adeone winked at Tancred. "I'll just deal with this, if you don't mind?"

"Not at all, Sire. I would never intentionally stop your duties."

Simkins entered and Adeone said softly, "Remind Henry that he isn't a member of my household to provide gossip to others. He's far too tardy leaving a room after announcing someone who's currently notorious. James and I might get a reputation for being too relaxed with each other."

Simkins smiled. "I'm sure only with practice, Your Majesty. He'll not be tardy again." As he left, he cursed. His son had just scuppered his chance of becoming Prince Tain's manservant.

When he'd gone, Adeone laughed. "We're causing disquiet, James. Uncle Lachlan would be pleased."

"His late Highness would, I suspect, have joined in."

Adeone pushed himself to his feet and poured them drinks. "More than likely. Now, I need a serious talk with you… How's Prince Tain's authority and attitude to power?"

"I cannot see a fault in it, sir. He is fair-minded and does not judge without knowing facts now, but surely, Sire, you know His Highness far better than I do. I cannot believe you hold doubts as to Prince Tain's character."

"No, you're right, I don't," admitted Adeone, "but I want you to test it. Lord Scanlon wasn't as vindictive and controlling until he knew that the authority he held was a truly powerful thing, that he could destroy men he disliked, and that he could, by exercising that power, bend men to his will."

"I do, sir, but I cannot see how I could ever test Prince Tain in that manner. His Highness has no part of him that is like Lord Scanlon."

"You could tell him your story, Your Honour."

Tancred paused. "I would rather not lose His Highness' trust or good opinion, Sire; it would break me."

Adeone looked Tancred in the eye. "That is the test, James. If he can cast off your teachings, then he is not the person I thought him."

"I beg you, sir, can I not use a hypothetical situation, Sire?"

"No. For in hypotheses is safety. You will do this, Judge Tancred, for all our sakes. In this test is the character of the future Justiciar, don't you wish to see it?"

"I think, Sire, I fear it, for I have had its making. It might be like looking into a mirror and not seeing the reflection one expected." He considered the King, seeing something haunting in his face, he gave in. "I will tell Prince Tain my story, but should his character not stand the test, what shall we do?"

Adeone collapsed into a chair, rubbing at his face. "I don't know, James. I just need some sort of assurance that he'll be a good man. Prince Arkyn is everything we could hope for, other than his health isn't the most robust, but Prince Tain…"

"Is still young, Sire." Tancred squeezed his shoulder. "His Highness' character may not be fixed for many years but, personally, I think it has a good start."

Adeone smiled sadly. "Thank you. Do you mind rearranging your lessons with the terror to Alunadai and Cisadai next week? I think he's picked up a cold. That or his age is showing."

Tancred relaxed. "Of course, sir. It is no trouble."

On Alunadai, seeing the Prince in a more subdued mood than normal, Judge Tancred decided to approach the subject that day, concluding that Tain was more likely to be honest if he had other things on his mind as well.

"I'm not feeling my best, Judge," admitted Tain candidly.

"I am sure we shall still manage something, Your Highness, but I shall bear it in mind. Do you mind if we start with something unconventional? I have been asked to tell you my story…"

Tain smiled. "I should like to hear it, Judge."

Tain listened with an open and ready visage. When Tancred finished the story, he said, "You ought to write that down, Judge."

"I had a traitor in my family, Your Highness."

Tain chewed at his lip and his gaze was frank. "So?"

"There is a huge disgrace with it, sir. My parents died of the shame. My family was torn apart by the strains put on it but in comparison to what my brother did in defying the empire and possibly leading to its destruction—"

"There was a doubt, you know," said Tain, still chewing at his lip, looking away.

Tancred stilled. "Sir?"

Tain turned back to him. "I found an account in Great-uncle Lachlan's diaries of the day your brother was executed. Two men were definite traitors, their initials are there alongside your brother's but it wasn't certain that your brother was a traitor, but they had to act to stop treachery. I'm sorry, Judge, but I've known about this for a while."

Tancred got up and moved over to the window, trying to compose himself. "Why did you not say something, sir?"

Tain paused. "Because I thought you'd rather I didn't know and I felt guilty for the knowledge. You'd spoken so often of Prince Lachlan I wanted to get to know him. I started reading his diaries but when I found that account and I'd read to the end of the rebellion and then I discovered about Lord Dunius I realised what I was finding out was damaging to people I care about; so, I've stopped reading his diaries. I thought it better. I'm sorry, Judge."

Tancred held his worried gaze. "You have done nothing to be sorry about, Your Highness. I promise you that. His Majesty, I believe, wants to know if you still wish for my tutelage when I have a traitorous brother in my past."

Tain shrugged. "Your brother's actions were not yours, Judge. I couldn't ever blame you for them. It's over forty years since the Bayan rebellion.

Time enough for your life to be your own." The Prince got up and crossed to the judge. He put a tentative hand against the older man's arm. "I'm sorry for all the pain this has caused, for all the pain my family has caused yours over the years. You've never deserved that."

Tancred looked at him searchingly. "Thank you, Your Highness. May we move on to a lighter subject?"

"Of course, Judge, but, at some point, can we discuss what the law requires when it comes to traitors' families and the measures that *must* be taken when treason's proved, either in a military camp or in civilian life?"

"We will, sir, but military law is the domain of the King."

"I know, but I'd like to understand where the definitive bounds are between my future responsibility and a king's when it comes to treason."

Pleased to have been asked, Tancred said, "Then I shall organise some lessons and reading into it, Your Highness; however, for now, I thought we would talk about something much more mundane: the layout of the Courthouse and its peculiarities."

"Sounds fascinating. We couldn't examine something else?"

Tancred smiled. "Not without taxing Your Highness' brain. Shall we start, sir? Then, after lunch, I am sure Your Highness can explain all the mad schemes that yourself and Master Calumiel are brewing."

Tain grinned. "It's a deal."

Chapter 87
PARDON?

Tretaldai, Week 4 – 24th Cearal, 3rd Middis 1213
Inner Office

A COUPLE OF DAYS LATER, a knock at the Inner Office door heralded Judge Tancred. Adeone greeted his friend and son's tutor as though there had never been any revelations about his past. After a few pleasantries, Adeone asked how he could help.

Tancred hesitated. "I've told Prince Tain my story, sir."

Adeone passed him a drink. "Ah. How did he react?"

"Rather unexpectedly, sir, but I do not think it is cause for concern. His Highness admitted to already knowing about my brother's actions, Sire, from reading Prince Lachlan's diaries."

Adeone stilled. "Oh. What was his actual reaction?"

"One of guilt for already knowing and then supreme indifference for the past, sir. I could almost go so far as to say the thought that it should bother him had never truly entered His Highness' head. He was concerned for me, but not about my story."

"Thank Alcis for that!"

"Quite, Sire; however, His Highness did mention one thing I am unsure if Your Majesty knows…" Tancred hesitated. "His Highness says that in the Prince's diary is a note to the effect that my brother's treason was not proved beyond all doubt. That action was taken to ensure the troops knew what would happen if they betrayed Your Majesty's family and the empire, not because my brother was a proven traitor."

Adeone whitened. "If that is true, you have my sincerest apologies."

"Your Majesty, they were the actions of your forebears in a different time and for good reason. If my brother's death can be seen as having been him laying down his life for the protection of the empire, then I am content."

"I am more than happy to consider it so. I have never known my son lie about anything outright. He'll skirt the truth but not lie. If he told you what he read, then you can be assured it is as my uncle understood it on the day. I will draft a pardon—"

"Sire, I am content to know the truth. A pardon would involve Lord Scanlon and, as His Lordship was probably responsible for the matter being brought to light, I rather think he would not sign it."

Adeone rolled his empty glass between his hands. "Your forgiveness and understanding humbles me."

Tancred took the King's glass to refill it. "Sire, maybe the traits one recognises in others are ones within oneself. The amount of times I have thought that Your Majesty would have acted differently are too numerous to count."

"I do it to wrong-foot people."

Tancred chuckled. "I cannot believe that completely, Sire, but sometimes I think you might."

Taking back his glass, Adeone said, "Just because my forebears acted a certain way in given situations doesn't mean I have to. So, James, other than surprising us, what else is my errant son up to?"

"Apparently still not feeling quite himself, sir. He was rather quiet."

"Has he been overworking again, do you think?"

"I rather suspect he may have been, and I am sorry, sir. It is my fault."

"Fault, no. Compare how much he hated law in 1211 to how hard he works now. Your inspiration has been extraordinary and surpassed my expectations. I'll go and see him at Ceardlann. He's been in Oedran often enough, but it's rather difficult to get time to see him properly."

Tancred smiled. "I suppose it must be, sir. Have you heard from Prince Arkyn recently? Has he reached Lord Faran's yet?"

Adeone settled down to talk about family matters. For these few minutes, he could forget he was anything else but a father and uncle. Tancred listened, pleased to see the empire's cares drift away from Adeone's features.

A short time later, a knock at the door heralded Simkins.

"Your Majesty… There's been a bandit attack in Lufian…"

CHARACTERS

FAMILIES

FITZALCIS	*KING ALTARIUS APOLINAR*	*King of the Oedranian Empire 1168-1204*
	KING ADEONE ALTARIUS	King of the Oedranian Empire 1204-present
	QUEEN IRA	*King Adeone's wife (deceased)*
	PRINCE ARKYN ADEONE	King Adeone's eldest son
	PRINCE TAIN LACHLAN	King Adeone's younger son
	PRINCESS ELIZA ELANIA (ELLA)	*King Adeone's daughter (deceased)*
	PRINCE LACHLAN AMARUS	*King Altarius' brother (deceased)*
	LADY AMARA TALITHA	King Altarius' sister
	LORD SCANLON AMARUS	Justiciar of the Empire
	LADY AELIA	*Lord Scanlon's wife (deceased)*
	LADY ELANTHA	Lord Scanlon's daughter
LANDIS	LORD FESTUS LANDIS	Lord of Oedran, Defender of the King's Life, Chief Advisor, nearfather to Adeone's children
	LADY CORNELIA LANDIS	Long-suffering, hardworking Lady of Oedran
	LORD JULIUS AND LADY JULIA	Eldest children, twins
	MARCELEA, ANTONIA, LUCIUS, IRA	Younger children
IRIS	LORD IGNATIUS IRIS	Lord of Oedran, Deputy Chief Advisor to the King
	LORD IDRIS IRIS	Lord Iris' son
	LADY LINA IRIS	Lord Iris' wed-daughter
	LORD IRVIN IRIS	Lord Iris' grandson
	LADY INDRIA IRIS	Lord Iris' granddaughter

RALE	Lord Finian Rale	Lord of Oedran
	Lord Finn Rale	*Lord Rale's father (deceased)*
	Lady Malinda Atgas	Lord Rale's mother (remarried)
PARA	Lord Joren Para	Lord of Oedran for Anapara
	Lord Kenelm	Son of Lord Para
	Lady Malandra	Daughter of Lord Para
GALDWIN	Master Galdwin	Cloth Merchant
	Madam Galdwin	Wife and mother
	Calumiel Galdwin (Cal)	Eldest son
	Haltern, Louisa, Crispin, Tabitha, Elsie	Younger children
WANDA	Laioril	A chief of the Wanda
	Miranda	Wise woman of the Wanda
	Sayre	Man of the Wanda

KING'S RETINUE

Judge James Tancred	Mentor to Prince Tain, Friend
Richardson	King's Administrator
Simkins	King's manservant
Doctor Chapa	King's Physician and cousin
Sergeant Marsh	Head of the King's Guard
Sergeant Hillbeck	Sergeant of the King's Guard
Smithers	Guard in the King's Guard
Lyne	Guard in the King's Guard
Kenton	King's Secretary
Advisor Rayburn	King's Military Advisor
Advisor Vanval	King's Court Advisor
Advisor Spellen Master Ewall	Tutors
Mistress Clayton	Lady Elantha's governess
Maria Wynfeld	FitzAlcis nurse

ARKYN'S RETINUE

KADEEM	Arkyn's manservant
EDWARD	Arkyn's administrator
THOMAS	Kadeem's deputy
ALAN	Footman
GUNN	Edward's deputy
HALIEN	A guard
SIMON	Groom

SCANLON'S RETINUE

BANTLING	Advisor
MILLAR	Manservant
DYER	Administrator

CEARDLANN

COMPTROLLER	Gentleman in charge of Ceardlann
SUSAN	Housekeeper
COOK	Cook
ALFRED	Chief groom
JOE, DAVID	Footmen
LUCY	Kitchen maid
SPECKLES	A crafty cat

LANDIS HOUSE

WILLIAM KADEEM	Lord Landis' manservant
ADAM KADEEM	Lord Julius' manservant
CLODACH	Chief groom
COOKIE	Cook
NURSIE	Children's nurse
BACKERY	Footman
COLBAN	Foreman in charge of rebuild

IN OEDRAN

COURT	Lord Fairson	Lord of Oedran for Tradere
	Lady Fairson	Lady of Oedran
	Lord Ryson	Lord of Oedran for Gerymor Provost of the Law School
	Lord Lux	Lord of Oedran for Lufian
	Lord Teran	Lord of Oedran for Terasia
	Lord Cearis	Lord of Oedran for Denshire
	Lord Rathgar	Lord of Oedran for Bayan
	Lord Rufus Rathgar	Husband of Lady Neassa
PALACE	Steward	Gentleman in charge of day-to-day running of the Palace
	Chamberlain	Gentleman in charge of the individual rooms in the Palace
	Herald	Gentleman in charge of the mail routes, runners and couriers
	Captain Pixney	Captain of the Palace Guard
	Denny	Chief Server of Upper Hall
CITY	Merchant Chapa	Merchant of Oedran and King Adeone's cousin
	Aldhouse	Chief Yeoman of Oedran, head of law enforcement
	Moonshi	Chief Alcia in Oedran
	Keeper of the Justice Hall	Superintendent of the Courthouse of Oedran
	Master Selth	Judge Tancred's scribe
ARMY	General Paturn	Head of the King's Army
	Major Wynfeld	Major of Oedran
	Major Axton	Major of the Northern Empire
	Captain Beaver	Captain of Intelligence
	Corporal Garron	Corporal of Intelligence

IN THE EMPIRE

PARAS	Lord Synclare	Domini of Paras, King's Representative
	Lord Kensal Parchi	Young lord studying history
	Castellan	Steward of Paras Castle
	Captain Jones	Domini's guard captain
	Sergeant Butterworth	Jones' deputy
TERA	Lord Percival Wealsman	Margrave of Terasia
	Lady Kristina Wealsman	Wealsman's wife
	Ernst	Deputy Governor of Terasia
	Lady Daia Sansky	King's ward
OTHER	Lord Aldwy	Tuchlin of the Low Plains
	Lord Daioch	Low Plains Deputy Governor
	Lady Feronia Daioch (Nia)	Lord Landis' sister
	Lord Eames	Sagamore of Lufian
	Lord Faran	Lord of Lufian, Adeone's friend and confidant
	Lord Ogilvie	Lord of Gerymor

Delvings

Lexicon

OF THE MOONS

ALUNA	The larger of the two Erinnan moons
ALUNA-MONTH	Four weeks
ALUNAN	The higher section of society
ALUNAN-AGE	Twenty years old. Alunan become adults in law
CISLUNA	The smaller of the two Erinnan moons
CISLUNA-MONTH	Three weeks
CISAN	The lower section of society
CISAN-AGE	Fifteen years old. Cisan become adults in law

FOR THE ANCESTORS

ALCIA	A guardian of the ancestor's memory
ALCIUM	A place to remember the ancestors, for blessing new life, for contemplation and for funerals.
MOONSHI	Chief Alcia in Oedran

ON RELATIONSHIPS

NEAR*	Named when a child is born, *nearparents* act as mentors for a child and would act as guardians should the child be left orphaned. Nearparents' children are *nearcousins*, unless the child lives in the same house, then they're *nearsiblings*
WED*	This prefix denotes relatives married into the family, rather like the suffix *in-law*
KINAKIN	Related by marriage but beyond the immediate family. So a child's wed-family would be kinakin to the child's parents.

IN OEDRAN

TRINICULUM	A formal dining room at the Palace
ETANES	The law making body, made up of the Lords of Oedran and twelve cisan members
EALDORMAN	The person keeping order in the Etanes debates
EMBASSADOR	A legal ambassador
AULNAGER	Chief cloth merchant

HONORIFICS

SIRE, MAJESTY	The King
GRACE	The Queen
HIGHNESS	Princes
ELEGANCE	Princesses
EXCELLENCY	King's Representatives
BENEVOLENCE	Moonshi
GREATNESS	Scanlon
MY LORD	Lords
MY LADY	Nobel Ladies

FEALTIES

FEALTY	A declaration of loyalty from one person to another: a declaration to take up the fight for the liege by the vassal
TRUTH- BINDING	In addition to fealty, the vassal swears to speak to the truth to the liege when required.
SPEECH- BINDING	In addition to truth-binding, the vassal swears never to reveal anything confidential, never to say anything to annoy the liege, to speak only for them not against them.
HONOUR-BINDING	In addition to truth-binding, the vassal swears only to work for the honour of the liege, not against them.
LIFE-BINDING	Melding all aspects of truth, speech and honour bindings, the vassal ties their life force to the wishes of the liege. If they annoy their liege, they feel pain. If they commit treason, the vassal will die immediately.
VALLEY-BINDING	Specific to the Rex Dallin, this binding is said to be life-binding but may stop short of death.
OTHER BINDINGS	There are oaths which fall short of the recognised fealties, that are sworn when taking on specific duties or when an employer requires it.

ON MONEY

DARL	Gold coins
TALENCE	Silver coins, twenty to a darl
CRESCENTS (RES)	Bronze coins, twelve to a talence

The Cearcall and Ull's Legacy

At the beginning of the reckoning of years, the Majistar Ull brought magic to Erinna. Twelve star sapphires controlled the creation of the magic. Ull gifted the star stones to twelve individuals, each with a magical spirit. For six hundred years they, and their successors, controlled magic on Erinna, formed laws around it and maintained peace. In the year 600, they died, blown to the winds when magic, wielded by the Tribility who held three spirits, destroyed the Cearcall Tower in Denshire. Since 600 magic has been weaker, almost dormant. Some stones were lost, their location hidden by history, along with some items related to the members of the Cearcall.

Title	Spirit	Stone Colour	Item
AMSER	TIMER	TURQUOISE	AMSER'S WATCH
BERAN	BEARER	BLACK	BERAN'S PENDANT
ESPIER	ESPIEN	YELLOW	ESPIER'S GLASS
JECI	ILLUSIONIST	BLUE	JECI'S RING
MEITHRIN	HEALER	PINK	MEITHRIN'S VIAL
MEMINI	MEMOR	GREY	MEMINI'S MANUSCRIPT
RHEOL	BALANCER	WHITE	RHEOL'S NEEDLE
SENNACHIE	SEER	GREEN	SENNACHIE'S BOWL
SENTIRE	SENSOR	RED	SENTIRE'S KNIFE
SKIFTA	SHIFTER	PURPLE	SKIFTA'S SWORD
SUNDRIAN	SPLITTER	ORANGE	SUNDRIAN'S WHISTLE
WRIGHT	MANIPULATOR	BROWN	WRIGHT'S BOX

Each magical spirit manifests differently from healing hurts to splitting the mind, from creating illusions to manipulating objects.

More than one person at any one time can hold a spirit, but only one spirit wielder can possess the star stone and unlock its full power.

Each spirit has a collection of *hues*, lesser forms of the spirit, which may manifest in anyone.

People who wield magic are said to be affected by Ull's Legacy.

Provincial Information

Province	Capital City	Lord of Oedran
ANAPARA	OEDRAN	PARA
AREAL	AMPHI	RALE
BAYAN	GARTH	RATHGAR
DENSHIRE	CEARDEN	CEARIS
GERYMOR	RY	RYSON
LOW PLAINS	EYLLYN	IRIS
LUFIAN	LUFIA	LUX
MACIAN ISLES	MACIA	MACARIA
PALE LANDS	MEITH	LANDIS
SERPENT ISLE	ANGUIN	ANGUIS
TERASIA	TERA	TERAN
TRADERE	BYFA	FAIRSON

Province	King's Representative	Chief Judge
ANAPARA	DOMINI OF PARAS	CHIEF JUDGE (PARAS)
AREAL	GOVERNOR	KENNER
BAYAN	EXARCH	ESCHERVIN
DENSHIRE	VISIR	HAKIM
GERYMOR	DEY	BORSHOLDER
LOW PLAINS	TUCHLIN	DOMESMAN
LUFIAN	SAGAMORE	DEEMSTER
MACIAN ISLES	FENCIBLE	DOMARE
PALE LANDS	JARL	LAGHMAN
SERPENT ISLE	PASHA	TUOMARI
TERASIA	MARGRAVE	TERAZI
TRADERE	SATRAP	ARCHON

Province	Symbol	Colour
ANAPARA	THREE CROSSED ARROWS	PURPLE
AREAL	A KEY	SILVER
BAYAN	A BIRD IN FLIGHT	ORANGE
DENSHIRE	A TWELVE-POINT MYSTIC ROSE	BROWN
GERYMOR	A SET OF SCALES	WHITE
LOW PLAINS	AN EYE	GREEN
LUFIAN	A FLOWER AND SNOWFLAKE	BLUE
MACIAN ISLES	A TRISKELE OF THREE SPIRALS	RED
PALE LANDS	A VIAL	PINK
SERPENT ISLE	A CURLED SNAKE	YELLOW
TERASIA	A BEAR'S PAW PRINT	BLACK
TRADERE	AN HOURGLASS	TURQUOISE

Notes on Time

WEEKDAYS		FESTIVALS		
	ALUNADAI		MUNEWID	FIRST DAY OF SUMMER
	CISADAI			FIRST DAY OF THE YEAR
	TRETALDAI		MUNPYRAM	FIRST DAY OF AUTUMN
	IMPERADAI		MUNDIMRI	FIRST DAY OF WINTER
	PENTADAI		MUNLUMEN	FIRST DAY OF SPRING
	HEXADAI		*These festivals are known as Alcis Days*	
	SEPTADAI		*and are marked by both moons being full*	

ON TIME

1 MINUTE	=	60 SECONDS
1 HOUR	=	72 MINUTES (12 X 6 MINUTES)
1 DAY	=	24 HOURS
1 WEEK	=	7 DAYS
COURT CYCLE	=	12 DAYS
1 FORTNIGHT	=	2 WEEKS

Season	Aluna-month	Week	Cisluna-month	Season	Aluna-month	Week	Cisluna-month
SUMMER	CEARAL	1	CEARCIS	WINTER	RALAL	25	RALIS
		2				26	
		3				27	
	TRADAL	4	MIDDIS		ANAPAL	28	NORIS
		5				29	
		6				30	
		7	TRADIS			31	ANAPCIS
		8				32	
	LOWAL	9	LOWIS		BAYAL	33	BAYIS
		10				34	
		11				35	
		12				36	
AUTUMN	MACIAL	13	MACIS	SPRING	TERAL	37	TERIS
		14				38	
		15				39	
	MEITHAL	16	EASIS		GERYAL	40	SOUIS
		17				41	
		18				42	
		19	MEITHIS			43	GERYIS
		20				44	
	SERAL	21	SERIS		LUFIAL	45	LUFIS
		22				46	
		23				47	
		24				48	

POSTSCRIPT

To you, my reader...

Thank you.

I hope you enjoyed *Trapped*, the third book in the *Treason and Truth* series.

Please consider leaving an honest review of this book wherever you feel most comfortable. Reviews really help readers find their next book and help authors find their next reader.

Acknowledgements

Authors rarely get to publication without help and support. They sit and write in snatched hours or minutes. Sometimes stories flow unceasingly from their fingers, clamouring to be heard amongst the din of everyday life. When the last scratch of the pen and click of the keyboard is done, then comes the editing, the interior design, the cover...

My journey has not been solo. From my friends and family who have read, re-read and given me honest feedback to you, the reader that got this far, I say thank you.

This book is dedicated to Gary, whose questions have been the basis of so much. The question referred to in the dedication was 'What have you hidden in books 1 and 2?' These books could not have been written without him, his insight, friendship and support.

Explore Erinna

Please visit https://erinna.co.uk for more about the Erinnan Legacy or sign up to The Court Newsletter for freebies and news.